Elfhunter

A Tale of Alterra: The World that Is

Kevin - Welcome to my world!

BY

C.S. MARKS

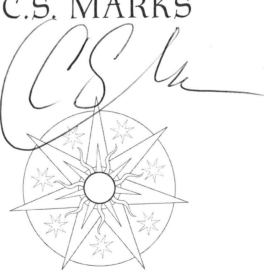

PARTHIAN PRESS

Elfhunter

The characters and events this book are entirely fictional. No similarity between any of the names, characters, persons, and/or institutions in this book with those of any living or dead person or institutions is intended, and any such similarity which may exist is purely coincidental.

Copyright © 2013 by C. S. Marks, Iron Elf, LLC

Cover Art and Frontispiece by Hope Hoover
Map and Interior Design by Carie Nixon
All other Illustrations by C.S. Marks

Edited by Leslie Wainger

All rights reserved. No part of this book may be reproduced in any form by any electronic or mechanical means including photocopying, recording, or information storage and retrieval without permission in writing from the author.

Published by Parthian Press, all rights reserved

PARTHIAN PRESS

ParthianPress.com
ISBN: 978-0-9859182-4-8

The Author's Website
CSMarks.com

Book Website
Elfhunter.net

Connect
Facebook.com/Alterra.CSMarks
Twitter.com/CSMarks_Alterra
Amazon.com/C.S.-Marks/e/B002CHYQR2/
Goodreads.com/author/show/521676.C_S_Marks

Contents

1 The Trail Begins	1
2 Of the Fishermen and the Rescue of Nelwyn	13
3 On the Trail Again	29
4 The Fate of Gelmyr	39
5 The Trail is Lost	45
6 The Path to the Greatwood	57
7 In the Halls of the King	71
8 The Path to Mountain-home Begins	81
9 Rogond Proves His Worth	95
10 Eros and Realta	121
11 The Tale of Galador	129
12 The Trail Grows Warm	139
13 The Fate of Nelwyn	159
14 In Which Some Friendships Are Renewed	173
15 Dark Heart	193
16 "He Who Waits"	215
17 Farewell to Mountain-home	225
18 The Pale Tower	237
19 The Dividing of the Company	251
20 Cos-domhain	261
21 The Stone of Léir	307
22 Gorgon's Army	329
23 Return to the Greatwood	349
24 The Mirror Revealed	375
25 Gaelen Undone	397
26 Out of the Darkness	415
27 The Plans Are Made	427
28 The Trap Is Set	447
29 Fire and Rain	461
30 The Trail Ends	493
GLOSSARY of NAMES	505
About C.S. Marks	526

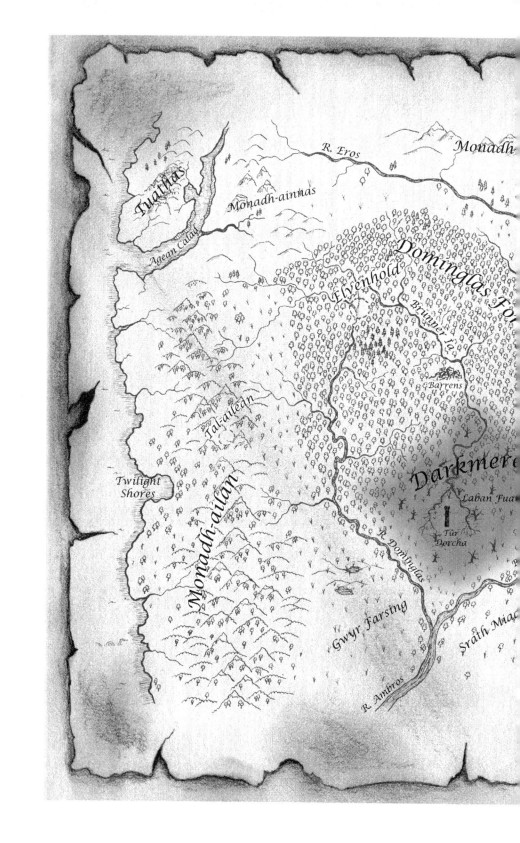

Two campfires come alight in the winter wood.

Both encircle their makers in welcome warmth. Each is a wild hearth—the gathering-place of friends.

One hears only laughter, good-natured argument, and the reassuring cry of an owl. The other bears witness to the tearing of breath from body, the loss of hope, and the triumph of hatred. No owl calls there, but the fire hears the cries of the innocent. It cannot answer, flaming in silence beneath a suffocating cloud of shadow.

It marks the return of a monster.

1

The Trail Begins

The darkness came early in midwinter, especially in the Greatwood. Even in the height of summer the forest was not a bright place. Very little sunlight penetrated the vast canopy, hence the overall effect of a cool, dark haven shot with green and gold. In winter more light could pass through the layers of skeletal branches, but it was a cold light, thin and grey. In the ever-present mists of winter, a traveler who ventured into the depths of the forest unprepared might find himself lost, chilled to death in the long dark. Fire, in this realm, was life.

Gaelen Taldin, a Wood-elf of the Greatwood Realm, was glad to have been sent out into the deep woods. As with most of her kind, Gaelen was most content among the trees, and she had dedicated herself to the guardianship of her forest home. She paused in her gathering of dead wood for the fire that she would soon need, appraising the leaden, tree-netted sky to the northwest. It looked as though it might start snowing at any minute.

She struck a spark to the tinder she had collected, carefully tending the fragile flame until it was truly kindled, and wrapped her winter cloak about her. She had lived through well over a thousand such winters and was not disquieted, for she was resistant to the elements and the cold bothered her little. Still, the fire was most welcome.

Just as Gaelen realized that she was truly hungry, her cousin Nelwyn appeared with two fine game-birds in her hand. She tossed them to Gaelen, who nodded in approval. Drawing a small, curved blade from the top of her boot, she split the breasts of the birds, pulling back the skin and removing it with a few expert strokes. She hated plucking feathers; they stuck to her fingers and would cling to her clothing for hours afterward. She tossed the skin aside with satisfaction and reached inside the birds, extracting the innards with strong, clever fingers. Tossing the carcasses to Nelwyn, she cleaned the blood from her hands by stripping a piece of fragrant bark from a nearby spice-bush. Then she settled down to watch her cousin at work. Nelwyn rubbed the meat with the previous summer's dried herbs, wrapped it in softened sheets of fire-birch bark sprinkled with sweet oil, and set them aside. She would roast them when the coals were just right.

In the depths of winter the sunrise would come late, but Gaelen didn't mind. The cold darkness was not to be feared, at least so long as the warmth of the fire continued. Her enemies were unlikely to be abroad in the cold, especially so deep within the boundaries of the Elven-realm. Even if they were, she had already noted the presence of at least one owl in the vicinity. Owls made excellent sentinels, and as long as these kept calling, she knew the area was secure. She and Nelwyn sat together in an enormous, hollow tree-trunk beside the well-concealed fire, quietly singing songs and telling tales, laughing and making merry until dawn.

The snow that Gaelen had sensed upon the wind finally came in the early morning, but by that time she was refreshed and ready to move on, hoping for a warmer day. She and Nelwyn had been sent by the King to patrol the eastern border of the realm, for Ri-Aruin appreciated information concerning who or what was abroad in his lands. Gaelen and Nelwyn were excellent scouts; they could travel without being seen or heard if they wished, and they had often warned the King of trespassers. They had permission to deal with certain of these on their own; Ulcas, in particular, would fall quickly.

Gaelen had always regarded these misbegotten creatures with a mixture of loathing and disgust, though she felt a small amount of pity for them. From a distance they almost looked human, but a closer look revealed their lumpy, discolored flesh, muddy, unintelligent eyes, and twisted limbs. Even more disturbing to the Elves was their utter hairlessness—Ulcas lacked even eyelashes. Gaelen had seen a bald man before, but he still had eyelashes, eyebrows, and hair on his exposed arms. She found the sight of Ulcas—especially unclothed—revolting. They reminded her of the blind, squirming things that lived under rotting logs.

She packed up her gear and made for the eastern boundary, the silent snow falling around her. She expected nothing out of the ordinary in the coming daylight, but would have to put some miles behind her if she and Nelwyn would reach their intended encampment by nightfall. Swift and silent, scanning the forest in all directions as she ran, Gaelen hoped for an interesting encounter. Her blood was up, and she was in the mood for adventure—hopefully her impetuous nature and irrepressible curiosity wouldn't result in more than she bargained for. Again.

After the sun had risen, Nelwyn, who was especially good at climbing, scaled one of the taller trees and surveyed the sky and the canopy, looking for signs. Gaelen, whose talents ran more to tracking, listening, and scenting, stayed on the ground. She put her sensitive nose to work, surprised to find the unmistakable tang of wood-smoke carried on the breeze from the southwest.

Nelwyn climbed back down and dropped lightly beside her cousin. "There's a fire burning southwest of here," she said.

"I know. I smelled it. I suppose we should investigate."

Nelwyn sighed. "Is there any more to be gained from the signs?"

Gaelen looked around her and shrugged. "Nothing that I can see…not here, anyway. What do you wish to do?"

"We must go and see who burns a wood-fire in the Greatwood. I don't believe our folk would be out this way, burning a campfire at mid-morning."

Wood-elves certainly didn't call attention to themselves in the deep forest by risking a smoky fire in daylight. At night it would be different, as a properly concealed campfire would be difficult to see from any distance. Gaelen wondered whether the fire was accidental—a remnant of the last night's camp that someone had failed to extinguish. If so, that someone was either careless, overconfident, or dead.

As they made their way toward the rising column of smoke, Nelwyn risked climbing again to see how near they were to it. Gaelen's heart sank as she picked up a darker, more sinister undercurrent beneath the odor of wood-smoke. She shivered, the hairs on her arms and the back of her neck raised in suppressed alarm. This was no longer a simple matter of a neglected campfire, and she knew it.

As if she could sense her cousin's distress, Nelwyn returned to her at once. "What is it?"

"I don't think we need to worry about whoever made that fire—we're too late. It's an old fire, made last night, if I am not mistaken, and now…" She wrinkled her nose in distaste. "…I smell burning flesh."

Nelwyn drew closer to her cousin, shuddering slightly at the thought. "I suppose it's a vain hope that you are mistaken?"

"Definitely flesh burning, and not Ulca-flesh, either. We'd best go carefully and see if anything can be done."

They proceeded to track their way to the source of the burning. There had been a properly made encampment there the previous night, much like their own. A fire had been built in concealment amid a ring of large stones in a fair clearing, where the occupants could have seen the stars until the clouds rolled in at midnight. The remains of the fire were still smoldering as Gaelen and Nelwyn crept in from downwind to behold a terrible scene.

Two Wood-elves lay dead in the clearing. One had fallen into the fire with an enormous, ungainly arrow in his chest. At least he would have perished quickly. The other appeared to have been hacked at with a dull blade...his blood was everywhere. From the look of it, he had died while trying to pull his companion out of the fire. Apparently, they had been caught completely unaware. Nelwyn, horrified, had started toward them when Gaelen grabbed her upper arm.

"No! It hasn't been that long since they were as alive as we are now. We must make sure that whoever did this is gone. You take the east, and I will circle west."

Gaelen surveyed the area, her senses sharpened and her body tense. Both she and Nelwyn had their bows at the ready; they would not be taken so easily. As Gaelen circled closer to the fire, she searched for signs--clues as to what had taken place, what might be lurking still--but she found none. As they drew near their fallen comrades, she saw tears of recognition in Nelwyn's eyes.

"Oh...Gaelen, it's Talrodin and...and Halrodin."

They were brothers, inseparable both in life and now in death. Gaelen gasped and ran to Halrodin's side. His strong, dead hands grasped his brother's arm with desperate effort. His sightless eyes stared up at the sky, but he was still warm enough that the snowflakes melted as they touched him. She brushed away tears and helped Nelwyn pull Talrodin from the smoldering ashes, noting the look of pure astonishment on his face.

Gaelen tried not to gag at the stench of charred flesh and fabric. She didn't know which was worse, that or the underlying smell of roasted meat, normally tantalizing and inviting. She bit her own lip, disgusted that she found it so.

She returned to Halrodin, who had been her friend, and knelt beside him, looking intently into his eyes and grasping his cold hands with her own. Gaelen possessed a unique talent—one she had revealed to no one except Nelwyn—and she searched Halrodin's eyes for what they might reveal. She knew that the dead may speak to the living and, if one could perceive it, the tale of their last moments lingered for a while. She concentrated and focused her will, locking her bright hazel-green eyes with Halrodin's glassy, lifeless ones. The violence of his last moments was clearly written there, but there was something else, as well. Revulsion, a kind of fascinated horror, came clearly to Gaelen's mind. Though she could not see the image of the enemy through Halrodin's eyes, she could feel his last thoughts. She could also feel some of the malevolence of the thing that had tortured and killed him.

At least the brothers hadn't been dragged off and eaten, and their few belongings remained with them—all except one. Halrodin's beautiful, elegant sword, his most prized possession, was missing, along with the curved, silver-clad leather sheath that had fitted it so well. Gaelen's slight frame shook with cold fury, and she looked over at Nelwyn with an expression of determination the younger Elf had seen before: Gaelen wouldn't rest until she had recovered that sword and restored it to Halrodin's family.

Nelwyn sighed, considering the immediate task before them. "We had best get to work. The carrion beasts will be drawn to blood on the wind."

Gaelen worked beside Nelwyn in silence, wrapping her fallen friends in their cloaks and covering them with stones to keep them safe from the scavengers. Then she sang a lament of the ancient line of High-elves known as the Èolar, for their sad songs were hauntingly beautiful. The anger smoldering within her did an excellent job of steadying her voice, which did not waver despite her grief. Nelwyn wept openly, especially for Talrodin. They had spent untold hours sharing herb-lore, and she had been fond of him.

When Gaelen had placed the last stone, and the last notes of her lament had faded into the forest, her thoughts turned to her new enemy. This was a wanton, senseless act against two innocents who had every right to be where they were. They weren't unwary travelers, but clever, wood-wise forest dwellers with keen senses and quick reflexes. That someone should have taken them unaware and with such crude weaponry was inexplicable. What sort of being could have strung a bow so powerful with an arrow so large that it had pinned Talrodin to the ground, and then hacked Halrodin to pieces—taking plenty of time about it—before vanishing with little trace? It had to be huge, heartless, and incredibly strong. Gaelen knew that she could track it, but not easily. The snow had not been falling long, but it covered what little sign had been left. Progress would be slow, as careful tracking took time and effort.

There was an unfamiliar and very unpleasant stench about the place, but it was fading rapidly, also blunted by the snow. Gaelen committed it to memory; she would know it if she ever encountered it again. She saw no blood other than that of the two brothers. Her small frame shuddered, momentarily overcome with a mixture of horror and rage.

Nelwyn placed a concerned hand on her arm. "I wonder if it would be best to return home…to tell our people what has happened. Then we could come back with many others to help us in hunting down this enemy."

Gaelen closed her eyes. "That will take too long. We might as well just say fare-thee-well and give up. If we want to hunt this…this thing, we must hunt it now!"

"But…"

Gaelen's eyes flashed. "Don't even consider delaying this."

In answer, Nelwyn's gaze hardened. "Just remember what this scene might have been had it taken place in a different encampment last night. You will not avenge our friends by falling to the same foe."

But Gaelen, as usual, had the last word. It was a single word, spoken through clenched teeth, and Nelwyn could offer no argument.

"Thaldallen."

Five days later, their tracking had turned them south near the eastern forest boundary, then eastward toward the River Ambros. Gaelen was determined to catch up with their quarry before they reached the Great River; she feared all signs would be lost in the crossing, and she knew they would be difficult to pick up again on the other side.

Her tracking efforts had confirmed that she pursued a lone enemy. That was of little comfort, but at least there was only one pair of eyes and ears that could turn back toward them. At first, she gritted her teeth at Nelwyn's constant admonitions that she not go too fast, that she would surely miss some sign, but these were getting harder to ignore. They had neither rested nor eaten, and both were weary from the tiresome, close work of tracking. The only good news was that the killer had become more careless as it drew farther away from the kill. That, and the simple fact that both Elves were becoming more familiar with their enemy, had increased the speed of the pursuit considerably.

"If we don't stop to rest and eat soon, I shall not be strong enough to contend with this marauder when we do catch it." Nelwyn had been trying to get Gaelen to stop for hours, undoubtedly wishing she had convinced her cousin to give in to the sensible suggestion to return home.

Gaelen snorted. "As if either of us would ever be strong enough to contend with a creature that could do what was done! My only plan is to get close enough to shoot the cursed evil wretch in the throat."

Still, Nelwyn's request made sense; Gaelen realized that she needed to rest and renew her strength, as she was becoming a bit reckless. She stretched her lithe form toward the cold, pale blue winter sky, and then rummaged in her food pouch for a few dried apples, some dried mushrooms, and strips of dried, salted venison that chewed rather like leather. She and Nelwyn ate quickly, washing down the dry, salty meal with refreshing cold draughts from their flasks. Then they rested a little, knowing they could not linger beyond sunset.

They had been tracking even in the dark, for it had been clear and moonlit these last nights, and they could see well enough. Nelwyn had noted that the creature moved much faster by night, though she estimated that it was now only one or two hours ahead of them. Once or twice it veered from its course, and they found the remains of a deer that had been slain and partially devoured, torn to pieces and eaten raw. No fire had been built, and if their enemy had taken rest, it was not obvious.

Nelwyn was the first to notice the column of smoke to the east, rising from a copse of trees very near the river. Gaelen shivered, as she was not comfortable with the idea of approaching from upwind. She didn't know whether the enemy could or would take notice of their scent, but they could not afford the risk. She directed Nelwyn to follow her, moving in a wide arc until she was satisfied with their position. Then they crept cautiously in.

This time the victims were not Elves, but men. Two of the fishermen who lived along the river lay dead amid the ruins of their camp. They had been slain with quiet efficiency; the brutal savagery with which the Elves had been attacked was not evident here. The stench of the creature still hung heavily in the air, as it had not been long gone.

A sudden thought struck Gaelen, who leaped up and sprinted toward the water, abandoning her prior caution. Fishermen are never very far from their boat and, as she feared, it had been taken. She mouthed a silent curse, gazing downstream at a massive figure paddling southward with the current, disappearing into far distant twilight. If only they had been quicker! Frustrated and weary, she sank down onto the bank as Nelwyn ran lightly up behind her. Peering into the gathering dark, Nelwyn realized that their enemy was beyond their reach.

She sat down beside Gaelen and shook her head in resignation. "I suppose that's the end then...we'll never catch up now. Did you get a look?"

"Yes, a brief one," said Gaelen, examining the riverbank. "It's tall—taller than any Ulca. Heavier, too...the boat rode quite low in the water."

Nelwyn nodded in appreciation of her cousin's keen sight; the boat was only a tiny speck by now. "A troll, maybe?"

"Doesn't smell like one. I could swear the thing was wearing armor. And besides, trolls don't like the water."

"Neither do Ulcas."

Gaelen cast her eyes heavenward. "Obviously, it's not an Ulca! I don't know what it is, and thanks to all my delays, I may never know."

She drew a deep breath in an attempt to quell her frustration. "We are now faced with a choice. Do we go on along the riverbank and follow the boat, or do we turn back for home?"

They regarded one another in silence for a long moment. At last, Nelwyn spoke.

"I keep thinking of Talrodin—the way he knew every leaf and blade in the forest. He was so quiet and gentle-natured, and he loved his sons. They will never learn any more of that herb-lore from him now. I fear for all who pass near this terrible enemy, and, though I counseled you to turn about, I wonder now whether I can live with what will happen if we do. I fear we must continue on...though we may not see home again."

Gaelen loved her cousin very much. She had been thinking similar thoughts, but the revelation that Nelwyn shared her determination to continue the pursuit was unexpected, and it filled her with relief and gratitude. Her desire to hunt down the creature had wavered a little, and she would have turned back for Nelwyn's sake if asked, but now they were united and strong in their resolve.

"Halrodin was left to bleed to death, yet he still tried to pull his brother from the fire," she said. "Such courage and devotion must be avenged. Halrodin would not have suffered his brother's killer to walk free, and neither will I."

She remembered Halrodin's sword, the one the killer had stolen. It was a prized heirloom of his house, and she bristled at the thought of it in the hands of his murderer. She made a silent vow to get it back.

Gaelen also understood what Nelwyn meant about what would happen if they turned from their pursuit. This creature killed everyone it encountered, seemingly for the most trivial of reasons. It could easily have stolen the boat from the fishermen; it didn't have to kill them. At least they had been taken quickly and had suffered little pain.

The brutal treatment of her friends had planted an irrefutable thought in Gaelen's mind. This creature, whatever it was, hated Elves above all others. She had read this in Halrodin's dead eyes, sensing it like the heavy, suffocating feeling of an approaching storm. Talrodin had been killed quickly enough, but the creature had gone out of its way to maim and inflict as much pain as possible upon his brother. It had taken his weapon, leaving him to die in agony and despair.

Gaelen knew this was not mindless, but by design. This enemy would go out of its way to kill Elves wherever it encountered them, and they would die in torment. No, she could not turn from the path now—she would continue the pursuit until her last arrow buried itself in the creature's black, hateful heart.

Nelwyn took one last swallow of water from her flask and rose to her feet. She ran her fingers through her hair and sighed. It would be another long night. There was nothing to do now except make their way southward with all speed and hope that the bright stars would shine upon their path.

In the realm of King Ri-Aruin, the discovery of the fate of Halrodin and his brother had not yet been made, though it was noted that both they and the She-elves were long overdue. It was not unusual for scouting parties to be gone for many weeks, but as the days continued with no word, a few of their kinsmen brought the matter to the attention of the King.

The news that four worthy hunter-scouts had failed to return or send word troubled Ri-Aruin. Gaelen and Nelwyn concerned him less, as they had a habit of returning when they pleased, but Talrodin would never inflict such anxiety upon his sons without dire cause.

There was nothing to do but send new scouts to find the brothers and help them if need be. Perhaps there was a harmless explanation for the delay, but of this Ri-Aruin was not hopeful. The rescue party left at sunset, well equipped and ready for anything—so they thought. When they returned nearly twelve days later, bearing the remains of Talrodin and Halrodin, they had only their sorrow to offer.

Ri-Aruin was both saddened and frustrated, and it was now apparent that Gaelen and Nelwyn had been involved. The manner in which the bodies had been cared for made that clear. In addition, Nelwyn had placed a small beech twig bearing a few perfect, copper-colored leaves in Talrodin's right hand. Of their whereabouts there was little clue, but the search party rightly guessed that they had gone off in pursuit of the unknown killers. Ri-Aruin grew impatient as he questioned his scouts. What sort of enemy had done such a thing? The scouts did not know and could not even speculate, as this was simply beyond their experience. Indeed, it would be a long time before any Wood-elf of the Greatwood would fully understand the nature of the threat that had passed through their lands.

Gorgon Elfhunter rested in the rocky scrub along the river bank, shaded by the long, windswept branches of an ancient willow, still basking in the satisfaction of his recent 'kill'. The suffering of Elves was about the only thing in the world that brought him pleasure—that, and the bizarre habit of inflicting scars upon his own flesh with his own blades. He settled back, unconcerned, confident in his ability not only to remain concealed, but to evade pursuit. After all, he had always made certain that those few who saw him clearly did not live to tell of him, hence he preferred to strike the Elves down as they traveled alone or in pairs.

He was as cunning as they, but larger and stronger, and his heart was filled with hatred of them and lust for their blood. He could point to every single one of his battle-scars with pride, knowing that the ones who wounded him had been far beyond healing when he had finished with them. It pleased him especially to see the look of horror on their faces when he revealed his true nature at the moment of their deaths.

He drew forth the short-sword he had taken from the Wood-elf, the foolish one who had been so concerned with trying to pull his dead companion from the fire, examining it in the dappled light. "Turantil. Tooo-rran-teeeel," he purred, reading the Elvish runes engraved in the pommel. The name meant "Scourge of the North". He chuckled, remembering the pathetic struggle its owner had put forth. "Not much of a scourge, were you? Well, no matter. You will certainly have the chance now, my pretty, pretty blade." He replaced the sword in its beautiful scabbard, thrumming deep in his broad chest like an enormous cat. Soon, he would rest.

He had lurked in the world long enough to have heard some of the stories about him—tales of his marauding came mostly from men, and even the Ulcas knew of him and feared him. Gorgon had no love for them either, and usually killed any he encountered as a matter of convenience. Ulcas were beneath his contempt—stupid, mindless creatures with little will of their own.

Gorgon spent much of his empty life in solitude deep under mountains, for such was his place of comfort, resting and planning his next foray. Sometimes, when pickings were lean, he would lapse into a state of torpor, usually while clutching a weapon or other reminder of a long-dead enemy. He stopped killing only long enough for people to doubt his existence, as he dreamed of the deaths of a thousand Elves. Then he would awaken, travel to his next killing-ground, and the tales would come alive again.

He had discovered the pleasure of carving his own flesh long ago—first cutting away his right ear and then his left, bit by bit. Now hardly an inch of his filthy, greyish flesh was left unmarred. His nose was a flat lump of misshapen cartilage with wide nostrils, his pale eyes gleamed from folds of scarred flesh. He felt no pain that he could not endure, and he knew no fear except that his life would end and he could kill no more. That was a thought he could not accept so long as Elves walked, sang their songs, and breathed of the free air.

2

Of the Fishermen and the Rescue of Nelwyn

Eventually, the creature would have to come out of the river. Gaelen reasoned that he would not go far, for he was clearly visible as long as he traveled by water. She had guessed that he would not spend long in the open if he could help it. Because they did not know on which side of the river their enemy would disembark, the Elves knew that they must track along both riverbanks for signs of the boat. If their enemy came ashore, they would know.

The first difficulty would be in getting one of them across the river, for although they both swam well, the swift water was far too cold. They decided to seek out the rest of the fishermen, tell them of the fate of their kin, and ask their help. First, they returned to the fallen ones and tended to them. They wrapped the bodies respectfully in their cloaks, laid them side by side, and covered them with dead winter leaves to hide them from unfriendly eyes. Then they went looking for the settlement.

They found it easily enough—several small, thatched earthen dwellings along the riverbank. They looked crude, but warm and comfortable. Gentle fires glowed from within, and a large rack of drying fish had been suspended over a bed of smoldering coals outside. There were boats, nets in various stages of mending, and other signs that a hardy people dwelt and thrived there.

Fisher-people were found along most of the flowing waters of Alterra. Some were men, while others were smaller, web-footed, secretive creatures known as Currgas. This was a settlement of men—honest, hard-working, and generally harmless. They would be wondering why their slain kinsmen had not returned, as it was raining again, and the wind promised a bad storm by nightfall.

It would probably not do for Gaelen and Nelwyn to appear from out of nowhere, for Elves would undoubtedly seem strange to these folk. It would be safer and wiser to approach cautiously, one at a time. Gaelen, who wasn't as tall as Nelwyn, wrapped her cloak about her, stooped over like an old woman with her hood hiding her face, and limped slowly toward the warm bed of coals. She leaned upon a walking-stick of yew wood that she had fashioned from a downed limb and stood near the fire, apparently trembling with cold, making herself as small as possible to the eye. Nelwyn stood hidden nearby, an arrow fitted to her bow. She would give Gaelen time to escape if things went amiss.

The strange, huddled figure drew the attention of the fishermen at once, and several of them came out of their dwellings, approaching with some reluctance. One called to Gaelen in the common-tongue:

"Old woman! Who are you, and what is your business here?"

Gaelen answered, for she knew the language that was used by most of the men of Alterra. "I should think, with such weather, that my intention to warm myself would be obvious. I mean no harm to you or your folk. However, I bear news that you will not find pleasing, and I must now ask if I may speak to you without fear."

The fishermen considered for a moment. They were very wary of Gaelen now. They didn't like the sound of bad news coming, and they sensed that she was not as she appeared. She could not disguise the Elven ring and clarity of her voice, even through the wind and the rain.

"No old woman ever had a voice like that. Perhaps she means to harm us, as she is not what she seems," said one.

Another replied, "If she had meant to harm us, would she have appeared so openly and without a weapon in hand? We could so easily kill her. What news does she bring, and why bring it, if her intent is to harm us?"

"Weapons can be hidden," said a stout, bearded man who appeared to command respect from the others. He straightened and raised his bow, fitting an arrow to the string, as Nelwyn drew on him silently. He called out: "Show yourself, for you are not as you seem. Then we shall decide your fate."

In reply, they heard Gaelen's soft, clear voice singing in the Elven-tongue. A mournful song, more beautiful than any they had ever heard, rose above the sound of the rain. The archer lowered his weapon, transfixed. The men stood astonished as Gaelen rose to her full height and, still singing, cast back her hood, revealing the light of her eyes. Though still grieving for her friends and weary with traveling, she radiated strength and purity of purpose. The fishermen had, of course, heard songs and tales of the Elàni, but they had never before known them or been among them. The song filled their hearts with both sadness and longing, so that they wished for it never to end, but knew if it did not, the sorrow in the song would consume them. When Gaelen stopped singing and held out both of her empty hands to show that she held no weapon, they remained as though frozen in a kind of fearful trance.

It was then that Nelwyn appeared at the edge of the trees, bow in hand, hood thrown back. She called to them: "Will you hear our tale? Choose now, or we will be gone."

The sight of Nelwyn, who was undoubtedly the most beautiful creature the fishermen had ever beheld, broke them from their trance. They knew then that they were in the presence of Elves, and they bowed in respect and reverence.

"Most fair bearers of ill news, please come and be warm and dry, and we shall hear your tale," said the archer, indicating the largest dwelling.

Inside there was warmth, light, and shelter from the wind. Several young children huddled together on the far side of a great wooden table set with small oil-lamps. The Elves were invited to sit there with the men-folk of the clan. As they removed their wet cloaks and hung them near the fire, the men and women marveled at their fine leather garments and elegant weapons.

The Elves wore little of ornamental design, for they were dressed as hunter-scouts of the Greatwood, presently in winter colors. Their cloaks were grey-brown lined with warm, soft fur of mottled brown and white that would conceal the wearer among winter trees or snow-covered rocks. They wore tall, soft-soled boots of worn, oiled leather. Gaelen's were brown, Nelwyn's a dull green.

Though their clothing was plain, their weapons had been made by Elven craftsmen and were of the finest quality. The blades were engraved with runes and images of warriors and huntsmen. The sheaths that held them were of worn, dark leather clad with traceries of silver. The fishermen had never seen their like, nor ever would again.

The bearded archer, named Maleck, seemed to be in charge of the others. He instructed the women to bring food and drink, but the Elves did not partake. "Our tale must first be told, for two of your folk are lost, and you will need to care for them. We will aid you in this," said Nelwyn.

With great sorrow the fishermen received the news of their fallen kinsmen and the theft of their boat, for these were men beloved of many. The Elves sat in silence, eyes downcast, as their gentle hosts wept for those lost. At last Maleck asked where his kinsmen could be found, and Gaelen answered him.

"We will show you where they are lying. We tended to them as we could, but we are tracking the one who killed them, and we have come here in part to ask for your aid."

"Take us there," growled Maleck. One of the fallen was the husband of his younger sister, and Maleck wanted to know all he could learn.

The fishermen bore the bodies back to their settlement intending to bury them beside their kin. Then they returned to the larger dwelling, inviting their guests once again to share food and drink. This time the Elves accepted with thanks, for they had not eaten a proper meal in days.

The men sat around the large wooden table, their faces grey and somber. "What sort of enemy killed our kinsmen, who were no threat?" asked Maleck, at once bitter and incredulous.

"We do not know," said Nelwyn sadly. She then told the tale of the discovery of the two Elvish brothers and of the savage nature of the attack upon them. "They were friends of ours, and we must pursue their killer. For this, we need your aid."

"What would you ask of us?"

"Only safe passage for one of us to the east bank of the river as soon as light dawns tomorrow," answered Nelwyn.

"And perhaps some provisions so that we may continue on our journey," put in Gaelen. "We will repay you, if you wish, with songs and tales tonight, so that your minds may rest from grief for a little while."

"No payment is necessary," Maleck replied. "You may take anything we can provide. Even so, I would listen to your tales and especially to your song. But please...less sorrowful than the last, for we are sorrowful enough."

Outside, a gale lashed at the small, sturdy dwelling. Two of the children whimpered with fear of the wind and icy rain, edging closer to Nelwyn, who spoke words of comfort in her soft, gentle voice.

Gaelen smiled. "You shall have your song. And it will be a song of hope...perhaps your fallen companions are still near enough to hear it as they journey to the Eternal Realm."

Maleck didn't entirely take her meaning, for it was his belief that his people were released to the river they loved upon their deaths, and that their voices could always be heard amid the flowing waters. Yet he nodded in respect as Gaelen began to sing.

When dawn came, the grey light chased away the last of the rain. Inside the warm and comfortable dwelling, the two Elves prepared to depart after a long but not unpleasant night. Gaelen and Nelwyn had comforted the people, especially the children sitting in their laps and at their feet, with tales and songs. Sorrows were forgotten for a time, and hearts were lightened.

Maleck was now determined to accompany them, but Gaelen and Nelwyn knew they could not afford his company. They thanked the people for the bread, honey, dried fish, and clear water, and set out for the river with Maleck and his brother, Unvar, who would ferry Gaelen across.

When they reached the boat, Gaelen, Maleck, and Unvar climbed in. Nelwyn lifted her eyebrows at Maleck, but said nothing. She would remain on the western bank to track along it, always keeping Gaelen in sight if possible. The river was swollen from the last night's rain, thus the boat might not be brought ashore until it had gone down river for a considerable way. Nelwyn would need to run swiftly. She stretched and warmed her limbs in preparation for the chase, eager to be away. She didn't much care for the idea of being separated from Gaelen, but she saw no other way to avoid missing their enemy. She only hoped Gaelen would dissuade Maleck without hurting his pride.

As it turned out, it wasn't so difficult. Unvar put the boat ashore about a mile down river. Gaelen could see Nelwyn running along the bank, keeping up with little effort. She gathered up her light provisions and turned to the two brothers:

"My thanks for your aid in bringing me across the river. Your part in this has been played. Return now to your homes; care for your fallen kin and your families. I would suggest you not tarry long, as your people need you. My cousin and I wish you well."

Maleck shouldered his pack. "It's not my intention to leave you, for I also would see my kinsmen avenged. Unvar is here to return with the boat."

Gaelen could see that he was determined, but in his eyes there was doubt. These were not adventurous folk, and they did not travel far from their own lands. It took great courage for Maleck even to consider this course. Gaelen shook her head and spoke gently, though her gaze was firm.

"You cannot go with us, Maleck. Your heart tells you so, brave heart though it is. You are a worthy man, and we respect you and your folk, but you simply cannot strive with us. You must aid your brother in returning with the boat—that is task enough. If I have still not convinced you, let me remind you of my friend Halrodin's fate at the hands of our enemy. He was hacked to pieces with a dull blade, and left to die in great pain and despair. This is an enemy beyond you. Take your honor, and depart."

Reluctantly, Maleck saw the wisdom in her words. "Farewell then, Gaelen, daughter of the Greatwood. We are thankful to have known you and wish you success in your quest. Take care that the enemy you seek does not find you first, for I would rather meet you again."

Gaelen bowed and smiled at him before she sprang away, leaping and sprinting along the river bank, keeping one eye on Nelwyn and one eye at the water's edge. Within moments, Maleck had difficulty spotting her, and then she was gone.

The air was as chill as the trail was cold. Nelwyn drew her cloak tighter as she gazed out at the dull grey river-water, now veiled with rain. The wind was coming up strong again from the northwest, and it rained or sleeted almost every day at this miserable time of year. She could just barely make out the form of Gaelen, who was carefully searching for signs on the other side of the river.

It had been nearly five days since their encounter with the slain fishermen and the escape of their enemy in the boat he had stolen. Nelwyn stood shivering on the riverbank, thinking of the coming storm, hoping that they would find signs of the boat being pulled from the water before the river rose high enough to wash them away. The enemy would undoubtedly cast the boat loose when he was finished with it, but even if he didn't bring it ashore, he would have to come ashore himself. Then they would find the signs if there were any to find. They were not as familiar with this section of the river—it was narrower, but deep and turbulent. As they both looked downstream, they observed some respectable rapids in the distance.

The rapids both cheered and worried Nelwyn. Surely their enemy would come ashore rather than risk crossing the wild water. If so, had they missed the evidence? Or was the enemy lurking just ahead, lying in wait? They hadn't exactly been vigilant about concealing themselves from view. At any rate, Nelwyn hoped that they would find something before they reached the rapids. She just hoped they would not find the enemy himself; they were not yet ready for such a confrontation. Nelwyn thought of Talrodin's astonished expression and shuddered. She didn't like being all alone by the river. At least it was getting warmer as she made her way south, and the cold wind would soon pass. For now, she was miserable.

The Elves had encountered only two others in the last four days, fishermen of a different clan from those up river. Both had been on the east bank. Gaelen had questioned them, but from her posture it was apparent that she had learned little or nothing from them.

Gaelen was wet and miserable herself. She felt her cousin's gaze, straightened, and waved at her. They would both go to shelter for the night facing the same dreary prospect—no dry wood, only a few remnants of food, and no nice, warm cousin to share cloaks and the pleasure of complaining with.

If they didn't find something soon, Nelwyn feared they both would lose heart, and she had no wish for that. But they were so far from home already! Grumbling to herself, she settled her back against some large stones that protected her from the wind. This was not much of a shelter, but it was better than nothing.

A few moments later, Nelwyn was startled by a cry from the east. Though it sounded rather like a large bird, she knew it was Gaelen—she must have found something. Nelwyn leaped to her feet, shaking off the cold, and peered into the rain. Gaelen was pointing down and across the river, gesturing for Nelwyn to investigate. Gaelen started down river herself, keeping a close watch on the far bank. The boat was there, about a quarter mile to the south.

There was no sound, scent, or sight of the enemy. Nelwyn could tell that he had left the boat in haste and was now making his way over land, for he had left plenty of sign for her to follow. This was encouraging, as it meant that he was probably not aware that anyone was tracking him. Either that, or he didn't care.

Though the second possibility frightened her, the first cheered Nelwyn as she climbed into the boat, which had been secured with a short rope to a nearby stone. She examined the small craft for signs, and there were plenty, if not very enlightening. A few remnants of food stolen from the fishermen and a few drops of strange, dark blood were left behind, not quite washed away by the rain. The same foul smell was now evident, but it was very faint, indicating that the creature had been gone for a while.

As she stood up to signal to Gaelen, the rear of the boat moving unsteadily under her feet, Nelwyn heard a sound from the brush at the edge of the trees. She spun around in surprise to behold a tall, shadowy figure moving rapidly toward her. It startled her enough to throw her off balance and, with a cry, she fell into the water. The cold numbed her senses for a moment, long enough for the current to pull her away from the bank.

Gaelen gave a cry of alarm, grabbed a slender cord she carried across her shoulders, uncoiled it, pulled a rather unique arrow from her quiver, and tied the cord to it. As she did so, she spotted the tall figure leaping after Nelwyn, who was floundering along a steep and rocky bank grasping at whatever she could. The unknown figure could not reach her, and it soon disappeared amid the thick scrub along the riverbank.

Gaelen held her breath, waiting until Nelwyn had fetched up against a large stone and clung to it, struggling against the wild water.

Seeing her chance, Gaelen drew back with all the strength and skill she could muster, and sent her shot across the river.

The stout, multi-barbed shaft lodged firmly among the stones several feet above Nelwyn's head. The cold had robbed her of her strength, and soon she would no longer be able to stay above water. She didn't dare try to grab the cord—Gaelen would have to help her.

Observing a stout young spruce that hung out over the water, Gaelen acted quickly. Taking only her weapons and one small pack, she tied up her winter cloak, flexed her cold fingers, and leaped up into the branches, securing the cord around the trunk to make a life-line across the river. She climbed hand over hand, swaying in the ever-rising wind, her heels hooked over the line.

The cord was strong, but it stretched under Gaelen's weight, lowering her toward the churning river. She gasped as the cold water soaked her back. It grabbed at her cloak, bow, and quiver and nearly tore her loose, but she hung on, grimacing, until she reached Nelwyn, who was by now exhausted. Gaelen grasped the back of her cousin's sodden cloak, heaved it out of the water, and slung it across one of her shoulders. At that exact moment, Nelwyn lost her grip on the cold stone and was then held to the world only by the sturdy clasp of her cloak. Her eyes were closed, her teeth were chattering, and her strength was gone. She turned over, moaning, as Gaelen's hand found hers and grasped it. The added weight of holding onto Nelwyn pulled Gaelen completely down into the water, and she didn't know whether she could hang on.

She looked up to behold the mysterious figure standing directly over them atop the rocks. It appeared to be either an Elf or a tall, strong young man; she could not yet tell. He threw a rope down to the water, cast off his own cloak, and began to climb toward them.

When he reached them, Gaelen saw that he was, in fact, an Elf. His hair was long and dark, and his grey eyes were anxious. Grasping Gaelen's wrist, he pulled her up and onto the rocks, along with Nelwyn, who was now unconscious. He removed Nelwyn's cloak, which had taken on enough water to weigh as much as Nelwyn herself, and cast it up onto the stones. Then he lifted her and slung her over his shoulder, as Gaelen followed his example with her own sodden cloak.

Gaelen watched as he struggled back up to the top of the rocks, then she grasped the rope with icy hands and climbed slowly and painfully up to join him. She had secured the rope around both of the wet cloaks, for they would be needed and could not easily be replaced. She was not afraid of the newcomer; her instincts told her that he could be trusted, for his eyes held no evil in them.

When she reached the top, Gaelen was pleased to find Nelwyn wrapped in the stranger's dry cloak. He had given her a draught from his flask, and her color was coming back. She would recover quickly once she was warm. The stranger waited for Gaelen, his anxiety and impatience obvious. "Follow me. I have a good shelter and a fire nearby."

"Wait! Who are you, and what is your business here?" asked Gaelen. In answer, the stranger rose to his feet, lifted Nelwyn, and began to walk away. Gaelen was weary, wet, and cold, and she didn't like having her question ignored. It was her opinion that the stranger had most likely startled Nelwyn into the water in the first place; it was the only thing that made sense. Her blood rose as she got to her feet, nocked an arrow, and drew on him, calling in a low, chilly voice:

"If I were you, O Nameless Elf, I wouldn't turn my back to Gaelen, daughter of Tarfion. I would show her the courtesy and respect that are warranted."

"Even if you had just saved her life and the life of her friend?" replied the stranger with a bemused glance over his shoulder. When he saw that he looked down the shaft of an arrow, his amusement faded. Gaelen was obviously in no mood for it.

"Put that away. My name is Galador. I am not your enemy, for if I were I would not have pulled you both from the river. You are obviously cold and weary, and your wits have left you."

"If you were not an enemy and were in possession of YOUR wits, you would not have startled my cousin into the water in the first place, making it necessary for you to pull us from the river," muttered Gaelen. But she lowered her bow and followed him without another word.

It was truly dark, and the weather was positively wretched by the time they reached Galador's promised shelter. It was a rare find—an unoccupied cave in the hillside with a smooth, dry floor. It only went back about twenty feet to a solid wall, but there was a small hole in the ceiling through which smoke from a dying fire was curling. There was another person in the cave, near the fire, wrapped up in a bundle of blankets. Three horses stood by outside, their tails turned to the wind, heads down. As soon as the three Elves entered, Galador spoke to Gaelen.

"Try to get the fire going again, will you?"

He lowered Nelwyn, who was by now reviving nicely, on the opposite side of the fire. He pulled two spare cloaks from a pack in the corner and tossed one to Gaelen, who busied herself with building the fire back up, glancing curiously at the prone figure on the floor nearby. It appeared to be a man, tall and strong, but presently either wounded or ill. She approached him, as Galador moved to join her.

"Who is he? A friend of yours?"

Galador observed the man with grave concern. "Yes, he is a very good friend, and he is very ill. I would help him, but I really don't know what to do for him. I was hoping one of you would be able to heal him."

Gaelen sniffed. "You'd have better luck with the fishermen than with us, I'm afraid. But let Nelwyn take a look when she is recovered. She has some knowledge of healing arts."

The man stirred again, moaning and opening his eyes. He looked right through Gaelen as she placed a hand on his forehead. "He is burning with fever. I have heard my folk speak of this when they have dealings with men. They say that men die of this. How is it that he is ill?"

Galador shrugged. "I don't know. He started getting weak about three days ago. He really isn't himself now. I fear for him, but don't know how to aid him." He looked helplessly at Gaelen. "Any suggestion would be welcomed..." She now understood why he had been in such a hurry to get back, and she would forgive his discourteous treatment of her. Besides, he had pulled them from the river. Her attention now focused on the man lying beside her.

"What is he called?"

"His name is Rogond. Neither he nor I know his heritage, other than as a man of the Tuathar, those of the lost northern realm."

"Tuathar?" Gaelen was intrigued. She had heard of these tall Northmen in stories, and she had even met a few of them when they found their way into the Greatwood. She knew them to be generally good and noble, but mysterious. She was now looking forward to learning more.

Both she and Galador turned at the sound of Nelwyn getting to her feet and moving to join them. She was still cold and weary, but her color had improved. If she rested she would be fine by morning. Gaelen told Nelwyn of all that had happened since the river, and of Galador's wish that they could heal Rogond.

Nelwyn was not hopeful. "Alas! I have no power or knowledge to heal such a sickness. It is beyond my experience," she said.

Gaelen agreed. In the case of a simple wound, they could have been of aid. Even a festering wound, which the Elves thankfully did not suffer, they could have dealt with. But this was a real sickness, of the kind that sometimes devastated whole populations of men.

Nelwyn needed to rest; she was looking a bit wobbly as she tried to rise to her feet. Galador laid hold of her shoulders to steady her, assisting her back to her place by the fire. He sat with her while she rested and ate the food that he offered her.

Gaelen drew the blankets back from the shivering man, recoiling from the stench of sickness that surrounded him. "*Ehyah!*" she exclaimed, and shook her head. Sometimes it seemed that mortal men began dying the minute they were born. She gently probed the man's neck, feeling large, hard lumps beneath his skin at the angle of his jaw. He was sweat-soaked and unshaven, and his face was pale, but she could see that he was a fine representative of his ancient line. He swallowed painfully, opening his eyes again—this time it seemed as though he actually perceived Gaelen for a moment. His brow furrowed and he moaned miserably, shaking with a sudden chill.

Warming up a basin of water, Gaelen gently cleaned the sweat and dirt from his face, speaking soothing words to him as his eyes wandered aimlessly, looking at nothing. They were a beautiful, calm grey, but right now they were red-rimmed and over-bright with fever. Gaelen tried to warm him with more blankets, but it seemed nothing could stop him from shaking.

As his fever burned higher he became delirious, speaking all manner of languages, including at least two rare Elven dialects. Gaelen was fascinated despite her concern. She tried to comfort him, and he would calm in response to her words. Then the chill would take him again, and he would rave incoherently until it passed.

Gaelen glanced over at Galador, who was still hoping that she would think of something to help his stricken friend. She didn't blame him for being anxious. With each episode of chills and delirium, Rogond grew weaker. Soon he would be too weak to fight off the sickness, and then he would be lost.

"I must calm you somehow...to help you ride out the storm of chills and madness. You are like a small ship at the mercy of very large waves. You need…you need an anchor. I will do all I can for you, Tuathan, for you are young, and you have a part to play yet. Now I must hold you to this world."

When the next hard chill came, she drew a deep breath and lay down beside him, steadying him with her hands and her voice. When the fever came on him and he raved at unseen enemies, Gaelen held him down while Nelwyn cooled his brow with clear water. They spoke soft words to him or shouted at him as needed. At times, it was more than a bit frightening.

Rogond was not seeing anything but his enemies, and they were terrifying. At such times he would twist and fight, grabbing Gaelen's slender arms so tightly that she cried out in pain as he tried to push her away. Then Galador would step in, for he was stronger than Gaelen and could easily hold Rogond down. Gaelen would sing her songs, and the enemies would draw away, leaving only peaceful sleep behind them.

Galador looked on in approval. Rogond's life might not be in their power to save, but he certainly had a better chance now. At least someone was doing something. Galador had not known what to do and had despaired, certain that his friend would die. He had thought to bring women to help, but knew that they would be unwilling to expose themselves to the sickness. She-elves were therefore his next choice, for although they knew no more of healing pestilence that he did, they still seemed to have unique instincts. Galador knew, for example, that Gaelen's idea of embracing a raving, sweat-soaked, delirious man would never have occurred to him, but it had certainly made a difference to Rogond.

By dawn's light, Gaelen was weary from serving as Rogond's anchor through the long night. She had sung songs of great power, and they had drained her. As she rested, Galador brought her food and drink, apologized for his initial discourtesy, and thanked her profusely for her effort.

Gaelen assured him that all was well between them. She was now hopeful that Rogond would live, but she knew that it would be awhile before he was strong again. Regardless, she knew that Galador would have to care for him without her.

"We cannot stay here. You will have to take care of him yourself as soon as the fever breaks."

Galador's eyes widened, his dismay obvious. "But...he will need more than I can give, probably for some time. He is a worthy man, worth saving! Why must you leave us in our need?"

"We were tracking the creature that brought the boat ashore. We have been in pursuit for many days, and the trail is cold enough already. I cannot risk losing it altogether."

"What creature? How came you to be tracking it?" asked Galador, who could not understand how the pursuit of an enemy could be more important than saving Rogond.

Gaelen told him the tale, leaving nothing to his imagination. She described the manner in which her friends were killed, the encounters with the fishermen, and the hardships she and Nelwyn had faced since. When she got to the end of the story, at the point that Nelwyn had been startled into the river, Galador's ears reddened and he looked at his hands.

Gaelen smiled at him. "It's all right. She has forgiven you already... at least I think she has."

Beside them, Rogond stirred. He opened his eyes, which looked clearer and more focused than Gaelen had yet seen them. She knew, though, that the fever would probably rise again after sunset. Now was a good time to get some food and drink into him if they could. Rogond needed her now, more than Halrodin did. She sighed, turning back to Galador.

"I will give you another night. If Nelwyn wishes to stay beyond it, that will be her choice. I must continue the hunt or all will be in vain."

Galador still did not understand. "What are you going to do, all by yourself, if you catch up with your enemy? From what you have told me, you won't have a chance. Your friends were experienced and wary, yet he took them with no effort and there were two of them."

"They were unaware of his existence, and I am not," she replied simply. In truth, she hoped Nelwyn would choose to go with her, as tackling the creature by herself had not been in her plan. "I must speak with my cousin. See what you can do to get him to take some food and drink. I will return soon."

Gaelen found Nelwyn stroking the neck of one of the horses—a proud, rough-coated dun animal such as the people of the north favored. The horse acknowledged Gaelen with a soft whicker of greeting, earning a friendly pat. After a moment of reluctance, she put forth her statement with her customary lack of fanfare. "We dare not leave the pursuit for long."

"If we had Galador and Rogond beside us, we would have a better chance of defeating the creature," said Nelwyn. "Have you considered waiting until Rogond is strong, and then asking for their help?"

"The longer we wait, the colder the trail," Gaelen stated with finality. "Will you go with me, then?"

Nelwyn considered for a moment. She turned back to the dun horse and resumed stroking it. "I am not certain of the wisdom of your course, but naturally I will go with you. Do you think I would leave you to face that...that *thing* by yourself?"

"I know that the fire of this chase has burned hotter in me than in you these past days," Gaelen replied.

Nelwyn took a half step back, incredulous. "I have already told you that I would never abandon you to fight this alone. You are the person in this world that I care most about, and you should know it! I won't ask you to break off the chase and go against the desire of your heart."

Gaelen sighed. "I know, and I'm glad to hear it. The only difficulty is that I will not lead you against the desire of *your* heart. I will wait at least one more day. Northmen are rare in these times, and this one is in need of us. I do feel for Galador. I...sort of...promised to stay until the fever breaks."

Nelwyn turned about. "Oh, you *did*, did you?" She quirked a bemused half-smile at Gaelen. "You never could resist a challenge involving the weak and helpless."

Gaelen looked annoyed, but it was obvious that she had kept her good humor. Rogond would have his anchor for at least another day. Tomorrow they would decide again whether to stay with their new allies or rejoin the pursuit of the dark creature that had so easily and successfully eluded them.

3

On the Trail Again

It was three days since they had found the boat by the river, and the Elves were ready to move on. Nelwyn was packing up her gear when Galador approached her, bringing provisions from his own stores. Gaelen had washed their clothing at the riverside and hung it to dry in the late winter sun and wind. In Nelwyn's opinion, Gaelen had used this as an excuse to return to the river and check the boat for herself, as when she returned she had seemed preoccupied and ever more eager to get away.

Before she would leave, however, Gaelen made certain that Rogond was no longer in danger of death. His fever had broken on the second night, after an exhausting delirium that had taxed them all as they fought to calm him. At last he had collapsed, soaked with sweat, and they all feared that he would never move again, until the dawn came and he stirred at last.

Gaelen had still been with him, singing quietly, warming and comforting him with her embrace. Hers was the first face he beheld on awakening, and he later told Galador that it was her voice that had pulled him back from the madness of his delirium as he fought with unseen demons. He started taking food the day after, and it seemed that all would be well provided that he and Galador could stay safely hidden until he was strong again. Gaelen and Nelwyn brought fresh meat from the forest, and they had plenty of good water and dry wood. Galador was reasonably confident that Rogond would be able to ride in a few days.

Now, as Galador handed Nelwyn the provisions he had brought, his grey eyes betrayed his disquiet. He didn't want Nelwyn to go. He was worried for her, and besides, he would miss both her company and her help in caring for Rogond. He spoke to her in his deep, gentle voice while gazing off into the trees.

"Must you leave us now? Why not stay until he is healed, and then we can go all the more swiftly because of the horses."

Nelwyn smiled, touched by his offer of aid. "The horses will not avail us here, Galador. We dare not make too much speed; we may miss some sign. Gaelen and I can move swiftly enough and attract less attention on foot. Rogond will not have his full strength for some time, and it would be unwise for him to leave your sanctuary until he is fully recovered." Then she added, "I would very much like to have your help, and your offer is received with thanks, but I fear that we cannot accept at this time. We have told you of the enemy we seek. Our only chance to defeat him is to catch him before the trail grows so cold that we never find it again."

She cast her eyes toward Gaelen, who was inside with Rogond. "She will never give up, and I cannot abandon her. And I also wish to prevent this monster from doing further harm to our people." She thought of her friend Talrodin and his two sons, remembering the stench of his charred flesh and the difficulty they had in prying his brother's hands from his arm. Her eyes and her voice grew cold. "I also wish vengeance for my friends."

She looked at Galador, and she could see that he was troubled. He did not know what he could say to dissuade her, though he felt an almost desperate urge to do so. "I sense that if you leave now, without me, it will mean your doom," he said quietly.

At this Nelwyn sighed and turned away. "Then doom it must be, for we are leaving."

Gaelen, who had approached without seeing Galador at first, had overheard this last exchange and now knew that Galador was trying to delay Nelwyn further.

"Take heart!" she said with false brightness. "We have tarried here so long that the trail is undoubtedly cold by now, and the doom you fear will be quite unlikely. Perhaps we'll come back when we realize that all efforts of the last fortnight have been in vain."

Galador bristled at her, as it seemed she would not take him seriously.

"You're so confident that you can handle this enemy yourselves. Tell me, Gaelen, have you ever seen real battle? Or is your experience limited to ambushing stray Ulcas in the forest? Do you not understand that my wish to delay you is grounded in the desire to help you?"

Nelwyn's eyes widened—these were bold questions. Gaelen stood before them, her face calm. She did not immediately answer

Galador, but set her pack down and unlaced the front of her shirt. Pulling it aside, she displayed a jagged scar that ran diagonally from her collarbone on her left shoulder.

"This was made by a blade forged by an evil hand. Ambushing Ulcas is sometimes a dangerous business. Our people have been fighting and dying for untold years trying to safeguard the Great Forest, yet it grows ever more perilous. None of us can be sure of returning home. In the north it is only safe to travel because of our vigilance and skill. Ask Nelwyn to show you the marks of *her* encounters. Our skills and experience are at least as valuable in dealing with an enemy that hides and strikes the unwary as those of one who has cut down his enemies in open battle."

Nelwyn remembered the origin of the mark on Gaelen's shoulder. She had come as close to dying as was possible before the healers had pulled her back. The wound still pained her at times, and it was not her only mark. Nelwyn, too, bore evidence of the perils they had faced. True, neither had seen the sort of warfare Galador was referring to, but they had certainly seen their share of battle.

Galador was abashed. "I meant no disrespect," he said, staring at Gaelen's shoulder. Only a dark blade would leave such a mark, and he knew what it had cost her. "And you're right. Open warfare would not prepare you for this enemy. I wonder, though, how you will fare when you finally encounter it. Have you any thought as to what sort of creature it is?"

Gaelen nodded in acknowledgment of his apology. "The signs left near the boat are confusing. There were traces of some sort of strange blood left behind. I tried to identify it, but it is outside my experience. I only know that it is not the blood of Ulca, or man, or Elf. It is…something else, but whether from the creature or some unknown victim, I cannot say." She lifted her light pack from the ground after re-lacing her shirt front, then slung her bow over her shoulder and turned to Nelwyn.

"Are you ready to depart?"

Nelwyn looked at Galador, who had by now lost all hope that she would stay but was still imploring her with his eyes. Nelwyn had made her intentions clear, and she did not waver. "Yes, I'm ready. Have you made your farewells to the Aridan?"

"No. I would rather not disturb him, as he is resting. Galador can say our farewells to him when he awakens and can explain why it was necessary to leave him. He will be all right with time and care; what he needs most is rest."

She said farewell to Galador and headed out toward the river without waiting for her cousin. Galador waited until she was out of sight, and turned then to Nelwyn.

"Since you feel you must leave, I bid you farewell, O Daughter of the Greatwood. May your steps be swift and your aim be true. May you both escape the fate that I fear awaits you...I would look upon you again."

Her expression encouraged him, and he took her in a stiff, somewhat awkward embrace. Then, with a last "Farewell," he turned and strode back to the cave so that he would not have to watch her go.

Rogond awoke in misery some hours later, his head pounding and his entire body wrung out and sore. He sat up slowly, groaned, reached for his water-skin, and took a long draught from it. The cool water felt good going down, but it did little to ease his discomfort. His friend Galador was stoking the fire. Rogond noticed that the Elf seemed tense; his movements were mechanical, not fluid and relaxed as they normally were. He started to ask Galador about it, but his head swam, and he suddenly felt ill enough to lie down again. He closed his eyes and breathed deeply until his head cleared. He opened his eyes again, at first focusing on Galador.

Then Rogond noticed that Gaelen and Nelwyn were nowhere in evidence, nor was their gear. He turned onto his side, trying to ignore the ache in his muscles and the vague tingling in his hands and feet, which went quite nicely with the ringing in his ears.

"Where is Gaelen?" he asked, knowing the answer already.

"She and Nelwyn have gone. You don't know the story of how they came to be by the river, and I fear it may distress you," replied Galador, pulling back his long, dark hair to keep it out of the fire as he leaned over to tend the coals.

Rogond propped himself up on one elbow. "So tell me, then. I'm already distressed that she is gone, without even a farewell." He was pale, still unshaven, and he trembled as he attempted to remain upright. Galador crossed to sit beside him, bade him lie back down, and told him all he knew of the Elves' tale. Gaelen had not left much out; Galador was able to paint a vivid picture for Rogond, who was dismayed and troubled by what he heard.

There was something disturbingly familiar about the story. As a child, Rogond had been fostered by a group of Elves who frequented the lower elevations of the Verdant Mountains. One memorable, tragic summer, four of them had died badly by an unknown hand. They had been set upon, tortured, disfigured, and left to be found by their horrified kinsmen. There had been the same strange odor and the same difficulty in tracking. Oh, it had been easy enough for a while, then the sign would fade and disappear altogether, as though the marauder had sprouted wings and flown from their grasp.

There had been other killings, other victims found, but only the Elves had been so tormented. No one in Rogond's foster family could make sense of it; they only knew that this enemy was a creature of hate. What if Gaelen and Nelwyn approached it armed only with their slender bows and fine arrows? What if the creature, in its cunning manner, caught them unawares? Rogond asked three questions, and received three answers.

"Do you care for them?"

"Yes, of course," Galador replied.

"Do you trust me?"

"Yes."

"How soon can we be ready to ride?"

Galador considered. "Let's wait until tomorrow morning. You will have a hard time staying mounted unless you rest for today at least."

Rogond took another long drink, curled up before the fire, and tried to will his pain to go away. Whether successful or not, he would be following Gaelen in the morning.

Rogond, who had not slept well, roused himself at dawn. He washed and dressed, shaved off his scruffy beard, and presented himself to his companion, who was readying the horses and packs. Galador looked at him in approval.

"You still resemble a walking carcass, but the shaving has helped. How do you feel?"

"Like a walking carcass. But if I don't tax myself I should be all right. I'm anxious to be riding again."

One of the horses, the strong dun, nickered softly at Rogond.

Galador chuckled. "It seems that Eros is eager to be away, as well. Let's hope for a gentle ride."

Rogond's horse had a streak of mischief in him that was occasionally inconvenient, but he stood patiently as Rogond mounted with some difficulty. The horse sensed that Rogond was not himself and bore him with care. Eros was a fine animal, one of a noble, hardy race prized in northern lands. He was thick-coated and proud of bearing, stronger than he was swift, but tireless and steady. The other two horses were Galador's own Réalta, a silver-white grey, more refined and swifter but less powerful than Eros, and Cronan, a sturdy chestnut pack-horse.

Following Nelwyn and Gaelen proved to be more difficult than Galador had foreseen. For one thing, the She-elves were not mounted and could therefore pass obstacles that horsemen would have to ride around. They could negotiate narrow paths, wend their way through tangled undergrowth, and climb sheer, rocky inclines where the horses could not go. For another, they were swift, hardy, and unencumbered by a comrade whose strength and endurance were in doubt. Galador didn't really hold much hope of catching them so long as Rogond was with him, but neither would he risk leaving his closest friend behind. He had observed that men were occasionally quite sensitive about the relative frailty of their bodies. It didn't help matters that many Elves weren't shy about reminding them; though most tried to be kind, they were often seen as patronizing. The last thing Galador wanted was to hurt his friend's dignity.

Rogond had managed to mount his horse with some help from Galador, but he could not make speed. He was still very weak, and Galador feared he would fall if pressed too hard. It fell to Galador to dismount and follow what signs there were; even after all this time there was more evidence of the passing of the enemy than of the two Wood-elves. Rogond trailed behind, keeping a watchful eye for any who would approach.

As the afternoon waned, Rogond suddenly swayed in the saddle as a wave of dizziness took him. He leaned over the horse's neck, clutching at the thick, black mane, fighting the darkness that clouded his sight as a deafening roar filled his ears. Perhaps this had not been such a wise idea, but there was no turning back now. Galador sensed his distress and was soon at his side, his face disquieted.

"Are you fit to continue? If not, we can rest for a while." He shook his head. "You look truly ill, my friend. It makes no sense to drain your strength in this pursuit. Let's make camp and continue tomorrow."

Rogond considered for a moment. Though he struggled against it, his body probably wasn't strong enough to continue. Yet to rest now would mean losing the She-elves, perhaps forever. They would need his aid—he was certain of it. He bit his lip, the pain bringing his thoughts back to clarity and his vision into focus. He knew that Galador would stop rather than risk his friend's return to health. Rogond would just have to convince him.

"I feel my strength coming back…I'll be fine to ride yet awhile. We dare not wait, Galador. You know it."

"Yes, they have gained ground on us since this morning, and I fear they will not rest or delay their pursuit," said Galador. "Our only hope lies in the enemy. If it reaches the river and decides to cross, they will lose the sign, for they cannot follow across the river on foot. For that they will need a boat…or horses."

He looked up at Rogond, whose face brightened at the prospect. If Gaelen or Nelwyn needed to cross the icy-cold river, they would have to wait until the horses arrived. From then on, all would travel together. The thought cheered both Rogond and Galador, and they continued their slow progress to the south and east, toward the River Ambros.

The twilight came on just as Gaelen and Nelwyn reached the western bank. They had passed through these lands before, carrying messages to and from the Elven-realm of Tal-sithian, which stood upon an island in the center of the great lake known as the Linnefionn. The river had widened out south of the rapids and was now steady and calm. They knew that it would soon begin its slow meandering through wide, green meadows that would give way again to woodlands. Then it would grow much broader as it received the waters of the River Artan.

Gaelen crept quietly through the scrub that flanked the river course, tracking their enemy right up to the water's edge. Incredibly, it appeared that the creature had waded into the cold water. Though she and Nelwyn searched both up and down the bank for some distance, there was no sign that it had ever come out again. That meant it had crossed the river under its own power, but how?

The brief look at its silhouette had suggested armor to Gaelen, and swimming would have been difficult. She had found no cast-off armor. Had it tried to make the crossing and failed? That was unlikely. It was probably safely on the other side of the river by now. What other strange powers did it possess? One thing was certain—something had drawn it to the eastern shore, because if that had been the original intent it would not have landed on the west bank in the first place. Gaelen feared for whatever, or whoever, had attracted it. If it was the promise of another victim, she knew that Elvish blood would be spilled before dawn. She had felt some of the malevolence of her enemy like a surge of ice water in her veins, once when she locked eyes with Halrodin, again when she beheld the creature going away down the river, and once again when she touched her fingers to the strange blood in the boat.

She was aroused from this dreadful thought by Nelwyn, who had found no sign of the enemy. So, the creature must have crossed. They could not follow it without a boat. They had been thwarted.

Nelwyn, ever the optimist, tried to salvage Gaelen's hopes. "Perhaps a boat will come down river, and we may ask whoever is guiding it to help us cross."

Gaelen looked over at her friend with a rather sour, sarcastic expression.

"Yes, Nelwyn, that will happen. But not before some great bird swoops down from the mountains, lifts us up, and carries us across. At any rate, I am tired, hungry, and discouraged. I need to lie back, listen to the river, and pretend that I am free of this terrible task and may go where I will. Perhaps the river will bring news."

At this, Gaelen dropped to her knees among the soft reeds before lying on her back, eyes raised toward the stars. She tried to clear her mind and fill it with the soothing song of the river, but she could not escape the feeling of dread that had come over her. As she looked toward the rising of Eádri, the evening star, and at the three bright stars in the belt of Fiana the Huntress, she was unaware that, at the same time, an Elf named Gelmyr was enjoying his last sight of those same stars from what he believed to be a secure resting place. And as Gelmyr met his doom at the hands of Gorgon Elfhunter, both Gaelen and Nelwyn shivered in the moonlight, suddenly overwhelmed with uneasiness and a profound sense of loss. It was as though the light of the stars had dimmed, and they would never be truly happy again.

In their own encampment, Galador and Rogond sat huddled together against the dark chill. Rogond was exhausted. Galador knew that when his friend was healthy he was as hard and tough as iron, but this sickness had really laid him low. He was shivering miserably, trying to sleep, as Galador kept watch. Eros was standing nearby, looking at them both rather intently with his large, liquid brown eyes.

"What are you looking at? Go on and graze with your companions," said Galador, indicating the other two horses. Eros ignored Galador, approaching until he stood right beside Rogond, then reached down and nuzzled the top of his head. Galador was about to wave him off when Eros sank to his knees, lying carefully down behind Rogond, who took advantage of the opportunity, resting back against the warm body of the animal. He stopped shivering almost at once, and Galador smiled before turning to regard Réalta.

"Now take a lesson in faithfulness! I have underestimated the depth of your character, Eros. If you will permit me, I, too, will share in your warmth." So saying, he joined Rogond and was soon warm and reasonably content. He maintained his watchfulness, though the horses would probably alert him if any evil creature came near. As the stars wheeled above him he grew uneasy, hearing what sounded like faint, distant cries, but he told himself that it was only the wind. He prayed that Nelwyn would be kept safe, and that he would soon find her again.

4

The Fate of Gelmyr

The river wove with lazy abandon among open meadows that were now the brown of winter. The nearby trees were both tall and strong, and would provide a refuge for the lone Elf who stood on the banks of the Ambros, surveying the landscape with satisfaction. His name was Gelmyr, and he had been journeying from the Linnefionn for only a short while. It was always pleasant there, even in winter, for the Elven-realm of Tal-sithian was evergreen and beautiful.

Gelmyr was in no particular hurry to reach the mountain-realm of Monadh-talam. In fact, he had diverted west, for he so loved the Great River. He would linger awhile before continuing north and then eastward, for he would need to cross the tall mountains known as the Monadh-hin. In winter, this would be difficult. The people of Tal-sithian had offered to send emissaries to accompany him, as they could certainly find business in Monadh-talam, and traveling alone in these times was unsafe. Gelmyr had declined the offer of an escort; he was a skilled and fearless warrior, had often traveled alone, and felt there was little left in Alterra to thwart him compared with what he had already endured.

Gelmyr was descended from the mighty, and he was counted mighty himself. He was of great age, having fought many times beneath the banner of the High King Ri-Elathan beside his friend Magra, who was one of the most renowned warriors of Alterra. Gelmyr was traveling to Mountain-home in the hope of reuniting with Magra, and he expected little difficulty on the journey. He was unlikely to encounter real danger until he crossed the mountains. For now, he enjoyed the shelter of trees and the soothing sound of the river as he prepared to rest and partake of food and drink. He did not realize that watchful eyes were upon him as dusk turned to deep twilight, and the first stars appeared.

Gelmyr made no fire, as he needed none. The weather had gentled down such that a winter cloak was more than adequate, and the ground was reasonably dry. All the same, he decided to climb a tree where he could pass the night in safety, relaxing and gazing at the ever-brightening winter stars.

Gorgon Elfhunter wasn't usually so lucky when he passed through the area between the mountains and the lake. At times he felt that, despite the misery of his life, he was blessed. Had not Gelmyr happened along just when he was needed? It was not typical of their kind to travel alone, yet here he was—perfect prey. Not a Wood-elf, either. Oh, no indeed! This was a powerful, seasoned warrior from the look of him. He had no doubt seen battle aplenty, but he would have little defense now. All the same, Gorgon would need to be cautious. The memory of the terror of the Wood-Elf in the forest, the one who had tried to defend his companion, was fading from Gorgon's mind. He needed a new victim to sustain him until he reached the mountains. Then he would go to ground for a while.

He waited until Gelmyr had relaxed in his tall sanctuary, gazing at the glittering stars, which promised to be so bright. All Elves were united in their love of starlight; they took great comfort in it and tried always to view the stars by night. Gorgon did not share Gelmyr's affection for them. He fitted a large, blunt-tipped arrow to his powerful bow, for he meant to cripple Gelmyr, not to kill him as yet. With his pale, sharp eyes, Gorgon located his intended target—the base of Gelmyr's spine was clearly visible as he lay half-reclining against a limb, eyes cast upward.

Gelmyr was just thinking of the cold, rushing waters of the Mountain-realm, and how pleasant it would be to see his friend Magra, when a violent blow struck him, knocking his relaxed body clear of its support so that he fell awkwardly to the ground, dazed and in pain. He gasped and tried to clear his head—what had happened? He felt a dull agony in the middle of his back and sharp, stabbing pains filling his shoulders, chest, and arms. Below his waist he felt nothing.

As soon as his head cleared he drew his blade, trying to listen for his enemy through the sound of his own labored breathing. His eyes were wide and filled with pain and confusion as he searched in all directions, moaning as he tried to turn over. When his legs would not answer, he knew his back was broken. He also knew that he would soon be dead even if his enemy never appeared, as he was now helpless and alone in the wild. No one would look for him, and some enemy or wild thing would surely take him. At least if the one who had felled him came near, he would be ready.

He gritted his teeth and waited, sword in hand, breath whistling in his throat. He could hear slow, cautious footsteps approaching and could smell an unpleasant odor on the wind. He first beheld his enemy— immense, dark, menacing, armored and helmeted, a curved sword in hand. Gelmyr's eyes fixed on Gorgon's—those strangely pale, cold eyes filled with malicious pleasure at the sight of his seemingly helpless foe.

Gelmyr waited, hoping the monster would draw near enough to strike, but Gorgon was not so easily lured close. He knew he had time, and he intended to take it. Gelmyr tried to remain still and silent, but a sudden wave of pain came over him, and he shuddered and groaned through clenched teeth. Gorgon smiled, though Gelmyr could not see his dark face well enough to perceive it.

"Put the sword aside, for it will not avail you, O Already Dead," he growled in an almost amiable tone.

Gelmyr snarled in answer. "Come but closer, and we shall see!" Then, in his own tongue, he said: "You are craven to cripple and then attack. You dared not challenge me until first rendering me helpless, but I am not so helpless as you think. It will take a greater warrior than you to defeat Gelmyr of the Èolar!" He spat at Gorgon, who actually chuckled in his deep, oily voice.

"You think I do not understand your tongue? I speak it as well as you do, Èolo!"

Gelmyr was both astonished and horrified, but did not completely lose his wits. As Gorgon approached him, he suddenly lashed out with his blade, thinking to strike the legs of his foe, but Gorgon leaped back and met the blade with his own. Trying to rise, Gelmyr propped himself on his elbow, frustrated and in pain, as Gorgon sought to disarm him. Their blades rang as they clashed together, for both were Elven-made. Each stroke was an agony of effort for Gelmyr, but still he fought, lashing out like an eagle cornered in a cage. At last, however, his strength waned, and Gorgon struck his sword-arm, disarming him and bringing fresh blood onto the grass.

Gelmyr now had only his long knife, which he pointed at Gorgon with a trembling left hand. Chest heaving, eyes desperate, he had dragged himself painfully backward until he came up against a tangle of roots at the base of the tree he had sheltered in and could go no further. Gorgon laughed at Gelmyr's desperation, but he still didn't like the look of the knife. Picking up a length of fallen limb from the ground, he swung hard at Gelmyr's left hand, connected with a satisfactory "crack", and knocked the knife free. Casually, he went to retrieve it knowing that his victim was not going anywhere.

Pain and hopelessness had blunted Gelmyr's senses; he was barely conscious by the time Gorgon returned to him. Gorgon shook his head and went to work binding Gelmyr's wrists together, having broken the left one with his disarming stroke. Throwing a rope over a low-hanging limb, he hoisted Gelmyr so that his feet dangled inches from the ground. Then he waited patiently for his prey to revive. Gelmyr would have done better to have died then, but he did not, for he was made of harder material than most. He came to with the rising of the moon, a great golden orb that hung low in the eastern sky. Soon the land would be nearly as bright as in twilight, which to the eyes of an Elf is as daylight to a man.

"I will not kill you, Elf, until you hear my tale. Then, if your response pleases me, I will kill you quickly. If not, I will leave you here to beg for death," said Gorgon.

Gelmyr knew that he had seen his last sunrise, whatever happened. He fought back the pain and stared stoically into the eyes of his enemy. Then he spoke, still defiant, still proud.

"Do as you will, you cannot break my spirit. I do not know of what vile race you were spawned, but know this: my kindred will avenge my death, and they will not be merciful."

Gorgon genuinely laughed at this, a horrible sound filled not with mirth, but with malice. "What vile race, indeed! You truly cannot know, cannot conceive. But you SHALL know ere death takes you. Then much may your pride avail you, Warrior-elf! As for your kin, I fervently hope they do seek vengeance, for that will bring them to me, and they shall suffer the same fate."

Gorgon brought his face close to Gelmyr's, so that Gelmyr nearly swooned from his foul breath and terrible disfigurement. Every inch of him was covered with a web of raised, tangled scars. Only his eyes appeared untouched. They were pale grey, clear, and bright with hostility. He spoke softly to Gelmyr, watching the Elf's expression change—from defiance to a sort of horror tinged with pity—as he heard Gorgon's tale.

By the time Gorgon had nearly finished his story, he had worked himself into a state of fury. He began striking Gelmyr with his curved blade, bringing blood but not death, as his victim writhed in pain and terror. Gorgon threw down the blade and stood panting and angry, consumed with hate. Grabbing Gelmyr's jaw he lifted the Elf's head so that their eyes met for the last time. Then, with his other hand, he removed his own helmet. Gelmyr might have cried out in horror had he the strength. With his last sight he beheld the true face of his enemy, and he knew then that the creature before him was terrible indeed.

Gorgon killed Gelmyr with a single stroke to the side of his neck, releasing a flood of bright blood and draining the life from him in a few moments. He had promised to do so if Gelmyr heard his tale, and the reaction to it had been more than fulfilling. Gorgon would leave the body where it was, after stripping it of weapons and provisions. Then he would continue west to one of his many underground resting places and lie low for a while. This had been a most uplifting encounter, better than he had hoped for. It cheered him that this was undoubtedly an important Elf, one who would be missed and mourned by many. The Èolar were already all but extinct, and Gorgon had just brought them one step closer. For now, his blood-lust was sated and he could rest.

He had some fine new weapons to add to his stores, and he had become especially fond of the sword he had taken from the Darkmere. He held it up in the moonlight, the blade of Turantil glittering through the blood of its victim. Gorgon wiped it on the brown grass before sheathing it again, gathered his stolen provisions, and headed toward the mountains. He paused before Gelmyr's body and gazed into his now-sightless eyes.

"Gelmyr. *Gel-meeer*," Gorgon muttered with disdainful sneer. "Your pride has always been your undoing, Èolo--how fortunate for you that I have taken it from you." He laughed and spat on the ground at Gelmyr's feet. It was always best when, at the end, their pride left them. With some difficulty he replaced his helmet and then disappeared into the night.

5

The Trail is Lost

Gaelen and Nelwyn were still lingering near the river bank when Galador found them on the following afternoon. He had left Rogond with Eros and galloped straight toward the river, intending to follow its course until he found them. Réalta ran with his tail in the air, for the slow going of yesterday was not to his liking, and he stretched himself and ran with enthusiasm. Galador reveled in the sound of his mount's swift feet on the grass and the wind in his long hair as he sat tall and proud, cloak unfurled behind him. He was alive, his friend was healing, and Nelwyn was waiting. At least, so he hoped.

Rogond had agreed to remain behind because he knew that catching Gaelen quickly was his best hope of ever seeing her again. He was stronger this morning, but still was not up to riding very far or very fast. Réalta was the swiftest, and when he was in full flight Eros could not keep up with him. Rogond patted the dun's shaggy neck and was rewarded with a nuzzle at his hip.

"Never mind, Eros, you have proven your usefulness on countless occasions. The efficient may prevail where the swift falter."

"Efficient" was a good word for Eros. He maintained on very little feed, unlike Réalta, who grew lean where the grazing was poor. He was very steady in his way of going; he did not tire his rider or his own legs with erratic movements and hard pounding. Eros flowed like water over nearly any terrain; hence he had been named for the gentle River Eros that fed into the Ambros from the north.

The first sign of trouble came as the horses raised their heads and turned them to the southeast, their ears pricked and their bodies tense as they stood motionless. Rogond also stood riveted, listening. A sudden whistling sound pierced the air as a dark arrow sped through the trees, startling all three of them. In the dim light of morning Rogond could only see that the arrow had flown from the direction of a large pile of rocks near their resting-place. He dropped quickly to the ground as a second arrow flew, striking the pack horse behind the elbow, felling him. This was a marksman of some skill, and Rogond feared for Eros. Taking shelter behind a large stump, he whistled and shouted to his mount, seeking to move him out of range.

"Run, Eros! Run toward the river until I call you!"

A third shaft flew, barely missing the animal's shaggy neck. Rogond flapped his cloak at the horse, crying, "RUN, I tell you!"

Looking just a little offended, Eros turned and trotted off toward the river as Rogond reached for his bow, only to remember that his quiver was still attached to the saddle. He swallowed hard and cursed his lack of alertness. Only his recent illness could explain it. How ironic for Galador to find Gaelen and Nelwyn at last, only to wait by the river for his friend who would never come. There were at least two reasons why Rogond could not let that happen. First, he would not look upon Gaelen or hear her song again. And second, his spirit would have to endure the knowledge that he had been picked off easily, as might a fool traveling without skill. For the pride and honor of his race, he would have to prevail.

He hoped there was but a single enemy, but as he leapt from the shelter of the stump and grabbed his spear, he was disheartened to see three Ulcas rush from their rocky concealment, yelling and waving their crude but deadly blades. Their dark, ugly faces were drawn into a snarl, and they squinted even in the dim light of dawn. Their strategy was clear: they had intended to kill both horses, undoubtedly to eat later, then to kill Rogond, whom they had rightly perceived as outnumbered. They would have eaten him, also.

What they had not known was that Rogond's lack of awareness was only momentary. He called back toward the river, sword in one hand and spear in the other, bracing for the fight.

"Eros! Eros! I need you! Come to me!"

The three Ulcas burst into the clearing, but they checked back at the sight of Rogond. What they had thought to be an unwary traveler appeared now as a tall warrior, well-armed and stern-faced, keen of eye and strong of limb. It was only partially true; Rogond was still weak from his illness. The Ulcas were deceived nonetheless, and they drew back for a moment.

"Come on, you miserable rats!" snarled Rogond. "It is time for you to join your pathetic ancestors in whatever forsaken pit they dwell!"

Without waiting for them to react, Rogond sent his spear straight into the heart of the first Ulca, and then lashed out with his long blade at the others, who leaped upon him, waving their dark and pitted weapons. Normally they would be no match for Rogond, who was skilled at arms and had seen real battle, but in his weakened state he was slow to react, and his strokes lacked their usual power. His skill was far superior to theirs, but his strength was ebbing quickly. It looked as though he would meet with a lowly fate, until Eros burst between Rogond and his enemies, trampling one handily while knocking both Rogond and the remaining Ulca to the ground.

Rogond had retained his grip on his sword-hilt. The Ulca was swifter to rise, and it leapt upon him as he dodged its last stroke. Rogond drove the sword into its belly, releasing its dark blood, and the encounter ended.

Winded, head swimming, Rogond lay for a while on the grass, praying that these were the only ones he would contend with this day. Eros approached him, nuzzling his face and tickling it with his long whiskers. Rogond blew hard into the horse's nostrils, causing him to step back, tossing his head in the air. Then, after getting rather gingerly to his feet, Rogond patted Eros' strong neck.

"Well done, my friend. May your forelock flourish and keep the flies from your face."

He surveyed the scene before him. Eros would now have to carry the packs, as Cronan lay dead where he had fallen. After instructing Eros to stay in the clearing, Rogond tracked the Ulcas back for a little way just to make certain there would be no further threats. He was not fearful, as he was now on his guard, and the dawn had truly broken.

What he found when he had gone back along the Ulcas' trail dismayed him. There were nearly a dozen dead, in two groups of five and six, killed with swift efficiency. The tracks that went away were confusing, but Rogond soon read them as Gaelen's and Nelwyn's mingled with those of the enemy they tracked. So, the creature was not a friend of Ulcas, either. The three that had attacked Rogond must have escaped its notice, or been away from the other groups when the attacks came. From the look of things, these unfortunate ones had been dead for five days or more.

Rogond was thankful for that, as Gaelen and Nelwyn were still on the trail of the enemy, but they were unlikely to catch up unless it had tarried near the river. All tracks did indeed go back to the Ambros. Rogond hoped that Galador had found the Elves already and would be waiting for him. Returning to Eros, he removed their gear from the body of Cronan and patted his still form with affectionate regret.

"Farewell, my sturdy friend. Rest here forever on the grass you loved." He packed their belongings onto Eros, who snorted and tossed his head. "It's no use complaining about it," said Rogond. "We both must go on feet today." He turned and led Eros westward, following the tracks of Réalta.

When evening came and there was still no sign of Rogond, Galador began to worry. The plan had been for Rogond to follow Réalta, mounted on Eros and leading Cronan, at a pace that would not tax him. He would therefore have been expected by now, as Galador had accomplished the task of locating Nelwyn and Gaelen by early afternoon. Even at a walk, Eros could have caught up. To Galador's delight, Nelwyn had been more than happy to see him.

Gaelen had also greeted him with enthusiasm, though she appeared even more delighted to see Réalta. Here was the answer to her river-crossing problem! She looked back north, hoping to see Rogond coming up from behind, but found no sign of him.

"Where is Rogond? He surely has not been lost, or you would not be in such good spirits."

"He is following, but slowly. I expect he will be here in a few hours. He leads the pack horse."

"How is he faring? Is he well? Surely he is not yet strong," said Gaelen, concerned at the thought of Rogond traveling alone. When she had last seen him, he had been fairly helpless.

"He is far from strong, yet is stronger than he was. He will recover if he is not overly taxed."

If Rogond had overheard, he might have wondered whether fighting off Ulcas and having to walk all those miles when he was supposed to be riding constituted being overly taxed. However, this seemed to satisfy Gaelen, who now occupied herself with thoughts of pursuing her enemy across the river on horseback and seeing Rogond again, in that order.

As they all waited for Rogond, Nelwyn and Galador renewed their friendship. Nelwyn told of all that had passed since their departure. She spoke of the slain Ulcas they had found, more of the creature's handiwork. They had been killed, but not tortured or maimed; it seemed that honor was reserved for Elves alone. Then Nelwyn asked Galador why they had followed so quickly.

"Rogond was insistent, as I told him of your enemy, and he feared for you. I believe he has known of this enemy before. He told me some dreadful tales about it."

Nelwyn grew agitated. "So he *knows* it? What did he tell you? Does he know its nature or how it may be killed?"

Galador calmed her. "Hush. The last thing we need to do is arouse Gaelen. She would probably run back on foot to find Rogond if she thought he had useful information. No, neither he nor his people had much insight into the creature that so terrorized them, but the pattern you described was so similar, he knew it was either the same creature or its twin brother."

Nelwyn looked over at her cousin, who was now sitting preoccupied on the river bank, staring fixedly out to the south and west, her thoughts clouded by an unshakable melancholy. Gaelen sensed that something evil had happened in the night, not far from their encampment. Though she normally did not sleep in the manner of men, she did sometimes experience a kind of waking dream. Last night's had been a bad one. As the moon rose high, Nelwyn had found her, trembling and pale, eyes wide and staring, mouthing the same words over and over: "Aontar release me, Aontar take me…"

Nelwyn had grasped her shoulders, shaking her lightly, calling her name. She came out of her trance-like state slowly, still whispering the name of Aontar. As Nelwyn looked deep into her cousin's eyes, they shared the same feeling—their enemy had killed again. They sat together in quiet sorrow for whatever poor soul they did not know, in hope that his spirit would find safe passage to its eternal home.

Now Gaelen turned and invited Nelwyn to sit beside her. The afternoon was waning into twilight, which came so early in the winter. After that would come the cold darkness, and there was still no sign of Rogond. They both looked over at Galador, who was saddling Réalta, preparing to backtrack and find his friend. His ageless face could not conceal the worry he felt, and Nelwyn didn't like it. She wanted to go along, but Réalta could not carry the three of them, and she didn't want to leave Gaelen alone. Galador promised to return as soon as he could and then was gone.

He had ridden about five anxious miles when he finally found Rogond. It was alarming to see that there was no pack horse, and that Eros was now carrying both Rogond and their gear. Rogond had walked until he could walk no more, then he had persuaded Eros to carry both himself and the packs, and told him to follow Réalta. Once mounted, he had slept. He was still asleep when Galador rode up; not even Réalta's loud greeting of Eros had awakened him. Galador jumped down from his horse and ran to Eros, taking hold of the bridle. The dun was undaunted by his heavy load and didn't seem to understand Galador's distress, but Galador didn't know whether Rogond was wounded, sleeping, or dead. The absence of Cronan was a bad sign.

He roused his friend with some difficulty; the strain of the encounter with the Ulcas and the long walk of so many miles had thoroughly worn him out. But now that he had slept a little, his mind and his eyes were clear. He was certainly happy to see Galador and began looking around for Gaelen at once.

"She is not here. We must ride back a few miles, but they are both safe. Tomorrow we will cross the river."

Galador then asked Rogond to tell what had happened. Where was Cronan? What had taken so long? Rogond told his tale as they made their way back to the river in the dark, ultimately falling asleep again as Eros walked with gentle, quiet care, his feet lighting softly on the hard ground.

The next day they crossed the river. It was deadly cold, and the current was treacherous, but the water was not as deep as they had feared. They made it with the help of the horses, leaving all that they could spare behind. The horses did have to swim, but not for long, and they got to the other side with most of the gear dry. Rogond had slept well indeed once he had been reunited with the Elves, as there were now many watchful eyes and he could do so without worry.

The four of them rode south as the river began her slow turning and meandering, and the grassy, shrubby banks backed by forest began to turn to open land with only scattered trees. They chose to stop for the night, sheltering under a bank where they could rest together. As Rogond began to drift off, he asked Gaelen to sing.

"No, Tuathan. I cannot sing tonight. A great evil has been done near here. Nelwyn and I both sensed it, and tomorrow I fear we will find the proof. Instead, I would hear your tale. Galador has told me that you know something of this enemy already. Will you not share with us?"

Rogond told all that he knew of the vile creature, and when he had finished, the Elves agreed that indeed it was, if not the same evil, at least of similar ilk. Galador wondered whether some of the stories he had heard told of mysterious disappearances in and around the Verdant Mountains had been related to the experiences of Rogond's people. There were reports of Elves who journeyed to the Twilight Shores, but did not reach them. Some had been found dead by their companions, and some had never been found at all. Those who were found had not died easily. In truth, Gorgon was not responsible for all of those lost ones, but he had a hand in many an unpleasant ending. These incidents, and the inevitable tales that resulted, had been going on for a long, long time.

Hearing of this again had unsettled Galador so that he could not rest. He rose and climbed up onto the bank where he could see and hear all around him. There he sat, alone and watchful, as Nelwyn regarded him, settling back against the bank next to Gaelen and Rogond, who was soon fast asleep.

When the wind shifted so that it blew from the south, the Elves' worst suspicions were confirmed. Galador caught it first as he stood watch. Nelwyn felt Gaelen tremble as she lifted her head, scenting the air. Then Nelwyn also detected it—the smell of blood and corruption, of suffering and death. As Nelwyn spoke comforting words to Gaelen to stop her trembling, she lifted her eyes up to Galador's. She was truly glad of his company, but she hoped that she had not led him into a situation from which none would escape.

The Elves could not rest after that, as each was lost in his or her own thoughts. Gaelen's dreams had unnerved her, and she dreaded the dawn. Nelwyn was afraid also, for all of them. Galador, who alone among the Elves had yet to actually experience the violence of this enemy, was nonetheless disquieted. His thoughts turned more and more often to Nelwyn and how he longed to tell her that he would defend her unto death, though he hoped it would not come to that.

They first caught sight of what remained of Gelmyr in the late morning. He was still hanging from the tall tree, swaying slightly in the wind. They debated as to whether it would be safe to approach him, but Gaelen could tell by the faintness of the enemy's scent that he was long gone. In fact, Gorgon had been gone for more than two full days. They were wary nonetheless as they approached Gelmyr, for his body had been left hanging for someone to find, and perhaps there were traps and snares. But they found none, and as they drew near to him Galador started back in dismay.

"But, he is of the Èolar!" he said, amazed.

"I remember him. He came as emissary to the Greatwood long ago, along with his friend Magra. His name is…Gelmyr, as I recall," said Gaelen.

"It was Gelmyr," said Nelwyn sadly. She, too, remembered Gelmyr together with Magra—two powerful Elf-lords at Ri-Aruin's table. How different he had looked then!

Rogond drew his long knife and cut Gelmyr down. They laid him gently on the ground, as Galador began to examine him. They were all horrified at the damage that had been done, as they pieced together the manner of death from the tale the ruined body told them.

"So, this enemy was clever enough to approach an Elf such as Gelmyr without being seen or heard, craven enough to break his back so that he is helpless, and then cruel enough to hack him to pieces while he is still alive. Yet at the last it kills quickly? It is almost as if there is some vestige of honor amidst the evil. It doesn't make sense," said Rogond.

"Perhaps it does," whispered Gaelen, as she bent over Gelmyr's ruined face. His once-beautiful blue eyes were difficult to read; they were clouded over like pale moons, but Gaelen put forth all her effort into searching their depths. Gelmyr had possessed a powerful spirit, and in spite of his being nearly three days gone, she could still sense a remnant of it. She took hold of his cold hands and searched harder. The icy feeling washed over her without warning, and she cried out in dismay, letting go of Gelmyr's hands as though they burned her.

Rogond caught her as she swooned back, her eyes closed, shaking with cold. None of them fully understood what she had done, and they were confused and worried for her. Rogond tried to lift her, but she suddenly came alive in his arms and pulled away, leaping to her feet with her hands flung up before her as though trying to ward something off.

"Gaelen!" Nelwyn cried, rushing to her side and forcing her to look into her eyes. "Come back to us!"

Gaelen buried her face in her hands for a moment, and then the shadow lifted from her as she turned to her friends, who were standing transfixed by what they had just witnessed.

Nelwyn approached her again, placing a hand on her shoulder. "Did...did Gelmyr speak to you? What did you learn?" Gaelen turned to Nelwyn with an expression of cold fury in her eyes.

"Yes, he spoke to me. What I learned is that this enemy will not stop until every one of us is dead, and that he would prefer to kill us one by one, at his leisure, in the worst possible way. What I did not learn is why. Though, at the end, Gelmyr thought he knew."

They did not know what to do with Gelmyr. In truth, he deserved to be brought back to Monadh-talam, where he was loved by many, and laid to rest there. But that was not in their plan. There were no stones to cover him with, and the ground here was soft and damp, not suitable for burial. In the end, they decided to give him to the chilly waters of the Ambros, which he loved. Gaelen sang for him as they released him into the grey water. It carried him gently until he finally slipped out of sight as it took him under.

After Gaelen finished singing for Gelmyr, she returned to the base of the tree where they had found him. Her steps were somewhat stiff as she walked to the base of the tall beech and without warning slammed her fist into it. None of them dared approach her for a few moments. Then Rogond placed a hand on her shoulder.

Her body stiffened, and he took his hand away. Turning from him, she returned to the horses and slung her bow, quiver, and other gear across her shoulders.

"What do you think you're doing?" asked Galador, incredulous.

"I'm tracking, Galador. I can bear my own things, since I will be on foot from now on," she replied, as though it should be obvious. She headed toward the mountains, determined in spite of her fears, leaving the others to stare after her. Rogond and Galador mounted the horses, pulling Nelwyn up behind Galador, and they trotted after Gaelen. Rogond drew nigh her, leaping off Eros and striding along at her side.

"Keep the horses behind me, Tuathan. They will trample and confuse the sign," she said.

He reached over and grabbed her upper arm, forcing her to stop. Her eyes flashed as she turned toward him. His gaze was gentle, and he smiled wryly at her. "You aren't, by chance, related to Aincor, are you?"

Gaelen just stood there with her mouth open. This was an insult of the highest order. Surely, Rogond knew the tale of Aincor Fireheart, the first High King, who grew so proud that he was driven to recklessness. Once he set upon a course no counsel would sway him—his stubbornness had resulted in mass genocide. Rogond dared compare Gaelen to *Aincor*? Unthinkable. Ridiculous. Gaelen stood in disbelief for a moment—what sort of point did he hope to make? Come to think of it, perhaps she *had* been just a little bit impetuous… and she did *sometimes* tend to be a little bit stubborn…

All at once, her stern façade gave way, and she laughed.

"No, Tuathan. I claim no kinship with him. But you certainly have made me see this with different eyes."

"Well, you would seem to possess some of the same determination. Come and sit with me awhile, for I would speak with you."

Gaelen agreed to parley with Rogond, and they sat upon the dry winter grass, talking and gesturing, for quite some time. At last she dropped her gaze, and he again placed a gentle hand on her shoulder, though she still did not appear to welcome his touch. They rose to their feet and approached the others, as Rogond told them that he had struck a bargain with Gaelen. They would continue to track the enemy for as long as possible, but when the signs vanished, which Rogond knew they would, Gaelen agreed to break off the pursuit until the trail grew warm again somewhere else. They would remain alert for rumors of the creature and would warn all who would listen of him, but they would break off the pursuit.

Gaelen turned and resumed tracking, unaware that exactly what Rogond had predicted would come to pass less than three days later, when it appeared that all sign of the creature had suddenly vanished from the land. It was as though it had sprouted wings and flown up and out of her grasp.

Had Gaelen known it, her enemy was not far away, but she would not find him. Gorgon lay, alone as ever, brooding in his dark lair deep underground. Here were provisions enough to last awhile; he would not have to leave his haven for several weeks. He had gone to ground beneath the Great Mountains, leaving no sign for anyone to follow. He would rest and think, and remember the anguished face of Gelmyr. He smiled a twisted smile, caressing the keen edge of Turantil. Lifting the blade, he drew it along his already-scarred forearm, imagining the pain he had inflicted upon his once-proud, once-mighty victim, his strange dark blood flowing freely, dripping onto the cold stone floor.

6

The Path to the Greatwood

Gaelen slid down from behind Rogond and surveyed their intended encampment. It was she who had decided the Company needed to stop for the night, for she could sense Rogond's weariness as he sat before her on Eros. Knowing his pride and not wishing to call attention to the fact that he was still not at full strength, she had feigned a need to stop and look to her gear.

"My blade is dull and my arrows few," she had said, "Let's stop while there's still daylight, so that I may replenish them." The others had agreed that a rest of a day or two would not hurt. The farther they rode from their enemy, the more relaxed and less driven they became. The pursuit had taken more energy than they were willing to admit. Now that they had diverted from it, a sort of weariness mixed with relief had washed over them.

They had decided to return to the Great Forest, there to inform the King of their recent hardships. Once they had made their report, Gaelen and Nelwyn desired to travel to Monadh-talam, also known as Mountain-home, for they wished to bring the news of Gelmyr's death to Magra, his friend. They would beg the King's leave to do so, but in their minds they had already resolved to go regardless of Ri-Aruin's decision. They kept this plan to themselves, not wishing to influence the intentions of Rogond or Galador. Gaelen, in particular, had the sense that Rogond, for some reason, had appointed himself her protector. As if she needed one!

The journey from the Greatwood to Mountain-home would be difficult, as it was not exactly the optimal time of year to cross the mountains. Spring was not far off, but winter still ruled the forest, and it would not relinquish its hold on the mountains for some time yet. It was true that there were fairly safe paths known to the Elves, otherwise the crossing could not have been attempted. Still, the weather would tax them, and the going would be slow and laborious.

Nelwyn, for once, did not suggest the sensible alternative of waiting until spring had softened the mountains. She had been profoundly affected by the death of Gelmyr and remembered his close friendship with Magra. She recalled the two of them at the King's table, tall and proud yet relaxed and merry, happy to be sharing in Ri-Aruin's hospitality.

Nelwyn thought of Magra waiting, but no word of his friend would come unless they brought it to him. The way from the Greatwood back to Mountain-home would not be so easy, but the promise of a new and likely perilous journey would be especially good for Gaelen. It would take her focus from their enemy, as there would be new challenges to be met. But first, they would have to return to the Greatwood. What Nelwyn dreaded most in all of this was facing Talrodin's two sons.

This dread was shared by Gaelen, who would rather have come back with the news that the creature had been slain and the sword Turantil recovered and returned to Halrodin's heir. She suspected that Turantil had been the very blade used to inflict such grievous damage upon Gelmyr, though how she knew it she could not say.

With this plan in mind, they had returned to the ford and crossed the river again, as this would be more difficult the farther north they traveled. They stayed close to the Ambros wherever possible and did not enter the forest, as the southern regions of the Darkmere were thoroughly dangerous places.

Now, Gaelen was searching in her pack for her whetstone, her bag of steel arrow-points, and the feathers she carried for fletching. Nelwyn had been sent to find the straightest and strongest material to manufacture the shafts. She was expert at this. She could find suitably straight-grained, seasoned branches where no one else could. She soon brought several back to camp, where Rogond and Galador took them and began the shaping of them. Gaelen watched Rogond intently, and it was soon apparent that he was skilled in this as in many other ways of woodcraft. Turning to the sharpening of her blade, she spoke to him.

"How is it that you know so much of the woodland way? And how came you to speak Elven-tongues as if born to them?"

Rogond paused in his shaping of the arrow-shaft, regarding Gaelen with a pleasant expression. "I would tell you my tale, but you may not wish to sit still long enough to hear it," he said, having noticed her tendency to be restive.

Gaelen snorted, favoring him with a wry look. What did he know about her abilities? She recalled a day the previous summer when she had been forced to hide herself for hours in a tall tree standing alone in a meadow on the western edge of the forest. A large, armed company of Ulcas had appeared suddenly and she had not the time to get out of the open. The Ulcas had chosen that tree as their resting-place, and they were there nearly four hours before they left to seek underground shelter from the coming dawn. For all that time Gaelen had to sit absolutely still and silent, listening to their horrid speech and smelling their rotten flesh, lest any one of two dozen pairs of eyes should detect her. In the flickering light of their fires, she had been glad she wore very little of silver, gold, or gem. She could certainly remain still if need be. "Tell your tale, Aridan. I'll sit still for it…if you make it interesting enough!"

"There's not much to tell, really," he said, his grey eyes shadowed by regret. "I don't know who my parents were, or whether I have any family yet living. I know my mother was killed by Ulcas when I was just a baby…she was running from the Plague that had overrun Dûn Bennas."

"I have heard the stories," said Gaelen. "It must have been terrible!"

"It was," said Rogond. "I can only assume that the rest of my family was felled by it…there were so few who lived. It spared no one—noble or journeyman, mother or child—it swept through the settlements of men like a wildfire. I was fostered by the Elves of the Verdant Mountains, who found me tucked away in a crevice of rock. Apparently, my mother hid me there before the Ulcas overwhelmed her. The Elves found this ring on what was left of her finger—it's the only thing of my family that I possess." He showed the ring to Gaelen, who admired it appropriately.

"This is of Dwarf-make," she said. "It's very beautiful, though rather massive for a woman's ring." She gave it back to Rogond, who replaced it on the smallest finger of his right hand. "It looks perfect on you, though," Gaelen added, not wishing to offend him. He smiled back at her.

"Well, that explains why you are so fluent in Elven-speech," said Gaelen, after a rather awkward silence. "So, if you grew up among the Elves, why are you not with them now? Did you offend someone? Did you grow weary of their company?"

"Not shy of asking personal questions, are you?" said Rogond good-naturedly. "Since you ask, I didn't *exactly* offend anyone...I was just behaving as any normal young man would."

Gaelen looked puzzled at first, then her eyes grew wide and she drew in a quick, sharp breath, lowering her voice to just above a whisper. "Did you cast your young man's eyes upon a She-elf?"

Rogond stared at her for a moment, seeing she was deadly serious. Then his face split in a broad grin, and he laughed. "You are remarkably perceptive for a hunter-scout."

"What *happened*?"

"Well, I had already learned so many things from the Elves—I had learned that I was mortal, that I would age and die, that I could get sick...that was a particularly difficult blow."

Gaelen nodded. She could only imagine. "But, what did they do to you when you cast your eyes on their daughters? They didn't drive you out or anything...did they?"

"They decided that I needed to learn my place, and that it wasn't in the Verdant Mountains. They sent me to Mountain-home to be educated, hoping that Lady Ordath could reunite me with others of my race. Mountain-home is a place where people of every sort gather to learn. It was a good idea."

"It got you away from their daughters," said Gaelen. "I'm sure they thought it was a grand idea. But why did they not just send you to Dûn Bennas, if your people came from there?"

"I am Tuathan. I guess they thought I would be more at home among the Northmen. There aren't very many of us left—only a small remnant still wanders in the North, and I am now one of them, a ranger sworn to defend the Light. I spent years studying and learning at the Sanctuary, and they were very happy years. I loved especially learning languages and lore. Even Ordath herself said I had a knack for it. When she finally introduced me to the rangers, they knew me as one of their own. I learned a lot from them, as well."

Gaelen nodded, her face solemn. She had met a few of the rangers when they passed through the Greatwood, which was not often. They were inclined to be rather grim and serious, and they followed a strict warrior code. With enough ale, however, they could be quite good-humored. Wrothgar hated them, and that was enough endorsement for Gaelen.

"I met Galador on…well, let's say it was an interesting day," said Rogond with a bemused expression. "We've been friends for, ohhh, six years at least, and we've had some adventures! But I'll save those tales for another time. You must tell me more of yourself, as well. It should be an interesting ride back to the Greatwood."

"Perhaps later," said Gaelen. "Thank you for trusting me with your story. It was well told." As she sheathed her blade, which was now sharp enough to split the bristles on a cricket's belly, she considered what he had told her. It was obvious that he longed to know more of his origins; she could hear it in his voice. It made her sad, really. He probably had little hope of answering any of the questions that troubled him, as most of those who had known of him would have been lost to the horror of the Plague.

Rogond handed her a perfect, straight arrow shaft, and as she began the work of fitting and finishing it, he asked her again to tell of her own beginnings. She smiled and shook her head.

"Perhaps later, Tuathan. My beginnings take some time to tell, and I sense that your tale has worn you out. Why not lie by the fire, and I will sing to you so that you may take rest. It appears that Nelwyn and Galador are keeping the watch tonight."

So saying, she moved to the fireside with him, and he rested while she sang of the Elves and the men of Tuathas, and of the great friendship between them.

Rogond rested for yet another day, and the Elves looked to replenishing their provisions as best they could. They now had plenty of arrows, which cheered Gaelen, as she had the feeling they would be needed before she would see King Ri-Aruin's halls. Food was another matter. There was little to be gleaned here, even if one ventured into this part of the forest, which lay a good ten leagues west of the river.

They still had some stores left from Galador's pack, but the going would be lean until Gaelen and Nelwyn drew closer to home. This did not concern the Elves, for they did not require much to keep their strength; but Rogond, who was still recovering, needed fuel.

When Nelwyn and Galador returned from foraging, they carried an assortment of roots, herbs, and tubers. Gaelen had obtained game in the form of a large bird—dark-bodied, with a broad, iridescent tail and naked, wrinkled red face. It was tough and stringy, but delicious! The tubers, roots, and herbs were roasted together among the coals and made a reasonable accompaniment for the meat. Rogond ate all he could hold and was soon asleep again.

In the morning they resumed their journey. There were two roads that ran from west to east across the forest, but the Elves would not take them, as they went too far to the south of Ri-Aruin's domain and were no longer safe. Besides, Galador and Rogond had the best possible guides. As they rode they kept silent, saving the telling of tales for the evening fire. Then they would all be entertained with some of their favorite legends, such the trials of the great warrior Aincor Fire-heart, and the love of Shandor the magic-user for Liathwyn of the Èolar. As Galador told of the terrible events brought about by Aincor, Rogond reflected that it takes far less time to acquire skill and knowledge than it takes to acquire real wisdom.

Sometimes they would tell tales of their own experiences, as well. Rogond and Galador spoke of their adventures in the far north, where evil creatures were now abroad in large numbers. Galador was the only one among them to have actually seen a winged dragon, and he spoke of the encounter which, though distant, was nonetheless frightening. He spoke also of the Bödvari, captains of Wrothgar, and their terrible power. These were chilling tales, and Gaelen and Nelwyn shuddered as they sat side by side, the firelight flickering in their large, bright eyes.

At last they came to the path through the forest that was made and maintained by the people of Ri-Aruin. Even with the trees not in full leaf, the Greatwood looked dark and forbidding. They had over a hundred- fifty miles to go through it to reach the halls of the King, but mounted they could average at least twenty miles a day, and the Elves could easily do this on foot. Gaelen and Nelwyn took charge as they entered the forest, with Nelwyn scouting ahead and Gaelen bringing up the rear. Every so often, Nelwyn would climb up and have a look around, but she saw nothing disturbing.

Rogond was thankful for their company, especially at night. It was so very dark that it unnerved him at times, for the ancient oaks still held their brown winter leaves. The Elves, however, always seemed to be able to find places to camp over which the stars were clearly visible. The oaks gave way to maples and beeches as they drew nearer to the Elvenhold, and the woodland became lighter and more welcoming. Gaelen and Nelwyn relaxed their vigilance somewhat, for their enemy was nowhere near to trouble them, and they were confident that the familiar perils of the Darkmere would not assail them unaware.

At such times they would sing together, to Rogond's delight. All three Elves had fine voices and sang songs of such beauty and harmony that occasionally he found himself with moist eyes, heart aching to hear more. Once in a while they became a bit over-merry, setting words to some of the songs that were never intended by their original composers. These Gaelen and Nelwyn found uproarious and, try as Galador might to keep his serious expression, he broke into laughter right along with them. Rogond was amused; he was unused to seeing three of these generally dignified folk shaking with laughter at their own silly humor, which he admittedly did not quite understand. Though he had been raised among them, and probably knew as much of them as any mortal man, they were still of different mind from himself.

The intuition that Gaelen would need her arrows was proven correct on the fourth day, as they approached the crossing of a swift, cold-water creek that was wide, but not deep. The Wood-elves made their way north along the bank, until they came to a place where the crossing would be easier.

"This place is sometimes under watch by enemies; we must make certain it is safe," said Nelwyn, as she and Gaelen disappeared into the underbrush. They circled the area, scouting it while Galador and Rogond remained with Eros and Réalta. For a time the two She-elves vanished entirely, leaving Galador and Rogond to wonder what had befallen them, when they suddenly reappeared from behind, startling Rogond into drawing his blade. Gaelen gave him a wry smile as he sheathed it again, shaking his head and looking somewhat annoyed.

"We have thoroughly explored the area near the clearing, and found no sign of danger," she said. "We think it's safe to try to cross. It is best if the horses attempt this with but one rider, so Nelwyn and I will cross on foot." Gaelen turned up the tops of her worn, brown boots as she spoke, lacing them about her thighs, and then waded into the swift water without another word.

"I won't hear of it," said Galador. "My lady, please accept the offer of dry passage." He bowed before Nelwyn, gesturing toward Réalta.

Nelwyn's ears reddened and she shook her head, a shy smile on her face. Galador then did something quite uncharacteristically foolish; he waded into the shallows and promptly sat down, his eyes widening as the icy water washed over him to the waist.

"Ahhh…refreshing!" he said, while trying to keep his teeth from chattering. "Now, since I am already wet, does it not make sense for me to wade, and for you to ride?"

Gaelen and Nelwyn looked at each other. Gaelen rolled her eyes and chuckled, gesturing toward Réalta as Galador had done. "Well, go on, my lady, you heard him! Hopefully the horse has more sense than he does."

They were nearly half-way across when Nelwyn first noticed the disturbance in the water. It was difficult to see because of the swift flow, but when she looked harder she beheld a roiling mass that was moving against the current. Gaelen was picking her way carefully, trying not to allow the water to wash over the tops of her boots, when she heard a cry of alarm from Nelwyn.

"*Aiyah*! Úlfar *are coming*! Gaelen, Galador, get out of the water, quickly! Gaelen…Úlfar are coming!"

Galador and Rogond looked at one another. They had not heard of such things, yet Nelwyn was terrified. She put her hand down to hoist Galador up, crying with fear. Gaelen had drawn her blades, shouting up at Rogond:

"Whatever you do, do not place any part of yourself in the water! One bite from these, and you are dead! We are much harder for them to kill…stay on your horse!"

The roiling mass was upon them even as Galador tried to swing aboard Réalta. He could not do so, both because of the water pulling at his legs and the unsteadiness of his mount, who was now surrounded by a writhing tangle of what appeared to be very slimy snakes. They were pinkish-grey and eyeless, with sharp teeth encased in a sucker-like mouth surrounded by long, fleshy feelers. They turned the water around them into a mire of slime, and the horses struggled against their tangling flesh and the thick, gluey morass in which they now found themselves.

Gaelen yelled fiercely as she swung her blades. The slime made piercing or cutting the Úlfar more difficult, still the water was bloodied about her.

"Keep the horses on their feet, no matter what!" she cried, drawing her bow and sending a swift arrow into the mass of Úlfar, which scattered temporarily.

"*Galador!*" cried Nelwyn as she saw the tall Elf fall to his knees, now up to his chest in the thick, unspeakable mire. It was like jelly; though the cold current tore at it, still it clung to the legs of the horses and to poor Galador, who went under quickly.

Gaelen and Nelwyn leaped to his aid, still shouting at Rogond to stay aboard Eros. The powerful horse was heavier and steadier than Réalta, but he was alarmed at the tangle of Úlfar and threw his head in the air, snorting, as Rogond tried to calm him and make his way shoreward. He looked back, horrified, as he saw Gaelen and Nelwyn pull Galador to his feet. There were at least four of the vile things attached to Gaelen's bare arms and twice that number upon Galador's neck, arms, and chest. Nelwyn threw Galador's arm around Réalta's neck and urged the horse from the water as Gaelen struggled after her. She had stopped trying to kill the Úlfar, for they were too many.

The Company struggled onto the bank, tearing the wretched things loose from their flesh and grimacing. Gaelen was unsteady on her feet, as was Galador, for they had each taken several envenomed bites. Nelwyn had been bitten once, on the back of her right hand, for her clothing covered most of the rest of her. Rogond vaulted from his horse and ran to aid them.

"Stay away from...from the water," said Gaelen as she sagged down onto the pebbly shore. The creatures were still there, lashing and writhing, frustrated at having been denied their prey. They turned upon those that had been wounded by Gaelen's blade; it was all they would get this day. A few attempted to wriggle out of the water, but decided differently, and at last they retreated.

"I have never heard of them to come so far north," said Nelwyn sadly. "This is ill news!" Indeed, it was. It was fortunate that Gaelen and Galador had taken only a few poisoned bites, for even Elves may be killed if enough venom is given them.

"It's terrible news," Gaelen agreed, breathing hard and trying to remain alert. "They have finally made their way here from Tûr Dorcha. Next they'll be swimming right into the Elven-hold."

Rogond was aghast. "What *are* those things? I have never seen them before."

"Then you've never been near Tûr Dorcha," said Nelwyn, trying to pry the last of the vile creatures from Galador's arm. "They attack anything that moves, but they can only attach to bare skin. The hair on the legs of horses will foil them, as will clothing. But when they entangle their victims and mire them in the thick slime they produce...well, you saw what happened."

Rogond took one look at Gaelen, whose pale face was turning a little green. "Are they...poisonous?"

Nelwyn nodded. "Once a victim has been subdued by the venom, and most likely drowned in the slime, the creatures work their way inside by rasping and tearing away the flesh, or they enter through the orifices of the body, consuming it from the inside out. It's one of the worst fates imaginable!" She recalled the hairless, bloated body of an Ulca that she and Gaelen had once found floating in the Darkmere. Gaelen had actually shot an arrow into it, believing it was still alive, before they both realized that it was only moving because it was filled with Úlfar. Nelwyn shuddered at the memory.

"But...why did you fear for me, and not yourselves?"

Nelwyn paused, turning from Galador long enough to look Rogond in the eye. "A single bite from an Úlfa would have killed you," she said. "Even if very little of the venom entered, you would die raving with fever, because the bite would fester beyond healing.

Even the greatest healers have found no remedy for an Úlfa bite—not in a mortal man."

"Thank heaven for the horses' hairy legs, then," said Rogond. He looked over at Galador and Gaelen. "Will they be all right?"

"Hopefully they'll be able to throw off the effects of the venom in a day or two," said Nelwyn. "Galador has taken more bites, but Gaelen is a lot smaller. They'll both need watching, and neither will be able to ride unaided." She examined the fading red mark on her own hand with disgust, but didn't seem concerned about it.

While Galador rested, Nelwyn and Rogond cleaned the slime from him as best they could. Regrettably, his hair had been sullied; some of the foul substance had dried there, and there would be no remedy other than cutting it off. He would need new clothing and, of course, he would despair at the loss of any of his beautiful long hair, of which he was quite vain.

In the morning they took stock of their situation, and though things could have been much worse, they were far from ideal. The going would be slow now, with only two of them in full possession of their wits. Nelwyn estimated about fifty miles and at least three or four more days at their current pace. Both Galador and Gaelen were insensible. Galador rode behind Nelwyn, his head resting on her shoulder. Twice he had slid to the ground before Nelwyn could grab him. Gaelen had finally felt the full effects of the venom, and she rode in front of Rogond, her head thrown back against his neck. She occasionally moaned and muttered fitfully as though in dark dreams. That night the chill took both of them, and they shook uncontrollably as Rogond and Nelwyn tried in vain to warm them. But in the morning they were much improved. Neither was in the best spirits—heads pounding, wits still muddled and bodies aching from the chill of the night. Yet they rode unaided, and by the time they approached the Elven-hold three days later, they were more alert and needed little assistance.

They were sighted first by two scouts, friends of Gaelen and Nelwyn, whom they recognized at once. They called to one another in the bird-voices used by hunter-scouts, and in a few moments they appeared: two Wood-elves, one male, one female, both with long, chestnut-brown hair and nearly identical light brown eyes. As they wondered at the newcomers, Nelwyn requested that they return and tell the King of their impending arrival. With one backward, slightly mistrustful glance at Rogond, they disappeared in the direction of the Elven-hold.

The King's emissaries met the Company as they drew within sight of the hidden gates. Rogond marveled at how cleverly the Wood-elves had concealed themselves; he stood on the doorstep of one of the great realms, yet if he did not know better he would have taken little notice. Ri-Aruin had improved upon the work done by his father, and although much of the fortress was below ground there were hilltop gardens, courtyards, and battlements that were concealed by the natural features surrounding them. The grassy hills that lay to the west of the fortress were wide and open. Rogond could hear horses and the sound of flowing waters.

The source of the Forest River, known as the Dominglas, was formed by the union of two cold springs to the north, and it flowed beside the underground realm.

In general, the reception was a warm one, for all had feared for Gaelen and Nelwyn and rejoiced that they still lived. To the newcomers they extended every possible courtesy, escorting them deep below ground, removing the horses to the capable care of those in the stables.

They were allowed to wash, rest, and dress in fresh clothing that was provided for them. There would be a feast tonight in their honor, but first Ri-Aruin had summoned Gaelen and Nelwyn, as he wanted to hear their news in private.

They stood before him, lean and somewhat travel-weary but still bright-eyed and clear of thought, and told him of all that had passed. He had been especially shocked and dismayed at the sorry fate of Gelmyr, who had been his honored guest on several occasions.

He sensed that Gaelen kept something back from her tale at first—she was reluctant to tell Ri-Aruin that she could read the eyes of the dead. She did not wish to recount the terrible tale she had read in the eyes of Gelmyr, but the King needed to know everything of this enemy, and she relented. Not even Nelwyn had been privy to all of it, and when the tale was finished, she and Ri-Aruin looked at Gaelen with new respect.

When they came to the point at which the trail had been lost, Gaelen hung her head. It still pained her that she had failed. But Ri-Aruin, though he sometimes found her exasperating, was fond of her and bade her not be troubled.

"It is more important," said he, "that you have returned through this peril to tell the tale. We all rejoice that you are found— let that satisfy you."

But Gaelen said, in a small but clear voice, "I would rejoice with you, my King, yet Nelwyn and I still must face the memory of the sight of our friends and the bereavement of their families. I hear your words, but I do not feel them in my heart." Ri-Aruin was grieved, knowing that the desire to pursue and slay this creature would never entirely disappear from her, and that she would be with her people only for a short while.

7

In the Halls of the King

There was a feast that night in celebration, for two thought lost had returned. Both Nelwyn and Gaelen would sit at the King's table, an honor they had each received only once before, and on separate occasions. Of course, one did not decline the invitation of Ri-Aruin, but Gaelen and Nelwyn would sooner have sat in less prominent positions among their friends and kin. Rogond and Galador were invited, of course, and were received as honored guests, though not at the King's table. Galador, who was of High-elven heritage, was treated with great respect, as was Rogond, for the people of the Greatwood had met and interacted with Rangers before and considered them to be allies.

Galador looked reasonably well, though in the end they had needed to trim off some of his hair in spite of his protests. A bit of rest, good food, and hot water had done wonders for Rogond, and he looked every inch the noble man of Tuathas. Clad in Elven-made garments of grey and white, clean-shaven, combed, and polished, he was so comely that Gaelen barely recognized him. He was hale and strong, for he had come to full vigor in the prime of young manhood. His dark hair was held back from his face by a circlet of silver, and his grey eyes were bright. Yet the tale of fifteen years in the wild could not be entirely erased from his face; sun, wind, and worry had left their marks on him. Still, sitting beside Galador, he could easily have been taken for an Elf-lord.

Nelwyn was attired in raiment of soft green, her golden hair set loose and flowing about her shoulders. She also wore a circlet on her brow, but it was of gold. Her cloak was of a warm, darker green, and she wore a brooch fashioned in the image of golden leaves, a gift from the King. She appeared as a morning in the green of spring, bringing to mind the freshness of new growth and the return of the sun, as she sat between her cousin and the King's son, Wellyn, who was recently returned from a foray in the lands to the east. He sat at the right hand of his father. Many remarked on Nelwyn's beauty; it seemed that she glowed with golden light.

Gaelen, by contrast, appeared more as a brooding storm cloud. She was dressed more for traveling than for celebrating, in plain, soft leather of very dark grey-brown, booted and cloaked. As ever, she wore little ornament. Her chestnut hair was cropped and wild, as though windblown. It was always so, no matter how she tried to tame it.

Her one concession to the occasion was a brooch that now fastened her dark red cloak at her shoulder. It was of silver, shaped as a running horse, with an eye of adamant. Ri-Aruin had given her this token, and she wore it to please him. She wore no other ornament, as weapons were not permitted at the King's table, but as he gazed at her, Rogond felt that she needed none. The brilliance and depth of Gaelen's hazel-green eyes would have overshadowed all the songs and beautiful words of the Èolar and all the bright gems and precious metals of the Rûmhar, in his opinion.

Rogond did not yet fully understand this wild Elfling—so childlike in some ways, and so sophisticated and worldly in others. Gaelen was wise, yet foolish, with a heart both loving and ferocious. He knew that a part of his heart was lost to her from the first time she sang to him in his need, that he would never be able to tell her so, and that she would never be his. That piece of his heart was gone nevertheless. He would settle for being her guardian and her friend when needed, for as long as she would have him, and this was reflected in his face. He could not stop gazing at her.

Several of the Elves, including Ri-Aruin, took notice of Rogond's attention to Gaelen, and they were troubled by it. Galador perceived their reaction, and grabbed Rogond's arm to gain his attention, speaking in a hissing whisper:

"Rogond! Do not gaze at her thus. Some of these folk may be her kin, and they are not looking on you with favor just now."

Rogond dropped his eyes, but then his gaze was drawn to Ri-Aruin, who sat tall and proud, in robes jeweled and embroidered, looking down at him with a rather stern expression. Even darker was the expression upon the young face of Wellyn, the King's son and heir. Rogond bowed his head in respect, as he did not wish to offend his hosts, and he looked no more upon Gaelen.

She, in fact, would have preferred his quiet company to the feasting and merrymaking. The music, no matter how pleasing, did not comfort her, and she did not sing in spite of the entreaty of many, including the King. The table of the house of Talrodin and Halrodin held two empty places, plates that were unfilled, goblets that held no wine. Nelwyn also took note of this with sadness, and it was as though a cloud had passed over her face and dimmed her light as a grey rain in the fullness of spring.

Deep under the Great Mountains, the creature Gorgon stirred and fretted, locked in a dark dream. He did not often truly sleep, as his dreams were seldom comforting, but an inexplicable weariness had come over him, and now the price would have to be paid. The dream had begun pleasantly enough, with visions of the Elf, Gelmyr, crying out in pain and horror as he died. But as Gorgon stood before the now-lifeless body, Gelmyr lifted his head, and life appeared in his dead eyes once again. He shook his head slowly, an expression of pitying amusement on his battered face. Gorgon could neither move, nor speak.

"The circle is tightening around you, and the fire draws near," said Gelmyr quite clearly, though his bloodied lips did not move. "Your killing will end and it will be as though you had never been, abomination of Wrothgar! And when the Elàni learn of you, they will pity you. They may even deem it worth a song, which they will sing as they pass to the Eternal Realm, where you cannot follow. You will not be counted as strong, but pathetic and miserable, the victim of your own mindless rage. And they will never fear you again." He swayed gently in the wind as he hung before Gorgon, who still could not move, though he could now speak.

"You're wrong! I will endure forever. I am timeless and I am to be feared. My sword will take uncounted numbers of your kind until none remain, and they and their folk will shed tears uncountable! You are *wrong!*"

Gelmyr smiled and replied, "You know you have been pursued. It is only the beginning. There are those who know of you and are now driven to destroy you. No one will mourn your passing, but they will weep for the wretchedness of you. You cannot escape this fate, no matter how much you hate them and yourself."

Suddenly, Gorgon's limbs became free and he took a violent swipe at Gelmyr, his mighty arm passing harmlessly through the apparition as if through smoke. Gelmyr faded from his sight like a mist, but his voice lingered for a moment. "Farewell, Gorgon, who once named himself 'Elfhunter'. You are the hunted now. Brood well in your lair while you can."

Gorgon jerked awake, breathing hard, a mixture of fury and fear on his dark, twisted face. He shook his head to clear his thoughts and erase all traces of the voice of Gelmyr, but he remained troubled for a long time after. Gorgon's dreams, though dark, had always been easily shaken off, but this dream had been different. He stormed about in the blackness of his stronghold, crying aloud in a terrible voice, attempting to subdue the feeling that this had been not a dream, but a prophecy. Who was pursuing him? He had felt it as he lingered on the banks of the river, before heading to the mountains. No, this could not be a prophecy. He would not allow it. He would not be prevented from his course of hatred, and he would not be pitied!

If he was vigilant, none could prevail against him. The Elves were too scattered—they clustered in their few remaining settlements like sheep in paddocks and would not unite against him. He would continue to take advantage of their foolish wanderings, but now he would be wary, at least for a time. If he detected any pursuers, and they drew too near, he would leave them such a vision of horror and death that they would think twice about continuing. The Èolo was wrong, and he was only a dream, after all. Gorgon muttered a dark battle-chant, repeating it over and over as though to ward off the prophecy of Gelmyr, until at last he grew weary and drew back within himself.

After many hours of revelry the King finally rose and left the Great Hall, signaling the official end of the feast. Although any were free to remain if they wished, they were also free to leave. Gaelen breathed a sigh of relief as she rose and turned to depart, her dark red cloak unfurled behind her, moving swiftly toward the main passageway. She was waylaid by Wellyn standing tall and elegant before her, clad all in white and silver, his raven-dark hair beautifully plaited, his blue-grey eyes intent.

He had just returned from a rather stressful foray into the east, where he and his companions had battled with two of the many groups of Anori-men that seemed to constantly harass the borderlands to the northeast. As such he was in need of merriment, and was not yet ready to retire. Gaelen was not unhappy to see him, as they had been good friends since a rather apocalyptic incident when Wellyn was seven years of age. Gaelen was far older than he, and she had shown him then what a true friend she could be. On the rare occasion that he found her, for they were rarely both in the same place at the same time, Wellyn often confided in Gaelen and sought her counsel, for he trusted her.

Now he faced her, eyes full of concern. "You were not celebrating with us in your heart tonight, Gaelen. Your people are overjoyed that you are found, and yet you are not content. What troubles you?"

Gaelen looked over at Rogond and Galador, who were still seated at their table, surrounded by those who wanted to hear more of their tale. They had been required to give only the barest account of it at the feast, as Ri-Aruin had seen how weary the full disclosure had made them. Rogond, in particular, was fending off a group of very curious Wood-elves, who wanted to know all about him. They were polite, but persistent, and they had him surrounded. Gaelen sighed, knowing that she would have to go and rescue him.

Turning back to Wellyn, she replied, "It is a long tale…one for which I haven't the strength tonight. I am retiring to the forest to rest in the trees near the river, where the sun may warm my dreams. Perhaps I will give you a full accounting when I return."

But Wellyn was not deceived, for he knew her well, and could sense that she meant to leave the Greatwood with little rest. She was being driven by something, and though he did not yet understand it, he knew that it was greater than simple desire for revenge against the killer of Halrodin. As she would not make eye contact, he knelt down before her, forcing her to look at him. He read her thoughts in her eyes and was disquieted.

"You cannot put me aside so easily," he said. "You would be long gone before I heard any of your tale. You carry a heavy doom upon you, and it worries me, for I would have you remain safely here. Your friend Wellyn would share this doom with you. Please... come with me now and tell what has befallen, that I may aid you."

As usual, Gaelen found Wellyn difficult to resist, especially as he knelt before her, beseeching her. This was not lost on the courtiers of the King, and Gaelen reflected that, in a way, Wellyn had done her a favor. Ri-Aruin had never approved of her friendship with him, and permission to travel to Mountain-home was now almost assured. Though she intended to do so in any case, it was always easier with the King's sanction than without it, as she had no wish to openly defy him. Now Ri-Aruin would probably pack her provisions for her.

The King would certainly *not* have his son on one knee pleading with a feral, disheveled Sylvan hunter-scout, who, while eminently useful and occasionally charming, was not an appropriate consort for the Prince of the Greatwood. As Gaelen appraised the expressions on those of the King's court who remained, she supposed that Ri-Aruin was probably being told about it already.

"I'm truly sorry to disappoint you, my friend," said Gaelen, and she meant it, "but I must go now and look to the Aridan. Otherwise, our people are so curious that they will be questioning him and pestering him until he falls over from exhaustion." So saying, she swept around Wellyn, close enough for the edge of her cloak to brush against his astonished face. He was unaccustomed to being dismissed in this manner, especially by Gaelen, and he rose and turned to regard her as she rounded on the group of Elves surrounding Rogond, parting the crowd as a stiff wind parts the tall grass. Rogond smiled at her with relief, rising to his feet and moving toward the corridor. She placed herself before the inquisitive Wood-elves, who turned back from the amiable yet fierce Gaelen Storm-cloud, temporary protector of Rogond the Aridan.

As Wellyn of the house of Ri-Aruin watched her turn and sweep down the corridor behind Rogond, his emotions were mixed. He was concerned that Gaelen really had called some dreadful doom upon herself. He was disappointed that she would not share this with him, and disquieted that she felt she could dismiss him in order to see to the comforts of a mortal man. And deep in his heart, he was resentful of Rogond, because he would probably hear what tales Gaelen had to tell this day—tales for which he, Wellyn, would have to wait, if indeed they would be heard by him at all. Thoroughly out of the mood for merrymaking, he turned on his heel and strode toward his own chambers, the beginnings of this resentment smoldering as a tiny spark that may, in time and under the right conditions, give rise to sudden flame.

Rogond had returned to the sumptuous chamber that had been prepared for him, gone directly to his bed, and fallen back upon it in a deep slumber. The wine brought dreamless, pleasant sleep, and his face was contented and peaceful as he lay stretched out before Gaelen, who regarded him with ever-increasing fascination. Cautiously, she approached him, tracing one index finger along the angle of his jaw, noting the already-emerging bristles of his beard. The feel of it was most peculiar. Not only that, but he often made strange sounds as he slept, a sort of deep rumbling that was occasionally quite loud. It was a wonder that he did not attract the attention of his enemies! Elves made no such sounds; in fact, they rarely slept unless healing or wearied by grief.

Wellyn need not have worried; no one would be treated to any tales from Gaelen this day. She did not intend to tell Rogond of her plan to leave the Greatwood—she and Nelwyn had agreed that it was best if Rogond and Galador were allowed to continue on whatever path they had taken before their meeting. Though they were hardy and skillful travelers, they were perceived as potentially burdensome, as Gaelen and Nelwyn had their own ideas about the best route over the mountains and were accustomed to traveling at their own pace. Rogond would bog down in the deep snows over the high mountain passes, and he was more vulnerable to the elements than the Elves.

That was their perception, but if they had known more of Rogond's people, they would have known that he was of a tough and hardy breed. Unless troubled by illness, he was at least their equal in withstanding the hardships of the mountains in winter. True, he could not step as lightly as they and would sink in the deep snow, but so also would Galador—High-elves had not the Wood-elves' gift of walking trackless over the snow.

There existed devices used by the men of the north, made of curved wood and leather that strapped to the feet, allowing them to walk as lightly as the Cúinar. Rogond's had been left behind during their travels, but he knew the craft of their making and could easily construct a new pair. But even wearing them, he could not travel with the swiftness of the light-footed Wood-elves. Again, neither could Galador.

It was with some misgiving that Gaelen considered her decision to leave Rogond behind, for she liked him and wished to learn more of him. She knew that her cousin was also fond of Galador, who, in her mind, was less likely to burden their going than Rogond. Gaelen could not deny that both had been very useful in their recent travels and were worthy companions for the most part, but she certainly did not wish for Rogond to accompany her, as he almost certainly would, out of a sense of duty, obligation, and the desire to protect her. She and Nelwyn would make their own way as they always had.

Though the task before them was daunting, they would see it done. Gaelen would find this murderer of Elves, and when she found him she would make certain he would never kill again. She looked for the last time that morning upon Rogond, and then she turned and went out into the dawn to take rest beside the river, where the late winter sun did eventually warm her dreams.

Gaelen and Nelwyn were summoned to the King's chambers that afternoon and were not surprised when he dismissed his attendants. "I wished to speak with you both in private," said he, "for I believe you have a request to make of me, and I would hear it before deciding whether others should know of it." Gaelen supposed that he was referring to Wellyn. She glanced over at Nelwyn, who bowed and stepped forward.

"We desire to travel to Mountain-home to speak with Lord Magra of the death of Gelmyr," she said. "They were great friends, and we fear that he will not learn of this unless we tell him. I would guess that he awaits Gelmyr's arrival even now. We would also warn the people of Mountain-home about this creature, for they may not know of him."

Ri-Aruin considered for a moment. "You plan to cross the mountains? The weather is immoderate at this time of year. Have you thoroughly prepared for this?"

Of course, he knew the answer already. They had probably thought of nothing else since their decision had been made, and they did know how to cross the mountains in winter—they had done it before. There was merit in telling Magra as soon as possible; though it would grieve him, at least he would know of his friend's fate. Still, the King was reluctant to sanction their request, as it would be more prudent to wait until spring. But the terrible violence that had taken Gelmyr had already grieved the Elves of the Greatwood, and Nelwyn was right—the people of Mountain-home had to be warned. Perhaps Magra would take up the quest to hunt and kill the creature, a task Ri-Aruin thought might be beyond Gaelen and Nelwyn alone.

The King wrestled with his conscience as he weighed the alternatives. If he sanctioned their request, providing them with supplies and sending them on their way with no word to anyone, he would be aiding them in a very risky endeavor from which they might not return. Even if they surmounted the crossing of the Monadh-hin and gained entry into Mountain-home, Ri-Aruin sensed that this path of vengeance might well claim their lives. He also knew that his son, Wellyn, who was close in friendship with Gaelen, might attempt some foolish action to protect her, and then he would be pulled down with them.

Ri-Aruin knew better than to refuse the request outright, as Gaelen and Nelwyn were determined and would almost certainly defy him. They would then have to secure their own supplies, destroying all hope of secrecy. He could not risk Wellyn's discovering their plan.

If Ri-Aruin encouraged them to wait for the weather to moderate, it would give him time to ensure that his son was far away on some errand and unable to accompany them when they finally did set out. But there was still the risk that they would grow tired of waiting and set out anyway, at a time of their own choosing. Ri-Aruin sighed. The best course was to grant their request, protecting their secrecy so they might proceed alone as they wished.

And what of their companions, the Ranger and the High-elf? They were hardy and steadfast, and would probably be of some help, but Ri-Aruin did not approve of Rogond's apparent fascination for Gaelen—it was obvious that he was traveling down a forbidden road. Ri-Aruin, though sympathetic, was inflexible concerning the union of the Elàni with those of mortal race. Galador was apparently in close comradeship with Rogond, and probably would not separate from him. And so it would have to be Gaelen and Nelwyn alone.

The King raised his eyes and regarded the two hunter-scouts standing calmly before him, reflecting that he was probably sending them to their deaths. They were worthy among his folk, and he would not have wished this, but he had made his choice. He told them that they were sanctioned to travel immediately to the Sanctuary, and that he would make sure they had provisions for the journey, but that all must be kept in secrecy.

"My heart is heavy that I must send you onto so perilous a road, but as you seem determined to follow it, I will aid you," he said.

He saw their faces brighten as they drew themselves up and squared their shoulders, ready to face any challenge. This simple gesture grieved him even more, as he felt they could not imagine what lay ahead. He shook his head slowly, his glossy black hair gleaming beneath his crown of silver. "Please do not have me regret this decision. Promise me that you will return when you can, as you are needed here."

In answer, they both bowed. Gaelen approached and knelt before the throne, taking the right hand of the King and pressing it to her forehead in a gesture of respectful obedience. Then she rose and, followed by Nelwyn, turned and left the council chamber as Ri-Aruin watched them in silence, wondering whether he regretted his decision already.

8

The Path to Mountain-home Begins

Galador shook his handsome head in frustration as he tried for the third time to secure his long hair back from his face. It had always been his custom to plait each side, parting it back from his ears, so that it never strayed before his eyes. Now it had been trimmed in such a way that plaiting it was difficult if not impossible, and parts of it were too short even to tie back behind his neck, which was what he normally did with the rest of it. There were several unruly strands that now insisted on hanging forward in his face; it was almost as though they were protesting their years of captivity and were intentionally making themselves as inconvenient as possible. There was nothing for Galador to do but put up with them until they grew long enough again.

Gaelen had playfully suggested a solution as she drew her long knife, nipping off a small bit of her own hair and grinning at him, eliciting a smile that did not reach his eyes.

Gaelen's hair was something of a mystery to all except Nelwyn; even Rogond had asked her about it. Elves usually did not cut their hair, and he had not yet seen such a shaggy, windblown look among the Elàni, who were inclined to be so vain of their long, silken tresses that cutting them short was unimaginable to most. They were often even named for their hair and identified by it. An Elf with cropped hair was the equivalent of a clean-shaven dwarf.

When Rogond had questioned Gaelen about it, she responded good-naturedly that there were aspects of her character that would simply have to remain a mystery. She did reveal that she had not always cropped her hair, not until she was about twenty years of age, but that it would remain her custom until her death. She leveled her gaze at him.

"Why do you ask, Tuathan? Does my appearance distress you?"

He smiled and shook his head. "No, it does not distress me. I only ask because I have never seen such hair on an Elf before. But I must also admit that it doesn't surprise me, Gaelen, as I sense there are many ways in which you are unique among your folk. I expect that you have an eminently sensible reason for the manner in which you wear your hair."

Gaelen nodded—she did, indeed. She remembered a terrible day...the day she witnessed her first death in battle. It was her dearest childhood friend, a delightful young male named Aran. They had done nearly everything together, and were as close as two friends could be. Aran had been nearly decapitated when a large Ulca had grabbed him from behind by his long hair, wrenched his head back, and cut his throat before he could blink. Gaelen closed her eyes, remembering his blood drenching her as she leaped forward to try to wrest him from the Ulca; she had spent her arrows and was now fighting hand-to-hand with the others of her group. The Ulca's head had at last been cloven by the heavy blade of her beloved uncle Tarmagil, who later met his death in battle during the Third Uprising.

Gaelen's mother, Gloranel, had found her daughter still holding her friend's body and crying as though her heart would break. From that day forward, Gaelen's hair was cropped short. She would listen to none of the admonitions of her kinsfolk and had never paid attention to any since. She saw no need to explain her choice to anyone.

Rogond, relaxing in his pleasantly warm, comfortable chamber, was mildly amused by Galador's attempts to govern his unruly hair. "Give it up, my friend," he chuckled. "You will just have to look like a vagabond until it grows back." Then he added, "It could be worse. At least you don't have to scrape your face with a blade every morning." This was true, and Galador was thankful for it. He looked over at Rogond, who had already grown enough hair since the day before to darken the lower half of his face. Giving up his hopeless task, Galador moved to sit beside his friend.

"Have you learned of their intentions?" he asked Rogond, referring to Gaelen and Nelwyn.

"Not a hint from either of them. You?"

"No, but I sense something in Nelwyn's manner that suggests she is planning some action soon. I believe she might want to confide in me, but is holding back."

"If she and Gaelen have agreed that we are to be kept from it, she will not tell you, though she might wish it," said Rogond. "They are getting ready to set out again, I just know it. If we want to follow them, we will have to be vigilant."

"Is that what you wish to do?"

Rogond considered. Their original plan had been to travel to Dûn Bennas, there to meet with King Hearndin and inform him of the rumor of ever-increasing activity in the Darkmere, until Rogond's fever and the ensuing events had diverted them. Now he could not shake the feeling that his destiny lay with the Elves. He would have died of the fever had Gaelen not aided him, of that he was certain. And she needed him now, whether she admitted it or not—the task before her was too great. A Ranger goes where he is most needed.

Rogond had his own reasons for seeing to the death of their enemy, though he had not made them known to his friends. Galador wanted to go with Nelwyn— that was plain. Rogond could only guess why the She-elves were trying to get away in secret. He suspected that Gaelen was behind it, worrying that Rogond, a mere mortal man, would prove too great a burden during the perilous winter crossing of the Great Mountains. He didn't know of the King's concerns.

He turned to Galador, who was patiently awaiting the answer to his question. "We cannot leave them now. They will have need of us before this is over, of that I am certain. Let us both keep watch over them until they depart, as I fear that if we miss their going, we will never catch up with them."

Galador nodded. "I will keep at least one of them in sight during the dark hours. You attend to them during the daylight. Agreed?"

Rogond agreed that this was a sensible plan. The moment it appeared that Gaelen and Nelwyn were making immediate preparations to leave, Rogond and Galador would be alerted. They would gather and pack their own provisions now, taking what they could carry, for the horses would have difficulty with the High Pass of the mountains. Rogond went below to the stable, where he found Eros and Réalta resting knee-deep in fragrant bedding and hay. He spoke to Eros as the powerful dun nuzzled his shoulder.

"I can't take you with me this time, and it may be that I will not return for a long while. You must remain here, in the service of the King, until I come for you. Behave yourself and try to be useful, my friend. I shall miss you."

Eros looked at him placidly enough, but seemed to know that he was being left behind, and he didn't much like it. He whinnied after Rogond as he turned to go, and Rogond called back over his shoulder.

"Remember, now, no mischief! I don't want to find you hitched to an ox-cart when I return."

Leaving Eros was difficult for Rogond, but necessary. He left written instructions for the keeper of the stables, saying that the Elves could make use of both horses to pay for their upkeep. He included a mild admonition concerning Eros:

> *"He sometimes has a roguish nature, and will not suffer those who are foolish, over-proud, or disrespectful to ride him easily, but he is a fine war animal and excellent for long journeys. His name is Eros. I will return for him—Rogond of the Tuathar."*

Gaelen and Nelwyn had made ready to leave at sunset. Their packs were ready, and they were clothed for winter travel as before. One side of their fur-trimmed cloaks was a dull brown, the other pure white, for there would be deep snow from the foothills to the far side of the mountain pass, and the white cloaks would conceal them well.

They wore new fur-lined boots, silken undergarments overlaid with dull grey leathers, and carried their weapons and various packs. Arrow-points and fletching, resin and sinew, whetstone, flint and steel, cord and rope, flasks of clear liquid that warmed like fire but refreshed like cold water, a few spare garments—Gaelen insisted on bringing her old boots along, just in case—and as much food as they could easily carry were packed into light leather bags and slung at shoulders and waist. As always, they favored dried venison and fruit, but nothing such as butter or honey that would need heavy containers. They suspected they would be quite a bit leaner once they reached the other side of the mountains. No matter, in Mountain-home they would be fed like royalty. It was Nelwyn's opinion that they would probably be ready to eat everything placed in front of them by then.

In addition, each carried a gift of great value for the Lady Ordath, tokens of King Ri-Aruin. They would have preferred to carry little of value—such things always seemed to attract the wrong sort of attention—but they could not refuse the King's request. Gaelen still wore the brooch he had given her, and as she turned to leave his chamber, he called out to both of them:

"Speed Well and Safe Journey, daughters of the Greatwood. May you find your way through peril to the journey's end. Stay steadfast upon your path and remember your promise to return to us. Farewell."

Gaelen and Nelwyn returned to their own quarters for the last time. Nelwyn began writing a message for Galador, concerned that he would not understand why she had left him behind. The sun was already down beyond the trees to the west. They needed to be away soon, but Gaelen had one more duty before her. "There is something I must do before we depart. Please don't be concerned, just wait for me." She removed her new winter cloak and fur-lined boots, pulling on her old ones so that she would not arouse suspicion.

Nelwyn nodded at her, saying "I know what it is you must do, and you are right to do it. Just don't take too long. He was down in the deeps when last I saw him."

Gaelen made her way down into the depths of the fortress, her shadow flickering and wavering along the torch-lit walls. She thought she knew where to find Wellyn, and she did indeed find him in the armory, practicing target shooting down the long, straight passageway. She crept near him, fitting her bow. When he loosed his next shaft straight and true to the exact center of the target, she shot past him, the arrow quivering in virtually the same location as his own. He was startled, and whirled around to regard her standing behind him.

"Well met, Wellyn, son of Ri-Aruin. May I speak with you for a little while?"

Wellyn laid down his bow, approaching her. His expression was mixed. "You are free to speak to whomever you choose, Gaelen," he said. "What do you want of me?"

He was glad to see her, but she could tell that he had not forgotten her treatment of him. She hoped that he would not make things any more difficult than they had to be. "I was wrong to dismiss you at the feast. I really was preoccupied and was not thinking clearly.

Please accept my apology, for you are a very dear friend and I would never intentionally cause you hurt."

Her sincerity was genuine, and Wellyn, who had always found her disarming, was taken aback. He took a step closer to her, as she continued.

"Because you are my friend, I felt I could do what I needed to do, because friends forgive each other when they mistakenly cause insult. I promised to tell you of my adventure, and I will keep that promise. I just don't know when." Wellyn stood quite close to her now, considering what she had said. Then, he spoke to her.

"You're leaving us again, aren't you?"

As Gaelen regarded her tall, handsome friend, she wanted more than anything to give up the quest and to remain in the warmth and safety of her home. Tears started in her eyes, and she quelled them, but not before sharp-eyed Wellyn beheld them.

"You're alarming me, Gaelen. Whatever you're thinking of doing... please don't do it."

Gaelen took a deep breath and found her courage again. "I go where I will, and do what I must, as always. But I *will* return, and then you shall be the first to hear my tale. Please, say nothing of this to anyone, especially the Aridan. He somehow feels obligated to protect me and will be unhappy when he finds I have gone. You must help me in this." She looked hard at Wellyn, who was torn between disappointment that Gaelen was leaving, and relief that at least Rogond was not going with her. His dejected expression transformed into firm resolution.

"I will keep your secret," he said, embracing her as a friend fearful of losing her, and her resolve wavered again at his comforting touch. Then she pulled back from him, eyes clear and bright as he bent to kiss her forehead. Taking both his hands in her own she spoke to him once more before turning to leave.

"So, am I forgiven?" She smiled, though her eyes still shone with unshed tears.

"You are forgiven... *this* time. But I shall *not* forgive you if you allow yourself to be taken beyond the borders of this world. You must safeguard yourself so that I may hear your tale at last. You owe me that much!"

"Then that I shall do. And you will no doubt have new tales of your own when next we meet. Farewell, my friend, and be content that when I return our reunion will be fair and sweet." So saying, she turned and left him again to his bow. But the next few arrows did not find their mark, and it took Wellyn many days to shake off the melancholy that came over him as Gaelen's footsteps faded and were heard no more.

At last all was made ready, and they departed in stealth as the dark of night loomed at their backs. They would see no stars; a gloomy late winter day would give way to a cold late winter night. Nelwyn looked back over her shoulder in regret as she and Gaelen made their way beyond the hidden gates of the Elven-hold, crossing into the forest beyond. While it was good that they were away at last, she hoped that Galador would find her message and would take it well, understanding the reason for her going without him. She would very much have preferred had it not been so, as in her eyes he was fair and worthy, and would have been of great comfort. She knew she would miss his company on the road, as they had spent much time together and learned much of each other in recent days.

The memory of those past days would have to be enough, however. Gaelen was right that they should not interfere with whatever plans had been made already by Rogond and Galador. This matter did not concern them. They had not lost friends to this enemy, and they had no doubt been charged with other duties. Perhaps she would meet Galador again when they both were unfettered by obligation and could simply be together in peace.

Nelwyn considered the task set before her. While she did not doubt that she and her cousin were up to crossing the High Pass in winter, as they had done once before, it would still have comforted her to have Galador's strong arms, stout bow, and keen blade beside her.

Gaelen, who strode beside her, was not thinking of Rogond, of Galador, or of Wellyn. Her mind was filled with thoughts of the chase, of seeking and bringing down her prey. She was high and glad to be away on that road, for it brought her closer to the realization of her goal: to find and destroy that which brought so much sorrow. It was with sharpened senses, then, that she perceived two intruders lurking before them beside the trail. She hissed a warning to Nelwyn and sprang aside into the understory, fitting her bow and calling out: "Show yourselves, trespassers, or die quickly! Elves of the Woodland command you!"

It was then that Nelwyn beheld the face of Galador much sooner than she had expected, as he and Rogond stepped out upon the path where they had been waiting. They were dressed and provisioned as for a journey, and looked not a little unnerved to be staring down the shafts of two bright arrows. The Elves knew them at once and lowered their weapons, looking them up and down.

"Why are you here, and why are you dressed as travelers? You are not coming with us," said Gaelen.

Rogond looked hard at her. "So you say, yet that is our intention. We will not have you face this alone. You will have to outrun us or kill us to prevent it. Why not just accept our company and be glad?"

Nelwyn did not have time to be polite. "You will burden us, Aridan. You cannot go in our footsteps and you know it. Don't make this any more difficult than it already is."

Rogond, who was used to being underestimated by Elves, took no offense. "If I am a burden, then may I fall into Darkness rather than interfere with your progress. But I will follow you with or without your leave. I do not ask it of you, anyway. Rogond of the Tuathar goes where he will, as does his friend Galador. But while we travel with you, we offer our swords and our aid. Whether you avail yourselves of them is your choice."

To this, Gaelen had no answer. She stood defiantly before Rogond, slowly shaking her head. "May you fall into Darkness, indeed! Fine, Aridan, share our road. But I, for one, will not wait for you, nor will I turn back to aid you when you find yourself alone in the freezing wilderness. Don't count on Gaelen of the Greatwood to protect you from your own foolishness!"

So saying, she re-slung her bow and nodded to Nelwyn, who sprang forward with her as the two of them bolted down the trail and out of sight. Rogond and Galador stared at one another for a moment, unsure of how to react.

"Come on! They mean to outrun us, and I expect they can do it unless something delays them. We must fly!" Galador yelled. They sprinted down the trail in the dark, each hoping that either Gaelen or

Nelwyn would relent, for that was probably the only way they would be caught ere they reached the foothills of the Monadh-hin.

Galador growled at Rogond between breaths as he ran. "You had to… suggest they outrun us. You couldn't just leave it… that they had to kill us. No. You had to… give them the idea… to outrun us."

Rogond was amused, though he, too, was regretting his statement. "Just be thankful… my friend… that killing us… wasn't presented… as their only option. I am not… so certain that I… at any rate… would be drawing breath right now."

At this Galador chuckled, though he could ill afford it. They would be running for days if he were any judge of the Wood-elves' plan. And Nelwyn and Gaelen knew the forest, whereas they did not. On and on they ran, seeing nothing but the trail ahead, hearing nothing but their own footfalls and their own breathing, until a sudden arrow shot straight before Galador's face and lodged, quivering, in a tree-trunk. Tied to it there was a scrap of parchment, which they warily removed after recognizing the arrow as one of Nelwyn's.

It was difficult for Rogond to read in the dark, but Galador had less difficulty.

> "You are off the trail. If you continue your course, you will run straight into a rather dreadful bog. We suggest that you turn back now, or if you will not, at least move due north until you find us. We will wait yet awhile."

Rogond looked over at Galador and shook his head. "Well, come on, then. Let's try to salvage what's left of our self-respect."

They had nearly caught their breath and stopped blaming each other for going off course when they found Gaelen and Nelwyn at last. The She-elves were relaxing in the shelter of a ring of stones in one of the clearings maintained for their own use when traveling the forest.

Nelwyn rose to greet them, saying, "Well-met, both of you. We have decided not to leave you helpless in the forest, for it is not our wish that you die by our hands, even indirectly. But we would counsel you to turn back, for we will not return for you again. What is your decision?"

Rogond was beginning to lose his good humor at this point. "Our thanks that you would save us from sinking into the mire, O Generous Ones, but since you're in such a hurry I'd suggest wasting no more time in debate. We did not set upon this path lightly, and we have no intention of turning back. I, for one, will be grateful if we do not have to run all the way to the Sanctuary. You must at least give me time to shave the beard from my face, or it will grow so long that I will be unable to run without treading on it."

To this, Gaelen replied: "Do not fear, Tuathan, for the mountains are infested with all manner of nasty, disgusting creatures…even in the chill of winter they are more than happy to relieve you of that burden by severing your head from your neck. Shaving your beard will be the least of your troubles before we are through."

"So be it, then," said Rogond.

Gaelen shook her head, her thoughts conflicted. Rogond was certainly courageous, strong, and fairly fleet-footed. But the crossing would tax him, and he would fall behind. When that happened would she be true to her word and leave him? The answer to that, she supposed, depended on the circumstances. If it meant failing in her task, turning back, or risking Nelwyn, Rogond might well be left behind. He and Galador would find their own way out of their difficulties. Still, she had grown quite fond of him, and in her own way she admired all that he had accomplished in the very short span of years that he had been alive. Rogond was not looking for answers from her, and he meant to go with her, whatever happened. Might as well make the best of it.

"Well, are you rested? We're ready to move on. If you are ready to go with us, come on, then."

Nelwyn looked surprised at this, and her eyes widened at Gaelen, but she said nothing. Galador gave a slight bow, indicating his readiness to proceed, and Rogond nodded as well.

"Let's make time while we still know the trail well. Things will become difficult soon enough," said Gaelen, turning and running lightly ahead with Nelwyn close behind. Rogond and Galador followed, keeping up easily with the more moderate, efficient pace set to eat up the distance between them and the mountains. As they ran, Galador reflected on the wisdom of their decision. They still had the river crossing and the mountains themselves, which he had never attempted at this time of year. But at least if he had to die a frozen death in the High Pass he would die beside Nelwyn, and that chased all further doubts from his mind.

The stable-hands were greeted with loud whinnying the next morning when they discovered that Eros and/or Réalta had demolished their stalls during the night. They were dismayed to find Eros, who had up to then been quite tractable, kicking unceasingly at the one barrier that still confined him, while Réalta circled his stall, pawing in the deep straw of the floor. Both horses were damp and steaming from the effort. At first the stable-hands wondered whether they were ill, and they summoned the Master of Horse, a wise and venerable Elf named Capellion. He observed them for a few minutes, concluding that they were not ill, but distressed at their confinement. They should probably be turned out to run free with companions in the wide grasslands east of the forest, but as neither animal belonged to the Elves, Capellion could not make that decision. Eros and Réalta were caught, haltered, and tied between two pillars while one of the stable-hands went to seek the strangers, to ask if they might allow the horses to be turned out.

When he returned, he brought news that not only could he not find either Rogond or Galador, but that their gear was gone as well. In the meantime, the message left by Rogond had been found, and as Capellion read it, he sighed and shook his head. Here, then, was the explanation. He looked at Eros, who was literally bouncing up and down off his front feet, tethered as he was between the pillars, shaking his long, dark forelock with frustration. Réalta was in no better mood, shifting his weight alternately between his forelegs with an occasional lash of his tail. It was odd that no one had told Capellion the strangers were departing and leaving their horses behind.

Just as the horse-master was trying to decide what to do, King Ri-Aruin appeared, dressed for the hunt along with several of his courtiers. He noticed the two restive horses tethered between the pillars.

"What animals are these, and why are they tethered thus?" he asked.

Capellion bowed. "They belong to the newcomers...the Aridan and the Elf. They are tethered because they have been trying to break out of the stables since early morning—I would guess because of this." He showed Rogond's message to the King, who read it quickly, his face darkening.

"I see," he said. So, Rogond and Galador had managed to find out about the departure of Gaelen and Nelwyn and had no doubt followed after them. That was why the horses had been left behind; they could not make the mountain crossing in winter.

Ri-Aruin turned quickly to his trusted horse-master. "Who else knows of this?"

"Only the stable-hands, my lord. I will summon them so that we may inquire of them."

The stable hands reported that they had not told anyone of the message. They had asked after the strangers and been directed to their chamber, but that was all. Ri-Aruin turned to the three of them. "Say nothing of this to anyone, especially my son. He is not to know that the strangers have left. This is of utmost importance! Do you understand?" They nodded and bowed before him.

"Keep these two animals in confinement until I return, and keep them as well as you may," said the King. "But do not allow Wellyn to view them, as he will ask too many questions. For now, help us to get on our way. This outing must now last longer than I had originally intended."

They rushed to attend to the King's wishes, carrying equipment and provisions to the eastern courtyard that faced the wide grasslands. Ri-Aruin could see Wellyn, mounted on his own horse with neither bridle nor saddle, calling and whistling to the other horses that followed behind him with their tails in the air, eager to be away. They trotted into the courtyard where they were caught and tacked up, for while the Elves did not need gear to ride or control their mounts, they often used it when hunting, as one needed places to secure things. Besides, Ri-Aruin nearly always went out in relative splendor, which was enhanced by the ornate intricacy of his beautiful equipment.

The King was a sight to behold as he sat mounted astride, his raven-dark hair held by an intricately woven crown of hard silver, his robes of sable and white. Beside him, his chosen courtiers and huntsmen were also attired in relative splendor, and some carried banners that bore the crest of the Woodland Elves upon it, shimmering in green and gold in the chill, early breeze.

Only Wellyn showed some reluctance. Ri-Aruin had detected a melancholy in him; no doubt he had somehow learned of Gaelen's departure. The King had decided that going on an extended hunt would accomplish both the task of distracting him and of raising his spirits, as Wellyn loved hunting with his father.

The King was certain that, should his son discover that Rogond had gone after Gaelen, even the orders of his father would not dissuade him from going after them as well. Rogond had been smitten to the heart, and both Ri-Aruin and Wellyn had seen it. The union of one of their own people with one of mortal race was unseemly and to be forbidden—Wellyn would never allow it. The last thing Ri-Aruin wanted was for his son to go haring off after Gaelen in order to safeguard her from Rogond's advances.

Wellyn moved slowly and deliberately as he made ready, turning back toward the stable and listening to the frustrated calling of Eros and Réalta. Ri-Aruin rode up before him, saying, "Make haste, my son, for all are ready save yourself. The dawn is growing and we are eager to run over the wide lands."

Wellyn made some adjustments to his own equipment and swung lightly up on his own horse, a clean-limbed grey mare. Were he in better spirits, he would have looked quite formidable, clad in grey and white, armed with bow and blade, his dark hair flowing behind him. But his blue-grey eyes were subdued beneath his dark brows.

"What animals are those, neighing and pawing in the stables? Why are they not looked after and calmed?"

"They belong to the Aridan and the High-elf. We have sent for them—I expect they are both still at breakfast. The horses are restive because they know we are going out, and they wish to accompany us. Once we're away, they will settle down. So, let us be away!"

Ri-Aruin turned and rode forth into the sunrise. Wellyn followed, but he sensed that his father had not told him everything, and he was troubled. Ri-Aruin now set about the task of distracting his son. He would allow Wellyn to return home only when the opportunity to follow his friend Gaelen, and the moon-struck Ranger who pursued her, had long since passed.

9
Rogond Proves His Worth

It looked as though Galador's thought of dying a frozen death beside Nelwyn might well come to pass. An unexpected storm had come over the mountains in late morning, and by mid-afternoon the snow was flying so thick and fast that the Company could not separate by more than a few feet, lest they lose sight of one another. They would need to find a place to weather the storm, and soon, or the combination of the screaming wind, bitter cold, and blinding snow might well be the death of all four of them.

They had been on the trail now for nearly nineteen days. The last five had been spent crawling painfully along toward the High Pass of the mountains. They had made great progress through the forest, skirting to the north of both the swift river and the wider Ambros, crossing instead the two broad streams that came down from the north. It was plain that the Wood-elves knew this route well, but it had meant going out of their way, as the High Pass lay considerably farther south. That did not seem to concern Gaelen and Nelwyn, who moved along at a consistent pace of about five miles an hour, covering a minimum of twenty miles a day. They would have gone farther and faster, except that they wanted to conserve their strength for the crossing and make time to procure fresh food where they could to save their stores.

Once on the eastern side of the Ambros, they had again followed the river south for a while, and then cut across the wide scrub forest to the foothills of the Monadh-hin, the Great Mountains. Rogond did not like the look of them. They were nearly always shrouded in a mist that told of cold, damp conditions, and on the rare occasions that they were clearly visible, they were seen to be clad in white from about halfway up the tree line. Rogond was wise in mountain lore, but he had been raised in the Verdant Mountains, which were near to the sea. The climate there was much more moderate.

He took advantage of one of many opportunities to sit before the fire and assemble two pairs of new snowshoes, as he and Galador would soon be in need of them. Gaelen was fascinated, as she had not seen them before. Rogond had soaked and bent the frames before setting out, so that they had cured and were ready to be strung with the rawhide strips he had procured from the Elves' tannery. These he soaked overnight to soften them and then proceeded to wrap the frames, weaving the long strips back and forth like a coarse net.

Gaelen's curiosity had gotten the best of her. "What are you constructing? Is that a thing for netting fish? Or perhaps some sort of trap?"

Rogond smiled. "You shall find before long, do not fear," said he. "I only hope I have constructed them well, for we shall have great need of them." He referred to himself and to Galador, who would also require snowshoes to keep up with the Wood-elves. The talents of High-elves did not include walking trackless in deep snow.

The chance to try them out came not four days later, as they worked their way up the rocky slopes through the tall spruce/fir forest into a world of white. Gaelen and Nelwyn watched in fascinated approval as Rogond strapped on his creations, which resembled rawhide-laced beaver tails. He could then walk nearly as lightly as they.

"Well done, clever Tuathan! I have underestimated you again. Those are ingenious! How fast can you travel in them?" Gaelen was impressed.

"Fast enough, I hope," replied Rogond, his eyes on Galador, who had seen him use the snowshoes before and knew that they would slow him down considerably. Galador would have less difficulty, for he was both hardier and more graceful than Rogond. The Elves would all have to slow their pace to allow Rogond to keep up, but he was determined not to hold them back, and he set off as fast as he could go. Though it tired him quickly, he would not say so. Fortunately for Rogond, the climb and the footing would slow the Elves down as well. Though these paths had been made by many travelers, they were still steep and treacherous, and one needed to use great care in traversing them.

One also needed to be watchful, especially during the dark hours, as there were many enemies living under the mountains. Therefore, the Company tried to find places of concealment before dusk where they could sit huddled together against the cold. Once in the mountains, there could be no fires except in dire need, as they could not risk discovery. Doing without a fire was not as difficult as it sounded at first, for the Elves and Rogond all were hardy in the cold, and their cloaks were warm, especially when shared. But the chilly, ever-present mists blocked the stars and dampened the spirits of the Elves, who loved always to renew their bond with the stars by night. So they huddled together in silence, listening only to the wind, the cracking and shifting of the rocks, and the occasional sound of snow sliding from the high peaks. At such times Gaelen felt Rogond tense beside her, and she understood his concern. To be caught in one such slide would probably finish them all.

The storm had come upon them on the fifth day. They had heard it approaching but had not seen it, as the mists were now so thick that it was like traveling through a cloud bank. The wind came up at midday, and it began snowing. Soon the blizzard was upon them, and they were all having difficulty moving in the wind and the snow that piled over Rogond's snowshoes faster than he could lift them. They could not hear one another for the wind, nor could they see one another beyond a few feet. Galador brought out a long rope, which he handed to Nelwyn, Gaelen, and Rogond, instructing all to keep hold of it. Then he took up his position behind Rogond so that he could watch over him. Nelwyn led the way, followed by Gaelen.

After a while, Gaelen shouted to Rogond over the screaming wind: "We are going to look for shelter. Nelwyn and I believe we know where to find it." She patted his snow-covered shoulder encouragingly, and he smiled beneath his frozen moustache, trying not to worry her. He had struggled valiantly but was losing ground, and by the time they stopped to rest under an overhang of rock, he was completely spent. Gaelen and Nelwyn debated with one another, trying to establish their location and the whereabouts of the shelter they sought. The fact that they did not agree was not encouraging.

Rogond lay panting, exhausted, and shivering with the cold, as Galador turned to Nelwyn. "We have to get him to some warmer place where he can rest. He is worn out with trying to walk in those snowshoes. You said you knew the mountains. Why can you not agree?"

Nelwyn cast a worried glance at Rogond. "I think the shelter is farther up the pass, but Gaelen thinks it has been passed by. She wishes to go back and look for it, but if she is wrong, it would be disastrous for Rogond. He cannot risk using any energy in a false pursuit. She would go back on her own, but I don't think we should separate." She looked pointedly at Gaelen, who shrugged at her.

"You're right, we should not separate," Galador agreed. "How certain are you of the location of the shelter?"

"Not certain at all, but neither is Gaelen. The mists and snow have made it difficult for us to keep our bearings on the trail. We are not exactly lost, but we're getting there."

Gaelen looked over at Rogond and shook her head. "Enough of this! While we stand here debating, the Aridan is freezing to death. I am going out to scout the way. You should all stay here…there is no point in risking more than one of us. If we don't find the shelter soon, we shall *all* freeze to death." She drew her cloak tightly about her, took a draught of the warming liquid from her flask, and headed out into the snow over the protests of Nelwyn and Galador. Then they lost sight of her, and there was nothing to do but wait and compare her again to the Fire-heart.

She reappeared not twenty minutes later, completely covered with snow and shivering, but elated. "Nelwyn, you were right! I found the shelter, and it's not far. I'm *so* glad you talked me out of going back." Moving to Rogond, she roused him and got him to his feet, pouring a quantity of the warming fluid down his throat. He stopped shivering and shook off his weariness, looking hale enough. "Up and onward!" cried Gaelen, in a voice charged with hope. "Forth, bold adventurers!" They each grabbed the rope and set out into the blizzard, trusting that Gaelen knew what she was doing. Thankfully, this time she did.

They soon reached their intended shelter, a most welcome little cave whose entrance was nearly concealed by the rapidly accumulating snow. It was a miracle that Gaelen had spotted it, but so she had, and they were now protected from the worst of the weather. It was a small cave, with a single narrow passage leading off the back into the darkness. It probably went back for miles to places best left unseen, and no one in the Company had any desire to explore it. But the small chamber in which they were now sitting was hospitable enough, with a smooth floor and a roof tall enough to stand beneath. Gaelen tested the air at the entrance to the passageway. It was clean of the smell of Ulcas or trolls, at any rate. This shelter had been used by many travelers at one time or another, and some had left evidence of their coming and going. Runes and letters adorned the walls, providing some entertainment until the light failed. There were also some old torches that had been used and discarded, and a ring of stones marked someone's attempt at a campfire.

The four companions rested together, and after a meager meal they settled back, listening to the howling wind and hoping they would not have to dig themselves out of too deep a drift in the morning. Turning two of their cloaks around backward, and two forward, the heat of their bodies was well-contained. A fire would have been wonderful, but it was out of the question as they had no fuel. The Elves kept watch while Rogond slept, resting in the cold darkness, imagining the warmth and light of a crackling fire under a sky filled with stars.

Gaelen reflected that Rogond had made a remarkable effort and actually had slowed them only a little. She patted his arm affectionately and whispered to his sleeping form: "Well done, Tuathan. It appears that we will not have to leave you on the ice after all." She shook her head and chuckled to herself. Snowshoes. What a clever idea! But Rogond could not hear her, as he was deep in unpleasant dreams of struggling to keep up with the Elves, who drew ever farther away from him no matter how hard he strove to catch them, hearing their scornful laughter drifting back upon the wind.

The Elves felt the tremor long before they heard it—a rumbling vibration so low that it was like a wave of pressure that brought an oppressively close feeling they could not shake off. This grew until they knew it for what it was, hearing the first roar of the hillside as it thundered down from the high peak above them. Rogond then felt and heard it too, and the four of them clutched each other tightly, fearing the collapse of their tiny cavern but not daring to emerge from it. They huddled together in the dark as the noise grew to a deafening thunder that seemed to fill the world, shaking the walls and floor so that dust and small stones rained down upon them. One struck Nelwyn, and she cried out in panic as Galador pulled her to his chest, trying to protect her.

Then, rather abruptly, it was over. They could feel the tremors receding down the mountainside, but outside the cavern there was dead silence. Slowly they separated, faces pale, hands trembling. Relieved that none had been hurt, they cautiously felt their way to the entrance of the cavern. It was now blocked with boulders, frozen soil, and what appeared to be the broken dead bough of a spruce tree. These they could feel but could not see, as they had been plunged into darkness so complete that even the eyes of the Elves could not pierce it. With growing dread they realized that they were probably now entombed in the tiny cavern and that the only way out was down the small, black passage that led into the mountain.

When daylight came, their suspicions were confirmed. The mountain snows had indeed slid down upon them in the night, bringing part of the mountainside with them. They would not be able to dig their way out until the snows melted in late spring. They were left now with one choice: they would have to take the passage and hope that it would not lead them to some dark doom. Only a tiny bit of grey light managed to filter through the impossible mass of ice, snow, and rock that now blocked their way.

They groped in the dark for the old torches, blessing the ones who had cast them aside, as they still had a bit of good pitch and would give light for a while if only they could be ignited. Gaelen produced her flint-and-steel, and, stripping some dry needles off the spruce bough that protruded into the cavern, she struck a spark to them, tending it carefully until it flared into flame. Then she touched the pitch to the tiny fire. At first she was not successful, but tried again twice before the old, dry pitch gave in and smoldered into life.

They had two torches to light their way, and this was encouraging, because they could not have risked the journey otherwise lest they fall into a sudden chasm or get hopelessly lost, unable to see what lay ahead or behind. But the torches would not last forever, and they would have perhaps a few hours of light from each, so they lit only one, trusting that they could light the other when it failed. Rogond bore the torch, holding it aloft for Gaelen, who walked ahead, and Nelwyn and Galador, who walked behind.

All three Elves had weapons at the ready, and Rogond could tell that they were ill-at-ease. This was not to their liking at all, and he could not blame them. They had all heard tales of the dark things that dwelled under the mountains, and the Elves felt disadvantaged in this unfamiliar environment, though their keen senses and quick-witted agility would still stand them in good stead.

They were all thankful that they would not have to face this peril alone, as four pairs of eyes and ears straining into the darkness were certainly better than one. The narrow passage widened out quickly and went fairly straight and smooth for a while, but then there were a few heart-stopping moments when the path fell into deep blackness, forcing them to shinny along narrow ledges and leap over wide gaps in the dark. They went as silently as they could, every now and then signaled to stop by Gaelen, who would check for any sign of strange scent before moving on. At such times Rogond watched her in fascination as she stood with her eyes closed, tensed and quivering, sampling the air in all directions. She found nothing amiss for a long while, but traveling with one's senses at fever pitch was exhausting even for the Elves.

As the light of their first torch faltered, they took stock of their situation. They had no idea where they were or where they were going. They had only a few hours of torch light left, and all were so tense that a sudden shadow on the wall was likely to have at least three arrows in it before any of them could draw their next breath. At least they would not die of thirst—the sound of water dripping into deep pools and empty caverns was all around them— and it was a great deal warmer going under the mountain than over it. Gaelen had detected no sign of fresh air as yet, but there had been relatively few choices to be made as to which passage to follow, and always she chose the one that smelled less stale.

They decided that they would find a suitable place to rest before the light of the first torch went out altogether, and then they would trust to Gaelen to get the second one going, as she had gleaned all she could of the wonderful dried spruce needles. They would rest in darkness, saving the second torch for when they continued their journey to who-knew-where. They found such a place just in time— the torchlight gave one last flicker and went out as they entered a small, round chamber with a pool of very cold, clear water in the exact center. The water looked wholesome enough. It seeped from a spring in the floor, and they drank of it gladly, for they had been rationing their water supply. They filled their water skins and then rested in the overwhelming darkness, taking comfort in their companions.

Rogond began to tell a tale in a soft, low voice, and all the Elves hearkened to him, for it was of the lost realm of Tuathas. Gaelen and Nelwyn both wept as Rogond described the cataclysmic upheaval of the Fire-mountain that covered the lands with ash and choking vapors, taking every life. So few escaped, and so much that was fair and good was lost. It seemed especially sad that Rogond, whose forebears had managed to escape that terrible fate, should tell the tale. "Do you think you will ever know whose blood is in your veins?" Gaelen asked.

Rogond reached out to Gaelen, who, for all her bravado, was a sensitive soul, and gently wiped her tears away. "If it is meant that I should know them, then I will," he replied, his voice betraying his great longing.

"I'm sorry, Rogond. It was not my place to ask."

At this he smiled in the darkness. "Do you realize that is the first time you have called me by my name since the journey began? Not 'The Aridan', or 'Tuathan', but by name?"

Gaelen was silent for a moment. Then, she replied, "My apologies, Aridan. I'll try not to let it happen again."

This was followed by a chuckle from Galador. "Let that be a lesson to you, Rogond. A proud mare does not give in so easily."

"True, but they are worth the effort in the end," answered Rogond, and to this the Elves had no reply.

The passage they had taken appeared to have been little-used for some time. Though travelers crossing the pass had often found and sheltered in the small cavern, Galador doubted that any had been inclined to explore the dark, narrow way behind it. He was thankful that no one had thought of blocking it up, as they would have been in a real fix. But the situation they were presently in was real enough.

They all knew that the mountains were infested with Ulcas, trolls, and all manner of enemies, though they had not seen, heard, or smelled any sign. But as they continued, the paths they took became broader, smoother, and well worn. This could either be a welcome indication that they might soon find another way out of the mountain, or it could be a sign that an unpleasant encounter was becoming more likely.

They crept along in silence in the last of the torchlight, hoping that Gaelen's nose was leading them well. Galador whispered to her as she paused again at an intersection of two stone passages, eyes wide in the flickering light, a look of uncertainty on her upturned face. "What is it? What sign do you read?"

Gaelen knelt down upon the stone floor and examined it. "Ulcas have passed this way within the past two days," she replied, wrinkling her nose slightly. "I would guess a dozen or so. And they had some sort of rotting carcass with them." The idea that the Ulcas were scavenging rotting meat was of no concern, but the thought that they had passed by within two days was discomfiting. Galador and Nelwyn listened down the passageway, hearing no sign of footfalls.

Rogond suggested that the carcass the Ulcas were carrying was likely to have come from outside the mountain. If so, perhaps the Company could back-track the Ulcas, and thus find a way out. The Elves were not convinced. "We don't know what sort of carcass it was, Rogond," said Galador. "It may have been that of a lost traveler who died alone in the dark, as we are likely to do if we make the wrong choice now."

Gaelen considered for a moment, and then spoke in defense of Rogond's idea. "The Aridan is right. This was not the body of a traveler. I would know the scent of rotting Elf or man-flesh, or Ulca for that matter. I think it was most likely an animal of some sort. That being said, it doesn't mean they found it outside. But it is at least a path we can follow, and I see no merit in any other choice."

"What about the merit of a path not recently traveled by Ulcas?" asked Nelwyn. "Where there are some, there are bound to be others, and once we are found, well…"

None of them liked to think about it. The Elves still had a sense of the passage of time and knew that it would be daylight for many hours yet. If there were a way out, it would be easier to find while the sun was up, as they would see the faintest trace of light filtering in. Of course, once back outside, they would probably have no idea where they were or how to get back on their course, as the mountain had inconveniently rearranged itself.

They were not thinking of such things just then; all they wanted was to emerge from under the mountain and see the daylight again. The image of what would happen if they encountered a large, well-armed group in the darkness was more than any of them wanted to face. Nelwyn was right—where there were any Ulcas there were bound to be many more. The dead carcass they were carrying could have come from anywhere, and they might have been carrying it for some time.

Therefore the Company decided to follow the course that had not been taken so recently by Ulcas, even though they could see the logic in Rogond's suggestion. As it was, they chose the path less traveled which, unbeknownst to them, led straight into the heart of the mountain.

The torch light would only last a brief while longer. They had seen no sign of any diversion, nor any hopeful glint of daylight. It was too late now to regret their choice, though they all wondered about it. They would just have to rely on their wits and trust that fate would not abandon them in the dark.

Rogond walked up behind Gaelen, who had paused as though she had noticed something interesting. "What is it? Have you caught something in the air?"

Gaelen turned. "It is not what I smell, but what I see!" She pointed ahead to a dim, bluish glow that could be clearly seen, though it was difficult to tell how far away it was. Only Gaelen had noticed it, because only she was walking in front of the torch, and thus it did not interfere. This was a beacon of hope, and Gaelen's elation was obvious, even in the waning glow of the torch-light.

"We must be cautious. Though I welcome the light, it may well mean enemies ahead," said Rogond. This was true, and they crept toward the light with senses attuned and hands straying toward weapons as the torch finally flickered and went out. After what seemed like ages, they reached an intersection of their own path with a much broader one, smooth and high-roofed, with regular, rounded walls.

The source of the light hung from the roof by a chain of steel. Its purpose was probably to mark the intersection. It was a blue lamp made of some sort of mineral crystal that captured light so effectively that it seemed to burn with its own flame. Looking both ways down the long, straight passage, they saw a faint blue glow indicating the placement of other lamps.

"I have seen these before," said Galador. "They were created originally by the Èolar for use in their underground realms."

"Well, I don't care who created them…they are marvelous!" said Gaelen. "I only wish they would help me gain my bearings. I have a vague sense that we are moving south, but I cannot vouch for it."

Rogond examined the area around the intersection with wonder. "These tunnels are not of Ulca-making— they were fashioned by dwarves. A path so well maintained probably is one of their main thoroughfares and therefore unlikely to be used by Ulcas, at any rate. Thralls of Wrothgar do not love the dwarves, who are fierce fighters and will not abide trespassers into their domains.

"You mean trespassers like us?" muttered Galador, whose dislike for dwarves was deep-rooted.

"If the dwarves keep the Ulcas away, I'm happy," said Rogond. "But I do not know which direction we should take. If even the Elves are confounded, what chance do we have of finding our way?"

"I can speak only for myself," said Gaelen, "but my sense of placement becomes muddled when I can see neither sun, nor stars, nor tree, nor glint of daylight. We are unlikely to be of much help down here, unless Galador has some extra sense of which I am unaware."

"First Ulcas, and now dwarves?" said Nelwyn, who was not comfortable with either. On very rare occasion she had met a few dwarves passing through the forest on their way eastward, where it was said they prospected for rare metals. Ri-Aruin sometimes exacted tribute from them in return for safe passage between his borders, and his treasury was thus begrudgingly enhanced. But the King provided them with food, drink, and protection and guidance to the borders of the forest. By the time they had crossed far enough in to encounter the Elves, most would have given nearly any of their belongings to escape the dark, dangerous woods, which were in no way to their liking.

Gaelen and Nelwyn had twice been assigned the wearisome task of conducting lost dwarves to the eastern border. The Elves viewed them as noisy malcontents. Gaelen in particular grew weary of their constant grumbling, and Nelwyn was appalled at their habit of cutting down beautiful, healthy young saplings for the sole purpose of procuring straight shafts for the making of arrows. They had scoffed at her when she suggested that they might glean seasoned branches from trees that had died and fallen.

"Why should we spend all that effort, when these young trees provide us with the perfect material? It's not as though you're lacking for trees here. Our axes could be busy for many months and never even dent this wretched tangle."

Gaelen had been required to grab one of Nelwyn's arms to prevent her from "explaining" matters to the dwarves, sending her away so that she would not forget the admonition of the King, which was to make certain they all reached the eastern border without incident. Then Gaelen had turned to the dwarves and informed them that only fools made arrow-shafts of green wood without spending hours curing them over coals, and that uncured shafts would warp and need to be re-shaped.

"Your saving of time is thus a false one," she told them, not even attempting to disguise her contempt. "Now I understand why so few of your arrows actually find their mark."

Unfortunately, dwarves do not suffer well the contempt of Elves, who are viewed as having unjustly superior attitudes. It was true that, although the Elves respected the skill of the dwarves, and some even formed friendships and partnerships with them, they were still regarded as ill-mannered, clumsy, and unattractive. The two peoples were simply too dissimilar to find much common ground, unless in the making of beautiful things by craft.

Now the Elves were in the dwarves' domain. And while they were thankful for the lamps and the probable scarcity of Ulcas, they were uncertain of how things would end should they encounter a large group of dwarvish folk. Some dwarves, particularly those that had grown from the remnant of the lost Dwarf-city of Rûmm, were especially dangerous. There had been a terrible war long ago between the dwarves of Rûmm and the Elves of Eádros—Galador's people. Any of the descendants of Rûmm would quite possibly do harm to Galador, and maybe even to Gaelen and Nelwyn, on principle.

The Company needed to decide which way to turn and, as usual, they did not agree. Galador wanted to go left, which he was convinced was "south". Rogond wanted to turn right. Gaelen and Nelwyn then joined in support of Rogond, as the last decision had gone counter to his wishes. "A fine group of frozen folk we shall make at the end of this road," muttered Galador as he strode along toward the next lamp.

"True enough," chuckled Rogond, who walked beside him. "But at least we won't rot until spring. And our friends the Ulcas will have fine eating in the meantime."

"You know better than that," Galador hissed back at him. Even Gaelen and Nelwyn had turned their eyes back at this. Rogond knew, of course, that Ulcas would not consume the flesh of Elves, although they would eat almost anything else, nor would they suffer the touch of objects that were Elven-made. Rogond also knew that the Elves were somewhat sensitive about it. And there was no question that he had once again been reminded of another difference between himself and his companions, for the Ulcas would consume his flesh with relish.

"Sorry...I forgot myself for a moment. I suppose that only I would provide nourishment for them."

"Well, should that come to pass, I hope you choke them!" said Gaelen, who then made deep gagging sounds and clutched at her throat, pretending to expire on the spot. Even Galador, who had momentarily lost his good humor, chuckled at the thought of Ulcas gagging on Rogond, though the idea was a bit morbid.

They continued in silence until they passed three more of the lamps, which seemed to be hung so that the cold light from at least one could always be seen. Rogond noticed that the fourth lamp was larger and more ornate than the others, yet there was no intersection, but only a recessed area of the passage wall, into which there appeared to be carved runes and ornate traceries that suggested both dwarvish and Èolarin origins.

"What can you make of this?" Rogond asked, staring intently at the runes. The Elves could read bits of it, but Rogond actually was more familiar with those runes used by dwarvish folk, as he had studied them in the Sanctuary. He had a fine gift for the learning of languages and a fascination with them. There was one old lore-master, a dwarf descended from the founders of the Great Cavern Realm of Cós-domhain, who had taken up residence in the Sanctuary as an advisor to Lady Ordath. His name was Fima, and from him Rogond had learned much concerning the ways of the dwarves, including some of their speech.

Unlike the Elves, who delighted in sharing and teaching their languages to any who would learn, the dwarves guarded their tongue jealously, and very few outside their race knew even the rudiments of it. Rogond had been in great favor with Fima, who taught him as much as he could learn. Rogond spoke many forms of Elvish, as well, and had studied the dialects of men in all their variety. He had accomplished much in his years at the Sanctuary, and he looked forward to returning there and renewing his friendship with Fima.

Now he studied the graven runes carefully, trying to make out the meaning of the inscription. At last, he nodded with satisfaction and pressed four of the images at the same time. With a sort of grinding "creak", a small fissure appeared along the right-hand edge of the panel. Rogond, with help from a very surprised Galador, pushed as hard as he could, moving the heavy stone panel inward until a small chamber was revealed.

As the door opened, another of the eerie blue lanterns caught the dim light and sparked into life. The chamber appeared to be a storehouse of goods left to provision the dwarves on their journeys through the mountains. There were earthenware jugs of food, barrels of wine and ale, spare garments and weapons, and…torches! Piles of them, the pitch wrapped with wax, stood in one corner.

The Company could hardly believe their good fortune. They had been rationing their food stores so carefully that their mouths began to water at the thought of the abundance before them. Rogond cautioned his friends. "The dwarves had laid this by for the provisioning of their own folk, and they will take none too kindly to our despoiling it. We should take only what we need for the immediate future."

This was greeted with silent stares from all three Elves, who were hoping to take at least two torches and several days' worth of food each. And they certainly wouldn't turn their noses up at the wine. "I don't see any dwarves here now," said Gaelen, looking all around her. "Let the dwarves ration their goods a little—I'm not about to pass up this bounty. Besides, we can pay for it." She ran her blade around the edge of the wax seal on one of the jugs and opened it to find sacks of nuts, tubers that filled as well as bread when roasted, and some hard, sweet cakes that tasted wonderful even if one risked breaking teeth on them. She tossed several of these to Nelwyn, who was busily investigating one of the smaller jugs, which turned out to be filled with wild honey.

To a Wood-elf, this substance is more precious than gold and more intoxicating than wine. Gaelen and Nelwyn wasted no time getting into the dark, sticky-sweet richness, and they were soon quite silly. Forgetting all caution, they sat giggling in one corner as they shared cakes covered with honey, both charged with exuberant energy.

Rogond had the feeling that, though it was better than nothing, the small pile of gold coins they left behind would not be considered adequate by the next party of dwarves to pass through. He hoped that they had left little other evidence behind as they finally packed what they could easily carry, lighted one of the eight torches they had taken, and pulled the heavy panel until it was nearly closed. Then Rogond repeated his action of touching four images simultaneously, and the panel closed with a grinding 'thud'.

The Company was much more cheerful after that, what with Gaelen and Nelwyn laughing and very nearly colliding with the walls, and at least one of their water-skins filled with good wine. They had plenty of food in their packs to see them for quite a number of days yet. In truth, they had not made much of a dent in the stores, but the dwarves still would have no sense of humor about it if they suspected that anyone other than their own folk had taken the provisions.

To that end, Rogond had at the last insisted that the Elves surrender one of the tokens sent by the Woodland King for Lady Ordath—a beautiful and incredibly lifelike golden replica of a dragon in flight, jeweled and enameled. It was meant to fasten and adorn a cloak and was of great worth, for it had come from the treasure-stores of the Eádram, though it was of dwarf-make. Gaelen and Nelwyn were fiercely opposed to the idea, but in the end they relented, as they still had one other token for the Lady. The dwarves would count themselves well paid. "Well, then I'm taking our coins back, at least," said Galador.

As the four travelers made their way north along the dwarf-passage, they were unaware that, a scant two miles away, Gorgon was stirring in his stony sanctuary, preparing to go abroad again. The disquieting visions of the Elf Gelmyr spouting prophetic nonsense from his dead lips had motivated Gorgon to seek new prey as quickly as possible. It was the only thing that would make the visions go away. He also had the uneasy feeling that the same pursuers he had sensed by the river were still close at hand, though he could not really explain why or how he knew it. Gorgon did not realize that his "sense" of Gaelen was coming from her already-intense hatred of him, nor did he understand that she, through her contact with his victims, now held a sense of him, as well. For a while, he contemplated seeking out those pursuers and making an end of them, but decided that would be imprudent, as he only knew that at least one Elf traveled with them. He strapped on his armor and various weapons, provisioned himself lightly, as he had no trouble finding sustenance on the trail, and placed his heavy helmet on his head.

Now to decide which of his killing-grounds would be most productive. He thought about returning to the Darkmere, as that area was still fresh in his experience and might prove interesting. But he felt that he had picked up his pursuers shortly after he had killed the two Wood-elves there, so at last he decided to make his way westward, toward the gentle lands near the sea. Hopefully it would not be too long until he could waylay one or two of the Elves passing through those pleasant lands and make a very unpleasant end of them. Then he would go to the Verdant Mountains and prowl for more. After all, he would have to apply himself to his murderous task if he hoped to erase the images of Gelmyr's sinister, smiling face and at the same time accomplish the goal of exterminating the Elves from the face of the world. Someday Gorgon would have an army, and then he would slay them all. He had foreseen it.

He glanced at his reflection in the mirror-bright, polished center of his dark shield, pausing to tuck away a few long strands of silken hair that had fallen across the thick, grey skin of his forehead. "Forth, Elfhunter, and good hunting," he growled. As he headed out he was in fairly high spirits, despite the vague, uneasy feeling of unyielding pursuit that gnawed at the back of his mind.

The Company had not gone more than a mile north of the dwarves' hidden cache when the first rumor of heavy-shod feet was heard down the passage ahead. All four of them froze in their tracks, listening intently, trying to determine the nature of the oncoming threat. "They do not sound like Ulcas…I would expect them to go more quietly, especially down dwarf-roads," said Galador.

"Dwarves then, I expect," said Rogond, looking at the three Elves, who appeared less than happy at the news.

"We cannot risk an encounter with them, Rogond," said Galador. "They are very likely to take offense to our presence here, and it sounds as though they are many. We shall have to find a hiding-place at once!"

"There *are* no hiding-places," said Gaelen with alarm. "We will have to outrun them back the way we came, and turn back up the other passageway, hoping that they will go straight on—it's our only chance." Without waiting for agreement, she turned to move quickly back the way they had come, going as quietly as she could, listening to the rumble of the approaching dwarves behind her. As she approached the hidden doorway, she froze in dismay. Similar dwarf-racket was now heard from in front of her, as well. Apparently, the Company had been caught between two groups of travelers who most likely meant to meet in the exact spot where they were now standing.

"Hurry!" whispered Nelwyn. "The other passage is not far… perhaps we can make it!" It was worth a try, though they all doubted they would make the passage before the dwarves did. As they hurried along, they caught their first sight of the north-bound dwarves. They were a group of about twelve, jogging easily, apparently relaxed and in a good humor, talking amiably with one another. This evaporated when they beheld the four interlopers, and they halted and became silent, twelve sets of hands gripping twelve axe handles.

"Well," whispered Gaelen with a sardonic shrug of her shoulders, "this explains why we haven't seen any Ulcas."

That was true enough. The dwarves approached with deliberate caution, stopping about a hundred feet from the Company, and called out to them in the common tongue: "Hail, wayfarers. Who are you, and by whose leave do you trespass upon the Great Dwarf Road?"

Galador spoke first. "We are lost travelers, waylaid on our way to the Sanctuary and driven underground from the High Pass. We do not wish to trespass, only to find our way out again. We had hoped this road would lead us there."

The dwarves muttered in low voices, as one stepped forward. "I am Dwim, son of Dolim," said he. "We do not usually brook Elves making use of the passages made by our folk. You will have to find another way out."

"Rogond of the Tuathar bows humbly before you," said Rogond, bowing low. "We have naught but praise for those who built this passage, for it is as fine and straight as one could hope for. However, unless I am wrong, Elves of the Èolar also had a hand in the building, and it was they who provided these lamps. Can my companions not claim a share, enough to travel in peace just this one time?"

The dwarves considered this, and then Dwim spoke again. "They are not of the Èolar. Hardly any of those folk remain. However, we have been set to meet a group of Dwarves from the Northern Mountains, and when they arrive we shall consider your request and decide your fate." Dwim and his folk approached the Company and surrounded them. Then they were conducted back to the carved stone door that marked the food cache, where the south-bound group had arrived and stood waiting. "Stand where you are!" said Dwim, as he went to greet them.

The group of dwarves coming south looked tired and travel-weary. A feeling of dread came over Rogond, as he expected they meant to break into their stores to replenish themselves. They would find what had been taken. Rogond's dread grew deeper when he noticed the crest of Rûmm emblazoned on their leather breast-plates. This made sense—the Northern Mountains had been settled by the survivors of the war that had destroyed both Rûmm and Eádros.

He hoped the dwarves would consider the dragon-brooch adequate payment, but since they would now know the stores had been plundered by Elves, sufficient payment might not be possible.

He spoke to Galador aside. "Whatever you do, don't speak to them again. They will know you for a High-elf, and they won't like it. You are now a Sylvan Elf of the Greatwood Realm." Galador would not need to be told twice—he, too, had noticed the crest of Rûmm on the dwarves' armor.

The Company was surrounded by a group of some two dozen dwarves, nearly all of whom were muttering in angry voices about the Elves, who were now trying to look as non-threatening as possible. Dwim hailed the leader of the northern dwarves, whose name was Noli.

"We are glad to have encountered you, Noli of the Northern Realm. Here you shall rest from your travels for a time, and then we shall escort you to Cós-domhain."

"It appears we're not the only ones you're escorting," growled Noli with a very unpleasant look at the Company.

"They are trespassers. What do you and your folk think of them?" asked Dwim.

"We don't like the look of them. We do not know the man, but Elves are not welcome here or in any of our lands to the north," said Noli. To this, all his folk agreed, nodding their heads and muttering. "Let's bind them until we learn more, and then decide their fate."

At this the Elves could keep quiet no longer. "We will not suffer ourselves to be bound and made helpless!" cried Nelwyn, who was becoming very nervous indeed. These dwarves were fierce, and outnumbered the Company by six to one.

Rogond placed a steadying hand on her shoulder. "You surely do not expect us to submit to being bound, O Reasonable and Courteous Dwarves, whose beards are indeed impressive. You may trust us to remain here quietly until our fate is decided." He shot a look at the Elves, who returned it with expressions of tension bordering on barely controlled panic.

"We might trust you, Aridan, if you had chosen better companions," said Noli. He was eyeing Galador with suspicion.

"I will vouch for them," said Rogond hopefully, but the dwarves were moving closer, and several had cords in their hands.

"I'm sorry, Aridan, for you are courteous, and I would trust you. However, we cannot trust *them*. They will be bound, and if they do not resist, no blood need be shed this day. If they do, we are ready to deal with them." Dwim patted the haft of his axe. He turned to his companions. "Bind them," he said. Then he turned back to Rogond.

"I sense that you lead this Company. Tell your companions to submit peacefully, or things will not go well with you."

Rogond did so, and the four of them were soon bound hand and foot, sitting in a row with their backs to the wall opposite the engraved stone door. As an extra precaution, they had been blindfolded. Gaelen trembled not with fear, but with indignation, as the dwarves bound her. She spoke under her breath to one of them; he did not understand her tongue, but the message was clear. He jerked the rawhide thongs painfully around her slender wrists, and she stifled a cry that he noted with satisfaction.

A few of the dwarves were inspecting the contents of their packs, and they became angry and suspicious as they noted the provisions that might very well have come from their own stores. They discussed this in low voices with Dwim and Noli, who immediately went to the carved panel, no doubt intent on investigating. They pressed the icons that opened the door to their storehouse, and several of the dwarves entered. The angry shouts began almost immediately, and the hearts of the Company sank into their boots. They knew the dwarves were in the storehouse; they had heard the door open.

Dwim stormed over to the captives, and jerked the blindfold from Rogond's eyes. "What do you mean, breaking into our stores and stealing from our folk? You neglected to mention this to us. Did you think we would not notice?"

"Let's just slay them and have done with it," growled Noli. His folk heard this and began to move toward the Elves, who were still blindfolded. Rogond searched frantically for a solution. Dwarves were not savages, but these were angry, and they were advancing on Galador.

Then the words of Lore-master Fima came to him, and he cried aloud: "Norúllu hadi Rûmhar! Ish menukurr ani belkur!" *Most noble Dwarves! Wait until you hear my tale!*

They froze in their tracks, regarding Rogond in astonishment. "I have rarely heard our tongue spoken by one such as you," said Dwim, looking Rogond in the eye. "How came you to learn it? Speak quickly!"

In answer, Rogond replied once again in the dwarf-tongue. What he said was apparently satisfactory, as many of the dwarves chuckled, and they seemed to relax a bit. They lowered their axes, at any rate.

"What did you say to them?" whispered Gaelen, who sat next to Rogond.

"I told them I learned the dwarf-tongue from one named Fima in the Sanctuary, so that we could talk about the Elves behind their backs," he replied. "I'm going to have to do some careful talking to get us out of this. None of you should pay heed to anything I am going to say." Gaelen was puzzled, but she trusted him.

Dwim and Noli questioned Rogond further. Dwim and the folk of Cós-domhain were familiar with Fima, and honored him even though he had gone to the Sanctuary at Mountain-home. The realm of Lady Ordath was possibly the one place in all of Alterra where good people of every race met and discoursed with freedom and respect. If Fima had deemed this man worthy of learning the dwarf-tongue, then he was indeed worthy. They would at least hear what he had to say. They took off Rogond's binding so that he might address them, over the protests of Noli, who would not have shown such courtesy.

There followed a long conversation in which Rogond told of the Company's travels and how they came to the Great Dwarf Road. He admitted that they had broken into the cache and taken supplies, but that they had left payment. The dragon-brooch was found and brought to Dwim, who examined it with awe.

"This was made by the folk of the ancient Dwarf-City of Rûmm, that was the Deep-delving," said he, turning the brooch this way and that so the various jewels caught the light and sent it back in rays of scarlet, green and gold. Noli stepped up for a closer look, and Rogond held his breath. Though Noli regarded it with wonder, he did not appear to associate the brooch with the Eádram and the ruination of Rûmm.

"From whence did this come?" asked Dwim. "Surely the Elves did not leave such a fair token in payment for food and a few torches."

"No, it was I who left it," replied Rogond. "I have been charged with leading these three Elves over the mountains, though I doubted the wisdom of it. And now, they must do as I direct them, for they are of the Cúinar, the Woodland folk, and are helpless underground. Had I known they would tax me so, I would have refused." The dwarves nodded, looking over at the three blindfolded Elves with disdain.

Rogond continued speaking to Dwim and Noli as though in confidence. "They're worthy enough in their own lands, I suppose. Good enough at climbing trees, feasting and singing, dressed all in their finery. Not much good at making anything by craft. Were it not for dwarves and men to make their ornaments and carve out their great halls, where would they be? They remember the days of the Èolar, who were mighty craftsmen among their people. Those smiths are long since gone, yet the haughtiness of their descendants remains. And the real frustration for us is that we cannot even escape their haughtiness by outliving them!"

The dwarves nodded in agreement as the Elves sat in silence. Their faces reddened a little, for there was a small grain of truth in Rogond's words. Dwim clapped Rogond on the elbow with a hearty laugh. Here, surely, was a kindred spirit.

Rogond glanced over at his friends before turning back to Dwim. "Actually, I'm reasonably fond of these, else I would not have agreed to help them in their folly, but would have abandoned them. I would appreciate your leaving them unharmed, as I promised to make every effort to conduct them safely."

Noli growled under his breath at this. It was clear that he was going to be difficult. Rogond thought quickly then raised his voice to the assembled dwarves: "Let's have music and song, avail ourselves of this excellent wine and ale, and rest from our labors. I'm happy to be in such pleasant company at last!"

The dwarves of Noli's group, who were weary and in need of just such a diversion, joined their fellows in a hearty cheer. Soon the wine and ale were flowing with abandon, and torches were lit all along the walls. The Elves had been moved out of the way of the merriment. Their captors took turns keeping an eye on them as they sat on the cold stone floor, still bound and blindfolded, but safe enough for the moment.

The dwarves had loosened up considerably and were nearly all in a good humor as they played their tunes and danced in the torchlight. They were surprisingly agile, hardy, and strong. "Perhaps we should play a bit of the music of the Elven-folk," said Rogond. "It might be enjoyable to watch them dance." The dwarves glowered at him, and Rogond looked around, and then feigned sudden understanding. "Oh, I see! You thought I meant to *untie* them first!"

At this the dwarves all burst into laughter, turning their heads to regard the three Elves, who were becoming quite uncomfortable. The dwarf who had been set to watch them actually clapped Galador on the shoulder, startling him such that he cried out.

Rogond gave Noli a look that said: *You see what I have to put up with?* There followed a long period of jesting, mostly at the expense of the Elves, and in the dwarf-tongue. Rogond missed some of the words, but he took much of the meaning. He was glad the Elves did not understand what was said about them, as he felt they had suffered enough already. They were a proud and worthy people, and Rogond knew and loved them well, but this would not serve their interests just now. Better he should at least pretend to join in the jest.

"What I would like to know is…how can they tell their men from their women? The men are at least as pretty!"

"Aye, some are even prettier!" The fact that male Elves were beardless had always been a joke to the dwarves.

"What I find dismaying is that they complain about the smell of dwarves and of men, but pay no heed to their own. It's as though they don't believe they have any smell!"

"Oh, that's a good one. I once had to walk into a room full of them. You can always tell where *Elves* have been."

To this, Rogond would give no argument, though he had always found the normal scent of Elvish folk pleasant, rather like fresh sage. They certainly didn't suffer from the same foul odors that afflicted men, even when they were unwashed and weary. Of dwarvish aroma, Rogond knew little, and wisely decided to forego comment.

"I marvel at the way they can talk out of both sides of their mouths at once," growled Noli, remembering the dwarves' version of the treachery of the High-elves and the subsequent fall of Rûmm. He was in a better humor, but he and his folk still presented a danger, and Rogond was waiting for the right time to suggest that perhaps they might go on their way. But then, one of the folk of Cós-domhain approached him and bade him stand in the torchlight.

"Show me that ring on your right hand," he asked Rogond, indicating the ring of gold with the black stone. Rogond removed it and handed it to the dwarf, who examined it with wonder. "I am Glomin, of Cós-domhain. How came you by this token?"

"It was taken from the hand of my mother as she lay dead, slain by Ulcas in the mountains," said Rogond. "The Elves gave it to me as an heirloom. It's the only thing of my family that I possess, for I know not even the names of my kin. It is my great desire to learn this," he added hopefully.

Glomin was amazed. "If this ring is that which I think it is, it belonged to one of the great among our folk, whose life was saved by a proud maiden of Dûn Bennas. If it is indeed that ring, the stone is like to very few that remain in this world, for the craft of their making is closely guarded. Come and look into the light of the Èolarin lamp. We must come away from the torchlight."

He led Rogond down the passage until they reached the next of the blue lamps, and only its light illuminated the ring. "Look deep into the depths of the stone. The image will appear only in this light." Rogond searched and was astonished to behold an inscription, tiny but legible, glowing blue in the black depths of the stone.

He translated the words aloud, to the wonder of Glomin. "I, Farin, declare the bearer to be Dwarf-friend and free in Dwarf Realms."

"He gave that not lightly, Aridan. Show it to Dwim and Noli. They will honor it," said Glomin.

"This Farin—does he still live?" Rogond was anxious. Could it be that this dwarf would shed some light on the mystery of his parentage? If so, Rogond would seek him out and learn all that he could.

"He does," said Glomin. "Farin has attained greatness among our people as a hardy warrior, and of his smith-work, you can see for yourself. Let's go back and show this to the others. Then I will tell the tale of Farin as I have heard it"

After Glomin had spoken to Dwim and Noli, they also marveled at the ring. "This changes everything, Aridan," said Dwim. "If you are Dwarf-friend, you are free to take any provisions you need while in our lands, with no need of payment. I give you back your token." He handed the dragon-brooch back to Rogond, who bowed, then gave it right back to him.

"I give it to you freely, but not as payment for provisions. I give it in ransom for the Elves, that they also may have provisions and leave to continue their journey."

"As your companions, they are free to leave with you," said Dwim, though Noli still glowered. "But no provisions will they take from our hands. You may take enough for all, but they must know that this generosity toward them comes from you and not from us."

"Then I still give this token in friendship, Dwim of Cós-domhain. May your beard grow to match those of the Five Founders and never grow thin. But I would stay and hear the tale of Glomin, as it concerns me closely."

He asked that the Elves be unbound and allowed to stretch their limbs and partake of food and drink before going on their way. To this, the dwarves did not agree.

"Let them lie there until you are ready to depart, Rogond. They will be allowed to proceed with you unharmed. Let that satisfy you."

Glomin stepped into the center of the circle to tell his tale, and they all attended him, for it was a tale some had not yet heard. "I will tell of Rosalin, the River-maiden, who was Dwarf-friend, and how she came to save the life of one of our greatest warriors and craftsmen, Farin son of Farlos."

Rogond was rapt, for he knew then that Rosalin, his mother, had been a proud woman of the Tuathar—a fierce fighter and worthy companion, friend of Elves, dwarves, and men. Of his father there was no mention, but Rogond held out hope that Farin would know something of him.

It was with such hope in his heart that Rogond prepared to lead the Elves from the mountain, at the direction of Dwim, who knew the quickest and easiest way to the Sanctuary. After saying their farewells, the dwarves left the Company and began the return journey south to Cós-domhain, together with Noli's folk. Only then could Rogond release the Elves.

Galador, Gaelen, and Nelwyn were nearly paralyzed from being trussed and immobile on the cold stone for so long, and they got up with some difficulty upon being released. Gaelen actually fell down twice, as she had no feeling in her feet for several minutes. Rogond braced her until she could walk, her face set and determined not to show the pain of a thousand hot needles flaring in her hands and feet as life returned to them. She glared at the dwarves' retreating backs, and would always remember their treatment of her.

Galador and Nelwyn were of similar mind. It was their opinion that Rogond had perhaps enjoyed his camaraderie with the dwarves a bit too much, particularly at the Elves' expense.

Their attitudes softened when Rogond pointed out that they now had their provisions, had found their way back to their destination, and still had all four of their lives. "Rogond, you have proven your worth far beyond my expectations," said Gaelen. "Forgive us our lack of gratitude. I will not underestimate you again."

Rogond smiled at her. "You will, you know...you will not be able to help yourself."

10

Eros and Réalta

Capellion, the Master of Horse in the Woodland Realm, had never before faced a situation such as this. Two fine animals had been left in his charge, and he had been instructed to keep them confined, but, try as he might, he could not get either of them to settle down.

Both horses were well used, had no doubt seen years of long travel and warfare, and had probably not often been in confinement. But it was a rare animal that did not eventually settle in to the comfortable accommodations provided in the King's stables. The stalls were roomy, the bedding fine and deep, and the feed superb, even at this time of year. Though the Elves did not cultivate their own fodder they traded for some of the best, and this year's crop had been excellent.

Capellion was Master of Horse because he had an innate sense of the minds of horses. Even so, he was puzzled by these two. At first he assumed they were unhappy at being left behind and would have preferred to follow their masters. But surely they would have gotten over that by now; even foals taken from their dams did not fret for so long. They had been in his keeping for three weeks, and though they had thankfully stopped their incessant neighing, they paced and circled, and simply would not rest.

Ri-Aruin and Wellyn had returned from the hunt, and Wellyn had been down in the stables once or twice since, but he had not been allowed access to Eros and Réalta on the King's orders. Apparently, Wellyn had been told that both strangers had gone, but as he had not seen their horses he had assumed that they had gone away mounted, attending to their own business. If he had known the horses were still there, he might have guessed his father's deception, and that would have been a very bad turn of events.

Capellion was unhappy with this situation, as he took great pride in the care shown to the horses in his charge. Eros and Réalta now looked lean and ill-kept. Though he tried to soothe them and keep them groomed, they would not stop pacing, nor eat more than a few mouthfuls of feed. Eros, in particular, looked much less fit than he had. His ribs were now easily felt, even through his thick hair, which was beginning to shed with the waning of winter into spring. Capellion wished that the King would relent and allow him to release the horses onto the wide plain, but he also knew that if they did so, Eros and Réalta would never see his stables again. Better that, than to watch them stress themselves until they sickened and died.

Capellion was struck especially by the mind of Eros. The Aridan had described him in his message as occasionally having a roguish nature. What Capellion observed was a calculating willfulness bordering on genius. They had stopped trusting him when he had nearly escaped from them on his third day of captivity. Eros had feigned an injury to one foreleg, compelling the stable hands to halter him and bring him out for Capellion to examine. He had stood placidly while the horse-master ran his experienced hands over the 'injured' leg. Eros waited for the Elves to take their attention from restraining him...after all, he wouldn't run off lame, would he?

Capellion had felt neither heat nor swelling, yet the horse would place no weight on the leg at all. Cradling the forefoot in his hands, Capellion called for steel pincers to test the hoof, for such deep lameness could only be detected in this manner. Eros nuzzled his back affectionately, convincing the Elves that he had relaxed and was now accepting their care. Two of the stable-hands had opened the large double doors to let in more light from the outside courtyard.

Eros lifted his head, turned it toward the doors, snorted once, and then leaped forward, knocking Capellion and one of his handlers to the ground. The other handler was determined to hang on, but Eros literally dragged him through the large double doors, slamming him into one of them so that he fell back, stunned. It was then that Eros discovered that he was in a wide, stone courtyard. There was only one gate, and it was closed. Dragging his long line, he called to Réalta anyway. Let the Elves try—they would not catch him. Réalta was screaming in his stall, rushing at the gate and slamming to a stop. Finally, with the grace of a gazelle and a tremendous effort, he lifted himself up and over the partition, barely avoiding the stone roof with his head and withers. Capellion and his aides tugged frantically at the stable doors, closing them just in time.

Réalta and Eros were both furious. Thank the stars that the King and his son were gone on the hunt. Who would fail to notice the frustrated screaming of the two foiled conspirators, one of which still ran wildly in the courtyard? Capellion noted the complete lack of lameness as Eros floated majestically back and forth before the gate, eyeing the "Master of Horse" in defiance, as though daring him to try to outwit him with his feeble, two-legged brain. Capellion would have given a great deal at that moment to have known Eros as a foal and to have raised him as his own. What a war-animal he must be!

Eros grew weary and thirsty about mid-afternoon and stood by the courtyard gate, his tail raised like a sable flag. Réalta was still calling out, but he had been caught and placed back in the stall, the gate of which had been fortified such that he could not jump it again. Such agility was rare, and Capellion would have liked to keep Réalta to cross over some of the mares in the band, as it would no doubt improve the quality of the foal crop. Eros, on the other hand...

Capellion would have worried a bit about the temperaments that would have resulted from that cross. There was such a thing as having too much intelligence. Eros was a horse that would be suited to relatively few riders. As Rogond had said, he would not suffer prideful or foolish behavior, and Ri-Aruin's people sometimes displayed plenty of one if not the other.

Capellion approached Eros now, no rope in hand, but with a small vessel of water. The tall, strong dun raised his head imperiously, eyeing Capellion with suspicion. If one had been privy to their thoughts, they might have gone something like this:

You will have to open this gate eventually, you know!

Not before you come into the stables to drink, Son of the North.

Try to outwit me, and you will regret it. I serve one master, and he has gone. I will find him, whatever comes.

Not without water. I will not harm you, but you must drink, and you know it. Your chance to outwit me again will come soon enough.

There is water in the Great River. That is where he has gone and where I must follow.

At that moment, Réalta called plaintively from his now-fortified captivity.

Your companion calls you, even now. Will you leave without him?

Eros stamped his "lame" foot once, raising the dust, snorted and flung his head in a circular motion. He took one step toward Capellion.

Set that water-vessel down, and we'll talk.

Indeed, we will talk, but not before the courtyard gate. The water is waiting, you have but to come and take it.

Eros was very thirsty. He wanted to drink, but he didn't want to approach Capellion, as he sensed that the Elf was his equal in cleverness and was now wise to his tricks. He knew Capellion would not be fooled again. Réalta was trapped inside the wretched stable, and Eros really didn't want to leave without him. Eros wondered what his friend Rogond would think of his usefulness to the Elven-king at this particular moment. Well, what did he expect? Rogond surely knew him better than that. He had sworn loyalty to only one and was of quite different temperament with any other. If any of the Elves tried to ride him they would find out!

These thoughts occupied him even as he followed the water-vessel, held before him by Capellion, until the stable doors closed behind him. He was allowed to drink his fill before being led to his own stall next to Réalta. Capellion stayed with him for a while, stroking him, speaking softly to him, and offering him bits of fruit, which he would not take at first.

Réalta snorted, envious. Capellion gave him a few dried apples, which he consumed with enthusiasm, dripping white froth upon the stall floor as he chewed with his eyes half closed. That was too much for Eros. After all, he didn't really have anything against the Elves, and Capellion was worthy of respect. It couldn't hurt to take a few dried apples. He nuzzled the pouch that hung at Capellion's belt, nickering.

All right…I will submit for the moment. May I please have some of those?

Capellion smiled and gave Eros most of the rest of the apples, sharing a few yet with Réalta. He patted Eros again, trusting that they understood one another. Eros lifted his proud head and looked the horse-master in the eye.

Don't think that this changes anything between us, Elf. You have your duty, and I have mine!

Capellion nodded to himself. They did indeed understand each other.

Now, weeks later, Capellion regarded both horses as they stood in their stalls, looking at him in forlorn silence. Eros gave a halfhearted toss of his head and resumed pacing. Réalta gave a low nicker at his companion through the partition that separated them, circling slowly in his own stall, first one way, then the other. Capellion was disheartened as he observed the uneaten feed in the mangers. Something would have to be done. He decided to go to the King and beg leave to turn the horses loose before their condition declined any further.

After Capellion had explained the situation, Ri-Aruin came down to the stables to see for himself. He agreed that Eros and Réalta needed exercise and fresh air, but he did not want them turned out to run loose, for he knew as well as Capellion that they would soon be gone. "The strangers left them in our care," said he, "and we cannot lose them. It is not in the manner of the Woodland to fail in such safekeeping when asked."

"I am keeping them, but I am not keeping them well," said Capellion. "They will not stand for it much longer, and they are worthy animals. It pains me to see them decline. Are they not better off running free than to be so put upon? When their masters return, they will hold us to blame if their mounts have wasted from grief."

Ri-Aruin considered the words of his trusted servant. "They will blame us the more if we have lost their mounts, and my son must not know that they are here. Allow me to send him on an errand to the west, to see to our interests there. The horses may then be used and ridden over the wide lands. That should cheer them. Will that satisfy you?"

Capellion bowed before the King, his right hand on his breast in a gesture of submission. Though this was not his preferred course, it was better than the present one, and he knew better than to press Ri-Aruin's generosity too much. "Thank you, my lord. Hopefully, the chance to exercise and feel the air will turn them around, though they will still need to be confined. You will inform me when Wellyn has departed?"

Ri-Aruin agreed to inform Capellion, and then left the stables. Wellyn set forth a few days later, and Eros and Réalta could then be ridden and exercised by the Wood-elves.

Four of the best horse-handlers were assigned this task, as Capellion still did not trust either of the horses, especially the wily Eros, not to slip their bonds and escape. He decided that perhaps it might not be safe to ride them as yet, so long lines were attached to the halters, and two handlers were mounted, one on each side, galloping either Eros or Réalta between them. They did this twice daily, and Eros' heart was gladdened, for he was beginning to wonder if he would ever see the sun and the grass again. He and Réalta bided their time, being as cooperative as lambs.

Spring was coming on in the wide lands, and though winter still held dominion it had lost most of its power. The four Elven handlers mounted up, took hold of the long lines securing Eros and Réalta, and went forth in the late morning. They anticipated no difficulty, as the weather was fine, and they were now well acquainted with their charges. Six horses ran over the plain as one, heads and tails high. The Elves were enjoying themselves as well, bent over the necks of their mounts, long hair flowing, long lines grasped firmly, enjoying the illusion of control.

Eros blew a great snort through his wide nostrils. *I believe we have convinced them to trust us...that we have submitted to their will.*

Agreed. They are becoming ever more lackadaisical. They have no idea what we're capable of. What say we show them something today?

Eros and Réalta had learned that it was they, not the handlers, who controlled their pace, and now they matched each other stride for stride. They stretched their forelegs before them, eating up the ground, and encouraged the horses that flanked them to do the same. The four handlers' illusion was about to be shattered in mid-stride.

Looks like this would be a good time to give these riders a thrill. Yes...any moment now...watch THIS!

Eros stopped abruptly, flinging his head in the air and slamming his forelegs into the ground. This startled the two horses beside him so that they swerved away, unbalancing their riders just enough that the sudden hard tug from the long lines unseated both of them. The Elves hit the ground hard, still holding on. Stunned and shaken, they clung with grim tenacity to the lines, but could not hold Eros for long, as he was now practically running backward, dragging them over the stony grass.

Let GO...of me...you...idiots!

Eros whipped around and galloped as fast as he could to the south, the lines flailing loosely around his legs.

Réalta had not been idle, either. When Eros stopped, both of Réalta's handlers were distracted and dismayed, and sought to slow him down. He reacted by lashing his head as hard as he could to the right, jerking the one off balance, then leaping sideways, nearly colliding with the other, who now had a lap full of loose line and no control. Then, Réalta showed them all the speed with which he was gifted.

Just try to keep up with me, you snails! Just TRY!

The flankers had no chance, and the handler on the left was pulled from his mount so handily that he actually landed on his feet for a moment. But of course, he could not hold the speeding, leaping Réalta, who then found himself held by only one white-faced but determined Elf. The two of them raced along the wide valley, leaping over stones, Réalta like a streak of silver flame unfettered by a rider. He drew ahead of the Elf's mount, straining at the line until the handler needed most of his strength just to hang on.

I believe it's time we parted company...

Réalta swerved to the left, and the line went slack as the Elf turned it loose. He would not have remained mounted otherwise. Réalta turned and went after Eros, catching him easily, for he had slowed to a trot.

Eros lifted his head and gave a loud call toward the stables. Capellion heard it with some dread, for he was very intuitive and perceived Eros' message clearly:

You have been as kind as you could be, worthy Elf, but we hold the mastery. Our duty is plain, as was yours. Only one of us could succeed.

Though Eros did not know where Rogond had gone, he would not stop until he had found him. At last he was free to go where he would. Réalta, who was having similar thoughts concerning Galador, was fussing over the troublesome halter with its dangling long lines. Soon they would deal with that problem and set about finding their masters.

The grass is coming on, thought Eros. *We'll be just fine.*

11

The Tale of Galador

It took the better part of nine more days for the Company to see daylight again. Dwim's instructions, complete with a hastily-drawn but reasonable map, had proven invaluable. The journey was not without its perils; Dwim had warned that the path they would now take was occasionally traveled by Ulcas as well, increasing the likelihood of an encounter. With that in mind, the Company proceeded with the greatest caution, thankful for the torch light that would at least prevent them from pitching forward into some abyss.

Not even an enormous party of well-armed Ulcas could have dampened Rogond's spirits. The Company rejoiced with him, as he had learned a great deal from the dwarves concerning the history of the woman he believed to have been his mother. As soon as he could manage it, Rogond intended to travel south to Cós-domhain to learn more from this dwarf named Farin, and perhaps fit a few more of the missing pieces into the mosaic of his personal history.

Now, though, there were other pressing matters at hand. The road to Mountain-home still stretched before them, and it would take a while to get there. Then there was the question of how they would proceed after that. Rogond had no doubt that Gaelen, at any rate, would want to take the most direct path that would lead her back onto the trail of her enemy. What would lead her to that path was as yet unforeseen.

Galador walked quietly behind Nelwyn, lost in thought. The mishap with the dwarves had unnerved him, as he had little doubt that Noli, the leader of the group from the Northern Mountains, would have ordered him killed had it not been for Rogond. The strife between the Elves of Eádros and the dwarves of Rûmm was bitter, and neither kindred had forgotten it.

Galador now anticipated Rogond's desire to travel to Cós-domhain, and he was concerned. He wouldn't have admitted it, but he was reluctant to enter this greatest of all underground dwarf-realms. Because he was of the Eádram, he feared he might encounter the same dislike from the dwarves of Cós-domhain. Though neither they nor their ancestors had anything to do with the fall of Eádros, dwarves were likely to share enmity in defense of their own. When he had the opportunity he would speak to Rogond about it; perhaps his friend could reassure him.

The other thought gnawing at the back of Galador's mind was the growing fascination and friendship between Rogond and Gaelen. Surely, Rogond knew that binding himself to one of the Elàni was ill-advised, yet Galador knew the looks cast at Gaelen for what they were. He should never have let her minister to Rogond during his illness—her songs carried power that she probably didn't even realize. If Galador was any judge, his friend's heart was now completely and irretrievably lost to her.

Gaelen, for her part, did not appear to reciprocate in the same manner, but she was fond of Rogond and obviously enjoyed his company. Galador worried that this friendship could escalate, knowing it could only end in tragedy for one or both of them. He was reluctant to speak with Rogond about it as yet, but knew the time would come soon. When it did, Galador would be forced to reveal a very old and painful part of his own past.

One of the things Galador and Rogond had in common was the fact that neither knew very much about the history of the other. In Rogond's case, this was because he knew almost nothing of it himself, whereas Galador had simply never elaborated much on his own lineage or what had happened to him in the last several-thousand-or-so years that he had been alive. Rogond had noticed that his friend often seemed distant and somewhat melancholy, and that he had only rarely joined in merrymaking until the advent of Nelwyn. Rogond was glad that Galador had found such a pleasing diversion, as he sensed that his friend had been a solitary wanderer for much of his life.

It had not always been so.

As he walked in silence beside Rogond, Galador's thoughts could not help straying back to the lost realm of Eádros, the place of his birth. Because of his love for a mortal woman, he had been banished from that beautiful place—sent far away from his friends, his family, and his home. He had never opened his heart to anyone since. The pain of his loss had been so bitter that, until he had come upon Nelwyn that day by the river, he had thought never to love again.

Now he saw his friend Rogond about to stray down the same path, but didn't know how to dissuade him. He was reluctant to reveal this most intimate and heart-wrenching account of his past.

He closed his eyes for a moment, recalling the security and splendor of the realm of Eádros, where he had once stood in high favor. His skill at arms, tempered by a gentle nature, had endeared him to the hearts of the King and the ruling council, and so he was often sent forth as emissary. His words were well chosen, and he was strong and swift. He had traveled to the other Elven-realms, and was sent also to help maintain relations with the various tribes of men.

Galador glanced over at Rogond, who was now his closest friend. Because of his role as ambassador to the realms of men, he had come to know them. He appreciated them from the first—far better than did most of his kindred—viewing them with both compassion and admiration. They accomplished much in their short span of years. Beset constantly by enemies, they dealt with pestilence and the decline of their bodies with age, yet they sang, danced, and loved one another in joy. Always, death stalked them. Their time in the world was as a single firebrand that kindles, burns brightly for a brief time, then fades and dies in the grey twilight. They would never know the seemingly endless span of days that he and his kindred enjoyed, just as he could not know or understand their mortality—or the fate that awaited them after death.

Galador had always known that Elves and men should not intermingle, but he also knew that awareness of what *should* be does not always govern the choice of one's heart as to what *will* be. The growing attraction of Rogond for Gaelen had brought back memories that he would have preferred to keep buried deep within, though he had never been truly successful at escaping them. He would never tell Rogond all the details of this most distressing part of his history, but he intended to impart enough that his friend would take the warning and pull back from Gaelen before he had gone too far. If Rogond would not listen, Galador would talk to Gaelen herself. After that, the choice would be theirs, but at least they would be armed with the foreknowledge he had lacked.

If Galador had been aware that his life would be shattered when he first cast eyes on the mortal woman named Gwynnyth, he would have set himself on a different path. But she had seemed so fair, and of such a pure and innocent nature, that he had been drawn into a hopeless, tragic, misguided bond resulting in naught but pain.

In those days, the Elves of Eádros were not well-disposed toward any of the kindred of men, some of whom had stood in battle beside Lord Wrothgar. King Doniol of Eádros, in particular, mistrusted them. Yet Galador wondered...if the Elves had afforded more protection to the children of men, might they have resisted the influence of evil? They were set upon from all sides by the minions of Wrothgar—who could blame them for giving in? Galador had never really approved of the King's attitude. It was all well and good to feel superior when Cuimir the Beautiful sat at your right hand. Cuimir, one of the original seven magic-users, was an ancient being whose enlightenment had graced Eádros from the beginning.

At the heart of most of the great Elven-realms there was a magic-user, one of the mysterious Asari. Such folk have ever been rare. Twelve were sent into the world when it was formed, and they held great power over certain matters. Yet they could choose to follow either the Light or the Darkness. Those who chose the Light favored the Elf-realms, for the Elves have rarely if ever served the Darkness, and then unwittingly. It was the Asari who kept those realms well hidden; one could not gain entrance without their leave. Eádros, which was underground, was so well concealed that men who lived in the surrounding regions wondered if it even existed, speculating that the Elves simply appeared out of thin air.

It was of the utmost importance that no outsiders were shown the way into the hidden realm, but this Galador did for the love of Gwynnyth. He remembered her impassioned plea, for she had wanted to see the wonders of the Elf-realm for herself. When she saw how secure and idyllic it was, she had then tried to persuade Galador to bring the remainder of her people, who were besieged by the enemy and had endured great suffering, into the hidden realm with her. They would live in peace as allies of the Elves.

Galador was uncertain, but he was yet young and his love for Gwynnyth was very great. To reassure her he promised that, at the very least, her family would be admitted. This unfortunate promise was overheard by one of the King's courtiers, who reported all that he had heard.

Galador shivered, remembering King Doniol's wrath. Guards had come, arresting him and dragging Gwynnyth off to a prison cell. Galador feared the worst—that Doniol might even have ordered Gwynnyth killed—until he stood before the throne to answer the charges against him.

The King had, of course, not killed Gwynnyth, but he was both grieved and wrathful at the perceived betrayal. "I will give to thee a choice," he said to Galador. "Your woman may remain forever within the boundaries of Eádros, but she will be confined here, never to roam free again."

"But she will not wish to abandon her people, and her freedom is precious," said Galador.

Doniol's voice was heavy with regret, but his eyes were hard. "If she refuses, then I have no choice but to banish you both from this realm. You will never be allowed to return."

Galador thought of his beloved, knowing he had only one choice to make if he truly loved her. She cared for her family and would pine for them. "I cannot condemn her to a life of imprisonment—no matter how comfortable the prison," he said.

"So be it. You know our laws, and what you have done is treason. Your choice is made, Galador, and you are hereby forbidden to ever set foot in the realm of Eádros."

The Asarla of Eádros, Cuimir the Beautiful, was saddened. But he obeyed the King's decree, closing the way to Galador, abandoning him to the dark and hostile world outside.

Galador would never forget the finality of those words spoken in judgment of him so many years ago. Those words were like a sharp blade cutting him loose from everything comforting and familiar. He fought to distract his troubled mind from remembering the terrible events that came after, but he could not. Instead he dropped back, allowing Rogond to stride on ahead of him.

Rogond paused and turned. "Are you all right?"

Galador could not look his tall friend in the eye. He pretended to fuss with the lacing on one of his tall boots, muttering a reply. "I'm good…this lacing has come loose. I'll catch you up."

If Rogond had looked into his friend's eyes, he would have seen the turmoil of emotion fighting to escape. He had seen it before, but not often. "Are you sure? Can I help?"

"I don't need help. Go on ahead…I would rather not delay. I'll only be a moment."

But the truth was that these memories had plagued Galador for over a thousand years. "A moment" would never be enough to really suppress them—even now he recalled the terrible day of his banishment, remembering how lost, how alone, and how helpless he had been.

Once outside the Elf-realm, the lovers had gone to Gwynnyth's folk, but found no welcome there. Gwynnyth's people mistrusted and feared the Elves, and they had driven Galador out of their settlement, chasing him with stones and wooden spears. He still remembered his pain and shame. Gwynnyth went into exile with him, and they wandered together in the wild.

Despite their uncertainty they were happy for a time, as their love sustained them, and in the spring Gwynnyth was with child. This brief, happy memory softened Galador's face and brought light back into his eyes, but the light faded as he remembered what came next.

Their happiness together came to an abrupt end when Gwynnyth was seven months into her childbearing, as autumn waned and winter drew near. She and Galador had prepared a place to spend the difficult months of cold and snow, and had laid by stores of food, for there would be little to be had.

Galador had gone out gathering, leaving Gwynnyth in the relative safety of their shelter. She had ventured forth to walk among the trees in twilight and had been set upon by Ulcas, even as Galador returned over the ridge and beheld her. He drew his bow and killed or drove off the Ulcas, but not before they had grievously wounded his beloved. Galador rushed to her side and bore her back into their shelter, but even as he did so, he knew her wounds were grave. He tended her as best he could, but as darkness came she roused herself, knowing what her fate would be. Her eyes filled with tears as she beheld his beautiful, anxious face.

"My love…sit here beside me, for I must leave you tonight."

Galador refused to face the truth. "Do not say such things…do not even think them! Your wounds will heal—I have tended them well so that they won't fester, but you must not think such black thoughts, for they will take your strength. As long as you stay strong, you will prevail. Tomorrow I will make you a healing poultice…and some… maybe some strengthening tea?"

Gwynnyth shook her head slowly, closing her eyes and shuddering with pain. "The wounds are poisoned," she muttered. "You have tended them as best you could, but…but they are beyond your power. Here, in this wild place, there is no help for me."

Galador's brows knitted together as he squeezed her hand… it was so cold, and he despaired. "Please, my love…don't give in."

"Listen to me, Galador, son of Galathar. Our child is dying in my womb…the poison in my blood is killing her. Please…I need you to be strong now, and take her from me while there is still a chance. Please, my brave one, take her while she still lives. I will not see the sun rise tomorrow, but she might."

Galador's eyes filled with grief and horror—he could never do such a thing. Sacrifice Gwynnyth to save the child? "You ask me to do the impossible," he whispered, and the anguish in her eyes pierced his heart and ripped it to pieces. He sat beside her, trying in vain to comfort and strengthen her, but he could not stop either her pain or her grief.

After a while, her eyes fluttered open, but she could no longer shed tears. "Our baby is dead," she whispered. "She has taken the last of my strength."

"Forgive me…I could not kill you with my own hands," said Galador, trying not to let her see the tears in his own eyes. "Forgive me…please?"

"Mother and child will go together into the hereafter," she said, attempting a weak smile. "I understand. I'm so sorry to leave you alone…and I would ask…no, I would *beg* you to keep watch over my family, though they may not love you. They will need your protection, and they are all that will be left of me. Promise me?"

"I will," said Galador, though his throat was closed up so tightly that no sound came from his lips.

"I know you will…I know. Now hold us, beloved…hold us until we leave you. We are not afraid…"

Gwynnyth died in the early morning, as he held her in his arms and wept. As she lay before him, cold yet still beautiful, Galador knew that he had lost all that he loved.

The Elves do not know the ultimate fate of men; they are only certain that this fate is different and entirely separate from their own. Galador knew that he would never be with Gwynnyth or with their child. Even so, he resolved to meet Gwynnyth on the misty, distant shores where the children of men go when their lives end, there to set out for their unknown and irrevocable fate. Surely, if he called to her, she would come back.

He arranged and tended the body of Gwynnyth, wrapping it in his own warm cloak. He then lay beside her, trying to will his spirit to follow her. For two days and nights he was still and cold as stone, his mind and heart focused on the task, but he could not achieve it, for he was only an Elf, and the way was closed to him. Finally, when cold and thirst had nearly claimed his life, he roused himself. The death of his body would not serve his purpose, as he knew that his fate would then be separated from Gwynnyth beyond hope. He ate and drank, and tended Gwynnyth, then tried again for two more days and nights to follow her, this time barely managing to escape death.

He knew then that his hope was vain and that Gwynnyth was truly gone. He wept for many days after that, wishing that death would now take him rather than allow him to live in misery, but such was not his fate. He remembered the desire of Gwynnyth that, in spite of their estrangement, she would have Galador keep watch over her folk from afar. To comfort her he had agreed, though in his heart he carried bitter resentment of their stones and spears.

Though Galador possessed a strong spirit, he was nearly consumed with grief. He lay in solitude in the small shelter, still trying in vain to reach out to Gwynnyth, wherever she had gone. He wept and slept fitfully, eating and drinking only enough to keep himself alive until spring. Gaunt and haggard, he finally emerged, but it was a long while before the light returned to his eyes.

He buried Gwynnyth in a grove of maple trees. The warmth of spring stirred new life all around him, but he was not cheered by it. For uncounted years he watched over Gwynnyth's folk as best he could, for he had promised her. His long bow and keen blade kept them safe, but then the east wind brought a dreadful pestilence that devastated men, women, and children without mercy. Galador sorrowed for them but could do nothing to aid them, and at the last he revealed himself to the few who remained. He sat beside them, speaking comforting words as they died, begging them to carry his message of love to Gwynnyth, if they should meet in the hereafter.

Stone-hearted and bitter-minded, Galador became a solitary wanderer for many an age, until his true nature prevailed and allowed him to walk again among Elves and men. During that time many things came to pass in Alterra: there was war between the dwarves of Rûmm and the Eádram, so that both realms were destroyed. King Doniol was slain, and Cuimir became so despondent that he gave up his own life. Galador fought beneath the banner of the High King in the Third Uprising of Lord Wrothgar. The northern land of Tuathas, home to the most enlightened of men, was laid in ruin, and the Plague spread its icy hand over all the western lands, taking far more than it spared. Throughout those long ages, Galador kept largely to himself.

Then, during his recent travels, he met and befriended Rogond, and they had traveled together for six years. It was this friendship—this slight opening in the stone of Galador's heart—that had allowed him to venture into the Light. But it was Nelwyn's light that truly gave him hope.

For the first time since his world was torn apart, his heart was swelling inside its stony shell. If he could but listen, he would escape the dark, loveless prison he had built for himself. Nelwyn was beautiful, and gentle-natured, and of Elven-kind. He could love her without fear, and be joined with her forever, if only she would have him. Galador took courage from his thoughts of happiness with Nelwyn, and for the time being he waited to see if his love would be returned.

Pushing his dark memories aside yet again, he made sure his eyes were dry before catching up with the rest of the Company. He had grown quite fond of Rogond in their travels together and would not let his friend make the same grievous choice. When the time was right, he would tell just enough to dissuade Rogond. He hoped that the inevitable rift that would result would not sunder him from Nelwyn before their love could flower, but better that, he told himself, than to allow Rogond to impale his heart upon bitter thorns.

12

The Trail Grows Warm

When the Elves and Rogond finally emerged into the light from the depths of the mountains, they rejoiced at the sights, sounds, and smells of the world outside. They could hear one of the two mighty streams that flowed near the Sanctuary and realized that their destination was very near at hand, though they were now south of it. Rogond, who had spent more time in these lands than any of the others, looked around with satisfaction. Though they would still have to negotiate treacherous footing along the rocky slopes, and undertake a precipitous climb over the pass that opened the hidden way into Ordath's realm, it would be nothing compared with what they had already been through. They were now below the tree line, and the snows here were old and tired. Spring would bring the land into flower before long, and they had actually made better time than they had planned.

Each of them now blessed the encounter with the dwarves, who had shown them the way out. Luck had been with them in that they had not encountered any significant threat along the way, but there was one rather queer sign at the tunnel exit. Crude gear, food stores, and weapons, apparently to provision a small company of Ulcan guards, lay abandoned. It was queer because the Ulcas that owned the provisions were nowhere in evidence, yet it was full daylight outside, and the Company had seen no sign of them back up the tunnel for a long distance. Galador guessed that they had gone out in the dark of night on some mischief and had either gotten lost or had fallen under misfortune.

"If they got anywhere near the Elven-realm, they will never return. That much is certain," said Rogond. "All the same, we must take care."

Gaelen and Nelwyn picked up the trail of the Ulcas without difficulty. They had gone south along the slope, avoiding the path toward Mountain-home, but for what purpose none could say. Curiosity had gotten the better of Gaelen; she wanted to know what had befallen them. A familiar prickling was growing in the back of her mind. She and Nelwyn tracked the Ulcas southward, despite the mild protestations of Rogond and Galador, who pointed out that they were getting farther from their destination. Finding themselves ignored by the She-elves, they followed behind, speaking in low voices to one another and keeping watch for enemies.

"We may encounter Elves of Mountain-home in these lands, hunter-scouts like yourselves," said Rogond. "They will welcome us once they know us, but they may be a bit twitchy if they cannot identify us quickly. Of that we must be wary, especially as evening draws down. I would suggest that we stop moving once night falls."

Gaelen nodded, though she had no intention of stopping until she discovered the fate of the Ulcas. The prickling in her mind had not gone away; it had turned instead into a low burning. She looked up at the sun-bright sky and smiled. She did this for two reasons. The first was that it was good to see the sky again, unclouded by snow or mist. The other was that the stars and moon would be bright tonight, and she would have good light for tracking. A short while later she was beginning to pick up scent on the wind, and in a few moments she knew that tracking the Ulcas would not need to extend into the darkness, as they were dead.

Their scent had carried for miles, and it was coming on toward twilight when they were found at last. Seven dark, rotting bodies, dead for several days, lay among the rocks. There was evidence of a struggle, and several of the Ulcas had fled upward toward the tree line in a vain attempt to escape their attacker. These had been killed quite effectively, lying face down with arrow-wounds in their backs. The others had been killed hand-to-hand using a keen blade. There was blood, but much of it had been washed away, apparently by a late winter rain. Several massive stones had been displaced, indicating that a large and heavy being had taken part in the fighting, yet was not among the dead.

Gaelen galvanized as she beheld the scene, then she had to sit down and wrap her arms about her shoulders to stop their trembling. This was the work of their enemy—of that she was certain. The scent was faint and nearly obliterated by the stench of the rotting Ulcas, but it was there. Nelwyn also recognized the pattern; it was becoming all too familiar. So, he had been in this very spot only a few days ago. Gaelen could not believe her luck!

They moved upwind of the decaying Ulcas and held a council. It was decided that Galador would make his way back to Mountain-home and deliver their message to Lady Ordath and Lord Magra. Then he would rejoin the others, who would continue tracking the enemy. With luck, he would bring aid.

"Rogond, I have some concern that I will not be able to find the way into the hidden gates, as I have never been to the Sanctuary without an escort," said Galador.

"But you have been there, and you are known to them," said Rogond. "The way will be opened to any Elf. Do not fear."

Gaelen knew they had to be swift. The sign could disappear at any time, and it was her sense that, somehow, this creature was dimly aware of them and would become more wary as they drew nearer. Her contact with Halrodin and Gelmyr had forged a bond, albeit a vague and tenuous one, with her enemy. As long as their mutual hatred flourished, this dim awareness would continue.

It was all she could do to restrain herself until morning, but she knew that this was the only wise course, as signs would be easy to miss in the rocky darkness. Tracking this enemy was not like tracking a group of unwary Ulcas, at least not when he was on his guard. She stood alert in the light of the crescent moon and waited.

Quite a number of miles away, Gorgon also found himself standing alert in the light of the crescent moon. He had emerged from the mountain many days ago, moving north along the slopes toward Mountain-home, hoping for prey. He would avoid the Sanctuary itself, for it was protected by a power that was beyond him. Having done so, he could then drop down along the western side of the mountains and cross the river into the great forest. There he might encounter stray Wood-elves as he moved ever westward, eventually gaining the Verdant Mountains, where he would go to ground again for a while once he was sated. He would be far, far away from anything to do with Gelmyr the Èolo, whom he had banished from his thoughts.

Gorgon lifted his proud, ugly head, turning it to the north as the breeze stirred his long hair. So, his pursuers had found him again; he was sure of it. He was both annoyed and impressed that they had somehow managed to intercept his course, but he felt it was high time to resolve the situation one way or another. He had a sense that there were Elves among them—one in particular— and now he intended to draw them close enough to get a good look at them. If there were but few, he would eliminate them, and if not, he would stage a demonstration that would make them think twice about the wisdom of meddling in his affairs.

He rose and stretched his massive arms and legs, replacing his helmet and gathering up his gear. There was a fair likelihood of finding prey nearby, as Gorgon had lingered near one of the main outposts used by the scouts of Mountain-home as they kept watch. He could still smell them. Like Gaelen, Gorgon possessed a keen sense of smell, and had trained himself to use it. If he waited yet awhile, they would return. For now he would find a place of concealment and be ready when they did.

"I am uncomfortable with the idea of your going to Mountain-home on your own, you know," said Nelwyn, as Galador made ready to depart. "I really think we should stay together. If we find the enemy, I sense it will take all we have to defeat him. And you may find unknown perils on the road, with no one to aid you. Will you not reconsider?"

"Someone must warn Lady Ordath and Lord Magra, and tell of the fate of Gelmyr. Who knows how far this road will take you? It is my intention to return to your side as soon as I can, hopefully with the power of the Elves of Mountain-home at my side." He sighed, and turned to face her. "It is not my desire to leave you, but I feel there is no other course. Do not fear. I will find you again." He smiled, intending to reassure her, but all it did was make her heart ache the more at the thought of his leaving. She embraced him as a cold wash of dread came over her.

"This can only end badly. I know it! I cannot leave Gaelen, but she is on a road that will take down all who travel upon it. Please,

Galador, return as quickly as you may, for you will be needed here. And take care that your own road ends safely…" Then, at the last, she whispered, "…for my heart goes with you." She turned and left him before he could reply.

At dawn's first light, Rogond, Gaelen, and Nelwyn set off on the trail of their enemy. They would remain on this trail for days, as the signs at first became fresher and more obvious, then faded, then picked up again. This was of some concern to Gaelen, for she wondered whether the creature was taunting them by making things too easy, and then making them so difficult that even her tracking skills were sorely tested. What was he playing at?

She picked up the first signs of the Elves of Mountain-home nearly four days into the pursuit. They had come along a track from the southeast and had been intercepted by the enemy, who apparently had rested nearby for several hours until they had appeared. There were three Elves in the group, and they were not being especially wary, for their sign was easy to follow. The creature was obviously in pursuit, and Gaelen feared for them. Rogond and Nelwyn were also dismayed; they did not wish to find another like Gelmyr. On the morning of the fourth day, they first beheld the Elf named Elethorn, as Gorgon had left him for them to find.

It was Nelwyn who first caught sight of Elethorn from her vantage point in the high boughs of a tall spruce. Her heart sank as she took notice of the limp form bound to a tall stone. There was no sign of any other living being as far as she could tell. Climbing carefully back down, she informed her friends of her discovery, and they all despaired, assuming that the unknown Elf would be dead when they found him. They wondered what had happened to the others, suspecting that they would soon learn the unhappy truth of them, also.

As they drew nearer to the stone where the Elf was bound, they relied on Gaelen to judge how recently the enemy had been there. She could not tell, as the scent was confused. Here it was faint, there it was still fairly strong, but still at least a day old in her estimation.

There was very little blood, but the tracks told the story. Two of the three companions had been dropped quickly; the third had been set upon and dragged away, struggling. Now there was blood. The sign was strong here, and the Company drew back, alarmed. Retreating to the shelter of stones, they discussed what to do next.

"We must attend to this poor soul and see whether he still lives, but I fear the enemy is near, and I am afraid," said Nelwyn.

"That poor soul was left there to lure us in, Nelwyn. You have every reason to be afraid," replied Gaelen, who could not seem to stop her hands from shaking.

"We don't know that," said Rogond, who had lived among the Elves of Mountain-home, and feared for what he might find. He was bent on rescuing the unfortunate Elf, though he did not as yet know him. "Perhaps it's the same as the last; the enemy just enjoys displaying his victims to any and all that pass."

Gaelen shook her head. "I trust Nelwyn's instincts, as they are seldom in error. If the creature had meant to arrange a display, this one would have been like Gelmyr— he would not have been left alive for us to attempt rescue. If this is not a trap, then I'm a dwarf!" She shook her windblown hair from her eyes, and turned to Rogond.

"What is your honest opinion of our ability to defeat whatever it was that killed Gelmyr?" She searched his anxious face.

"I don't know," he said at last. "But we cannot just leave the Elf. We don't know that he is dead...what if he is yet alive?" He looked imploringly at Gaelen.

"This is a chance to do what I have longed for these many weeks, to get close enough to get a good look at the creature and hopefully get off a shot that will remove his stench from this world forever," she stated, as though this should be obvious. "I'm willing to take the risk, for I, too, would prevent another needless death if I can. And I'm weary of this chase. I certainly will not waver...not when I am so close. But let's at least make a plan first."

They spoke in hushed voices, quickly formulating a plan to rescue the unknown Elf. Nelwyn, who had the steadiest hands and was best at shooting from high places, would climb a tall spruce where she could survey the area with ease, her bow ready to deal with the enemy should he appear. Gaelen, who was the smallest, lightest, and most stealthy on the ground would steal in and release the Elf, while Rogond remained concealed until they were certain the area was secure. If the enemy evaded Nelwyn's bow and attacked Gaelen, Rogond would come to her aid with sword and spear. Then they would all work together to defeat the creature.

Gaelen wore her curved short sword across her back in addition to her bow and quiver, and she carried two long daggers that she could throw with deadly accuracy. Nelwyn embraced her before being hoisted onto her shoulders and springing up into the convenient spruce tree. She disappeared into its green heights, and Gaelen felt much safer. Nelwyn's marksmanship was almost infallible—nothing would get past her.

Rogond and Gaelen drew as near to the tall stone as they dared before Rogond crouched down among the moss-covered boulders, preparing to defend Gaelen and himself. The two of them could now see the strange Elf clearly, and Rogond stifled a frustrated moan, for he recognized Elethorn, who was one of the scouts of Ordath, and a friend. Rogond and Elethorn had once enjoyed roaming the marches of Mountain-home together with several other companions, escaping the civility of the realm for a time. Rogond was more determined now than ever, as anger burned within him on behalf of his friend. He squeezed Gaelen's arm as she prepared to leave.

"Be wary, Gaelen, but be swift. I sense that if Elethorn is alive, he will not be so much longer. I'll watch over you with Nelwyn, but if the creature appears, fall back and do not linger. I will take him if I can."

Gaelen gave Rogond a look that told him she was not likely to fall back and that she would linger until the end, but she understood him. Just before she left cover, she turned to him and took his face in her hands, running her fingers curiously against the grain of his ever-present whiskers. Then she smiled and whispered: "Just be there when I need you, Aridan. That's all I ask. I'll try to leave something for you to do. Now, let's fall into the trap!" She turned before he could see that this bravado did not extend to her mind or heart, and crept carefully toward Elethorn.

Rogond and Nelwyn were both tensed and ready; Nelwyn's bow was fitted, but not yet drawn, and Rogond gripped his sword-hilt with one hand and the shaft of his spear with the other. They jumped as a small but noisy tumble of rock came rolling down the hillside. All turned their attention to it for several minutes, straining to see what had set it off, but found no sign of the enemy. By this time Gaelen had nearly reached Elethorn, and she rejoiced as he stirred and moaned in his pain, his face haggard and drawn. So, he was alive! She paused, straining to hear all around her, but heard nothing but her own breathing and rapid heartbeat.

Elethorn was unconscious as she approached him, but he roused himself as she gently took hold of one of his feet and squeezed it. His eyes opened, then focused on her and grew wide with fear. Speaking in a low voice, she reassured him as she quickly took in his condition. There was blood on the stone behind Elethorn's legs; apparently the enemy had not felt confident enough to bind him without first crippling him. Otherwise he had no obvious deadly wound, though he had been bound to the stone without water or warmth for some time and had very little strength left. Gaelen drew one of her long knives, and as she cut him from the stone he fell into her arms.

Lowering him gently to the ground, she replaced her blade, looking back over her shoulder as a sound from the tall spruce caught her attention. To her horror, she observed the slender body of her cousin Nelwyn as it fell, limp and lifeless, to catch in the branches of the tall tree. It was fortunate that she did not fall all the way to the ground. Gaelen cried out in alarm, leaping to her feet, but she would not be able to find out what had happened to Nelwyn just yet.

Another sound distracted her and she turned, gasping as she beheld for the first time the shadowed figure that seemed to emerge as from the very stones, making straight for her. The next few seconds were a blur of motion and speed, as Gaelen drew her bow without thinking and loosed an arrow at the huge, dark enemy. It was easily deflected by his black armor, and she drew her curved blade, leaping back just in time as he was upon her, his sword ringing against hers with a force that was like a great tree that crashes to the ground during a storm. She knew then that she was outmatched, and that even the strength of one such as Rogond might not be enough.

Gorgon had not been idle. For over two days he had been lying in wait, concealed by his grey cloak among the stones, taking only an occasional sip of water, sitting still and silent as though made of stone himself. His scent he had disguised with that of the two now-dead companions of Elethorn; this was a trick he had learned long ago and it had always served him well. He first noted the approach of those that tracked him in the late morning. *Ha. It is as I had hoped… there are but three. And only two are Elven. The third, though he has the look of a warrior, is a mortal man. This will not prove too challenging.* Then he had remembered the words of Gelmyr. Was this the pursuit of which the Elf had warned? Ha! Trust an overconfident dead Èolo to make a prophecy of two Wood-elves and one mortal man.

Gorgon watched as Nelwyn, Gaelen, and Rogond took up their positions, and he quickly guessed their plan. The one in the tree was the lookout, and the man was there to back up the other, who had apparently been appointed rescuer. The first part of Gorgon's plan was to quietly eliminate one of them from the fight. Moving as one in slow motion, he drew forth a weapon of which he was most proud, as it had proved its worth on countless occasions, and he had constructed it himself. It was a stout, Y-shaped creation of supple yew wood, highly polished and balanced, with a thong of leather strung between the branches. In the center of the thong was a concave piece of hard silver into which he placed a rounded piece of steel about the size of the end of his own index finger. It remained only for him to decide which of his enemies to strike first.

Gorgon smiled as he beheld Nelwyn's small bow; though she was undoubtedly skilled, her weapon would lack the power to penetrate his armor. He would have to be careful never to turn his face to her, as she might wound him sorely if she hit him in the eye, but he reckoned that was about the only way she could do much more than annoy him. Gorgon was not only well armored, his skin was as thick and tough as several layers of leather, and there was precious little of it exposed. He was positioned so that, if he wished, he could shoot any or all of his pursuers, but in the end he decided that, as the lookout, Nelwyn would be his first choice of target. Then he would not have to concern himself with her darts and could turn his eyes where he would.

His plan was to incapacitate or kill Nelwyn with his marvelous weapon, and then to engage Gaelen and Rogond. He had already assessed his risk and found it acceptable. Rogond would probably put up a stimulating if brief struggle, and as for Gaelen, he would swat her as a fly, perhaps after toying with her first. He would keep her alive long enough to ensure that there were no others to trouble him, at least.

He drew silently on Nelwyn, hoping that her sharp eyes would not detect the movement until he could get the shot off. He pulled back, straining against the tough yew wood, sighting in on Nelwyn's forehead. At this distance, he would be satisfied with any head shot, as it would accomplish his purpose. Nelwyn tensed—had she heard something over the wind in the spruce boughs? Gorgon's thick, black fingers released the weapon. The steel projectile hurtled straight to its target, and Nelwyn knew no more.

Gorgon had then leaped to his feet and rushed toward Gaelen as she beheld Nelwyn with alarm. As he had guessed, she was quick to get off a shot at him, but his armor deflected her arrows even at close range. Sword drawn, he met her pathetic attempt at fending him off with about half the force he was capable of. There followed a violent but somewhat awkward bit of swordplay, during which Gorgon slashed so hard and fast at Gaelen that it was all she could do to leap out of the way. The few times that he made contact with her blade he nearly bore her to the ground with the power of his great arm.

Rogond had also reacted with alarm when Nelwyn fell from her perch, but Gaelen's cry of dismay had turned his attention back as Gorgon rounded on her. He leaped up and made toward the enemy, his heart sinking as he took notice of Gorgon's size and power. Gaelen would be crushed quickly, even as the enemy toyed with her. As Rogond rushed toward them, he brandished his spear, which had always served him well; it was rare armor that it would not pierce. Gorgon was moving much too fast to risk hurling it, so Rogond sprang in front of him, striking at his enemy's heart with all his strength.

Regrettably, Gorgon's armor *was* rare. It was made of a most unusual material—the carapace of a gigantic beetle that dwelled only in the deepest caverns beneath the great northern wastes. The beetles fed on large prey, including one another, and the really enormous ones were not only rare, but nearly impossible to kill. Wrothgar's most skilled armorers had shaped the armor, which was relatively light yet harder than steel. Even so, its weight would have daunted any mortal man or bright Elf, though it meant nothing to Gorgon, who was so seldom without it that it seemed a part of his own skin. The best quality was the stealth it afforded—metal armor clanked and creaked and rattled with every movement, but this armor was utterly silent, allowing Gorgon to approach as quietly as if he wore none. The plain black surface was dented and pitted from many battles, despite the natural resilience of the carapace. Most weapons would simply bounce off.

Rogond's spear, though a worthy weapon, made little impact on it, but at least for the moment Gorgon had to pay careful attention, as he now faced two foes. Rogond was taken aback and struck again as hard as he could, ducking under a sweeping stroke of Gorgon's broadsword. This time the spear point snapped against the black armor, to Rogond's dismay. He cast aside the broken weapon and brandished his sword as Gaelen deflected a fresh attack. She had thrown both of her daggers, but Gorgon was incredibly quick and agile, and he had managed to evade them.

Confident that he was more than a match for these two, Gorgon raised his heavy, polished shield. It was mirror-bright in contrast to the dull black of his armor. The man's favored weapon was now useless, and he would soon fall. The Elf would present no difficulty, for though she was quick and apparently possessed of a certain amount of skill and stamina, Gorgon's strength would wear her down. He drew himself up and brandished his long sword in the air, roaring like a beast and displaying his long, sharp teeth. Both of his adversaries froze, staring at him in horror. Then, he chuckled at them. He certainly was fearsome, wasn't he?

Rogond was first to recover, as he realized that Gorgon was toying with him. This enemy was no doubt quite intelligent, but he was twisted and malicious, and altogether evil. Rogond fought with all the skill he had been able to acquire in his short lifetime, but Gorgon more than matched him, even with Gaelen's help.

She had managed to place no fewer than three arrows in Gorgon's flesh, a difficult task considering the speed with which the creature moved. Two had pierced his sword-arm at the inside elbow, but he had ripped them out quickly, as they had not gone deep.

The one that now lodged under his left arm had been more troublesome; it had caused him to drop his shield, though he felt little pain as yet. It was time to put an end to this annoyance. Abruptly, Gorgon came alive before them with all his strength, roaring and slashing at Rogond until he was overwhelmed, finally striking him with such force that he was flung aside to land hard among the rocks, insensible.

Gorgon paused as though catching his breath, though Gaelen could see that his strength was far from spent. They stared at one another for a moment, Gorgon now breathing easily, Gaelen still panting hard. She had never seen anything quite like him, and for a moment she forgot that he was a mortal enemy as she regarded him with fascinated revulsion. His pale eyes narrowed, and he bared his sharp, yellow teeth in a sort of sneering smile. He was only slightly taller than Rogond, but much more massive. His limbs were all corded muscle beneath his armor, and his weapons and bright shield gleamed. Though he brandished a broadsword that he had taken from Gelmyr, Turantil hung at his side, and as Gaelen beheld it, she snarled back at him.

He noted this with satisfaction, and then he spoke to her in a voice that made her skin crawl: "Well met, Elf of the Darkmere. You are kin of he that owned this sword?"

Gaelen put forth every effort to keep the tremor out of her voice. "Not kin, but friend. One who would see you dead at any rate!"

Gorgon's pale eyes narrowed. "We don't always receive what we desire, She-elf. If that were so, neither you nor any of your accursed race would yet exist. Regrettably, I must wait for the fulfillment of my desires. As for yours, it will be a long time indeed ere I perish at the hands of one such as you."

Of this, Gaelen now had little doubt. Still, she gritted her teeth and faced him, trying to make herself appear to be as large and menacing as possible. "I know of your desires, Hateful Horror," she replied. "Gelmyr has told me of them."

At the mention of Gelmyr, Gorgon's eyes flickered and his lip curled just slightly. Gaelen sensed that he was uncomfortable with the mention of Gelmyr's name. She glanced over at Rogond, who had not yet stirred, an action that did not go unnoticed.

"Hoping for the Aridan to save you? I don't blame you, Hapless One. That sword you carry is not your preferred weapon—you have the look of an archer to me, and I would say a fairly apt one, but your bow will not avail you here. Your mortal friend may not yet be dead, but he soon will be. He is no match for my strength. And as for Gelmyr, you are a liar. He was as dead as stone long before I left him and was not in a position to reveal anything of my desires, or aught else."

Gaelen had caught her breath, and she tightened her grip on her sword-hilt. "I will not bandy words with such a friendless monstrosity. Come on then, and let us finish this! I know you have been toying with me. Taste of victory against me if you can, and may I at least prove to be troublesome."

Without waiting for him to respond she flew at him, blade flashing in the now-bright sunlight of late morning, taking him off guard for just a moment. He still had not retrieved his shield, and she managed to inflict a rather deep wound across the back of his left hand, which bore no armor. It was a mistake, and he drove her back, enraged, all thoughts of toying with her forgotten. He slashed at her with such ferocity that she knew her time had come. She could not stand against this—she found herself thinking of Nelwyn and, oddly, of Rogond. Her strength spent, she tripped and fell backward before the feet of her enemy, as he raised his weapon to strike her from the world.

Her arm was shaking as she held her blade before her face in what was surely a futile effort to protect herself. As she did so, the brightly polished surface caught the light of the full sun, reflecting it into Gorgon's strange, pale eyes. To her surprise, he flinched back, squinting and blinking, turning his flat, ugly face away for a moment. So! He was vulnerable, at least, to something. Taking advantage of his brief moment of distraction, she crawled backward just as Rogond appeared before Gorgon, sword in hand, looking a bit dazed, but still very much a force to be reckoned with. Gorgon snarled and met Rogond's blade with his own.

Gorgon had underestimated Rogond's skill and determination, and for a moment it looked as though the Aridan might actually prevail. But Rogond could not keep up the level of strength necessary to hold off this enemy, and he soon flagged as Gorgon, sensing weakness, pressed ever harder. Gaelen thought to shoot at Gorgon's eyes, though his helmet would make this difficult, but she found she could no longer pull her bow, much less hold it with the required steadiness. She dropped it in frustration, picked up her short sword, and tried to distract her enemy from Rogond, but Gorgon struck her against the ground so hard that she did not get up again.

Rogond raised his blade for what he guessed might be the last time, wavering on unsteady feet, breath whistling in his throat. He had held off the enemy alone for several minutes, a feat not often accomplished in all of Gorgon's long years, but his strength was spent at last. As Gorgon raised his weapon to strike, a bright arrow flew out of nowhere to lodge under his right arm, and he actually cried out in pain. Nelwyn, wan and shaking but determined, had come up behind Rogond and now stood in his defense. Gorgon gripped the shaft of the arrow and yanked it hard from his flesh, grimacing, before casting it aside. He was still confident that he would prevail, as the Aridan would give no further trouble, and the golden-haired She-elf would be taken easily—she could hardly even focus on him.

"Back away from him, Dark Horror, or the next one flies straight to your foul eyes," said Nelwyn, still trying to distract Gorgon from finishing both of her friends.

In answer, Gorgon's blade cut hard toward Rogond, who found it all he could do to deflect the blow before the next one came, aimed straight at his neck. He ducked under it, but his head swam and he sank to the ground, fighting to remain conscious. Nelwyn's arrow struck Gorgon's helmet harmlessly, and he rushed at her intending to make an end of her. Nelwyn staggered back, defenseless, as she had no blade.

At that moment, Gaelen appeared behind her cousin, clutching Gorgon's mirror-bright shield, aiming the reflected beam of brilliant sunlight directly into his eyes. Gorgon roared with pain and drew back, flinging his arm before his face. Gaelen continued to focus the reflected light from the shield on him as he turned about, trying in vain to escape it. This had never happened to him in all his dark years! Fury welled within him—he could never let the prophecy of Gelmyr prove true. He turned back to face his enemies, left hand trying to shade his burning, streaming eyes, and now beheld not three foes, but four. Galador stood with drawn sword, a fierce light in his eyes, and at full strength.

Despite all expectation to the contrary, Gorgon felt for the first time that he might not prevail this day. He engaged Galador, and they fought for a few tense moments, as the Elf became aware of the magnitude of the enemy he faced. Gorgon's strength was returning, and his confidence showed dangerous signs of renewing itself. If that happened, Galador knew that they might likely all be killed. He backed away for a moment, and addressed his foe:

"Now is your chance. Take your honor, if indeed you have any, and live to defeat us another day. You cannot prevail here."

"No Elf engages Gorgon Elfhunter and lives," said Gorgon. "Your companions are all but dead from trying to defeat me. As for yourself, you're already living beyond your time. This fight will not end until none of you draws breath." He looked quite capable of making good on this threat, drawing himself up to his full height. Without warning, he rushed at Galador who, like Rogond, would not have the strength to hold him off for very long.

"Gaelen! The shield!" cried Galador as the rocks rang with the sound of clashing blades. Gaelen could no longer lift the heavy shield by herself, and as she cried out in frustration, Rogond's strong hands gripped it. Together they tossed it to Galador, who, to Gorgon's horror, turned the bright sunlight upon him. Gorgon staggered back, lashing out blindly, but his enemy easily avoided him. This was not in his plan at all. He could not prevail with that accursed fire burning his eyes. He had but one choice now—to turn and flee.

Gorgon fought through his burning pain as he tried to grasp the reality of his situation. Never before had he engaged an enemy and left him standing, always he had made certain that the odds were so overwhelmingly in his favor. But now, he must turn or die. Later he would deal with this humiliation, of a magnitude that he had not felt for a very long time.

At first backing up before Galador's onslaught, he finally turned and sprinted for the safety of the dark mountains. Galador started after him, but he heard Rogond call out: "No! Do not pursue him alone! He goes to ground, where the bright shield will fail. Do not pursue him alone!"

Rogond was right. Gorgon had escaped, and they were in no condition to follow him. He was so incredibly fast for one so large! With one last look after his enemy, Galador turned and went to see to his companions.

Galador found the three Elves and Rogond all lying together among the stones. They were bloody, battered, and exhausted. Gaelen and Nelwyn were both weeping quietly in the realization of what might have happened. Rogond's face was grim and weary, and a few of his wounds were fairly deep. They would have to be cleaned and dressed, as the flesh of men sometimes harbored corruption if not properly tended. Nelwyn's head was pounding, and she felt very shaky and ill as she lay upon the ground. Gorgon's missile had struck her just over her left eyebrow, where a deep indentation had appeared. Blood was flowing from her left ear as well; she would have to be carried to Mountain-home. She moaned miserably in Gaelen's embrace.

Gaelen was not in much better condition. She was pale and shaking, and she had taken several wounds. Though most were not deep, it would be awhile before she pulled her bow again. What Galador concluded when he assessed the condition of his friends was that they were all in for a slow, painful journey.

Then there was the matter of Elethorn. Gorgon had cut the cords behind both of his knees so that he could not stand and had left him without water for nearly three days. He was bruised and battered, lying unconscious as Galador tried to get him to take some water. Rogond was so exhausted that he was not able to be of much help. Galador gathered wood, built a fire, and set about the task of comforting his friends. He kept ladling water down Elethorn, wrapping him in a warm cloak and positioning him near the fire.

Gaelen, Nelwyn, and Rogond lay senseless and unmoving. Galador went to each in turn throughout the night, tending them carefully until the dawn came.

He had never been so thankful that he had followed his instincts. He had been well on the way to Mountain-home when the nagging doubts as to the wisdom of leaving his companions suddenly gave way to a feeling of dread. He was compelled to return to them as quickly as he might, and a good thing, too. Had he lingered in debate or chosen to remain on the path appointed, he had no doubt that no living Elf or man would have been here to greet him. He shuddered as he thought of his friends overpowered at last by Gorgon, dying at his hands. Nelwyn lost! He could not have borne it. He vowed never to leave her again.

Elethorn fretted and moaned as Galador soothed him with gentle words. He could only imagine the horrors Elethorn had witnessed. The other two scouts were undoubtedly lost, and Galador would not waste time or energy in looking for their remains. If the Elves of Mountain-home wished to recover what they could, they were welcome. Galador didn't really want to know the grisly details of their fate.

Rogond awoke as dawn broke, feeling as though he would never move again. He gazed at Gaelen's inert form lying next to him, disheveled and bloody, her pale, bruised face drawn with anxiety. His heart was filled with both loathing of Gorgon and fear of his return. Thank the stars Galador had returned, although Rogond wished that he had not called Gaelen's name aloud.

They needed to be on their way as quickly as they could manage, lest Gorgon return and finish them. It would be so easy, especially after nightfall. With sudden urgency, Rogond roused Galador, who was dozing in the early light of dawn, and held a brief parley. Then they began preparations to depart.

It was indeed a sorry procession making its way along the rocky and difficult slopes toward Mountain-home. This beautiful refuge, shielded by the mists of the Monadh-hin, was the hidden realm of Lady Ordath. It was a fair place for all folk of good will to gather, study and learn, and rest from the cares of the world outside. Within its borders rose the renowned University known only as "The Sanctuary".

Lady Ordath was widely acknowledged as the greatest master of the Healing Arts in all the world, for though her mother was of

Elven-kind, her father was a powerful Asarla. He was the mighty Shandor, silver-haired and with eyes like ice. He founded the realm of Mountain-home with his beloved Liathwyn of the Èolar, and Ordath was their child. She had inherited the strength and ageless nature of the Elves, together with the magical abilities of the Asari. Her power had grown very great, so that the people of Mountain-home had little to fear. Because Ordath was descended of both the Èolar and the Asari, she was devoted to learning and knowing—the Sanctuary was unrivaled as a place of study. Because of her vigilance, the way into Mountain-home was shown only to those of good will and open mind.

Though Shandor and Liathwyn had gone, Ordath would see that the realm they had founded was kept safe. Outside, the mountains could rage as they would, but they dared not challenge the power of the Lady.

As the Company struggled painfully toward their destination, it looked as though the skills of Lady Ordath would be sorely needed. Galador walked at the fore, carrying Nelwyn, who was grievously hurt. Behind him went Gaelen and Rogond, bearing Elethorn between them. Neither had strength in their arms; Gaelen's shoulders were torn, and Rogond had simply spent his strength to the point that he would need time to recover. In addition, he had taken several wounds and lost sufficient blood to further drain his strength. As such, they had rigged a sling of Galador's cloak and some of their light cord, suspending Elethorn between them. Gaelen bore her part across her chest, Rogond behind his shoulders. It was not an efficient or a pleasant strategy, but the only one available to them.

Elethorn was now conscious, and he lamented as he beheld the pain of those who bore him, but he could not walk on his own. When he suggested that they leave him behind, sending others to return for him later, they dismissed the idea as absurd. Who knew when Gorgon would decide to return by dark of night? He would certainly kill Elethorn, who would be helpless against him. They got very little enlightenment from Elethorn concerning Gorgon, for the creature had revealed almost nothing of himself.

With each time they stopped to rest, it became more and more difficult to rise again and continue. Though they had only a few leagues left to travel, it would take at least one more day at the rate they were going. Galador was by now very anxious. Nelwyn needed the services of a competent healer, and soon. The wound on her forehead was small, but deep, and Galador suspected that her skull was cracked, as she kept bleeding from her left ear. Her eyes appeared to sink into dark purple wells, and she was rarely conscious. When she did manage to rouse herself, she muttered quietly in words that made no sense at all.

Galador was right to be concerned, for Nelwyn had taken deadly hurt. Her chances grew less with each passing hour. Frustrated, he called back to his friends, whose pace had slowed such that they had fallen way behind again. "Why do you tarry? We must make haste, for Nelwyn's sake, as she is in grave need. Can you not come faster?"

Gaelen and Rogond had spent much of the last hour chastising one another for every misstep that delayed them or threw them off balance. Elethorn tried to be helpful, but there really was nothing he could do. They were all exhausted, especially Rogond, who felt that his feet were literally constructed of lead. Gaelen was in a significant amount of pain and worn out. Neither was in the mood to be admonished by Galador, though they understood his urgency.

Gaelen grew silent, set her jaw, and fixed her eyes straight ahead, willing herself into a sort of half trance that no pain or weariness could assail. She would make it to Mountain-home with Elethorn on her back if she had to.

Rogond had already seen more hardship than many mortal men could have endured. He focused on the back of Gaelen's head, trying not to think about the way the cord was cutting across her already-damaged shoulders, or the deep, sickening ache in his own.

His mind wandered back to the encounter with the enemy. Gaelen had really come through for them, discovering Gorgon's weakness and exploiting it, but he sensed that her spirits were severely dampened by the incident, and he knew that she was terribly worried for Nelwyn. He also sensed a deep guilt that had welled up within her, as though this whole affair had been her idea, and the outcome was therefore her fault. Gaelen would probably never forgive herself should Nelwyn die. This would, of course, have displeased Nelwyn, because she made the choice to pursue Gorgon and was a willing participant in the search and in the confrontation. She would not have Gaelen bear this burden, for it was not hers to bear.

As the afternoon waned and twilight came, Rogond took a bad step onto a loose stone, his left leg turned from under him, and he fell hard upon the rocky ground. He lay, panting, head swimming, as the evening sky wheeled unpleasantly above him. Gaelen's anxious face appeared, and when he focused on her beautiful eyes the world stopped spinning. Galador gently set Nelwyn down and ran back up the slope to his fallen friends. Rogond tried to rise, but his body simply would not respond. Elethorn and Gaelen reassured him, but they had all reached the conclusion that Rogond had taken his last step for a while. They were now so close to Mountain-home that perhaps it would be prudent for Galador to go on with Nelwyn and send back help for the others. It was less likely that Gorgon would come so near to the Realm of Ordath, where they could once again hear the rushing waters that flowed forth from the mountainside.

Elethorn, whose strength had increased with rest and water, would keep watch over Gaelen and Rogond. They would build no fire and would need none, for the warmth of spring was in the southerly breeze that stirred the tall trees, bringing the scent of growth and burgeoning life. Galador promised to return as quickly as he could, lifted Nelwyn, who had neither moved nor spoken in many hours, and disappeared into the grey twilight.

Gaelen shrugged out of the cord that bound her to Elethorn, grimacing at the deep crease it had made in the flesh across her chest and shoulders. She somehow made her way to lie beside Rogond, who was already beyond awareness, his eyes closed, his breathing shallow and irregular. Her vision blurred with weariness, so she closed her eyes and the darkness took her out of the reach of pain. Elethorn lay beside them, taking Gaelen's cold hand to warm it, knowing the debt that he owed and vowing to repay it when he could.

13

The Fate of Nelwyn

Gaelen awoke to the sound of flowing water and soft, pleasant voices. She was in a dark, warm place, and although she did not yet know its name, she knew somehow that it was safe. It was night, and the lamps were lit, but as she looked up toward the open roof of her chamber she could see the stars. She tried to sit up, but this was difficult given the lack of strength in her arms. Rolling painfully onto her side, she dropped both legs over the edge of the pallet on which she had been carefully laid and then jerked her body upright. This was a mistake, as she overbalanced and fell to the floor, her vision occluded by a black cloud and her head ringing as she fought to remain conscious. This gained the immediate attention of two of the Elves of Mountain-home, who rushed to her side, speaking in soothing voices. They lifted her with gentle hands and replaced her on the pallet.

Through the darkness that clouded her vision, Gaelen still managed to ask a few breathless questions. Was she in Mountain-home? Where was Rogond? Had these people encountered Galador and Nelwyn? Had they summoned the Lady Ordath? The Elves did their best to answer, while calming Gaelen as they could. Yes, she had been brought to Mountain-home along with Rogond and Elethorn. Galador had arrived with Nelwyn, and the Lady had sent back rescuers who had borne everyone to safety. Of Nelwyn's condition they could not yet tell.

"Rest and recover, for your strength is spent and you have taken serious hurt. There will be time for questions and answers from all as you are able. Lady Ordath has not yet tended you or your friend the Tuathan, for she is occupied with your other companion. Rest until she comes to you. Then you will learn the truths you seek."

Gaelen was not satisfied. She wanted to see Rogond and Nelwyn, and protested even as she was covered with warm, woolen blankets and given a strengthening liquor from a silver flask. Her attendants were determined to prevent her from trying to get up again.

"The Lady Ordath would not be pleased should we allow you to harm yourself," they said. "You must respect our wishes, and remain here until she has seen to you. Close your eyes and rest, for the liquor you just drank also contained a sleeping-draught, and you will not remain aware for long. Don't fear, Elf of the Greatwood. No harm will come to you or your friends." Gaelen muttered something about the unscrupulous nature of Elves who would conceal a sleeping-draught and give it to her unaware, just before she sank once again into the long dark.

Galador sat unmoving beside Nelwyn, who was fighting for her life. She had worsened during the journey to Mountain-home, and had barely moved or made a sound for two days and nights. Lady Ordath, great healer though she was, could do nothing further for her. This sort of hurt was not of the sort that lay within her power. If Nelwyn wanted to live, she would have to recover mostly on her own.

Galador was nearly beside himself with worry, and he had neither slept nor eaten. He didn't know whether he could bear the loss of Nelwyn, just when he had opened his heart and allowed himself to love again. Now their happiness would be snatched away before it could take root and grow. No, he decided, it would be unbearable, and therefore unthinkable. He stayed at her side, gently stroking her hair and speaking words of comfort. He even sang a little, but he found he could not keep his voice from breaking, so he sang no more. She did not respond, but he kept trying, pouring very small sips of water through her lips every few minutes. He told her some of his favorite tales, ones he had learned of old, but she was pale and cold. At times he wept, but quietly so she would not hear.

He found himself cursing Gaelen and her blind, headstrong tenacity. Nelwyn had chosen to follow Gaelen on her obstinate course despite doubts as to the wisdom of it. Were it not for Gaelen, and Nelwyn's desire to protect her, they would probably still be safely in the great forest. Galador came close to wishing that Gaelen had gone off alone to face Gorgon. Perhaps they would have killed each other, thus ridding the world of two driven, self-willed personalities.

He knew this wasn't really fair. Gaelen had not anticipated the cleverness and might of this enemy. If she had, she might have chosen differently. But no, Galador thought, she had seen Gelmyr. They all had. It did not daunt her that an Elf with five times her power and experience had fallen victim. She had to be related to Aincor. *Had* to be.

As Galador sat brooding on these dark thoughts, Gaelen appeared in the doorway, looking small, pale, and hurt. She had roused herself, found her clothing, dressed with great difficulty, and somehow made her way to Nelwyn. She said not a word to Galador, but crossed to Nelwyn's bedside and sat nearby, both hands twisting in her lap. She looked for a moment into Galador's eyes and read his thoughts in them: *Do you see what you have done?*

She did not weep, but stared back at him, her message clear. *You're right, Galador. This is my doing. I do not blame you for your thoughts of me.* She turned her attention back to Nelwyn, who lay unmoving, her eyes sunken and dark, her breathing slow and shallow. She had been well tended, for all the good it would do.

Gaelen would make no further eye contact with Galador, but sat still as stone, her eyes lifeless and miserable. Though Galador tried to hold on to his resentment, he was not used to the light being gone from Gaelen's eyes, and it worried him. She had encountered a terrible foe and had battled with valor, and were it not for her they would all have been lost. She had not expected what had happened to Nelwyn…she had taken the greatest risk upon herself.

Galador also knew that Gaelen felt quite bad enough without enmity from him. She probably believed that she had failed Nelwyn, who was the person she was closest to in the world. Galador was well acquainted with such feelings, and a wave of sympathy came over him, quelling some of his animosity.

As though she could sense his thoughts, Gaelen turned her pale face toward him. Though miserable, she was still proud, even in the midst of her helplessness. "Do not pity me, Galador. Give me your ill will, if you wish. I cannot alter my nature, or whatever fate drives me. I would give anything now to take back the thing that I said to Nelwyn upon that day when we stood by the graves of our friends and decided to pursue this Dark Horror. But I cannot. I can only wish and regret, while enduring the knowledge that all has been in vain. For all of this, Gorgon Elfhunter is still free to kill our kind as he will. Keep your pity, Elf of the Light!"

She dropped her eyes, and both Elves understood each other. Galador rose and crossed to sit beside Gaelen, laying his hand very gently on her shoulder, for he knew that otherwise it would pain her. She accepted the gesture, but did not acknowledge it, as she was deep in her own thoughts. Galador shook his head in sorrow. He knew what it was to live with regret and torment. At that moment, he took back most of his dark thoughts concerning her. After all, she was deserving of some consideration. Even the Fire-heart had needed it in the end.

Rogond of the Tuathar had been greeted as a beloved comrade who returns home after a long journey. He had lived in Mountain-home for five years, had made many friends, and had gained the respect of most who came to know him, including Lady Ordath herself. Now he had slept, with the help of the Elves' healing elixirs, for two days and nights. His strength was returning, and his wounds were healing rapidly, for he was a hardy man. He had met with Lady Ordath and learned that Galador and Gaelen were watching over Nelwyn. Ordath had questioned Rogond about their travels, especially about the encounter with Gorgon, as Galador had been able to provide only a partial account. Rogond had promised that he would tell all he could, but now he must see to his friends. Ordath nodded, her wise face solemn.

Soon Rogond was also at Nelwyn's side, ready to assist if needed. He did not like the look of Nelwyn either, and he was not hopeful. He was also concerned about Gaelen and Galador, neither of whom had rested or eaten. Gaelen, in particular, could ill afford this, as she was still battle-weary, and her wounds would not heal until she had gained strength. Her face was drawn, her eyes held no light, and she did not move or acknowledge Rogond's presence.

Gaelen was still thinking of Nelwyn and of the day they began their pursuit of Gorgon Elfhunter. She had spoken a single word to Nelwyn then—a word that had set her upon this course that might well result in her death:

"Thaldallen."

The word, literally translated, meant "steadfast oak". To understand it, one needed to go back to an incident that happened when Nelwyn was only sixteen years of age. She had befriended an attractive, engaging young Elf named Talrodin. He was handsome and lively, and she adored him. She and Gaelen, who had been about forty and six at the time, enjoyed roaming the forest with Talrodin and his older brother Halrodin, who was also quite likeable. They hunted and gathered, and made merry in the manner of young Wood-elves.

Nelwyn followed after Talrodin, racing along the edge of the forest in the deep twilight on her uncle Tarmagil's great horse, Anlon. Talrodin was a superb rider, but he could not evade Nelwyn, who swept around him, snatching from his hand the banner of his house. She urged Anlon to pull away in front of Talrodin, looking back over her shoulder and laughing.

She did not see the shadowy, dark figures that rose up suddenly on either side of her, pulling taut a fine rope between them. The figures braced themselves as the great horse, running full tilt into the rope, was neatly tripped and sent flying onto the grass, throwing Nelwyn hard against the ground. Talrodin pulled up in alarm and called Nelwyn's name in panic, for he had seen only that her mount had fallen. The tall grass was suddenly alive with fierce, snarling Ulcas who rushed toward him.

Talrodin saw them drag Nelwyn into the forest, but he could do nothing alone against such a horde. He turned and fled, his mount flying as fast as she could, and the Ulcas were denied a second captive. But they had Nelwyn, and Talrodin knew that she was doomed unless he could rescue her in the immediate future. His only hope came in the knowledge that sometimes Ulcas were instructed to take Elven captives to be delivered alive to Lord Wrothgar, the Shadowmancer, for purposes unknown. If that was the fate that awaited Nelwyn it was the blackest imaginable, but at least it would buy time.

He almost literally ran into his brother Halrodin, who was following with Gaelen, intending to spend the evening watching the stars once they caught up with their friends. Talrodin told them in a panicked, desperate voice of what had befallen Nelwyn. There was no one to aid them, and they would have to act at once. They tracked the Ulcas as carefully as they could, turning Talrodin's mare loose, instructing her to return to the stables. Anlon had been killed and dismembered where he had fallen. The Ulcas would feast well this night.

The Elves finally caught up with the Ulcas as dawn was breaking. Nelwyn had been taken south through the deep forest to a clearing near a small stream where grew a great oak, standing alone, believed to be the oldest and tallest in the forest. The Elves called it Thaldallen, and it was a venerable landmark. Nelwyn had been bound tightly to it and gagged so that she could not cry out. The Ulcas were sheltering from the sun in the surrounding undergrowth, but watchers had been set. The Elves counted about fifteen of the enemy, but in fact there were eighteen. Gaelen and the brothers had about thirty arrows between them.

Their greatest fear was that Nelwyn would be slain before she could be rescued, as they did not yet know what was planned for her. They crept quietly around the group of Ulcas, taking up various positions where they had reasonably clear targets. Nelwyn heard several "bird calls" emanating from the forest that were not made by any bird of Alterra. Her spirits rose, knowing that her friends were near, for though she feared for them she now hoped desperately for rescue. The first arrows flew, and before the Ulcas could gain their feet, each Elf had taken three. That left nine to contend with, six of which rushed toward the source of the arrows while drawing their own weapons and shooting into the undergrowth. Several near misses forced Talrodin into the open, and as Gaelen tried to draw the attention of the enemy from him, Halrodin made toward Nelwyn. She was surrounded by three of the remaining Ulcas, who were now intent on making an end of her.

Halrodin had drawn his sword, and he leaped into the fray with a ferocious yell. He was skilled with a blade, large and strong, and more than a match for the Ulcas, who have not the size, speed or strength of Elves. Still, there were three of them, and they were fairly adept. Halrodin was hard put to deal with all of them together. He slew two of them after several moments of fierce fighting, but his heart sank as he turned to regard the third standing with its blade at Nelwyn's throat. Intentions were clear: if Halrodin didn't back off, she would die.

Halrodin was instructed to throw his sword into the brush, and he did so despite Nelwyn's shaking her head in anxious protest. The Ulca then told Halrodin to lie down with his hands clasped behind his head. This Halrodin did, though his eyes never left the enemy. Laughing in a hideous, malicious manner, the Ulca told Halrodin that he had been deceived, and Nelwyn closed her eyes in anticipation of having her neck slashed. But the stroke never fell.

Two arrows, one with white fletching and one with black, cut through the air. The first struck the Ulca's sword hand, knocking the blade free even as the second buried itself in the Ulca's throat. Gaelen and Talrodin ran into the clearing and cut Nelwyn from the massive trunk of Thaldallen. Her knees gave way, for she was very young and had been through a terrible ordeal. She had indeed been destined for the Black Flame; a worse fate they could not imagine! Talrodin and Halrodin, together with Gaelen, had saved her from that fate at great risk to themselves. Thus, when Gaelen had spoken the name of the great oak as they stood by the remains of the two gallant brothers, who had been true and lifelong friends, Nelwyn could offer no argument to the pursuit of their killer. She remembered their courage and sacrifice so long ago.

Gaelen would have given anything to take back the mention of Thaldallen. She had spoken it knowing that Nelwyn could not refuse her. Now, Nelwyn had certainly paid any debt she might have owed. Gaelen sensed that her closest friend was held to the world only by the slenderest of threads, and if that thread broke, Gaelen would have only herself to blame.

Rogond was losing hope that Nelwyn would recover. Her breathing had slowed so much that each one led to anxious moments until the next finally came. Galador died a little each time; Rogond had never seen him look so careworn. Rogond was also terribly concerned for Gaelen, who had not moved in several hours. She had not been caring for herself at all, and she now sat upon the floor at Nelwyn's right side, knees drawn up before her, staring unblinking through eyes that Rogond now regarded with alarm. He knelt beside her, took her chin in his hands, and raised her gaze to his. His heart sank as he looked into her lifeless eyes. They were glassy, unfocused, and dead. Though Gaelen was still breathing, and her body technically still living, she was not there.

Nelwyn looked down with wonder at her own hands, which seemed now to glow with a cool, soft light. She did not know this place; a thick grey mist enveloped everything so that she could not see. She could still hear Galador's voice, and she perceived the desperate sorrow in it, but it grew fainter with each moment that passed. Soon, she would be unable to hear him at all. She took a few tentative steps, and as she did so the wind rose, or at least it seemed so, for she felt a pull at her clothing and heard the soft sighing of the breeze as it lifted her golden hair.

With her next step the breeze grew stronger. She could hear other sounds as well, but she could not identify them. Were they voices? She felt a great desire to move toward them. As she took her next step, the strange land grew darker, as though building to a storm, though she still could see nothing through the mist. She was not frightened and was no longer in pain. The struggle had been so hard just a short while ago, yet now she breathed with no effort, and seemed feather-light as she took another few steps through the darkening mist. Her own inner light glowed ever brighter in the gloom. What was this place?

The pull of the wind grew greater, and the voices more clear. Behind her, there was nothing. She could no longer hear Galador, but she was transfixed, and it did not distress her. Another step and the wind rose yet higher, pulling her toward the voices. But one voice drifted from behind. It was small, yet insistent. Nelwyn paused, and turned to look over her right shoulder, her hair blown back. Whose voice was this, calling her name so that she could not ignore it? She stood now against the pull of the wind, listening.

The voice called again: *Nelwyn, daughter of Elwyn, beloved of Galador, and protector of things that grow in the earth, stay your flight from those who love you!* It was Gaelen's voice, and she was drawing nearer. Nelwyn turned all the way around, despite the persistent forces pulling at her, and beheld a radiant red-orange glow that pierced the swirling darkness of the mist. Her cousin appeared a few moments later, leaning into the wind, her inner light flaming around her. It seemed that the forces drawing Nelwyn were battling Gaelen, for her thick, tousled hair blew back from her face, and her cloak was torn back from her shoulders.

Gaelen! What are you doing here? I sense you should not tread this way with me. Nelwyn's own light flared blue-white as she said this, as though confirming her intuition. Whatever forces were drawing her, she was being directed to a destination where Gaelen could not go. Gaelen's outline was wavering and indistinct, as though she gave off tremendous heat. Her eyes blazed as she reached out, trying to take Nelwyn's hand.

You go to the end of your life, and I came to return you to those who love you. Find your strength and come back with me. You can do it!

Nelwyn stared at her, mesmerized, but the pull of the tempest at her back became so intense that she knew she could not stand against it for long. The cacophony of voices mingled with the roar of the wind and swelled to a deafening pitch. Nelwyn shook her head sadly at Gaelen.

I cannot go back with you, for I am called to the Far Shores. My time has come, and I must go where I am bidden. She turned her face back toward the voices, and her inner light dimmed.

You must not leave Galador! He will grieve forever and never love again! There was a dark doom upon his heart until you came—I sensed it. You have healed him from hurts so deep that he would dwell ever in the dark without you, yet you would now leave him without even a fight? Take my hand—I will aid you! Gaelen raised her voice to be heard over the dark grey gale that tore at Nelwyn and stretched her hand out, burning as though with fire. When Nelwyn turned her face back toward her, Gaelen saw her eyes fill with tears. She reached out to Gaelen and took her hand, feeling the heat wash over her, and the wind and the voices ceased.

They found themselves standing in a misty silence now, almost floating, hands still locked together. The light that had surrounded them was nearly gone, only the dimmest flicker illuminated their faces. Gaelen did not understand what had happened, but she didn't care. She was bent on bringing Nelwyn back, and the thought of failure had not even entered her mind.

Gaelen had actually been gone for some time when Rogond discovered her near-lifeless state. He looked desperately up at Galador, still holding Gaelen's face in his hands. Galador regarded Rogond with concern.

"What is it? What's the matter with her?"

Rogond shook his head. He did not yet know. "She is not with us, Galador. I do not know where she has gone, but she is not with us."

Galador crossed to Rogond and knelt beside him, examining Gaelen for himself. What he saw made him draw back in alarm. Gaelen's eyes still reacted to light, but there was no spirit behind them.

Rogond took her in his arms, despairing at the stiffness and coldness of her skin against his, almost as though she were made of wood.

"She is dying," said Galador. "We need Lady Ordath." Surely, Ordath would be able to put her right. Rogond had been prepared to lose Nelwyn and to deal with Galador's grief, or so he thought. But the thought of losing Gaelen had not really entered his mind until now. His eyes implored Galador, who rose and went to seek the help of the Elves of Mountain-home.

Lady Ordath was found and brought to them. She entered to find Galador once again beside Nelwyn as Rogond called in vain to Gaelen, trying to revive her. Gaelen's dead eyes stared at the carved ceiling as Ordath bent over her, studying her with grave intensity. She searched the anxious face of Rogond and realized the depth of his feelings, for she was very wise in the ways of the attractions that could sometimes arise between Elves and men.

She shook her head. "Your affection for her is ill-fated, Rogond. Still, it is deep, and I sorrow for you. This will be a difficult night." Then she examined Nelwyn, turned to Galador, and confirmed his worst fears.

"Nelwyn is leaving us. She has not long until her last breath."

Galador's face was set, but Rogond knew he struggled to keep his strength at this news. "Is there no hope? Nothing that can restore her?" Galador's voice broke as he asked this question, because he knew the answer already.

Ordath spoke quietly to Galador. "Everything in our power has been done. I have seen far less take those I would have thought stronger; the fact that Nelwyn remains here is a tribute to her strength of will. But her best and only hope now rests with the one who wanders in shadow with her."

She turned to Rogond. "That is where Gaelen has gone. She is trying to keep Nelwyn here against the directive of fate. If she cannot, and Nelwyn's strength fails, it is likely that neither will return."

Both Rogond and Galador tried to grasp the full meaning of Ordath's words. Rogond closed his eyes and clung to Gaelen's now graceless form, trying to reach out to her in thought. But the door was closed, and she could not hear him. He opened his eyes again and addressed Ordath with calm stoicism. "I can do nothing?"

"She has gone where you cannot aid her," Ordath replied. "She is determined to bring Nelwyn back, or to follow her. I do not know Gaelen well, but from Galador's thoughts concerning her, I sense that she will not accept failure. And the alternative to failure, in this case, is death. Hold on to her, and if the time comes, you may yet aid her. I cannot know as yet."

She turned to Galador and spoke to him in sympathy, though her gentle rebuke was clear. "Gaelen's devotion to Nelwyn is strong indeed. You must rid your heart of the unworthy thoughts you have held toward her—this hurt is Gorgon's doing. Without Gaelen to hold her here, Nelwyn will surely leave you. They both possess great inner strength, but they will need more before the end. Let's hope that Gaelen is as persuasive as she is tenacious."

Galador's face reddened as he recalled his resentment of Gaelen. His eyes were unnaturally bright as he faced Ordath. "How may I aid her?"

"Remain vigilant, Galador, for the opportunity may yet come," said Ordath, who knew that Galador and Rogond might well be able to assist Gaelen when the time was right. "I will remain with you until this ends, whatever happens." She made her way to sit beside Galador and fixed her gaze upon Nelwyn's pale face, awaiting the inevitable.

Gaelen and Nelwyn stood together in the darkness, as the wind began to rise again. Nelwyn appreciated this last opportunity to speak with her cousin, as she knew that she must soon follow to the land of her forebears, and nothing would detain her. Even as Gaelen tried to persuade her, she had closed her mind. She was so weary, and the promise of rest was too strong.

Gaelen sensed this, the fire of her spirit flickering brighter as she strengthened her resolve. *You cannot give in, Nelwyn. You must prevail and come back with me. Do you not hear me? You must prevail!*

No, Gaelen, I cannot. They that have gone before are calling to me even now. Release my hand, for I must go where you cannot follow. She sorrowed at the despair in Gaelen's face, but her own light now flared around her as she attempted to pull away from Gaelen, who would not let her go. *Release me! You cannot come with me, and you cannot hold me here. Do not endanger yourself thus.*

Gaelen would not let go of Nelwyn's hand. *Do you not understand what you are asking of me? I will never let go! Aontar Himself will have to come and strike me down. I will not let you leave us so long as my strength holds.* She meant this with all her heart, though her strength was waning even as she spoke the words. Her fiery aura was diminishing as Nelwyn's grew brighter.

Take not so lightly the name of Aontar. It is useless to resist. Let go! I will not be the instrument of your death, Nelwyn cried, pulling back with all her strength. Gaelen hung on with grim resolve.

I will not let you go without me. If I must follow you into the Eternal Realm, so be it. May I be imprisoned together with the spirit of Aincor forever—I will not leave you. But even as Gaelen said this, Nelwyn slipped from her grasp…

…and drew her last breath.

Lady Ordath stiffened, waiting for Nelwyn's next breath, which did not come. She reached across to Galador, gripping his arm. "You said you wanted to aid Gaelen, and now is your chance. Call to Nelwyn. Call her back to you and make certain she can hear you from the shadows. Rogond, do not call to Gaelen—her greatest test is at hand and you must not distract her. But focus your will and your fortitude, that she may gain strength from your devotion."

Galador called to Nelwyn, even as her spirit drew farther from him, in a desperate, broken voice. In the dark, swirling chaos Gaelen cried out to Nelwyn, even as she began to turn away. *Listen! Do you hear*

Galador? This is the cry of forlorn hope! Can you not hear it? Turn back and face me! I would speak with you one last time. The fire of her spirit flared for a moment, so that she was difficult for Nelwyn to look upon, but it faded rapidly until all Nelwyn beheld was Gaelen standing before her, her face grim and sad.

Speak, Gaelen, for I must leave soon. I hear Galador's cries… they wrench my heart. But I must go now to my fate, as it cannot be denied.

Then the fire flared again in Gaelen, until Nelwyn had to close her eyes against the brightness of this final effort to hold her.

You are not so fated! You just refuse to see it! Where is your strength, daughter of Turanen? Where is the love of Galador? Where is your love of Gaelen, the one for whom you endured the black ditch? Do you not remember? We did not care as we both leaped into that foul, stinking mire together so long ago. Is that not stronger than this? And when you saved my life in the dark when we drew too near the Pale Tower? Will that spirit not prevail? Will you leave us to die in despair without you? My spirit is spent with effort. I cannot return without you, for I have gone too far. Galador, though he may not die of grief, might as well do so rather than live forever without love. Will you let Gorgon succeed in killing the spirit of three more worthy Elàni? I think not, daughter of the Greatwood. I KNOW not!

Nelwyn shuddered, trying to grasp the impact of Gaelen's words. She could not let Galador suffer such a fate. And Gaelen, who had gone so far to save her that she herself would be lost, what of her? The pull of death was so strong, and the promise of rest so tempting. She was so weary! Then, as if sensing Nelwyn's wavering, Gaelen spoke one last time:

If you deny me, and go to this fate, I shall have no choice but to go with you. And I was not ready to give up my life, Nelwyn, not until my quest is fulfilled. I love you and would return with you to the wide world, where so much yet awaits us. But if you insist on death then I shall make certain that you never, EVER hear the end of it! Even as she said this, her spirit faded and flickered.

Rogond moaned in despair as he sensed Gaelen's fading spirit. At the bidding of Ordath he did not call to her, and he knew that there was nothing he could really do for her, as she was unaware of the depth of his devotion. He sat in grim silence, focusing his will on thoughts of her returning, bringing Nelwyn with her, and reuniting with him. He thought of the adventures they would yet have together and how she would come to know him better. And he thought of how he would give all the strength he had at this moment to ensure that he could behold the light of her eyes and hear the clear sound of her voice again.

NO! cried Nelwyn. She would not tear Galador's fragile heart with grief, and Gaelen would not be lost. Her resolve hardened as she turned at last from the voices, and reached out with both hands toward Gaelen's rapidly diminishing light.

I don't want to leave any of you! I WILL try. Help me! Nelwyn, her own inner fire flaring blue-white, struggled forward against the forces pulling at her, clutching at Gaelen. They combined and renewed their strength, clinging to one another in the gale, taking first one step, then another. The voices of Gaelen and Galador filled Nelwyn's ears, sustaining her resolve and drowning out the voices calling at her back.

Remember the Black Ditch! Remember the Dark Tower! Remember Talrodin and Thaldallen and your vow of vengeance! Find the strength to live, for your work is unfinished! Hearken to Galador, who loves you!

The darkness faded, and the wind grew less. Gaelen closed her eyes as warmth returned to her limbs, and she grew vital again in Rogond's embrace. Nelwyn once again drew breath, and Ordath smiled.

14

In Which Some Friendships Are Renewed

With the return of Gaelen and Nelwyn, the darkness passed from the Company, and the peace and healing of Mountain-home could be enjoyed at last. All Elves are quick healers, but it would be awhile before Gaelen or Nelwyn regained full strength, probably late spring at least.

As soon as she was able, Gaelen met with Ordath and Magra to tell them her tale from the beginning. Magra was especially dismayed by the tale of Gelmyr and the horror Gaelen read in his eyes. She told Magra this knowing it would distress him, for she hoped to enlist his aid.

Magra was an Elf-lord of the Èolar, and his name means "Mighty", for so he was. One of the chief advisors to Lady Ordath, he also commanded her forces in battle. He had fought beside Ri-Elathan during the Third Uprising of Wrothgar; in fact, Magra was probably the closest thing the High King had to a friend. Gaelen was hopeful that with one such as Magra to aid her, Gorgon would be overthrown and destroyed at last. In the meantime, she resolved to accomplish two things while in Mountain-home: to acquire a larger, more powerful bow and to regain her ability to pull it.

Nelwyn and Galador were nearly always together. They rejoiced as they came to learn more of each other, and Nelwyn thrived under Galador's excellent care. She slept well and often, as Elves do when they are healing, and at such times Galador would rest with her, though he did not sleep.

Rogond did not dare appear too solicitous of Gaelen, for though he knew that Ordath had perceived the truth of his feelings, he did not wish to make them the subject of widespread speculation in Mountain-home. Gaelen initially had needed rest, as the journey of her spirit had exhausted her nearly beyond recovery. She had slept beside Nelwyn for a day or two, and Galador had not begrudged her this, knowing that he owed her a great debt.

Gaelen's recovery was swifter than Nelwyn's, and she was soon on her feet and wandering about. Though both she and Nelwyn had been in this realm before, they had never been afforded the status of honored guests. Now Lady Ordath announced that there would be a celebration in honor of the Company, for their courage and devotion in bringing their grim news as quickly as possible and at such great risk. The feast would occur during the new moon in three days' time, for the stars would be most bright above Mountain-home, and no mist would cloud them. The Lady would see to it.

Those three days passed quickly. On the morning of the celebration, Nelwyn, Galador, and Rogond were brought before the Lady, where they listened with fascination as Nelwyn told them of her encounter with Gaelen in the Spirit Realm. Galador chuckled at Rogond as Nelwyn described her own blue-white aura and Gaelen's fiery one.

"You see? I told you. She is a foundling descended of the house of Aincor!"

Rogond smiled back at him. "A good thing, my friend, as the blood of the Fire-heart must have been an asset. Gaelen accomplished a difficult task."

To this, Ordath agreed. "It was indeed difficult for both of them. Nelwyn also has a strong will, though it lies more deeply hidden—like a swift current beneath calm waters. You shall all sit at my table tonight with Lord Magra. This reminds me...I must seek him now, as there are things I would discuss with him. You will please pardon me."

She rose gracefully to her feet and bowed before taking her leave, pausing in the doorway to address Rogond. "There is a friend here who would see you; he was in the second floor library, I believe."

Rogond knew at once who she referred to. Fima, the dwarvish lore-master, was waiting for him; the library had been their favorite place to meet and study together. Rogond said farewell to Galador and Nelwyn, and prepared to greet his old friend.

Magra found Gaelen perched on one of the high walls overlooking the rushing waters of Monadh-talam. Her hair was ruffled in the early morning wind, her eyes distant, looking out to the west. She appeared to be lost in thought. Magra didn't really know why he wanted to speak with her, but he sensed that she had not yet told him everything of Gorgon and the death of Gelmyr. He also wanted to give her a token to show his appreciation for her efforts. He had one for Nelwyn, as well. Gaelen had not yet detected his presence, and he stood for a moment, gazing at her, as she sat motionless as though made of stone. He didn't wish to risk startling her from her perch, so he made certain she could hear his approach. She turned quickly to face him, and then relaxed.

Gaelen had been edgy all morning for some reason, maybe something in the wind or a movement in the earth? She did not know why.

"Gaelen, may I sit with you awhile?" Magra drew nigh her, his long flaxen hair blown back and his piercing blue eyes fixed on her. For a moment, they took one another in. Gaelen admired Magra's broad, strong shoulders and powerful, tall frame. Magra's gaze was drawn to Gaelen's large, bright eyes and rather long, elegant ears, which were swept back along the sides of her head in a most attractive manner. Most male Elves would agree that Gaelen's eyes were beautiful, but her ears were considered stunning and highly sensuous. They more than made up for her shortcomings: her slight stature, her cropped hair, and her reluctance to wear any but masculine attire. Magra wondered…would she make an exception for him?

Gaelen dropped down from the wall onto the ground, and they walked a few paces to an intricately carved wooden bench. Sitting beside Magra, Gaelen waited to hear what he had to say, for she knew there was some purpose to his coming. First, he drew forth the longbow he had slung at his back and presented it to her. It was a thing of beauty, plain but elegant, of Èolarin design.

"Word reached me that you wanted a more powerful bow. Please accept this as a gift for your invaluable service. I would say that you will not be able to pull it as yet, for it is a powerful weapon with a very long range. It was recovered from the battle-plain and has been kept wrapped with oil for many long years. May you have better fortune than he who bore it last."

Gaelen was delighted. She could hardly wait to try out her gift. She would make certain, however, that she was unobserved, as she sensed that Magra was right. She would not be able to pull this massive weapon for quite some time. She accepted it with thanks, still waiting to learn why he had sought her out.

"I would speak with you of Gelmyr. What became of his remains? Are they where they might be recovered?"

"Alas, they are not. We gave him to the Ambros, as I remembered him speaking of how much he loved the sound of it."

"When did he speak of this? I was not aware that you knew him well," said Magra, his eyes and his voice solemn and sad. His heart ached for the loss of his friend, and Gaelen's mention of this personal detail grieved him, for she was quite right about Gelmyr's affection for flowing waters.

"I did not know him, but he came once to the Greatwood, and I remember you sitting with him at feast. He must have mentioned it then. My lord, is there anything else you would learn of me?"

Magra nodded. "I felt a great dread come over me, a fear that I could not name. I don't recall now when it happened, but I expect it was about the same time as Gelmyr's death. I dreamed of a large, dark enemy coming for Gelmyr, for me—for every Elf who lives. We could not stand against it. Gaelen…what *was* this thing you fought with on our southern borders?"

She took a deep breath. "What was the moon like on the night of your dream?"

He considered for a moment. "It was full, or nearly so. I remember that it had risen when the dread struck me, and I grew cold and did not know why."

Gaelen nodded, and then confirmed his suspicions. "Gelmyr died under that moon. You felt it. As to the nature of the enemy, I do not know."

He pressed her, perceiving that she held back. "You have sensed something. I know it! Please, tell me what you think."

"I thank you for your gift, Lord Magra. I cannot tell you my beliefs, as they have little foundation, but it is clear to me that this enemy is formidable to the point that the next time we encounter him, it had best be with as much strength as our people can muster."

"Certainly you shall have the resources of Mountain-home to aid you. You intend to continue pursuit?"

"Eventually. I must now wait until my friends are strong and the trail grows warm again. But we may at least warn the people of Tal-sithian and of the Verdant Mountains. If we are wary, we can ensure that we are not taken so easily. Perhaps then we can force the creature out into the open, though I don't know...he is very clever."

Magra smiled inwardly at Gaelen's expressing the need to wait until her *friends* were strong. He also agreed that warning the Elves would be most prudent. He rose and turned to leave her, but spoke to her once more: "My thanks for your enlightenment, though it was not all that I desired. I notice that your friend Nelwyn has a companion in Galador. Will you allow me to be your companion tonight?"

Gaelen considered for a moment. This was an appealing notion, as she liked Magra, though she was a bit in awe of him. "But what of Rogond? Surely I must escort him, as he has been a worthy traveling companion, and a doughty warrior. He must not feel as though he has been cast aside."

Magra took her point. "Then at least you shall sit at my right hand. Your friend Rogond can sit then at yours. Will that be satisfactory?"

Gaelen nodded. Magra then added a parting comment: "I will send raiment for you...it would please me if you would favor me by wearing it."

Gaelen's beautiful ears turned red as she stared at his retreating back.

Rogond returned to his chamber to find a complete ensemble of very elegant attire all laid out for him. He had spent a very pleasant afternoon renewing his acquaintance with Fima, the dwarf, who had been delighted to see him and hear of his adventures. Fima was particularly impressed with Rogond's tale of the encounter with Dwim and Noli, and either nodded sagely or chuckled heartily in all the right places. He was surprised to learn the hidden secret of Rogond's ring; he had known it as an outstanding example of dwarvish smith work, but had not known to place it under an Eolarin lamp to reveal the message within.

He frowned as Rogond told him of the encounter with Gorgon and what had happened when Gaelen had flashed the reflected sunlight into the creature's eyes. "This sounds like a formidable enemy indeed," said Fima. "I wonder if any light makes him react thus, or whether only sunlight will do? If so, you had best never pursue him below ground. He sounds vaguely Ulca-like, and Ulcas can tolerate bright light other than sunlight, though they do not love it. Still, I wonder."

"He was no Ulca, Lore-master," said Rogond. "He was larger and stronger, and much more clever and adept than any Ulca."

"You might be surprised," said Fima. "When first the Ulcas were spawned, there were those among them that were mighty. Their kind has diminished with the passage of time and distance from their forebears. But you are right to believe that this creature, if he were of such mighty lineage, would be indeed ancient, and therefore that is unlikely. Most of the great Ulcas perished in the First Uprising of Wrothgar, and their like has not been seen in Alterra since. But come and see for yourself—some knowledge of them has been recorded."

Fima drew an ancient manuscript from a battered leather case containing many such old parchments. He thumbed through it until he found a description of large, powerful dark warriors that wreaked havoc in ancient times, complete with illustrations.

Rogond studied them intently. He concluded that while there were certainly similarities between Gorgon and the depiction in the manuscript, there were several very significant differences. Gorgon's legs were straight and powerful, not bowed and crooked as in the drawing. Gorgon stood tall and proud—in no way was he ungainly. In addition, no Ulca has either eyebrows or eyelashes, and Rogond had seen both upon Gorgon.

The manuscript described these ancient Ulcan warriors as "reasonably adept with weaponry, clever and crafty, but not swift." Gorgon was clever and crafty, but he also was fabulously skilled with a blade, and, for his size, swifter than anything Rogond had seen that moved on two feet. He concluded that Gorgon was not an Ulca, even a mighty one, but something else. He discussed this with Fima, who then agreed that Gorgon seemed unlike any other creature.

As the afternoon waned, Rogond begged leave to go and prepare for the celebration. "You will be there, of course?" he asked Fima.

"I never miss a good feast in Mountain-home. I'm sure you remember that the food here is absolutely superb—we are in for a real treat. But by all means, go and make ready. After all, we of the mortal kindreds of Alterra must make an impressive showing, mustn't we?"

Rogond chuckled. "If that's true, my undersized friend, we're in trouble. It will take the rest of the afternoon for me to repair some of the holes in my garments."

"You will not have to repair your garments. I am certain of it. Lady Ordath provides well for her honored guests. I shall be present tonight, and if you grow weary of Elven tongues, come to my table and we shall see what you remember of Rûmhul." Then, in a sly voice, he added "They hate it when I do that."

Once Rogond had gone, Fima pondered for a few moments, his wise, weathered face looking troubled. He rose, moved to a stack of tall cases, and climbed the ladder attached to one of them. It took him a few minutes of searching to find the old manuscript, and then he fetched it down, settled into a comfortable chair, and began to read. "I wonder," he muttered, contemplating Rogond's words. "I wonder…"

Gaelen sank thankfully into a tub of very hot water. She relished the feel of it as it relaxed every muscle in her body, particularly her stiff, sore shoulders, which were still healing. The water had been scented with fragrant oils, some of which were medicinal. The vapors felt wonderful as she breathed them in, filling her lungs and soothing her spirits.

When the water began to grow chill, she emerged with some reluctance and wrapped herself in the silken robe that had been left for her, shaking her wet hair from her eyes. She ran her fingers through it to tame it, to little avail. Frustrated, she glowered at her reflection in the glass, and then was startled as a tall, brown-haired Elf-maiden approached her from behind, a basket under her arm. The maiden was momentarily flustered when she beheld Gaelen's lack of readiness.

"Good heavens! We have much to do to make ready, and the hour is late. My name is Nasülle, and I am an apprentice healer. I have been sent to prepare you for tonight."

"Yes, I've seen you before. You have some skill in the healing arts. You are the one who gave me the sleeping-draught, I believe. Quite unprincipled of you to take advantage of my weakness...restorative draught, indeed! But I see you have other skills as well." Gaelen was looking rather pointedly at Nasülle's perfect hair.

Nasülle drew a comb from her basket and approached Gaelen.

"Let's see what we can do with this. When I am finished, you will not know yourself. You sit at Lord Magra's right hand tonight—you should look the part."

Gaelen sighed, resigned to Nasülle's attentions. It took a while to tame Gaelen's hair into a satisfactory form, and Nasülle changed her tactics several times before she was finally satisfied. When she had finished, even Nelwyn might have needed to look twice to recognize her cousin. "Come on, then, and let us get you dressed and ready," said Nasülle, admiring her handiwork. She brought in the attire that Magra had sent, and Gaelen snorted most inappropriately.

"I cannot wear this! I shall look absurd. This was made for some high-and-mighty personage that I'm certain bore little resemblance to myself. Besides, it's too long for me, and I shall no doubt stumble over it."

"You can wear it, and you *shall*," Nasülle insisted. "It's my job to make certain that it is a perfect fit. You needn't worry about stumbling over it. What, would you appear at this gathering in your traveling clothes? Do you understand the honor done you by Lord Magra? You shall be admired by all tonight and envied by a few. I have labored long already to make you presentable, and you shall be presentable!"

There commenced a brief verbal struggle over whether Gaelen would suffer herself to be thus attired, but she gave in and endured Nasülle's attentions once again. When she had finished, Gaelen looked magnificent. As predicted, she did not know herself. Who was this strange, elegant creature staring wide-eyed from the glass?

"Hurry along, for the feast may have started by now," said Nasülle. "They are most likely waiting for you. Hurry along!"

Gaelen made her way to the wide veranda where the feast would be held, hoping her late arrival would not be noticed.

The veranda was positively grand. Tables had been set with glittering crystal and silver, and laden with delicacies of all sorts. Everyone looked resplendent, especially Magra, who was arrayed all in sky blue and silver. Strong and silent, his blue eyes were serene as he surveyed the scene before him. Beside him was an empty place at the table, undoubtedly intended for Gaelen. To the right of this sat Rogond, darkly handsome in tailored, elegant slate blue trimmed with black. Lady Ordath sat at Magra's left on a slightly raised dais, as befitted her station, and was attired in white and gold, her long dark tresses woven and set with wildflowers. Beside her sat Galador, then Nelwyn, and finally Elethorn. Galador wore light grey trimmed in a deep purple, which was pleasing next to the silky lavender gown worn by Nelwyn. Her golden hair was also adorned with spring flowers, and she looked both strong and radiant.

Gaelen's hope of an inconspicuous entrance was dashed as Magra beheld her and rose to his feet. Rogond looked over at her, and his jaw dropped. He had never seen Gaelen attired as anything other than a hunter-scout in breeches, boots, tunic, and cloak. She lifted her chin as all eyes turned to her for a moment, responding to Magra's rising to greet her. She flushed as he indicated the seat at his right, but as she approached she smiled at Rogond, who had by now also risen to his feet, cocking one eyebrow at the purple evening sky. Her expression in return was clear—what did he think he was staring at? He lowered his eyes in respect.

Gaelen's gown was of pale ivory, trimmed with silver and pearl, and her soft, shining hair was perfectly arranged, garlanded with pale blue and white flowers and held in place by an intricately woven circlet of silver. Her large, bright eyes shone with an inner light, and the ivory gown contrasted with her tawny complexion. She was positively lustrous. Nelwyn and Galador both nodded in greeting as Magra took Gaelen's arm, directing her to sit beside him and smiling in approval. When he sat back down, all turned their attention to Lady Ordath.

The Lady rose to her feet, proclaiming the purpose of the celebration. All lifted their goblets in honor of the visitors, whose courage and sacrifice had restored Elethorn to them, and bowed their heads in remembrance of those lost. When Ordath finished, she called for the feast to begin. Everyone ate and drank and talked for hours.

Gaelen wondered at the empty plate and goblet that had been set beside Magra, and then she realized that it was in honor of Gelmyr. Magra took his own goblet, filled it, and poured half of the wine into that set for Gelmyr. Then he lifted his glass and drained it, speaking too softly for any but Gaelen to hear. When he set his own goblet back down, he sat for a moment with his eyes closed and his head bowed. Gaelen did not disturb him, for she knew the pain of his loss.

At last he turned to her, as music filled the skies, and some began dancing. Galador and Nelwyn were already among them, stately and graceful, moving as though of one body. Gaelen watched them wistfully, her heart aching for the kind of devotion that Nelwyn had found in Galador. She had once known such devotion, but it had been taken from her.

Magra mistook this wistfulness as a sign that Gaelen simply wanted to join the dance. Rogond, who by now knew her fairly well and was attuned to her feelings, started to ask her, but was too late. Lord Magra took Gaelen's hand and led her to the floor.

Rogond watched the Elves as they performed their elegant, refined dances, male and female moving together as one. He looked with misty eyes upon Nelwyn and Galador, who had eyes only for one another, and upon Gaelen and Magra, tonight impossibly beautiful, powerful, and… Elven. More than ever, Rogond wished that he had been numbered among those of immortal race and could share in their fate, forsaking death and what lay beyond it for the endless days they enjoyed. He desired Gaelen deep in his heart, wishing that he could trade places with Magra and thus be free to court her openly.

The combination of the wine, the music, the sight of Gaelen so attired, and the keen glance of Magra kindled a boldness in Rogond that he had seldom allowed in the presence of the Elves. He was dismayed and sought to quell his impulses before he gave in to them, for he knew they would not be well received. Magra was in total possession of Gaelen tonight, or at least, so it appeared. Rogond noted with some uneasiness that his hands were clenched in his lap. This was most unworthy—to be jealous of the attention of an Elf-lord to one such as Gaelen. Why would Magra not turn his attention to her? She was the most radiant, most perfect, most spirited of all the

Elàni in Rogond's eyes. Perhaps another glass of wine would relax him and turn his thoughts aside.

This strategy did not work, however, as the wine only seemed to further embolden Rogond, and he realized that he should drink no more of it. Pushing his crystal goblet away, he surveyed the scene, looking for anything that would divert him. Then his gaze fell on Fima, who was still at the table, eating and drinking with another dwarf and one of the Elvish healers. This appeared to be a merry gathering, exactly what Rogond needed to take his mind from the tall Elf-lord who was presently occupying the attentions of his only love. He rose and moved to join Fima and the healer, who made him welcome.

Fima suspected that sitting alone watching Magra with Gaelen would not be to Rogond's liking. "You are very subdued tonight, my young Aridan," he said, watching Rogond look sidelong at Magra, who was at that moment being disgustingly charming.

Rogond drew a deep breath. "I have never been one for this sort of formal revelry. Perhaps I should excuse myself and return to my chamber, for tomorrow will be a very long day, and I have much to think about."

Fima smiled and shook his head, then leaned over and spoke quietly to Rogond. "First think about this—running away won't solve your dilemma, my friend. If you want that Elf, go and take her. If you ask, and she accepts, you shall have your answer. Magra cannot interfere with her choices, lord though he is. You are as worthy as are any of these folk, but they have trained you well, so that you do not see it. Go on and take her! If you don't, you'll regret it. I suspect that Magra only toys with her anyway, as she is but a Sylvan rustic, and he is a powerful Elf-lord. You must trust her. Think of all you have seen and been through with her; she will honor it. Besides," he added with a sly wink, "I would very much like to see the two of you dance together. It would gladden my heart."

Rogond's eyes flashed at the thought of Magra's toying with Gaelen. He wondered how the great Elf-lord would have fared against Gorgon—would he have discovered the creature's hidden weakness, as had the Sylvan rustic? He resolved to take Fima's advice. "Then you shall see it," he declared, getting to his feet.

Fima nodded in approval and clapped Rogond on the arm, sending him forth. "Go on and take her, my friend," he repeated, then rose and worked his way over to the musicians. He spoke urgently to one of them, pressing a few coins into his hand.

Magra and Gaelen were standing together, speaking in low voices, waiting for the music to resume. Magra had been entirely focused on his companion, ignoring all attempts at distraction by the Elves of Mountain-home, several of whom also desired his company.

Nelwyn and Galador, flushed with the excitement of the evening, approached Gaelen, who asked if they had seen Rogond. Then she heard a voice from behind her right shoulder.

"He is here," said Rogond as she turned to face him, "and he would dance with you. Will you have him?"

Things grew quiet around them for a moment, as Gaelen considered. Several of the Elves of Mountain-home had ceased their conversation and turned their attention to Lord Magra and his companion, who had just been asked to dance by Rogond of the Tuathar. Rogond and Magra knew one another, and there was no enmity between them, at least not until now. But the Elves were understandably curious as to Gaelen's choice and the reaction of either Magra or Rogond to it.

Gaelen, who in her naïveté had no idea of the significance of her next act, took Rogond's hand and followed him without so much as a backward glance at the tall Elf-lord. Magra was somewhat taken aback, though he did not reveal it.

Galador quickly stepped in. "They are good friends, Lord Magra, but friends only. It was generous of you to allow this intrusion."

"It is of no consequence," replied Magra with a dismissive wave of his hand. "I must speak with Lady Ordath at any rate, and this time alone is appreciated. But your friend Rogond, I fear, takes an ill-fated path, for I know Gaelen of old, and I know her heart's desire. She longs for that which she cannot have. All hope of winning her is vain." He looked hard at Galador, and his next remark was chilly. "It would be best if your friend became aware of this, as I sense his interests in her are far less casual than are mine." So saying, he returned to the table, there to occupy himself in conversation with Ordath.

As soon as Lord Magra had gone, Galador turned to Nelwyn. "What did he mean by all that?" he asked, puzzled.

Nelwyn shook her head. "You will have to learn it from Gaelen herself, if you want to know, but even Magra does not hold all the knowledge of her that he believes he does. Though it is possibly true that Gaelen will never fully give herself to another of Elven-kind, Rogond's hopes are not in vain." She embraced Galador, who was more confused than ever. "Do not try to make sense of this now, as I will speak no more of it," she implored him. "Let's return to the dance."

At last the musicians resumed playing, but rather than the slow, cadenced, deliberate tempo that had dominated much of the evening, this was faster, lighter, and more abandoned. Such music was favored by the Wood-elves of the Greatwood and of the Verdant Mountains, though it seemed a bit out of place in the court of Mountain-home. Rogond and Gaelen knew it at once. Gaelen tossed her head, knocking her garland askew, and was soon dancing in the manner of her people—a lively, springy dance with much elaborate footwork. Rogond also knew this dance (as Fima had been perfectly aware) and they moved expertly together.

The Elves of Mountain-home delighted in watching their energetic performance, and some even joined them. The others clapped their hands and sang snatches of the tune as they could. The level of merriment reached its peak, and the song ended.

Rogond and Gaelen were now flushed and breathing hard from their efforts, but both felt much better for it. Gaelen's perfect hair had come undone and now displayed its usual windblown untidiness; she looked very much the Sylvan rustic.

Rogond bowed before her, turned toward his good friend Fima with a nod and, with a last acknowledgment of Nelwyn and Galador, he took his leave. He paused to bid good evening to Lady Ordath and to thank her. Ordath nodded, but her gaze, though gentle, was stern. Magra also nodded toward him. "Aridan," he said, with a courtesy in his voice that did not extend to his eyes.

Many thoughts grew in many hearts that night in Mountain-home. Rogond returned alone to his chamber, his courage waning with the influence of the wine. He began to doubt the wisdom of his bold possession of Gaelen at the feast. She would almost certainly ask him about it. What in the world had Fima been thinking? "Go and take her," indeed! Now he would have to explain himself to her satisfaction and at least partly reveal his desires to her. What, then, would she do? What if she rejected him utterly? He supposed she would insist that he leave her to face Gorgon without him. On the other hand, he did not believe that she would scorn him. She had gone willingly to the dance, the light of her eyes was not tainted by disdain, and her voice held no derision of him as she said goodnight. On the *other* hand, she was no mortal.

Rogond had not meant to show discourtesy to Lord Magra, either. Despite Fima's insinuations, there was no evidence that Magra's affection for Gaelen was anything but genuine. Tomorrow Rogond would find him and apologize. His face burned as he thought of it.

Ordath knew the truth of Rogond's feelings, and she had always been kind to him, even somewhat motherly. Perhaps it would be prudent to seek her advice in this matter, though he thought he knew what she would say, and he dreaded hearing it. Once given, such advice would be difficult to disregard. Rogond wished for a moment that he had just a bit more of Gaelen's self-willed nature; she didn't balk at disregarding advice from anyone, but followed the desires of her heart. She judged all advice on its merit and always against the standard of her opinion, whether it came from Elf-lord, Sylvan rustic, or mortal man.

Rogond truly loved the civility of Mountain-home, but he found himself wishing for the wilderness and for the company of his own people. They judged him always by his actions and not by his heritage. They were now so few, and there was much work to be done.

Shaking these thoughts from his mind, Rogond tried to take rest before the dawn came, but found that it eluded him. His main comfort came from thoughts of finding Fima in the morning and having a few words with him concerning his manipulation of the actions of a certain wine-besotted Aridan, playing on his feelings for one fair, immortal, headstrong Sylvan rustic.

Gaelen had settled in a warm, moss-covered niche overlooking the water. She drew her battered cloak around her, relishing the feel of her familiar clothing, and settled back to rest, though she found that she could not. She had taken leave of Magra, Galador, and Nelwyn not long after Rogond's departure. She stayed long enough to dance with Magra again, promising to teach him some of the Sylvan way, as he in turn offered to aid her in mastering the longbow. With a last, gentle farewell, she had left him, pausing and bowing before Lady Ordath. The Lady's expression was enigmatic. Gaelen could not tell whether she was displeased, concerned, or attempting to be dispassionate, but she read something there. Certainly Gaelen did not wish to offend the Lady, but she could not imagine how she might have done so.

She wondered about her friend Rogond, who knew so much of the ways of her people. She liked him immensely, even loved him in her way. She had grown so fond of him in the past few months that she was beginning to be unable to imagine traveling without him, as though he had always been at her side. He was faithful, courageous, considerate, and not in the least arrogant or willful. She admired his skill in battle, but even more the complex workings of his mind and the seeming simplicity of his heart. Alas that he was of mortal race, for he would remain in her world only for a brief while. And where he went after, she could not follow.

Tears sprang unbidden to her eyes as she thought of that parting, which would come no matter what their fates held. She thought it very likely that one or both of them would perish in the upcoming struggle with the Dark Horror that brooded now beneath the mountain. She wiped the tears away quickly, though none would witness them. Did she cry for Rogond, at the thought of saying goodbye, or for herself? The answer to that question lay in her past, in a land far to the north of the Greatwood, and in the Vault of Eternity.

Nelwyn and Galador lay together in a fair glade beside gently flowing waters, breathing in the heady scent of the new spring blooms and embracing beneath the stars. Galador had given himself over completely to this deeply passionate, beautiful maiden who now declared her love for him. She had reached into his very soul, extracted the poisoned dart of his suffering, and cleansed his heart, opening it anew. Though he would always carry his love for Gwynnyth, he had learned that there was room in his heart also for Nelwyn, whose light would fill the emptiness of his life both now and through eternity. His joy could not be quenched, and he threw his head back and laughed aloud, as Nelwyn smiled back at him. "Why do you laugh, my love?"

"Because I am filled with joy at this fate, which though it had seemed so desolate, I would not now trade with any in this world. It has been long since I laughed in joy, as I do now." This said, he held her in a passionate embrace, and they kissed for the first of many times that night. As Galador beheld his perfect, loving companion who now held absolute dominion over the desire of his heart, he knew that he was ready to dedicate himself to her utterly, to die for her if need be.

As for Gaelen, foundling descendent of the Fire-heart, Galador could never repay the debt he owed her. What had Magra meant when he had spoken of her heart's desire that could never be attained? Nelwyn would not tell him, but Magra had intimated that it was something Rogond should be made aware of. Tomorrow Galador would seek to learn the truth of this from Magra, or perhaps from Ordath. Nelwyn had said that Gaelen would never give herself to another of Elven-kind. Did this mean her heart was given already? If so, how sad that her desire was unattainable, but how fortunate that his own was not.

Oh, Happy Elf of Eádros! Galador exulted, closing his thoughts of Gaelen and submitting once more to the loving attentions of her gentler cousin, of whose origins in the Greatwood there was absolutely no doubt.

Rogond found Magra in the armory the next morning. He seemed quite genial as he approached. "Ah! There you are, Aridan...now I shall not have to go in search of you. Come and have a look at this." He held out Rogond's spear, which had been restored with a new blackened steel point. The shaft, finely balanced so that it rested lightly in his hand, would fly straight and true. "What do you think? Is it to your liking?"

Rogond's expression left no doubt that it was very much to his liking. He bowed courteously, and then raised his eyes to meet Magra's.

"This weapon has never been tended with such skill. My thanks are insufficient," he said, and meant it.

Magra favored him with a good-natured smile. "You restored Elethorn to us, and helped bring the news of Gelmyr and this creature, Gorgon. It is we who are in your debt. Besides, Gaelen and Nelwyn should not be the only ones with fine weapons. You will need your spear, Aridan, before all is ended."

He turned and lifted Gorgon's shield, which they had brought with them slung across Galador's back. Magra shuddered as he touched it. "If the armor is of the same material, it is no wonder that your spearhead was turned." He handed the shield to Rogond, who had not as yet examined it closely. The weight of it was daunting. No weapon that he knew of in Alterra would penetrate it. There were many dents, each no doubt a reminder of some desperate and ineffective fight for an Elven life. Rogond suddenly felt ill, and he lowered the shield to the ground.

Magra looked at him with concern. "I don't blame you, Rogond. I had the same feeling and would sooner not handle anything that has been touched by this creature. Gaelen said that you held it off for several minutes in single combat. That's an impressive feat, for any creature that could bear that shield must be mighty indeed."

Rogond smiled. "He slung it around as a leaf in the wind. Its weight burdened him not at all. It is a good thing Gaelen is as quick as she is, or neither of us would have been favored with her company last night." He searched uncomfortably for the right words to say to Magra, but the Elf saved him the trouble.

"Rogond, I must apologize for last night. Gaelen had told me that she wanted you to be her companion, but somehow when she was sitting at my right hand I simply forgot myself. We have known each other for quite a long time, and I do enjoy her company. At any rate, I had no right to force such a choice upon her. It is obvious that she is very fond of you. You definitely have her respect, and that's not easily earned." He inclined his head in a gesture of esteem.

Rogond was taken aback, as he had expected to be the one apologizing. Before he could stop himself, he asked a rather bold question of Magra—one that caused him to raise both eyebrows in mild surprise.

"Forgive me, but what does a great Elf-lord see in a simple Wood-elf such as Gaelen? I know that she is considered worthy in her way, but surely there are countless others more worthy to consort with one such as you. Please don't be offended…I'm merely curious, and intend no disrespect."

Magra took a deep breath, as though formulating his reply. "Gaelen and I do not 'consort', Tuathan. We might be considered friends, and I enjoy her company, but there are things I know of her that would preclude my consorting with her. And as for being a simple Wood-elf, you should know by now that Gaelen is anything but simple, and her worth is not for the folk of Mountain-home to judge. I am not offended by the question, as it has been asked by many here. But I would caution you against getting too deeply involved with her. I will speak no more of this matter."

Then, his eyes grew wide for a moment as though he had just remembered something. "I was to give a message to you from Lore-master Fima, should I encounter you. He asks that you meet with him this morning in his underground chamber. You know it, of course?"

Rogond nodded. "I shall go now; I have a few words for him as well. Thank you again for this." He indicated the spear, which he placed carefully among the others in the armory. He would have no need of it while in the Sanctuary.

Magra turned to leave, but Rogond delayed him with a last question.

"I don't suppose you are willing to tell me *why* you caution me against involvement with Gaelen?"

Magra turned back for a moment and replied, "No, I am uncomfortable revealing such matters. If you wish to learn more, inquire of Ordath if you cannot ask Gaelen directly. I don't know how Gaelen would react to such an inquiry." Before Rogond could reply, Magra had gone.

Rogond found Fima sitting amid the clutter of his underground study. Rogond looked around, bemused. This place hadn't changed a bit since his last visit over a decade ago. His friend was poring over a manuscript, muttering to himself, and had not heard Rogond until he shouted, "Go and Take the Elf, *INDEED!*" whereupon Fima was very nearly startled to death. Rogond slumped down in the only man-sized chair in the room, opposite Fima, who was looking daggers at him and smiling at the same time. They both chuckled good-naturedly like the true friends they were.

"Ah, Rogond, you are still as willing to be manipulated as ever. It was good for Magra. Somebody has to remind him occasionally that he breathes the same air as the rest of us. And I noticed that your friend didn't even ask his leave! Some were still speaking of it this morning. How very marvelous!"

Rogond gave him a wry look, as Fima continued. "At any rate, I have no time to discuss the humbling of Magra by a Wood-elf. I have something important and remarkable to share with you, a gift that will stand you in good stead. I have been thinking about your enemy and the fact that you may need to pursue him below ground or in the dark of night. This will aid you, but I warn you that it is a powerful gift and dangerous if mishandled."

He drew forth a glass phial containing a small mass of what looked like soft, white metal suspended in a clear amber fluid. "The phial contains oil, and this material must be kept inside until needed. To use it, you will need a tiny bit of water. I have arranged a small demonstration." He indicated a clay saucer in which a tiny shaving of the metal was lying. "Shield your eyes," he cautioned, as he took a drop of water, applying it to the edge of the saucer so that it ran down onto the metal.

The result was immediate and startling. Rogond flinched as a tiny explosion, accompanied by blinding white light, forced him back a few paces. It was incredible. The reaction lasted for several seconds. When it had faded, Rogond gaped at Fima, speechless.

"What dwarvish devilry was *that*? What is it called? How did you get it? What would happen if you did that to a larger quantity?"

Fima raised his hand. "We call it maglos. As to how I acquired it, that is mine to know. It is very rare…difficult to mine and refine to this form. As to what would happen if you added a larger quantity, you had best not find out, unless in imminent danger from your enemy. Then, may you have the good sense to gain some distance from it quickly!"

"Maglos," muttered Rogond. The name meant "mighty light". True enough! Fima handed him the phial.

"The oil prevents moisture from accidentally contacting the maglos. That would be a catastrophe. When you need it, simply shave a bit off and add water. You have seen the result. The light will serve you well against this enemy. If he looks directly into it he will be blinded for several minutes, if I am any judge. It's definitely something he will not expect."

Rogond bowed before Fima. "Immeasurable thanks, my dear friend. This will be a difficult road, and you have given us a weapon that will allow us to walk with less fear in the dark."

Fima returned the bow, but his face was grim. "Yes, Rogond, walk with less fear, but with fear nevertheless. I have my own thoughts concerning the nature of your enemy, and if I am right, he has abilities as yet unseen. Beware! I did not go to all the trouble of teaching you our tongue so that you could take the knowledge to an early death."

Rogond was intrigued. "Will you not share your insights with me? I would hear them, for you are wise beyond any here save Lady Ordath herself. Please, favor me with your speculation."

Fima nodded and then spent nearly an hour explaining his view concerning the nature of Gorgon and the reasoning behind it. When he had finished, Rogond thanked him and took his leave. Though Fima's hypothesis was horrific, it was unassailably logical. As Rogond made his way back up the long stair, the phial of maglos tucked safely away, he reflected that Fima's theory definitely made sense. It actually made very good sense.

15

Dark Heart

Gorgon had fled into the cool, dark haven beneath the mountain, nursing wounds to his body, his mind, and his pride. He had never been thus routed in all the long years since he had been turned loose upon the world. He was among the mightiest of all the misbegotten children of Darkness, and the labor of producing him had begun long ago.

Wrothgar had decided to fashion the perfect evil warrior—an invincible creature of such stature and might that none could stand against it. Ultimately, he succeeded, having learned from the horrible failures that had come before. The result was Gorgon, and Wrothgar was at first pleased with his success. But when he learned that Gorgon would not be controlled and served no master but himself, Wrothgar had set him loose to cause as much suffering as he could manage, to the satisfaction of both. Wrothgar was perhaps the only being in Alterra who hated the Elves even more than Gorgon did.

This "invincible warrior" had been thwarted by two Wood-elves, a man, and a third Elf of unknown origin. Though he had not anticipated this third Elf, Gorgon still could not believe that such a pathetic force had defeated him. The arrows of the accursed Wood-elves had damaged him, especially the last that had lodged beneath his right arm. He had pulled it out immediately, but it had gone deep. The other that still pained him had gone under the left arm. The point had come free of the shaft and remained deep within his flesh. His head was still pounding from the searing blast of light that had nearly blinded him. He cursed himself for his carelessness. Why had he not made certain that he struck the lookout with enough force to kill her outright?

And what of the others? They knew Gorgon's weakness now; the accursed She-elf had discovered it. It would be no good attacking in daylight from now on. He had lost his shield, as well. One thing was certain—the next shield would have no mirrored surface that could be turned upon him. The mirrored shield had allowed Gorgon to delight in the fact that his victims could see their own desperate, doomed faces reflected in it as he vanquished them.

For the first time in untold centuries, Gorgon despaired. He knew that these Elves would not rest until they had hunted him down, and in the meantime they no doubt intended to warn all who would hear of him, betraying his weakness. Deep within his flesh, the Elven arrow-point burned him. Would he now carry that reminder forever? He cursed the one who had given it to him, knowing it was she whose relentless pursuit he had sensed from the beginning. How could he have let this happen?

You let it happen because you were careless. It is your destiny to be defeated by these foes. Gorgon jumped, startled by the voice to his immediate left. Gelmyr was sitting beside him, as he often did these days, glowing vaguely blue in the darkness. He wasn't looking too hale, but considering the length of time he had been dead, he was managing admirably. *I warned you of this, you know. You didn't listen because of your pride. Up until the last, it blinded you to the truth. You said once that you had taken my pride and that it had been my undoing. That was true, but your own pride will bring about your downfall as well. After all,* he added with a knowing smile, *it comes from the same source.*

Gorgon closed his eyes, trying to will Gelmyr to go and leave him alone with his pain. He growled at the empty chamber in which he was lying.

"Wretched Èolo, you are wrong. This is but a minor inconvenience. I will slay them all when next we meet. And do not dare to compare yourself to me."

Gelmyr truly laughed then, as he did more and more frequently as time passed.

Why not? It is apt in some ways. But I will not compare myself to you again, for you are weakening day by day, and soon the fire will take you. And while it is true that I no longer count myself among the living, at least I did not have to die awash in pity, as you will, and at least I fell before a once-mighty foe, not whimpering before an undersized She-elf.

This last enraged Gorgon so much that he turned and swung hard with his right arm at the apparition beside him, releasing a bolt of pain through his entire right side. He groaned and clenched his teeth, squeezing his eyes shut against the pain of the wound and the scornful laughter that rose, fell, and faded away. When he opened his eyes again, Gelmyr was gone.

Gorgon lay, breathing painfully, humiliated in his defeat. He thought of trying to rest again and closed his eyes. He had removed his armor, and the blood that had flowed from his wounds might draw enemies, but he was too discouraged right now to concern himself with such things. Not even his ever-present rage and resentment would sustain him. He curled up on his left side, drawing his legs close to his belly. His breath came in shallow gasps as he tried to sleep. He would heal if he found his strength, and sleep would help.

As he drifted off, he thought he heard a deep, sonorous voice beckoning him. It was familiar, though he had not heard it for time out of mind. He roused himself, waiting for it to come again. When it did, he realized that he was feeling the voice rather than hearing it. After a moment of silence, Gorgon spoke softly into the dark.

"Are these the words of the Dark Master, whose voice I have not heard in so long?"

Gorgon waited in the dark, and soon the reply came.

Yes, it is I. Thou hast done well in thy task, Gorgon Elfhunter, until now. I have heard thy desperate call and have come to aid thee. Do not fear Me, for I am thy friend. For much time have I watched over thee, rejoicing in the accomplishment of thy purpose, yet discontented, for there is so much more that could be done if thou would accept My help. Now, in the depths of thy despair I sense that thou art ready. Heal thyself Elfhunter, and come to Me. Thou wilt find Me in Tûr Dorcha. My strength is not as yet restored, but I have strength enough to aid thee in thy purpose. Come thou, then, and receive My blessing and aid. Thou art as a son to Me. Return to thy place at My side.

Gorgon spoke quietly in the darkness. "Yea, Lord Wrothgar, it has been so long since I have been aware of Thee. Yet I wonder... why have I heard not from Thee in all this time? What force has drawn Thee here now?"

The force of thy destiny draws Me hither. As I have spoken to thee in the pit of thy despair, thou art ready at last. Come to Me and accomplish thy purpose. I will give to thee a gift that will vanquish thy foes, and they and their kind shall weep long ere thy purpose is fulfilled. Come to Me and nourish again thy hatred. Remember thy name and recall what thou art!

At these words, the familiar rage welled again in Gorgon, and he answered Wrothgar with words of his own. "Yea, Lord, I will. I will not promise to submit to Thy bidding, even as I could not before, but I will hear Thy council."

Let it be so. Heal thyself, and come to Me as soon as thy strength is recovered. I will await thee.

Gorgon waited for a moment, but the voice of Wrothgar came no more. Gorgon truly slept then, as the pain of his wounds seemed to grow less. The Black Flame had called him and offered to aid him in the defeat of his enemies. Gorgon hated and feared Wrothgar, and with reason aplenty, but he also revered his power and purpose. His pride had welled in him once again, and he would not let fear stay him in slaying the Elves and wreaking his vengeance. Now he would will himself into a long, deep sleep, as his body healed itself. When he regained his strength he would turn aside from his intended path and make his way back the way he had come, toward Tûr Dorcha in the south of the Darkmere.

Lady Ordath, daughter of Shandor the Asarla and Liathwyn of the Èolar, understood the ways of many races and possessed unique insights into the hearts of Elves and men. She had known of rare unions between the Elàni and the Aridani, and so it was to her that Rogond finally decided to go for counsel. The innuendoes given by Magra concerning Gaelen could only be explained by Ordath, who apparently understood the nature of them. Ordath herself had stated that Rogond's desire for Gaelen was "ill-fated". All such unions were considered to be ill-fated. Why, then, had Ordath been compelled to point this out to him? It was time to make matters plain.

Mountain-home was indeed a wondrous realm. Sheltered and hidden by the surrounding mountain peaks it should have been clouded, cold and grey, but it was not so, for magic had shaped it, and the Lady now kept it. Her influence could be seen in the open-air courtyards, tall trees, and foliage reminiscent of a carefully-tended garden. This contrasted with the Sanctuary itself—a massive white granite structure rising from amidst the green.

Lord Shandor had designed this monument to learning, and, like its founder, it was stark and cold. Yet he had made it strong and enduring to remind all who beheld it of the power of knowledge.

Two bright springs arose from the center of the realm, flowing musically along to the southeast and southwest before disappearing beneath the rocks. Outside they emerged as two mighty watercourses, enlarged by the melting snow, crashing down the mountainside to be reunited into the clear but always-chill river Artan. Within the influence of Mountain-home the air was warm and the stars were bright, despite the cold mists of winter still clinging to the mountains outside.

Rogond found Ordath relaxing in one of her light, airy courtyards surrounded by flowering vines that filled the air with their fragrance. She looked up from the manuscript she had been studying, for she knew of his approach almost before he did. "Come and sit with me, Tuathan, for I would speak with you awhile." Rogond bowed, and then moved to sit across the small table from Ordath, who watched him intently.

After a moment, Rogond spoke. "It is well that you wish to speak with me, Lady, as I also have matters I would discuss with you. However, I am not certain how to broach them, as they are... somewhat delicate."

Ordath smiled to herself, as she had always favored Rogond and found his awkward manner in the present situation rather disarming. "Perhaps you would do better to wait until I have brought up my own concerns, as they may be closely tied to your own," she said. Rogond looked hopefully at her and nodded.

"I have always been fond of you, young Aridan, and have taken a special interest in you since you were first brought to the Sanctuary. I have heard good things about your exploits since you left us years ago, and I am pleased that you have done so well in the company of your own people. I would state that I take some pride in having had a hand in your education. Therefore, if I see you going down a path that I would deem unwise, I must at least make you aware of my concerns. Do you understand?"

Rogond nodded, though he was beginning to worry that the "unwise path" to which Ordath referred was precisely the one he had come to inquire of himself. Abruptly, Ordath startled Rogond with a very direct question:

"Exactly what is the nature of your desired relationship with Gaelen Taldin?"

Rogond drew back from Ordath's straightforward gaze, dropping his eyes for a moment. He had been hoping to lead gradually up to this sort of question, but the Lady was obviously unwilling to allow him that luxury. After collecting his thoughts, he looked again upon Ordath's very perceptive countenance.

"I'm not quite certain how I should answer that," he said.

"Then allow me to put it another way," said Ordath gently. She did not wish to make Rogond uncomfortable, but she needed to get to the truth. "Is Gaelen merely your friend, or are you enamored of her? Is she but an attractive plaything, or are you hoping to make her yours, so that you might be bound to her forever?"

Rogond thought for a moment. Was that really what he wanted? Did he love Gaelen enough to bind himself to her?

"She is much more than a plaything, and yes, she is my friend. But I cannot now imagine life without her. You ask if I hope to bind myself to her. I love her more with each day that passes, and the more I learn of her, the stronger my attachment becomes. So I suppose the answer to the question is, yes, I think."

Ordath's mouth twitched in a suppressed smile. "You *think*? Are you uncertain of this?"

Rogond looked flustered for a moment. "I am only uncertain because I have been trained well to never consider the possibility of such a union. I...I was hoping for some insight from you into such matters."

Ordath nodded thoughtfully. "Rogond, will you tell me how this love for Gaelen came to be, and how it has progressed? What has drawn you to her, such that you would consider binding yourself to one of Elven-kind, against all the advice you have ever been given?"

Then Rogond told Ordath all he could about his attachment to Gaelen, from the moment she first sang to him as he lay in the deadly grip of fever, to the journeys they had taken together and the perils they had faced.

"When I thought Gaelen might be lost in her effort to save Nelwyn, I felt the life drain out of me, as though my heart would be wrenched from me. I want to be with her always, even if it means keeping my feelings hidden."

His face had flushed bright red by then, and he dropped his eyes. "Just being there to protect and defend her would be preferable to being without her. The worst fate I can imagine at that moment would be…to be sent away, never to see her again. And she will *need* protection! I love and admire her spirit, but she…well, she must have someone to moderate her. She will need my strength and my spear and blade, as well. Please do not counsel that I must leave her, for I will not, at least not without her command. And having sought your wisdom, I shall not wish to gainsay it."

"Does she know anything of this?" asked Ordath. "She is obviously fond of you, but does she have any idea of the depth of your devotion to her?"

Rogond considered. "I don't know. I haven't told her, but I don't know what she may have guessed already."

"My suspicion is that she is still fairly naïve concerning you, gentle Aridan. Otherwise she might have left you already. She is wise and experienced in the way of the wild, as you are aware, but she knows little of the intricacies of the heart. Gaelen tends to see everything as either right or wrong. She may have some difficulty seeing this union as being 'right'."

Rogond nodded, but his expression indicated that he did not think Gaelen would leave him, at least not without explanation. After a brief silence, he found the courage to ask the question that had prompted his visit.

"Magra has indicated that I would be quite unwise to involve myself with Gaelen, and I sense that this warning goes beyond the obvious. He will not explain, but tells me I should inquire of you if I wish to learn more. Will you enlighten me?"

Ordath raised one dark, elegant eyebrow. "I am not certain that all should be told here. Galador has also expressed concerns to me of this. Apparently, Magra and Nelwyn have spoken to him concerning your attachment to Gaelen. Do not be wrathful! Galador is a true friend, and he wishes to stay his friend from folly. He did gain some enlightenment from me, though not as much as he would have wished for. I will tell you now that you will need to learn much of it from Gaelen herself. Magra was also acting in your behalf, for he thinks well of you…*despite* your shameless effrontery!" She paused and shot a stern look at Rogond, though there was amusement beneath the surface.

Rogond flushed at the gentle rebuke. "It was not entirely shameless, my lady, not by morning, at any rate. But though I regret the affront, I would not take back my action. I would still have risked denting Magra's pride for a dance with Gaelen."

"Admit it, my friend. You were marking your claim. Your demeanor made that clear from the first. We all took note of it. In your situation it is understandable; men live for such a short span of years that patience and forbearance may not number among their virtues. Yet this is so unlike your usual comportment…it was this that concerned Magra. As to your request for enlightenment, to you I will give that which I feel it is my right to give. But first, I would speak plainly with you concerning the Elàni and the Aridani, and why it is that the union of one with the other is ill-advised. I know that you may have been told of this already, but hear me and take heed."

Ordath then told of those unions of Elves and men that were known to her and of the devastating results. None could deny the fate that awaited every man, and Rogond would indeed pass out of the realm of reckoning when death took him. Gaelen could not follow him, and she would be forever apart from him with no hope of reunion. Should she give up her life before him, her spirit would go to Elysia, the eternal realm set aside for the Elves by Aontar. Rogond would never see her again.

"One of the things that makes death bearable is the hope of being reunited with those we love who have gone before," she said. "To bind yourself to one of Elven-kind may mean happiness for your brief span of days, but loneliness and longing on the part of both for eternity. You shall be separated beyond hope. Ask your friend Galador about the agony of such a loss, and you shall be enlightened. And I judge there will be no exception made for you, or for Gaelen." Her eyes filled with deep sadness as she continued. "Not even the mightiest Asarla can gain entry into Elysia."

Rogond knew that this simple truth had doomed her father, Shandor, to an eternity of longing for his beloved Liathwyn, such that he had lost his reason. This had no doubt grieved Ordath greatly, for she had loved her father. And what fate had been ordained for Ordath herself, who was both Elf and Asarla, upon her passing? Not even the wise could say.

Rogond could not hope to escape this eternal parting, for Gaelen could not follow him into death. But neither would she choose to do so, no matter how much she came to care for him, said Ordath. "There is one who awaits her on the shores of Elysia—one to whom her heart has already been given. He will await their reunion until she can follow him, or until the End of Days. Her heart has been given."

The color drained from Rogond's face, and he fought to maintain the steadiness of his gaze into the eyes of the Lady. The pain of being the deliverer of this news was clearly written there.

"Oh. I see. And who is this fortunate one for whom she holds her heart in reserve?"

"That I cannot tell you, as Gaelen herself must reveal it. But I will say this—do not count him fortunate, for much of his life was hard nearly beyond enduring. And he did not become acquainted with Gaelen until the very end of it. They had precious little time together—a matter of hours, I would say. He died a hard death, Rogond, for many reasons." Ordath looked into the distance for a moment, her face drawn with the painful memory.

Rogond looked bewildered. "Hours, you say? How could a strong heart such as Gaelen's be given so quickly? How could such a brief bond be so unbreakable?"

Ordath sighed. "Have you not heard what I have said concerning her? She sees all things as right or wrong. And he was much the same. You should know that such immediate attractions occasionally happen among the Elàni. They bonded forever by the end of their first meeting, though neither of them intended or wished for it. He, in particular, was filled with both joy and regret, for he had foreknowledge of his impending doom. She would have followed him then, had he allowed it." She shook her head. "As I have said, do not count him fortunate. He lived most of his life in grim solitude only to find the one he would share it with in the last days. Imagine the knowledge that you would have such a short-lived relationship."

To this, Rogond answered: "But it was not short-lived—she carries him in her heart even now! I would sooner have her for a brief while, knowing that one day we would be together for eternity, than never have known her at all."

Ordath lifted her chin and raised both of her eyebrows. "Ah! Hear your own words, my friend. They speak more to the wisdom of this choice than I could ever reveal. For you *cannot* be with her for eternity. If you choose to bind to her, knowing that she is already bound to another, then so be it. We will not interfere. But you will have to content yourself with whatever time you have in *this* world, for beyond that you shall be forever apart. Do you now see that it is not concern for Gaelen that drives us to question your wisdom, but concern for *you*? And unless I am mistaken, she will not sanction this union for your sake. Consider carefully your choice."

Ordath rose and extended her hand to Rogond, placing it on his shoulder. "I must leave you now with your thoughts, my friend. I do not envy you the decision you will have to make. But I will give you one gift ere I depart. If you would know the identity of He Who Waits, look for the small, flat pouch she wears always across her heart. It contains a token given to her upon his death. Take notice of the design upon it, as it once belonged to him. You may then learn the truth." She turned, and left Rogond alone.

His thoughts were in turmoil; he had not expected anything like these revelations. More than anything he wished that he had not heard them, as he honestly didn't know how he would address them. His despair welled at the thought of Gaelen's heart being given irretrievably to another. He felt at once the desire to confront her, and the desire to turn from her forever. He did not yet know in which direction his choice would lead.

Gaelen sat once again atop the wall overlooking the peaks to the west, weighing her choices in her mind. She had grabbed an early meal from the pantry before going out and had now settled herself on her stony perch. She had a sense that something of importance was about to happen, a sort of anticipation rather than foreboding. Something compelled her to take this vantage point, and she kept scanning the approach route to the north, as her sense was that whatever was coming would first appear there. She had already eaten most of her meal, which had consisted of a small loaf of fresh-baked bread that she had cut open and stuffed with a mixture of butter, honey, and cream. This would sustain her until tomorrow if need be. She chewed thoughtfully, relishing the taste of the wild honey, and considered her course.

There was much that could be done. Someone would need to travel to Tal-sithian, to the Verdant Mountains, and to the lands west to warn the Elves there of the existence of Gorgon. His next path was unknown to all save himself—he could go anywhere.

She thought of her promise to Ri-Aruin. In truth, they should return to the Greatwood, and the thought of going there was very attractive to Gaelen, as she missed her friends, especially Wellyn. She did not like the thought of Wellyn worrying about her, and though they were quite accustomed to being apart, she would ease his mind. The circumstances under which she had left him were far from ideal.

And what of Rogond's desire to travel to Cós-domhain to learn more of his origins? She would want to accompany him there, should he choose to go. She shuddered at the thought of walking willingly into the greatest of all dwarf-realms, but as long as Rogond walked beside her she would not fear.

She would go and seek counsel from Ordath and Magra as soon as was practical, as there was some urgency in the need to warn as many as possible of this dark threat. Perhaps she and Nelwyn could travel to Tal-sithian, though it had been a very long time indeed since they had carried messages there. It was a long journey, and these days the more perilous.

Gaelen also wished to make use of Magra in the best possible way, as he might be a match for Gorgon should they meet. He was as tall as Rogond, but of greater substance, and he had seen more of battle than perhaps any Elf yet living. She remembered Gelmyr, who had been taken so easily despite his experience, but Magra had the greater power, and he was aware of his enemy. Gaelen felt quite certain that he would not find himself sharing Gelmyr's fate.

It was with such thoughts turning in her mind that she first heard the horns of the scouts who patrolled the rim of the mountains to the north. They announced the arrival of strangers, but not of enemies. She strained to see the tiny path leading down into Mountain-home, and her keen eyes quickly spotted five horses: two ridden, one laden, and two led. There were two tall men astride the horses, but they dismounted when the going became treacherous, turning the two other horses loose to make their way carefully before them. These two looked familiar, especially the dun, who stopped and lifted his head into the wind, then gave a loud whinny.

Eros! Gaelen whispered his name, then stood up, balancing atop the wall, and called out in a loud, clear voice. Eros and Réalta both heard Gaelen's call as it carried to them on the wind, and they broke into a careful trot, taking the difficult path without hesitating. Gaelen was very happy to see them, and she knew that Rogond would want to be told right away.

She looked carefully at the two figures that now led their mounts and pack horse. Even from here, she could tell that they were men, Northmen most likely. Both had dark hair and were unshaven. They looked hale, but were probably travel-weary. Gaelen would go at once and find Ordath and Rogond, as well as Galador and Nelwyn. She rejoiced as she sprang lightly from the wall and sprinted back down the twisting, narrow path to Ordath's dwelling. Here, perhaps, were more allies! She would count three hardy Tuathar as a definite asset.

"Vile, black-hearted creature, you will spill no more Elven blood before long. Gaelen and her army are coming for you!" She entertained an amusing thought of herself, clad in kingly armor and brandishing every sort of weapon, leading an army. By the time she reached the lower courtyard she was laughing out loud.

She found Ordath in the upper courtyard, and ran up before her, flushed with excitement. "Two Rangers are coming down into the valley from the north! They have Rogond's horse with them. He will no doubt want to be there when they arrive—do you know where I may find him?"

Ordath held up her hand in an attempt to calm Gaelen. "I will summon Rogond. Why don't you find Nelwyn and Galador?"

Gaelen seemed not to hear. "So, where is Rogond?" she asked, literally bouncing up and down on the balls of her feet with suppressed excitement.

Ordath placed a hand on her shoulder to quiet her. "Please, Gaelen, you are making me dizzy. Perhaps you would do me the favor of alerting those in the stables, and I will fetch Rogond. It will be an excellent use of your apparently boundless energy."

Gaelen started to protest, but Ordath held up her hand again. "You are in my house, Elf of Greatwood. Here, you will do as I request." Gaelen flushed and dropped her eyes in submission. Ordath did not tell her that she had an excellent reason for keeping her from Rogond just now. When Ordath had last seen him, he had been in no condition to confront Gaelen.

Nelwyn and Galador were first to arrive in the lower courtyard, followed closely by Gaelen, who had practically flown to the stables to inform the caretakers of the five new arrivals. She ran breathlessly up to Nelwyn as Eros and Réalta first made their appearance. Eros trotted right up to Gaelen, ears forward, nickering softly. Réalta nearly knocked Galador down, shoving his head under the Elf's right arm. Galador accommodated him, scratching the base of his neck at the withers, while Réalta nibbled affectionately at Galador's back, an expression of bliss on his finely chiseled face.

"They appear to be a bit lean, but otherwise in fine condition," Nelwyn observed.

Gaelen agreed as she rubbed Eros' neck and face with practiced hands. She swung astride him, and as Rogond appeared in the courtyard she called out: "See what I have found!"

Eros turned about and faced the outside entrance, ignoring Rogond completely. Gaelen laughed and slid down as the rest of the party arrived—two tall men and three horses; a bay, a chestnut, and a black.

"It appears our good friend Rogond has been shunned by his noble mount," said Nelwyn.

Rogond returned the insult, walking right past Eros to meet his friends. They exchanged warm greetings, then Rogond turned and introduced them to all assembled. "This is Thorndil, and this is Belegund. They are two very good friends, come to look after me, I expect." The Elves bowed courteously. A few of them had met Thorndil and Belegund before.

Thorndil chuckled. He looked older and far more careworn than either Rogond or Belegund. "Indeed, we know that you are less than capable of looking after yourself on occasion. But you seem to be faring well enough now, though Eros still begrudges you."

"Ah, well, Eros doesn't understand that I must sometimes leave him behind. When he is thus abandoned he gets rather non-sociable until I do something to appease him. It may take a while this time," Rogond observed, taking note of the look of disdain in Eros' eye. He wasn't really worried, though. By tomorrow morning they would be the best of friends again.

Rogond turned then to his recently-arrived comrades. "How came you to the Sanctuary? You must have passed through the Greatwood, for that is where we left the horses. They still wear the King's mark on their halters."

Thorndil explained that the horses had come in search of them after escaping their handlers. "Because the halters bore the mark, we went looking for you in Ri-Aruin's realm, as we knew Eros would never intentionally leave you and Galador, and feared some ill fate had befallen you. It's a relief to find you alive and well!"

Thorndil observed the still-healing wound on the left side of Rogond's neck, where Gorgon's sword had brushed him as he had deflected it. "It appears as though someone has tried to remove your head," he said, his expression more serious. "You must tell us your tale."

"Not until you are fed and rested, my friends. Then I shall take you to Lady Ordath, for she would know of your purpose. Now that you are here, we would all like to know your immediate plans, for a matter has arisen that we must deal with, and your help would be most welcome."

"Our plan was simply to find you. We have no other—unless Thorndil keeps it from me," said Belegund. "And you know we will always aid one of our own when needed. We are also counted in the service of Lady Ordath and the Elves of Monadh-talam."

Rogond clapped each of them on the shoulder. "Then let us see to your welfare. Your horses will be looked after, and your things sent to your chambers. I will conduct you."

He turned to Gaelen, who had been standing by, hoping to be introduced to Rogond's friends, but instead he merely instructed her to see to the horses. She noticed that he would not look her in the eye as he spoke. Confused, she nodded and took the reins from Thorndil and Belegund, who bowed respectfully before following Rogond from the courtyard. Gaelen looked over at Nelwyn, shrugged her shoulders, and led the horses down toward the stables. Eros and Réalta followed willingly; they had seen quite enough of the wild for the time being.

After Gaelen had gone, Nelwyn turned to Galador. "What do you suppose has gotten into Rogond? You haven't been telling him of things you don't really understand, have you?"

Galador had not informed Nelwyn that he had been in conference with Ordath concerning the matter of Rogond and his affections, but he still took slight offense that she hadn't credited him with more sense.

"Of course I haven't. But I wonder whether someone else has. Perhaps I should inquire of him."

"Best wait and give it more time; it may be nothing," said Nelwyn. "For the moment we should occupy ourselves with more pressing matters—we should enlist the aid of these men in our quest. Let's go and help Gaelen, then we will all await Rogond and his two friends, whereupon tales will be both heard and told." She turned and strode toward the stables, with Galador close behind. She hadn't cared for the look in Rogond's eyes as he had turned from Gaelen. For a brief moment, pain was graven there.

That evening tales were told, counsel was given, and acquaintances were renewed. Thorndil and Belegund enjoyed the hospitality of Mountain-home after many months in the wild, and they listened with great interest to the tale of Gorgon, which was told from the beginning by Nelwyn. Thorndil was especially interested in the details of Gelmyr's fate, as he had once discovered the body of an Elf during his travels near the Ambros.

The Elf had been stricken with a blunt-tipped arrow, but the force of it had been too great, and it had killed him outright rather than merely crippling him. The arrow appeared to have broken the great vessel that runs along the spine, and the Elf had bled to death in a matter of moments. The signs had been confusing. The body had not been molested, although someone had gone to the trouble of hanging it head-downwards. Thorndil had cut it down and tended it, giving it to the waters as they had done with Gelmyr. That had taken place nearly sixty years ago and had remained a mystery. Now they all wondered whether Gorgon had been responsible for this death as well.

It was with such unsettling thoughts, and after much debate over the course of action that should now be taken, that the group disbanded for the night and went to their resting places. Thorndil and Belegund would sleep more comfortably than they had in many months, as the security of Mountain-home was a thing they rarely knew—they could never relax their vigilance in the wild. Rogond found that he was quite weary and took his leave. He passed by Gaelen, who rose and started to follow him, but he raised a hand to halt her.

"Do not follow me, Gaelen. I am simply going to rest, and I need to be left alone. If I need you, I will find you."

Gaelen was not used to such curtness from Rogond. He had barely acknowledged her presence all evening. "Why are you reproachful? Have I offended you in some way?" she asked. She was confused and hurt, and Rogond knew that his treatment of her was undeserved.

His expression softened, and he spoke to her again. "I'm sorry, Gaelen. I simply am very weary and have many thoughts in my mind that I must work through. It's nothing you have done. I just need to rest in solitude for a while." This seemed to satisfy her, though her eyes still bore some of the hurt.

"If I can help sort out your thoughts, please ask. That's one of the things friends do for each other. I will leave you alone until you tell me I should do otherwise. Rest well."

She turned and left him standing in the corridor. He wished that he could follow her and be with her this night, and that he was still blissfully unaware of the existence of "He Who Waits".

After leaving Rogond, Gaelen decided to go down to the stables and look in on Eros and Réalta. It was one place where she could express her feelings to a living being without having to listen to anyone's advice. She found Eros lying comfortably on his thick bed of straw. He nickered when he saw her.

"Well met, Eros…at least someone seems glad of my company." She entered the stall and knelt down beside the great horse, stroking his neck, and began to tell him all of her feelings concerning Rogond and his recent behavior. She was confused and filled with foreboding, trying to imagine what she had done to offend him. "Eros, I don't know how I feel about him. I just know that I would rather lose my right arm than not have him beside me in the conflict to come. I had thought he was content…but now I sense that he is thinking of abandoning us. I don't understand."

She was suddenly overcome with emotion at the thought of losing Rogond, and she hugged Eros' neck and buried her face in his mane, shedding silent tears. "You must not let him leave without telling me, Eros. He won't go without you. Promise that you will not bear him from me."

Eros didn't understand what Gaelen was saying, but he knew that she wept. He truly liked Gaelen and nudged her gently, trying to cheer her. She stayed with him for a few more minutes, then stood, brushed the straw and the tears away, and left the stables. Eros rose to his feet, watching her with some concern as she disappeared into the darkness.

The new day dawned chill, damp, and grey. Rogond still had not slept. He paced the floor of his chamber for the fiftieth time, weighing his alternatives. He was no closer to a decision now than he had been in the beginning—he needed another opinion. After a few hours had passed, he would seek out the advice of the one friend in Mountain-home whose perspective lay outside the world of both Elves and men. Fima, the dwarvish lore-master, would help sort things out and certainly would tell Rogond exactly what he thought in the situation. He could also be trusted to keep matters in confidence. Rogond lay back down on his bed, looking at the ceiling, counting the hours until he could go and find Fima in the hope that the dwarf's practical wisdom would suggest the right path.

Rogond found Fima in his study in the late morning. The dwarf was not known to arise early, as he was usually awake through most of the dark hours, reading and studying. He greeted Rogond, inviting him to sit opposite him as he ate and drank. He offered food and drink to Rogond, which was politely declined.

"Something weighs heavily on you, my friend," said Fima through a mouthful of bread and sausage. "Have you come for counsel?"

Rogond nodded. Fima continued eating, as Rogond waited patiently for him to finish. At last, Fima pushed his empty plate away and settled back in his chair.

"This is about that She-elf isn't it? I thought as much. Well, let's have it, and don't leave anything out. I'll try to be as helpful as I may."

Rogond began his tale, and it took some time to tell. He painted a vivid picture for Fima, explaining the nature of his feelings, telling of his conversation with Ordath and of all the thoughts he had since. When he had finished, Rogond looked at the dwarf in hopeful silence.

"Elves and men, men and Elves," said Fima, clucking and shaking his head. "Rarely have I heard a tale of a situation so simple turned into something so complicated. This entire matter rests on your answer to a single question, by which you may succeed, or be doomed to fail. Consider carefully."

Rogond nodded, awaiting the question. After several long moments of silence, it came.

"Do you desire to be free to love Gaelen, or do you wish to possess her?"

Rogond was taken aback. He had never really thought to possess Gaelen, but he realized that his despair at the discovery of her lost love was rooted in such desires. A wise, warm smile crossed Fima's face as he took note of the understanding dawning in Rogond's eyes.

"Ah! You see, don't you? This Elf who was lost cannot love her in life, as you cannot love her after death. She may yet love him, but cannot be with him until she leaves this world, which may be a long time coming. Surely there is room in her heart for you as well, for she has been alone for a great span of years. One day you must leave her, but she will carry the memory of you to whatever fate awaits her. This situation doesn't really change anything unless you must possess her, for that you cannot do. But I sense that you may love her and find your love returned. I have observed this one. She may be worth the effort."

"She is," replied Rogond. "And the answer to the question is no, I did not really wish to possess her. I know that's not possible. I don't know if she can love me, though, and I am afraid to declare my feeling lest she send me away before our quest to bring down Gorgon is achieved. Such is Ordath's belief. That would sadden me greatly, for I fear she will be lost in that conflict without me to aid her."

"So, what's your hurry, my friend?" said Fima. "Who says you must declare your feelings until you are comfortable doing so? Court her if you wish and see how she responds. You will know when the time is right. And don't listen to the advice of any Elf, as they almost never approve of their kind consorting with mortals, however worthy. One cannot blame them entirely, as it isn't the perfect situation. Certainly, you would be far better off with a mortal woman. Yet the situation exists, and you cannot now take back the desire of your heart. One fact should cheer you—your friend Gaelen will not ever give herself completely to another of immortal race. You actually are in an excellent position to gain her love, my friend, for she knows it cannot extend beyond this life. In my opinion, your differences are exactly what will allow you to come together, if only for a brief while."

Fima paused as though in reflection. "I wonder who she gave her heart to so long ago…and after only a few hours? How regrettable."

Rogond agreed that it was indeed regrettable. "Tell me Fima, does this sort of thing happen often? And if so, do you know how or why it happens?"

"My real understanding of Elves is somewhat limited, though I know a great deal of their history and lore. I can tell you that they are often very passionate and very much driven by destiny. It is their belief that there are certain attractions that cannot be denied, and that these are immediately apparent. In other words, you meet the one you are destined for, and you know it. You cannot deny it, and you are forever bound by it. They call it "The Perception", and it happens only once in a lifetime. That is apparently what happened to Gaelen and her lost love. They say that the stronger the spirit, the more likely it is to resist other attractions until the one for whom it is destined becomes clear. Gaelen certainly has a strong spirit, and I suspect he did, also. Ordath said he died a hard death, and he had foreknowledge of it? No doubt he was some High-elven warrior who perished in some great battle. They were, in general, quite strong in spirit. Yes, indeed."

Fima looked intently at Rogond. "I have given you something to think about. I trust it has been helpful?"

"As ever, very helpful," Rogond replied. "My gratitude cannot be expressed, as this was weighing heavily on me. I know now what I must do." Fima nodded in approval, and then spoke as Rogond prepared to take his leave.

"If you find out the identity of this lost Elf, will you come and tell me? I'm understandably curious as to whether my theory is correct."

Rogond assented to this, then turned and left the study, climbing the stairs to the lower courtyard. Though it was raining, he was in fairly good spirits as he went now in search of food and drink. He hoped he would not encounter Gaelen just yet, as he needed to prepare his response carefully. If all went well, she would forget about his recent treatment of her, as though it had never been.

Wrothgar, Lord of Black Flame, awaited the arrival of his wayward creation with anticipation. Not that such an evil being would ever be capable of true creation, for that is the province of the Light. Gorgon was a perversion, not a creation; the result of the union of two beings so diverse that such a thing seemed inconceivable.

Wrothgar had somehow managed to bring forth the Ulcas, whose name means "evil", to serve as his minions, but how they came to be was unknown to most. They had some things in common with Elves, and some with men, but few outside the Dark Fortress knew of the material from which they originally sprang. They multiplied rapidly, but as they drew farther from their origins, many grew weak and became less formidable in battle. They had always been creatures of the dark shadows; sunlight, in particular, pained and sickened them. Although they would certainly fight if ordered, they were inherently cowardly, and therefore relatively easy to defeat unless they attacked in large numbers. This had not always been so. As Fima had pointed out to Rogond, there had been those among them that were mighty, especially in the early days.

Wrothgar desired an invincible army, and thus he sought to create the perfect warrior-race. He used only the largest and most ferocious as the foundation for these efforts. Still, they were lacking in speed, grace, and cleverness. Wrothgar needed to imbue them with those qualities, together with the courage they lacked. He devised a plan to unite the largest and strongest of his evil brood with the blood of the fairest beings in Alterra and, if possible, to select those among the Elàni that possessed the greatest strength of heart, body, and will. The Èolar were the obvious choice, as they were renowned for their vitality and stamina, for their skill in battle, and for their intelligence. They were the tallest and most powerfully made of the Elves of Alterra. A creature that would result from the union of two such mighty progenitors would be formidable indeed, provided it could be nurtured and molded by the hand of evil.

There were obvious difficulties in the beginning, as ensnaring a worthy Elven representative without killing it was difficult. The Elves hated Wrothgar and everything to do with him, and they would not be beguiled. Any would die rather than subvert to his will. Then there was the matter of actually accomplishing the union.

The Shadowmancer had many Elven captives in his fortress, but the two races were so dissimilar that interbreeding them was not possible. They did not produce offspring in similar fashion; the Ulcas had lost that ability long before. Of their spawning little is known or recorded, and no Elf would willingly participate in such an unclean, horrific joining. In addition, She-elves could bear children only of their perceived life-mates.

The attempts made by Wrothgar and his servants were vile and contemptible, resulting in nothing but suffering. There were no offspring, and any Elves who faced the terrible fate of being chosen for this endeavor died as a result, either because of the hideous process itself or by their own hand.

Throughout these failures, Wrothgar noted the cause and devised a new plan. The few times that his Dark scholars managed to accomplish the blending of the flesh, it became clear that such an offspring could not be spawned in the manner of Ulcas; it would have to be carried by its mother in the manner of the Elves. This was tried several times, but none could bear the hideous offspring, as they grew so large so quickly that they overwhelmed and destroyed their would-be mothers long before they could survive on their own. These unlucky females, though their deaths were agony, relinquished their spirits gladly, for to be the bearer of such an abomination would be unthinkable. Their cries, and the cries of all who knew of them, echoed in the dark pits of the Shadowmancer's realm.

Wrothgar eventually put aside the idea and turned his thoughts in other directions, as he did have quite a mighty army. His forces included the Bödvari, dragons, trolls and innumerable hosts of Ulcas. Yet he did not entirely abandon the notion of breeding the ultimate warrior, and eventually he sought to continue the work begun so long before. He had learned enough from the earlier vain attempts that he felt ready to try again. It was such an attractive prospect should he succeed, and he had such a likely candidate in the Ulca that eventually turned out to be the sire of Gorgon that he simply could not resist. The origin of this mighty one is uncertain; even Wrothgar himself did not know. He was discovered deep under the Monadh-hin and brought before Wrothgar, whose power and influence were nearly at their peak.

This Ulca stood taller than any man, as broad as a great oak, with skin as dark as pitch. His eyes, yellow and feral, gleamed with a rare intelligence, and his crooked fangs were sharp and long. In spite of his age he was both powerful and enduring, but Gorgon would later outstrip him in both agility and swiftness.

To this impressive bloodline Wrothgar now sought to add the influence of the Elves, and he sent his spies abroad to search for it. They found her outside the Lake-realm of Tal-sithian, and there she was lost. Her people never saw her again, that golden-haired maiden whose own child grew in her womb unaware that it would serve as the raw material for one of the mightiest yet most forlorn of beings. Wrothgar crafted this abomination carefully, for he thought to set Gorgon at his right hand—the perfect general of his mighty army. Gorgon and others like him would lead the dark host to a victory that would result in the ultimate destruction of the Elves, as well as any of the race of men who would not bend to his will. Such was his design, but it would not come to pass, for Wrothgar did not reckon with the fierce independence and stubbornness of the Èolarin heart, and Gorgon answered to no purposes save his own.

16

"He Who Waits"

The rain ceased by late afternoon, clearing to a sky that promised bright stars. Rogond sought out Nelwyn to learn more of the truth of Gaelen's history, knowing that Nelwyn, who was closer in friendship with Gaelen than anyone, would have much to reveal. He knew also that Nelwyn both loved and trusted him, and would be kindly disposed to his request for enlightenment. He didn't need to worry about Gaelen—she had gone with Magra, Thorndil, and Belegund on a foray to the south, from which she would not return until dawn.

Rogond had allowed her to ride Eros, to their mutual delight. Rogond wondered for a moment whether he had lost his favorite mount, but when the great horse nuzzled him as Gaelen rode up to bid him farewell, he knew his friend was forever faithful.

"Why will you not come with us? I can choose another mount for tonight," said Gaelen.

Rogond looked away from her for a moment. "I need the time to meet with Fima and ponder our next course. He always seems to know what to do in any situation. Besides, I have been looking forward to spending some time with him."

Gaelen wondered whether he was being truly forthcoming, but the others were waiting and she could not delay.

When Rogond was certain that she had gone, he spent a few brief moments in a last debate with himself, then found his resolve and went in search of Galador and Nelwyn.

He strode out in the early evening, seeking the gentle, golden-haired Nelwyn in one of her favorite haunts: a quiet glade surrounded by fragrant vines, carpeted with moss and soft grass. Here he found her in quiet conversation with Galador, who rose protectively to his feet until he recognized Rogond. He greeted his friend and then started to ask if there was some pressing purpose to his coming, as he sensed some urgency in Rogond's manner. Rogond held up a hand to quiet him.

"I have come on a matter of some concern to me, yes, but I need to speak with Nelwyn. You are welcome to remain if you wish, as this may or may not take long. You, I believe, are aware of most of it anyway, having been in counsel with Lady Ordath."

Galador looked down at his hands, muttering something about the inability of some folk to keep matters in confidence. "Please do not be wrathful…I merely wanted to seek answers to questions that would help me to guide you, as I always have when you have sought my aid. I didn't mean to pry too deeply, and in truth I learned very little from the Lady."

Rogond smiled wryly at Galador, who still would not look directly at him. "And what matters did you not pry deeply into, my friend? If you refer to the unfortunate history of Gaelen and her lost love, then be content, as I'm here to seek enlightenment from Nelwyn on this very subject. I no longer have time for veiled insinuations." He turned to Nelwyn and drew a deep breath.

"I love Gaelen and would seek happiness with her, if only in this life, for I know that is the best I may hope for. It's time I knew the nature of the obstacle I must overcome to win her. You are well aware of the workings of Gaelen's heart. Will you aid me?"

Nelwyn was somewhat taken aback by this bold declaration. She looked briefly at Galador and thought for a moment. Then she looked into the eyes of Rogond the Aridan. In them she saw much the same longing that she had beheld in the eyes of Galador that day on the western slopes of the mountain, before he had left her to seek the aid of Mountain-home. *Rogond…he is so young,* she thought, *yet he has such a brief span of years before him. He has not the luxury of patience over long years of waiting, as we do. I can't blame him for wanting to know the truth, yet why he does he not ask it of Gaelen herself?* She posed this question to him, and he looked away from her for a moment.

"Because…I am not yet ready to face her. I cannot know how she will react, as I do not yet comprehend the matter myself. I thought that if I knew the truth, I could more carefully craft my inquiry, and be more cautious of her feelings."

Nelwyn chuckled in spite of herself, for she took his meaning. "I believe you've just told me you are afraid of her reaction should you speak too plainly with her. That's quite understandable. Gaelen has gone to some lengths to establish herself as less than approachable, and make no mistake—she can be somewhat prickly, especially when it comes to matters that make her uncomfortable, as this surely will. Still, she admires you, and appreciates your forthrightness. If you truly love her, you had better get used to dealing with her."

She looked over at Galador again, rejoicing in the hope of enjoying his company for a long span of years. Would she now deny Rogond the chance at the same joy? She could not send him to face Gaelen unprepared, even though it might mean incurring the wrath of her occasionally difficult cousin. And she had a sense that Gaelen, who clearly was very fond of Rogond, would quickly forgive the indiscretion, for she had always disliked veiled insinuations and innuendoes. She preferred honesty and clarity of purpose.

"Sit down, my friend, and I will tell you what I know. Having learned of it, may you choose wisely."

Gorgon Elfhunter, the Half-elven, was stirring once again in his dark sanctuary. His wounds still pained him, but grew less with each day that passed. He had risen and sought one of the pools of icy water that formed in the deep caverns, washing the blood and Elf-stench from his body, now charged with the new hope of aid from the Shadowmancer. Gelmyr had not appeared since Gorgon had heard the voice of Wrothgar in his despair. It was likely that the wretched dead Elf had been banished forever. This thought cheered Gorgon immensely as he stood beneath a cascade of snow-melt that poured through a rocky fissure in the cavern's roof. It took his breath for a moment, but he felt his own malevolent energy surging deep within him as the icy water pounded his shoulders and turned his long hair—the fine, silky hair of his mother's kin—into a river of gold.

Soon he would once again don his black armor and set forth into the wide world. There he would move cautiously to Tûr Dorcha to meet with the One who knew and understood his nature more completely than any other. The Shadowmancer had promised aid, and though Gorgon was still wary and mistrustful, the promise of some new power that would help vanquish his pursuers and achieve his hateful purpose went a long way toward dispelling all doubt. His lip curled with contempt as he spoke the name of the She-elf who, along with her companions, was surely doomed to die by his hand.

"Gaelen…Gaehhlehhnnn…you have wounded me, little maidrin. But the hurts I have received from you will be as nothing compared with your fate. Enjoy each breath you take while you may." Gelmyr did not appear to offer argument. So long as Gorgon's resolve was strong, he would come no more.

Rogond and Galador had listened with fascination to Nelwyn's tale, recounting all she knew of the nature of Gaelen's lost love. Nelwyn had never met him, or even seen him, but she knew of him—they all did. Rogond had seen several renderings of him here in Mountain-home, paintings depicting various heroic acts. All were similar: a very tall, powerfully built, dark-haired Elf-lord, stern-faced and keen-eyed. Above his head there was a banner of sable and blue, bearing the design of a field of silver stars encircling a sunburst of gold.

The same design was barely discernible on the worn leather pouch Gaelen wore always. It had been passed down an ancient line, adorning the banners of some of the mightiest and most wise, and it took a moment for Rogond to comprehend that little Gaelen, lowly Sylvan Elf of the Greatwood, had given her heart to none less than Ri-Elathan, the last of the High-elven Kings.

Galador shook his head in disbelief. How could it be so? Yet he recalled now an incident that had occurred during the feast in the hall of Ri-Aruin, and again in Monadh-talam. "The Tragic Fate of Ri-Elathan" had been harped and sung by the fine minstrels in both realms, and each time Gaelen would rise and take her leave, as though she would not suffer herself to hear it. Galador had not understood or really taken notice at the time, but now the reason was quite clear.

Rogond now recalled the words of Ordath. *Do not count him fortunate. His life was hard nearly beyond enduring, and he did not become acquainted with Gaelen until the very end of it. He died a hard death, for many reasons.* Rogond was overcome for a moment, and his heart ached with empathy for Ri-Elathan. He knew that the High King had lived most of his life in solitude, burdened with the responsibilities of his office and the dreadful doom that lay before him. At last he had been allowed to open his great heart to the one unlikely spirit who was to be bound forever to him, only to leave her until death reunited them. Rogond could not imagine the grief that this grim fate had wrought.

Nelwyn recounted all that Gaelen had told of her first encounter with Ri-Elathan, where she gave her heart forever to him, and of their reunion at the gathering of the Great Host as it moved northward, going forth to engage the armies of Darkness. Then she told what she knew of their final parting. Ri-Elathan had left Gaelen behind; insisting that she return to the Greatwood, promising to come for her should he survive the war. But he had known then that this was not likely, as he had foreseen his own terrible death. He spoke without much hope, yet Gaelen kept faith in her heart that he would return, for she was very young and could not allow herself to think otherwise.

Together with the hosts of Tal-sithian and the Woodland, Ri-Elathan succeeded in routing Wrothgar's army, but the effort and the losses were great, lasting for several years. During that time, many of the Sylvan Elves were lost. Nelwyn's father Turanen and her uncle Tarmagil both perished in the final great assault. Wrothgar was finally defeated, but at the cost of the High King.

Even though they were far from the battle-plain, Nelwyn and Gaelen had both known when this final, desperate stand occurred, for as Ri-Elathan gave up his life, Gaelen's heart was torn from her. She had fallen to her knees as though stricken, unable to breathe, an expression of horror in her over-bright eyes. Nelwyn had reacted with alarm, not knowing what had befallen her cousin, and called Gaelen's name over and over.

Gaelen's eyes met Nelwyn's then, and she had covered her face with both hands and wailed—the high, keening sound of a heart that has been forever diminished by unfathomable loss. Nelwyn backed away in fear, for she did not yet understand, and Gaelen turned from her, still wailing, calling the name of her beloved as though to stop his flight from the world. But of course, she could not. Her faith had been ill-founded, and his doom the stronger, for she would never lay eyes upon him again in this world.

Her face somber and voice breaking as she recalled that dreadful day, Nelwyn finished her tale. She would later learn of the deaths of her father and uncle, and of the outcome of the assault and the defeat of Wrothgar, but all she knew then was that her closest friend had been overcome with grief. She had tried to comfort Gaelen, and in the days that followed she was of great help, but right then it made no difference; Gaelen was alone in her devastation, beyond all reach.

It was of no surprise to either Gaelen or Nelwyn when Tarfion, the only one of the three brothers to survive, returned at last to the Greatwood, bearing with him the blade of Tarmagil and the bow of Turanen. With him came the mighty Magra, his pain and empathy clearly visible as he returned to Gaelen the scorched and tattered remnant of the silken banner that she now preserved and cherished, carefully folded, next to her heart.

Rogond despaired at the thought of Gaelen in such pain, and he could not imagine it having ever been so, for she now seemed cheerful, strong, and self-possessed. Yet, Nelwyn cautioned him, the pain was still there, and Gaelen had been forever diminished by it. Though much time had passed, and her spirit was nearly whole again, the sun would fall into the sea before Gaelen would ever forget either her love for Ri-Elathan or her pain at his loss.

"This is the chasm that you must cross," she told Rogond, clasping his hands in gentle concern. "It is both wide and deep. I hope the way has been made clearer for you with this knowledge and that I have not daunted you beyond trying, for I would see Gaelen's heart truly glad again. This knowledge must be guarded closely; none now know of it who remain in this world save few—Magra, Lady Ordath, and, of course, myself. What Magra knows he learned from Ri-Elathan, for they were great friends."

Rogond looked discouraged. "A deep, wide chasm, indeed. Is there any hope that she might love me, Nelwyn? How can I compete with the High-elven King? How can she find room in her heart when it is filled with so much pain?"

"She did not love the High King; she loved the soul of Farahin, for such was his name before he took the scepter. And love that fills the heart will overcome and diminish the pain. It will never be gone, but it may be assuaged, at least that is my hope. She has resigned to living her life in waiting, but I pray that it will not always be so. She holds some love for you, of that I am certain. Whether the love she has to give will be enough to sustain you is another matter, and something that only you may decide. At any rate, I have done as you asked, for good or ill. Take the knowledge and hold it close in your heart, and follow your desires wherever they lead. Know that I am your friend and confidante, Rogond, so long as you have Gaelen's welfare in mind."

Rogond nodded and managed a weak smile, though his eyes were haunted. This was a lot for him to absorb all at once. Galador and Nelwyn turned to leave, but Galador lingered for a moment, turning back toward his friend as though he wanted to remain. He spoke quietly to Nelwyn and embraced her ere she left them. Then he approached Rogond, placing a hand upon his shoulder.

"I would speak with you awhile, my friend. Know that I am as surprised as you are by the things I have learned this day, but there is a matter of concern to me, and it cannot wait any longer. This will be difficult for me to say, and perhaps difficult for you to hear, but hear it you must."

Rogond shrugged, resigned to hearing yet another disquieting tale. "As you wish. I expect I know the nature of your concern. I have heard enough already today, such that my senses are numb and my heart knows not where to turn. Speak your mind and guide me if you will. I know you are a true friend."

"That I am. But now I must pain you by warning you to back away from Gaelen. I have feared that you loved her from the first, and now you have spoken of it not only with me, but also with Ordath." He paused and drew a deep breath. "I have more knowledge of these matters than you know. The greatest sorrow of my life has been brought about through the love of a mortal woman, and my grief has been difficult to bear. I loved her long ago, with all of my heart, and she was taken cruelly from me. I will never see her, share her spirit, or hear her voice again, as she has gone where I cannot. The pain of this loss nearly took my life."

He looked into Rogond's surprised, distressed face. "You have only considered your feelings in this matter. What of Gaelen? Even should she bind herself to you, despite her love for Ri-Elathan, you will be with her for only a short while. Then death will take you beyond hope of reunion. She has been grieved for much of her life. Would you now afflict her heart with such despair?"

Rogond's face was drawn in an expression of pain, and his eyes were bright as he answered his friend. "Would you rather see her alone for the rest of her life? She has known real love for only a short while; her grief and loss have afflicted her for a thousand years. Yet she continues—an indomitable spirit determined to live happily. That is what has made her different from you, who have lived these long ages in sorrow. Gaelen will decide for herself, but know this: my heart is given to her, whether she will have it or no. And I will love no other."

Galador's face was stony. "So said I to my love so long ago. If I had known then what would befall, I would have chosen differently... for both my sake, and hers. I am different from Gaelen because she lives in the knowledge that, one day, she will see her love again. I have no such hope." He cast his eyes downward for a moment, drawing a deep breath. Then the moment passed, and his confidence returned.

"My happiness with Nelwyn has made me the most fortunate of souls, for she is of Elven-kind, and I am of Elven-kind, and we shall be together not only in this life, but the next. That is what Gaelen had of Ri-Elathan, however briefly. That is the order of things as they should be. I love you as a friend, and I will not interfere with your choice, but consider carefully, for you threaten not only your own happiness, but hers as well. Farewell, Rogond."

At this he rose and left the glade, where Rogond was now alone with his thoughts. He was having some difficulty taking in the impact of Nelwyn's revelation and Galador's warning. *Ri-Elathan—the last High King.* Rogond sighed. He was certainly in impressive company in his affection for Gaelen. There was much to know about this "simple Sylvan rustic', this occasionally exasperating but irrepressible Wood-elf to whom his heart had been irretrievably given. She would be returning soon, he supposed, as he noticed the first light of dawn dimming the stars in the east, over the mountains. *Will she have enough love to give me? Do I dare risk telling her how I feel, for fear of hurting her? Can I be sustained, knowing that not only would her love be one day lost, but that I must share it with another? Is there room in my own heart for this?*

He remembered the words of Fima, those wise words that sprang from pure friendship and not from any concerns over the ways of men or Elves. *This situation doesn't really change anything unless you must possess her, for that you cannot do. But I sense that you may love her and find your love returned. I have observed this one. She may be worth the effort.*

And Rogond remembered his own reply: *She is*.

He considered Galador's words once more before putting them forever from his mind. He could walk away now, leaving Gaelen hurt and confused, and live the rest of his life in grief and longing to spare them both the pain of their inevitable parting. Or, he could continue to love her and see whether his love would one day be returned, allowing her to choose.

Rogond closed his eyes and whispered: "Most noble Farahin, I do not know what thoughts you are permitted as you await her on the shores of Elysia. But if you can, know this—you must share your affections for Gaelen of the Greatwood with Rogond, a mortal man, for as long as he can give them. You cannot gladden her heart, or strengthen her resolve, or protect her from the dark hand of fate, though I know that you would. I hope you will welcome my efforts in this common purpose, for one day you shall be reunited with her, and I will be forever sundered from her. Then well may you remember Rogond and his love for the one you hold dear."

He left the glade and mounted the steps to the watch-tower overlooking the south march, so that he might look for her return.

17

Farewell to Mountain-home

Seven horses stood waiting in the courtyard as the Company prepared to depart. Their decision to leave Mountain-home had been made after a long council that had included Lady Ordath and Lord Magra. It was decided that Gaelen, Nelwyn, Rogond, and Galador would now travel south to the Lake-realm of Tal-sithian, taking with them Belegund and Thorndil. Magra would ride west to the Verdant Mountains and the sea, ensuring that as many as possible were warned of Gorgon. At least some deaths might be prevented if their people were aware of the threat.

Rogond intended to investigate more of his heritage in Cós-domhain, which lay between Mountain-home and Tal-sithian, and he hoped that Gaelen would go with him. Her attitude toward dwarves had mellowed since she had spent some time with Rogond's friend and mentor, Fima. She found him funny, even charming, very direct and earthy. He was neither arrogant nor false and was thoroughly interesting in most respects. He in turn warmed quickly to her, for he was already far more open-minded with respect to Elves. After a few afternoons spent gaining mutual trust, he actually taught her a few words in the dwarf-tongue, emphasizing that she was to use them only when needed. She was not to reveal their meaning to any others of her own race. Rogond approved of this new friendship, as he truly liked Fima and was looking forward to learning more from the folk of Cós-domhain. This would be much easier without a hostile Elf at his side.

As they made their final preparations, Fima appeared in the courtyard. He was provisioned for a long journey, and to the surprise of Rogond and all assembled, he announced that he would be traveling with them as far as Cós-domhain. They marveled at his appearance, for he had seemed old and rather soft while poring over his manuscripts in Mountain-home. Now he stood clad in dwarf-mail, carrying his weapons and packs. In fact, he would have looked fierce were it not for the gentle good humor in his eyes.

Then he saw the horses.

Fima had a long-standing mistrust of horses that bordered on antipathy. Although many dwarves could ride, and ride well, Fima preferred to go upon his own feet whenever possible. The tall horses standing in the courtyard might as well have been fire-breathing dragons as far as he was concerned, and it showed on his face. He had never forgotten the humiliation a horse had once brought upon him, and, regrettably, neither had certain of the Elves of Mountain-home. Fima had been taught a hard lesson, and he would long remember it.

Rogond took notice of his friend's dour expression, realizing the nature of it. "We're all truly glad that you have chosen to come with us, Fima, but I'm afraid you have no choice but to ride with one of us. I know the horses are too tall for you to handle without aid."

Fima grumbled and growled, but Rogond saw also the fear behind his complaining. "Don't worry," he said. "I'm sure that whoever you choose to ride with will make certain you're perfectly safe and comfortable…"

"There *is* no way to be comfortable on those unpredictable, excitable jackrabbits! Why can I not walk beside you? Are you in that much of a hurry?"

Rogond knelt down, looked Fima in the eye, and spoke so that no one else could hear. "If you want to come with us, Lore-master, you will have to ride. There's no use arguing—I'm afraid that's all there is to it. Now, make your choice."

"Here, Fima, ride with me!" said Galador, stepping forward. "Réalta is more than strong enough to carry us both. I would be honored to have you."

Nelwyn smiled in approval, though she wondered about the wisdom of selecting Réalta to bear one such as Fima. The dwarf was in apparent agreement as he eyed the restive, spirited silver-grey charger, whose head was lifted to the wind and was taking in great draughts of air through his wide nostrils, eager to be away.

"My thanks, Galador, but I believe I shall ride with one of the Aridani. Their mounts do not appear to be as fiery as yours."

"Fair enough," said Galador, bowing and swinging gracefully aboard Réalta, his grey cloak thrown back in the morning breeze.

Rogond stowed Fima's pack with their other gear as Lady Ordath entered the courtyard to say her farewells. She approached Rogond, who bowed before her, and spoke to him aside. "Go forth, my friend, and keep safe. I wish you success in your quest. Take care, especially, of your heart…I pray it will remain unbroken." She looked over at Gaelen, who stood by. "Do not expect too much of her, my young Tuathan. Take care."

She moved next to Nelwyn, favoring her with a gentle smile. "I rejoice that you have been restored, fair daughter of Turanen. May you and your beloved keep safe upon the journey. Perhaps a happy union of the Eádram and the Woodland will be forthcoming?"

Nelwyn blushed, and glanced over at Galador, then raised her beautiful green eyes to meet Lady Ordath's. "We shall see, my lady. We thank you for your hospitality and your aid. I would hope to visit your fair lands again."

Ordath then approached Gaelen as she sat already upon her mount. Gaelen bowed her head and placed her right hand upon her breast in a gesture of farewell. "I give my thanks for your aid in our need, O Lady of Mountain-home, and for the gift of the horses. Perhaps one day you will receive our aid in time of peril, for it shall always be given to you."

Lady Ordath returned the farewell gesture. In Gaelen's eyes she saw the honest spirit and the strength of purpose that had no doubt appealed so strongly to Ri-Elathan, and she felt a sudden pang of grief as she remembered the High King, who had been both kin and friend.

Gaelen looked around the courtyard, hoping to see Magra, but he was nowhere in evidence. She recalled her farewell to him the previous evening, as he had promised to travel to the lands of Tal-ailean and to the Twilight Shores, to give warning of Gorgon Elfhunter. At the last Magra had turned back to her, as she stood alone in the dark courtyard, and when he looked upward toward the stars, she saw his eyes fill with sorrow. In a voice heavy with regret, he had spoken to her.

"I could not save him, Gaelen, though I tried. Please forgive me…I could not save him." He had drawn back the sleeve of his tunic, displaying horrific scars that covered his right arm. These extended all the way to his neck; they had been made by the fires of the Bödvari. Gaelen could not speak for a moment, but as Magra replaced his sleeve and turned to leave her, she called after him:

"There is nothing to forgive. One day we will both see him again." Magra had paused, and bowed his head for a moment in acknowledgment.

Now, as she prepared to depart, Gaelen wanted to look upon him once more, as she cared for him and would miss his pleasant company.

Lady Ordath took notice and reassured her. "Magra prepares for his own journey. He wishes you safe passage, and reminds you to be cautious. I will add my own voice to his in that admonition, for I sense that you embark on a path fraught with difficulty. Guard our friend Rogond, and take good care of my lore-master. Farewell."

The Company rode from Mountain-home in the fair light of morning, some never to return. Others would see that fair land again, but only after years of hardship had assailed them, wearing down their spirits and their hopes. Gaelen had vowed that Gorgon Elfhunter would be defeated utterly before she saw Mountain-home again; but that, of course, remained to be seen.

Many days had passed since Gorgon had gone forth, and he was nearing the south of Darkmere, a gnarled tangle of forest with trees dead and dying, old and forbidding, now full of evil creatures that lurked unseen. He would stand before his Lord soon. He estimated that the journey would take only a few more days at his current pace, which had been swift and sure. None of the perils of Darkmere would waylay him. He had no fear of Ulcas or beasts, except for the most fierce and fell, for he knew that he traveled under the protection of Wrothgar. He had been summoned.

His pain had diminished to the point that it bothered him little, excepting the arrow-point that still burned deep under his left arm. It would not daunt him beyond annoyance, however, and perhaps Lord Wrothgar could rid him of it. For now, he plunged into the depths of the forest, the dank gloom enveloping and concealing him. The creatures that roamed the Darkmere would have more to fear from him than he from them, and once Lord Wrothgar favored him as promised, he would be invincible. He only hoped he would cross paths with the ones who had so shaken his confidence, as he would utterly destroy them, after first ensuring that they suffered long and painfully.

The Elfhunter's hand strayed to the sword taken from the Greatwood, the one the accursed She-elf had recognized. He would be certain to use it on her, but not to kill her—not until he paid her back a hundredfold for the pain she and her kind had wrought upon his life.

"Yes, my little maidrin...you will beg for death ere I release you from torment—you and that accursed Aridan and the others of your Company. You shall see this sword again. You will gaze on it through your own blood ere I put your bright eyes out with it. It shall be your payment for the burning of mine!"

Swift and silent, Gorgon moved on his large, heavy feet, toward the Pale Tower. The She-elf may have discovered his only real weakness, but he would come on her in the darkness where it would not avail her. Darkness was more to his liking, anyway.

In the misted fortress of Tûr Dorcha, Wrothgar the Great, now known as the Shadowmancer, awaited the arrival of his wayward creation with anticipation. Gorgon was being drawn as a fly to honey by the promise of a powerful new weapon, one that would make him invincible. Wrothgar smiled inwardly as he thought of it. The gift that he had in mind would indeed make it possible for the Elfhunter to wreak more havoc than ever before. In addition, it would increase Wrothgar's hold upon Gorgon, perhaps to the point that Gorgon would submit to his will. This was a task never before accomplished in spite of Wrothgar's great power.

Even when he was young and fairly naïve, Gorgon had resisted control and would not bend. It was a pity...he would have made such an excellent captain had it not been so. Perhaps now this would be possible, and that would please Wrothgar to no end. The Èolarin spirit with which Gorgon had been endowed would serve well, but only if it could be subjugated and diverted into Wrothgar's design. The Shadowmancer settled back amid the fires surrounding his dark lair, and awaited his opportunity.

"Rogond, I beg of you, stop this accursed animal!"

Fima had degenerated in the last half hour from growling to pleading. Eros shook his head in annoyance as the dwarf came down hard upon his loins for about the hundredth time in the past several hours. Rogond sighed, wincing at the death grip Fima had about his waist, and signaled for a halt. Eros was only too happy to oblige, since Rogond had forbidden him to launch Fima with a powerful thrust of his hindquarters, as was his desire.

Gaelen pulled up beside them, concern in her eyes. "Fima, you shall ride with me next. Perhaps I can soften your journey."

Rogond looked at her. "How do you propose to do that, Gaelen? If you have some magical method I would love to learn it."

Gaelen cocked an eyebrow at him. "I do not have a magic method, only an idea. But it may be worth trying. Let's rest for a while first."

Fima was a little insulted that Gaelen suggested he needed to rest. "I wouldn't have to stop if I could go on my own feet and not rely on this fur-covered mountain of beefsteaks. At least I may predict where my own feet will take me and in what manner!"

Rogond swung his right leg across Eros' neck and dropped to the ground, then helped Fima to dismount. "Well, you may not need rest, Fima, but I do! Your constant growling and grabbing of my midsection has tired me. Let's hope Gaelen's idea increases your comfort sufficiently."

When they had rested, Gaelen took Rogond's bedroll and tied it to the front of her saddle, draping it across her horse's shoulders. She preferred mares, though she was very fond of Eros, and had chosen a small, tough grey from among those offered her in Mountain-home. The mare was fine-haired and sinewy, nearly pure white, and of a type favored by the desert folk of the far southern lands. In Gaelen's experience, these were often the toughest and most enduring horses to be found anywhere, despite their small size. The mare's name was Siva, meaning "grey".

Siva stirred restively as Gaelen assisted Fima onto the soft, thick cushion at the front of the saddle and then swung up behind him. Fima was not convinced of his security on the small, agile mare that could so easily jump from under him, but at a word from Gaelen they set off at a lovely, rolling canter that Fima found almost tolerable, especially with Gaelen steadying him from behind. The cushioning helped as well; it seemed to minimize the bouncing and discomfort to both the rider and the horse.

Rogond nodded in approval. "Well, Fima, has your outlook improved now?"

"It has, though I still would rather feel the ground under my feet," the dwarf replied. "But your friend the Wood-elf has me under her protection, and so I will bear it." He looked over at Rogond, Belegund, and Thorndil, who rode beside him, and winked. Rogond smiled back at him before sending Eros forward to catch Galador, who was leading the company along with Nelwyn. She rode a fiery chestnut appropriately named Gryffa the Red, who was of similar type to Siva, but a bit larger.

Fima rewarded Gaelen for her patience by regaling her with all sorts of captivating tales as they rode. He had lived a much more interesting life than might have been imagined, and he knew so much of history and lore that his supply was inexhaustible. He knew the answers to nearly all her questions concerning events of significance in Alterra, and the day's journey passed quickly. So pleasant was their discourse that Fima forgot all about his discomfort.

At last they stopped to camp for the night. Fima drew Rogond aside as they prepared to sleep. "Oh, yes, she's *worth* it, my friend. You have my permission to court her, and if you don't, I will!" He nudged Rogond in the ribs, saying, "I think I love her…at least my backside loves her!"

Rogond chuckled at him. "Well, that would be the most vital part of you. Have a care, my stout-hearted Fima. You would be in way, way over your head with her!"

Fima drew back, feigning insult. "Why, Tuathan…how little you estimate the power of my dwarvish charm." Then he drew near and spoke in a low voice. "Remember, you said you would reveal to me the identity of her Lost One. Are you nearer to discovering it?"

Rogond flushed, for he had forgotten his promise to Fima, but now he was uncertain whether he should honor their agreement. "I have discovered it, Lore-master," he said, "and perhaps later I will reveal it, but not just now, I beg you."

Rogond looked back toward the encampment where Gaelen was preparing the fire. He knew he could trust Fima with the information, but he was still uncomfortable. He and Galador were now privy to a secret that few were left alive to know.

Fima sighed. He knew that his friend would tell him when he was ready. He also sensed that his instinct concerning the identity of Gaelen's beloved had been correct, and thus this news would be of some significance. He would suppress his curiosity until the time was right. It would probably be worth the wait.

That evening Nelwyn and Galador lay together in the soft spring grass, gazing up at the bright stars and thinking of Lady Ordath's parting words to Nelwyn. Would there be a happy union between the Woodland and the Eádram? Galador could see no reason it should not be so, as they both were happy in each other's company, and their love grew deeper each day. Yet, Nelwyn was troubled. She had foreseen dark times ahead, when evil would disrupt the Company and tear it asunder.

She had clung to Galador one night in Mountain-home, crying in fear. It had taken him some time to quiet her, and in fact she would not be satisfied until she had found Gaelen and Rogond, who were, of course, perfectly safe. But Gaelen had looked into the eyes of her cousin with alarm. Though Nelwyn would not reveal all of the nature of her dark foresight, enough became known to make Gaelen uneasy for several days. Nelwyn had already told Galador that she would not consider any betrothal until their journey's end, when they would be once again in the Greatwood and could be at peace.

Now she shivered in his embrace, not so much with chill as with disquiet. He responded by enfolding her in his arms, drawing her golden head to his chest. Once again she felt safe and warm. Nelwyn knew that Galador would not go beneath the mountains; he had seen quite enough of them. Of the four of them, he had been the most ill at ease traversing the darkness beneath the Monadh-hin. She sensed that some horror of the deep darkness had assailed him on a time, for he would suffer neither himself nor Nelwyn to go there again. Thus she had agreed to go with him to Tal-sithian, there to await the arrival of Rogond and Gaelen. Fima would remain in Cós-domhain through the next winter, as he had not seen his kin in quite a span of years. What course Thorndil and Belegund would take was unknown.

Nelwyn was not happy being separated from Gaelen, and she had tried to talk Galador into going under the mountains, but he really was not comfortable with the idea of entering the dwarf realm, though he liked Fima well enough. "I would sooner go over the mountains than ever go under them again. I know Fima is quite open-minded, but many dwarves still considered Elves to be their bitter enemies—especially Elves like me. I don't know what sort of welcome I would have in the deeps of Cós-domhain."

Nelwyn had asked Gaelen about her choice to remain beside Rogond, even though it meant walking willingly into Cós-domhain. Gaelen had thought for a moment before answering. "I know he does not need my protection, as he is far more adept in dwarf-realms than I, but I sense he has placed great store by the information he expects to get from this dwarf, Farin. I fear it may not be all that he hopes for, and if he is disappointed I want to be there beside him. He seems vulnerable when it comes to the discovery of his history. He stayed by my side when I faced difficulty in Mountain-home—I now wish to do the same for him. Besides, I truly enjoy his company. Are you certain that you will not come with us? Fima has told me that this dwarf-realm is something to see."

Nelwyn shook her head. "I would go with you, Gaelen, but I must stay with Galador, and he will not go under the mountain. Since you will not come with me to Tal-sithian, we must wait for you there."

Gaelen laughed. "A fine waiting-place it will be in late spring! I cannot feel too sorry for your waiting. I shall be glad to see those lands again."

Nelwyn agreed. "Yes, but I shall be the more glad to see you again. There is an evil that stalks us, and though it does not yet draw near, it will. I'm certain of it."

At this, Gaelen grew somber. She knew that Nelwyn had held some sort of premonition, and it frightened her. The realization of how formidable Gorgon really was— that he had nearly succeeded in killing them all—had unnerved her, yet she was now more determined than ever to bring him down. She reached out to Nelwyn and embraced her, trying to convey a confidence she did not truly feel. She hadn't really been separated from her cousin in a long reckoning.

"It will be all right, Nelwyn. I shall come to Tal-sithian as quickly as I may. And you must take care in the mountain crossing, as it may be dangerous enough. In the meantime let us enjoy our time together. It will be many days ere we reach the mountain gate, then we shall say farewell for a while."

Now Gaelen sat by the fire that she had built, gazing into the depths of the flames. Her mind was far away as Rogond sat beside her; she did not appear to take notice of him at first. He wondered whether she was casting her thoughts toward her beloved Ri-Elathan; her eyes were full of longing that Rogond could see through the reflected firelight. In truth, she was lost in a memory of another time, when she had cast her thoughts to one in need of them.

It happened in the forest as she had settled for the night in a clearing, when the stars were so bright that the sight of them gladdened and inspired her spirit into song. It was so with all the Cúinar, to whom the stars are beloved.

It had been three long years since Rain had left her. As she sang on that night, she could see him standing alone on a hilltop overlooking the choked, poisonous ruin that was the battle-plain, and he had lifted his eyes to the heavens in despair. He had not seen the stars clearly for time interminable, and his heart was sick and weary. Her song somehow reached him, and as he gazed heavenward he closed his eyes, and her visions filled his mind with an indigo field of silver lights so bright that he gasped in surprise and delight. Here, at last, were his beloved stars, millions of brilliant jewels that filled his spirit with joy. He saw her as well, bright eyes raised skyward, clear voice ringing, singing a beautiful song of hope and love…and of longing. The wonderful vision could not last, but it was such a gift that when it faded he did not despair, but treasured the memory of it until the end. It was his last clear sight of the stars, and the moment did not come again; though she often tried to call to him, he could not hear.

Now Gaelen was startled from her memory by the arrival of Belegund and Thorndil, who were preparing to settle by the fire for the night, as it was turning chill. Thorndil commented that they really were unused to the luxury of such a well-rested journey while in the wild, as the Elves, who needed no sleep, would keep the watch. They sat side-by-side, wrapped in their cloaks, hard men who had faced perils without number. Rogond asked Gaelen if she would sing for the three of them, as his friends had not yet been favored with her song. Gaelen obliged, and the sound that came from her was so beautiful and sad that the hearts of the Tuathar were torn by it, making Rogond wonder still whether she called out to the one who waited for her.

Had Gorgon heard that song in the depths of the Darkmere, he would have been filled with loathing. The song of Elves, no matter how fair, was to him abhorrent, for it served to remind him of the rejection of his existence by his mother's people and of his lonely life full of hatred. He neither loved nor appreciated the beauty of anything Elven. The pain he felt as he raised new scars upon his own flesh was at times the only thing that made him know he was even alive. Yet alive he was, and now he was filled with hopeful anticipation, as he drew ever nearer to Tûr Dorcha and the Realm of the Shadowmancer.

18

The Pale Tower

The next several days passed quickly and proved enjoyable as the weather had turned fine and warm, and the Company was in no hurry to reach their destination. Though they did not tarry, they set a relaxed pace.

Nelwyn and Gaelen were both fascinated by Fima, who never seemed to run out of surprises. Neither of them had ever allowed more than a minimal acquaintance with any of Fima's race before, and they now regretted it, as it appeared that at least some dwarves were truly worth knowing. Fima, who was much more enlightened concerning Elves, was gladdened at this change in attitude. He taught Nelwyn a little of the dwarf-tongue and shared with her his people's conception of the beginning of the world. Gaelen would hear all that Fima knew of the history of the Èolar. She also wanted to hear more tales of the fabled northern realm of Tuathas, and she became rather close in friendship with old Thorndil, who shared a wealth of such tales with her.

When they were not sharing tales, they were practicing their skill at arms. Nelwyn's artistry with a bow was amazing. Her green eyes narrowed in concentration as she placed shaft after shaft exactly where she wished to. It was as though she merely had to look to a target, and the shaft appeared there. Galador and Rogond sparred with Thorndil and Belegund, their long swords ringing, as Gaelen sharpened her short sword and long daggers, humming softly to herself and enjoying the sight of them. Belegund was the most powerful, and Thorndil the most efficient and accurate. Rogond, the youngest of the three Tuathar, was the quickest and most graceful on his feet, for he had been well trained by the Elves who raised him. His swordplay was impressive, but even more so was his skill with the spear, which he could hurl with a precision nearly as great as Nelwyn's arrows. Such abilities were rare even among Elves. Galador was Rogond's equal when it came to the sword. In addition he was nearly as adept with the bow as Nelwyn, and his shots were far more powerful.

On one such day, Fima sat beside Gaelen, watching these displays with admiration. "Little Wood-elf, I notice you are not vying with your companions, yet I know that you must have some skill. What is your strength at arms?"

Gaelen turned to him and smiled. It was amusing being called "little" by one whose head did not reach her shoulders. "Bring your axe, Master Dwarf, and you shall know."

Fima was delighted at the prospect and grabbed his axe. Gaelen then led him to a small clearing nearby, where an old tree-stump stood about as high as Fima's head. They stopped about fifteen yards from it, and Gaelen held up her hand. "Cast your weapon, Child of Fior, and then watch and learn."

"Hmmm…" said Fima, as he sized up the target. Then he drew back, axe in hand, and let it fly swift and sure. It turned gracefully over thrice before coming to rest, quivering, in the exact center of the stump. Gaelen clapped with delight, patting Fima on the shoulder.

"Well thrown! That was a beautiful thing to behold. Now see where my skills lie." She drew a long dagger quick as thinking, leaped in the air and turned about, landing catlike, bright eyes focused on the axe. She let the dagger fly, striking the stump in the same fissure made by Fima. She dropped and somersaulted, throwing a second blade to again strike the fissure upon the opposite side of the axe. Fima's weapon wavered and sagged, and Gaelen rolled and caught it as it dropped to the ground. Then, she tossed it to Fima in a blur of motion. "Defend yourself!" she cried, drawing her short sword and leaping upon him before he could blink.

The next few seconds were alarming for Fima, as Gaelen's short sword met his axe time and again; it was all he could do to fend her off. He forgot that she was a Sylvan rustic; here was a whirlwind of sinew and steel. At last he lay winded upon the ground, her blade held harmlessly at his throat for the sixth time. She drew back and smiled at him, her face flushed, eyes full of excitement. Drawing a deep breath, she sheathed her blade then held out her hand to help him to his feet.

"That was amazing! I thought you preferred the bow," said Fima, catching his breath.

"I do prefer it, Master Fima, but I cannot vie with either Nelwyn or Galador in tests of archery. The blade is my second choice, as I do not possess great power, so I must make up for it in speed and accuracy. What do you think? Are my skills satisfactory?"

Fima eyed her ruefully, brushing the leaves and dead grass from his jacket. "I would not want to be your enemy, Gaelen of the Greatwood. Now let us return; this exercise has made me feel slow, old, and very mortal, not to mention hungry and thirsty!" At this he chuckled, then laughed heartily as they made their way back to the encampment.

Rogond met up with them, still somewhat winded and sweating from his contest with Belgund. Fima drew him aside. "I have now concluded that our Gaelen is much too quick for the likes of you, Rogond. Watch her, my friend, or I will steal her from you. She obviously finds me fascinating!"

Rogond looked sidelong at him. "Of that I have no doubt, Fima. Yet many things in this world might be described as fascinating. I will leave it to you to think of them."

Fima laughed again and clapped Rogond on the elbow. "Fair enough. I still think she is too quick for you. Alas that she was not born a dwarf; it is the only thing that would truly improve her, though she would no doubt still cut her hair."

Rogond smiled. "No doubt—and she would probably shave her beard as well!" At this, Fima shuddered, being unable to imagine such a thing.

Fima went in search of food and drink as Rogond took stock of his own condition. He was sweating in the heat of mid-day, and was in need of a good soaking. There was a deep pool of cool water nearby that would be perfect for such an application. After all, it certainly would not do to be unclean in such company. His clothing he could wash as well; the sun would dry it quickly.

He eased himself into the soothing, green depths, ducking under so that his long hair was thoroughly wetted. Removing his clothing, he scrubbed it beneath the water, and then tossed it upon the bank. He swam beneath the surface, reveling in the feel of the water as it traveled across his skin. After warming and stretching his limbs with slow, powerful strokes, he came up at the edge of a reed bed, and was surprised to see Gaelen entering the water from the opposite side. She was unclothed, her soft skin flawless save for the scars that she bore. She lowered herself gracefully into the water, then disappeared beneath the surface, raising hardly a ripple.

Rogond held his breath, not knowing what her reaction would be to his presence, as she surfaced again. As though she had suddenly become aware of him, her head turned and she met his gaze. Her expression was calm as she swam toward him, but Rogond flushed and dropped his eyes. Then she was right in front of him, standing waist-deep among the reeds, her left arm across her breasts. She tossed the wet hair from her eyes, her expression quizzical, as if standing before him unclothed was the most natural thing in the world.

"Are you all right? You look distressed. Does my presence here disquiet you? If so, then I will permit you your privacy."

Rogond still would not look directly at her, as he feared she would read his thoughts in his eyes. Her skin was like fine alabaster, and the light of her eyes smote him to the heart. He felt such an incredible longing for her in that moment that it was nearly unbearable. He wanted to declare his feelings right there and take her in his arms upon the warm, soft grass. He wanted to feel her soft skin next to his own and become one with her until they were both spent. No, he had best not look directly at her just now. He muttered some words that she could not understand, then turned from her and waded through the tall reeds, paying little heed to the black sediment that now coated his legs from the knees downward. He only wanted to escape his predicament, but in his haste he had forgotten about his clothing, which was lying in a wet heap quite some distance away.

Gaelen knew that he was distressed, though she was uncertain of the cause. She called to him: "Rogond! I am going now, so that you may enjoy your time undisturbed. I merely wished to cool myself, and have done so." She had no idea that Rogond would be so easily mortified; he had always seemed self-confident and secure. Ah, well, there was surely an explanation. She called to him again. "I will meet you back at the encampment, where we may eat and drink in a little while. Will that suit you?"

Rogond called back to her. "Yes, of course. I won't be long—wait for me and I will eat and drink with you." But what he really thought was that it did not suit him. What would have suited him at that moment, he could not reveal to her. And he wondered whether he ever would have the courage to do so.

Gorgon first beheld the pale vision of Tûr Dorcha, stark and full of foreboding, as it stood shrouded in a sickly grey vapor. All around was desolation—a terrible, fetid bog surrounded it where no tree or leaf would grow. Yet he did not fear the Tower, as his coming was anticipated. His pride sustained him as he approached it, standing unafraid before the gates. He called out to the guards that drew their crossbows on him from atop the outer wall: "Lay aside your weapons and tell your master that Gorgon Elfhunter has come."

The guards looked upon him with puzzlement and not without awe; they had not beheld him before, this massive figure that could withstand so easily the evil energies radiating from the Tower. If an ordinary foe, such as Elf or man, came nigh to this place, he would be sickened and weakened merely from drawing breath. His vision would be clouded by a thick mist of confusion and despair, and he would either turn aside or die. An enemy that could approach so boldly was formidable indeed.

The massive gates opened, and a small retinue of well-armed Ulcas appeared, approaching Gorgon as he looked down at them with disdain. Gorgon held nothing but contempt for them. He had once respected his own mighty sire, but he had been exceptional. Gorgon despised ordinary Ulcas for their weakness, their inability to travel well in daylight, and their distorted, twisted bodies. In truth, were it not for his armor, which effectively blocked the sunlight from much of his flesh, he would have experienced some of the same difficulty, for he did not love the sun. His pale eyes were still quite vulnerable, as the accursed She-elf had noticed.

Well, there was surely a remedy for that! When she and her companions were all dead there would be no need to worry. He snarled at the Ulcas.

"Lay down your weapons!" he thundered at them, and they took several steps back from him as he drew Gelmyr's blade. The Elvish steel glinted in the misty twilight.

They retreated farther, snarling and arguing among themselves in their foul tongue. Gorgon laughed. "I am expected, you pathetic descendants of worms. One of you direct me to the Lord Wrothgar, for he is waiting. Otherwise I shall exercise my blade on your scrawny necks." He swept the head from the nearest guard without even looking at it.

The others took his point immediately, and began to flee toward the Tower and its great black doors. The doors opened as they reached it, but, rather than providing sanctuary, a burst of fire came forth, felling them as they shrieked and rolled upon the ground to no avail. Gorgon drew back a little, though he was untouched. The flames gentled down, and now burned softly, hanging inexplicably in the air before him. They went from golden to black, with peculiar green flickers edging and tipping them, as the deep, malevolent voice of Lord Wrothgar invaded Gorgon's mind.

"Thou art as prideful and strong as ever I made thee, Elfhunter. Have a care as thou wouldst enter My fortress, and lower thy proud gaze, if thou wouldst have My aid. Thou art as a wayward child returned. Show thou respect to thy Father."

Gorgon dropped his eyes then, though he did not submit within his heart. "Yea, Lord Wrothgar, I have returned as Thou willed. Yet Thy offer of aid was not made with the price of my pride, or assurance of my submission. I cannot promise this to Thee, and if it is Thy price, now may I know of Thy gift that I may judge its worth? My pride and resistance to Thy will may be of the greater value to me."

Unpleasant, malicious laughter emanated from the flames, and they burned hotter and brighter—showing their blood-gold hearts—before Gorgon. "How like to thy mother's kin, Elfhunter. And how foolish, though I take pride in thy strength. Thou dost not comprehend thy peril at this moment; never hast thou done so. But I will grant thy request. Come unto Me, and then we will parley, O Wayward Son. Then might thou understand the value of My promises."

Gorgon nodded, and the flames died back to a small flicker that still burned brightly in the grey mist. The flame drew back through the great doors, with Gorgon following its reddish glow. It led him down the dark passages and up many winding stairs. There was no light inside, only the small amount from the guiding flame. Gorgon had no difficulty, as he was most at home in the blackness, yet the screams and cries of the prisoners of the Pale Tower disquieted him. Down in the depths, unfortunate souls captured by the minions of Wrothgar could be heard even now, writhing and shrieking in their agony. It had always been so.

The first sounds Gorgon had heard ever in his life were the helpless wails of his Elven mother as he was forcibly taken from her womb, and the first sight he had beheld in his innocence was her horrified expression as she looked upon his hideousness with her dying sight. He had inherited her perceptive nature, and knew from the first that he was a ghastly abomination in her eyes. She held pity for him as well, but she rejected him utterly even as he was placed in her arms as she lay dying. She held him once to her breast, then cried out in revulsion and pushed him away.

He would never know a warm embrace again, and would never be willingly accepted by any being in Alterra. The Elves would hate him, and the Ulcas would fear him. Both would find him repulsive, loathsome, and monstrous. Still, he had cried out to his mother in the darkness, yearning for her warmth and the comfort and security of her breast, for he had not yet understood his own nature, or his purpose. He understood it well enough now, however, and he would soon be in the presence of the One whose power, added to his own, would allow him to achieve that purpose.

He followed the flame into a large chamber lit with torches placed along the walls which, like the floor, were jet-black and highly polished, reflecting the flickering torchlight as would a mirror. Gorgon saw his own dim reflection there as well and drew himself up, throwing out his powerful chest and placing his hand on his sword-hilt in readiness. Then, the voice of Wrothgar came again.

"Remove thy helmet, Elfhunter."

Gorgon hesitated for a moment, then reached up and pulled off his heavy helmet with his left hand, releasing the flood of golden hair from beneath it. Gorgon's hair was beautiful. It was as fine and soft as spun golden thread, and it lifted like silk in the fiery breeze. Wrothgar appeared in the midst of his own unnatural, dark fire as a black, shadowy figure seated upon a massive throne. Where he actually was and what he really looked like would remain unknown to Gorgon, who realized that this was merely a vision planted in his mind.

Then the vision of Wrothgar spoke: "Thou wouldst visit death upon thy foes, those of thy mother's kin, yet taking them singly by chance meeting will not further thy cause. They are aware of thee—they ride even now to Tal-sithian and to the lands west. If thou wouldst destroy them, take heed of this gift."

From the depths of the peculiar greenish-black flame came a vision of a small, golden disc, hanging in the air before Gorgon's vision and turning gently. As Gorgon looked on in wonder, the cover snapped open to reveal a round mirror, winking and flashing in the flickering green light.

"Take it, and rejoice, for it will aid thee."

Gorgon hesitated, for he was wary. There were objects in the world that held powers unknown to him, and he did not wish to be ensnared. This one appeared to be of Elven-make; Gorgon could see some form of beautiful engraving upon it. It had in fact been made by Dardis, the greatest of the Èolarin craftsmen, who had been killed during the Second Uprising. Objects forged by his hand were known to contain great power, and this mirror had been collected and corrupted by Wrothgar. Who knew what terrible fate would befall one who possessed it or tried to use it? Wrothgar read Gorgon's thoughts, and answered them.

"Do not fear. The mirror will not subvert thee to My will. It has but one power that has been placed within it, though that is not small. Take it, and I will explain it to thee."

Still, Gorgon hesitated, torn between distrust of his Dark Master and desire for the power the mirror would give.

"Dost thou wish to vanquish thine enemies, or dost thou wish to be vanquished by them? The choice is open to thee."

Gorgon knew the black flames would not burn him—not unless Wrothgar wished them to. He reached out into them and took hold of the mirror. It was warm in his hand as he turned it over, gazing into the smooth surface of the glass. Its depths were bottomless and filled with many-colored lights.

"Now I will tell thee of how it may be used. If upon learning of the power of the mirror thou wouldst take it unto thee, it will become thine, such that no other may use it until thy death. I give this not lightly, as its like shall not be made again."

Gorgon nodded. "I understand, Lord. What is this power?"

Wrothgar explained that, once possessed by its master, the mirror would allow him to see and hear through the eyes and ears of one of his enemies. The master would determine which of his enemies would be bound to the mirror, and to do this, he needed either a part of the body of the enemy, such as hair or blood, or some possession that had passed through the enemy's hands, the more recently the better. Wrothgar waited as Gorgon absorbed the impact of this information. If he could see and hear though the eyes and ears of one of his enemies, he could know all they were planning and could easily come on them unaware. In addition, they would lead him to more of his foes that he could prey upon by dark of night. They would not be able to evade him, as he would know their every move and plan as it was made.

"There is a warning, Elfhunter. Thou must choose the one whom thou wilt bind to the power of the mirror, and must then ensure that this one remains alive, for if slain then the mirror is useless. It will not work again for thee in thy lifetime, and may be used by another only upon thy death. Therefore, choose well!"

"But how do I choose, Lord? Wilt Thou not guide me? I wish to slay them all and leave none alive. How may I reconcile this?"

Wrothgar answered. "Thou wilt visit sorrow and pain enough upon the unfortunate one chosen, as they will be the instrument of death for those they love. Reserve thy final vengeance upon them until the last, when the mirror is of no further use to thee. Then reveal thyself to them, that the pain of their unwitting complicity in thy purpose may drive them mad. They may then welcome death at thy hands." Wrothgar laughed then, a horrible mirthless laugh that raised chills even upon Gorgon. "Which of thy foes is best known to thee?"

Gorgon considered. He knew precious little of any of them and had spoken only briefly with two of them: the tall, dark-haired Elf and the small She-elf, the one who had first discovered his weakness. Her name was known to him, and his lip curled as he spoke it aloud: "Gaelen... bright-eyed Elf of the Greatwood, how little I know of thee, and yet perhaps enough."

Wrothgar searched Gorgon's thoughts and produced an image of Gaelen, hovering in the center of the dark flame. She was as she had appeared when speaking to Gorgon—teeth clenched, blade held before her, an expression of desperate hatred in her eyes. Gorgon snarled back at her in spite of himself.

"Dost thou have any item that has passed through her hands, or a bit of her blood?" Gorgon did not know. In fact, some of the blood upon his sword had been Gaelen's, but it was mingled with that of Rogond. Gorgon had wiped the blade clean after tasting of it.

"Lord, I have no blood of this enemy of which I may be certain. The blood of the Aridan mingles with it."

Wrothgar reflected for a moment before speaking once more. "Thou hast something that has passed through her hands—carried deep within thy flesh. Raise thy left arm, Elfhunter."

Gorgon did so, approaching nearer the flame, as the arrow-point deep within his flesh stirred painfully, drawn by the power of Darkness. Gorgon cried with pain and gritted his teeth as the steel worked slowly toward the surface. Suddenly, he was free of it, and it hovered in the air before him, dripping with his strange blood.

"Take it, my errant son, and hold it in thy hand." Gorgon gasped as he lowered his arm; the pain grew less with each moment until it was nearly gone. He reached out and took the bloody arrow-point in his right hand. It burned hot in his grasp, but its touch was bearable.

"It is the heat of thy hatred, Gorgon Elfhunter. Revel in it and speak her name, if thou would bind her to the mirror."

All Gorgon had to do was speak Gaelen's name, and the power would be his. He could track them down and slay them—all except Gaelen herself. Would that satisfy him? He really wanted to kill her most of all; he had promised it to himself. He had vowed to put her eyes out with Turantil, but now her eyes would be central to his purpose. If he confronted her, would he be able to resist killing her? Almost immediately, he knew the answer. To slay her companions with her unwitting aid would be far worse than killing her. He knew this deep within his black heart. She was the one who pursued him with the greatest passion, bent on laying him low. How delicious that he should subvert her desires into the deaths of those she loved! Gorgon clutched the arrow-point, as the burning heat of it increased with the swell of hatred within him.

"Yea, Lord, I will accept this gift. May I be successful in the hunt, as it will also aid Thee in Thy purpose. But what would Thou ask of me in return?"

"Only to accomplish thy desire to kill as many of the Elàni as possible… that will please Me greatly. Upon a time, I may ask more of thee, but be assured that the boon will involve nothing beyond the slaying of Elves. Does that reassure thee?" Gorgon considered for a moment longer, then, slowly, he nodded agreement.

"Then speak her name, and she will be thy eyes and ears until her death…or thine."

Gorgon glared at Gaelen's bright eyes as the vision still hovered before him. "They shall be my bright eyes now, unwitting She-elf. Guard them well." Then he spoke her name.

On the other side of the mountains, Gaelen suddenly fell from her mount to lie unconscious upon the ground. The Company, having resumed their progress toward the gates of Cós-domhain, was breezing along at a fair pace. Thorndil, who rode beside Gaelen, called out in alarm as he reined in his mount. Rogond looked back over his shoulder, then wheeled about and galloped Eros back, leaping off to kneel beside Nelwyn, who was already there. She was calling to Gaelen, who had not yet stirred. Her graceless fall had resulted in her striking her head upon a stone. A trickle of blood flowed from a small gash in the left side of her forehead. Fima appeared then, a small phial in his hand.

"Stand aside, both of you. This will bring her around." He held the phial before her face, and as she breathed the vapors emanating from it, she suddenly opened her eyes, turning her head from them and moaning.

Rogond took her hand. "It's all right, Gaelen. You have fallen from your horse, but you are not hurt badly, just shaken a bit. Lie still until you find your wits." Gaelen closed her eyes and shuddered. Nelwyn looked at her with concern.

"Something happened to her, Rogond. She would not simply fall off her horse. Something happened."

Rogond took Nelwyn's point. He turned to Thorndil, who had been nearest. "Can you shed any light on this, my friend?"

Thorndil shook his head. "Not really. She was riding well, then suddenly I noticed her sagging sideways, and a moment later she was on the ground. I believe she was unconscious long before she came off the horse." Rogond agreed, but until Gaelen could enlighten them, they still had no idea as to why this had occurred. Gaelen moaned again, and Rogond squeezed her hand.

"Come on, my little Gaelen. Come back to us, it's all right." He helped her to sit up, wiping the blood from her pale face.

She took the flask of water from Nelwyn and drank gratefully. Then, she looked around as though confused. "What happened? Why am I sitting on the ground? And *why* does everyone keep calling me 'little'?"

"You fell from your horse. We don't know why. Something must have come over you," said Nelwyn. "Do you have any memory of what might have happened?"

Gaelen shook her head. Her color was coming back, and she felt strong again. She got to her feet, shrugging off the fall, but Rogond and Nelwyn insisted that they all stop for the night anyway, to Gaelen's immense annoyance. "I'm just fine. I do not need to rest. It's too early to stop for the night," she said. But Nelwyn, in particular, was not convinced.

"You do not just fall from your horse for no reason, Gaelen, something happened to you. Besides, you struck your head, and we should make certain you are truly all right before we proceed. Tomorrow will be soon enough."

Gaelen went to sit beside the fire, grumbling under her breath. She could not know that Gorgon Elfhunter, her mortal enemy, had just had his first taste of the power of the mirror as he stood with his back against the wall of Wrothgar's chamber, staring into the same fire.

Wrothgar had warned him that the mirror would take some getting used to. He would refine and improve his vision as he gazed into it, but at first, things might appear clouded and indistinct. After all, he was adjusting to input from senses other than his own. What Wrothgar had neglected to mention was the pain experienced while using it. Gorgon had gasped and staggered back against the wall, as his skull seemed to reel with nearly unbearable pressure. Tears of pain flowed from his eyes. Then Wrothgar's voice was heard once again:

"Focus on thy hatred, Elfhunter. The Maker did not intend the mirror to be used thus! It must be dominated and subverted to thy purpose. The pain will remain, but it will be lessened. In the future, thou wilt choose the time to use it, for it will tire thee, but the reward will be great! Concentrate on achieving thy purpose."

Gorgon did so, focusing all his thoughts on finding and eliminating the Elves one by one. He began breathing normally again, concentrating on dominating the mirror. It was his now and would serve his purpose. It would always pain him, but he would bear it.

At first, all was blackness, but slowly his vision came into focus. Then he heard Gaelen's name being called repeatedly, followed by a blurred, wavering vision of the faces of the fair-haired She-elf and the tall Aridan. Gorgon witnessed the revival of Gaelen with a sort of pained fascination. He could see the others in the party: an old dwarf and two other men. And there was the dark-haired Elf, the one who had finally run him underground.

They appeared to be concerned for Gaelen, though Gorgon did not know why. He could hear her muttering as she stared at the fire. This was going to be trickier than he thought, as he would not be able to bear the mirror for more than a short period at any given time. Whether he saw or heard anything of real importance would be largely a matter of luck. Yet this ability would aid him, no doubt about that.

He stood with his eyes closed against the pain, still focusing on the vision in his mind. Gaelen had lifted her eyes from the fire, and was now looking at Rogond, who offered her food and drink. "Perhaps later," she said. The Aridan then sat beside her, placing his cloak about her shoulders. "Stop fussing over me, Rogond. I told you, I'm all right. I would rather have made more progress today; we will never get to Cós-domhain if we keep this pace."

Gorgon galvanized. Cós-domhain—how very interesting. He smiled in spite of his pain. Only a few minutes, and he had already learned of their destination…how excellent! Deep within his fortress, Lord Wrothgar was satisfied. Gorgon was impressed with his gift already, and as time passed he would become more adept at using it. The Elves would never know what had befallen them, and he would pick them off one by one. He would know of their whereabouts and when they were getting too close, should they suspect his presence. They would never catch him if he remained cautious. Who knew what sort of information Gorgon would discover? Wrothgar was, in general, pleased with this plan. It seemed that the labor of creating Gorgon might prove to have been worthwhile after all.

19

The Dividing of the Company

Nelwyn was lost in thought as she stood upon the hilltop, keeping the watch over the encampment, for this land was not without its perils. They had come to the separation of their paths, and tomorrow they would decide who among them would turn west to cross the mountains and who would go beneath them. Nelwyn had volunteered for the watch this night, and Galador would no doubt be joining her soon, for it was his habit. At such times they would speak quietly with one another, sharing their thoughts, and she had learned much of him in this way. But now she was unhappy about the upcoming division of the Company, yet she could not sway Galador in his determination to part ways with the others.

Nelwyn knew that he was deeply troubled and fearful of the passage under the mountains, though she did not yet know why. He had certainly been uncomfortable when they had been forced under the Monadh-hin, and not without reason, yet they all had, even Rogond. Galador was keeping something from them, something that made it necessary for him to turn from his companions even if they faced grave peril without him. Nelwyn knew that he was very old compared with the rest of them and had lived in places and seen things they could only imagine; yet it would take a lot to turn him from Rogond.

It was with such thoughts in her mind that Nelwyn sensed a presence behind her and turned to investigate. Gaelen was standing there. She had left the others and gone out walking, alone among the stars.

"Where is Galador? I would have thought he would be with you, as always," Gaelen said, with only a hint of resentment in her voice. She had precious little time alone with Nelwyn since the coming of Galador.

She liked him, and rejoiced that he had found love and happiness at last, but she also wished that he would not have come between Nelwyn and herself to such an extent. Nelwyn heard this in Gaelen's voice, and she sorrowed, for she knew that Gaelen had been largely shut out of her life of late. They had nearly always depended on each other, had saved each other's lives on several occasions, and had been inseparable until now. Nelwyn didn't like the prospect of taking separate paths any more than Gaelen did.

"He is not here at present, but I expect he soon will be," Nelwyn answered. "It's just as well, for I would speak with him. There is something troubling him that he has not told me about, something that prevents him from going under the mountain. But I suppose it is well that we are not all going, as someone must get the horses across to Talsithian." She sat down beside her cousin, and they shared their cloaks against the chill, for the wind was rising.

"I thought Thorndil and Belegund were to travel across with the horses," said Gaelen, who was unwilling to admit that there was a positive side to Galador's reluctance.

"The intentions of Thorndil and Belegund are as yet unknown. Perhaps they are bent on staying with Rogond," said Nelwyn.

Gaelen sniffed. "I thought Galador was Rogond's dearest friend and thus would be bent on staying with him. I just do not understand."

Nelwyn loved her cousin, but she was beginning to get annoyed, and was inclined to speak in defense of Galador. "You are *my* dearest friend, Gaelen, and yet you will separate from me to stay with Rogond. You will not cross the mountains with us, but instead will remain with the Tuathan and the dwarf? And what is your lofty motive for this course? Admit it! You wish to get beneath the mountains in the hope that you will pick up the trail of your enemy, the sooner to pursue him with foolish overconfidence. I love you, Gaelen, and would fall defending you. But sometimes you frighten me." As soon as the words escaped her, she regretted them. Gaelen was not likely to forget them, either.

"My motives are not lofty. I simply feel compelled to remain with Rogond. This encounter he seeks may bring him great joy or make him very unhappy and disappointed. And to whom shall he turn then? His friend Galador, with whom he shares his thoughts, will be in Tal-sithian, along with you. My motives are no more lofty than that. As for finding the trail of the enemy, you have listened too long to Galador if you believe that I would pursue him lightly now that I understand his nature. I would correct you on one other point, as well. He is not merely my enemy. He is the enemy of our race and our very way of life. The sooner he is dead, the better, but I will not confront him again until I have considerably more power beside me. I thank you for your vote of confidence." She rose somewhat stiffly, and turned to Nelwyn, cutting off her apology.

"Galador is coming. Perhaps he will enlighten you as to the real reason he chooses to abandon his friends. In the meantime, I know you did not mean to say what was said, but sometimes what we do not mean to say expresses our true feelings. I will take my leave of you now, for my presence here will interfere with your ability to inquire of Galador. I would very much like to know of his motives, if he has them. Perhaps you will share them with me on a time."

Nelwyn watched her go as Galador approached from the other side of the hill. Gaelen had been hurt by Nelwyn's words and had left without giving her a chance to explain or take them back. There was nothing to do for it now. Galador came up behind Nelwyn, embraced her, and they sat down together. Now she would try to learn the real motive for his reluctance to enter Cós-domhain. She hoped he would trust her sufficiently to tell her of it and that Gaelen would understand.

Some time later, Nelwyn sat with Galador's head in her lap, stroking his long, dark hair, still wondering how best to broach the subject of his underlying fears. None of the ideas she had entertained up to now seemed right. She could just imagine Gaelen's approach: *So, Galador, what is the REAL reason that you choose to abandon your friends?* She smiled in the darkness. No, that approach would not do at all. But she finally decided to simply ask him directly, as he loved her, and she knew she needn't fear his reaction to an honest question.

"Galador, my love, why will you not go under the mountain? I know there is something else besides uncertainty of the descendants of Rûmm. Will you not make this clear to me? We are leaving our friends in what I have foreseen to be a time of peril. Please, beloved, open your heart and let me help you if I may."

Galador stiffened, and his eyes met Nelwyn's in the deep starlight. She had never known anyone so beautiful, or so complicated. She was unswerving in her love and would never abandon him. "I will always love you, no matter what may befall us," she whispered.

"Your heart and its secrets are safe. I will not disparage you. Please, help me to understand."

He sat up then and threw his cloak across her shoulders, drawing her close. "Ah, Nelwyn. I will tell you, but you must not reveal what I am going to say to anyone. Rogond knows it already. And you must promise not to turn from your course and to stay with me on the path to Tal-sithian. I believe you will understand once I have told you."

Nelwyn nodded, promising to keep his secret, though she did not look forward to informing Gaelen that she could not share with her. Galador then proceeded to tell her a tale of two events: one that had happened in a time long past and another that had happened much more recently in Mountain-home. When he had finished, Nelwyn did indeed understand his motive, and she knew that she could not turn from her course beside him, for to do so would break his heart.

She prayed that her friends would find their way safely beneath the mountain and would meet them in Tal-sithian, but that was not what Galador had foreseen. He had seen death stalking the Company beneath the mountain, and would no more go there now with Nelwyn than kill her himself.

"Something lurks under the mountain, and at least one of our friends may not come out again. One thing is certain—if you go with them, you will die. I have foreseen it." He held Nelwyn as she wept with fear for her friends.

"Then, we must stay them all from this course! I would not lose any of them!" she cried. "How can you let Rogond go?"

Galador tried to calm her. "Hush, Nelwyn. Rogond knows of this, as I have told him. Yet he would not be diverted from his path, for it is of great importance to him, and he knows that my visions do not always come to pass. Besides, it was only *your* death that was foreseen."

Nelwyn could not stop trembling. "But surely, we must warn them all of this! Perhaps they might choose differently."

Galador shook his head. "It is enough that Rogond knows. He will discourage Thorndil and Belegund."

Nelwyn drew back from him and looked into his eyes. "And what of Gaelen? Would you have her walk unknowingly into peril?"

"Of course not, but...I sensed from my vision that she was not in danger. Rogond might be, though, and you most of all. I tried to turn Rogond from his path, but he is set upon it; he so desperately searches for answers to his identity. This is a hard burden for me to bear, for I would not abandon Rogond if I had any other choice. But to protect you from this fate is the only choice I can make. Fear of the enmity of dwarves is just a façade." He sighed. "I'm sincerely tired of Fima's reaction to it…he teases me without mercy."

"He is merely trying to reassure you by making you see that your fears are groundless. You would be quite safe in Cós-domhain with both Fima and Rogond at your side."

"I would not be entirely sure of that, Nelwyn. But you now know that my fears are not of the dwarves. Remember that night in Mountain-home, when you dreamed of the great evil that stalks us? My vision was much the same. You could not stop crying until we found Gaelen and Rogond. What you do not realize is that I wept for YOU as you lay beside me. I have seldom had such a vivid and frightening vision before, but when they happen, I have learned to pay attention to them."

Nelwyn looked into his face and saw deep anxiety written there. She held him in a reassuring embrace. "I will go with you, my love, do not fear. Yet I am troubled and afraid for my friends. Can we not tell them all of this, so that they may choose? They will not disparage you, for they love and respect you. Please, Galador, at least let me tell Gaelen that she must be ever watchful of Rogond."

Galador stiffened in her embrace. "Gaelen? You want to tell *her* that I've dragged you away because of a bad dream? You want me to open my deepest thoughts and fears to her? Oh, most certainly!" His sarcasm was obvious, and he knew immediately that it was a mistake. Nelwyn drew back from him, and in a moment she had broken free of his embrace and stood before him. It was the first time he had ever seen her truly angry.

"And you decry her for *her* pride! You would let her walk into this darkness alone and uninformed rather than explain yourself to her? Well, here is a bitter truth for you: she would never do the same to you. She would care more for your safety. You had better confront her, Galador, unless you love this hilltop, for here you will stay until you do. And I will not take one step toward Tal-sithian until you have spoken with her. I promised not to reveal your secret, but you *shall*. Only then will I go with you to the Lake-realm."

She turned and strode back down into the encampment, leaving Galador to keep the watch alone. He contemplated her words, the blood ringing in his ears as he considered them. He was not certain that Gaelen would have cared more for his safety than for her pride were their situations reversed, but the important thing was that Nelwyn thought she would. He was humbled by her words and by her simple faith in her cousin's integrity. Had he been vying with Gaelen for Nelwyn's affections? If so, he should have known better.

Galador dropped back onto the grass and gazed at the stars, the watch forgotten for the moment. Then he realized that he was not alone. He started up in alarm to find Gaelen standing before him. He cursed himself for taking his eyes from the watch, as she surely had an even higher estimation of his worth than before. She did not comment, but leveled her gaze at him, knowing he would wonder why she had appeared.

"I came up here because Nelwyn has just gone back down into the encampment, and she is unhappy about something. She seems angry, Galador, and that does not happen without cause. I came to ask you about it." Her tone was neither accusing nor combative—she simply wanted to know. In that moment, as Galador looked into her artless face, he knew he had to tell her.

"Sit down, Gaelen, friend of my beloved, for I would reveal much to you."

Gaelen did so, and Galador told her everything of his thoughts and fears, of his frightening vision and his dread of Nelwyn's death beneath the mountain. He found her surprisingly easy to talk to, as she gave her full attention, and did not scoff at him or grow impatient. When he had finished, he took a deep breath and looked into her eyes. "Well, Gaelen, do you have any thoughts?"

In answer, she surprised him with a tentative embrace, for she had misjudged him.

"I'm so sorry, Galador, for my unworthy thoughts concerning you. I hope that you may forgive them—I just did not know. I will watch over Rogond. You must promise to watch over Nelwyn for me. You are a worthy companion and a stout friend. I hope we may see one another again in Tal-sithian, but if not, remember me as one who loves you and wishes you joy. You shall be as a brother to me." Then she broke her embrace, looking into his eyes once more.

"I truly am not descended of Aincor Fire-heart, you know. You think I cannot hear your comments to Rogond? It is really quite unseemly of you to keep suggesting it."

Galador smiled at her. "Of *course* you aren't," he said, in a sarcastic tone. This earned him a half-hearted punch to his upper arm, just before she turned to go. She couldn't resist one parting remark over her shoulder.

"If you ever want lessons in how to approach someone without making such a racket, ask either Nelwyn or myself. That skill is somewhat necessary to hunter-scouts in the Greatwood."

Galador chuckled at her, shaking his head. He was pleased with the outcome of this conversation, now assured that Nelwyn would accompany him to Tal-sithian and that he and Gaelen would be on much better terms from that point on. He was relieved, not knowing that the evil he feared beneath the mountain was moving toward them even now, and that Gaelen could prove to be its unwitting instrument.

Gorgon had been released from Tûr Dorcha and was now making his way back toward the mountains. He knew the way quite well. He also rejoiced to learn of his foes' intention to go deep into Cós-domhain, for at least some of those paths were fairly well known to him. It was immense, the greatest dwarf-realm that had ever been. The name meant "Deep Cavern," and it was an ancient and impressive excavation. Gorgon neither hated nor feared the dwarves, for he was clever and could avoid being seen if he wished. Yet he had no objection to killing them.

His tentative plan was to follow his enemies deep under the mountain, where he would hold the mastery, and then kill all save Gaelen. She would grieve for them, but in time she would seek out more of her kind, and he could then prey on them as well. With luck, she would return to Mountain-home. Then she would provide him with plenty of opportunity, as she would know when various Elves were leaving and where they were going. There were mighty Elves there, and he could almost taste of his coming victory over them.

Gorgon sat alone under the stars, his evening meal before him. He had worked up an appetite, and he tore enthusiastically into the raw flesh of the ewe he had strangled a short while ago. The meat was tough, but tasty. Gorgon relished raw flesh; this was a tendency he had inherited from his father. He stopped short of consuming the flesh of Ulcas or men, however, and as for Elves, other than occasionally tasting their blood out of curiosity, he left their ruined flesh untouched. Somewhat fastidious, he preferred fresh meat that he had killed himself, and he disliked scavenging. But he seldom went hungry, for it did not take much to sustain him. These were qualities of his mother's folk, though Elves did not eat raw meat of any sort unless desperate.

He wiped the blood of the ewe from his mouth and lay back upon the grass, flattening it beneath his tremendous weight. He thought to try the mirror again and view what was happening in Gaelen's world. Drawing it from a small pouch on his belt, he turned it over, admiring it in the starlight. The engraved golden cover glittered as he beheld it—it picked up nearly every trace of light and shot it back in every color imaginable. He cautioned himself not to look at it in full sunlight.

Carefully, he pressed the tiny pin that released the cover, flipping it open to reveal the magical surface of the glass. He looked into the misty grey depths, steeling himself against the pain that would follow. It slammed into his head like a bolt, and he squeezed his eyes closed, focusing hard on subduing it. Gradually, it subsided until he could bear it. He could hear voices inside his own head, speaking in Elven-tongues. They were speaking of plans to separate and go to Tal-sithian as well as to Cós Domhain. Gaelen and Rogond were still going under the mountains, and Gorgon could wait until later to pick off the others. Gorgon smiled as he listened to Galador's recounting of his terrifying vision of death beneath the mountain, imagining that it surely would not be as bad as the reality! But now the pain in Gorgon's head increased, nearly blinding him, and as Gaelen embraced Galador, and Gorgon beheld the disgusting sentiment they shared, his gorge rose and he looked away, lest the effort spent in obtaining his excellent meal should be in vain.

The day dawned with the arrival of grey, chilly weather that brought with it the promise of rain by mid-day. The Company had packed up their gear, and they were now sitting around the fire, cloaks wrapped about their shoulders, warming themselves. Which of them would now go beneath the mountain? Rogond and Gaelen would go with Fima; that much was certain, but the choice of Belegund and Thorndil remained unknown. Rogond had of course told them both of Galador's fears, and Gaelen hoped that at least one of them would go with Nelwyn. It might be somewhat difficult leading seven horses over the mountains, especially when one of them was Eros, who would be intent on following Rogond.

In the end, it was decided that Thorndil, the older and more experienced of the Tuathar, would go with Galador and Nelwyn, as he had walked in Cós-domhain before, but never in Tal-sithian. Belegund, who had not yet seen the great halls of the Deep-caverns, wished to go with Rogond despite Galador's warning.

The time had come to go separate ways. Nelwyn shivered as she sat astride her restive mount. She had already embraced Gaelen and Rogond, and even Fima, tears welling in her beautiful green eyes. Fima had blushed and muttered something about the overly emotional nature of Elves. Gaelen also had tears in her eyes for a moment, but she quelled them. Galador sat in stony silence upon Réalta; he alone had seen the vision of death in Cós-domhain, and he prayed that it would not come to pass. He looked hard into the eyes of his dearest friend.

"Farewell, Rogond. Keep safe and remain ever vigilant, as this journey you undertake is perilous. Safeguard my little sister, she who denies being of the House of Aincor." He looked sidelong at Gaelen and smiled as he said this, and she muttered something disparaging under her breath.

Rogond answered Galador: "It will not be the first time you have been wrong, Elf of Eádros! Take heart and remain watchful yourself, for your way is no less perilous. Thorndil—take care of these Elves for me, won't you?"

Thorndil nodded, raising his right hand in farewell. He turned his stout black horse toward the mountains, leading Eros. Nelwyn looked once more into Gaelen's eyes, then turned Gryffa and Siva to follow Thorndil. Galador remained for a moment longer, his expression grave. He nodded once more to Rogond, then turned Réalta, Belegund's chestnut horse, and the bay horse that bore their gear, and trotted off after Nelwyn. Galador prayed that he would see his friends again, even the dwarf, whom he had come to like and respect.

It would be a long and hard journey, for although winter's hold upon the mountains was well and truly broken, it would still require skill and a bit of luck to reach Tal-sithian. Galador was glad that Thorndil had chosen to accompany them, for he was worthy and was now out of harm's way. Belegund had made his choice even after knowing of Galador's grim vision. He was still fairly young, and his desire to see the Cavern-realm was great. Galador hoped he would not fall, as he was steadfast and quite likeable, with a ready sense of humor. As though sensing Galador's misgivings, the rain began to fall as they departed. Even the horses felt the melancholy that had settled over the now-divided Company, as they hung their heads and trotted away, with some reluctance, into the cold, damp gloom.

20

Cos-domhain

It took several days of careful going for Rogond, Gaelen, Belegund, and Fima to draw near the gates of Cós-domhain. They traveled along steep cliffs that rose straight up on both sides of a narrow footpath. There was no sign of activity anywhere.

"It would seem that this path has been well-used on a time, yet I see no sign of any gate or entrance," said Belegund. "Are we there yet?"

"No, my good Aridan," replied Fima. "But your concern is well taken. The eastern gates are difficult to find and nearly impossible to enter unless one knows the password. That password is well-known to me, do not fear!" Fima was obviously enjoying his role as trusted guide. They were approaching the underground realm from the east, where the way was little-known, rarely used, and kept in secret. The Great Gates on the western side were large, ornate and much easier to find, but they offered only limited access to the wonders within. Enemies would find little value in storming them. Fima laughed at Gaelen's worried expression.

"Don't fear, little one. You are in safe hands! The realm of Cós-domhain is a bright and hospitable place. You will be welcome, as you are in my company. No servant of Darkness is allowed to enter. We have never been deceived by Wrothgar nor by any of his minions, though he has tried through all his long years to win us over to his will. For this reason, because we resisted, he hates us."

"You're in good company there," said Gaelen. "Wrothgar has always hated the Elàni. For many an age have we warred with him."

"True enough," said Fima, "yet the Elàni have also formed partnerships with those who turned to the Darkness. My people never were favored with the presence of magic-users in our realms, and although we are thus considered less enlightened, it turned out to be a blessing in my opinion. Take Dardis, for example. He was perhaps the most beloved and skilled of all the Èolar, and my people still revere him. He wrought some of the most wondrous things ever seen in

Alterra—mirrors that could see the truth and tell enemy from friend, magical rings and blades, and even a shield that was said to be able to turn back the very fires of Wrothgar. He learned this craft from no less than three Asari. There was Léiras, the far-sighted, Baelta the bright, and Lord Kotos, whose name means power. Dardis was the maker of what has become the most powerful magical object known in Alterra, and that, of course, is the Stone of Léir. But Dardis was deceived by Kotos, and unwittingly by Baelta—only too late did he discover it. All of the Èolar were taken in, for they trusted the magic-users."

Fima shook his head. "The desire to know all things was the curse of the Èolar, and it was also the thing that doomed several of the Asari to Darkness. They were lured to Wrothgar with promises of answers to all mysteries, and once ensnared they could not escape. It is thought that Kotos alone survives among the Dark Asari, and he has lost much of his power, yet he is still a terrible and dangerous enemy. Dardis discovered the treachery of Kotos, and for that Kotos killed him. My people wept at his passing and never since have maintained friendship with the Elves, which is a pity. The downfall of the Èolar was a time of great sorrow."

Gaelen knew that Fima was well over two hundred years old, but not remotely old enough to have known many of the Èolar save those remaining in Monadh-talam. Still, she could not help but ask what he knew of the High Kings.

"Ah! Now THERE was an interesting and noble collection of Elves. There were only four, and all came to spectacular but bad endings." Fima could not conceal his admiration. "Yes, if you're going to throw your life away, do it with style. They didn't seem to have any sense of their own limits. Most notably so, of course, was Aincor Fire-heart. It was said that once he decided upon a course of action, nothing would sway him. Aincor was said to be of brilliant mind, but he allowed his passion to override his judgment one time too many, and as a result Wrothgar's forces nearly prevailed. When Aincor was killed, his elder son, Asgar, refused the throne. Instead, he supported his cousin, Aldamar of the Èolar."

"I thought the Èolar were supposed to be the wisest of all Elves," said Belegund, who had been drawn into the tale.

"They of all Elves held the greatest knowledge, but knowledge is a thing separate from wisdom," said Fima sadly. "The Dwarves, for example, are unenlightened according to the High-elves, and yet we have never been taken in by the Dark Power. This is a characteristic that we share with the Elves of the Greatwood." He winked at Gaelen.

"At any rate, Ri-Aldamar was said to be a wise and a good king, and he produced two sons named Iomar and Farahin. Iomar was heir to the throne, and he stayed with his father, but it was decided that Farahin should be sent to the Sanctuary to be educated. That, of course, is the great University founded by Shandor, who was said to be the mightiest and most noble of the Asari.

Ri-Aldamar thought Tal-elathas would withstand any onslaught, alas that he was misguided. It was indeed fortunate that Farahin was safe in the Sanctuary, for Iomar was lost in the Second Battle along with his father. Thus Farahin, the second-born, reluctantly took the mantle of High King and the name of Ri-Elathan. Yet he was as ill-fated as the rest of them, and his death was perhaps the most horrific of all."

"I have heard the stories," said Belegund. "It is said that he was killed in the Third Battle by Wrothgar's own hand. No Elf or man had ever before met Wrothgar directly, not in single combat." He shuddered as he thought of it. "That must have been terrible."

"Oh, I have no doubt of it," said Fima. "Wrothgar probably thought that, if he brought about the death of the King, the Elves would fall back in disarray and he would defeat them. So he commanded his Bödvari to surround Ri-Elathan such that none could interfere, and then engaged him. At the last, they fought hand-to-hand. Ri-Elathan was burned alive by the Black Flame as his power faded and his strength finally failed. He died in pain and despair, but that wasn't the worst of it."

"What could possibly be worse?" asked Belegund.

"It is said that the King had foreknowledge of his fate, that he knew he would die in agony," said Fima quietly. "He looked into the Stone of Léir before he went forth to battle, and Lord Shandor showed him his doom. Imagine having learned that you would face such a trial, knowing how it would end!"

"If he knew of it, why did he allow himself to be taken? Why did he not guard himself such that Wrothgar could not engage him?" asked Belegund, incredulous.

"It seems a fair question," replied Fima, "and I have a hard answer. He could not guard himself, because he knew that if he did not fulfill his destiny all would be lost. His sacrifice was not in vain—when he fell, the Elves were so enraged that they found their courage. They rose up and slew the Bödvari, and drove Wrothgar back into shadow where he still remains. At the same time, Belegund, your forefathers saw to the defeat of Kotos' vile armies as they tried to overwhelm Tuathas. Alduinar, your King, fought valiantly and survived the battle, but he was terribly grieved by the loss of Ri-Elathan, who was his friend."

Rogond, who had been following behind, overheard the mention of Ri-Elathan and had been horrified to hear Fima discussing the details of his undoubtedly agonizing death. He prayed that this was not the first time Gaelen had learned of them. He strode forward, silencing Fima with a hand on his shoulder, looking pointedly toward Gaelen. Fima was shocked to see that she fought back tears.

Suddenly she halted, eyes closed, as a great weakness came on her. She sat upon the ground as Rogond knelt beside her. Gaelen was quite vulnerable to reminders of Ri-Elathan's death, as she had felt some of his anguish as his spirit was torn from his body. Her sorrow had drained her strength for a moment, but she reassured Rogond that all would be well.

"Perhaps I need to rest for a brief while, and partake of some water," she said, as Rogond handed her his water-skin, then left her, drawing Fima aside so that, with luck, she would not hear.

"Do not speak of such things again, my friend. You have opened a wound that is old and deep. I beg you, do not mention Ri-Elathan in her presence again." Fima looked over at Gaelen, who sat with her back to them, her head resting on her arms, which were folded across her knees. Understanding dawned in his lined, intelligent face, and he looked at Rogond with wonder.

"You don't *mean* it! This concerns her Lost One, doesn't it?"

At this, Rogond looked at his hands, and would not look Fima in the eye. "Just leave it, Fima," he muttered without much hope that the dwarf would hear him.

"By Grundin's Beard! I had thought him to be a person of importance, but…I had no idea. The High King himself and our little Wood-elf?" Fima could hardly contain his excitement and babbled on for a few moments, to the dismay of Rogond.

"Of course, from what I know of Ri-Elathan, he would be just the type to be subject to giving his heart on first meeting at the directive of destiny. He was very passionate, I'm told. That explains so much that I have seen in the eyes of Magra, and of Ordath, and the way they react to Gaelen. Of course! Why had I not seen it before?" Then, his expression grew melancholy. "Alas! I would not have wished such a fate for anyone, let alone Gaelen. Such sorrow she must have known."

Rogond turned then and spoke sharply to Fima. "Hush! If she hears you, all is lost. I will neither confirm nor deny your speculation. But do not ever mention it again in front of her."

Fima grew solemn. "Of course, my friend. I surely did not mean to hurt her and will avoid doing so in future. But I am more concerned for *you* right now. Winning her love may be more difficult than I first predicted."

Then his weathered face brightened and he smiled at Rogond. "Never mind. You are up to the challenge…and she needs one such as you. I have complete confidence that you will prevail."

Gaelen had lifted her head and turned her sharp ears toward them. Rogond grew anxious.

"Be still, Fima! I will have no chance at all if you force my hand now, so for the love of Aontar, *hush!*"

He left Fima and returned to Gaelen, who appeared now to have mastered herself; her color had returned, and her eyes were dry. She rose and gave him back his water-skin, but as they continued on their way to finding the gate, she asked no more questions of Fima. In fact, she did not speak for several hours, until they reached at last the doorway of Cós-domhain.

It was indeed lucky that Fima knew where to find the gateway, because it could not be easily seen. "You will see it as it opens, but not before," said Fima. "Now, if you will forgive me, I must concentrate." He uttered a complex incantation in a tongue that none of the others had ever heard before, an ancient version of the dwarf-tongue that had not seen common usage in time out of mind. Fima struggled with it at first, and had to repeat himself once, but in the end two sentinels appeared atop the rocks, raising their hands in greeting. A rather small opening appeared in the very rock. They would have searched for an eternity and never found it.

"That's one of the cleverest illusions I've ever seen, Fima!" said Rogond as Fima stepped back, beaming at all of them.

"Actually, I could see the entrance clearly, but then, I knew where to look! The incantation is uttered merely to keep the guards from… ummm, from not opening the door."

"Ah. By that, you mean to keep them from shooting us?" said Gaelen.

"Not at all," Fima replied, his face reddening a little. "We aren't nearly as suspicious as we have been in the past, after all." He forced a small chuckle, and then extended a short, sturdy arm dramatically toward the rocky doorway. "Well, what are you waiting for? Enter and marvel at the Realm of the Rûmhar!"

Belegund, who was eager to see this great sight, entered first. Rogond then stepped through the great doors, looking back at Gaelen and beckoning to her. Still, she hesitated. There was something about this that she didn't like.

Fima came up behind her. "Go on, little Wood-elf. You shall be most welcome, I promise! Don't be afraid. Surely, you wouldn't wish to hurt my feelings?" That much was true. For Fima's sake, and for Rogond, she took a deep breath, squared her shoulders, and stepped through the doors into the greatest underground realm that had ever been.

It was three days since the Company had divided, and as Rogond, Fima, Belegund, and Gaelen arrived at the mountain gate, the others were making their way slowly toward the pass known as the Iolari, or "Way of Eagles". This was a steep and winding path between two very tall peaks to the west, which dropped down into the foothills and the valley beyond, wherein could be found the great lake known as the Linnefionn. The Elven-realm of Tal-sithian was located on an island in the midst of that lake.

There would still be snow in the upper elevations of the mountains, but with any luck the path would be mostly clear now, as the Iolari was considerably farther south than the High Pass they had attempted to take into Mountain-home earlier. Summer was approaching, and that meant there would be many swift, churning streams of snow-melt. Immersion in them would freeze the life from man or Elf in a few minutes. The other hazards of traversing the mountains lay in those inhabitants that lurked below ground during the daylight hours. Ulcas and Trolls were known to take the unwary, but they did not occur in large numbers due to the vigilance of the dwarves, whose realm was so vast that it easily encompassed the entire area beneath the pass.

One source of difficulty had come, not unexpectedly, from Eros. He was unhappy at being separated from Rogond and demonstrated this by stubbornly refusing to follow Thorndil, pulling and tugging at his long line and generally making matters difficult. Thorndil knew Eros well, but had not been treated to the complete demonstration of his displeasure before. It was difficult enough negotiating the tricky footing without being pulled off balance by over a thousand pounds of reluctant animal, and Thorndil's tolerance was wearing thin. Handing the two horses he was leading to Nelwyn, Galador dropped in behind them, and when Eros lagged and tried to pull Thorndil off balance, Galador drove Réalta forward, bowling into Eros from behind and startling him into leaping forward.

Eros shook his head at Galador and lashed his tail, daring the Elf to repeat *that* maneuver! In reply, Galador rode up beside him and swung a coil of rope at his hindquarters, slapping him with it. Réalta neatly dodged both of Eros' hind feet as the big dun lashed out at the irritating Galador, who then had the unbridled temerity to laugh at him.

"Get along, now, Eros, and stop your playing! You cannot follow Rogond; you must await him on the western side of the mountains. I shall tan your backside if you do not behave!" To reinforce this point, he slapped Eros again with the rope. "Go ON, now! Don't try my patience." If Eros could have grumbled, he would have done so. As it was he sulked along, plotting his next opportunity to escape and return to Rogond.

"You have my thanks, Galador, for setting him upon the straight path. I thought he was going to pull me over once or twice. He seems much more cooperative now," said Thorndil.

"Yes, it would seem so. But I would not trust him...he is biding his time. Watch him carefully!" With that admonition, Galador turned and made his way back to where Nelwyn waited with the other three horses. Galador took hold of the lines again, and they set off.

In time, they stopped for the night. They would light no watch-fires, as their enemies would be drawn to them, so they sheltered under an overhang of rock that made an excellent vantage point for the watch. The horses were hungry, for there was not much grazing to be had, but at their current pace it would take only a few days to reach the western valley, where there was grass aplenty. The horses would survive until then, as at least there was plenty of water. They picketed the horses to keep them from roaming and shared some of the provisions they had brought from Mountain-home.

Thorndil slept as Nelwyn and Galador sat atop the rock shelf, each taking turns resting while the other kept the watch. At times they would talk quietly together, but they were weary from the long day's ride. The path was treacherous; sometimes it seemed to disappear altogether, and sometimes it wound along the mountainside with heart-stopping drops on one side. At such times the horses were led in single file, tied head to tail, and Eros forgot all about escaping Thorndil, concentrating on the task before him like the sensible, sane animal he generally was.

At present, the sensible, sane animal was working diligently at freeing himself from the picket line. Thorndil had secured him with a difficult knot and had double-secured him with two lines about his neck, but there weren't many knots that Eros could not undo when he applied himself. He was gifted with great dexterity, and he used this gift in such mischief as breaking into Rogond's food stores and helping himself to the dried fruit that was usually found there. Rogond had thwarted the horse in the past by placing several dried apples stuffed with ground red pepper in the food sack, then turning a blind eye as his wayward animal broke into them, receiving a valuable lesson. This resulted in Eros' developing an uncanny knack for detecting dried fruits that were stuffed with pepper and thenceforth avoiding them.

Now, as Eros worked the second knot loose, he considered his choices. In a few moments he would be free to go where he would. And though he did not relish the thought of traveling the mountains at night by himself, he truly did want to get back to Rogond. Besides, Galador had thrown the gauntlet in his face, slapping him from behind like a common mule! He would show that Elf a few things. The memory of the indignity inflicted on him by Galador decided him, and he walked quietly from behind the picket line, ducking his head under and lifting it so that he could proceed back down the path the way he had come.

Nelwyn, who kept the watch, heard his quiet footfalls, though he trod quite softly indeed. Then, all the horses began nickering after him, especially Réalta, who nearly always wanted to follow Eros into mischief, but was not as adept at untying himself. Suspicious, Nelwyn roused Galador from his rest, and they both rose to their feet and peered into the darkness, just in time to observe the light golden body of Eros disappearing back toward the east.

Cursing, Galador leaped down from the rock shelf, grabbed Réalta, and swung onto his back. Eros heard the galloping feet of his pursuer, and the chase was on!

It was fortunate that both Elves and horses see as well in the dark, as the mountain pass was difficult enough in the daylight! Eros ran swiftly along, leaping over stones and gaps in the path, followed closely by Réalta, who thankfully was the swifter, even carrying a rider. Galador held his breath several times as the trail dropped away beneath him and Réalta leaped into the night; his life was literally hanging on the agility and sure-footedness of his mount. If he could keep up with Eros long enough to reach the point where the path widened, he could get alongside him and catch hold of him. Then he and Réalta would drive Eros into the cliff-face, halting him.

Without warning, Eros slammed to a stop, wheeled about and charged back up the path, nearly barreling into Réalta. Galador came very close to flying over his mount's head, sitting astride his neck before pushing himself back into proper position. He spat an oath at Eros, who was now fighting to get past him on the narrow trail. A loud bellow from behind Eros told the tale—a huge mountain-troll was striding purposefully toward them. Galador was in no position to engage it, as he had only his sword, and even if he had brought his longbow, it would have been of limited use. Trolls are nearly impossible to kill, as they are vulnerable only in the eyes and through the mouth. In the dark, on a moving horse, such a shot would be difficult at best.

Trolls are tireless, but fortunately, they are not swift. Galador caught hold of Eros' lines as he tried to crowd past, then turned Réalta and galloped back up the trail with the troll in pursuit. Drawing near to their encampment, Galador looked back over his shoulder, and was dismayed to see that, though it was far outdistanced, the troll still followed. Galador called out a warning to Nelwyn and Thorndil, and then galloped under the rock shelf to find them arming themselves and releasing the horses, preparing to ride. The troll's heavy feet could now be heard taking great, slow strides; it would be upon them in a few moments.

"Hoist me up, Galador," said Nelwyn, grabbing her longbow. Galador knew he did not have time to argue, and taking Nelwyn's left foot in his hand he tossed her up onto the rock shelf, where she knelt, drew an arrow, and bent her bow.

The troll caught sight of its quarry and dropped into a low, crouching run. It was charging them, intending on crushing them with its great arms. The horses cried in terror and backed into the wall as Thorndil and Galador struggled to control them.

Nelwyn peered into the darkness, drawing the powerful bow back to the limit of her strength. Then, holding her breath and praying, she released it. The shaft flew straight to its mark, burying itself in the troll's tiny left eye. It pitched forward, dead before it hit the ground, churning up the rock with its heavy body. It nearly slid into the frightened horses and their caretakers. Had it done so, it would have crushed them, but thankfully it ground to a halt before doing any real damage.

Nelwyn exhaled, her knees weak and shaky, and sat down upon the rock. Galador and Thorndil were still occupied with calming and subduing the horses, who seemed to know that they had just come perilously close to becoming provender for a troll's larder. Galador cast a jaundiced eye at Eros, who stood quietly without restraint as though truly repentant.

"Now, you nearly worthless animal, see what you have done! Do not try my patience again! If you ever even consider such a course I will forget that Rogond actually likes you. He will find another mount, believe me!"

Eros was humbled and nickered softly at Galador, then tried to approach Thorndil, who shunned him as well. "Don't try to appease me, Eros. You know Galador is right. Behave yourself from now on and prove that you're still worthy. We will find Rogond again."

Eros looked so forlorn that Thorndil took pity on him. "Don't worry, you will regain favor soon enough. Rogond's faith in you is well placed, but sometimes you allow your loyalty to get in the way of your judgment." Eros nuzzled Thorndil's sleeve and was rewarded with a pat on the neck.

Galador had climbed up to congratulate Nelwyn, and witnessed Thorndil's kind-hearted treatment of Eros. "So now you *reward* him? I would prefer to tie his head to his tail for a few hours. Worthless animal!" He chuckled in spite of himself. "He nearly succeeded in his escape plan. I am quite glad that I do not have to tell Rogond that his favorite mount was eaten by a troll. He is quite fond of the scoundrel. Why that is so, I cannot imagine!"

But in truth, Galador had no trouble imagining it. When he was with Rogond, Eros was one of the finest, steadiest animals alive. Rogond had ridden him into battle, where he seemed to have an innate sense of what to do and how to do it. He had saved Rogond's life several times, and he was courageous and steadfast. Galador knew that his friend's trust in Eros was well deserved.

The stench coming from the dead troll was incredible, so they elected to move some distance before once again settling down until dawn. They found a good, wide semicircle in the rock that would be perfect for sheltering. The wind was rising and they could smell rain on the air. It would probably roll in before dawn, so best to take rest while they could.

The ordeal with Eros and the troll had tired Galador, and he sat with Nelwyn as Thorndil took the watch. As he looked back toward the west, where the weather was building, he wondered how their friends were faring. They had most likely reached the Gateway by now. Galador fixed his eyes on the heavens, imagining the stars shining there, and entered the realm of waking dreams, where Elves regain their strength in time of weariness. After a few moments, his thoughts moved in a very unpleasant direction, drifting…drifting…

…Galador looked for the last time into the eyes of Rogond as his friend died in his arms. There were signs of struggle all around them, but Rogond had been bested, run through with a formidable blade, and was now bleeding to death. Galador had come too late to aid him. Galador called his friend's name, and Rogond roused himself, his grey eyes focusing with some effort. He beheld Galador, whereupon his brow furrowed with exertion as he breathed a final, single word—*Gorgon*. Then he died, his body at first going rigid in Galador's arms, then limp and lifeless, his eyes staring unfocused and sightless, his last breath rattling in his throat. Galador could not weep, but set his friend's body down gently, a sudden sense of panic and urgency gripping him: he had to find Nelwyn!

He tracked the bloody footprints leading from Rogond's body down a dark corridor that seemed to go on forever, until he beheld a dim glow in the distance. Running recklessly now, he flew toward it, turning to his left into a large underground chamber to behold a horrifying sight. There was blood everywhere—Elven blood. Nelwyn was lying in a crumpled heap in the center of the floor, and she was covered with it. Gaelen knelt beside her, her back turned toward Galador, who cried Nelwyn's name in horror. He could not move toward her—it was as though his feet were rooted to the floor. He called to Gaelen through his panic, tears flowing from his eyes. Nelwyn's head was turned such that he could not see her pale face. Gaelen's left hand was bloody, entangled in Nelwyn's hair. Was she bent with weeping?

"Gaelen…Gaelen! Does Nelwyn live? Does she still live? *Gaelen!*"

Slowly Gaelen rose to her feet, her hand still gripping Nelwyn's long, golden hair. As she turned, to Galador's horror, she tightened her grip and lifted her arm. Galador moaned as Nelwyn's head came away from her body; it had been severed by the same blade that had killed Rogond. Gaelen looked up at Galador then, confusion in her hazel-green eyes.

Then her eyes rolled back into her head, and when they reappeared they were pale, nearly colorless, with tiny pinpricks of black at the center, and full of malice. She chuckled in a voice other than her own.

"Does Nelwyn live? No, my 'brother'. I think not!"

Galador wanted to cry out in horror, but he could not; his strength had left him. Gaelen started toward him, now laughing in Gorgon's voice, and he knew no more…

"Galador…Galador? Come back to me, my love. It's all right… come back!"

Galador jerked upright with a sharp intake of breath. He was sweat-soaked, pale, and trembling. "Calm yourself, my beloved. It's all right," Nelwyn's soothing voice reached out to him in his terror. He opened his eyes and beheld her, then pulled her to him, enfolding her in his arms, shaking and silent. His hair and tunic were wet with sweat, and he clutched her so tightly that breathing was difficult. She endured his embrace, fearing for him, and spoke words of comfort until he finally mastered himself and relaxed his hold on her. She looked into his eyes and reached up to stroke his damp hair as he drew slow, deep breaths. His trembling stopped.

"What happened? You were crying and calling my name. What has so terrified you?"

Galador's vision was so horrible that he was unable to speak of it. "I…I cannot say. Please don't press me about it…I could not bear to relive it. I must try to wipe it from my mind; otherwise it will torment me. Please understand."

Nelwyn nodded, but she was afraid. She knew that Galador's vision had concerned her—he had been calling her name. She settled back against the moss-covered boulder she had been sheltering behind, pulling him down to lie against her breast. His breathing had slowed, but there was a tension in his body that she didn't like. She tried to relax, to show him there was nothing to fear, but she could not. The premonition she had while in Mountain-home still troubled her. Was Galador's much the same?

Nelwyn sighed and stroked his hair, looking up at the clouded night sky. No stars to comfort them tonight. As Nelwyn thought of the stars, her thoughts turned to Gaelen and Rogond, who would not see the stars for a long while.

Galador's dream had wearied him, and though he rested at last, the tension never entirely left him. He struggled to rid himself of the sight of Gaelen, pale malicious eyes gleaming, speaking in Gorgon's voice and clutching Nelwyn's hair in her bloodied hand. He did not understand—Gaelen loved Nelwyn more than did anyone save himself, and would never harm her. Why Gorgon's eyes and voice? That question would remain to trouble him for a long time after.

Rogond, who was still very much alive, reflected that he had never seen Fima so elated as he led them through the passageways of the underground realm of Cós-domhain. Fima still appeared to know his way around, even though he had not seen the inside of the mountains for a very long time. This place was so vast and complex that even one living there might conceivably lose himself in the maze of passages, chambers, halls, and stairways. Belegund walked beside Fima, who led their small party. Rogond walked behind with Gaelen. She was wary, looking and listening all around her, though she was truly impressed with the intricacies of this enormous excavation. Fima stressed that they had seen nothing as yet; the Great Halls were at least two days' journey away.

As Fima had promised, the passageways were well lighted by means of torches and cleverly placed shafts and mirrors that reflected and magnified light from the surface, as well as many of the blue Elven lamps. These cheered Gaelen, as they reminded her that these folk had once been great friends of the Èolarin Elves. The four of them made their way along corridors and climbed endless, wide stairs, meeting dwarves as they went. Each time, the dwarves acknowledged Fima. Some appeared quite happy to see him, greeting him enthusiastically and welcoming the visitors, but they all looked somewhat sidelong at Gaelen.

It was no mystery when dwarves approached either from the front or from behind, as they are not remotely stealthy, and the corridors were frequently alive with echoing voices. Gaelen took some comfort in this, as she did not need to worry about being taken unaware. She still did not relax, as more than one hand strayed to an axe-handle upon beholding her. This hostility did not extend beyond her introduction by Fima, however, and the dwarves then greeted her almost warmly, removing their hoods and bowing in a humble display that she politely returned.

One stout fellow in a green jacket bowed before her, and, to her surprise, addressed her in rather stilted High-elven speech: "Hail, Gaelen of the Greatwood. Thy presence honors us, though many will not know it. I shall hope to converse further with thee on a time, if thou art remaining among us?"

Gaelen kept her tone serious as she replied to him: "Alas, we are but passing through this great realm, O worthy Disciple of Fior. Yet we may speak awhile, as I deem we will be here for at least a few days' time. I shall look forward to conversing with one who speaks our tongue so well." The dwarf bowed low and took his leave, pausing once to look back over his shoulder at Gaelen.

Fima muttered to Belegund, "That's just old Tibo. He loves Elves. He'll be a bit disappointed when he learns that our Gaelen is a Wood-elf, and not of the Èolar, though I cannot imagine anyone being truly disappointed in her." He turned back and smiled. "Well, my little Wood-elf, have you found your confidence in my realm? What is your impression thus far?"

"Truly, it is impressive beyond my estimation, Fima. I shall be most eager to see the Great Halls. And your people are, for the most part, accepting of my presence here, though I sense were we not with you, things might be different."

Fima nodded. "Of that there is little doubt. Were it not for me, you would have been brought before the Council of Elders in bonds until we learned of your business. As it is, I expect a delegation to meet us directly. Then, you shall taste of our hospitality in full!" He gave a hearty laugh and rubbed his hands together in anticipation of good times to come.

Gaelen had heard of dwarvish hospitality while in Mountainhome. Dwarves were earthy folk, and they delighted in such pleasures as feasting and drinking, dancing and even singing, though their song was much different from that of the Elves. She knew that both Fima and Rogond were hoping she would sing for their hosts, as the dwarves would have rarely heard such song.

Fima's prediction proved true a short while later as a delegation of rather impressive-looking dwarves met them at the junction of two passageways. They were immaculate compared with Fima, who was somewhat travel worn, but they greeted him with great respect. They wore many beautiful ornaments of gold, and their tunics and cloaks were of finest make in various splendid colors. After introducing themselves, they escorted Fima and his guests to a large, well-appointed chamber where they could wash, change, eat and drink. It would take another day to journey to the Great Halls, where the Council of Elders would receive them and hear their tale. Fima was well known to them, and they were always hungry for news of the wide world.

Rogond rejoiced, as surely these great persons could tell him where Farin, the smith who had known his mother, might be found. Thus he waited patiently, though Gaelen could see that he was anxious.

The Company settled back on their soft beds, all except Gaelen, who stalked quietly up and down the floor. She did not like being closed in underground and would take no rest. Rogond and Belegund had some difficulty, as the beds, though designed for guests, were still too short for their tall frames. Their feet hung over the edge a little, but they were comfortable, especially after a couple of meat pies and two flagons of beer each.

"Gaelen...would you please stop pacing? You're making me nervous," said Fima, who could not understand why anyone should be uncomfortable in such eminently hospitable surroundings.

Rogond raised himself up and called to her outside Fima's hearing. "Come and sit with me awhile and be content, for I will tell you a tale. I know this place isn't to your liking, but we will be here for only a few days. Please, come and sit with me."

Gaelen did so, and Rogond settled her back upon the bed beside him, lying with her head upon his chest. He could feel the tension in her body, and reaching around the back of her head he took one of her ears in his hand and gently began massaging it. At first she resisted his attentions, but he reassured her. After a few moments, she sagged into a completely relaxed state, her eyes half closed, all interest in hearing tales forgotten.

"Where did you learn such a thing as that?" asked Fima, quite fascinated with the action of Rogond's fingers on Gaelen's ear and her reaction to it.

"In Mountain-home," Rogond replied as Gaelen stretched her lithe form in contentment. If she had been a cat, she would have been purring loudly. "This comes in handy on a time when you must quiet or comfort someone. It is especially valuable when they are stressed or in pain." He turned to Gaelen. "You're not in any pain, are you, my friend?"

Gaelen stretched out again beside him, then spoke in a languid, drowsy voice: "Oh, yes, Tuathan. I am in considerable pain. I think you had better not stop doing that for a while."

Rogond smiled, and the time passed more pleasantly. He treasured the feel of her warmth and vitality as she lay beside him, and he did not sleep, for he did not want to miss a single moment of it.

Tibo could not remember having been so excited in recent memory. It was so rare that any of the Elàni came into this realm, and it was rarer still that he happened to encounter them. The She-elf had promised to speak with him later, and this pleased him, as he loved Elves and Elven lore. He loved especially the language of the Èolar, which he had taught himself after a fashion, and if he did say so, his High-elven wasn't too bad. The She-elf had responded politely and appropriately to it, at any rate. Many of his folk thought his desire to know and interact with Elves was strange, yet he would do so whenever the opportunity arose. Now he was looking forward to a nice, long conversation with Gaelen. She had been so courteous to him! She even called him a "Worthy Disciple of Fior," and had said that she looked forward to conversing with him.

He bustled down the passageway, having promised to meet his friends later. He would now go and put on his finest garments, then find where Gaelen was being kept so that perhaps he might speak with her awhile. As he drew near the intersection of two passageways, he heard a deep voice speaking softly in Èolarin Elvish. He stopped and listened, entranced for a moment, as the deep voice was actually addressing him.

"Ah, Tibo of Cós-domhain, at last we meet. Thy name is known to us, as is thy love of our people. The She-elf you met, though worthy enough, is but a Wood-elf of the Sylvan folk, whereas I am of the Èolar." (Regrettably, this was true.) "Come to me and we will speak of all the old tales. I shall delight in conversing with one such as thou, who speaks my tongue so fluently. I will await thee—follow my voice and all shall be revealed."

Tibo could hardly believe his good fortune. The deep, enchanting voice, speaking such beautiful words, held him in thrall. He followed it to the end of the corridor, stopping as he heard the voice again from the shadows.

"Well met, Tibo of Grundin's Realm. How fortunate that thou lovest the tongue of the Èolar, as it will be the last sound in thy hearing." Tibo did not yet grasp the impact of these words, but he briefly beheld the shadowy figure as it emerged from the darkness, wielding a glittering blade that neatly severed his astonished head from his neck. The beautiful words of the Elven-speech may have been the last in Tibo's hearing, but his last sight was horrifying, and definitely anything but Elven.

Gorgon tended the body of the dwarf, intending to take it along, as he had a use for it. It would probably keep fairly well, as it was cool in the deeps, and the flesh of dwarves decays but slowly, returning at last to the earth from which it was originally formed. Gorgon knew little of dwarvish history or myth, and he was really not interested in learning more. He needed to concern himself with the considerable difficulty he would find himself in should he arouse their wrath, and he would have to go about his business with discretion.

Gorgon had learned that the Company was expected to stand before the Council of Elders and might possibly be brought before Lord Grundin himself, although Fima had intimated that this was not likely. Although Grundin got along reasonably well with friendly visitors, he cared little for news of the outside world that did not directly concern his own realm.

For the time being, Gorgon would content himself with waylaying and killing one of the Company before they emerged from the West Gate in a few days. He settled on Belegund, because he wanted to be free to torture and kill Rogond at his leisure, not when he was in danger of arousing the dwarves. He would leave Belegund and Tibo for the rest of them to find, by which time he would be long gone. He could go as far away as he wished, because his wondrous mirror would allow him to find and rejoin his prey at a time of his choosing. He was not in any particular hurry now that he held the upper hand, and he thought briefly about killing Fima, the old dwarf, as he was a friend to both the She-elf and the Aridan. But Fima was also in great favor with the dwarves of this realm, and Gorgon was unwilling to risk arousing their vengeful natures.

Gorgon would move toward the West Gate, taking paths little used by the dwarves, until he became aware that the Company was preparing to leave. Then he would strike. In one of his brief encounters with his mirror, Gorgon had learned that Belegund had been warned against going into Cós-domhain, yet had chosen to do so because he so desired to see the great realm for himself. Gorgon smiled and shook his head. "Enjoy the sight while you may, Aridan. The warning you were given will prove true ere long. I shall look forward to our meeting." Slinging Tibo over his shoulder, he made his way silently and with great caution, lest he be discovered before he could put his plans into motion.

None of the Company save Fima had walked in the depths of Cós-domhain before. In fact, only Galador had seen the wonders of which dwarves are capable, as they had a hand in the creation of the Elf-realms of Eádros and Tal-elathas. Both of these great realms were now lost, but Galador remembered Eádros well, with its beautiful, majestic halls full of bright fountains and magnificent carvings. He had been polite enough in the halls of Ri-Aruin in the Greatwood, for it was plain that the Woodland King desired an underground realm to rival those that were lost, but the comparison was not favorable.

The difference between Eádros and the Sylvan Elves' unsuccessful attempt to re-create it was, in a word, dwarves. The Cúinar had not the skills of the Rûmhar to aid them.

Gaelen was awed beyond words at the sights before her. She had not spoken since they had resumed their progress toward the Great Halls, though she would stop occasionally and examine some glittering crystal or vein of bright metal twisting along the living rock of the walls. At such times Fima would approach her, identifying the substance so that she would know its name, and she would nod in silence as she committed it to memory.

Belegund, on the other hand, was anything but silent. He wanted to know how the dwarves had constructed the excavation without burying themselves, how they achieved such symmetry and smoothness of design, how they cut the rock to form bridges that spanned deep chasms, how they caught so much of the light, and so on. Fima put a hand to his brow.

"Please, my good Belegund! You are making me weary with your constant questions, which I have neither the time nor inclination to explain. Just remember that these walls were excavated over a vast span of time, and not all at once! We had the greatest smiths, masons and excavators at our service, including not a few Elves, though I'm certain they learned more of us than we gained from them. They were better at creating ornamental things, some of which you shall soon see. They did invent these lights, which are quite useful."

He indicated the blue lamps, placed strategically to catch and return light diverted down from the surface, along with that of the ever-present torches, thus the passage was quite adequately bright.

Gaelen normally did not fear heights, as she spent considerable time in the tops of very tall trees, but she became quite dizzy looking down into some of the deep chasms, where the blackness was so vast it seemed bottomless. She swayed a little on one of the narrow bridges, and Fima steadied her.

"Easy, my little Wood-elf. Best not to look too deeply, as you will not be able to find the bottom, and it can make you giddy. Your folk are unused to such sights."

That was true enough. Rogond, who walked behind the two dwarves sent to conduct them to the Council, dropped back beside

Fima and Gaelen. He too was ill-at-ease with some of the narrow going over such black depths.

"I have heard of a black passage to the West Gate that is so narrow that only one may move through at a time," he said to Fima in a worried tone. "Is there no other way out?" Fima shook his head. "Such devices are common in dwarf-realms. It's nearly impossible to evade our archers; no enemy attempting to invade from the west has ever been successful largely due to the existence of that passage. It's barely tall enough for a dwarf, and it's the only way in here, if one can even find it!" Here, he smiled up at Rogond. "You see, my very tall friend, there are some advantages to being made closer to the ground."

Rogond shuddered a little at the thought of the narrow passage, which he would most likely have to take on his hands and knees.

They stopped twice to refresh themselves, eating and drinking and chatting with the ever-present dwarves. They were everywhere, and Gaelen was greeted with reasonable courtesy, though a few could not conceal their mistrust. Gaelen turned to Fima. "Why do they look at me thus? They are not of Rûmm, and I am not of Eádros. What ill have my people done them? I am in good company, and obviously not a prisoner in shackles. It hurts me to see the look in their eyes, as though they would push me into the deeps if they had half the chance."

To this Fima replied, "And how have your people looked upon my folk when they have strayed across your borders? Honestly, now…"

Gaelen was silent for a few moments. "Dwarves cut healthy trees for no good reason, and they do not respect the forest, which we are sworn to protect. Our races have so little in common that it is difficult to understand each other. The Èolar were friends of the dwarves, but only because they delighted in smith work and the making of things by craft. In all other matters, they were apart."

Fima nodded wisely. "Yes, and don't think the Elves did not constantly remind them of this. I have lived many years in Monadhtalam, Gaelen, and I see the way your folk look upon one such as myself. Even I, who have earned the respect of Lady Ordath herself, must occasionally endure the condescending attitudes held by some of the very tall folk of that realm. I have done nothing to earn their scorn, except be what I am. You are different, Gaelen, as you do not equate your ideal of beauty with worth. Many cannot say as much."

Gaelen continued to walk beside Fima in silence. She knew that he was right about the superior attitudes held by some of her people; she had endured them herself. In Mountain-home the whispers and quick looks of disdain had not gone unnoticed. There were those who could not imagine why Magra would even acknowledge one such as Gaelen, and they had made this opinion known. Gaelen had no difficulty dealing with them, as she was quite sure of herself and cared not for the opinions of those who judge others using only those characters visible to the eye. There were many evil souls that wore a fair semblance.

She considered Fima for a moment. He was true of heart and ready of mind, with a marvelous sense of humor. She truly liked him and would rather have had him at her side than many who were considered beautiful. Rather abruptly, she told him so.

He smiled at her. "But, I *am* beautiful, Gaelen. Did you not realize it? It is your people who are lacking. Not even a whisker on any of them!"

Rogond, who had overheard much of their conversation, smiled to himself. Gaelen was learning some lessons from kindly professor Fima; she would take a different view of the dwarves ever after.

"Ah! Wait a moment, this is something worth seeing," said Fima, calling the guides to a halt. He led them down a wide passage to the left, where Gaelen could hear the rushing and splashing of water ahead. They entered a spacious cavern, in the center of which a sparkling, bubbling jet of crystal clear, cold water rose from the very floor to cascade down among the stones, which were as smooth as glass. The blue light that illuminated the cavern was caught by the bright waters of this marvelous fountain, and was then sent back in spangles and rippling waves upon the walls. Gaelen saw huge crystals, some clear, some milky white, growing and glittering from nearly every surface. She was breathless, as were Belegund and Rogond. What a magical realm indeed!

She hated to leave the cavern, but they needed to continue their journey. Fima insisted that they all partake of the waters of the fountain, which they found to be among the purest and sweetest they had ever tasted. Gaelen cast one longing look back over her shoulder as they departed, for she loved flowing waters and would have remained awhile. They saw many wonderful and strange sights on their way to the Council of Elders, but Gaelen would always remember that chamber with its cold, clear waters and fabulous glittering walls. The ornamental lamp hung from the vaulted roof was an outstanding example of the beauty that results from the combined skills of the Èolar and the Rûmhar. It was immense, wrought and engraved with images of mighty Dwarf-lords, combined with the emblems of the great High-elven realms. Here were the Stars and-Sunburst of the Èolar, and the White Flame of Monadh-talam, as well as the single bright Star of the Eádram.

At long last they entered the Great Halls of Cós-domhain, which were so immense and impressive that they said not a word, but walked in silent awe among the bustling dwarves until they were brought before the Council of Elders. Seven of the very wisest of the folk of Grundin's realm regarded them importantly from heavily carved oaken chairs, set upon a raised platform hung with tapestries. Their eyes were bright in their weathered faces, their beards were immaculate, and they were richly dressed. Chief among them was a dwarf named Ular, who rose to his feet and bowed.

Rogond and Company bowed as well, as Fima stepped forward, introducing his companions as Rogond and Belegund of the Tuathar, and Gaelen Taldin of the Greatwood Realm. Ular gave a warm welcome to Fima, who had once been a member of the Council himself, but had left it for other pursuits. It had been nearly fifty years since he had seen the inside of Cós-domhain, as he found Mountain-home a better place to indulge his considerable curiosity, exchanging ideas and lore with learned representatives of many races. Still, it was good to be home again, among his own folk.

Ular asked Fima why Rogond and his companions had come, and Fima gestured to Rogond, directing him to stand beside him and tell his tale. Rogond did so, at least the important points of it, emphasizing the encounter with Glomin and the revealing of the message contained within his mother's ring.

"I have come seeking Farin, the maker of the ring, in the hope that I may learn more of my origins. Much have I learned already from Glomin that I thought never to know…it is of great importance to me to hear all that may be told."

The Elders nodded in understanding. To a dwarf, as to an Elf or a man, heritage is important.

"Why bring the Elf? What is her purpose in this quest?" asked a stern-faced dwarf sitting to the left of Ular. His name was Nimo, and he wore a brooch fashioned with the emblem of the lost city of Rûmm.

"She is my friend and companion, and hoped to find welcome here," replied Rogond, but Nimo held up his hand to silence him.

"I would hear from her, Tuathan. Speak, Elf, and tell me why you have come and what you hope to gain from your entry into our domain."

Gaelen lifted her chin and met Nimo's gaze, as Fima interceded. "She is simply traveling with us, as Rogond has indicated. She comes with my friendship as well. I have found her to be trustworthy and steadfast." He glanced at Gaelen and smiled. "She is a true and fine friend. Surely you do not wish to have her doubt our hospitality and reinforce the unfortunate mistrust that so often exists between us."

Nimo was undaunted by Fima's words. "Be silent, Lore-master of Ordath, for you no longer sit upon this Council. You have never understood the enmity between my ancestors and theirs. You have gone soft in the Mountain-realm, exposed to their influence, and have been beguiled. I would not expect you to be wary of them now. Let me hear from her!"

At this Fima bristled, and his hand strayed to his axe. His voice was low and menacing, with none of its usual gentle patience, as he spoke. "You dare to suggest that I forget my origins, while I merely point out that blaming the She-elf for the troubles of the Dwarves of Rûmm is inappropriate and wrong? My feet are firmly rooted in the rock, Nimo, and my heart burns fierce right now. Have a care."

The other dwarves remained motionless, appearing impassive. This was between Fima and Nimo, and none would interfere. Things might have gone ill had Gaelen not chosen that moment to speak. She used the High-elven tongue, reminding the dwarves of the friendship they had once held with the Èolar. Her clear voice rang through the vastness of the huge hall, where once many such voices were heard, though not in the reckoning of any then assembled.

"O Ye Children of Fior, who is revered by both thy people and mine, hear what I have to say. I came here willingly that I might gaze upon the greatness of Cós-domhain, for I am of the Woodland, and know of it only through tales that have truly understated its grandeur. Never have my eyes beheld such wonders. Wouldst thou deny me the chance for such enlightenment? I have received warm welcome from thy folk, and understand thy trepidation, though I was long unborn when the War of Betrayal estranged our peoples."

At this the dwarves muttered among themselves; hundreds of voices could be heard, but one rose above the others. Noli stepped forward, asking to be heard. He spoke of his encounter with Rogond and his three companions upon the Great Dwarf Road, and told that they had been caught stealing by his and Dwim's folk. Rogond bristled.

"*Not* stealing! We left more than adequate payment. Surely the dragon-brooch was sufficient for a little food and a few torches to lost travelers wandering hungry in the dark."

Noli seemed not to hear, but looked directly at Nimo, who was in fact his cousin. "I do not forget the fate of the Great Smiths of Rûmm so easily. At least one of the Elves was of Eádros—did you think I would not hear it in his voice? We spared the three of them only because of the Tuathan, who at the time seemed burdened with the task of conducting them and had little praise for them."

"We are in the Realm of Grundin, not in Rûmm," said Gaelen, who was sincerely tired of Noli, and struggled to hold her temper as she remembered her ill treatment at his hands. "We suffered your hostility when we had done little to earn it. Will the folk of Grundin thus fail in their hospitality to one who has come seeking only enlightenment? I came willingly, and do humbly ask your pardon for any insult I or my folk have caused. Fima has called me 'friend', and I would fall defending him. At least allow me the chance to prove my worth. I mean no harm. Besides, I would learn from the descendants of Rûmm, as well as from Grundin's folk. Will you not share with one who knows so little?" This request, made with such apparent humility, seemed reasonable to the Council, but Nimo remained stern.

Noli glowered at Gaelen. "If you think you can beg my pardon, Elf, for such grievous wrongs, then think longer and harder. You cannot escape the misdeeds of your ancestors. I will teach you something of our way, as you have asked, and it is this: our memories are long and our pardon difficult to obtain. We do not forget the wrongs of the past, even as you do not. My trust you will never earn."

Then a new voice, deep and powerful and old as the mountain, rose again amid a somewhat uncomfortable silence. They turned to regard Grundin himself, who stood above them upon a ledge that flanked his private chamber, from which he could attend to the business of the Council if he so wished. He was magnificent. Gaelen beheld in his eyes the same regal bearing and wisdom she had seen in those of the High King and Lord Magra.

"Peace, Noli," said Grundin. "Though the Council understands the grudge you bear, we will not permit you to deny welcome to this Elf, who has herself done nothing to your folk, or to ours. Payment for the provisions was left, and this man is Dwarf-friend, and therefore entitled. She is his companion, and is a friend of Fima. You will not deny her the welcome of Cós-domhain." He turned to Gaelen. "Worthy Elf, your words are well chosen. Walk freely in my realm as did your folk of old." With that, he turned and left them, and there would be no disagreement, not even from the descendants of Rûmm.

The Company was now officially made welcome by Grundin's folk, and Rogond drew Gaelen aside, whispering quietly in her ear. "Well spoken! Perhaps you are not of Aincor's house after all."

But both Gaelen and Fima were still troubled. They had seen the enmity in the eyes of both Noli and Nimo, and knew that despite what Grundin had proclaimed, she was not welcome in the hearts of some of the folk of the Cavern-realm. Nor would she ever be.

The next few days passed pleasantly enough, as the Company enjoyed the hospitality of the dwarves, avoiding Noli and his folk as best they could. Fima renewed his bond with his family, and he insisted on introducing his friends to each and every one of them. Rogond was introduced to Farin down in the deep smithies where the forges burned hot and the hammers were rarely silent. This venerable dwarf greeted Rogond, embracing him as a long-lost cousin.

"You have your mother's eyes," he told Rogond to his delight, "but your father's hair, I expect. Hers was a dark reddish hue. How well I remember it! And who is your friend?" He looked over at Gaelen, who stood by.

Rogond introduced her, and they both sat upon the polished stone floor at Farin's feet. "Please, Master Farin, they tell me that you know something of my family. This ring was taken from my mother's hand as she lay dead, slain by Ulcas in the Verdant Mountains."

Farin cast his eyes downward, his expression both shocked and saddened. After a moment he met Rogond's eyes again, and spoke in a soft voice. "Rosalin slain by Ulcas? That is ill news and hard to imagine. She would not have been easily taken." He wrapped his fingers in the long hair of his grey beard and tore a rather large bit of it off, then dropped it into the forge. It went up in a flash of flame as Farin spoke soft words unheard by any save himself. He turned to Rogond.

"You have heard the tale of how my life was saved?"

"Yes," Rogond replied, "but not yet from you. Glomin has told us of it." Gaelen reflected that she would have been better able to attend the telling of Glomin's tale had she not been trussed and blindfolded on cold stone.

Rogond now tried to subdue the pleading in his voice, to little avail. "Please, I would learn all you can tell me. I basically know nothing of my family history. I…I do not even know my given name. Rogond is the name given me by the Elves."

Farin looked confused. "Rosalin had a son, she told me, of whom she was most proud. She said he was much like to his father in appearance and temperament, but never mentioned his name. He was in his twenties, living in the north. That would have been, let me see…about sixty years ago. You most certainly are not he."

Rogond nodded. "I am but one and fifty. I was a babe in arms when my mother's people were killed." So, he had once had a brother, possibly yet living. Perhaps they even had met, as his brother would probably be unaware of him and so would not think to search for him. Yet there were so few of the descendants of Tuathas left, for so many were taken by the Plague. Rogond sighed. His brother had no doubt perished with them.

Gaelen observed the mix of emotions that played across Rogond's face. "Don't be discouraged," she said, placing a hand on his shoulder, "but hear the rest of what Farin can tell." She turned to the dwarf. "I would hear of it, also, if my presence does not disquiet either of you." Rogond gripped her hand tightly, and she patted his arm. He was so tense that he could hardly remain still. She turned to Farin. "You had best tell him all you can. He has waited long for enlightenment." Neither she nor Rogond moved or spoke until Farin had finished.

"Is there nothing more?" said Gaelen. "We have learned precious little other than what we already knew."

Farin shook his head. "I knew nothing of Rogond's father, not even his name. I did know that Rosalin had a son who would be in his eighties if yet living—a son who resembled his father."

Rogond now knew that he had his mother's eyes and probably his father's hair. He knew the full tale of the rescue of Farin by his mother and of the gift of Farin's ring to her, but there was so much left unlearned. Farin sensed his disappointment.

"I'm sorry, Rogond. I wish I could enlighten you further, but I have told you all that I remember. It seems your mother did mention the name of her beloved, presumably your father, but I cannot now recall it."

Rogond took a deep breath and faced Farin with brightness in his voice that he did not feel. "Never mind…you've been of great help. I never thought to learn even this much. I now know that I may yet have a brother, and now that I know my mother's name it will be easier to learn whether he still lives."

"Just think," said Gaelen, attempting to cheer him, "you may even have met your brother unaware! Perhaps now you will find him. He will surely know much of your family history."

Rogond nodded, though he would not look Gaelen or Farin in the eye for a moment. The dwarf sensed that Rogond wanted to speak to Gaelen in private. Muttering something about the need to see to the forge, he rose and busied himself elsewhere, leaving Rogond and Gaelen alone.

Rogond turned to her, his eyes downcast. "I was wrong to expect more. I should be grateful for that which I have been given," he said.

"Spoken as a man raised in the company of Elves, who have forever to learn the truths of their history," she replied, concern in her voice. "I know you are disappointed, but know that if I can, I will help you find your brother. Then you will surely learn the truths you seek. This has only been delayed a while. Take heart!"

She caressed his cheek with a hand that was soft save for the callused fingers that pulled her bow. Rogond cast his eyes downward. The anticipation of talking with Farin had built up an incredible tension within him, and now that it was over he felt empty and drained. Gaelen put her arms about him in a rather stiff embrace, as though she felt at a loss for words to comfort him.

Suddenly the dam of his feelings broke, and he gripped her tightly with both arms, holding her to him as though clinging to life. He squeezed his eyes shut and held her, riding the tide of his emotions until they calmed. He did not weep, but neither did he release his hold on her until the storm had passed. Then, he whispered to her as the hammers rang about them.

"Gaelen, my friend, my love, thank you for being here."

Belegund had finished an excellent meal and decided to leave the Great Hall to do a bit of exploring. He had been told of a wondrous cavern with a well-shaft in the center that led not to water, but to the great forges of the dwarven-smiths below. The red light from those forges was said to give the walls of the cavern an eerie glow, and if one concentrated upon them one could perceive the faces of his ancestors, and maybe even receive messages from them. Belegund doubted the veracity of this tale, thinking that perhaps too much wine had been involved in its making, but he wanted to see for himself just the same.

The dwarves gave some direction, but told him the easiest way to find the red cavern was to be drawn by the distinctive smell of the great forges. He made his way along several long, dim corridors; these passageways were rarely used. His excitement grew as he approached a chamber lit from within by an eerie red light, reeking of the sulfurous, metallic vapors of the forges. He was tentative as he entered the chamber, but he found it to be all that was promised.

The weird red light seemed to move across the rough walls, creating all sorts of shapes and shadows.

Yet it was the scent that most confused him, as he was not aware that the forges would smell so...odd. There was an undercurrent of foulness in the air, a corruption that was new to his senses. As he turned slowly, taking in the full view of the chamber, the source of the strange odor became apparent as he beheld a massive dark figure moving silently up behind him, holding a blade that flashed red in the dim light.

As Belegund was entering the cavern, Gaelen Taldin of the Greatwood was walking the dim passageways, trying to sort out the meaning of Rogond's words. After hearing Farin's tale they had parted, and Rogond had gone with Fima to the Great Hall to forget disappointment by indulging in food, drink, tales, and song. Gaelen smiled. Fima would sort him out. She had never before seen Rogond's spirits dampened so, and Fima's humor and good sense would be of great benefit. But Rogond's final words in the chamber of Farin had troubled her.

"Gaelen, my friend, my love..."

Was he declaring love for her? She shook her head. Surely, he was simply overcome with emotion and meant only that she was a beloved friend. It was best not to read too much into it. But what would she do if it were not so, if he really was telling her that he loved her? He was vulnerable at that moment and was not on his guard—in her experience it was at such times that hidden feelings are revealed. She had felt much in his embrace; he clung to her as though he could not bear to be parted from her.

Gaelen was worried. Did he understand the nature of the mingling of the Elàni with the Aridani? And what of her own feelings? She had not allowed herself to open her heart to anyone save Farahin—her beloved Rain. She loved her friend Wellyn in a way, but she would never bind to him even if he wished it. She loved Nelwyn, certainly, but as one loves a blood relative and closest friend. She looked within herself. Could she ever love anyone the way she had loved Rain? Was she even capable?

She decided to let some time pass before being with Rogond again. Tomorrow she would observe the way he reacted to her. If she suspected that there was more to be told of this tale she would bide her time, waiting until he felt comfortable again, and then she would speak with him…perhaps.

She was so uncertain of her own feelings and of what her course should be that she did not at first notice the dark, unclean scent drifting upon the cool air of the passageway. She continued on until the scent grew stronger, and she heard a sound that startled her from her confused contemplation. The scent was distinctive, and she knew it at once. Gorgon was here! Here in Cós-domhain…but why? It didn't make sense. He would have no way of knowing they were here, and he certainly would find no welcome. The rumor of heavy feet and the clash of steel blades came to her ears, and she ran toward the sound, approaching carefully as she drew nigh it.

Gorgon and Belegund battled in a large, dimly lit chamber. Belegund, whose strokes held more power even than Rogond's, was fighting with all his skill, but he had been wounded several times already. Gorgon was in his element here in this dim red light and sulfurous air. He had a fine new shield, the surface of which was as dull black as the rest of his armor. Gaelen wondered where and how he had acquired it. He still wielded Gelmyr's broadsword, and still carried Turantil at his side.

A cry from Belegund startled Gaelen into action, and she rushed forward, drawing her own blade. Her bow, quiver, and long knives she had laid under the pallet on which she slept, which was a pity, for they would have been of great use. She leaped in to defend Belegund, who was proving much more difficult to kill than Gorgon had anticipated. Gorgon had precious few dealings with the descendants of Tuathas, and, excepting Rogond, he had never experienced combat with any of them. Gorgon was confident now and was in fact rather enjoying his encounter with Belegund, who wore no armor.

When Gaelen appeared, Gorgon was distracted for a moment; this was not as he had planned. She ducked under his blade and slashed at him as he aimed a deadly blow at Belegund. The wound went deep, and Belegund's blood was flowing in a crimson flood from his right shoulder. This sudden and severe loss of blood caused him to stumble and drop to his knees as much of his strength left him.

Gorgon was trying to subdue Gaelen; he could easily have killed her, or so he thought, but he was constrained by the knowledge that his mirror would be of no further use once she was dead.

Belegund rallied and struggled to his feet, wielding his blade with his left hand, trying to strike Gorgon's unprotected face. Gaelen cried out as Gorgon swept his shield-arm toward her, releasing the heavy metal disc to strike her so hard that it knocked her off her feet. Then he aimed a second killing stroke at Belegund, whose strength was flowing away with the bright blood still sheeting down his right side. Belegund gave an agonized cry as the broadsword was buried halfway to the hilt in the center of his belly. He gripped Gorgon's sword arm in a vain attempt to push himself away, and sagged to the ground.

Gorgon withdrew the sword as Gaelen stared, horrified, at the dying man. She called Belegund's name, then cursed aloud in a terrible voice. She flew at Gorgon again, but with only her short sword it was difficult, as he was her equal in speed and held a much longer reach.

Why did he not kill her? He had missed several opportunities already. Perhaps Belegund had wearied him to the point that he was severely off his form. Then, as she darted in to try to bury her blade under his right arm, he suddenly dropped his sword and grabbed her by the throat, lifting her from the floor.

He squeezed his huge fingers tightly around her slender neck, gazing into her bright, bulging eyes. He had only to close his fist and she would be dead, her windpipe crushed. He could imagine the blood pouring from her mouth as he did so; it was a sight that he greatly desired to see. Gaelen could not breathe at all as she gazed into the eyes of her enemy. She struggled, swiping at him with her blade, but she could do little as he held her suspended. The harder she fought the tighter he gripped her until at last she went limp in his hand.

Her ears rang with a deafening roar, and her vision went dark. Gorgon knew he could crush her quickly, or choke the life from her slowly, or simply shake her like a rat and break her neck. He lowered her to the floor, but did not let go of her throat. A small trickle of blood flowed from the corner of her mouth, touching the topmost of his fingers. The warmth of it shocked him into the realization that he would kill her in seconds if he did not release her.

He struggled with his own feelings of hatred for Gaelen and her kind, which he weighed against the promise of the mirror. Sitting heavily upon the stone floor, he kept one eye on Belegund, who was now so weak that he could no longer move or speak, but could only watch in silence as the last of his life flowed away.

Gorgon drew Turantil, placing the gleaming tip of the blade near Gaelen's pale face. It would be so easy to put out her eyes, as he had once vowed to do. He traced the upper lid of the left eye with the keen blade, drawing a fine line of blood. So easy…and so sweet!

Belegund closed his eyes, for he did not wish to see what would befall. Then, suddenly, Gorgon came to himself. What could he have been thinking? He released Gaelen abruptly, then shook her limp form and slapped her face to get her breathing again. She had a great deal of trouble, as he had done a fair job of flattening her windpipe, but she finally struggled back to lie unconscious, breath whistling but regular. Gorgon nodded in approval. She may have been undersized, but she was tenacious.

Now he went to sit beside Belegund, and, as the light slowly faded from his eyes, the Ranger heard all Gorgon would tell. He explained why he had not killed Gaelen and what his intentions were for the future. If he was lucky enough, perhaps he could even bring about the downfall of Mountain-home, or even Tal-sithian! Wrothgar had promised him an army should either opportunity arise.

Belegund listened to this talk with horrified fascination. Certainly it was madness. His pain was very great, and he squeezed his eyes closed against the tears of agony that welled in them. Gorgon seemed almost solicitous as he spoke to Belegund for the last time.

"I have nothing against you, Tuathan, and you proved to be a stimulating and worthy adversary. I will ease your passing now. You should have listened to the warnings you were given." With those words, he turned Belegund's head almost tenderly before cutting his throat, killing him in a few seconds.

The She-elf was still unconscious, but her color was coming back and Gorgon had decided that she would live. He removed Belegund's cloak and wrapped his body in it, then dragged it away and hid it among the rocks. He would return for it later. He came back for Gaelen, slung her over his shoulder like a sack, and carried her deep into little-used passageways where the dwarves seldom walked.

Thorndil, Galador, and Nelwyn had descended into the western valley, from which the mists that shrouded the Linnefionn could be seen in the distance. The horses had given no difficulty. Eros, in fact, remained close to Thorndil as though reluctant to interact in any way with Galador. The Elf had forgiven him—Eros' devotion to Rogond was commendable, if occasionally bothersome— but for now Eros preferred the company of Thorndil, who very much resembled Rogond in appearance and manner of speech.

Nelwyn rode before them upon Gryffa, who was fine of limb and proud of bearing, his red mane blown back. He called to the horses of Tal-sithian that pastured in the outlying lands to the southeast. The Company would first proceed there, crossing the cold stream that flowed from the Iolari Pass, and leave the animals to run with those of Tal-sithian, continuing on foot.

Thorndil patted Eros, who appeared anxious at being left behind. "Don't worry, my noble friend. Rogond will soon be approaching from the east, even as we did. You will see him again if you remain here! Do not stray from these lands and you shall be reunited."

Eros did not understand many of Thorndil's words, but took much of his meaning. He nuzzled the Ranger affectionately while sniffing his pockets.

"Ah! You have found them, I see," chuckled Thorndil, extracting a handful of dried apples. He gave some to Eros, then patted him again, and left him standing alone in the tall grass. The powerful dun chewed thoughtfully, wondering whether he would ever see any of his friends again. This place had a strangeness about it that unsettled him. He called once to Thorndil, who turned and shouted: "Stay *here*, Eros. You'd best be easy to find when Rogond arrives!"

Eros shook a fly from his ear. Of course his friends would return; they always had before. He looked forward to seeing Rogond, Gaelen, Belegund, and Thorndil again. The lure of the tall grass after so many days of poor forage decided him—this would be a fair waiting-place, and he would remain until Rogond came for him.

Nelwyn had been to Tal-sithian once before, but that had been many years ago. She and Gaelen had carried a message from Ri-Aruin to Lord Airan. In truth, the Elves of Tal-sithian had very little to do with the Greatwood, for they were High-elves of the Eádram under the protection of Lady Arialde, an Asarla of legendary beauty and grace. She and Lord Airan had founded the realm long ago, placing it upon an island in the center of the largest, deepest, and clearest lake in the west of Alterra. The Lady kept it hidden from enemies by virtue of a thick mist that would confuse and confound them such that they would turn aside. No creature of Darkness loves clear waters, and there was no Ulca living that even knew the Linnefionn had an island in it, though they were no doubt aware of the many sentinels keeping watch over the borders of the outlands around it. In fact, Nelwyn and her companions had already been sighted by them, hence the Lady knew of their arrival almost before they did.

Galador knew of Lord Airan, for he was a kinsman of Eádros. He was reasonably confident that the three of them would find welcome, though he was a little concerned for Thorndil. The Elves of Tal-sithian were known to be very secretive and protective of their borders, but once the Company explained their purpose, Galador was confident of a gracious reception. Nelwyn's sharp eyes had already spotted one or two grey-clad sentinels as they approached the cloud of mist that obscured the lake. She held up her hand to halt and then spoke:

"Elves of the Lake-realm, I am Nelwyn, daughter of Turanen of the Greatwood. I bear news and a dire warning, and would counsel with those who rule this realm. Stay your hands upon your bowstrings, but show yourselves that we may parley with you."

Thorndil was taken aback as about a dozen of the Elves appeared as though from the very air. Their raiment was grey to blend in with the mists and the grey waters of the lake, in contrast to the hunter-scouts of the Greatwood, who favored greens and browns to better conceal themselves in the dappled green sunlight of the forest.

The sentinels spoke briefly among themselves before one of them addressed the Company.

"Farath-talam. You are known to the Lady, and you are welcome. We will conduct you."

The Elves led the Company through the layer of mist, which seemed to vanish before them to reveal a brilliant sapphire-blue lake and the distant green isle of Tal-sithian. They were taken there in beautifully-made boats, and the way was made smooth as glass. There was a peace that lay over this place, a sense that no ill would befall while the Elves remained vigilant, a power that could not be seen, but could be felt. It was the same in Mountain-home, where evil things need not be feared.

The name Tal-sithian means "Realm of Deer-roaming', and as they drew near to the island they could see many delicate and beautiful deer of a light dappled golden color, much smaller than the deer of the Greatwood, gathering beside the waters. There were wonderful meadows and tall trees on the island, which was much larger than they had thought at first. The Elves here lived as they liked; some stayed belowground surrounded by carved stone, while others lived more as the Cúinar, preferring to remain among the trees.

In the center of the island there was a high hill where stood a dwelling that appeared to be made of white marble with many pillars and columns. This was the home of the Lady, and as they drew nearer, the columns were seen to be as carved white trees with intricately woven branches. Lady Arialde never strayed from the island, and soon the Company would stand in her presence, so that they might tell all that they knew of Gorgon. Then they would most likely be free to enjoy the beauty and peace of the Lake-realm. Any lands under the protection of Arialde would be as a paradise; the lands were in flower and the scent in the air was intoxicating.

Nelwyn cast her thoughts toward Cós-domhain, hoping for the safety of the remainder of the Company, praying that Gaelen could soon share the wonders of Tal-sithian with her.

They would not have nearly as long a stay here as they would have liked, for Nelwyn had resolved to return to the Greatwood as she and Gaelen had promised, that they might warn their own people of Gorgon. Nelwyn hoped that the creature had not already turned his path there.

If she had known better, she would not have worried for the Greatwood, as Gorgon was nowhere near it. He was at that moment leaving Gaelen in a dark corner of Cós-domhain, where she would soon awake to find that the warm welcome extended her by Grundin's folk had run out.

Rogond was beginning to become concerned as he sat with Fima and some of his kin in the Great Hall. He had not seen Gaelen in many hours, and though he assumed that she had gotten up to some activity with the dwarves, he wondered. He didn't like the thought of her being without his or Fima's protection, but Grundin himself had decreed that she might walk freely, and thus she would be quite safe. Belegund had gone off in search of this strange chamber leading to the forges, with its weird red light and moving shadows of dwarvish ancestors. Rogond smiled, as he, like Belegund, also suspected the involvement of wine, or perhaps beer, in the creation of that rumor. If Belegund found it truly wondrous, perhaps Rogond would go and have a look for himself.

Fima was just sitting down to a large plate of roasted mutton and potatoes when several grim-faced dwarves approached and surrounded him.

"Lore-master, you and the Tuathan must come with us. Something has happened…Lord Grundin commands your presence in his private chambers."

Fima put down the lamb shank he had just begun to enjoy with a sigh of regret, then fastidiously dipped his fingers in his water-goblet, a habit he had picked up in Mountain-home. He wiped them on the edge of the table-drape before turning to Rogond.

"This will be an important matter, I'm fear. We must go at once. I pray that no ill has befallen." His expression told Rogond he was not hopeful; they would not have been summoned unless the matter was very serious. They both rose and followed the dwarves to Grundin's private chamber.

Grundin was grave as he explained why they had been brought before him. "Ular will lead you; there is something you must see. When you have seen it, my folk will conduct you back here. I must ask you to return at once as I will need to speak with you of it. I do not understand the nature of what has happened here, but I warn you that it is quite grim, and I will want enlightenment from you." He turned to Fima. "One thing is certain—I fear for your Wood-elf. Her whereabouts are unknown at present, but there are signs that she was involved. I will say no more for now." He turned away, making it clear that the conversation was at an end.

Ular led Rogond and Fima down a long series of passages, and Rogond had the sense that they were going west. A large collection of dwarves had gathered at the end of the corridor, and Fima could hear not a few of them muttering and weeping. The crowd parted, and Rogond gasped in horror as he beheld the sight that had been so carefully arranged for him.

Three bodies hung from stakes driven into the rock of the wall. Two were dwarves, and the third was a tall man. One of the dwarves had been beheaded, and Fima recognized poor Tibo immediately by his green jacket. The other dwarf, to Fima's dismay, was Noli. He had not been beheaded, but hung limp upon the spike with his eyes and mouth open in astonishment. He had been killed with a single stroke to the neck.

Rogond had eyes only for Belegund. His friend was as dead as stone, with terrible wounds to his shoulder and midsection; he had apparently battled fiercely before being overcome at last. His sword had been broken and placed at his feet. All three bodies were covered with blood; the corridor reeked with the smell of it.

The dwarves moaned and muttered in their grief and horror, and many were becoming angry. One of the Elders stepped from the crowd, tears of sorrow and rage welling in his dark eyes. Rogond recognized him as Nimo, Noli's cousin.

"So much for the trust placed in strangers," he said to the assembled dwarves. "These have brought naught but sorrow among us. Their very presence here threatens us. And where is the She-elf? No one knows her whereabouts, and none may account for them. If she has been lost, why is she not among the dead? I'll warrant Noli's neck met with an Elven blade!"

Several of the dwarves muttered amongst themselves at this. None could doubt the sense of Nimo's words.

"Wait, wait good people," said Fima. We are all shocked and saddened by what has happened. Please, let's not turn upon our guests until we know the truth! The Tuathan was a good friend of all in our Company, and old Tibo was known for his love of the Elves. This was done by an enemy that is the enemy of all! If he has found the She-elf, I fear she is dead."

Rogond had never feared so much for anyone as he now feared for Gaelen. Fima was right—killing her would please Gorgon to no end.

"I must go in search of her," he cried, clutching at Fima's arm. "She will be easily taken if she is alone. I must find her at once!"

"No, Rogond. You cannot until we return to speak again with Grundin. Please, my friend—you would not wish to make an enemy of him. If you did so, neither you nor Gaelen would ever see the light again—that is certain. I sense that if Gaelen will die this day, then she is dead already. Come along, now."

Nimo looked as though he would also like to go in search of Gaelen, but with a very different purpose in mind. "Yes, Fima, return to Grundin, for he has something else he would share with you. Mark it well! It's possible that you and I will yet come to an agreement this day. If not, we will know that you have forever been corrupted by Ordath and the Elves of Mountain-home!"

Fima said nothing, as he did not yet know what Nimo was referring to.

"Leave them," Nimo called to some of the dwarves, who were trying to take the bodies down and tend them. "Leave them until all is made plain. We may wish to examine them again. There will be time later to care for them."

Rogond closed his eyes. Belegund had been his friend through many adventures. He muttered softly in the High-elven tongue, calling to Aontar, asking that his friend would find safe passage to the lands of his ancestors.

"I'm sorry, Rogond," said Fima, who also had liked and respected Belegund. "There's no time now. We must return and face Grundin." He sighed, a great melancholy in his lined face, looking every bit of his age. "I now very much regret that I did not answer Belegund's questions when he asked them. May he receive his enlightenment in the hereafter and remain forever young and strong."

Rogond nodded, though he could not speak. He was consumed with a mixture of grief and panic as he was once again escorted back to stand before Grundin.

The great Dwarf-lord faced them, his expression difficult to read. He handed a parchment to Fima, who showed it to Rogond. It was written in an unlovely but competent hand, and the message was understandably upsetting to the dwarves of Grundin's realm.

> "See, then, what fate awaits the Elf-friend in this Realm.
> Learn, also, of the fate of her Enemies.
> Noli was cloven by an Elven blade.
> I, Gorgon Elfhunter, send this warning."

Rogond and Fima stood confounded by the message. Gorgon would not know that Tibo fancied himself Elf-friend, any more than he would know that Noli was Gaelen's enemy or be able to call him by name. How could he know this unless he was far cleverer than they had imagined, or was somehow in league with Grundin's folk, which was absurd? Fima had to sit down for a moment. Grundin looked them both up and down.

"Well?" he said at last. "What does it mean to you?"

Fima was the first to react. "Surely, Wise One, you do not believe that Noli was killed by the She-elf! Obviously this enemy wishes you to believe it, but she could not have done so. Please tell me you are not beguiled by the lies in this self-serving parchment!"

Grundin's reply was stony. "I will not say what I believe until the Elf is found, Fima Lore-master. Noli's neck WAS cloven with an Elven blade; that much we have determined."

Rogond broke in. "Forgive me, my lord, but many may wield an Elven blade. I know this enemy, who calls himself 'Elfhunter'. I have fought with him before, and I know that he carries several blades of Elven make, taken from his victims. You cannot blame Gaelen for this."

"Can you account for her whereabouts, Rogond of the Tuathar? Unless I am wrong, neither you nor anyone else was in sight of her when this happened. Until she is found, I will hold back my judgment."

Ular appeared in the doorway at that moment, begging leave to speak with Grundin, who left the chamber for a brief while. When he returned, his face was grimmer than ever.

"Come with me, both of you, and we shall all be enlightened."

They followed him into an antechamber, and Rogond was both shocked and relieved to see the miserable, shivering Elf that now looked up at him with bright eyes full of pain, though she could not speak. Rogond started toward her, and as she beheld him she wept with grief, pain, and frustration. Grundin held up his hand, and two of the dwarf-guards stepped in front of Rogond, preventing him from reaching her. He halted, but looked around the guards into her frightened eyes, reaching over their heads to touch her outstretched hand. The guards pressed him, and he backed off, speaking soothing words to her and maintaining eye contact.

She had been ill-used and nearly killed—that was plain. Her clothing was torn and bloodied, her face battered and cut, and her throat was so bruised that it was a dark purplish-black. The imprint of Gorgon's fingers could be clearly seen. So, that was the reason she could not speak. She was in considerable pain; her neck felt as though filled with hot shards of metal, and the slightest movement caused her to gasp and grit her teeth. Her red, swollen eyes showed that she had been crying for some time. Rogond could smell Gorgon all over her, even from this distance. He tried not to show the horror and rage he felt as he looked at her.

Grundin's expression was difficult to read as he regarded Gaelen in silence. She in turn looked at Rogond, mouthing the same words over and over:

"Belegund…what of Belegund?"

Grundin spoke then to her. "Your friend Belegund is dead, apparently killed fighting an unknown enemy. What do you know of this?" Gaelen closed her eyes. She had known Belegund was gravely wounded, but she had not witnessed his death. She looked up at Grundin, her tear-streaked face hot with fury and frustration, and tried to speak, but no sound came from her other than a harsh, halting whisper.

"Belegund fought a terrible enemy. He calls himself Gorgon Elfhunter. We were journeying to Tal-sithian to warn our people of him, but did not know he was in Cós-domhain. When last we saw him, he was near to Monadh-talam, and we had wounded him. I never dreamed he would dare to come here…it doesn't make any sense."

Grundin then approached Gaelen so that he looked directly into her eyes. "Two of my people are slain as well. Tibo and Noli. What have you to say to this?" He studied her reaction carefully, and it was obvious from her surprised, saddened expression that she had not known. He turned then to Rogond. "I believe that she had nothing to do with this. You may attend her now."

Grundin felt a hand touching the hem of his cloak and turned to regard Gaelen, who whispered, "You thought I had a hand in this? Why would you think such things?"

Grundin handed her the parchment, explaining that it had been found clutched in Noli's dead hand. She held it before her face and read the words, her jaw working, eyes bright with hatred. She handed it back to Grundin and closed her eyes.

"I am truly sorry about Noli, though there was no love between us. I deeply regret the death of Tibo, who loved my people and seemed gentle and harmless. It is ironic that he was chosen for death, as the enemy could not have known these things."

Rogond now knelt beside her, concern in his eyes. "But somehow Gorgon knew that Noli did not love the Elves. That is clear from the parchment. How could he have known this?"

Grundin replied, "Noli wore the emblem of Rûmm. Your enemy must have seen it and knows enough of history to determine that Noli and Gaelen were not friends."

Gaelen clutched Rogond's arm. "Why am I not dead? I fought beside Belegund, though I could not aid him. If only I had my longbow…" She burst into tears again, and Rogond held her gently, trying not to hurt her.

"Hush, Gaelen, hush. What's done is done. You fought to your limit with what you had. It is obvious that he left you for dead…he thought you were dead. Thank the stars that you are not!"

Gaelen stopped crying and struggled to her feet, pain graven into her face. She faced Grundin and tried as best she could to address him.

"My Lord Grundin, we must leave now—today. Your people will be safe once we are gone. Our enemy follows us, though we did not know it. He will not rest until we are dead. So far as I know, he holds no enmity toward your people, but so long as we are here and you shelter us and show us kindness, he will hold you to blame."

"You are not ready to leave, little Wood-elf," said Fima. "You would never make it to Tal-sithian without aid." He turned to Grundin. "She must remain here until she is strong. Our people will be watchful now, as they are aware of the enemy."

But Gaelen again tried to speak. "You do not know Gorgon! He has killed untold numbers of Elves over the years, and he is clever, stealthy, and swift. He is a coward, striking from the shadows, and he only attacks when he is certain he will prevail. Merely being aware of him will not prevent him from taking vengeance upon Grundin's folk, and I will not stay here to be a danger to them."

Grundin held up his hand to silence them. "Here is my decision," he said to Gaelen. "You and Rogond are free to leave when you choose. I would encourage you to stay until you are healed, but I sense that you have already decided your course. Should you choose to leave us, you will be provided with an escort as far as the Lake-realm. If the enemy is as cowardly as you say, he will not dare attack you. After that, I cannot vouch for your safety. But your enemy does not understand the nature of Grundin's folk if by this action he expects we will turn you away out of fear of him! A coward understands only cowardice, and he thinks you will no longer be welcomed here. For your courage and willingness to place yourself at risk to protect my people, I name you Dwarf-friend. You are ever welcome in my realm."

Grundin bowed low, as did the other dwarves in attendance, and Gaelen tried her best to return the gesture, though it pained her. Grundin smiled.

"It has been long since I so named an Elf, Gaelen of the Greatwood. You have the heart of the Èolar. Guard it well."

Fima and Rogond helped Gaelen return to their chambers, where their few belongings were gathered. Gaelen would take no food, as she could not yet swallow it, but Rogond and Fima availed themselves of one last meal and a rest before departing. Rogond would be glad to see the outside world again, and he now wrestled with his own feelings of guilt and responsibility. Had he not disregarded Galador's warning, all would have been well. He certainly had not expected Gorgon to turn up in Cós-domhain. He had learned so little from Farin—certainly not worth the three lives that were lost. He mourned Belegund in silence, though no one was there to hear.

Fima went to see his kin, explaining that he would accompany his friends at least as far as Tal-sithian. From there his path was yet undecided, but he told them that it might be awhile ere he returned. They were saddened, as Fima was well loved and would be missed. Each hoped that they would see him again, for news of this new enemy had spread quickly, and they feared for him.

As Fima made his way back to the Great Hall, Nimo and several of the kin of Noli appeared out of the dark, blocking the way. They stood before him with stern faces. Fima sighed. "Pardon me, Nimo, for I am in a hurry to return to my chamber and prepare to leave with my friends. I have no time for your ill temper just now."

That made no difference to Nimo. "Well and good, Lore-master, leave with your friends. They brought this evil here, and while they may have the favor of Grundin, they had best never return so long as I or any of my kin are here. And they had best never go near the Northern Mountains. You may give them that message from me. We will never forget the loss of Noli. That Elf had better never show her face here again."

Fima nodded at him, his eyes cold and hard. "Very well. I will tell them. Shall I also inform Grundin that perhaps he should take back his designation of Dwarf-friend from the Elf so that it does not displease you? I'm certain Grundin would not wish to upset you or your kin, Nimo. And while I'm about it, perhaps I should alert Farin and his folk in the smithies that their friendship is wasted on Rogond, as well. After all, they certainly would not want to displease you, as there are only about a hundred of them. The last person who displeased Farin, as I recall, received the loving attentions of his hammer and required significant healing time. I shall certainly relay your threats to those who should hear of them."

Nimo and his kin responded with anger to Fima's bold words, for he was alone among them. They moved toward him, apparently meaning to do harm, when out of the shadows emerged about twenty of Farin's folk, bare-chested in leather aprons, their beards divided and plaited and tied behind their necks to keep them from the fire. They carried large hammers in their hands, and their eyes were alight with the possibility of mayhem. Farin himself stood among them.

"So, these folk think they can threaten our friends and gainsay the pronouncements of Grundin, do they? How very foolish! I would imagine, Nimo, that if you reflect for a moment, you will realize the folly of your words. After all, you sit on the Council of Elders. You must have some wisdom. If I were you, I would think on it, as you would not wish to deal with us."

This was true, as Farin's folk worked the forges, and were incredibly strong. They were also in high favor with Grundin. Nimo realized that he was outmatched, and he bowed before Farin, though his eyes were hard.

"Your pardon," he growled. "We shall rethink our stance in this matter, but expect no love for the Elf or the Tuathan from us. My warning to them concerning the Northern Mountains is still clear, Fima. Tell them so from me, won't you?" At this, Nimo and his kinsmen turned and retreated down the long corridor, grumbling as they went. Fima and Farin watched them go, and then Farin escorted Fima back to his chamber, as he wanted to wish Rogond well.

Fima looked in on Gaelen to see whether she needed anything. He found her standing as though entranced, eyes closed, mouthing a long stream of words that he could not fully understand. He did not comprehend what she was doing, and feared for her. She heard him approach and opened her eyes.

"What is it, Fima?"

The dwarf looked uncomfortably at his feet, as though he knew that he had witnessed something very private and spiritual.

"Nothing, ah, I just wanted to see if you were all right," he muttered. Then he looked up at her. "I hope I wasn't interrupting anything."

A sad, sweet smile crossed Gaelen's face. "I was just reciting a prayer in High-elven. I thought Tibo would have liked it."

Fima nodded. "That he would have. It was a fine and fitting tribute to his passion for the Èolar. I always said old Tibo was simply born at the wrong time. Gaelen, you are a tender-hearted little spirit deep down, aren't you?"

Gaelen sighed, grimacing as she tried unsuccessfully to turn her head toward him. "Yes, I suppose I am. But don't you go around telling anyone—otherwise these constant jests referring to my being descended of the Fire-heart might cease. That would break my heart." She rolled her eyes heavenward for emphasis.

Fima chuckled. "Yes, I've no doubt it would. Do not fear; I shall tell no living soul. Take some rest, little one. Tomorrow we depart for Tal-sithian, and I do not envy you the task of traversing the black passage—bending over will be difficult when you cannot move your head to look down!"

Gaelen smiled at him. "Rogond is the one I worry about—are you certain he will fit?"

"Ha! Of course he will, though he'll look somewhat undignified crawling along. We've entertained many tall guests over the ages… but few are as tall as our Rogond! But do not fear. You are high in favor with Grundin; he will see you both safely through. I bid you good evening. Rest well." He turned to go, but paused in the doorway. "Gaelen…?"

She turned to him and raised both eyebrows, indicating that she awaited whatever he had to say.

"Thank you for the prayer. I am certain Tibo would have loved it." Then he left her to her solitude.

21

The Stone of Léir

It was not long before Nelwyn and Galador were brought before the Lord and Lady of Tal-sithian, whose place of counsel was high atop the Greenwood Hill that stood in the center of the island. Nelwyn was quite at home in this place, as she loved all things green and growing, and Tal-sithian was presently in full flower and leaf, with beautiful tall forests that covered much of the land. Galador was likewise at ease, for he was surrounded by Elves of the Eádram, who were his distant kin. Thorndil, who knew little of Gorgon Elfhunter, did not need to present himself before the council and had remained beside the lakeshore, for such was his preference. He conversed politely with the sentinels as he awaited the return of his friends.

Lord Airan, who was a venerable and mighty Elf of the Eádram, had long, flaxen hair and wise, calm grey eyes. Nelwyn had spoken with him before, when she and Gaelen had delivered a message from King Ri- Aruin of the Greatwood. But Nelwyn had not yet beheld the Lady Arialde, whose deep blue eyes were unfathomable. Her hair, as with many of the Asari, was of flowing silver, and she had the most beautiful features Nelwyn had ever seen; it was as though some sort of divine light hovered about her in a glowing veil. Nelwyn had never actually met one of the twelve ancient Magic-users, and she was quite overwhelmed for a moment.

Now Arialde greeted her guests warmly, but with concern in her eyes. She maintained a close relationship with Lady Ordath, who was in fact her close kin, and they could share thoughts when they wished. Therefore, she knew why Nelwyn and Galador had come. She bade them tell their tale, and it was Nelwyn who stepped forward. She told what she knew of Gorgon and of her travels since leaving the Woodland in pursuit of him. She and Gaelen had probably traveled farther in less time and seen more of Alterra than any two Wood-elves in reckoning. When she came to the point at which the Company had been divided, she faltered and then fell silent.

Arialde looked at her with understanding. "I know why your tale falters. You are right to be concerned for your companions. I have seen great difficulties beneath the mountain."

Nelwyn's heart sank. She and Galador had both known that it would be so, though they had hoped otherwise. Arialde turned then to Airan.

"We must summon Amandir. This concerns him closely."

Airan shook his head. "Perhaps that should wait until the others arrive. We need to hear all that will be told before involving Amandir, as this will grieve him, and we must make certain that we have learned all that we may."

"There will be little to learn that has not yet been told, as I am already reasonably certain of the origins of this enemy," said Arialde. "Yet we cannot act until the others arrive, so I see no harm in waiting."

Nelwyn became agitated. "Do you mean to say that you know the nature of this creature that has so afflicted our people? I beg you to enlighten us!"

Arialde regarded her with an expression of deep melancholy. "Be careful what you wish for, daughter of the Greatwood. You may regret the knowledge once you have been given it. This is truly a tale of woe." She rose then and bade her guests refresh themselves with food and drink, as she and Airan wanted to speak in private.

But Nelwyn was not easily dismissed. "You have said that you have foreseen difficulties for my friends. I wish to return to the mountain and find them, and aid them if I may. I beg your leave to do this," she said, to Galador's dismay.

Arialde closed her eyes for a moment. "They are already on their way here." She looked into Nelwyn's eyes. "There are but three. A company of dwarves leads them. I am sorry, Nelwyn."

"But, my lady…of course there are only three. One of our companions is a dwarf, and was destined to remain in Cós-domhain. So, all is well."

"All is not well. Fima, the Lore-master of Ordath, travels with them. There is also an Elf, and a man. One remains forever entombed within the stone. I cannot tell more as yet."

The color drained from Nelwyn's face as Galador steadied her. He bowed his head before Arialde as both he and Nelwyn placed their right hands upon their hearts in a gesture of grief. Either Rogond or Belegund lay dead beneath the mountain just as Galador had foreseen. He felt the blood rise in his face as he stepped forward, addressing Arialde and Lord Airan.

"In that case, I wish to beg your leave to go to my friends, to see whether I may aid them. One of the men of the Company is a close friend, and I fear for him. If it please you, may I return to them?"

Arialde nodded. "Your friends will approach the lakeshore by the rising of the moon. There, they will rest, for one is in need of healing." She looked at Nelwyn, who was now even more distressed. "You will go with Galador?"

Nelwyn bowed her head, then met Arialde's gaze. She nodded once, her face pale, as Galador spoke again to Arialde. "My lady… can you not tell me any more of the man who still walks with our companions? Can you not describe him to us so that we may know which of our friends lies dead? Rogond is very tall—taller than I am, with dark hair and clothing."

Arialde nodded. "That is a fair description, but was not your other friend of similar form and coloring?" Galador dropped his eyes, for Arialde was right. Belegund and Rogond were quite similar save that Belegund was a bit more broadly made.

"Does he carry a spear?" asked Nelwyn, who was very fond of Rogond and was nearly as anxious as Galador.

Arialde considered for a moment. "I do not know. You will learn the truth soon enough. Our folk will guide you."

Airan had summoned an Elf who would conduct them back across the waters. Arialde addressed the guide as he stood before her. "There is an old dwarf with the Company—Fima is his name. He is the Loremaster of Monadh-talam and is welcome here. No other dwarf may enter. Please see our guests safely back to their friends, and take food and healing herbs to aid them. Return as quickly as you may."

The Elf bowed low, his right hand over his breast. Then Nelwyn and Galador took their leave, with many thanks to Arialde. They told Thorndil what they had learned, and the news grieved him sorely. Both Rogond and Belegund were dear comrades, and as Thorndil gathered his belongings, preparing to accompany Galador and Nelwyn, his lined face was grim and sad.

"This is indeed cruel news," he said. "There are so few of my people left that the loss of any is especially hard to bear. I fear the blood of Tuathas will one day disappear from the kindred of men. Belegund and Rogond were still young, and neither had taken a wife or left an heir. They were both worthy defenders and friends."

Nelwyn shivered as she gathered her gear. She could understand Thorndil's despair, and she feared for Rogond; in addition, Arialde had said that one of the Company was in need of healing. Perhaps Gaelen had been hurt! She wished more than anything at that moment that the four of them had not left the Greatwood, but had remained there until the spring had clothed the beech woods in new green leaves. She longed for the relative peace and comfort of her beautiful woodland home and for the company of her friends and kin. Not so far away, her cousin Gaelen would have stood in agreement.

As evening fell, Rogond first beheld the fair waters of the Linnefionn. There was a clear, cold stream that flowed into it from the mountains, and the dwarves decided to camp beside it that they all might be refreshed. Gaelen and Rogond were weary and heartsick from their experience, and they were pleased to rest beside the flowing waters.

Gaelen made her way carefully upstream until she was concealed from the eyes of the dwarves, who sat together eating and drinking and in general making a great deal of noise. She removed most of her clothing with some difficulty, for she was badly bruised and still could not move her head upon her neck, and then lowered herself gingerly into the invigorating waters, gasping a little as they washed over her.

Almost immediately her pain eased as she lay back, letting the water flow around her throat, her eyes closed. The stench of Gorgon was washed away, and at least a part of her spirit was renewed. She heard Rogond calling to her, but she could not answer, as her voice had not yet returned.

Taking small sips of the healing waters, she let them soothe her throat, hoping for improvement. She was rewarded; her pain was lessened and she drew breath more easily. When she next tried to speak, her voice, though strained and hoarse, could at last be heard.

She looked up and saw Rogond approaching, smiling as he drew nigh her. His expression was relieved as he waded in to stand beside her, taking the hand that she offered him.

"Are you all right, Gaelen? Please do not wander off so; Fima and I were afraid for you. Does the water ease your pain?"

Gaelen was pleased to note that she could now nod her head with much less discomfort. "I am sorry for worrying you; I did not wish to call attention to myself, and if you don't mind I will remain here yet awhile." Then, she looked up at him. "Will you stay nearby and aid me? I do not know if I can rise easily by myself."

Rogond nodded, pleased that she could now be heard. "Of course I will. First I will go back and get us some food and drink. Then, when you are ready, I will aid you in rising from the water." He turned to go, and as he mounted the stream bank Gaelen called to him once more.

"Umm…Rogond?"

Rogond turned back to her, smiling slightly at her use of his name. "Yes?"

She looked sidelong at him, blushing. "Ah…when you get back, could you do that…that thing with my ears again?" Rogond's smile grew broader. At that moment, he could not think of any duty that he would rather perform.

"I shall be delighted to do this for you, O Dwarf-friend of Grundin. I will return soon." So saying, he strode off into the gathering dark, noticing that the stars were emerging in the heavens, feeling that in spite of his recent disappointment and grief there was much that was still right with the world.

Nelwyn, Galador, and Thorndil reached their friends hours later, as the stars burned bright. They crept in so as not to arouse the dwarves, who had insisted on remaining where they were until dawn. They did not wish to approach the mists of the Lake in darkness.

Fima knew that the dwarves were less at ease as they drew nearer to the Elven-realm. In those days there was still some communication between Grundin's folk and the Elves of Tal-sithian, but it was rare. Strange tales abounded on both sides. Save for the Èolar, who were most like-minded to themselves, the dwarves found Elves to be thoroughly mysterious and puzzling creatures that were not to be trusted. Likewise the Elves viewed Grundin's folk as strange, stunted, and unattractive, with little to offer them save skill at craft. Out of such poor understanding comes disquiet, and both races had, over the long years, fabricated tales with only the barest truth to them. Regrettably, there were now few of the Eólar remaining to set things right.

Although both the Lake-realm and the Deep-caverns had been founded long before, the Elves had few dealings with the folk of Grundin. Likewise the dwarves of Cós-domhain had largely kept out of Elvish affairs for thousands of years and wished it to remain so. Only when their lands were directly threatened would the dwarves join the Elves in battle, and at those times they were counted as fierce allies. Yet their participation and their losses were minor compared with those of Elves and men.

In order to truly understand the enmity between the dwarves and most especially the Elves of the Eádram, one needed to know of the War of Betrayal, in which the dwarves of Rûmm laid siege to and finally overcame the Elven-realm of Eádros. Because the Elves of Tal-sithian were, for the most part, of the Eádram, dwarves were not welcome there, with few exceptions. Fima, who was known to both Lady Arialde and to Lord Airan, and stood high in the favor of Lady Ordath, would be admitted without question.

Galador, Nelwyn, and Thorndil crept silently toward the group of dwarves, but did not see Rogond or Gaelen among them. They quickly spotted Fima, who was sitting near the firelight, apparently lost in thought. Fima raised his head for a moment and gazed off in the direction of the flowing stream and a small copse of trees; Nelwyn guessed that she would find her friends there. She and Galador approached the little grove to observe Gaelen lying on her back with Rogond half-reclining beside her.

Though they were saddened at the apparent loss of Belegund, Galador and Nelwyn both sighed with relief at the sight of Rogond apparently ministering aid to Gaelen, who must have been the one in need of healing. Nelwyn gave a call that Gaelen would know at once; they had used it in the Greatwood forever and it was distinctive.

Rogond looked up and turned his gaze toward them, but Gaelen did not move. Nelwyn panicked then and rose to her feet, calling Gaelen's name, as Rogond held up a hand in greeting. Gaelen had not responded as she had been in a half-stupor caused by Rogond's attentions to her right ear. She had nearly fallen asleep, as the waters had taken her pain away such that she could finally relax. She could speak, but not yet well; her voice sounded hoarse and rasping, and she preferred to whisper. The moment she laid eyes on Nelwyn, the tears started in them.

Nelwyn embraced Rogond with relief, as did Thorndil and finally Galador, though his embrace was somewhat stiff, as though he was unaccustomed to such intimacy. When Galador pulled back, his face was grave.

"I am truly sorry about Belegund. I hope he died well, and trust that he now walks in the Light of Aontar," he said. Thorndil nodded in agreement.

Rogond's eyes were wide. "How came you to know of Belegund?" He asked in wonder.

"Arialde had seen only one man emerging from the under the mountain. We did not know which of you still lay beneath it," said Galador.

"I would know the details of Belegund's fate, for he was a great friend and comrade," said Thorndil. "I trust his remains were properly tended?"

Rogond nodded. By the decree of Grundin, Belegund was laid to rest with great honor, and his remains would be forever undisturbed. This death had been hard for Rogond, and his eyes were downcast. He recalled the calm, young face of Belegund as the dwarves placed the stone over him. He looked as though he had fallen asleep, his cares gone and his soul at peace. Gaelen had wept bitterly, though it pained her, and she had turned from Rogond when he tried to comfort her. He had understood her reaction, as he knew she blamed herself for not being able to save Belegund, and thus would not allow herself to be comforted.

Now she sat up, determined to face Thorndil and tell what she could of Belegund's ending. "He fell in single combat with Gorgon. Though his pain was great, he died well, but I fear needlessly. I failed to aid him when the time came…though I tried. I must now add Belegund to those I mean to avenge. He had no chance against Gorgon, yet held him off for several minutes…" She began to weep at the memory, and this time she allowed Rogond to comfort her. He took her in his arms and spoke quietly to his friends.

"This is a tale that must wait until she is stronger. Gorgon nearly killed her—he thought he had done so. When we are rested and recovered we will tell of our journey. For now, let us hear of your adventures! Perhaps Fima would like to join us, and I'm sure the dwarves would enjoy the telling as well."

They rose and made their way to the firelight, where introductions were made. The sentinel Elves, who had waited nearby at Galador's request, were invited to join the circle as the telling of the mountain crossing began. Rogond shook his head in exasperated sympathy as Galador described the mischievous and somewhat reckless behavior of his favorite mount.

"Eros, Eros. You impossible animal. Wait until I get my hands on him! I'll threaten him with sale to the Elves of Greatwood."

Galador drew back in mock dismay. "Ha! As if they would have him. I'll wager the King is not having kind thoughts of him right now. Thorndil tells me that there was some difficulty between Ri-Aruin and his son, Wellyn, over the reappearance of Eros. I didn't really understand it, but perhaps he'll be kind enough to explain."

Gaelen was puzzled. "Why would Wellyn care about Eros?"

Thorndil shrugged. "I don't know, Gaelen. But I do know that he very much wished to cross the mountains into Mountain-home with us. He seemed quite set on it, and his father would not allow it under any circumstances. When we left, they were both decidedly unhappy."

Gaelen wished, for a moment, that she could make her way home to set things right. She worried about Wellyn and missed him. But she could not turn from the task at hand—she would enlist the aid of Arialde and Airan in the pursuit and defeat of Gorgon. She hoped that she would be able to adequately describe his vile ferocity—the more avenging feet she could set upon his trail, the better. After that, she didn't know where the task would lead her.

Gorgon Elfhunter sat brooding in his temporary lair in a small cavern under the foothills of the western Monadh-hin. He was generally pleased with the outcome of his foray into Cós-domhain, for it would be a long while before Gaelen or Rogond would step again into the realm of Grundin. This had been Gorgon's aim, as Gaelen was fairly well protected in the dwarf-realm, and he would learn little of use from her so long as she was there. His purpose would be much better served once she got into Tal-sithian, or such was his belief.

He had used the mirror twice since leaving the bodies for the dwarves to find and had witnessed the meeting with Grundin, rejoicing as Gaelen declared her desire to leave immediately to spare the dwarves further harm. She was so disgustingly noble and therefore predictable. Gorgon considered it a major weakness, one to which he certainly would not fall prey.

There was a current of cool air drifting through the passageway that led into his cavern, and he removed his helmet, allowing it to lift the silken gold of his hair. It was really quite curious. Not in recent memory had he enjoyed such simple pleasures as the wind in his hair; always he had been content to lurk in the darkness, alone with his hatred, neither feeling nor considering any discomfort. Could his exposure to Gaelen's world have anything to do with his renewed interest in such things? If so, he must guard himself carefully. The desire to live in harmony with the world and seek the company of others was definitely counter to his purposes—a weakness of the highest order. He concentrated for a moment on the image of the Shadowmancer hovering in the flames. He drew strength and resolve from the presence of Wrothgar and at the same time felt a gnawing fear deep within, for he knew that much was expected of him.

Gorgon had known Wrothgar very well indeed upon a time, and had learned not to disappoint him. The Shadowmancer had played a large role in educating Gorgon and had molded much of his thinking, though in the end he could neither rule Gorgon's thoughts nor dominate his actions.

As though to prove to himself the mastery of the mirror, Gorgon opened the cover and gazed into it. He saw a fire burning by a flowing stream, and the dwarves camped for the night. Tomorrow the Company would enter Tal-sithian, and Gorgon would eagerly await the insights that would follow. He had never beheld the Lake-realm, nor the Lord and Lady, but perhaps he would now learn the secret way in past the well-guarded shores. If not, he could certainly lie in wait for any that he knew were venturing forth outside them. He realized for a moment that he was trembling at the prospect, and then renewed his concentration by focusing on the face of the tall Elf whose name, apparently, was Galador. Gaelen was speaking to him in the firelight, where she was attempting to warm herself. Gorgon noticed that she was shivering as she looked into Galador's eyes.

"My brother, I will never doubt you again. Had Nelwyn gone beneath the Mountains with us, I know she would have been lost."

Gorgon smiled at this. *Too right, she would have.*

The She-elf apparently took notice of the pain in Galador's face, and knew that she had spoken true. "We must now reassure Rogond, for he learned little in Cós-domhain, and now feels the weight of Belegund's death," she said. "Though we did not know the Dark Horror had somehow tracked us beneath the mountains, it was our choice to go there despite your warning. Rogond thus feels responsible."

Gorgon actually chuckled then. "Dark Horror" indeed! Gorgon was flattered. The Tuathan needn't have regretted his choice—Cós-domhain had little to do with Belegund's death. Gorgon would have found the Company and set upon at least one of them by now regardless of their path. He might not have chosen Belegund, for he was more interested in the other She-elf and possibly the tall Elf, neither of whom had been within his grasp as yet. He meant to remedy that problem in the near future.

He shuddered and snapped the mirror-cover closed as Gaelen embraced Galador, who whispered soft words of comfort and reassurance. Gorgon truly wished these emotional Elves would cease their nearly endless displays of sentiment, as he was uncomfortable with them. Gorgon had never experienced a simple embrace and had heard precious few kindly words in his lifetime. The one person who had cared for him long ago he had slain at the bidding of Wrothgar, and it was just as well. Sentiment was a weakness that he could ill afford, and now there was little chance of his ever allowing himself to experience it.

Rogond had never before seen the wonders of Tal-sithian, and when he first beheld it he could not speak for several minutes. Though he had seen some of the most beautiful places in Alterra, including Mountain-home, he had spent much of his recent life in the wild, and the beauty of that fair green isle surrounded by crystal-blue water took his breath away. Gaelen had been here before, but not when the wood was flowering; she was likewise awed by the majestic elegance of the trees and the intoxicating scent of the blossoms. With each step she took she felt her spirits rising. Though she could not remain long in this place, Gaelen hoped that the Company would be renewed by the time they moved on toward the Greatwood.

A sudden chill came over Gaelen, and she shivered a little. This was becoming a common occurrence, and she wondered what the cause could be. She knew that contact with Gorgon often chilled her thus, but he was far away, and she had not had a scent of him since cleansing herself in the waters by the lake.

Nelwyn had stayed by her side, as though she could sense that all was not well with her cousin. She had wept at the sight of the dark marks on Gaelen's neck, imagining the look of smug satisfaction on Gorgon's ugly face as he choked the life from her. It was nothing short of miraculous that he had not succeeded. Now she met Gaelen at the base of the Greenwood Hill, for they had been summoned. They ascended to the chambers of Arialde and Airan, their faces set and determined. It would now be up to Gaelen to communicate the horrible events she had witnessed in Cós-domhain and to try to enlist the aid of the Elves of the Lake-realm.

When they stood at last before the Lord and Lady, Gaelen stepped forward and started to speak, but Arialde held up her hand to silence her. She closed her eyes for a moment, then opened them, searching Gaelen's bright, unflinching gaze. The smaller Elf lifted her chin in defiance, but her expression softened as Arialde's voice was heard inside her mind:

Proud Elf of the Greatwood, soften thy grieving heart. I know why you have come to us, and I know of your pain and sorrow. You lie under a dark doom, Gaelen Taldin of the Cúinar, whose heart was given to One Who Waits. Though I cannot see the nature of it, I know that greater sorrow and hardship will befall you before all is ended. Now we must parley, and much will be revealed both to you and to us. Soften thy heart!

Gaelen nodded, though she did not drop her gaze. "There is one other who needs to hear your tale," said Arialde, indicating a tall Elf who stood by, hidden in shadow. He approached and stood behind the Lady. Gaelen thought he looked vaguely familiar. He was golden-haired, with keen blue eyes and a handsome but weary face that had seen much sorrow and trial. Lord Airan introduced him as "Amandir", and he bowed slightly to Gaelen, who returned the polite gesture before beginning her tale. Their discourse lasted into the evening, as Arialde, Airan, and Amandir had many questions.

"Why do you think Gorgon failed to achieve your death in Cós-domhain, Gaelen?" asked Arialde. This apparently troubled her, as she could not imagine the creature failing in such an important task.

Gaelen shook her head. "I don't know. I suppose I shall never know, but I do know this: he will regret his lack of thoroughness before all is ended. I mean to bring him down with the help of the Elves of Mountain-home and of the Greatwood. I am hopeful of your aid as well."

The Lady drew a deep breath, and Amandir dropped his gaze, refusing to look at Gaelen for several minutes. It seemed that he struggled with some deep pain that he could not reveal, and Gaelen was diverted for a long moment as she regarded him curiously.

"Look at me, Elf of the Greatwood!" Lord Airan's voice brought her back sharply to the matter at hand. "This creature is more closely tied to the Elves of Tal-sithian than to any others. Listen, now, to our tale of woe."

When Airan had finished, Gaelen and Nelwyn both stood in horror at what he had revealed. Nelwyn was the first to speak. "You cannot mean that creature is...of Elven blood?"

Arialde nodded. "Alas, he is Half-elven, the ill-gotten son of my handmaiden, the spouse of Amandir. Her name was Brinneal, and she was both beautiful and strong, a proud maiden of the Èolar. She was a survivor of the Second Uprising and chose to come here to the Lake rather than remain with the others in Mountain-home. Alas that she chose such! Her death was both tragic and welcomed, but the spawn of Darkness persists. I cannot imagine the evil nurturing and shaping he has received. We had hoped that the child had died, or been lost, but now we know that it was not so. Your story has confirmed it. We have wondered on occasion, but now we know it to be true, to our sorrow. This is ill news you bring, daughter of the Greatwood."

Indeed, Amandir looked as though his heart had been torn apart as he stood with an expression of blank horror and grief upon his fair but careworn face. His sorrow was unimaginable even to Gaelen, who had known deep sorrow in her lifetime. She wanted nothing more at that moment than to comfort him, but knew that there were no words or feelings she could express that would be of any benefit. She simply could not take her gaze from his downcast eyes, so full of pain. Before Arialde or Lord Airan could stop her, she approached him, reaching out with a gentle hand, placing it upon his arm. He drew back from her as though stung, cold fury burning in his eyes.

"What would you know of it, Elf? How dare you try to comfort me, when you cannot even imagine my pain. Keep your distance!" He turned to the Lord and Lady, saying, "I will not suffer myself to be in her presence, and I beg your leave to go. I must inform my son and my daughter that their half-brother has been found alive at last. I'm sure they await this joyful news even now. So, if you will pardon me, I will take my leave."

Without a word from either Arialde or Airan, Amandir turned and strode from their company, nodding to Nelwyn as he passed. He would not look at Gaelen, who stood shocked and hurt by his words. Whatever did he mean? What evil? She did not understand. When he had gone, Arialde sighed and shook her head, her deep blue eyes filled with grief. Gaelen looked to her, hoping for an explanation, but none came.

"I cannot explain Amandir's actions, worthy daughter of Tarfion. I only know that what he has felt, I have felt also. Guard yourself well, and perhaps things will be made plain in time. For now, you must forget Amandir's harsh words. He is not himself, and his pain has made him discourteous. Please do not let this trouble you, but rest and heal yourself, for you are welcome in the Lake-realm."

Gaelen stared at her. "Forget his words? He practically accused me of being in league with Gorgon! No one desires that creature's death more than I!"

But to this Arialde did not agree. "Were you in the place of Amandir, you would desire it even more, Gaelen. You know what it is to love someone deeply to the exclusion of all others. Imagine the pain he has endured because of this abomination, and you will forgive him his harsh words."

Gaelen was mollified for the moment, and she and Nelwyn bowed and turned to leave, but Arialde stayed them. "Amandir has insisted that when you leave to pursue the creature Gorgon that he be allowed to accompany you. I have granted this to him."

Gaelen bristled. "But I have *not* granted it, nor have any of my companions. You do not rule my actions outside of this realm, Lady, and right now I am not inclined to be thus burdened with one such as Amandir. This gift was not yours to grant." She drew herself up before Arialde, who, to her surprise, smiled at her.

"Fair enough, Elf of the Woodland. But I would beg you to reconsider. Amandir has a part to play in this, and you cannot deny him his chance for vengeance. Search your heart and tell me that you do not agree."

The Lady stared hard at Gaelen, who, to the relief of Nelwyn, dropped her gaze and muttered something under her breath. They did not need to challenge the Lord and Lady of the Lake, at least not while within their realm.

After the Company had been fed and rested, they sat listening to the haunting music of the Eádram, which filled the starry skies and echoed amid the gentle whispering of the leaves in the tall trees. Gaelen began to shiver, though the weather was warm. Rogond placed her cloak tenderly about her shoulders. She had been cold for much of the evening and could not seem to warm herself. Rogond added his own cloak to hers, but she still could not stop shivering.

Nelwyn had filled them all in on what had transpired, and they were predictable in their reaction. Galador was shocked that Gaelen would so defy Arialde. Rogond was angered at the response of Amandir to Gaelen's attempt to comfort him. They all wanted to know what was meant by this "dark doom" that supposedly lay heavily upon Gaelen, who muttered something under her breath about being tired of confusing predictions and mysterious pronouncements. Fima was the first to agree with her.

"Elves! If they cannot make themselves plain, they should say nothing at all," he said, patting Gaelen's shoulder. "Don't be concerned. I'll warrant there is nothing much behind it, probably just someone's bad dream." He looked pointedly at Galador as he spoke. "And I, for one, wish I had been there when you dared stand up to the Lady. You were quite right that it was not her place to grant Amandir's request."

Rogond nodded. "Perhaps not the wisest course, Gaelen, but certainly an honest one. And I will tell you one thing—no Elf who thinks ill of you will I suffer at MY side, no matter the decree of the Lady. Amandir had best relent if he wishes to travel with us."

Nelwyn also stood in agreement. "The Company shall remain devoted to its own," she said, "and will accept no one of ill will toward any among us." Thorndil and Galador added their voices in assent, and the six friends raised their glasses together, vowing to defend the Company to the last.

Gorgon cried out in frustration as the pain of the mirror hammered at his already exhausted brain. He had been trying for several hours to perceive the goings-on in Tal-sithian, but he could not see clearly, nor could he hear any but the barest snatches of conversation. What was wrong? It had been bad enough that the accursed mist had prevented him from knowing how to enter the realm, but now he could not even see clearly in the mirror. His powerful weapon was failing him even now. He grew dizzy and ill with trying to make sense of the distorted images that flickered across his vision and prayed that this did not mean that the power of the mirror was fading for some reason. Without it, he would once again be reduced to hiding and ambushing stray Elves by chance, and all of his grand plans would be in vain. What would Wrothgar have to say about this? Gorgon did not wish to consider it.

Ha! Having a bit of difficulty, are we? said a voice to his immediate left.

Gorgon was somewhat distressed to see that Gelmyr had returned, still as dead as ever, his blue glowing face displaying an ill-natured smile.

"Oh, go away, you wretched Èolo! I thought I had banished you from my presence at last. You are the last person I ever wish to encounter again. Why will you not leave me in peace?"

Gelmyr shrugged. *I am here because you willed it, whether you know it or not. I am very much looking forward to watching you unwittingly planning your own downfall. I hope I don't miss anything,* he replied.

Gorgon turned from him, concentrating once more on the mirror and the vague, unreadable images channeling through it.

The mirror will not work in the great Elf-realms, because you are using it for evil, said Gelmyr. *I'm sure an intelligent creature such as yourself has realized it. So much for your grand plans! Did you really think you could gain the downfall of Lady Arialde so easily? The Dark Power Himself has failed in this task. How very prideful of you to have such a hope!* He shook his head, his long, tangled hair matted with blood, which appeared silver in the blue light. *I thought I warned you about that, didn't I? I'll warrant my people won't have to do much to defeat you; your pride will do it for them!*

"Tell that to Belegund and those wretched dwarves," growled Gorgon, wishing with all his heart that Gelmyr would disappear and quit distracting him.

Ah, yes! Well, another victory for cowardice, after all. And then you nearly choked the life out of the one person who can aid you in accomplishing your purpose. How very savage and predictable! You know she is quite bent on destroying you. They all are. And they are gathering strength, Gorgon. You had better figure out a way to lay them all low, and soon. Wrothgar expects a return for His fine gift, and from what I have heard He does not suffer disappointment well. No, indeed!

Gorgon then closed the mirror, taking a swipe at Gelmyr, who was shaking his head and smiling ill-naturedly, mocking Gorgon all the while.

"Begone, you dead, helpless, vanquished pathetic excuse for an Elf!" Gorgon roared. "Begone and come to me no more!" Then he sank heavily down upon his knees, exhausted by the mirror and the effort of banishing Gelmyr, as the Elf's laughter faded slowly from his hearing at last, and he was gone.

The Company remained in Tal-sithian for several weeks, though Gaelen grew increasingly restive and anxious to set forth toward the Greatwood. It would be a pleasant journey with horses and fine summer weather to aid them, and Gaelen was looking forward to seeing her home again. Nelwyn was likewise anxious, and it was all Galador could do to keep her contained. She and Gaelen spent endless hours provisioning themselves for the journey—refitting their weapons, practicing with bow and blade. Gaelen enlisted Fima's help in training her to use his dwarvish axe, which she wielded with her customary grace, though she lacked Fima's power.

They saw little of Amandir, though he still planned to accompany them. Rogond had drawn him aside one morning, and though courteous, Rogond was direct. He told Amandir that no ill will toward Gaelen would be tolerated should the Company allow him to proceed with them, and it might be best if he apologized to her before they departed. Amandir returned Rogond's courtesy, stating that he did indeed regret his harsh words to Gaelen, but that the feeling of her unwitting complicity with their enemy remained. Rogond shook his head.

"You could not be more wrong, Amandir. She, of all the Company, holds the most hatred of him. She has been the force that has driven this quest. She will not give up until he is dead. You cannot have a stronger ally!"

Amandir shook his head. "These things you say may be true in your reckoning. I only know that some evil stalks her even now. It grows less with time in the Sithian, but I fear it will grow strong again once she leaves the protection of the Lady. And many Elven lives will be lost—I know it, because I have seen it. Now I ride with you because I know this enemy will not stray far from your Gaelen; the road leading to him lies where she has gone."

Rogond knew better than to scoff at Amandir, and he was worried. "What have you seen, and where did you see it?"

Amandir then told Rogond of the fabled Stone of Léir, now kept by the Lady, in whose depths many things could be seen. He had looked into it three days before the arrival of Galador and Nelwyn, at the request of Arialde. What he saw there had disquieted him.

"I presume that a man educated in Mountain-home knows much of the Stone's history already," he said. "The terrible war that surrounded the Third Uprising had begun because it was rumored that

Wrothgar would march on Mountain-home to overrun it and seize the Stone for his own. The Stone was then moved to the Lake-realm, for should its power be turned to the service of Darkness, the consequences would be devastating."

Rogond nodded, for he did know quite a lot about the Stone. It had been created by the Elf, Dardis, together with Léiras the Asarla. Initially its use had been completely benevolent and harmless; it enabled any who looked into its depths to re-live past moments that had brought joy and contentment. It had been especially useful in healing the troubled hearts of those damaged by grief. When the Second Uprising of Wrothgar destroyed most of the Èolar, the Stone had been taken to Monadh-talam under the protection of Shandor and Liathwyn. Wrothgar did not yet desire it, for its power at that time was of little use.

Liathwyn had been so grieved at the loss of her people that she relinquished her spirit, and she was accepted into Elysia, the Elves' eternal home. But Lord Shandor, mightiest of the Asari, could not follow her there, and he loved her so deeply that his great spirit was broken.

He grieved long and bitterly for his beloved and at last sought relief by gazing into the Stone, where he could re-live his happy years with Liathwyn. But memories are only reminders of what can no longer be, and Shandor's attempts to escape his grief and to heal himself were of little avail. It was said that he gazed so long and with such longing that at last he was drawn into the crystal. His body remained outside and has never withered, though it is without life. It is kept in a tomb of glass beneath Monadh-talam, for Shandor is the father of Lady Ordath, who rules that realm.

When the mightiest spirit in Alterra entered the stone, its power grew very great. It became at once the most magical and potentially the most dangerous object remaining in the world. Its use now is strictly governed by the Lady Arialde, and to look into the Stone outside the grace of the Lady is to court disaster. Shandor is a powerful but bitter soul, grieving for his beloved Liathwyn with whom he cannot be reunited, and in his wounded state he cares not for the pain of others. The visions he sends to those who should not behold them can drive them mad. Yet Shandor can, if he chooses, reveal the destiny of those who seek to learn it.

"It is difficult to imagine the terrible advantage that would be gained should such a power fall into the hands of Wrothgar," said Amandir. "He would be able to know the minds and deeds of his enemies, and discover the outcome of battles ere they were fought. The forces of Darkness have not yet discovered the present whereabouts of the Stone, but as they slowly regain their strength this would become more likely, and there might come a day when we will need to defend our great treasure to the last. I believe Gaelen is somehow aiding the enemy. I gained this insight from gazing into the Stone."

Rogond was disquieted, for he had been taught that visions perceived in the Stone were true. He was not the only one who wondered about the meaning of Amandir's vision.

Not far away, Nelwyn had paused on her way to find Gaelen as she overheard Rogond speaking to Amandir. Intending at first to make her presence known so that she might add her voice in support of her cousin, she now hung back in the shadows, listening to Amandir's tale of his encounter with the Stone. Lady Arialde had said that she had shared Amandir's concern—did she know of his vision? Fima probably knew of such matters; Nelwyn decided to ask him later. She remained still and silent until Rogond and Amandir departed, after Rogond had reminded Amandir that he still needed to set things right with Gaelen.

Nelwyn went back to their quarters in search of Fima, but instead found Gaelen preparing to ride. She had been granted permission to go to the mainland and ride Siva over the plains surrounding the lake, and she invited Nelwyn to join her. Though the past weeks had been enjoyable, Nelwyn compared them to being in a beautiful, very comfortable cage. She rejoiced as she readied herself for this excursion, and she and Gaelen went forth together.

Once they had gained the far shore, they called for the horses, reveling in their freedom as they rode, truly unfettered for the first time since the Company had divided. The weather was clear and warm, though there was the promise of rain in the coming evening. At last they met a group of Elves traveling toward the foothills where flowed the cold stream in which Gaelen had healed herself after her last encounter with Gorgon. A few of the Elves were planning to relieve the guard there, and several brought fishing nets and baskets with them, for there were huge dewberry bushes growing on both sides of the stream nearby, and the berries would be prime for picking.

They greeted Gaelen and Nelwyn warmly once they were recognized. Having little to fear in the daylight, they bore only light armaments, and they spread their cloaks upon the grass, inviting their guests to join them in an early meal. Gaelen was disinclined at first, until a jar of honey appeared beside the bread, cake, and fruit the Elves had laid out. She and Nelwyn swung down from their horses without another word, and they spent nearly an hour feasting and making merry with the lighthearted Elves of the Lake. Songs were sung then, as the sun rose high in the blue sky. One of the Elves sighed and looked at the towering white clouds that were beginning to make their way toward them from the west.

"It will be a chilly, wet night I fear," said he. "Just the time for me to relieve my brother at guard. Ah, well. At least I will enjoy the afternoon until I reach him. Save some of the food for us, for we shall have need of it!"

At this the others laughed. "Food there is yet aplenty, Lindor, but no honey will you take to the watch. It seems our Woodland cousins are as fond of it as we!"

This set Gaelen and Nelwyn to giggling, as they had just about polished off the honey-jar.

Lindor nodded. "Just as well, for we will have need of our wits. I suppose we should get to it, or there will be no time for berry-picking." He rose and bowed to Gaelen and Nelwyn. "Enjoy your stay with us and your ride in the fine summer air, and I hope that you shall now be able to sit your mounts and not fall off from laughing."

This, of course, made Gaelen and Nelwyn laugh all the more, along with their new companions, though Gaelen suddenly felt her good humor drain away, as though something was amiss. She rose and scanned the horizon in all directions, scenting the air, but found nothing. Probably just the honey wearing off, she thought. The Elves of Tal-sithian were not dismayed, and they knew the lands hereabout. If anything threatened them, they would be alerted. As they prepared to go on their way, they called back to Gaelen and Nelwyn:

"Farewell, new friends. We shall meet again and feast with you before you depart these lands. For now, we are off to the Cold-spring!

Dewberries are only ripe for so long. Farewell!" They went on their way again, singing as they went, for their hearts were light.

Nelwyn and Gaelen raised their hands in farewell. Nelwyn was still smiling and inclined to laugh without provocation, though the effects of the wild honey were waning. She glanced over at Gaelen, wondering at the serious expression on her cousin's face. Gaelen couldn't have explained had Nelwyn asked, and she turned away. She swung aboard Siva, shaking with the chill that had somehow found her once again.

22

Gorgon's Army

Gorgon had learned of Wrothgar's intention to send him the beginnings of an army soon after Gelmyr had reappeared. He had despaired upon discovering that the mirror would not work within the influence of Tal-sithian, but Wrothgar was not dismayed, and simply reminded Gorgon to remain vigilant. Gaelen would eventually emerge, and then he might learn something of interest. This was a somewhat frustrating task, as Gorgon felt compelled for quite some time to gaze into the mirror almost constantly lest he miss his opportunity. He was so weary after a few days that he was forced to relax, and after that things were more bearable.

Wrothgar assured him that all was well, and that he was pleased with Gorgon's progress. He instructed Gorgon to await the arrival of the Ulcas, to train with them, and then to venture forth and bring ruin upon as many of his foes as possible. This Gorgon happily anticipated, although he was still not comfortable with the idea of collaborating with such lowly minions. He would soon change his mind, however, when sixteen Elves lay dead with barely a struggle. He would only regret that neither they nor their kin would know from whence death came on that day. No matter. They would all learn soon enough.

Kharsh had been in the service of the Dark Powers for as long as he could remember. He was one of thirty Ulcas hand-picked from the descendants of the survivors of the Third Uprising, but only he was old enough to have actually lived through that great battle. Most of Wrothgar's army had withered as dry grass before a flame, but Kharsh had managed to escape with a few others when his Master was laid low.

He was old indeed for one of his race, though it was not truly known how long Ulcas could live if they were not killed. It was rare for one to live much longer than a few hundred years, for they so frequently fell victim to enemies, including each other. Kharsh was now well into his second millennium. Truly, he was exceptional.

Kharsh had been selected for his abilities as diplomat and tactician, not for youth or physical prowess. He stood about chest-high to Gorgon, if he did not stoop. His skin was a mottled grey-black; his face was as very old, worn leather with two yellowish-brown eyes peering intelligently from the folds of ancient flesh. His eight remaining fingers bore yellowed, curved claws. His teeth were few, but sharp and still surprisingly strong, though they could no longer crack even small rib bones the way they used to.

He had been instructed to educate and guide Gorgon, a task he did not relish, though it would no doubt provide an interesting challenge. The Elfhunter was difficult from the first, as he was proud and not inclined to take direction, no matter how well advised. In addition, Gorgon despised nearly everything and everyone—though he hated most the Elves, neither did he love the Ulcas.

Kharsh remembered having briefly met Gorgon's impressive sire, who was one of the most formidable and savage Ulcas spawned since the First Reckoning. Wrothgar had eventually set Gorgon against him in combat three times. The first two times, Gorgon would have been defeated had Wrothgar not intervened, but the third time Gorgon was victorious. Kharsh had heard tales of this conflict; it was said among his folk that the battle between Gorgon and his sire went on for days. In truth, it lasted several hours, and at the end of it, Gorgon stood triumphant, a look of utter contempt upon his then relatively unscarred face. This contempt for his father's race had grown with time, and thus Kharsh faced a daunting challenge.

He reflected that such talent and such a difficult creation as Gorgon had been wasted for too many years in hiding and striking down a few Elves. It was time to unleash the power Wrothgar had labored so long to develop, and to do this effectively Gorgon would need to learn the ways of a field commander.

Along with Kharsh, Wrothgar had sent nearly thirty Warrior-Ulcas that would make a worthy force against a relatively small host of men or Elves. They wielded various weapons; some were adept archers, others were more formidable with blades, axes, or clubs. They did not love Gorgon either, but in fear of Wrothgar they would do as they were told. Gorgon's obvious disdain for the Ulcas and his (in their eyes) glaringly Elven features and mannerisms made for an uncooperative beginning.

Kharsh knew that although Gorgon understood Ulcan speech quite well, he would not use it. Communication had been difficult at first, for none of the Ulcas save Kharsh spoke or understood any form of Elven-tongue, which Gorgon preferred. He stubbornly refused to address them in the common tongue, until Kharsh had pointed out that Wrothgar would indeed be disappointed should his hand-picked army fail for lack of clear direction. Gorgon then wisely reconsidered. He had actually killed two of his own Ulcas before their purpose was made plain to him, and Kharsh worried that Gorgon might be so undisciplined that he might not be able to carry out Wrothgar's commands

Then Kharsh became aware that Gorgon really did fear Wrothgar, and the situation eased. Regardless of his prideful nature, Gorgon would not openly defy the Shadowmancer, and thus, in spite of himself he would submit and allow Kharsh to complete his task. Kharsh tried to win Gorgon's begrudging acceptance by tantalizing him with promises of the destructive capabilities of his new command. Now Gorgon could, with planning and insights provided by the mirror, do considerably more damage upon the Elves, to his anticipated delight. Kharsh hoped that they would soon have an opportunity for mayhem, as both Gorgon and the Ulcas were growing restless.

Kharsh and the Ulcas had spent several weeks training with their new commander, and now they were ready to venture forth, for they had been presented with an opportunity. Gorgon had learned that a group of about a dozen Elves were traveling to the Cold-spring to relieve those on the far watch. Gorgon and Kharsh had some trouble convincing the Ulcas that they could endure the daylight even for so short a time, but that day the sun was dimmed by clouds, and their armor shielded them.

The Elves were taken unaware. Two of the sentinels were felled by Gorgon's weapon as they stood watch in the tree-tops. The others fell quickly enough, though two of the Ulcas were slain by the Elves' bows before they were taken. Soon the anticipated group of twelve appeared, and they were surrounded. They were utterly surprised and put up only as much struggle as their light armaments would allow, standing no chance against this well-armed and armored force. The dead Elves were dragged off and hidden deep underground. When the host departed there was very little sign for anyone to read, and there would be even less two days later, when a small party came from Tal-sithian to investigate. This attack bore none of the usual signs or methods Gorgon normally employed, and the Elves were confused and mystified. Gorgon was now much more appreciative of his "lowly minions".

Nelwyn finally found Fima in the early evening as he sat down to an evening repast with several of the Elves of Tal-sithian. They were enjoying their food, drink, and conversation, and Nelwyn did not wish to disturb them, but she wanted to ask Fima about the Stone of Léir without anyone else overhearing.

She hung back in the shadows behind a large vine-covered rock until Fima noticed her and invited her to join him. She approached and sat between Fima and the Elves, who were engaged in a lively discussion regarding the Time of Mystery and the interpretations that had been recorded since. Nelwyn listened with fascination, for she knew little of such things.

Eventually the Elves took their leave, and Nelwyn and Fima were alone. After a brief but awkward silence, Nelwyn turned to the dwarf, who had already guessed that she had not come only to socialize with him.

"You know a great deal about the history and lore of the Elves, Fima. Have you much knowledge of the people of Tal-sithian?"

Fima shrugged. "Some, Nelwyn, but they have kept many of their secrets well. What would you seek to learn of them?"

Nelwyn came directly to the point, for she knew that was Fima's preferred way in all things. "This is said to be the resting-place of the Stone of Léir. Do you know of and understand its workings? If so, what knowledge can you share with me?"

Fima looked at her with a mixture of curiosity and interest. "It is one of the things of Tal-sithian that I do know a little about, Nelwyn, though perhaps not as much as needed. How came you to learn of it, and why do you wish to know?"

Nelwyn told him of the conversation she had overheard between Rogond and Amandir, flushing a little as she admitted listening in secret. Fima smiled slightly at her—he did not blame Nelwyn for her action and was now enjoying the fact that he, too, was privy to the conversation. When she revealed Amandir's words concerning Gaelen, Fima's eyes hardened and he made a deep rumbling sound in his throat which Nelwyn interpreted as disapproval. He let her finish her tale, then drew a long breath.

"Good for Rogond. Someone needed to inform that fellow Amandir that he had best watch his step and curb his unworthy opinions of your little cousin. In league with Gorgon, is she? He obviously didn't see her in Cós-domhain. She fought off that armored giant with only her short sword—I still marvel that she escaped with her life. Alas that Belegund was not so fortunate. At any rate, this Amandir sounds like a load of confusing rubbish to me—typical vague Elvish nonsense, begging your pardon."

Nelwyn smiled, as no offense had been taken. She was inclined to agree with Fima.

"I will reveal what I know of the Stone," Fima continued. "It is kept in seclusion near the Greenwood Hill; you have probably passed close by without realizing it."

He paused and drew out his long clay pipe and a leather tobacco-pouch, filled the pipe and lighted it. Soon he was drawing contentedly, sending fine wisps of blue smoke heavenward. Nelwyn tensed as she became aware of a presence only a few feet away from Fima, but then relaxed as Gaelen's tousled head and bright eyes appeared among the leaves. She smiled as Fima gave a startled gasp, and then glared at her.

"Well, Lore-master! You have relaxed your vigilance in the Lake-realm, I see," Gaelen observed.

Fima shook his head. "I do wish you would stop doing that! You will startle me once too often one day." Ignoring the comment, Gaelen crossed to sit beside Nelwyn, apparently in quite a cheerful mood.

"Continue your tale, O Wise Dwarf, if you can pause long enough from your pipe. I would also hear of the Stone. It sounds interesting! What does it do?"

Fima sent forth a long curl of smoke before responding. "It shows the past, the present, and some say the future. Lord Shandor controls it...I would not look into such a thing for any amount of wealth! From what I've heard, the visions may be enlightening, but are often confusing, are always unpredictable, and are seldom uplifting. Not a few have gone mad upon viewing them. Thus Lady Arialde guards the Stone, and she will not permit its use outside her presence. She also sees what is seen by those who look into it, so unless you wish to share your visions with her, I would suggest you abandon doing what I believe you are thinking of doing."

Gaelen and Nelwyn looked innocently at one another. "And what is that, Fima?" they responded in perfect unison.

"You are planning to have a look and see whether you can gain any insights into your course in pursuit of Gorgon, is what! And neither of you were intending to ask permission if I am any judge. But you must, for if you disturb Lord Shandor without leave, you'll regret it! I would advise against this course, because I fear for both of you. You will see nothing encouraging." So saying, he rose and went from the glade, taking his pipe and a vessel of wine to pass the night in cheerful solitude. But he threw one last look back at Gaelen, for he could read the desire in her face. "Do not go looking for the Stone... you will not find it."

Gaelen and Nelwyn watched him go then turned to one another, both their faces set. "I would not object to any insight the Stone might give as to where our enemy is hiding," said Gaelen.

"But you heard Fima—the Stone is unpredictable. Lord Shandor does not perform on command, showing us what we desire to see. If we look, we may even go mad!" said Nelwyn with a shiver.

She was right to worry. Yet she had sought the information because Fima was correct—Nelwyn had wanted to look into the Stone and gain what it had to give. She turned to Gaelen. "Let us seek out Arialde, and see whether she will agree. If so, and she does not advise strongly against it, I would look into the Stone with you."

"Fine, then let us seek her tomorrow evening. I am pleasantly weary from riding—it felt so good to roam free again! I hope we can soon leave for the Greatwood. This is a delightful place, and I am grateful for the time of healing, but we must move on. So long as that creature exists, I will not truly rest. For now, let's ascend into the tree-tops. The rain has passed, and the stars are bright tonight!"

"First, I must find Galador. He worries when he does not know my whereabouts," said Nelwyn.

Gaelen shook her head. "What harm could befall you in Talsithian? Does he fear you will fall from a tree and break your neck?"

"Stop it, Gaelen! You know he simply wants to keep me safe. We may both find you later. The stars will be no less bright then, you know."

Gaelen rose and turned from her. "Don't bother to find me later, Nelwyn. I'm certain Galador would much rather spend time alone with you…yet again. I shall amuse myself on this fine evening. I am merely grateful that he allowed you to ride with me across such dangerous lands. We might have encountered some fierce groundsquirrel, or you might have fallen from your horse, who knows?"

Gaelen knew that her words and the mildly disgusted tone of her voice pained Nelwyn, but she didn't care. She left her gentle, good-natured cousin standing alone with nothing to say to her as she went in search of Rogond.

Gaelen was still worried about Rogond's reference to her in Cós-domhain as his "love". She had not yet spoken of it with him, but she knew that she must soon do so. Tonight was not the time to bring up such things, however. The fact that Rogond was nearby, and would no doubt be delighted to share the stars with her, brought great comfort. She hoped he was not too weary, but if so she would lie beside him and sing to him until the dawn came.

Nelwyn found Galador almost immediately. He had, in fact, been searching for her, not out of concern for her safety but simply because he wished for her company. He embraced her, and she expressed the desire to climb a tree and see the stars, which, as Gaelen had predicted, were very bright now that the rain had cleared and the moon had set.

"I suppose you will want to find Gaelen and ask her to join us," said Galador good-naturedly. He normally enjoyed Gaelen's company, even if he did prefer being alone with Nelwyn.

Nelwyn shook her head. "She does not want our company tonight. I do so wish she did not begrudge my time with you. She's probably sulking right now. No matter, she will be in a better mind by morning. She has not been herself since we rode out today and met the Elves going to the Cold-spring. She felt something, and it wasn't good."

From their vantage-point beneath the stars, Nelwyn told Galador of her intention to seek Arialde and request permission to look into the Stone of Léir.

Galador frowned at her. "From what I've heard, the Stone reveals little of joy and much of grief. It can be very frightening and can even mislead if misinterpreted. Do as you will, but know that my advice is to stay away from the Stone of Léir. And by all means, keep Gaelen from it! She has no business being anywhere near an object of such power." Then he shook his head, for he knew there was about as much chance of Gaelen's taking this excellent advice as the Lord of Eádros giving the hand of his only daughter to one of the dwarves of Rûmm.

Gaelen paused in her search for Rogond as she found herself near the tall trees that surrounded the home of Arialde and Lord Airan. Her curiosity had been awakened, and her hunter-scout's nature insisted that she should investigate the area, just in case. Gaelen's inquisitiveness was considered overdeveloped, even for a Wood-elf, and Fima had practically dared her to try to find the Stone, which she correctly guessed would not be too far away from the abode of Arialde.

She moved through the darkness in absolute silence until she finally caught a scent of the Lady, then she followed the scent until it led her into a glade surrounded by thick, fragrant cedars. Gaelen had hoped to find Arialde, but as she shyly entered the glade her breath was taken by the sight of thousands of fireflies flashing and hovering in the night air like gentle golden sparks. She had never seen so many! They were obviously drawn to the enormous crystal that stood upon a pedestal of carved red granite, emitting a soft glow in the reflected light of the fireflies and the bright stars.

Gaelen was drawn irresistibly toward it, despite her feeling that not only should she avoid looking into its depths, but that she probably should not have invaded the glade in the first place. Still, she approached until she was near enough to mount the base of the pedestal. The crystal glowed white before her, as if sensing her desire, yet there was a slightly menacing aspect emanating from it, as though it warned her to keep her eyes elsewhere. Gaelen stood helpless for a moment, eyes shut tight, her hands cold and her heart pounding. It was not too late to turn about; but alas, she was the victim of her own inescapable curiosity. After all, she probably would see nothing—hadn't Fima suggested that, outside the presence of the Lady, the Stone was nothing but a large rock?

Gaelen opened her eyes and looked at the crystal with a mixture of apprehension and wonder. What she saw was both beautiful and intriguing. There were an infinite number of flat, silvery planes within; they reflected the light in a myriad of interesting ways. Gaelen wondered how the Stone would appear in sunlight, and her eyes shone with delight at the thought of it.

A sudden feeling of foreboding came over her, and she knew that she should look no further, but the crystal shifted even as she tried to turn from it. An image began to form, and she began to hear voices. The clear surface roiled as though under tremendous heat, engulfing her senses with a vision so intense that she tried to reel back from it. It was too late to turn aside, and she was drawn into the grasp of the Stone, afflicted by a sight that she should never have seen.

She felt her senses blurring and whirling in a mass of light and sound, and she struggled to control the feeling that she was falling headlong into a maelstrom. This terrible, unsettling feeling of falling came to an abrupt end, but she was no longer in the glade—she was standing on a battlefield. The vision proceeded with inexorable, blinding speed. The Elves were beleaguered by thousands of enemies—banners from many realms waved their tattered, ghostly colors in a wind that stank of blood and sulfur. Gaelen looked down at her hands, which were now encased in armored gauntlets, realizing that she viewed this terrible scene through the eyes of one of the warriors who had actually been there. She could not control her body, not tear her eyes from the scene before her.

There were many dark and evil creatures, wearing black robes that glowed and flickered as though with fire. She could not see their faces. Their fingers were long and gnarled, with sharp claws, and they drove back the host of Elves with flames that burst forth from their hands. Gaelen recognized Magra among the Elves. He was struggling valiantly to get past the creatures, to no avail. All about them was a suffocating cloud of fear.

In the center of the fray, two warriors strove with one another to the death. One was immense, a terrible, monstrous entity engulfed in peculiar dark flames that sprang from the core of his own being. He wrestled in mortal combat with a smaller being of no less brilliance—an Elven-lord, blue-white and blinding to behold. Gaelen knew him at once! Her beloved Ri-Elathan strove against the Lord of Black Flame, and she could neither aid him nor prevent his terrible death.

The circle of demonic creatures kept any aid from reaching the Elvenking, yet he fought to the limits of his considerable power, and Wrothgar was weakening. But then, the Shadowmancer opened his great maw, showing terrible sharp teeth, and brought his flaming jaws down upon Ri-Elathan, biting hard into his right shoulder. The flames spread from the wound, overpowering the Light of truth, of courage and freedom, and Ri-Elathan was slowly consumed by it, overcome by the power of Wrothgar's evil. Gaelen could smell the stench of brimstone and burning flesh.

Still Ri-Elathan fought, despite unspeakable pain, screaming as the flames took him. Gaelen saw him turn his determined, agonized face toward her, and she looked into the eyes of her beloved Rain as Wrothgar overcame the last of his waning power, quenching his light forever. Ri-Elathan continued to fight as his life was ripped from him, his eyes unseeing, his jaws locked in a final grimace of determination, but even as he died Gaelen felt his bitter disappointment, for he knew that he had failed. Wrothgar then threw his head back and laughed, hurling the body of his victim past the dark circle of fire that surrounded them. It landed, still aflame, at the feet of Magra.

Gaelen gave a heart-wrenching cry of despair, her hands reaching toward the fading image of Farahin's ruined, smoldering body, cast aside by Wrothgar. She looked into his dead eyes and read his despair in them. She also read his longing for her. She cried again, screaming his name, horrified almost beyond return...

then she felt hands grasping her shoulders as someone pulled her back from the Stone, turned her around, and called her name in a powerful voice.

"Gaelen! Gaelen! Do not keep this vision in thy mind! Turn from it and come back to me. Come back! This horror is long past. Come back. Shandor, *RELEASE HER!*"

The battlefield vanished. Gaelen opened her eyes and beheld Arialde, whose eyes were filled with a reflection of the same horror. She had known Ri-Elathan of old and had called him friend. She held Gaelen for a moment, trying to calm her. Gaelen quickly pulled herself away and stared into the eyes of perhaps the most powerful being remaining in Alterra, knowing that Arialde had shared this horrific vision with her. Though they had lasted only a few moments, these images would remain forever etched in Gaelen's mind.

Look into my eyes, Gaelen Taldin!

The Lady searched the depths of Gaelen's bright eyes for a moment, and when she beheld no madness in them, she was relieved. Arialde gripped Gaelen's shoulders, chiding her gently, though she was clearly sympathetic.

"You have a most unfortunate curiosity, Elf of Greatwood. You should not have looked into the Stone without my leave. Luckily I was nearby to aid you. I sorrow for your pain, but you must never look into its depths again without my leave. Do you understand?"

This admonition was completely unnecessary; Gaelen had never understood anything so well. She was still trembling as she spoke to Arialde.

"It…it was as though I actually stood in that dreadful place! That was the most terrible sight I have ever beheld. Does this mean that it actually happened in this manner? My only love died so horribly and in such pain? Long have I known it in my heart. I felt it upon that day, but never had I seen the flames…or heard him screaming. Please, Lady, tell me that it did not happen so, that this is some dreadful punishment for my indiscretion."

But Arialde shook her head, her eyes full of regret. "You *were* there, Gaelen, in a way. What you have witnessed came to pass. In this case the truth was more than adequate punishment for your transgression. Now, I would have you come to my chambers, for

I would assuage your pain and try to gladden your heart, though I know I may not."

Arialde would lead Gaelen to the beautiful dwelling of marble, where she would soothe her with tales of Farahin as she had known him, before the shadow fell upon him. But as the Lady turned to leave, she reached back to caress the Stone, as if to calm the turbulence within it.

Shandor…beloved brother, what have you become?

The following day Nelwyn saw very little of her cousin. Though Gaelen did have a somewhat volatile personality, she was not known to sulk for more than an hour or two, and Nelwyn began to become concerned when late afternoon came and she still had not appeared. Nelwyn found Rogond relaxing with Thorndil and Fima, and asked him whether he had seen Gaelen.

"No, I have not seen her since early yesterday, before she went riding with you," replied Rogond, who was honing his blade on an oil-stone. "She mentioned that she is now eager to be away, and I am inclined to agree. The Greatwood lies many leagues from here, and the journey may be difficult. The sooner we reach it, the better. I hope I will find welcome there." Rogond remembered the disapproving looks he had received from some of the Sylvan folk, including the King. "I am not certain where we should plan to spend the winter, but I would prefer to avoid crossing the mountains again!"

At this, Fima laughed. "Indeed! What sensible being crosses the mountains in late winter? Proof that Elves have a short supply of wits, if you ask me," he said, winking at Nelwyn, who drew herself up and lifted her chin in mock hauteur.

"We would have made it without incident except that, well, there were a few incidents." She began to giggle, and Fima, Rogond, and Thorndil chuckled along with her.

"True enough," said Rogond. "At least we did find our way to Mountain-home, that's really all that matters. Hopefully we'll see Gaelen before long—I would like to have her company tonight. She sings to me while I sleep, and it is the most relaxing and comforting thing you can imagine. In the meantime, let us prepare for departure."

"So, we're finally leaving?" said Gaelen, who had approached them unaware. Fima jumped.

"By the Beards of my Fathers! You did it *again*. Rogond, can we not attach a bell to her or something so that she cannot sneak up on me constantly? It is my fondest wish at this moment."

Gaelen forced a smile. "If that is your fondest wish, Lore-master, then I pity you," she said. "But be not pained; I will make more sound in future. So, are we finally leaving? If so, then I'm glad. I would very much like to be gone from here."

Rogond was distressed at her expression, as she looked very weary and unhappy considering the pleasant situation they were in at the moment. Her hands kept straying to the leather pouch about her neck, fluttering in uncertainty until they touched it and knew that it was still there. Something had happened, and he hoped that she would trust him enough to tell him of it. For now, it was best to reassure her.

"Yes Gaelen; I think we should leave within a day or two. Which of us should inform the Lord and Lady?"

"I will see to that," said Nelwyn, as she had another motive for seeking Arialde. She hoped to gain permission to look into the Stone of Léir and learn what it could tell. She turned to Gaelen. "Do you remember what we spoke about? Let us go and see the Lady together, then."

"I have had a change of heart, Nelwyn," Gaelen replied, refusing to look Nelwyn in the eye. "Pursue the matter if you wish. I do not wish to have anything to do with the Stone of Léir."

Fima looked at her with dawning understanding. *Oh, Gaelen... surely you didn't gainsay all my good advice and go looking in the Stone without permission, did you? But, of course you did.* He shook his head as she turned and left them to wonder what had come over her. Yet Fima knew exactly what Gaelen had done, and that the Stone had so disquieted her that she now wanted to run away from Tal-sithian as fast as she could possibly do so.

Nelwyn sought out Arialde in the early evening and found her relaxing in one of many beautiful gardens amid the tall trees. Arialde welcomed Nelwyn into her presence, asking her why she had come, though Nelwyn somehow had the feeling that the Lady already knew.

"I've been asked to tell you that the Company will be leaving your fine hospitality tomorrow, to our great regret," said Nelwyn.

Arialde smiled. "I think that not all of you regret it, Nelwyn. You and Gaelen have seemed restless for many days now. I am somewhat surprised you have lingered this long, though, of course, you are welcome." She searched Nelwyn's gaze, as though she knew there was another question forthcoming. "Is there anything more you would ask of me, daughter of Turanen?"

Nelwyn raised her eyes to meet those of the Lady. "There is one thing I would ask. I hope you will not think me presumptuous, but I would learn all I may in this realm ere I leave it. Our quest is difficult. Can the Stone of Léir provide some insight? I would ask your leave to find out."

Arialde smiled gently. "I have expected this request. It will take some courage to look within the Stone…most find it quite unsettling. You are welcome to it, but I warn you that it may not be all that you expect or hope for. I will aid you as I may, but you alone must decide how any revelation should be interpreted."

Nelwyn took a deep breath. "Is it not better to proceed with insight, though it may be unpleasant? If the Stone can help guide our actions so that we may avoid peril, then it is worth the risk. I am willing to accept it. By your leave, Lady, may we go now?"

Arialde nodded, but she did not smile. She rose and led Nelwyn to the glade where the great crystal still rested upon its pedestal. It appeared harmless enough, but Arialde insisted on approaching it first, closing her eyes and caressing the surface. She murmured an incantation in a strange tongue before backing away. This time the mist Gaelen had seen did not appear; Nelwyn beheld only a beautiful, many-faceted crystal as she stepped forward to look into its calm depths.

At first, there was nothing, and for a moment Nelwyn feared that she would be deemed unworthy of any insight, for a lowly Wood-elf might not be fit to gaze into the Stone of Léir. Then, with almost frightening suddenness, the same whirling confusion that had afflicted Gaelen overtook her. She fell into the vision as Gaelen had, as images—fleeting, but clear—came to her bewildered senses. Talrodin smiling at her as he had when she had last seen him alive. Talrodin lying dead in the fire with Gorgon's arrow in his breast.

Halrodin battling Gorgon, being slashed to pieces, crying out in pain. Gorgon stooping to take Turantil, the sword of Halrodin, and performing the rather bizarre act of removing a part of his armor and slicing his own forearm with it before smiling in horrible approval. Gelmyr's terrified face as he tried in vain to defend himself against the very same blade. An unknown She-elf crying in panic, just before Gorgon took her life.

Nelwyn stifled a cry of dismay as she kept on falling, but the terrible images were far from over. Now she saw Belegund. Gorgon had slashed his throat, and he was dead. Now Gorgon had Gaelen by the neck. To Nelwyn's horror her cousin appeared lifeless, then to her wonder Gorgon released her and slapped her face, hard and repeatedly. Gaelen drew several difficult, painful breaths, and Gorgon smiled in cruel satisfaction.

At last, she stopped falling.

She was standing in the Greatwood, and her heart rejoiced when she realized that she was home. A small kernel of dread smoldered within her as she looked around to behold King Ri-Aruin, his son Wellyn, and many of their friends and kin. Why were they so bloodied and weary? They were equipped as for battle—here was Gaelen and the rest of the Company, including Galador. She knew the answer when the battle-cry of a large, fierce host of Ulcas came up from the south—they had advanced all the way to the stronghold of the King, where the battle had been joined.

Gorgon led the Ulcas. As he advanced toward her, his eyes turned to meet hers—but they were not his eyes at all. They were Elven eyes, hazel-green and glittering brightly—Gaelen's eyes! Then Gorgon revealed a small, round object in his hand. When he concealed it, the familiar cold, pale grey eyes reappeared. He gave a terrible cry, and the evil army surged forward. Wellyn fell, pierced by an arrow. Ri-Aruin, surrounded by defenders, battled to the last. Rogond and Thorndil lay dead beside Galador, who was calling Nelwyn's name with his last strength. Where was Gaelen? The Greatwood was falling to the power of Darkness, and the Elves were helpless to save it. Nelwyn fitted her bow again and again, trying to overcome the enemy, to no avail. She could hear and smell the forest burning behind her…and cried in terror.

Then she heard Arialde's voice: *"Enough!"* The visions ceased, and the Stone went dark. Nelwyn was pulled back into the glade in a rush of wailing voices and crackling flames. She would behold nothing more. Arialde approached her, an expression of grave concern on her face. She let Nelwyn recover for a moment before addressing her.

"These visions are grim, Nelwyn, and they are in some ways similar to those held by Amandir and myself. Now do you understand his warning? Gaelen and Gorgon are tied together somehow, and I suspect that it has something to do with the golden object in Gorgon's hand. He has become powerful and threatens all you hold dear. We of Tal-sithian sorrow for the very fact of his existence and would aid you in your quest to rid the world of him, for he is beyond redeeming. There will be war before all is ended."

Nelwyn was still pale, and she trembled as she stood before the Lady. "I'm afraid to share these terrible visions with anyone. How shall I avoid bringing doubt and shame upon Gaelen, who of all the Company has been the most steadfast in pursuit of this horror? I do not understand the meaning, and I now regret my choice to look into the Stone. What must I do now?"

Arialde nodded; she did not blame Nelwyn. "Yet the choice was made and cannot be undone. Just remember that the Stone will aid you, if only you do not stray from the task of defeating Gorgon and ridding this world of him. Thus far, you have accepted it faithfully. Do not turn from it now! You will share the visions as you may, Nelwyn, but some you will keep. I will bring some gladness to your heart now. I also beheld a vision when I last consulted the Stone, and though much was grim, there was also some of joy. If the Company is successful, you will bear a child of Galador, and her name will be…'Gwynnyth'."

Arialde smiled at the astonished look on Nelwyn's face, and then turned and left her alone in the glade. Nelwyn stared after her and did not move from the spot for a long time. She would have to consider what she had just seen for some time before sharing any of it with Galador. And much of it, she reflected, could never be shared with anyone at all.

The Company departed the next morning, heading north along the Ambros. The Lord and Lady came to bid them farewell ere they set forth, for Arialde would not leave the island. They stood beside the boats, which were laden with provisions, as the cool mists of dawn veiled the flat, steel-grey waters and clung to the shore. Amandir waited there also, and Fima rumbled in disapproval as he passed by this unwelcome addition to the Company.

The Lady went to each of the Company in turn, imparting an unspoken message, heard only by the heart of the recipient. She gave to Thorndil a glass through which he could see things clearly at great distance. *For the piercing gaze of eagles are you named; now you shall see with their eyes.* To Fima she gave a small volume that had been set down by Odo, the most revered of all dwarvish lore-masters. Fima bowed in respect, promising to treasure it. *You may surpass Odo one day, Fima son of Khima.*

To Galador she gave a small but elegant white horn mounted with silver. He winded it and they all marveled at the clear, mellow tone that sounded as though it would carry for miles. *Do not let your love of Nelwyn blind you to your purpose, for you will never attain the happiness and peace that you desire until that purpose is fulfilled. Every one of the Company has a part to play; you must permit each to play it.* She looked into the distance for a moment and then closed her eyes, as though collecting her thoughts. *The slaying of Elf by Elf is not to be permitted, even in an effort to protect those we love. Do not give in to such desires, Galador. All must play their part.* Then she moved on, leaving him somewhat bewildered by her message.

Next she stood before Nelwyn, smiling as she looked into her compelling green eyes. She drew forth a small, beautifully engraved silver cylinder with an enlarged end containing many tiny bells. When it was shaken, it sounded delightful—much like the water in Arialde's fountain. *This was a plaything of the Lady Ordath when she was a child, and she loved it on a time. I give it now for Gwynnyth, in the hope that she will love it also.*

Nelwyn took the gift with both wonder and reverence. "May it be so, Lady. I thank you with all my heart," she said in a voice only the Lady could hear.

Then Arialde approached Rogond, who stood tall and watchful, his gaze clear and his heart strong. She asked for his hands, and he offered them to her. She took them and held them together between her own. *You are a worthy man, Rogond. The desire of your heart you may yet attain, if you remain steadfast. Do not let anyone dissuade you, for she is of worth, and she will have great need of you before all is ended. Take this small gift, and hold hope in your heart.*

When she withdrew her hands Rogond found that there was a tiny stone, plain-looking at first, but when it caught the light it flashed many colors, fiery reds and gold, deep, cool green and intense vibrant blue. *This is like to her spirit, young Tuathan. Plain and unassuming it first appears, but the brilliance and beauty shines forth to those who know and understand its heart of fire.* She looked into his eyes, and he took her meaning.

She went last to Gaelen, who was restive and fidgeting as ever, anxious to depart. She calmed as Arialde approached her. *Last I come to you, Gaelen of the Greatwood, beloved of Ri-Elathan. I would bestow a special gift, for the road before you will be the hardest to bear.* She held out her hand, and Gaelen took the gift she offered. It was a brooch of silver graven with the crest of the High King.

This once belonged to Ri-Elathan. He left it accidentally in my keeping, and I never had the chance to restore it to him. You shall wear it now, in remembrance of him. Do not dwell on the terrible visions you beheld, rather remember him as he was when you were bound to him in Mountain-home. Take care of your heart, and do not keep it closed forever. This is not what he would have wanted. Farewell, little Silent-foot.

Gaelen could not find words to say as she took the silver brooch in her hands, warming it. She bowed her head before Arialde, and then looked up into her eyes. "Farewell, Lady. I do not suppose we shall meet again, though we may. I thank you for your aid in my grief, and I shall always remember the tales you told. Farewell."

Gaelen bowed once more to the Lord and Lady before climbing into the boat with Rogond and Fima. The Elves of Tal-sithian watched them as they departed, disappearing slowly into the mist. Once ashore, the horses were summoned and laden. Gaelen looked once more back toward the island, for though she could not see her, she knew that Arialde was there. She raised her hand in farewell, then wheeled about and cantered slowly toward the river, where she and the Company would turn north, toward the Greatwood.

Arialde raised her hand in return as they departed, her heart heavy with foreboding. This was not going to be a pleasant road, and it would be long and painful. It was likely that some would not live to see the end of it. At last she turned to go, after wishing good fortune and steady hearts upon the Company, hoping especially for the eventual happiness of Gaelen and Nelwyn, and of Gwynnyth.

At last Gorgon was rewarded for his vigilance. The Company had left the Lake-realm, and his vision was now unfettered. He rejoiced even in his pain as he beheld the solemn, thoughtful face of Nelwyn and the resolute expressions of Rogond and Thorndil. He could not, of course, view Gaelen; if he had been able to do so he would have seen the determination in her bright eyes, determination that did not quite conceal the haunted look buried deep within, the result of her encounter with the Stone.

It was indeed fortunate that Gorgon had not been privy to Nelwyn's vision. It would have disturbed him; his course would have been different if he had known that she had gained such insight. As it was, he continued with confidence, secure in the knowledge that the Company had no inkling of his ability, nor of the destructive force he now commanded. He summoned Kharsh—it was time to get this rabble organized and moving north. He looked once more through Gaelen's eyes as she rode alone at the rear of the Company, shivering slightly with the cold and pulling her cloak about her, though it was a bright, warm day.

23
Return to the Greatwood

The Company rode north along the Ambros, the horses stretching their legs and taking advantage of the flat going. Réalta and Eros ran side by side with Galador and Rogond astride them, and Réalta, at any rate, was happy to put his tail toward the lands near the Lake-realm. He had not fared so well there; in fact he now bore several wounds inflicted upon him by the herd stallion, a large, imposing fellow named Wodon. Réalta had discovered that Wodon, who had been in possession of the mares of Tal-sithian for quite a number of years, had very little tolerance for strange stallions.

Wodon had made that plain soon after Eros and Réalta had been left to forage nearby. They had been drawn to investigate the fine group of mares, who seemed friendly enough. The herd leader, a venerable chestnut mare named Elda, had looked them up and down, laying her ears back and lashing her tail, making it plain that she would tolerate no foolishness from either of them. Just then, Wodon had come galloping over the hilltop calling loudly; he had been away seeking water and now found two strangers among his precious mares. Eros backed off at once, but Réalta arched his neck and trumpeted back at Wodon, for he resented the stallion's attitude. Wodon didn't even know of their intentions as yet.

Eros watched his impressive friend engage in brief challenge with Wodon, but Réalta realized quickly that he was outmatched. He had a few chunks of his hide missing when he at last turned his tail and galloped off with Eros, who trotted sensibly behind him.

Once night had fallen, Eros encouraged Réalta to follow him back to the herd of mares. Wodon was keeping watch, facing south as the wind was in the north today, thus his nose would alert him from one direction and his eyes from the other. Evading Wodon would not be easy, but Eros had a compelling reason for wanting to approach the mares.

There was a young mare named Iduna in the band, and Eros fancied her. She was coming into prime breeding condition; tonight or tomorrow she would be most fertile, and Eros held a great desire to be alone with her. To accomplish this, he knew that he would have to distract Wodon, and he thought he knew just how to do it. First, he took notice of Iduna's position in the herd; regrettably she was nearly in the center under the watchful eye of Elda. It would have been so much easier had she been near the perimeter.

Now for the distraction of Wodon. The stallion already had his nose in the air and was moving restively back and forth on his vantage point, shaking his head. He had caught wind of them, apparently. Good! Eros needed to lure him down to where he might be engaged. Then Eros would exploit the pride and impetuous nature of his hapless companion, Réalta. Eros liked Réalta, but occasionally found him annoying with his superior attitude and flashy appearance. Réalta was both swifter and more graceful than Eros, and often reminded him of it. Réalta was also rather predictable, and he was not nearly so clever as Eros. Now his pride and predictable nature would serve Eros well.

Eros called once to Iduna, nickering in his most alluring way. The young mare lifted her head, as did many of the others. Réalta trotted up to make certain that he was not left out of anything, though he thought his friend's behavior somewhat rash considering the proximity of Wodon. Eros then approached the perimeter of the herd, still calling softly to Iduna, who was now making her way toward him. Wodon beheld Eros and Réalta approaching his mares, and threatened them from the hill-top. *Intruders! You have no business here! Back off or I shall teach you a hard lesson!* Wodon practically flew down the hillside, striding up before Réalta who stood nearest, as Eros had backed away again, dropping his head and trying to appear non-threatening.

Réalta was taken aback. Where was Eros? No matter, he could handle this situation himself. He would explain to Wodon, but would not bow to him.

I mean no intrusion, but do not press me or you shall have more of a fight than perhaps you need, Old One. He arched his proud neck and shook his long white forelock at Wodon.

No intrusion? Only I hold rights to the mares here. You were calling to Iduna. She is ripe for breeding. Do not try to deceive me, young fool!

Wodon struck hard with one foreleg, arching his massive neck and giving a sort of deep-throated squeal. Réalta didn't much like being called foolish, and regrettably his anger was about to make him so. He strode forward, challenging Wodon.

Do not press me, Old One. I am young and strong, the favored mount of a tall, proud Elf. I have seen battle, and am more than capable of defending myself!

Wodon snorted and tossed his head, dismissing all thoughts of diplomacy in that moment. Without another word, he flew at Réalta, and both stallions were screaming, rearing and plunging, striking at forelegs, biting at throats and ears. The mares turned to watch; they had not seen a strange stallion challenge Wodon in a long time. Most knew better. Réalta was holding his own, but he was tiring before the relentless onslaught of the old stallion, who had far more to lose should the battle go ill.

Eros had meanwhile returned quietly to the perimeter of the herd of mares and called again to Iduna, who was now quite near. She approached him even as Elda stood distracted by the combative stallions. Eros nuzzled her, chortling and arching his proud neck. What he lacked in sheer beauty he made up in finesse. She nipped him playfully, returning courtship. She had not really cared for Wodon anyway; he was far too serious and demanding. This good-natured one was more to her taste, and she followed him willingly under the moonlight.

Eros accomplished his purpose after a bit more courtship. Taking a deep breath and shaking his entire body, Eros now turned his attention to the rescue of his proud companion. While only a few minutes had passed, the two stallions were weary and both had taken several wounds.

Réalta was beginning to worry; perhaps he really was outmatched. And where in the world was Eros? His question was answered as the strong dun bowled into Wodon from behind, knocking him off balance.

He called to Réalta: *Come on! Now is your chance to run for it!* Eros kicked Wodon in the chest, receiving a savage bite to the hindquarters, but was otherwise unscathed as he and Réalta fled at last, leaving Wodon calling after them, warning them to never intrude upon his mares again.

As they ran back to where their companions waited Eros had turned to Réalta, amused. *Well, you certainly sorted him out! Your High-elf would be most impressed.*

Réalta, who was in some pain from his wounds, did not reply. He never did ask his friend Eros where he had been during the melee. Had Eros known it, he was nearly as predictable as Réalta. Luckily, unlike Wodon, Réalta did possess a sense of humor, and the friendship between Eros and himself was strong.

The Company had been riding for two days when Thorndil first sighted distant riders through the glass Arialde had given him. He called the Company to a halt, alerting them to the party of eight heavily armed and provisioned Elves, bearing the banner of the Lake-realm, who now rode up from the south. Their faces were grim as they approached, and their horses had clearly been ridden hard. Amandir rode out to meet them as they hailed him, followed by the Company.

It seemed that they had been sent by the Lord and Lady upon discovering the sad truth that sixteen of their kinsmen had disappeared from near the Cold-spring. There had been very little clue as to their fate, but enough sign had been left that they were presumed slain or taken by the Dark Powers. The Elves had tracked them as they could, and had eventually come upon some evidence that a rather large and well-armed company of Ulcas had camped nearby. Then the Elves had separated, with these eight being designated to ride out in search of the Company to warn and aid them.

"The Ulcas, it seems, were on a course that might well intercept your own," said a fair-haired Elf named Oryan. He looked earnestly into the eyes of Amandir. "We have been sent to accompany you on your quest, for our people are tracking these Ulcas even now, and there are nearly thirty accomplished archers, warriors, and trackers among them. They hope to overtake and slay the Ulcas before they can waylay us. I expect they will have little difficulty, as the Ulcas will be unaware that they are being pursued."

Amandir nodded, but he had a feeling of foreboding growing in his breast. He looked over at Gaelen, who stood by, shivering slightly in the late morning breeze, and his eyes narrowed.

"Say nothing more in front of her!" he whispered to Oryan. Then, he spoke aloud. "It is well you have come, for we shall have need of you. Are you set to ride all the way to the Greatwood with us?"

Oryan nodded. "We are provisioned for several weeks. The Lady asked us to see you safely there. She has a message for you, Gaelen Taldin. She says to please submit to our company. We promise to fight beside you to the end and we will not interfere in your purpose."

Gaelen smiled. Arialde obviously remembered her unfavorable reaction when she learned of Amandir having been granted leave to join them. She inclined her head to Oryan.

"You are more than welcome. I'm glad of your company, for we shall need your skills and courageous hearts in this task. I pray that you may thank the Lady from me one day."

Oryan bowed his head in return, though he looked sidelong at Amandir, who was regarding Gaelen with a mistrustful look on his proud face. Oryan was confused; the Lady had said nothing to him about Gaelen's being untrustworthy. Gaelen had certainly not given the Elves of Tal-sithian any reason to believe otherwise.

Amandir drew Oryan aside as the Company made ready to resume their course northward. Though he could not exactly explain how he knew it, Amandir told Oryan that the less Gaelen knew of matters of importance to their enemy, the better. In his heart he feared for the Elves who now tracked the "unwary Ulcas," wondering if the same fate awaited them as had befallen the Elves near the Cold-spring.

Nelwyn was saddened by the news of the disappearance of those merry Elves of Tal-sithian. They had seemed so free of worries on that bright afternoon, and now had almost assuredly met with some ill fate.

Gaelen was lost in thoughts of Gorgon; she wondered whether he had any association with the company of Ulcas that apparently had set out to intercept her Company. She did not suspect so, as Gorgon had given every indication that he disliked Ulcas and that he worked alone.

Nelwyn, on the other hand, knew better. She had seen Gorgon in command of a host of fierce Ulcas in the Stone of Léir, and that host would be set against the might of the Elves of the Greatwood. She had not yet shared the nature of what she had seen with anyone, not even Galador. Gaelen, to her surprise, had not asked it of her. Nelwyn did not know what had happened to her cousin, but she suspected that the Stone had been involved, and she now knew that Gaelen wanted nothing whatever to do with even the mention of it. As for Gorgon, Nelwyn hoped that the Stone was wrong, and that this was just a group of ordinary, sun-hating, unwary Ulcas that would give a well-armed group of Elves very little reason to fear. Even as she rode, she prayed it would be so.

Many leagues away from the Company, Gorgon stowed the mirror away, turned to Kharsh, who stood beside him, and wiped the sweat from his dark brow.

"We are being pursued by a host of about thirty Elves from Tal-sithian. They do not know that we are aware of them as yet." Gorgon scanned the surrounding countryside. It was full of hiding-places, and he knew it well. "I have a plan in mind that will surprise them most unpleasantly. Listen well, and then get these vermin moving. We do not have much time."

Kharsh listened to Gorgon's idea, which, he had to admit, was inspired. He bowed to his commander, and then hurried to carry out his orders. This was going to be most enjoyable. Though Kharsh did not burn with hatred of anything, he did not love the Elves, and he was looking forward to the looks on their astonished faces. Gorgon instructed his army to leave several alive, for he wanted to deal personally with them. Soon the trap was set, and the Ulcas lay in wait, their archers at the ready.

The Elves appeared as the afternoon waned and evening approached. The Ulcas had been hunkered down for several hours. The sign they had left for the Elves to follow was clear, but the Elves had to make up a lot of ground to catch up with them and were approaching with caution. Gorgon trembled as he first caught sight of them. He had let it be known that any under his command who did not show proper restraint and alerted the Elves to their presence would soon breathe his last, hence the Ulcas remained in complete concealment as their wary yet obliging victims walked into the trap.

When the last of the Elves had passed the appropriate point, the rearmost archers loosed their bows. This was the signal for the others to do likewise, and before the startled Elves could react they were felled from all directions. At least twelve perished in that first volley. The others had drawn their bows, but alas, the Ulcas were well protected in their rocky hiding places. Many more fine archers fell quickly, and their blood flowed red upon the ground as the Ulcas drew their blades and engaged those who remained. The Elves were now vastly outnumbered and were rapidly overcome. Six were left alive and brought before Gorgon, who was delighted to view their pained, hopeless faces as he instructed the Ulcas to tie them securely and hang them from the branches of nearby trees.

Gorgon then walked among them, savoring their pain and terror, enduring their proud glance. He explained how he had trapped them. Gorgon's folk had proceeded quite some way north before separating into two groups, one moving east and one moving west. They had circled back and set this trap for the Elves, who simply followed their trail north unaware that they had deviated from it in any way. "I do not blame you for having been so easily taken, proud Elves of Tal-sithian. You were expecting ordinary Ulcas, not those under the command of Gorgon Elfhunter!"

At this he removed his helmet, releasing his golden hair. The Elves despaired at the sight of him, for they had learned of his origins, and at least one had known Brinneal, his mother. This only seemed to enrage him.

"I will not be pitied by the likes of you!" he roared at them. "Only your hatred will I take. And you shall have an equal measure of mine."

So saying, he drew Turantil, which he wielded like a butcher's knife, and spent the next several minutes inflicting as much pain as possible upon the Elves who still lived. Kharsh watched this with fascination, as did the other remaining Ulcas in the Company. By the time Gorgon had finished with them, the Elves were in agony, no doubt longing for death.

Kharsh had learned one thing from this experience: the Shadowmancer had saddled him with a fearsome task. Gorgon was a force beyond many in his long experience. Yet Kharsh felt a foreboding deep within—this consuming hatred his new commander felt for the Elves would be his undoing somehow. Kharsh would have to be very, very careful. Gorgon was a master at inflicting pain and would feel no qualms at all about inflicting it upon anyone who displeased him. This lesson was not lost on Kharsh or on any others of the Black Command.

When the order to depart came, the Ulcas quickly gathered their provisions, moving north once more, leaving the dying Elves to suffer until their end came. As Kharsh heard the last of their agonized cries drifting behind him on the wind, he felt a most disturbing surge of emotion that might almost have been pity. For one such as Kharsh, that, indeed, was saying something.

The Lady Arialde had summoned the Lord Airan, for her mind's eye had revealed things that were disturbing, and she had need of his counsel. She turned to him, eyes full of sorrow.

"The enemy has taken our people...none of those we sent in pursuit of him will return. I hear their cries drifting upon an ill wind that blows from the Darkmere, and I have sent the Company upon its way to complete a task that I fear is beyond them, though my heart tells me otherwise."

Airan was dismayed at her pronouncement, but then he answered her: "Trust your heart, for it has always spoken true, even when your mind says otherwise. If your heart would have faith in these souls that have been set upon this path, then that faith is well placed."

Arialde sighed. Lord Airan's gentle words had reassured her, yet she remained troubled. While it was true that her heart held much faith in the Company, her mind recalled that which the Stone had revealed, and she knew the sorrow that would be visited upon them by Gorgon was just beginning.

As night fell, the Company prepared to rest. Fima, Rogond, and Thorndil saw to the fires, as the Elves busied themselves with caring for the horses and in general making themselves useful. Now that the group numbered fifteen, they felt that there was little to fear in this country, though they would still keep a watchful eye. It would be rare for any but the most determined or foolhardy Ulcas to attack such a large and well-armed company of Elves, even after sundown. Soon they were relaxing in small groups, eating and drinking, but the overall mood was rather subdued.

Gaelen rose and walked west, toward the setting of the moon, until she was far away from the firelight. Climbing a tall tree, she settled back to look up at the brilliant stars, which blazed so brightly that her heart ached with longing for them. If only she could share this vision with someone. Of course, her beloved Rain had shared them with her on a time, and she willed with all her strength that he might once again behold them. She called to him, but he did not answer. The realm in which his spirit resided was closed to her.

At that moment, Gorgon Elfhunter looked deep into the mirror. For a moment he swayed as the usual wave of pain shot through his body, making him shudder. Then his vision came suddenly, filling his world with a field of brilliant stars. He had never seen such incredible beauty! He was completely rapt, and stared at them in spite of himself, hardly daring to breathe. He heard Gaelen muttering in her soft, clear voice:

"If only you could know how beautifully the stars burn tonight… if only you could feel the longing in my heart for them… and for you."

"But…I *do* feel it," Gorgon muttered in reply, though he was not aware of doing so. His eyes were closed now, for he concentrated entirely upon the brilliant field of silver lights that wheeled above him. "Such beautiful lights...so bright...so cold. Like cold fire burning for eternity...."

At that moment, Kharsh approached. He cleared his throat, trying to gain Gorgon's attention without offending or startling him. Gorgon's eyes jerked open, and he quickly concealed the mirror in its leather pouch. The beautiful stars vanished, as did the sound of Gaelen's voice. Gorgon looked bewildered for a moment, then his own eyes focused on Kharsh and the familiar contempt returned to them.

"What do you want? I thought I told you never to disturb me while I am spying on the Elves. You had best have good reason for doing so."

He advanced on Kharsh, menacing him. To his credit Kharsh stood his ground, though he was justifiably afraid.

"Please, my lord...I understand little of Elven-tongues. May I speak plainly? My folk are wanting to make time as the moon has set and it is a cool, dark night. We really do not enjoy traveling in sunlight, and the Elves will stop to rest by night, for they are mounted, and their horses require rest. Should we make ready to move on?"

"Yes, good idea. But don't let them think they will not have to travel by day. I mean to keep up with those accursed Elves, though they are mounted and we are not. Tell the rabble to make ready. We move on within the hour."

Kharsh bowed and left Gorgon to gather his few possessions. When he had done so, Gorgon paused, recalling his vision of the stars and his reaction to it. When he looked heavenward now, he saw only an ordinary night sky—unremarkable, and certainly not worthy of the ecstasy it had engendered in him a few moments ago. When seen through the eyes of the Wood-elf, however... He was momentarily alarmed. What was happening to him? How was it that he had felt such longing when he looked through her eyes? He had better guard himself more carefully from now on, lest he become more and more alike to his mother's kin. He could not bear the thought of it! Even more alarming—he shared her vision even when his own eyes were closed. He did not even need to look into the mirror anymore, but only to hold it in his hand. The connection between them was becoming stronger.

What had the She-elf been saying at the end? "Cold…so cold, like death, like being forever alone…."

He did not understand her meaning. Perhaps she referred to the coldness of the fiery lights, burning everlastingly in the heavens. Perhaps she referred to the coldness of her own heart—Gorgon did not know.

The truth was that at that moment Gaelen had been overcome with the chill of Gorgon's presence, as she nearly always did when he was looking through her eyes. She had wished to share the stars with someone, and she had unwittingly done so, but her heart had been nearly overwhelmed with loneliness. Had she felt this emanating from Gorgon, who was surely one of the most lonely souls yet living? Or was it in fact the coldness and loneliness of her own life, her life without Rain, without the love that had once so filled her heart? She could not know the answer, even as Gorgon could not.

Gaelen stopped shivering as she clasped the largest tree-branch with both arms. It was warm and smooth, and she felt its vitality as she laid her cheek against it. Her tears came freely then, and she wept for several minutes. Her thoughts were released by those tears: fear of what the future would bring as well as the horror of what had already come to pass.

She held a fleeting vision of the lifeless eyes of Farahin, heard his voice calling to her as his spirit faded, but she could not bear it and drew her long dagger from the sheath without thinking, slicing into the flesh of one of her slender arms and crying in pain. This effectively banished the visions from her mind, bringing her world back into focus, and as she gripped her arm, gritting her teeth, she heard Rogond's voice calling her name. He sounded frightened…no doubt he had heard her cry and was now searching for her.

She climbed down from her perch to find him running toward her in alarm. "Why did you wander off? I have been worried for you. What happened to your arm?" He took it tenderly in his hands and examined it. "This will need healing. What happened?"

"I cut myself with one of my daggers. It was unintentional, and the cut is not deep. I shall have to be more careful," she replied. Rogond knelt before her, trying to get her to look at him.

"You've been crying," he observed. "What troubles you? Please, tell me. I want to help."

She allowed him to hold her then, but she would not tell him why she had wept, for she could not find words to express what she had been feeling. She only knew that she felt more secure in his arms than she had since the quest began. Now she wished only to keep silent as he rocked her gently, stroking her hair as tears flowed again from her bright eyes, dampening Rogond's tunic, wrenching his heart.

There were other troubled hearts that night in the encampment. Galador kept mulling over the parting words of Lady Arialde, and he did not understand their meaning. Nelwyn, who lay beside him, was yet troubled by the visions she had held in the Stone, especially that of the object in Gorgon's hand, a thing that somehow bound his fate to that of Gaelen.

Her dearest friend and cousin had been overtaken by a deep melancholy, one that not even Fima could assuage. Was Gorgon somehow reaching into her mind, wearing her down? Nelwyn could not say. She wondered whether she should share this vision with Galador, or with Rogond. But she could not bring doubt upon Gaelen, and that vision would surely do so. Nelwyn resolved to wait until her course was made plain, until revealing the vision truly became necessary.

Amandir was bent with silent weeping, as he had done often since Gorgon had surfaced. He was going out to hunt and slay the abomination whose creation had resulted in the death of his beloved Brinneal—a creature of which he had only recently been made aware. He could not imagine the abject horror Brinneal had suffered at the hands of the Shadowmancer. He remembered the day she went missing; he had rarely left her alone, as she was newly with child, and she had chided him for it.

"I'm only going out to enjoy the air and the feel of the grass on my feet, and to gather lily-bulbs for the garden. You would think I was going into some terrible peril," she had said, laughing musically and tossing her golden hair at him.

"I shall go and help you to gather them," he had replied, hoping that she would accept his company, though he knew she would think him foolish for worrying so.

"Did you not say that you wished to carve a cradle for our son? As meticulous as you are, he will be here before you finish it, so get to work! I will be back before the sun rises to its full height. Now, don't worry. And I am not going alone…Aureth is going with me."

He had laughed then.

"Oh, I see! You wish to go off with Aureth so that you may discuss matters of female importance. My company would not be sufficiently enlightening. Well, so be it, but I beg you, take care. You know that I worry so when you venture from the island."

She had given him her promise of caution, then turned and left him forever. Her fate remained unknown for many years, though they found Aureth cruelly slain, apparently while trying to protect Brinneal. When the Elves finally learned of Brinneal's terrible fate, Amandir was nearly destroyed by grief and horror at the thought of it. He hoped desperately that the vile experiment would go awry, that Gorgon would not survive, or that Wrothgar would not be pleased with him and would destroy him ere he could mature. Now those hopes were dashed, and he, Amandir, was set upon a path that would destroy Gorgon, the last child of Brinneal.

Amandir had not known it, but a part of him had gone into the creation of Gorgon as well. It would not have altered Amandir's resolve, however, for though Gorgon may once have been innocent, he was now a hateful, murderous monster, beyond hope of redemption. For the sake of his beloved Brinneal, Amandir would see Gorgon destroyed, and his memory erased from reckoning. Amandir raised his eyes, which were red from weeping, and beheld the stars, reaching out even as Gaelen had done, but Brinneal, like Farahin, could not answer.

The Company lingered at the junction of the River Artan for days, camped on the banks of the Ambros. This was the rendezvous point where the Elves of Tal-sithian expected to be reunited with those who had been set to track and slay the Ulcas. Yet their comrades did not appear, and the Company wondered whether they had been ill-fated, or whether perhaps the Ulcas had turned from their course, deciding to go beneath the mountains. But if that were so, their trackers would still have made the rendezvous, as they had been instructed to break off pursuit should the Ulcas turn from the Company. Everyone grew restless, for they had not anticipated this delay.

Rogond approached Oryan in the late afternoon of the fourth day, suggesting that the Company would move on slowly, allowing the Elves of Tal-sithian to catch up once they had been reunited with their friends.

"I am troubled, Tuathan," said Oryan, and his face was grave. "It is not like the Elves of Tal-sithian to fail in such a task, for we are more than able to defeat a small host of ordinary Ulcas, even if we are outnumbered. Is it possible that the Ulcas were joined by more of their fellows, or even by something darker and more powerful than they? My brother was one of the Elves set to track them, and I do not sense his presence any more; in fact I have not for some time. This is an unhappy riddle!"

Rogond placed a hand on Oryan's shoulder, and the Elf stiffened beneath it, for he was clearly distressed.

"The Company must move on," Rogond said, "though we would also like to know the solution to this riddle, for it no doubt concerns us all. But we must continue toward the Greatwood. Each delay provides opportunity for our enemy. Gaelen will leave on her own ere long if we do not make ready. I'm sure you have taken notice of her restive nature."

They had all taken notice, as Gaelen hadn't exactly been subtle about her desire to keep moving. Oryan turned and looked at Rogond, then asked a difficult question of him.

"I'm worried for you and your quest. Amandir has indicated that trust in Gaelen is ill-advised, that we should reveal nothing of our plans in front of her. This both confounds and distresses me, Tuathan. Can you shed any light on it? It is obvious that she is a trusted and worthy member of your Company, yet there is a Darkness that seems ever to stalk her and surround her. I mean no disrespect," he added, seeing the ominous look forming on Rogond's face.

"Perhaps not, Oryan, but nevertheless I am becoming very weary of Amandir's continual undermining of Gaelen. He somehow thinks her to be in league with Gorgon, which tells me that his mind is addled. Either that, or he has been listening to one mysterious prophecy too many. I shall have words with him before long."

Oryan shook his head. "You cannot know what Amandir has endured, or what drives him. You are young and have seen nothing like the long years of pain he has borne. I would pay attention to Amandir if I were you; he has looked into the Stone, which has set him now upon this path. He is not deluded. You, on the other hand, are blinded to any thoughts of evil things being associated with Gaelen, who is your beloved. Don't think we have not taken notice."

Rogond sighed. "I freely admit that I love her, Oryan. Will you now lecture me as to my folly? Do not trouble yourself; I have heard such advice from Greatwood to Mountain-home! Even my closest friend lectures me. It will make no difference in my resolve, nor dampen my desire, so save your breath."

Oryan smiled. "Peace, Tuathan. The Lady is aware of your heart's desire, and she has blessed it. Believe me, that is blessing enough for the Elves of Tal-sithian. I merely point out that we are aware of your bias concerning Gaelen. I would never presume to lecture you, for I sense that you are possessed of a ready mind and are more than capable of assessing your own folly."

At this, Rogond smiled back at him. "That I am, Oryan. And should I fail to assess my folly adequately, I pray that there will always be one of your folk nearby to remind me of it." They chuckled amiably, the tension broken between them.

"We will linger for one more day," said Oryan. "If you would leave, by all means do so, but look for us to catch you by noon five days from now. I will send our best scouts back to try and find what has happened. They will then make all haste to rejoin us. We may then learn the answer to the riddle. Yet I would counsel you to speak gently with Amandir. He may have some enlightenment to share that concerns your Company quite closely. Remember that his pain is very great, and treat him with compassion. He is not your enemy."

The Company left the next morning, and the two scouts were sent back to look for the Elves. Amandir, of course, went with the Company, his face set in its usual grim expression as he sat astride his tall horse. Gaelen's arm had nearly healed already, to the wonder of Rogond. There would be no scar from such a blade. Rogond shuddered as he considered the nature of the wound that had left the mark upon her shoulder. What sort of blade had left such a scar upon the flesh of Elves? He hoped never to know.

Gaelen and Nelwyn rode together, and the closer they drew to the Greatwood, the lighter their spirits became. Rogond knew how they felt; it was difficult to be away from one's home for so many months on such a difficult road.

Suddenly the cousins both reined their horses in as though of one mind, halting and staring into the edge of the forest on the opposite side of the river. The rest of the Company followed suit, and some drew their weapons in the belief that Gaelen and Nelwyn had spotted enemies lurking among the trees. Rogond rode up beside them, with Fima balanced precariously in front of him.

"What have you seen?" Rogond asked, scanning the forest in vain. Nelwyn pointed into the tree-tops, and after a few moments Rogond chuckled.

"Ah! I see," he said, shaking his head. "Do not fear, my friends. We shall no doubt be stopping in this very spot for the night. Am I correct?" He looked over at Gaelen, who nodded and swung down from her mount. She and Nelwyn were already making plans as to how they were going to spend their evening, for they had a task before them. Galador rode up beside Rogond, confused until Rogond pointed out the bole of the tall oak that grew beside the water, with the small, dark hole about twenty feet from the ground. Galador smiled and set about gathering firewood. Fima could not make it out until he borrowed Thorndil's glass; then he saw them, tiny dark shapes buzzing in and out of the hole. After the spring flowering, the combs would be so full of honey that the temptation to the Wood-elves was irresistible.

The tree was inconveniently on the wrong side of the Ambros, but luckily the weather had been very dry, hence the river was quieter and the current less swift than usual. The span was not as broad as in some areas, still the Elves remembered that it grew even narrower about a quarter mile to the south of them, and Gaelen and Nelwyn headed for the spot as night fell, accompanied by a curious Rogond, Thorndil, and Fima. Galador and Amandir remained behind to watch the horses and tend the fire. The Elves drew nigh to the narrows of the river, and Rogond wondered as to the wisdom of crossing it, for wherever a river grows narrow, it grows deep and swift. He pointed this out to Gaelen, who shrugged.

"It is our intention to cross without wetting ourselves in the water. Watch and learn!"

She strung her bow and sent a slender rope across into the trees, where it lodged obligingly. Then she tied the opposite end around the stout limb of a tall tree. Slinging a leather pack across her back, she swung hand over hand across the narrow span. This was much easier than the crossing had been when she had attempted the rescue of Nelwyn so many months ago, for then she had lowered herself into the water, and the current had been both swift and cold. She smiled at the memory. She had not yet become acquainted with Rogond, but would soon meet him and tend to him in his illness. She blessed the day she came to him, for she could no longer imagine traveling without him. She threw a wry smile back over her shoulder just before she dropped lightly down upon the far bank with Nelwyn close behind her. Then the two of them made their way to the honey-tree.

Fima was frustrated as he could not see what they were doing, especially now that darkness had fallen. He stood with Galador and Rogond on the riverbank, eyes trained on the two Wood-elves, who were experts in the extraction of honey and certainly would not be denied now. The oak was not suitable for climbing, but its brother that stood next to it was perfect. Gaelen and Nelwyn scrambled up like squirrels, each carrying a smoldering green branch with them. Rogond knew the purpose of it; he had seen the Elves use this trick before. The darkness and the smoke would confuse and stupefy the bees, rendering them virtually defenseless.

They could hear the Elves laughing then speaking to one another in serious tones as they drew near to their goal. Then, they heard Gaelen singing as she reached into the hive and reverently withdrew six large slabs of honeycomb while Nelwyn waved the green wood-smoke into the hole. It must have been a honey-gathering song, for it praised the bees for their industry, thanked them for their gift, and assured them that there would be plenty of time to rebuild the winter stores. Fima chuckled. Only an Elf would sing to a bunch of bees!

Carefully, the two Elves withdrew from the hive then climbed back down and doused the green branches in the river. They traveled back south to the crossing, where Gaelen returned first, carrying the honey-pack. Fima sighed.

"A shame to lose a good rope, though I suppose you think it was worth it," he said to Gaelen.

"Lose the rope, not to mention a perfectly serviceable arrow? What an absurd thought! Now you shall see why we tied it so high and over such a narrows. No one does this as well as Nelwyn—watch her!"

Nelwyn appeared in the tall tree on the other side, Gaelen's arrow in her hand. She crept out to the end of the largest branch that overhung the water, coiling the rope as she went. Then she gripped it with both hands, secured the coiled end to her belt, and swung gracefully across to join them while rapidly climbing the rope. Gaelen cheered as Nelwyn just missed wetting her feet in the churning water, landing unceremoniously on the bank between Rogond and a very suitably impressed Fima.

The two Wood-elves held the honey pack aloft in triumph as they embraced each other. From the look of that pack it appeared that the evening was going to be very merry indeed! It would be the first of several merry evenings, such as they had not known in a long, long time. A good thing, for when Oryan and the Elves of Tal-sithian finally rejoined them there were but six, and their news would put all thoughts of merriment aside.

They appeared nearly a full day after they had promised, and their horses had been ridden hard and long. Rogond knew from the first that they would bear grim news, for there were but six of them, and two he recognized as the scouts that had been sent back. What had befallen the ones who were missing? They would all soon find out, as the Company gathered to hear the news. The horses were tended as the two scouts and Oryan sat upon the ground with Rogond, Thorndil, Gaelen, and Fima. Nelwyn and Galador stood together, and Amandir, as always, stood alone. The two missing Elves had been sent back to the Lake-realm with grim tidings, and the scouts warned the Company that their news would be hard to bear.

They described in broken voices that which they had seen when their comrades were found at last. They were drawn to them by carrion-birds, cresting a hilltop to view a horrible sight in the valley below: nearly thirty of the worthy Elves of Tal-sithian lay dead, and six had been tortured horribly and left to die. Nelwyn wept aloud as the scouts described them, imagining the suffering of their last hours. Gaelen stared ahead in stony silence, for she now knew the cause of that suffering. She looked up at Amandir, who was staring hard at her with an expression of loathing on his face. She turned to the scouts.

"I am now certain that Gorgon Elfhunter was responsible for their deaths, for this is the way he deals with unlucky captives. Gelmyr was left in similar fashion, though we believe Gorgon killed him before leaving his body for us to find. These apparently were not deemed worthy of such merciful consideration."

Rogond placed a hand on her shoulder to steady her, as she was rapidly becoming enraged. Amandir's look of loathing did not fade from his face as he answered her.

"Gorgon is only partly responsible, if I'm right. If not for you, Elf, he would not have succeeded. I do not know how you are managing it, but he is learning of our plans through you somehow. If it is all the same, I would prefer that you not be present at this council."

"It is *not* the same to us!" roared Rogond, gripping Gaelen's shoulder. She was looking at Amandir in shock. The scouts and Oryan wore similar expressions, as though they could not imagine such a thing, but then Amandir spoke to them.

"How was it that our people were taken? Did you investigate?"

The scouts nodded. "It appears that the Ulcas traveled north, split into two groups and doubled back to lie in wait for our people, who followed the tracks right into the trap," they said. "It was obvious that the Ulcas knew they were being tracked."

Amandir questioned them further. "And how long do you believe it took for this trap to be laid?"

"At least a few hours; they went quite a distance out of their way to accomplish it." Understanding dawned in their faces, and they continued. "They must have known of our plan, though the signs indicate that our people were never directly detected; they did not get close enough until the trap was already in place."

Rogond and Fima stood in defense of Gaelen. "The Ulcas no doubt assumed you would pursue them when you found your other friends missing. It is not that difficult an assumption to make," said Fima. "The idea that Gaelen would do anything to aid Gorgon is absurd. And if you even suggest such a thing again, I shall need to fetch my axe and teach you some manners, along with a measure of common sense!"

Amandir drew himself up proudly before Fima, and things might indeed have gone ill had not Gaelen chosen that moment to stand between them.

"Enough, both of you! All right, everyone, I must now confess. I have been sending messages to Gorgon via trained carrier-bats. If it displeases you to have my presence at council, Amandir, then feel free to leave it. Your behavior is only partly excused by your grief, and I am tired of it. And though I appreciate your offer of courtesy lessons from your dwarvish axe, Fima, I am more than capable of defending myself from one such as Amandir. Do not abase yourself thus!" She turned to the scouts. "Where were the Ulcas headed?"

The scouts were taken aback for a moment, as they had just witnessed two of the Company nearly coming to blows. "They appeared to be continuing north," they answered.

"Then I suggest that we all cross the river as soon as possible. Ulcas loathe the water, and they will not cross for many leagues yet, until it broadens out and becomes quite shallow. We shall need to be swift if we wish to muster the forces of the Greatwood, for that is what I intend to try to do." She turned to Nelwyn.

"Are you taking this down? I shall need a suitable message for my carrier-bat this evening." Gaelen turned and strode off, furious, and began to make ready.

Fima chuckled after her, but Nelwyn's face was pale. Things were beginning to fall into place. If somehow Amandir was right, they all had much to fear from Gaelen, and Nelwyn had no idea how she would ever break the news to her friend. Nelwyn would have to be certain her fears were well founded before she told Gaelen of them. She planned to have a discussion very soon with Lore-master Fima concerning the golden object that she had seen clutched in Gorgon's hand.

The river crossing did not prove too difficult for the mounted Company, though Fima swore he would never sit a horse again as Eros plunged across; it was all Rogond could do to keep the terrified dwarf from pitching off. Dwarves do not swim well, and they ordinarily do not place themselves in the position of needing to. Although the crossing proceeded without much further incident, the accidental but regrettable soaking of the remainder of the honeycomb set the tone for the next several days.

Gaelen was especially disappointed, as she had been saving it to give to Ri-Aruin and Wellyn, for wild honey was considered to be a delicacy, and she knew that Wellyn, in particular, relished it. They had no other gift to bring. Gaelen suspected that they might need a peace offering for the King, who would no doubt be displeased that she and Nelwyn had not returned as quickly as they had promised when they left for Mountain-home.

At any rate, Gaelen was in a dark mood for much of the rest of the journey. Rogond and Fima both tried to cheer her, but she spent much of her time alone, brooding and avoiding contact with Amandir, who had stubbornly refused to apologize to her for his accusations. Neither Rogond nor Fima would speak directly to him.

Rogond, in particular, was dismayed by Gaelen's behavior. She would not sing, and she would not sit with them around the evening fire when tales were heard and told. Normally Gaelen loved such things, but now she sat alone under the stars, usually in some tall tree, until dawn came. Rogond noted with dismay that her arm was bound one morning—had she cut herself again? It was not like her to be so careless, and he worried for her.

Nelwyn was cordial enough to Amandir, as was Galador, but Amandir remained distant, preferring to speak only to Oryan and the Elves of Tal-sithian. He would not deign to speak with Thorndil, either, which did not dismay the Ranger in the least. Nelwyn noticed that Amandir's eyes were often red and his face pale, as though he had been weeping, but she wisely refrained from asking him about it.

Amandir and Gaelen did share one behavior in common: they both practiced with their various weapons at every opportunity, and the Company came to admire Amandir's impressive skill with a blade. They wondered what was going through his mind as he whirled and slashed at his invisible enemy. Gaelen's formerly slender arms and shoulders were becoming increasingly well-muscled as she sought to gain power in the use of Fima's axe. She drew her bow with greater power as well and had suffered no loss of accuracy. When next she engaged the enemy in battle, she would be ready.

They kept a slightly different course toward the Elven-hold than the one familiar to Rogond and Galador, and Nelwyn estimated that the journey would take about eight more days at their present pace. One evening, she sought out Fima, who was sitting by himself at the base of an enormous oak, smoking his clay pipe and looking thoughtful. Nelwyn approached and sat beside him as he turned to greet her.

"Hello, Nelwyn. What brings you to me this fine evening? I sense you would ask a favor."

"That I would, Lore-master, for I came seeking wisdom. What do you know of objects that…that carry enchantment?"

Fima blinked at her. "Enchantment? You will be in want of knowledge then, Nelwyn, not wisdom. Why do you wish to know?"

Nelwyn looked at her hands, which lay clasped in her lap. She turned to Fima, her green eyes beseeching him. "Please, Fima, I must trust you now to keep this in confidence. I beg you, do not be angry. I want to know the truth of Amandir's accusations, and I suspect that there is something going on that Gaelen does not know about."

She hesitated for a moment, then plunged ahead. Fima might as well know everything—he would need all information if he would be of any help. "In Tal-sithian I looked into the Stone of Léir and saw Gorgon with something in his hand. He was looking at me with…with Gaelen's eyes. When he put the thing away, his own eyes reappeared."

Fima was looking at her with an expression of dismayed fascination. "Go on," he said. "What else did you see?"

Nelwyn drew a deep breath. "Is that not enough? I tell you, he had Gaelen's eyes while he held the object…it was small, and made of gold. At one point it almost looked like…like a mirror. Was there ever a mirror that enabled the wearer to…to see what their enemies were seeing?"

Fima considered before rummaging in one of his many pockets, drawing forth the small worn leather volume that Arialde had given him. He thumbed through it for a few minutes, muttering to himself. Nelwyn was nearly bursting.

"Well? Are you going to help me, or are you just going to sit there reading that book?"

Fima was unfazed. "In time, my impatient Nelwyn, in time. Arialde has given a useful gift. This entire section of this very, very old manuscript is devoted to just such a question. Here the works of Dardis are described in detail, and there are many mirrors mentioned—Dardis had a fondness for them, you see. One of the first made by him was tiny and kept within a golden casing. It was said to confer the power to see and hear through the senses of one's designated emissary. It would have been quite useful in war, or in peace. These writings state that the mirror was never put to use, because Dardis was uncertain of its effects on the bearer, or on the emissary. The author mentions that it had to be bound by the bearer to the chosen emissary using either a bit of their flesh or some possession of theirs." He continued to look into the manuscript.

"It says here that the mirror was among those objects crafted by Dardis that were unaccounted for after the Second Battle, where Dardis was so cruelly betrayed and slain. Such a great gifted hand, so tragically taken." He paused, bowing his head reverently, then began again. "The scholars believe that it was taken by Lord Wrothgar. If so, then it has been corrupted. Yet if it fell into the hands of the Dark Powers, why have we not seen it used before? Surely it was not kept all this time merely for Gorgon's use."

"Who knows?" replied Nelwyn, who was now becoming alarmed. "What did this mirror look like? Is there a description in your manuscript?"

Fima looked deeper, and his eyes darkened. "There is," he said, "but to myself I will keep it, until you disclose the nature of the object in your vision. I will then know if they are the same."

Nelwyn closed her eyes, recalling the image as best she could. "It is difficult—I saw the mirror for only a few moments, and it was a blur most of the time. But I do remember this: it was of gold, with a clever lid that flipped open to reveal the mirror within."

Fima grew pale as he read the description of the mirror in the manuscript. "Nelwyn, this is very important, so think carefully. Was the cover engraved? Were you able to see any imagery upon it, and if so, what was it?"

Nelwyn did not care for the expression on Fima's face, and she cared even less for the one that replaced it as she answered. "I thought...I thought I saw a seven-pointed star."

Fima's face was now very grim. "Are you certain? Because if you are, I may have to apologize to that haughty Amandir, and our dear Gaelen will not be able to bear it. You must be absolutely certain." He sighed, and handed her the book. "Look upon this image, and tell me whether you have seen it before."

Nelwyn took one glance at the drawing and, to her horror, recognized the mirror at once. She thought quickly—she would have to put Fima off for now. She needed time to consider.

"I...I'm not sure. It might have been...different. I'm not certain." But she could not look Fima in the eye. "I must take my leave of you, Lore-master, though I am grateful for your aid and enlightenment. Please forgive me." She rose and left abruptly, before Fima could see the tears of panic that now welled in her beautiful green eyes, escaping into the forest to be alone with her thoughts.

Fima watched her go, a deep dread in his heart. He did not envy her those thoughts, for he knew that she was now aware that her dearest friend and kin was quite possibly ensnared in a web set by Gorgon, a situation that might soon devour her sanity. Fima considered. Everything was falling into place now—the reason that Gorgon had shown up in Grundin's Realm in the first place, the slaying of Tibo, the survival of Gaelen, and the death of the Elves of Tal-sithian. Everything made sense. Fima wept quietly for the first time in many, many years. He would keep Nelwyn's secret as he had promised, but Nelwyn herself would have to come to grips with it, and then they would have to act. Fima loved both Nelwyn and Gaelen dearly, and he could not imagine the sorrow that would be set loose upon the day this awful truth would be revealed.

Nelwyn wept bitterly for some time, alone in the dark forest. This was indeed cruel news, and she could not fathom how she would act on it if it were true. She tried to catch her breath, which was coming in great gasps. With some effort, she mastered herself; she would not get any closer to the truth by weeping. In her heart she now resolved to lay a trap for Gorgon, one that would confirm her suspicions once and for all. She suspected that Gaelen's recurring chills had something to do with Gorgon and the mirror, and she thought she knew just how to ensure that her suspicions were correct and that the Stone had indeed shown the truth.

Steeling herself for the coming task, she set about laying plans to carry it out, hoping that she was wrong. She vowed to tell no one, not even Galador, until she was absolutely certain one way or the other.

24

The Mirror Revealed

The Company made their way through the deep forest without further incident, though there were times when it seemed as though strange creatures surrounded them on all sides, especially at night. Fima was not comfortable in this deep gloom at all, surrounded by ancient, moss-covered trees that seemed to resent his mere presence. The Elves of Tal-sithian were also ill at ease at first; they were accustomed to the light, open forests of the Deer-roaming, and this dark, oppressive tangle was not really to their liking.

Gaelen and Nelwyn, who were born and bred in the Greatwood, had seen the advance of evil in their beloved forest, spreading outward from the Darkmere, with its evil-smelling bogs full of misshapen, horrid creatures. Gaelen and Nelwyn, as hunter-scouts, surveyed and guarded the borders of the Elven-realm, and as such were constantly exposed to the perils of the Darkmere. So long as they were not disquieted, the others knew they had little to fear.

Rogond was relieved to see that the closer Gaelen drew to the Realm of Ri-Aruin, the happier she became. Though she still seemed subject to occasional chills, she laughed and played alongside Nelwyn, and she even sang a little.

One starlit night he heard her voice echoing among the ancient oaks. The great trees sighed and rustled their leaves almost as though they could hear. The Elves of Tal-sithian, who were accustomed to beautiful singing, were nevertheless enchanted by the haunting, soulful notes that seemed to hang in the air, lingering until the last of their sweetness faded from hearing. No one made a sound until the song ended. Rogond, who had closed his eyes in a waking dream, was startled by the sight of Amandir standing before him as Gaelen's song ended, and all was silent again.

"I would speak with you, Tuathan," he said, his eyes hard in the firelight. Rogond regarded him for a moment, wondering what the Elf could possibly have to say to him. Rather than inviting Amandir to sit beside him, Rogond rose somewhat stiffly and faced him.

"Fine, Amandir. You are free to speak with me if you wish, but recall that I will hear no evil spoken of Gaelen. So if that is what you have come to say, then leave without saying it, for I will not suffer it in my presence. What have you to say?"

"Only this. Your love for the Wood-elf is admirable, as is your loyalty. I will not comment on the wisdom of either, but I would say to you do not be blinded by it, for your lives hang in the balance." Rogond drew himself up before Amandir, and his grey eyes narrowed, glinting in the firelight as the Elf continued.

"Stay your wrath, and hear the rest of my tale, for I do not hold your beloved to blame. She is unwitting in her support of the enemy, but it makes her no less dangerous. Say nothing of importance in front of her. The enemy somehow knows what she knows. I no longer care for my own life, as there is but one purpose remaining in it, but I would not see you or your friends destroyed. In fact, I fear for Ri-Aruin and those of the Greatwood. It brings me no pleasure to tell you these things, for I hold no grudge against the Wood-elf, but I know her to be an instrument of the enemy, and therefore I must speak these words, though I earn only your enmity. You cannot now say that you have not been warned, and my conscience is clear. I will leave you now to your unhappy thoughts."

"You will not leave until I have said *my* piece," said Rogond. "I sorrow for your loss and for your pain. I see a heart that is empty save for grief, and I despair for you. I once thought that none could be as driven to destroy Gorgon as Gaelen has been, yet I see my error; your loathing of him is deeper and more consuming than hers could ever be. She has held onto her spirit; yours has been lost and overwhelmed by your pain. You are now just a vessel for grief, Amandir, and it has made you wretched. I truly sorrow for you. You still have not revealed to me the nature of this 'knowledge' that you possess concerning Gaelen's complicity with Gorgon. It's easy to make such claims, but far more difficult to support them with evidence and allow the facts to decide opinion."

To his credit, Amandir allowed Rogond to finish. Then he bowed his head and closed his eyes for a moment. When he opened them, they were resigned and empty.

"Do you think I care any at all for your opinion of me? Very well, Tuathan," he sighed. "We shall sit down together, and I will reveal the evidence to you. Then try to deny it, though your heart despair."

At that moment, Fima approached them from Rogond's left, his hand on his axe-handle.

"And what is the nature of this discussion?" he said. "I can see that my friend Rogond is disquieted; surely no ill is being said of Gaelen, as I am certain a wise Elf such as Amandir would have taken my meaning earlier."

Amandir addressed Rogond, ignoring Fima completely. "At such time as we are alone and I decide again to enlighten you, I will. Until then, remember my words and my warning. Share no secrets with her."

Fima growled deep in his throat at Amandir's retreating back. Rogond sighed. Fima was one of his dearest friends, but his appearance had indeed been untimely. There was nothing to do for it now, though.

Fima muttered under his breath: "The idiot probably thinks I do not understand his tongue. How little he appreciates my abilities! I hope it continues, as he will say something to truly provoke me one day, and then I shall have an excuse."

Rogond was tired of enmity. "Stop it, Fima," he said, eliciting a confused look from the dwarf. "At present, I don't wish to discuss Amandir or even acknowledge that he exists, if it is the same to you."

"Well said!" Fima enthused, lapsing back into the common tongue. "Let us take some rest ere dawn comes. I don't think the nightingale will favor us again tonight. What a beautiful song she sings. It was good to hear her again; it means her spirits are lifted. Will you go and find her now?"

Rogond considered. "No, Fima, I believe from the sound of it that she is keeping the watch in the trees tonight. I cannot rest sitting in tree tops, though I might wish it. I shall stay on the ground, for I am weary. Goodnight, my stalwart friend." Rogond sat down beside Thorndil at the base of a large oak tree and closed his eyes, and Fima moved to join them.

Neither Rogond nor his friend the dwarf truly rested that evening, as Rogond was troubled with thoughts of what Amandir would reveal to him, while Fima was troubled with thoughts of Dardis' mirror and what they would all do should Nelwyn's vision prove true.

Later, as Fima slept, he found himself caught in the grip of a nightmare in which he had to apologize to Amandir over and over, but try as he might to speak the Elven-tongue, the words just would not come to him. The dream-Amandir laughed as the normally eloquent Fima was forced to use the common tongue, and even this was halting and awkward, to his extreme humiliation.

They reached the borders of Ri-Aruin's Realm four days later. Another day and they would be escorted into the halls of the King. Gaelen and Nelwyn were joyful but anxious, as they would indeed have a long and involved tale to tell Ri-Aruin when they finally found themselves in his presence. The two She-elves greeted the hunter-scouts who met their party as long lost friends, which, in fact, they were, and they spent the remaining travel time catching up on news.

There were many in the Greatwood, it seemed, who were anxiously awaiting their return, including the kin of Talrodin and Halrodin. Wellyn had somehow fallen out of favor with his father, though none knew why. This was somewhat distressing to the people of the Greatwood, as the King normally got on very well with his eldest son and heir. Gaelen shook her head as she rode. It would surely be an interesting reunion. Impatient and anxious, she rode out ahead.

As soon as she drew near to the Elven-hold, Gaelen saw a familiar figure standing tall upon the hilltop, his cloak unfurled behind him, his dark hair lifting in the wind. Gaelen knew him at once, and her heart leapt. She spurred Siva forward, galloping with all speed toward him, calling his name and waving. Wellyn broke into a wide grin and leaped down from his perch, striding out to meet her, and as the guards stood aside to let the mare pass, Gaelen dismounted and ran to him. They embraced joyfully and long, true friends reunited at last. In recent memory Gaelen had not been nearly as happy to see anyone as she was to see Wellyn.

She buried her face in his tunic and breathed in his familiar scent, comforted by the warmth and strength of his arms and the gentle, clear sound of his voice. She really was home, Wellyn was really here, and she was surrounded by all that she knew and loved. In those few moments, weariness and despair seemed to fall away to be replaced with hope.

Wellyn had been somewhat alarmed at the sight of her, but he kept it hidden. Gaelen was lean, hard, and travel-worn. She had aged; though her face was as young as ever, her eyes betrayed her. They shone with an almost desperate brightness, as though determined now to be happy after months of hardship and grief. She shivered slightly in his embrace.

The rest of the Company, including Rogond, arrived a few minutes later. Gaelen and Wellyn were now talking with one another in excited voices, as Gaelen promised to tell him of her adventures.

"Yes, Gaelen, remember you must keep nothing from me. You vowed to share all of your tales upon your return, and if I am any judge there will be too much to reveal in one night. We shall have several enjoyable nights in the telling…I look forward to it more than you can know."

Gaelen smiled. "And I shall look forward to the telling. How I have missed you! Wait until I show you my skill with the longbow. I have been practicing!" She drew the weapon from over her shoulder to show him. It was beautifully made, and he was appreciative.

"Ah, Gaelen. You are ever hopeful of besting me. Yet I must tell you that I have also been training since you left us, and you have little chance, though I am impressed that you are strong enough to pull this bow. Tomorrow we shall see!"

Gaelen laughed as Nelwyn, Galador, Rogond, and the remainder of the Company drew nigh. Wellyn took his leave, stating that he wanted to inform Ri-Aruin of their arrival.

"I will see you at the feast tonight, Gaelen. You shall sit at the King's table, at my right hand." He shot a look at Rogond, his eyes telling a different tale from his smiling face. "I see the Tuathan followed you across the mountains. It is to his credit that he survived the crossing; you must have aided him greatly. I am relieved to see that he is still with you."

Gaelen looked over at Rogond and winked. "Oh, he burdened us but little, my friend. We only had to save him once or twice."

Rogond smiled, but his heart was troubled. He had not been aware of Gaelen's deep affection for Wellyn, whose enmity toward him was obvious. Rogond had noticed that Wellyn would not address him directly, and he imagined Ri-Aruin's attitude would probably be even worse. At least Gaelen seemed not to notice. She and Nelwyn were happy and excited as they spoke of the feast to come, and of their plans to reunite with their other friends. Gaelen took Rogond's arm, her familiar spirited nature in full force once again, and went forward with him.

The horses were taken to the stables, and the travelers were escorted to chambers where they could rest and refresh themselves until called before the King. Gaelen came to fetch Rogond, explaining that Ri-Aruin had requested an audience with him as well. He quickly made himself presentable, and they proceeded to the King's private audience-chamber, where Nelwyn and Galador were already waiting.

They would not have the time for the full telling of the tale until the following day, when the King would also hear from the Elves of Tal-sithian. Nevertheless, Ri-Aruin wanted to hear from them as soon as they arrived. He greeted the Company with a grave countenance, and listened in silence as they began.

Afterward, Gaelen bowed before the King and spoke in a small, quiet voice: "We have returned as promised, my lord, and we seek the aid of the Elves of the Greatwood, for this is an enemy that will require the strength of many to be defeated. That is our purpose and that of our companions. The Elves of Tal-sithian were sent by the Lady of the Lake to see us safely home. Yet they have said they will remain and aid us in our quest to rid the world of this abhorrent creature. Please, my lord, will you aid us?"

She raised her eyes to meet his, and though her posture still indicated submission, her spirit burned in her bright, unflinching gaze. Ri-Aruin smiled in spite of himself. She and Nelwyn had done him credit, by the sound of things. He could not help liking them, though their news was grave and their request somewhat bold. When he spoke, his voice was stern, but gentle.

"I cannot answer, Gaelen, until I have heard all you and your companions have to tell. But we recognize the need to defeat this enemy, and will not turn our backs on that need. Take heart."

He dismissed them soon after, bidding them take their rest so that they might feast long and merrily. "The four of you shall sit at my table tonight. You have done honor to the folk of the Greatwood. Now, rest and forget your cares, for you are safely in our realm. Tomorrow we shall speak more of your adventures and of your plans. Enjoy the full measure of our hospitality until then," he said, looking at Rogond in particular.

The Ranger saw no enmity in Ri-Aruin's glance, to his relief. Perhaps the King had realized that Rogond was an ally, or perhaps he had simply grown accustomed to the idea of him. Either way, Rogond thought, the acceptance of Ri-Aruin would make his stay in the Greatwood much less stressful. Of Wellyn, Rogond was far less certain, but he was content for now to deal with one problem at a time. Tonight he would feast with Gaelen and his friends, and he would not worry about the security of his heart's desire before this tall Prince of the Realm. At least, not until tomorrow.

Early summer was a wonderful time in the Greatwood. The weather was warm, but not oppressive, the nights were clear, and cool breezes stirred the trees and whispered gently in the reeds and tall grasses by the gently running river. The air smelled fresh, full of life and growth that would culminate in fruit and seed. As the Company prepared for the evening's festivities, they already felt renewed and relaxed. Warm baths, clean, shining hair, and new, fresh clothing had lifted their spirits.

Gaelen and Nelwyn brought out their finery for the occasion, and Rogond and Galador were likewise provided with tailored attire suitable for honored guests. But Gaelen noticed that Fima had not been provided for. He had packed a spare cloak, but his clothes were stained and travel-weary. Gaelen went with Nelwyn to see the King concerning this matter, and after waiting for what seemed an age, they were brought before him. Gaelen expressed her concerns, recalling that there had been no mention of Fima and Thorndil being included at the King's table.

Ri-Aruin corrected the situation at once, requesting that Fima be brought before him so that the King might explain his oversight. The dwarf was most gracious, chuckling to himself as Ri-Aruin explained that they had no spare raiment on hand that would likely fit him, but that all haste would be made to provide it. Thus it was that Fima found himself seated at the King's table—the first of his race to do so—wearing drastically altered garments of blue and gold that had once been worn by the King himself. The alterations were difficult and had taken much of the afternoon, but Fima looked positively splendid, eliciting many curious looks from the Greatwood Elves. He sat to the right of Rogond, who sat at the right of Gaelen. Wellyn sat at her left, beside his father. Galador, Nelwyn, and Thorndil sat at the left hand of the King. To the left of Thorndil was an empty place, set for Belegund.

The Elves of Tal-sithian had been given a royal welcome and were seated at their own long table in a position of honor, to the right of the King. Oryan and Amandir sat at the head, flanked by their companions, and they rose and drank the health of the King and of the people of the Greatwood. Amandir looked hard at Rogond as he spoke, and Rogond heard his voice as though inside his head: *I will drink your health, Tuathan, for you will have need of it. We must speak of this matter, and soon.* Rogond nodded slightly toward him, though his eyes did not show reaction to the message.

There was a somber underlayment to this merry gathering, because Gorgon still lived, and the Elves of the Greatwood would soon be enlisted to aid in hunting him down. This task would be a daunting one, as they all knew, and lives would be lost.

Gaelen lifted her glass in remembrance of Belegund; only she had witnessed his last moments, and she still felt that she had failed him. "I am sorry, my friend, that I came too late and with too little skill to aid you," she murmured in a soft voice. Wellyn perceived the hurt behind her closed eyes, and he placed a comforting hand on her arm.

He tried to cheer her. "Let us begin our tale-telling tonight. Meet me by the river, beside the great stones, at the setting of the moon. I will bring food and wine, and we shall pass the time until the dawn."

Gaelen smiled at him. "Most assuredly, we shall. And I hope I am strong enough to do justice in the telling. This is a long, long story my friend. I may need some help—perhaps Nelwyn could join us, or Rogond and Fima? They also have much to tell."

"Not tonight, Gaelen. This is our time to renew our friendship and share thoughts and memories. Tomorrow will be soon enough for the others. Come alone, if you would enlighten me as promised. I shall await you."

Gaelen nodded. She had indeed promised him this time, so many months ago. She then looked at the heavily laden table before her. "Food we shall not need, Wellyn, but wine may be welcome. Until the setting of the moon, then." They lifted their glasses in acknowledgment of the plan.

Fima was truly happy to find himself at a table laden with delicacies of Elven creation, as over the years he had grown unaccustomed to being without it. The fare in the Greatwood was similar to that of Mountain-home, but simpler. The Wood-elves had not the same access to exotic spices and flavorings, but instead relied on the herbs and flowers that grew nearby. The wine, however, was among the best Fima had tasted. The meats were savory and tender, the greens fresh, and… the mushrooms! They were the most succulent and flavorful in Fima's experience, and were black in color. Finally, huge trays of honey-cakes stuffed with cream and nuts were set at each table, and the gathering became as merry as it could be.

Soon the feasting subsided and the telling of tales began. The Elves of Tal-sithian began to recount stories of the Lake-realm, and of their adventures since leaving it, including the frightening account of the disappearance of their friends, and the finding of the unfortunate remains of those that had been sent after Gorgon. The Wood-elves were dismayed and clamored to hear more about this enemy, who had already caused grief among their people. They feared that he was on a course set for the Greatwood, and they wished to be counted among those set to defeat him. There were not a few fierce, resolute expressions among them, for they were accustomed to defending their lands from all who would threaten them.

Using the mirror, Gorgon witnessed some of this activity as he crouched with his followers near the borders of the Forest Realm. He would not enter it, as it was simply thick with Wood-elves, whose arrows were deadly and could do serious damage to his rather small army. The last thing he wanted was to allow Gaelen and Company to know of his presence there—he could not risk it. There was too much to be gained in secrecy, and he would not reveal himself until he was in the position to do the greatest amount of damage. Besides, it was a warm night, and the Barrens were not far away.

This was a rather mysterious area of desolate rock set in the midst of the forest, with many dark hiding places. Gorgon had decided that for the sake of the Ulcas in his command, he would set up headquarters there, as the lands were more to their liking. Kharsh noted this with satisfaction; it was the first time Gorgon had thought to see to the comforts of his underlings. Of course, his reasons were purely selfish, as he wanted them fit and ready for battle, yet Kharsh saw this as Gorgon's showing some promise as a field commander.

Normally Ulcas are driven only by fear, and these had much to fear from Gorgon, but he had realized that they would work harder and fight better if they were not overly stressed. With this in mind he arranged to remain in a place where they could hide from the sun and where water was relatively plentiful. They had made their way slowly through the north and west of the Darkmere, taking an entirely different course from that of the Company, for they knew their ultimate destination. The north of the Darkmere held little to fear for Gorgon and his Ulcas, and they would reach the Barrens in a few days' time.

Gorgon listened to the tale of the Elves of Tal-sithian. It cheered him to hear the dread in their voices and to see the dismay on the faces of those assembled. Gorgon reflected that they had good reason to fear, and chuckled through his pain as the Elves vowed vengeance. Gorgon was happy to see that Gaelen had become a person of some importance and was now a central figure in their planning, for she knew more of Gorgon than anyone. He had only to remain vigilant, and he would learn what he needed to know.

The She-elf was beginning to relax and perk up a little, though it seemed that she was always cold. Gorgon wondered—did his intrusion affect her thus? So long as the Company never became aware of the existence of the mirror, they would never make the connection. Still, he wondered. Even now, full of food and wine, she drew her cloak about her.

Gorgon would not need to further avail himself of the mirror this night, as Gaelen would be engaged in telling the tale of her adventures. He needed to save his strength for more important matters, as the mirror both pained him and drew his strength—especially if he opened it and looked within. Luckily, that had become unnecessary. The connection between Gaelen and himself had become stronger with time—all he had to do now was hold the mirror in his hand. In fact, Gaelen's vision and hearing vanished completely only when he placed the mirror safely in the small pouch at his belt.

His own Dark Company would be traveling toward the Barrens, and he would need the use of his own senses. While Gorgon held the mirror, he literally could not see through his own eyes, but was obliged to view only what was seen by Gaelen. He could still hear through both her ears and his own, though Kharsh had learned that it was sometimes difficult to gain his attention.

Surmising that he would learn nothing of use this night, Gorgon put the mirror away, sighing with relief as the pain left him. He strode out into the night, his minions in tow. They were well-rested and ready for mayhem, but Kharsh cautioned them that they needed to remain wary. Even as distant from the King's halls as they were, they did not dare risk a chance encounter. They made their way toward the north and the welcoming Barrens, thoughts of mayhem put aside for the moment.

Rogond was apprehensive as he stood quietly in the armory, awaiting the arrival of Amandir. The Elf had indicated that he wished to continue the conversation that had been interrupted by Fima some days earlier, and that now was as good a time as any, as Gaelen had gone to spend the night with Wellyn. It gladdened Rogond's heart to see her thus occupied; there was nothing like being home again. Gaelen was accustomed to spending long weeks away from her friends and kin, but the intense pursuit over so many months had drained her, and this had worsened since leaving Mountain-home.

The tips of Rogond's fingers were tingling in anticipation of Amandir's arrival, and he dreaded the news the Elf would bring. When Amandir stood before him at last, his expression was unreadable. Rogond moved to the armory doors, which were of heavy oak fitted with iron, and pulled them closed with some difficulty.

"All right, Amandir. Say what you have come to say. My mind and my heart are open to you."

Amandir drew a weary hand across his eyes, brushing an errant strand of his long hair from his face. "I wish you to know that this brings me no pleasure, Tuathan. Having heard what I have to tell, may you act wisely and quickly, before any more Elven lives are lost. Remember also your friend who was lost in Cós-domhain. Gorgon takes victims of all races."

"I have not forgotten him, Amandir," Rogond muttered. "Get on with it."

Amandir told his tale in a few minutes, leaving nothing out. When he had finished, Rogond stood, white-faced and shaken, horrified by what he had heard. Though Amandir's conclusions were based mostly on insights gained through the Stone of Léir, his logic concerning events that had occurred since their arrival in Tal-sithian was unassailable. For example, Rogond had not known that the Elves lost near the Cold-spring had met Gaelen and Nelwyn earlier on the very day they were lost.

Amandir pointed out that Gaelen had witnessed the conversation regarding the pursuit of the Ulcas by the hapless Elves of Tal-sithian, so that they were taken by Gorgon, who had then known of their course. Rogond was now drawing conclusions of his own concerning events in Cós-domhain. Of course, Gorgon had known about Tibo, and probably about Noli. This explained why Gorgon had not killed Gaelen when his chance had come.

What Amandir did not know was how Gorgon was accomplishing the link with Gaelen, as the Stone had provided no specifics. Rogond knew that there were many mysteries in Alterra of which he was unaware, and he wished at that moment that his knowledge was vast enough to gain understanding. But alas, only one such as Fima, who had spent much of his life studying such things, might possess the insight needed to enlighten them. Suddenly Rogond brightened—he would seek Fima's aid at once. He turned to Amandir.

"I now understand your concerns, Amandir, although I still disapprove of your treatment of Gaelen. I would appreciate it if, in the future, you would at least attempt to conceal your ill feelings toward her—it would make things so much easier for everyone. It might keep you from the wrong end of an axe, as well. I must go now and seek wisdom so that I may know how to proceed. Thank you for finally revealing this matter to me, though I hear it with great pain and doubt."

Amandir looked upon Rogond with disdain. "You would not have heard me had I chosen earlier to impart it to you, Tuathan. And as for the dwarf, I will not waste my time worrying for my safety. He is an insignificant player in this affair. I enlighten you because you are at serious risk, as are any of my race who stand within her sight and hearing. As for concealing my feelings, do not fear, for I intend to place myself as far from her influence as I possibly can. It is my expectation that she will eventually draw this creature forth to where he may be killed. That is my sole reason for being among you. I pray only that few lives will be lost as a result, though I hold little hope."

Rogond shook his head. "You are determined that I shall not ever find you winsome, aren't you? Very well, distance yourself if you will. Again, my sympathy lies with you in this matter, and I would aid you if I could."

Amandir suppressed a cold smile at Rogond's sarcasm, his ancient eyes gleaming from his young, unmarred face. "You cannot fathom the nature of my grief, and I neither want nor need your sympathy. I have lived without it through the long years, and I shall not require it now. When Gorgon is dead, I shall go to join my beloved, and we shall at last give up our pain. Save your sympathy for those who will have need of it, including yourself." He turned and moved the armory doors with strength that surpassed Rogond's. Then, with one last look over his shoulder, he left.

Rogond went in search of Fima, but he was not in his chamber, and his whereabouts were unknown to anyone Rogond found to ask. In fact, he would not find Fima until the morning of the following day, as the dwarf was at that moment engaged in serious conspiracy with Nelwyn, laying plans to trap Gorgon into revealing the truth of the mirror.

"I know this will work, Fima," Nelwyn insisted. "Gorgon wanted to kill me in Cós-domhain. Galador had foreseen it…that's why he would not go under the mountains. He wanted to take me straight to Tal-sithian so that I would be protected. We must tempt Gorgon into revealing himself. If I must serve as the bait, then so be it. I will not jeopardize Gaelen until I am absolutely certain that this horrible mirror exists and that she is bound by it. If we are wrong, then I have little to fear."

"And if we're right, you have everything to fear!" said Fima. "Besides that, I'm not comfortable with using Gaelen for this...this manipulation of her enemy without her knowledge."

"I know...and I've thought quite long and hard about it," said Nelwyn. "But there's no way we can let her in on our plan without telling her everything. I can't do that until I'm absolutely certain that the mirror exists. Gaelen isn't ready to hear about it, Fima, and I'm not certain I should even be the one to tell her. For now, she cannot know what we're planning."

Fima shook his head. He was decidedly uneasy at the thought of confronting the same creature that had so easily slain the mighty Belegund, and he felt guilty hiding the plan from Gaelen, but Nelwyn's words made sense. It was the only way to be sure.

Tomorrow they would find Gaelen and watch her carefully. Nelwyn suspected that the cold chills Gaelen seemed to feel at inappropriate times might indicate Gorgon's presence, and if so, they could lay their bait.

Nelwyn intended to make herself available and vulnerable to attack, and therefore irresistible to Gorgon. Then she and Fima would lie in wait for him. If he appeared, they would know they were right about the mirror. Nelwyn had the feeling that Gorgon would not be far away, though she suspected that he would not enter the borders of the Elven-king's realm. She would need to travel far from the Elven-hold to lure him, as his cowardice would prevent him from taking much risk.

She and Fima talked until dawn, crafting their plan. When they had finished, Fima shook his head. "Nelwyn, are you certain there is no other way? The chance you are taking...if Galador knew...."

"And so he must *not*, Fima! I most certainly will not tell him. Remember, this plan is of our design, not Gorgon's. I know the forest, and he does not. We have the upper hand."

"He has an army," said Fima quietly. "You and I will be no match for an army of Ulcas."

"He will not bring his army to kill one Elf, Fima. I don't know how I know it, but I do. It would ruin the sport, somehow. And I sense he does not wish to reveal the presence of his army until he can do a great deal of damage."

"For some reason, I can't imagine Gorgon as the sporting type," said Fima, shaking his head again, his long, white beard waving to and fro.

"You know what I meant. This is too important for jesting, my friend. Gaelen's very life, and the lives of many others, may hang in the balance. We must be certain of this matter before we consider what to do next."

"If you thought I was jesting, then you know less of me than I thought," said Fima. He paused as he considered his next question. "Have you thought about what our course of action will be should this prove true? Suppose your plan works and we lure Gorgon in, and our fears are confirmed. What, then, will you do?"

"I am hopeful that he may be taken unaware, and perhaps I can pierce his armor with this," she said, indicating her powerful longbow. "If not, I will at least frighten him into retreating. He knows the forest is thick with deadly archers; he will probably withdraw if I chase him with a shaft or two."

"That's not what I meant, and you know it," said Fima, his voice deadly serious.

"I know," said Nelwyn. But she could not answer further, as she had no idea what she would do. They would have to tell Gaelen, and that simple fact caused such dread in Nelwyn that she shook the thought from her mind. She could not imagine the impact of such knowledge upon her dearest friend and cousin; it would surely devastate her. She turned back to Fima.

"One difficulty at a time. Let's first confirm our fears, and then I will consider our next course."

"Someone will have to tell her, you know," said the Dwarf.

"I know, Fima. Believe me, I know," Nelwyn replied, her eyes filling with tears at the mere thought of it. She turned and made her way back toward the King's halls just as dawn was breaking. The skies were on fire with the rising sun. The sight was beautiful, but it brought little comfort to Nelwyn, and she did not smile.

Thus it was that Gorgon Elfhunter found his journey toward the Barrens interrupted. He now addressed two of his underlings as they stood before him, Kharsh at his side.

"There is a She-elf, with golden hair. She and her companion have been sent by the King on some errand to the southern border of the Elf-realm, along the east bank of the Forest River north of where it crosses the old northern road. Do you know it?" The Ulcas nodded. They had been selected because they were most familiar with the Darkmere, but they were uneasy, as they had no desire to cross into the domain of Ri-Aruin.

Gorgon continued. "They will arrive in three days' time, as they are mounted. We must move swiftly, as they indicated that they would only be there for a short while. Make ready, for we leave at once. I will accompany you as far as the border; from there you will approach them, take them unaware, and bring the golden-haired one to me. Kill the other if you will, but bring the Elf alive and unharmed. I shall wish to take my time with her." Gorgon remembered the pain he had suffered as a result of his last encounter with Nelwyn. This would be a most pleasant diversion for him.

The Ulcas looked knowingly at one another. Their commander was intending to torture his victim as he had the Elves of Tal-sithian, no doubt in similar fashion. While they did not understand Gorgon beyond the bare minimum, they did appreciate his hatred of the Elves and would look forward to witnessing his terrible vengeance. It might almost make up for the danger involved in crossing into the Elven-realm. They bowed before Gorgon and went to gather their provisions, as they would need strength for this chase. Gorgon left Kharsh in command of the remainder of the Black Company, instructing him to continue toward the Barrens, there to await Gorgon's return.

Kharsh drew Gorgon aside before he departed. "Forgive me, my lord, but are you certain this course is wise? It seems to carry great risk. Why place yourself in peril just to kill one Elf, when soon you shall hold the mastery over many?"

Gorgon smiled sardonically at Kharsh. "I was not aware that you cared so for me; it touches my heart. This is not just an Elf—this is an Elf upon whom I have vowed vengeance. She once did harm to me, and I shall have her! Do not try to dissuade me, for it will not avail you."

"But, my lord, what if you are pursued? There may be many Elves nearby, and they may not be easily taken. I am unhappy with the thought of your going so near to the Elves' domain without your army to protect you." This was true, as Kharsh knew his own life would be forfeit should Wrothgar learn that his highly valuable creation was lost in some reckless pursuit because Kharsh failed to prevent it.

"If I didn't know that it is Wrothgar you fear, I would worry that you were becoming sentimental," Gorgon growled. "I warn you, Kharsh, do not suggest thwarting me, as you will draw breath once, perhaps twice, after I get wind of it." He drew Turantil with a speed that Kharsh could not even follow with his eyes and placed it at Kharsh's grey-wattled throat before he could move. Kharsh said nothing more, which was very wise.

Three days later, Nelwyn and Fima were in position, and the stage was set. Nelwyn's horse was tethered near the river in a small clearing. Their gear was placed so that it would appear as if they had gone collecting herbs by the waterside, for that was their professed purpose. According to Nelwyn's plan, Gorgon had been led to believe that Ri-Aruin's herb-master had sent Nelwyn to gather evening-bloom, a valuable plant with various medicinal properties. It was only known to grow in this area, and Nelwyn, who was quite knowledgeable in herb-lore, was a logical choice to collect it. Fima had stated that he would accompany her because he wished to learn more of the herb-lore of the Greatwood. In truth, Fima was not especially fascinated with herb-lore, but no one save Rogond knew this. Galador did not discover that Nelwyn had gone missing until late afternoon the day of her departure, though he had been searching for her.

He did not understand why Nelwyn should go off to gather herbs without him. And why take Fima along? He had asked Gaelen about it, and she had seemed uncertain as well. Galador had spoken then with Rogond, who had, in fact, been searching for Fima, and also found the whole affair rather odd.

The puzzle grew deeper when Gaelen went to speak with Ri-Aruin's herb-master. He had informed her, somewhat stiffly, that he had plenty of evening-bloom among his stores, and he most certainly had not sent Nelwyn and Fima to gather more.

Gaelen, Rogond and Galador were disquieted, and they left as soon as they could make ready. Nelwyn would now have to hope that Gorgon appeared in a timely manner, as she would have only about a day's head start on her friends.

Gorgon lurked within sight of the path that marked the boundary of the Elven-realm. His two companions had gone on ahead toward the river, where they might discover the whereabouts of Nelwyn and Fima, capture Nelwyn, and return her to the spot where Gorgon waited. They could do whatever they wished with Fima. Gorgon had promised them great reward if they succeeded, yet they were uneasy, eyes turned ever to the trees in the dim twilight. Soon it would be dark, but not soon enough for the Ulcas, who were very uncomfortable with the thought of sharp-eyed Wood-elves training their bows on them in the grey half-light. They muttered to one another in harsh voices as they drew nigh the camp.

"D'you see anyone?"

The other grunted and shook his head. "That makes me uneasy. Can't we just go back and tell 'His Highness' they weren't here after all?"

"What, you want to try to lie to him? Besides, we've been sent to catch that She-elf, and I'm betting he won't take 'no' for an answer. What was it he said? Don't bother coming back without her?"

"Yeah. An' I'll wager he meant it, curse his miserable Elf-hide. Why he hates 'em so much is beyond me—one look at him an' you can see he's practically one himself!"

"Well, don't know about lookin' at him, but he sure enough ACTS like one of 'em. He'll turn his back once too often, I'm thinkin'. But Kharsh says there's big plans afoot, and he's right in the middle of 'em, so we'd best get on with it."

They drew a bit closer to the encampment, listening intently for signs of life, but all they heard was the whistling sound made by two lethal shafts speeding toward them, and then they knew nothing more. Neither of Gorgon's luckless minions would have to worry about returning empty-handed to their disappointed commander.

Nelwyn made certain that the camp was secure before joining Fima in the clearing. She had killed both Ulcas on his signal, and now as she approached him, she knew that her worst fears would be confirmed. Fima had heard every word spoken by the unwary Ulcas, who, of course, had no idea they had been anticipated.

Fima's face was pale, his eyes full of despair. "So, it's true, then," said Nelwyn tonelessly. She had known it in her heart, and so had Fima. Still, it was a difficult thing to face. He recounted every word he had heard. Then he and Nelwyn sat in despair upon the ground, after collecting and packing their gear. Even though there would be no further need to maintain the pretense, Nelwyn had gathered enough herbs to convince Gaelen and Galador that she had been on an honest errand. She sat unmoving beside Fima, trembling as she considered the implications of what they had now learned.

How could she ever tell Gaelen? She began to weep, and Fima, to her surprise, suddenly rose to his feet and cast his axe into the trunk of a nearby tree, uttering a terrible, frustrated cry. He did not try to comfort Nelwyn, as he could not, so he sat alone in the shadows on the opposite side of the clearing, and his thoughts were his alone.

The night drew down around Gorgon, enfolding him in darkness, as he waited for the return of his two henchmen. Doubt was beginning to grow in the back of his mind; surely it would not take so long to trap one Elf and kill one dwarf. He had instructed the Ulcas to return with all haste, bringing the She-elf to him alive. They most certainly would not have dared defy him; Gorgon knew that the Ulcas under his command both loathed and feared him. He strained into the blackness of the forest, trying to hear, but he heard no rumor of any returning minions.

He grew impatient and decided to make a few preparations for the arrival of Nelwyn. He took the rope from his shoulders and threw the free end over a convenient, sturdy tree-branch, preparing to tie her and suspend her as he had the others, so that he might torment her at his leisure. As he made fast the rope, estimating the length he would require, a familiar voice startled him from behind.

You won't be needing that rope, you know. They are not coming back. Your plan has gone awry, and the Elves have held the mastery. She no doubt met companions on the road, and they have dispatched your pathetic would-be abductors. You might as well turn tail and go back to the rest of your rabble right now. Ha!

Gorgon did not want to turn around, for he knew what he would see. "Go away, Èolo, for I do not wish to bandy words with you tonight. I have nothing to say to you."

Gelmyr then appeared in front of Gorgon, forcing him to look into his dead, rotting face. *No doubt, Dreaded Horror! However, I have a few things to say to you. My people have proven their superiority once again. Even with every advantage—the mirror that allows you to know what they are planning, as well as large, strong minions handpicked by the Black Flame—you cannot prevail against one She-elf. This is the second time that she and her friends have bested you, I believe. And here you are, alone, a perfect target for their bows, and in one moment all of Wrothgar's well-laid plans could come to nothing! If that happens, you will indeed be glad that they have killed you.*

"What would you know about it? The Black Flame is beyond anything in your experience. You Elves have no stomach for the kind of dread power He wields. You are dead, Èolo, and you have no power over me. Why do you torment me thus? Does it give you so much pleasure that you will not rest?"

Indeed it does, O Fearsome Hand of Death! I appear when you are in doubt of yourself, and rightly so, I might add. I will not rest until you summon me no more. Gelmyr paused, and his blue glowing face twisted slightly into a vague, sardonic smile. *By the way,* he said in a soft, rather menacing voice, *have you regretted killing me yet? If you had simply left me alone that night by the Ambros, I would not be here tormenting you right now.*

"That I most assuredly have *NOT!*" roared Gorgon, as Gelmyr threw his head back and laughed aloud.

You know, 'Elfhunter', I would keep my voice lower if I were you. The Elves of Greatwood have deadly aim, and they see quite well in the dark. You are more than close enough to their borders to risk being taken. Give up waiting for your toadies; they were unwary and died without a struggle. Go back to your pathetic army. You may find their confidence in your abilities somewhat shaken, however. Most regrettable. I wonder how long before they turn on you and murder you some dark night?

"They will never do such a thing, as Wrothgar will have them, and they fear Him," said Gorgon. He had to admit that going back to the Black Company in failure was not something he looked forward to.

I expect you'll simply lie to them, won't you? You'll make up some story of your victory over the She-elf, alas that your two minions were lost, but you certainly enjoyed tormenting her. Isn't that about right? You are so utterly pathetic! You are an embarrassment to the name of Elves. Even your father's people would laugh if they could see and hear you right now. Elfhunter, indeed!

Gelmyr's laughter filled Gorgon's senses, and Gorgon wondered for a moment whether he was going mad. Then, mercifully, the laughter faded. As Gelmyr slowly disappeared from view, he spoke one last time:

So long as you continue to doubt yourself, I shall be with you. It appears that I shall have little rest. Ha! Farewell, pathetic underling of Wrothgar. Enjoy the rest of your night alone...dawn is nearly upon you. Farewell.

In that moment, as Gelmyr faded at last from his sight and hearing, Gorgon knew that the Elf was right. The Ulcas would not return, as dawn was nearly breaking, and he would now have to make his way alone to the Barrens. For a moment he considered going after Nelwyn himself, but he dared not. Once inside the Elf-realm he would be at great risk, and he did not know what peril had taken the Ulcas. It was possible that a large company of Elves lay waiting for him, and he could not risk being killed, not before he had the chance to visit disaster upon them.

No, Lord Wrothgar had placed this power at his command, and it would not be wasted. He would await his chance to lay them all low; it would come soon enough. He had escaped their notice, and therefore their wrath, for all these ages. The She-elf was not worth throwing all that caution away in one vengeful, foolish moment. He would wait yet awhile, but if the Ulcas did not appear he would continue back toward the Barrens, there to rendezvous with Kharsh and his army. He already had a suitably impressive response planned should Kharsh ask him what had befallen the Ulcas. If Wrothgar had been privy to Gorgon's thoughts then, he would have rejoiced. His wayward creation was coming into maturity at last.

25

Gaelen Undone

Rogond, Galador and Gaelen had stopped for the night to rest their horses, for they preferred traveling in the deep forest while the sun was up. It was obvious that Nelwyn and Fima had stopped in this very spot the previous evening, obvious to Gaelen at any rate, for she could detect the signs, though they were few. As they rested, they tried to imagine the purpose that had driven Nelwyn and Fima to this place, and in particular, why Nelwyn had felt it necessary to lie to Gaelen about it.

This was not Nelwyn's habit, and Gaelen remarked to the others that Nelwyn had lied easily and well, seeming quite in earnest and not at all uncomfortable. This was perplexing, as normally Nelwyn had a great deal of difficulty lying convincingly to anyone. Rogond likewise could not imagine what Fima was doing going off with Nelwyn on some unknown errand. Herb-lore did not interest the dwarf, and he loathed traveling on horseback. Yet here he was, riding for nearly three days with Nelwyn, to what end? Galador's distress was predictable, for he was both hurt and angry that Nelwyn had gone off without even telling him.

"Don't be angry with her, Galador," said Gaelen. "I'm sure that Nelwyn has an innocent motive...perhaps she and Fima are planning something to surprise you, and therefore kept it from you." Galador looked at her with a jaundiced eye, and she looked away, knowing how unlikely her argument sounded.

Galador had grown fond of Gaelen in recent weeks. Now, like everyone else who knew her well, he perceived that she was deeply troubled, and he relented. "Perhaps you're right," he said. "I pray that you are, for although it distresses me to admit it, I am really more afraid than angry. I am thankful for your reassurance...it is helpful."

Rogond had not been himself since the day before Nelwyn had left with Fima. He had been seeking the dwarf, and had finally found him that morning, but Fima had brushed him off, saying that he had no time for any discussions then, but would find Rogond later. Then he went off with Nelwyn unbeknownst to anyone save Gaelen. It was obvious to Rogond that Fima was avoiding him, but why? A deep, gnawing dread was growing in his heart. Did Fima already know something of Amandir's revelation? He had seemed rather grim and subdued for several days now, quite unlike his usual demeanor, and this would be a reasonable explanation.

Gaelen had built a small fire, which Galador was now tending. Rogond looked over his shoulder to observe her approaching a nearby tree, then he heard the soft rustling of branches as she climbed up to keep the watch. Rogond was suddenly overwhelmed with the need to speak to her, as though he might never get another chance. He did not especially relish joining her in the top of the tall tree, but this he would do, for his need was great and would not be suppressed.

He rose and bade Galador good night, making his way to where Gaelen had gone, though he could not see her. Then her soft voice drifted down, and she moved just enough that he could see her among the middle branches.

"I would speak with you, Gaelen. Shall I come up, or will you come down?"

"I will come down if it is an urgent matter, for it will be no use keeping the watch from here if you join me, as you will be both seen and heard. It's not the best vantage point, anyway." She dropped from her perch to land lightly beside him; he had not even seen her climb down.

"Fima is right. You are quite the furtive one! No wonder he complains so about your startling him constantly."

She ignored his comment. "I am here, Tuathan. What would you say to me?" She was direct, as always.

Rogond's resolve was beginning to waver, but he drew a deep breath and steeled himself—it was time. "Gaelen, please sit down, as this will be difficult for me to say, but I have long wanted to say it. I don't know why, but I must say it now… tonight."

She appeared apprehensive and took both his hands in her own, sinking down upon the ground before him. He then sat beside her and reached up to stroke her hair, gazing into her concerned face. Several long moments passed in silence ere he spoke, sometimes halting, sometimes very eloquent, but always genuine. "Gaelen…I have struggled long with this matter, for all have told me that my path leads only to sorrow, and that it is folly. I am a mortal man and one day I must leave this world and go to the place prepared for my kindred. There, you cannot follow. I will never be with you again. All have warned me of the grief this will bring, even Lady Ordath and Galador, but though I hear their words, my heart does not. My heart…"

Here he paused, as his voice broke and his hands were shaking slightly. He drew another deep breath, and looked once more into her bright eyes.

"My heart is given, Gaelen. It is given forever, and I will love no other. I cannot take back my choice even should I wish to. All have admonished me that my hope is vain and my desire is doomed, but I cannot undo them. Please understand that I love you, that I will always love you, and that I will stay by your side for as long as you will have me."

He watched her expression change from shock to distress as her eyes filled with tears. She did not know what to say to him, but sat before him in silence, her hands now limp in his grasp.

"Gaelen, please do not be grieved at this knowledge. You cannot know how difficult this has been for me to say, but I cannot keep silent any longer. Things are happening, my love, and our future is uncertain. I would have you know of my devotion, for I sense you will have need of it." Gaelen stared at him in silence, her face expressionless save for the tears that stood in her bright eyes.

"Please, Gaelen, have you nothing to say?"

She closed her eyes then, as though collecting herself, and a tear trickled slowly down her cheek. Rogond reached up and gently wiped it away, despairing as she stiffened at his touch. At last she spoke:

"I have been wondering about this since Cós-domhain, but lacked the courage to speak of it. I do not wish to hurt you, as I care for you deeply, but can you not see that Ordath and Galador are right? This cannot be, though we might wish it. You…you are the most wonderful person I know, the most caring and steadfast. You deserve a love that will be given fully to you and will follow you hereafter, until the ending of the world. You deserve better than Gaelen of the Greatwood."

Rogond's heart ached so much for her in that moment that he could hardly bear it. There was no one better. There never would be. Not for him. "Did you not hear? I will have no other. You are my love, Gaelen, to whom my heart is given. I cannot retrieve it even if I so wished. Do you not hear me? My heart is given. I am doomed to spend my days in longing for you, and I don't know if I can bear it."

She truly wept then, tears flowing freely from her eyes, and pulled her hands away from him with some difficulty. She rose to her knees, reeling back from him as he tried to stay her. "Rogond…I cannot sustain your heart. I do not know if I can ever love anyone the way you would want me to. You deserve better. I am not capable of giving my heart to anyone. Not now, not ever again. You cannot understand!"

He gripped her upper arms then, gently but firmly. "Stay and hear me, Gaelen, before you decide what you must do. I…I know your heart was given."

She looked at him with wide eyes. She had not expected this.

"Gaelen, I know about Rain."

At the mention of Ri-Elathan, Rogond saw pain and desperate longing flickering in the depths of her eyes, and he despaired for her. "Who has told you of him? This is knowledge that I have guarded even from my own kin. How did you learn of it?"

"It doesn't matter. In truth, I have known for some time, since Mountain-home. I know the whole tale, Gaelen, and I know the grief of your heart. I only want the chance to aid you and to love you with all my being for the duration of my days. I ask nothing more. Give me only what you can, Gaelen. I am not Ri-Elathan. I would never presume to take his place in your heart."

"That is well, Rogond, for that you cannot do. What I do not know is whether there is room in my heart to love anyone, especially someone as deserving and worthy of love as you. I do care for you, very deeply. I have despaired at the thought of your leaving me, for my life would be so much less without you. But I do not know whether I can love you the way you want me to. You must give me time to consider your words. I shall then give you my answer."

"That I will, beloved. But consider these words as well: I have no choice left to me. I must either live for the days of my life with the one I love and then part from her forever, or live the days of my life in bitter disappointment, alone in longing for her, and then part from her forever. Consider also your choices, Gaelen. You can allow me to love you, to my great joy, for the days allotted to us, and we can live happily until our parting. Or you can remain as you have been, and live in grief and longing until you are slain, or choose to give up your life. Your beloved, who awaits you even now, what choice would he have you make? From what I have heard of him, I cannot imagine that he would not have you choose to open your heart and not live in grief for him as you have done already for so many, many years. Tell me that is not so!"

Gaelen's eyes flashed. "If Farahin were here, Rogond, he could explain his choice to us. But he is not, and I cannot speak for him. I can only consider my own choices."

Rogond spoke gently to her. "That's right, Gaelen...Farahin is not here. He has not been by your side since the Third Battle. Look into my eyes and tell me that he would choose a lifetime of grief for you!"

Gaelen looked hard at Rogond, but she could not answer, and she looked away. "I need time to consider your words," she said, pulling back from him and rising rather ungracefully to her feet. "Do not say anything more until I have had time. If you press me, I shall turn from you. Do you understand?"

He bowed his head in acknowledgment, and she turned and ran from the glade. Rogond knew that he had upset her, for her footfalls were easily heard. He drew a long, shuddering breath, fear and doubt gnawing in the pit of his stomach, and returned to the firelight. He could not rest and began pacing the clearing, muttering occasionally to himself as Galador watched from his place by the fire.

"Rogond, your incessant pacing is unsettling to me. Please, come and sit in one place for a while and try to calm yourself. You will arouse the attention of our enemies with all this motion and noise."

Rogond looked over at his friend, whose steady gaze drew him back down. He moved to sit beside Galador in silence, as the Elf slowly stirred the glowing embers.

"Well, you've gone and done it now, haven't you, my friend?"

"Yes, Galador, I have done it. Though exactly what I have done, I'm not certain. I only hope that Gaelen will consider well my words and not send me from her. I don't know whether I will ever be happy again if that happens." He sighed, quelling the tears that threatened to fill his earnest grey eyes.

"I warned you, Rogond, and so did Ordath. Now you have come too far to turn back. I hope your heart survives unbroken, for I love you as a brother…a wayward brother who doesn't heed wise advice when it is given."

"Perhaps not, Galador, but I am a wayward brother who is true to his own heart despite wise advice. I simply do not know any other way. I am sorry that I cannot learn from the experiences of my elder brother, but I rejoice that he loves me nonetheless." He sighed, resigned to stirring the fire. Galador smiled for a moment, but the red firelight flickering in the cool grey depths of his eyes revealed the doubt that lay within.

Nelwyn and Fima had remained near their camp for a while longer, in case Gorgon should appear, but Nelwyn doubted that he would show himself as he had obviously not felt comfortable entering the Wood-elves' domain in the first place. The two hapless Ulcas lay dead. Nelwyn had shivered as Fima related every word of their conversation to her. So, they had been sent to capture her and take her to Gorgon. And the Ulcas had mentioned "big plans" in which Gorgon was heavily involved. What sort of evil mischief was brewing? It would be best to return to the Woodland stronghold as soon as possible.

They had just about finished their preparations when Nelwyn heard sounds in the undergrowth, followed by a familiar call that she recognized at once. It was Gaelen, asking whether the area was secure so that they might approach. Nelwyn replied with a distinctive call of her own.

She and Gaelen had developed a complex series of whistles and soft hoots that formed a sort of code. They and the other hunter-scouts often used such codes in the performance of their duties. Many an unwary traveler wondered at the strange sounds, which, though unfamiliar, seemed to fit perfectly into the ambiance of the forest. Enemies would find them the last sounds in hearing, just before the whistling of arrow-shafts ended their misbegotten lives.

The Wood-elves had no mercy upon the servants of evil, and showed little tolerance for trespass into their domain.

In a few moments Gryffa heralded the approach of Rogond, Galador, and Gaelen. They were relieved to see Nelwyn and Fima apparently alive and healthy; nothing seemed amiss in the area until Gaelen suddenly went rigid, scenting the air.

"Ulcas!" she hissed, turning toward the west, her bow fitted in a blur of motion.

Nelwyn grabbed her arm. "They're dead, Gaelen, and there were but two of them. There have been no others; I just returned from the watch."

Gaelen scented the air again. "Dead, eh? So they are. It is sometimes difficult to tell with Ulcas, as they often smell worse alive."

Nelwyn and Fima continued to occupy themselves with making ready to leave, and neither of them would make eye contact with either Rogond or Galador. "I learned something about you recently, Lore-master," said Rogond, who was following Fima around, trying to get him to look at him. "I was not aware that herb-lore interested you in the slightest. This must be a recent fascination. After all, what else could explain the sudden desire to travel swiftly for three days on horseback to this distant corner of the Elven-realm? You wouldn't care to enlighten us, would you?"

Fima continued his pretense of packing up his already well-secured belongings. "Not at this time, thank you," he replied. "Perhaps I will have some things to tell you when we return to the Elven-halls. Until then, my friend, I would suggest you not press either of us.'" He shot a knowing look at Rogond, who knew then that Fima had every intention of sharing his insights, but this was not the time.

Nelwyn was having far worse luck with Galador, who was angry with her for worrying him. Rogond could hear their voices from the undergrowth, engaged in a lively argument. Nelwyn, like Fima, was reluctant to explain herself, and pleaded with Galador to wait until a better time. He was indignant; Rogond heard the prideful tone of his voice as he lectured Nelwyn concerning the folly of going so far from the safe areas of the realm without him. Rogond winced at this. Nelwyn had lived for hundreds of years as a hunter-scout and had dealt quite well with the hazards of traveling in the Greatwood without Galador, and her annoyance was apparent as she so informed him. Then she accused him of suffocating her, which hurt his feelings. Rogond would not suffer himself to hear more, and went in search of Gaelen, who had disappeared into the forest, apparently in search of the Ulcas.

When he finally discovered her she was indeed tending to the dead Ulcas. She had dragged them into a clearing with some difficulty, as they were large and heavy, but she had grown stronger of late with her preparations for battle. For some reason Rogond felt reluctant to approach her, and as he watched he beheld a sight to chill his blood.

She had taken some stout vines and bound the wrists of the dead Ulcas. Then, straining with all her might, she hoisted them from sturdy branches to dangle grotesquely before her. Rogond was strongly reminded of Gelmyr. She had tied small pieces of parchment onto the arrow-shafts that protruded from their dead flesh; written upon each was the word "Trespassers!"

Rogond remembered Noli with the parchment clutched in his dead hand, and he suddenly felt ill as he beheld the satisfied expression on Gaelen's face. He could imagine the same expression upon Gorgon as he hung Belegund, Noli and Tibo in Cós-domhain. Gaelen's sharp ears detected Rogond's presence and she turned to him, looking somewhat quizzical at the look of trepidation on his face.

"What is it, Aridan? Is something wrong?"

He was not quite sure what to say to her. "Ahh...I suppose not... it's just that I had never seen you arrange such a display before. What is the meaning of it?"

She looked back at the Ulcas with satisfaction, then turned to him as though he were an untutored child. "They will be left to warn any of their fellows that an ill fate awaits trespassers in the Realm of Ri-Aruin," she stated, as though it should be obvious and there was nothing sinister about it. "It's our custom sometimes, especially in this remote area. Better to warn them now than to deal with them later."

This explanation seemed to satisfy Rogond, but Gaelen had not cared for his expression when she had first turned to him. He had plainly been horrified, and she did not understand. What was so horrifying about two dead Ulcas?

Rogond returned to the glade to find Nelwyn, who was obviously unhappy as she prepared to ride. He drew her aside for a moment, and then led her to the place where the Ulcas were hung. Gaelen was by now looking to Siva, making ready to leave with her companions. Nelwyn stopped in her tracks when she saw the Ulcas, and Rogond could tell from the look on her face that if this was indeed a custom followed by the Elves of the Greatwood, it was a very, very uncommon custom. She turned to Rogond with an expression of consternation.

"Gaelen did this?" she asked in a small voice. Rogond had not often seen such a look of disquiet upon Nelwyn. She shuddered, then turned and made her way back to where Gryffa was saddled and waiting for her.

The Company rode through the long afternoon, until they decided to stop and refresh themselves. Nelwyn and Galador were not speaking, and would barely even acknowledge each other. Gaelen sat by the small fire they had built; it was obvious to Nelwyn that she was not really speaking to Rogond, either, though Nelwyn did not know why.

Nelwyn was overcome with melancholy and wandered away from her friends to stand alone in the forest, silent tears glistening in her eyes. She did not hear Galador come up behind her, and was startled as he placed a hand upon her shoulder. She was in desperate need of comforting, and when she turned and beheld him, she fell into his embrace, muttering apologies over and over. Galador responded in kind, for he had come to try to heal the rift between them. He knew that Nelwyn was deeply troubled.

"What has so upset you, my beloved? Why did you lie to Gaelen and hide the truth from me? What brought you here if not the order of the herb-master? Please tell me, that I might understand."

Nelwyn drew back and faced him. She could not keep this inside any longer; she needed to confide in Galador. Perhaps he would be able to suggest a wise course of action, for he was true of heart and he cared for Gaelen. Perhaps Galador would know what to do.

"I have a tale to tell you, but you must promise not to reveal it to anyone, not even Rogond. Fima has agreed to tell him when the time is right. Do you understand?"

Galador nodded, but he was afraid. This tale of Nelwyn's would tell of naught but sorrow and pain; he could see it in her eyes. Then Nelwyn told Galador all that she had learned. When she finished, Galador was white-faced and shaken. He had expected a tale of woe, but his expectations fell far short of reality.

"Will you think on this, my love, and help to guide me? I cannot imagine what my course should be—how can I ever tell Gaelen? She will not be able to handle this dreadful news. And yet, she will have to be told. We all risk our lives and the lives of others whenever we are near her. What, then, must we do?" She implored Galador, desperation in her eyes. Galador had no answer for her.

"I...I will think on it, Nelwyn," he muttered, then turned from her and went off alone to collect his thoughts and absorb the impact of what he had learned.

Back in the encampment, Rogond and Fima sat on either side of Gaelen, partaking of bread and water. Fima kept looking over at Gaelen, who stared straight ahead into the fire, and neither moved nor spoke. Tomorrow they would reach the King's halls once again, but this did not cheer her. She did not understand why Nelwyn had lied to her about her errand, or why no one was speaking to anyone else, or why Rogond and Fima kept looking at her as though she were dying of some pestilence that would no doubt be transmitted to anyone who drew near. She sighed and rose from the fireside, crossing to where Siva was tethered. She stroked the mare's neck, running her fingers through her silken mane, and found some comfort.

They headed back north along the Forest River, a deep and fairly swift watercourse that flowed from north to south and passed directly beside the Elven-hold. They were not more than a few hours' journey away when they decided to stop for the night, as Nelwyn was more weary than Galador had seen her since their time in Mountain-home. In truth, she was heartsick. She was no closer to a solution to the terrible dilemma of what to do about Gaelen, and the strain was graven into her face, especially her eyes.

Galador wanted desperately to help her, but did not know what could be done. He had been frightened to his very marrow when Nelwyn told him why she had come to the borderlands of the realm with only Fima for protection. Gorgon had known through Gaelen, and he had sent his Ulcas to capture Nelwyn and bring her before him. What if they had succeeded? Galador shuddered, feeling shaky and ill at the very thought. For a moment he pictured Nelwyn hanging from a tree in the manner of Gelmyr, and his vision swam until he closed his eyes and banished the vision, attempting to clear his thoughts. They were all in dreadful danger. What if they let something slip in front of Gaelen such that Gorgon was privy to information that would lead him to accomplish some undoubtedly horrific end? What if the next time Nelwyn was not prepared and Gorgon took her? What if...?

Galador found himself wandering in the deepening darkness. He needed to be careful, as the forest was so dark and forbidding at night that it would be easy to lose one's bearings. Though the forest was actually quite beautiful within the Elf-realm, Galador knew that it could still bewilder him in the dark. This was not his home, and he knew that he would never be truly at ease here without Nelwyn beside him.

It was with such unsettling thoughts in his mind that he came upon Gaelen sitting alone, a single shaft of moonlight filtering down through the canopy to illuminate her pale, upturned face. Galador could see that she was struggling with thoughts of her own. Then she began to shiver despite the warmth of the evening, and Galador knew that, if Nelwyn was right, Gorgon was now privy to whatever she saw or heard. Galador was overcome with revulsion for a moment. The risk of Gaelen revealing information to Gorgon that would bring sorrow and death upon Nelwyn was more than he could allow. He had to protect Nelwyn, whatever the cost. He knew in his heart that if Gaelen learned of this terrible invasion of her senses she would most likely go mad. Mad enough, he supposed, to accomplish her own death. He gazed at her for a moment, imagining her reaction to this dreadful news. His heart welled over with pity then, and his trembling hands strayed to his bow.

The visions of Nelwyn hanging like Gelmyr, cut to ribbons and dying horribly, would not leave his mind. Before he was even aware of it he had fitted an arrow to the string, and, crouching silently in the dark, he drew on Gaelen, aiming the point of the arrow at her slender throat. All he had to do was release, and the nightmare would end. She would be gone, and Gorgon would have no power over her. He would not be able to harm Nelwyn, would not be able to visit sorrow and death upon the Elves using information gleaned unwittingly from Gaelen. She would go to Ri-Elathan, her beloved, with what remained of her sanity intact. She would never know the terrible truth of her complicity with the enemy. Yes, he thought, his right hand trembling as it held Gaelen's life on the tips of three fingers, this would be kinder. He could take her from all reach of pain and keep Nelwyn safe. All he had to do was release.

The words of Lady Arialde came to him then, as clearly as on the day she had sent them. *The slaying of Elf by Elf is not to be permitted, even in an effort to protect those we love. Do not give in to such desires, Galador. All must play their part.* His hands shook harder than ever as he struggled, his thoughts at an impasse. Arialde was right. He could not take Gaelen's life, even to save Nelwyn or preserve her own sanity. It was not his place to do so. He turned the bow skyward, releasing the arrow straight into the treetops, uttering a small cry of frustration as he did so, which caused Gaelen to turn and wonder what had come over him.

The next morning, as the Company assembled at first light and prepared to make the relatively short journey back to the Elven-hold, Galador drew Fima aside. "Nelwyn has told me of your discovery, Fima. I know the truth about Gorgon's mirror. You have been charged with telling Rogond, have you not?"

"Yes, but I thought I might wait until we are safely back in civilized company, as I really do not know how he will react. Gaelen will have to be told as well, and the sooner the better. I am uncertain as to which of us will draw that painful duty." Fima shook his head.

"You are aware that Rogond has declared his love for Gaelen and pledged himself to her?" asked Galador.

Fima's eyes grew wide for an instant. "I was wondering whether some such thing might have occurred. She seems very distant from him…how did she take it?"

"She is considering her choices, but from what I gather, her response was not at all what Rogond would have wished for. She has asked him not to press her, and so he has not. His timing was less than ideal, given the circumstances. I fear they shall both have their hearts broken. But Fima, there is something that troubles me. We must not wait until we enter the Elf-realm, as we dare not risk Gorgon's discovering any information that might aid him in doing harm to Ri-Aruin's folk. You must tell Rogond at once. I would prefer to tell Gaelen as well, but I know this will be very delicate and we must wait until the time and circumstances are right. At least Rogond may be able to keep her from being privy to the King's secret councils, or showing Gorgon the layout of the underground fortress. My advice would be to get her out into the forest as quickly as possible."

"We shall need Nelwyn for that," said Fima.

Galador was adamant. "No! I don't want Nelwyn anywhere alone with Gaelen, especially in the forest. Gorgon has already revealed his desire to take her! I will not allow it."

Fima raised both eyebrows at this. "I was not aware that you controlled her movements, Galador. Be careful, my friend. She has an independent mind. That is one of the things you love about her—do not attempt to govern her." He sighed, shaking his head. "But I take your point. It will be better if Rogond knows. I shall seek him now."

Fima found Rogond extinguishing the remnants of their small fire. The moment the Ranger looked into the eyes of his friend the dwarf, his heart grew cold. Surely, there was bad news coming. "What is it, Fima?" he asked, his voice anxious.

"Come with me, Rogond. I have some ill news that I must bring you, but you must hear it. Come with me. We cannot risk being overheard." Rogond rose from beside the fire as Nelwyn came into the clearing leading Gryffa.

"Where is Gaelen?" asked Fima, as he thought Nelwyn would know.

"She is watering Siva and Eros. She will bring them here when they are finished," Nelwyn replied, a note of trepidation in her voice.

"When she does, keep her here, will you?" said Fima, gesturing to Rogond to follow him.

Nelwyn knew then what Fima was about to do, and she grieved for her friend Rogond, who would surely be devastated. She nodded to Fima, knowing the importance of her task. She must occupy

Gaelen long enough for Fima to deliver his message, and for Rogond to react to it.

Fima bade Rogond sit upon a moss-covered log, as he stood before him, eye to eye. Then, he drew a deep breath and began his tale of the mirror. Rogond, who thanks to Amandir's warning was not entirely unprepared, listened with grave intensity, his face fixed in a calm expression that belied the horror in his eyes.

"So, that's how Gorgon came to take Belegund, and Tibo and Noli, and the Elves of Tal-sithian," he said.

"Yes, and that's why he did not kill Gaelen in Cós-domhain," said Fima, "though he came perilously close!"

"This will be a heavy burden for her to bear," said Rogond. "And I have not made things any easier by forcing her to consider her feelings for me at this point. Alas that I did not know better!"

"There is much that you still do not know, Rogond. Nelwyn held a vision in the Stone of Léir. It showed Gorgon using Gaelen's eyes to bring down the Realm of the Greatwood. You were dead, as was Thorndil, and Wellyn, and even Galador was near death. The Woodland was overcome by Darkness, and Gorgon was leading a mighty host. This is a grim vision indeed."

At that moment, they heard a sound behind them in the undergrowth. It was a sort of frightened, strangled moan, an expression of pain so deep that it sounded as though it had welled up from the very soul and could not be suppressed. At the same time, back at the encampment, Nelwyn was horror-stricken to see Galador leading Réalta, Eros, and Siva into the clearing before her, for she realized that Gaelen was somewhere else.

Rogond rose abruptly and turned about with Fima, hearing a rustling and thrashing in the undergrowth, followed by another small cry that might have been a sort of repressed wail. It tore at their hearts as they guessed its origins. Against all design, Gaelen had approached them silently, as was her habit, and had heard all that was said. She had left the horses in the care of Galador, who knew of no reason to refuse her, and had gone in search of Rogond, as she had been fighting back a feeling of dread concerning him and wanted to make sure of his safety. She heard voices, and they sounded distressed, so she approached in her usual stealthy manner, stopping as she heard her name.

She had thought to turn about, but she was drawn to the conversation and had heard all Fima had to tell, standing as still and silent as stone with icy water in her veins. There was a roaring in her ears, her heart was hammering, and she could hardly dare to breathe as Fima described Nelwyn's vision in the Stone. Gaelen possessed a ready mind, and she quickly assembled the pieces of the puzzle, to her abject and utter consternation.

A small cry had escaped her, and as Rogond and Fima turned toward her, she staggered back through the undergrowth, blundering away from them, trying not to cry out. She heard Rogond call her name in a panicked voice that tore the heart. She turned and ran then, as she could not face him, could never face any of them ever again.

When she encountered Nelwyn and Galador, they both guessed what had befallen. Nelwyn reached out toward her, but in her anguish Gaelen could only cry out and back away, both hands flung up before her. They heard Rogond call her name again, and a moment later he appeared with Fima at his side. Gaelen looked around like a trapped animal as her four friends tried in vain to calm her. She could not grasp the reality of what had been revealed—it was simply too horrific.

Her eyes went cold and hard, and she stopped trembling, backing away from them. Sweat-soaked, she took in great gasps of air, and the color returned to her face. She was gathering and collecting herself for some course of action, and they stopped their approach, hardly daring to breathe lest they drive her to something reckless. Nelwyn called out, trying to calm her.

"Gaelen…don't be afraid. It will be all right. You couldn't help this fate, and it wasn't your fault. Please come to your friends, so that we may aid you. We all love you. Please come to us."

Gaelen looked at Nelwyn then, silent tears flowing from her eyes. "How long have you known of this? Was this whole errand a test? Did you risk being captured by Gorgon so that you could be sure? Is that right?"

Nelwyn nodded. Gaelen moaned again and closed her eyes, her hands clutching at the pouch that hung around her neck. "I have brought death to so many, and if your vision is true, the Greatwood will fall because of me." She drew her long knives from their sheaths. "Stay away from me," she cried in a soft, menacing voice, brandishing the blades. "To be seen or heard by me is to walk into a nest of vipers. You dare not risk it! Do not hinder me now, for I know what I must do." Though her voice was resolute, her eyes were terrified.

Rogond and Nelwyn both knew that she planned to do harm to herself, and they tried to take her from both sides, but she lashed out at them with the daggers, crying in a terrible voice, *"Do not hinder me!"* Her skill with those razor-sharp blades forced them back, for she might have slashed them both rather than let them take her. They stood for a moment, frozen at the sight of Gaelen, the Warrior-elf, knowing that her sanity hung by the barest of threads. Her eyes softened as she looked upon Rogond, and her face twisted into a grimace of pain.

"How can you love me?" she asked him in a small, pitiful voice. "How could you ever have loved me?" To his horror, she drew her blades along both forearms, bringing blood onto the grass at her feet. She did not appear to feel the pain. With a last look at Nelwyn, she moaned once more, then turned from them and ran through the dappled forest light. Nelwyn and Rogond both called after her, to no avail.

"We must go after her, Rogond! She means to harm herself. She may put out her own eyes, or…or even kill herself. She is not rational! We must pursue her, for she is swift and knows the forest." Nelwyn turned to Galador. "Can you take the horses and Fima back to the Elven-hold?"

"Nelwyn…please don't go into the deep wood without me. I fear you will not return! Please don't go without me."

Nelwyn shook her head. "Fima cannot manage the horses. You must do this--for me. I will be all right."

"Leave the horses! I would see to your safety," said Galador, panic in his face. "And I would aid you in your pursuit of Gaelen, for I love her even as you do."

"If you love her, then do as I ask, and do not delay us further. Fima cannot strive with us, and we cannot leave him here alone. Please, my love, do as I bid! We will return as soon as we may."

She embraced him then, and turned to Rogond. "Follow me, Aridan. She is swift, but I am taller and swifter. Let us be away!"

They sprang forward through the trees, following Gaelen's trail. At first it was easy to follow, for though she ran lightly, the blood from her slashed forearms was clearly visible. Nelwyn cursed as she made her way amid the thick, tangled undergrowth that Gaelen had intentionally run through to block their way. Here, size was a disadvantage, and Gaelen drew farther and farther ahead of them, to their dismay. "She knows what she is doing," said Nelwyn ruefully. "We must be swift, for she is gaining ground."

The signs grew fainter as they went northward, but eventually they led back to the river. As they looked up and down for signs of Gaelen, a sudden insight, followed by a look of horror, came upon Nelwyn.

"She is headed for the Narrows, I just know it! Oh, Rogond… if she reaches them we won't be able to save her. She means to cast herself in. We must fly!"

She turned north and sped along the river's edge, as the land rose into two great bluffs on either side. They could hear the rushing waters of the Narrows, a deep, swift section of the river quite unlike the gentle, serene waters that flowed past the Elven-hold. As Nelwyn had feared, they spotted a lone figure standing erect on top of the bluff overlooking the water. Gaelen looked small and forlorn, but her shoulders were thrown back, her hair was lifted in the wind, and her head was not bowed.

They raced toward her, calling and begging her to turn about. She looked over her shoulder and beheld them, then raised her hand in farewell. Her friends had come too late. She bent over, picked up a large stone and clutched it to her chest with both arms. Rogond called frantically to try to stop her, but she seemed not to hear. She was afraid, that was plain in the way she shrank back just a little from the edge. Rogond saw her take several deep breaths, as though gathering herself. Then, to his horror, she simply stepped off the edge, plummeting toward the churning water, as Nelwyn screamed her name.

Gaelen gasped as the cold waters took her breath away, filling her mouth and throat. Her eyes were tightly shut, for she knew there would be nothing to see as she sank into the churning depths, aided by the stone. She released it and was swept along in the current of the Narrows, her body occasionally fetching painfully against the boulders that were strewn along the riverbed, but this brought only a dull ache to her numbed limbs. She had been holding her breath, certainly a natural response, but then she remembered her purpose and forced all the remaining air from her lungs in a silver torrent that rose rapidly to the surface, lost in the foam. Her eyes opened then—the roaring in her ears and the pounding of her heart were lost in a black tunnel that closed in around her, and she saw and heard nothing more.

26

Out of the Darkness

Gaelen could see nothing but blackness, and could hear nothing but the roaring in her ears. Then she heard voices calling, voices that were familiar. She was reliving significant moments in her past that had elicited particularly strong emotions, and she was riveted.

Well, done, Gaelen! You will surpass your uncle Turanen one day if your eye and hand continue to improve.

You have a new cousin! Her name is Nelwyn. Come and see!

Aran is dead. He is dead, Gaelen, and you must let him go. Let him go, my daughter. You could not have prevented it.

She is but a Sylvan hunter-scout, my son. She is not a fitting consort for you, this undersized, boyish rustic with no respect for convention. And she is certainly no beauty. Whatever do you see in her?

I am certain that you go whither you will even when forbidden, O Free Spirit. I would have your company; will you ride with me?

Even were you the mightiest Elf-maiden ever to draw breath and capable of great skill at arms, I would not have you stay. The thought of losing you would be too great for me to bear. Do you understand?

I will wait for you—one day we will be together again. But in the meantime, you must live your life! And you must not live it alone, in grief for me.

You will not cross the mountains with us, but instead will remain with the Tuathan and the dwarf? And what is your lofty motive for this course?

Gaelen, my friend, my love, thank you for being here.

You carry an evil before you. Keep your distance!

Did you not hear? I will have no other. You are my love, Gaelen, to whom my heart is given.

That is why he did not kill Gaelen in Cós-domhain, though he came perilously close.

We all love you. Please come to us.

Then she heard Ri-Elathan's cries of anguish as Wrothgar took his life. She heard his voice in her mind, as she had in the Greatwood:

Gaelen… Gaelen! My heart is torn from me…I cannot stay with you, my love! I am sorry…I cannot stay with you…Oh, my love…

Her eyes flew open, but there was only darkness around her. She was lying upon a soft, dry bed of sand near a body of calm water, over which a thick mist was hanging. The voices…they must have been coming from the mist. For a moment she forgot all about Gorgon, the mirror, and the Narrows, as she sat up to survey the strange, lonely landscape before her. There were weird lights in the mist. She had seen such lights hovering around bogs and marshes, but these did not seem as sinister, somehow. The water lapped gently at the sand, and there was very little other sound in her hearing, save for the voices, which were now so distant and indistinct that she could no longer decipher them.

One of the lights in the mist was growing larger, and it seemed to be coming toward her. She rose to her feet and approached the shore, straining into the blackness, to try to make out the nature of the light. It was a figure, tall and strong, with a red-orange light like a halo around it. Gaelen looked down at her own hands; they glowed and flickered with the same sort of fiery light. Her blood ran cold as she realized that she was now standing upon the shores where the shades of both the Elàni and the Aridani await transport to their respective fates. So, she was dead, then? Her memories of the Narrows and the events leading to it came back to her in a rush, and she was afraid. Then, she heard a voice calling gently; it was the fiery figure that drew ever nearer as it seemed to float across the surface of the waters.

Gaelen Taldin…my love, do not fear. I have been sent to give aid and counsel. Do not fear. It was the voice of Farahin, her beloved, and her heart leapt as she beheld his strong, grim face for the first time in well over a thousand years. She wanted to run to him, to fall into his arms and let him take her pain away. She reached out with both hands, trembling, her fiery aura burning bright around her, but he stopped just out of her reach. As she looked into his melancholy eyes, she knew there would be no opportunity to embrace him.

Rain…Rain, why won't you hold me?

I cannot. I have been sent here for a single purpose, and I must not turn from it, though my heart would desire otherwise.

What purpose? I am dead, or I would not be here. No one has come to stay me. Are you not here to guide me to the Far Shores? I'm afraid... please guide me. Take me with you!

Ri-Elathan smiled sadly at her and shook his head, the gentle glow flaming out around him. *That is not my purpose. I want nothing more than to take you with me, but I cannot. You must return to your life. It is not your time, and you have a purpose to accomplish before your end comes.*

What purpose? I am dead, Rain, and I cannot return. I am dead because I willed it to be so. I have made it my time.

So you say, but it is not the will of destiny that you go with me now. I have been sent here only to waylay you, to make certain that you return at once. Though I long to be united with you again, I know that it is not to be. Not yet. This is not your choice to make. You must return, and accomplish your purpose. You are the instrument by which the evil that stalks the Elàni will end.

Gaelen let out a moan of misery, remembering the events that had driven her to take her own life. *I am the instrument by which that vile creature works his evil! If I am gone, then he can no longer prey on our people using the mirror. The Greatwood will fall because of me. I cannot go back!*

She reached out to him again, and he extended a tentative hand toward her. They were so close now, she could almost touch him. Then he drew back and closed his eyes. When he opened them again, the fire flared around him.

You cannot turn away from your fate, Gaelen, even as I could not. The Tuathan knows how the creature may be defeated. You will work together to vanquish him and his army. Rogond is true of heart and steadfast in his love for you. Open your heart again, my love. I sorrow for you in your loneliness. He will fill your days and gladden them as I cannot. I shall await you, but only when the time is right will I rejoice in our union. That time is not now. Remember my words at our parting? Grieve for me no more.

His head lifted as though hearing a distant call. *There is not much time. You must return now, my beloved. Your task remains, and soon it will be too late. Go back now, and remember that I love you.*

No! Do not turn from me! Hold me, please, just hold me for a little while. I will go back, if you will only hold me now. She reached for him in desperation, but he drew farther from her.

No, Gaelen, I cannot. If I embrace you, there will be no returning. Go back now, little Taldin. Go and accomplish your task and rid our people of this scourge. You are strong in spirit, and resolute. You will prevail. I will welcome you into my arms when the time is right. He began to fade from her vision then. Gaelen could hear the voices calling him back.

Who calls to you, Beloved? Tell them that you would stay with me yet awhile. I have so many things I would know…do you hear me when I sing to you? Can you feel my heart as it cries for you in the darkness? Do you know what comes to pass in the world of the living? Are you lonely in the Vault of Eternity?

I can answer none of your questions directly, as it is not permitted. Continue to sing to me if it brings you aid, but do not grieve. Remember the Aridan. He knows how the creature may be vanquished. Go back to him, and let your heart be glad!

He faded slowly from her sight, even as her plaintive cries echoed after him, begging him to stay. Gaelen knew that he was right, she had to go back now, and time had run out. But somehow she simply could not lose him again, and without considering the consequences, she plunged into the cold, dark water, following the fading sound of his voice.

Immediately the surface became turbulent, and the once-calm waters threatened to engulf her. She blundered away from the shoreline, still calling after him, as his voice faded completely from her hearing. The water was very deep and very cold, and there was a sense that it resented this invasion, for it felt somehow hostile, as though it would either expel her or drag her under. She called Ri-Elathan's name with failing strength, floundering in the water, choking and gasping. She knew then that she could not follow him; she had to go back. She struggled to the shore once again, the waters casting her up into the shallows, where she lay senseless and unmoving in a dark, silent world.

Rogond and Nelwyn had watched in horror as Gaelen plunged into the Narrows. They ran to the top of the bluffs to see if, against all hope, they might find where she had gone and attempt a rescue. But there was nothing to be seen save the wild water, and they despaired. Still neither would give her up as yet, and they made their way down the perilous climb to the water's edge.

"We must be swift; the current will take her far downstream in a matter of minutes. She has not long to live!" Nelwyn wept at Rogond's words, for she knew he was right. But for some miracle, Gaelen was surely lost to them.

Galador and Fima had gone with all speed toward the Elvenhold, arriving just as Nelwyn and Rogond caught sight of Gaelen at the Narrows. They were met by Wellyn, son of Ri-Aruin, for he had been stricken by a feeling of foreboding bordering on panic, and he would know all they could tell him. A few minutes later Wellyn, who knew Gaelen well, had swung aboard Gryffa, and the three of them were heading southward along the river, toward the Narrows.

Many minutes had gone by, and Rogond's hope was failing. He would never retrieve Gaelen from this swift water, so cold and deep. They could see nothing beneath the surface, or along the shore. Still they kept their southward course, and soon the Narrows ended, broadening into a gentler flow. Nelwyn gave a cry, for she had seen something on the far bank that just might have been Gaelen's faded green tunic. Then she beheld a brief, tiny glint of metal as the sunlight hit Ri-Elathan's silver brooch, the gift of Arialde. Nelwyn gripped Rogond's arm and pointed. With a cry, they both plunged into the icy waters. The crossing was difficult, and they had to make their way back north to where Gaelen lay, for the current had drawn them downstream. They approached her as quickly as they could, but as they drew nigh her they both suspected that they had come too late.

Gaelen's face was expressionless, her sightless eyes were open, and her lips were blue. She was dead; Nelwyn knew it as she took Gaelen's cold, lifeless hand. There was no spirit there, no spark of life. Nelwyn sat still as stone as Rogond knelt beside her, calling Gaelen's name as though she had merely fallen asleep and he would awaken her. Nelwyn began to weep, wrapping both arms around her shoulders, rocking back and forth on her knees. Rogond lifted Gaelen and held her, after searching for signs of life and finding none. There was an expression of determination on his face as he carried her from the rocky waters and laid her upon the sand. He began to compress her chest with his hands, trying to expel the water from her lungs. Murky river water gurgled ominously from her mouth and nostrils, and his hopes sank, but he kept trying. He worked on her for several minutes, now breathing for her, now trying to start her heart beating, but she was cold and still, and his hopes were in vain.

Nelwyn wrapped her arms around him, trying to stay him from his fruitless effort to bring her back, speaking soft, gentle words. "Rogond… Rogond, she is gone. She is with Farahin, and we cannot reach her. Leave her in peace. Rogond, my friend, it's all right. She is beyond grief and pain. Let her be at peace."

Rogond seemed not to hear, and he kept trying. Nelwyn persisted, and all at once he stopped his efforts, lifted Gaelen, and held her to him, weeping quietly. Nelwyn spoke words of comfort, but his heart was broken and he did not hear.

Gaelen could feel the cold sand under her body, but could neither move nor speak. Her eyes were open, but they saw only blackness, and she heard only the waters of the Dark Lake. Then she heard Rogond's voice. He was weeping, calling her name, saying he was sorry that he had come too late, that he had failed her. She could not respond, and her senses would give her nothing more. She then remembered her purpose, and that she had to return from this dark realm, as she was not yet welcome in it. She mustered all the strength of her spirit and tried to will herself back into Rogond's world. Slowly and with great effort, she began to perceive the sights and sounds around her. First, she felt Rogond holding her and heard his voice. She longed for him in her heart and struggled back to him as he held her and wept. She could not breathe. She needed to breathe!

She gave a convulsive heave, constricting her chest in an all-out effort, and was rewarded with a torrent of murky water issuing from her mouth and nose, soaking Rogond's tunic. She took in a great gasp of air, and then heaved again, clearing more water as Rogond and Nelwyn both cried out in astonishment. She had spent her strength then, but Rogond grasped her with gentle hands to aid her in expelling enough of the remaining water that she could more easily draw air into her lungs. She was freezing cold and began shuddering violently, her teeth chattering between bouts of coughing and gasping. She grasped Rogond's arm with failing strength. He held her and wept, but this time his tears were of relief, not sorrow.

"We must warm her at once, or we may yet lose her," said Nelwyn. They looked around for any way to accomplish this, but there was nothing promising as they were all soaking wet from the crossing. If only they had a dry cloak! Gaelen had stopped shivering but was as cold as death, and her eyes were losing their focus. This did not bode well. Then, Rogond heard a familiar sound carried on the breeze from the north. He rose to his feet, still holding Gaelen, and gave a loud whistle.

"Eros! Come to me, my friend! I need you!"

It was not five minutes later that the ever-faithful Eros appeared, still bearing Rogond's saddle-pack. Behind him rode Galador and Fima on Réalta, and Wellyn, mounted on Gryffa. Gaelen was saved by the devotion of her friends, for they provided dry, warm cloaks to wrap her in as Rogond held her, rocking her gently and speaking to her in a soft voice.

"Gaelen, my beloved, it will be all right. Your friends are here, and no one holds you to blame. We will get through this terrible time, my beautiful, stalwart Gaelen. I have a plan that will trap the creature Gorgon, who has wrought so much misery. I cannot carry it out without your help, my friend, my love. Take strength from those who love you."

Nelwyn, Galador, Fima, and Wellyn each spoke to Gaelen then. Wellyn took her hand and kissed it. Rogond looked into his ageless face and saw the shock and anxiety in his clear, blue eyes. Fima had told him everything, and it was a lot for him to take in all at once.

Rogond handed the bundle of cloaks that was Gaelen over to him, saying, "Take her, Wellyn, for you are dry and warm, and can aid her better than I." The Elf looked somewhat surprised, then appreciative, as he held Gaelen to him, his eyes closed. Perhaps the Aridan was trustworthy after all.

They waited until Gaelen was warm and enough of her strength had returned such that the journey back to the Elven-hold would not tax her too much. Then they placed her in Rogond's arms, and Eros bore them both to the safety and comfort of the underground fortress. Gaelen was laid in a warm chamber upon a soft bed and given warming liquids to strengthen her. She remained unmoving and inert until the following day. When she roused herself, the first sight before her was the relieved face of Rogond. His eyes were red-rimmed, and it was obvious that he had not slept. She had not yet spoken, and as he sat by her side holding her hand, she turned to him.

Her hand strayed to her throat, her fingers searching for her familiar talisman, and Rogond suddenly realized that the leather pouch containing the banner of Ri-Elathan was not there. Had someone removed it? No, now that he thought about it, it had not been around her neck when he had ministered to her on the riverbank. He guessed that it must have broken free during her tumultuous trip along the river-bottom. Evidently, Gaelen had arrived at the same conclusion—he could see it in her eyes. She looked lost and incomplete without it; the loss of this token grieved her more than he could ever know. She sensed him looking at her and withdrew her hand, attempting in vain to hide the depth of her sorrow. After a moment, she spoke to him.

"Did you mean what you said about a plan to bring down Gorgon?" she whispered, her voice shaky and weak.

"Yes, Beloved. I do mean it. But now we must devise a way that we may converse without risking the chance of his knowing our minds. Let me take your arm. I think I know a way."

She extended her arm, and he drew his fingertip carefully across the flesh of her inside forearm in a series of graceful curves and lines. She shook her head, frowning, then understanding dawned, and her eyes grew wide. Of course! He was drawing characters upon her arm—runes that were used for the writing of lore. She smiled, and it was a sight that lifted Rogond's spirits beyond measure.

"Do you perceive, my love?"

Gaelen nodded. "I do," she replied.

Then Rogond began to trace a message so that he might be sure that she understood him.

I L-O-V-E Y-O-U L-I-T-T-L-E O-N-E.

"To whom do you refer as *little*, Aridan?" she whispered, just before her eyes closed with weariness, and she slept.

Rogond finally fell into sleep himself, but was awakened after only a few hours to the sound of anguished cries. He jerked upright and rose to his feet as he beheld Gaelen, who had fallen to the floor and was now screaming in terror. Her eyes were wide open, but she did not see him or anything else around her, and he concluded that she had gone into the realm of waking dreams and was now in the grip of a very unpleasant nightmare. He tried to restrain her as she fought him with surprising strength, still screaming.

"*Leave me, Dark Horror! Leave me and come no more!*"

She drove her clenched fists into her eyes, as though trying to drive Gorgon from her. Rogond gripped her arms and lifted her, placing her back on the soft bed, though she continued to struggle. Her face was twisted with pain as well, as she was badly bruised from her trip through the Narrows. Though Rogond tried not to hurt her, it was difficult.

He spoke urgently: "Gaelen, Gaelen! Don't be afraid. It's all right!" She sagged sideways, her eyes glazed, unblinking. Then she closed them, and when she began to weep, he knew that she had awakened. He covered her with blankets, stroking her hair and soothing her with his voice. It took time to master herself, and he knew that she would fight this battle time and again, probably for a long while. Rage welled within his gentle heart, and he resolved to arrange a council with the King as soon as he could find someone to relieve him from the watch; he did not want to ever leave Gaelen alone.

As if sensing his thoughts, she opened her eyes again, and to his relief they were clear and lucid, though dark shadows had already begun to appear around them. "It's all right, Rogond. The horror has passed for now, and I shall rest. Do what you must do. I'll be all right."

"Of course you will, but I would still see you attended to. You are badly hurt and your strength is uncertain. I shall go and fetch Nelwyn. Perhaps she will tell you a tale."

Gaelen nodded, as she would like that very much. She sighed and drew the blankets around her as Rogond kissed her damp forehead, then turned and left her. He had not been gone long when a sudden wave of cold overtook her, and she shivered. She wondered whether Gorgon could be the cause of it, and squeezed her eyes tightly shut, disgusted and heartsick.

She realized that Gorgon must not find out that anyone knew of the existence of the mirror, and so she suppressed the urge to cry out. Her enemy would hear only silence and would see only darkness. She was filled with loathing, desiring more than anything to tell the vile creature of her hatred, but for now she lay, sweat-soaked and shaking, wondering how she would ever survive this dreadful presence, this contemptible violation of her senses. The words of Farahin came back to her—she was to be the instrument by which Gorgon would be vanquished.

She thought of the plight of Duinar, the Magic-user who had tried in vain to contain the eruption of the Fire-mountain that had destroyed Tuathas, and settled herself to her own seemingly impossible task.

Rogond found Nelwyn soon after, as she would not go far from her cousin until Gaelen was back on her feet. Galador was there also, and he spoke to Rogond.

"I am ashamed, my friend. All this is my fault; I did not know that I should not have taken the horses from Gaelen, but if I had thought about it, I would have been wiser. I'm so terribly sorry."

Rogond reassured him. "She had to find out, Galador. Though I might have chosen a better time and place, she still would not have taken it well. You are not to blame."

Nelwyn went to attend Gaelen, but Rogond stayed Galador from accompanying her. "Nay, my friend. They need time alone. Besides, I need you with me—you and Fima. We must go and see the King at once, for he must know all that we can tell. And I would bring a proposal before him."

Galador nodded, as he had expected this. Rogond had some sort of plan to throw down Gorgon and his army before they could threaten the Elves of the Greatwood. Galador had learned that his friend the Aridan possessed a creative intelligence that, when he was motivated, was extraordinary. Galador doubted that Rogond would ever be more motivated than he was at present, and he went in search of Fima so that they might stand before the King.

Gorgon had at last come in sight of the Barrens, which were in fact a group of rather formidable rock formations rising from the forest that surrounded them. Nothing grew there aside from a few small trees and shrubs that struggled up from the sparse, rocky soil. No traveler would venture there, and it was a secure refuge for his army of Ulcas, who were no doubt awaiting him. He had already crafted his response to the inevitable question of what had befallen the two unfortunates that had accompanied him on his foray into the Elven-realm. Indeed, he could not tell them the truth—that his henchmen had been taken by wary Elves and that he, Gorgon, had gone away disappointed rather than face the same fate. They would begin to lose some of their fear of him if that happened, and he must appear to be invincible. Gelmyr's question of whether he would find himself with one of their blades in his back some dark night had already occurred to Gorgon.

Aided by the stench of the Ulcan army, Gorgon drew near their camp, where he was greeted by Kharsh. They hailed each other with upraised fists, then Gorgon stalked by without speaking, for he would eat and drink and rest himself ere he made any of his tale known. Kharsh followed him, joined by several others, until at last he sat before them in the cave that the Ulcas had designated as their command post. He tore into the meat and bread they offered him, still not deigning to speak. At last, Kharsh asked how the encounter with Nelwyn had gone.

"Did you obtain satisfaction, my lord? Was the diversion as fulfilling as you had hoped?"

Gorgon's eyes narrowed, and he paused from his meal. He shot an icy glare at Kharsh, who dropped his gaze, though he knew somehow in his black heart that his commander was more vulnerable than he appeared. "No, Kharsh, thank you for asking," Gorgon said in a sarcastic tone. "It was a complete waste of time, as I sent the wrong two idiots to retrieve her for me. They were not gentle and had difficulty with her, and she was insensible when they brought her to me. She died quickly and in little pain. At least I accomplished her death, but I derived little enjoyment from it."

Then one of the Ulcas who stood by asked what had happened to the two that had gone with Gorgon.

Gorgon set down his meal and rose to his considerable height, a mass of taut muscle and sinew, radiating incredible aggressive power. He faced the Ulcas, who shrank back from his threatening glance. "Where do you *think* they are? They have paid the price for their incompetence," he growled in a menacing tone, a look of absolute disgust on his face. The Ulcas asked no further questions of him.

27

The Plans Are Made

Rogond, Fima, and Galador stood patiently in the corridor, awaiting an audience with the Elven-king. They had been waiting for over an hour, and Fima was growing restive.

"Do you suppose they will ever get around to letting us in there? I do hope we don't have to stand here much longer, as I have never appreciated wasting my time in waiting. In Mountain-home it used to drive me to distraction sometimes. It was as if the Elves had all the time in the world to waste."

Galador smiled at him. "But, we *do*, Fima. When you have lived as long as I have, you learn to be patient. Still, your point is taken, for our friend Rogond has a matter of grave importance to discuss. I would have thought Ri-Aruin would be a bit more anxious to hear of it."

"You would be surprised at what goes on in the mind of the King," said a voice from down the corridor. They turned to observe Wellyn striding toward them, his blue-grey eyes keen and unwavering. "How long have you been waiting?" he asked Rogond, who replied, "not long" at the exact moment Fima said "nearly forever!" Wellyn smiled. As with most of his people he had never been fond of dwarves, but Fima was an obvious exception.

Wellyn glanced over at the closed, guarded door to the King's council-chamber. "You are here to discuss the matter of Gorgon and the mirror, are you not?"

"Yes," Rogond replied. "I have a plan to trap him, but I need the King's aid. The Greatwood Realm will be at grave risk unless we can draw him into a confrontation that he is not ready for, before he can amass too great a force. This has been foretold. It is this matter that most concerns Ri-Aruin, and I would counsel with him as soon as possible, for we will need to lay our plans quickly should he agree to aid us."

"He will agree," said Wellyn, his jaw set, face determined. "Do not fear, my good dwarf. You shall wait no longer." He strode to the doors of the council chamber and, after a brief exchange with the guards, was admitted. Rogond, Fima, and Galador were escorted into the presence of the King almost immediately, which was of no surprise. Wellyn had looked quite resolute.

Ri-Aruin received them graciously, inviting them to sit before him. "My apologies for keeping you waiting, but I sensed that your errand will keep you here for some time, and so I was dispensing with some important but easily completed tasks. Please make yourselves comfortable, for I would hear both your tale and your plan."

As the others settled themselves in beautifully-carved wooden chairs, Rogond stood before Ri-Aruin and began to tell him all that he could of Gorgon and the mirror. When Rogond came to Nelwyn's vision in the Stone of Léir, the King closed his eyes as though pained at the very thought. Wellyn stood beside the throne of his father, his young face impassive. He had heard most of the story already. After he had finished, Rogond drew a deep breath.

"That is the tale as I can best relate it, my Lord Ri-Aruin. Now I would ask you to hear of a plan I have devised to trap the creature, for I will need your aid. Will you hear me?"

Ri-Aruin nodded. They certainly would need to do something, and he had perceived that the Tuathan was highly intelligent and had taken the folk of the Greatwood to his heart. His plan was no doubt worth hearing. When Rogond had finished describing it, the King was no longer certain; the plan was very risky, and if the creature was as clever as they believed, it would be very difficult to set the trap without alerting him. Gaelen was a prime player in the plan, and Ri-Aruin wondered whether she would have the strength to stand under the pressure, and see it through to its completion. He muttered under his breath, forgetting for the moment that his son stood by and had heard every word.

"She'll manage, father. She will not fail in this task—I know it. Having set herself against this enemy, she will not rest until he is brought low."

Ri-Aruin nodded, then turned to his son and smiled. "You have such faith in her, my son. Let us hope that it is well placed." He addressed Rogond and his friends. "I shall need time to consider your plan. In the meantime, rest and recover your strength, for this ordeal has been difficult. I will summon you after I have considered."

When they had left the King's chambers Fima stopped Rogond in the corridor. "That was one of the most harebrained ideas I have ever heard. What are you thinking? One slip and we are all dead!"

"Then we must make certain that we do not slip," said Wellyn.

"Tell me how I may be helpful, Aridan." The more Rogond came to know Wellyn, the better he liked him.

"If you have some time now, I would seek aid in refining the plan. What do you know of the Barrens? Are you familiar with their design?" Wellyn nodded.

"Then let us speak further, my friends," said Rogond. "We shall need to work this out quickly, for our enemy is gathering strength."

Wellyn led them to a quiet chamber, where they spent the next several hours in planning. Rogond hoped that Gaelen was well, and that Nelwyn would not run out of tales to tell her.

Nelwyn had brought Gaelen food and drink, and then told her the story of how the magical realm of Monadh-talam came to be. She told of Shandor the Asarla, and Liathwyn, who was said to have been the most beautiful of all the Èolar. The story was perhaps not the best choice, as it ended in tragedy, and Nelwyn's tale faltered as she described Shandor's terrible, consuming grief. She looked into the eyes of her friend Gaelen, those deep, honest eyes reflecting a spirit that had never failed her, and imagined Gorgon looking through them. Nelwyn's face reflected her horror at this notion for only a moment, but it was enough for Gaelen to notice. She turned away, and her eyes were filled with tears.

"Go on, Nelwyn, aren't you going to finish your tale? This is the part where Shandor goes mad." Gaelen's voice betrayed her anxiety, and Nelwyn knew that she was terribly afraid of going mad herself.

"Gaelen, you are not Shandor. You have already endured the loss of your beloved, and your sanity overcame your grief. You will not stray down the same path."

Still, Gaelen wept as Nelwyn tried to calm her. Gaelen was afraid to say anything about her fears, lest Gorgon be listening. This was going to be incredibly difficult, as she didn't know how long she could keep everything locked inside. Her crying intensified as Nelwyn tried to comfort her.

"It will be all right, Gaelen. I should not have told you of Liathwyn…it always makes you weep."

But Gaelen did not weep for Liathwyn, or for Shandor; she wept at that moment for Belegund, and the dwarves, and the lost Elves of Tal-sithian. And she wept for herself, because she knew she would not be able to bear the burden of one more death.

Nelwyn knew she had to distract her, and she did so with a question that, though she knew it was incredibly bold, had been weighing on her mind.

"Gaelen…you died that day by the river. There was no doubt in my mind or my heart that you were dead. Tell me, how is it that you were allowed to return to us? Was it like to the time when you and I walked together in the Spirit Realm?"

Gaelen stopped crying and turned to face her. "No, Nelwyn, the circumstances were different, as you well know. You wanted to live. You were fighting to live. I was fighting to die."

Nelwyn was abashed, for of course Gaelen's words were true, and they no doubt pained her. Nelwyn need not have worried, for Gaelen did not hold it against her, and she continued though her eyes were haunted at the memory.

"I was sent back. I can say no more of that, only…" Here she paused, and her voice was small and distant. "…Only that Rain came to me, and spoke to me, though we could not touch. He could not hold me; he could only send me back. I was on the shores of the waters that lead to the Eternal Realm, but there was no ship to bear me…only Rain. He left me again, Nelwyn, though he did not wish it. And I could not prevent it. I had to come back."

Nelwyn was overcome by this revelation, and she bent down and hugged Gaelen, who stared straight ahead, trying not to cry again. They remained so for several moments in silent affirmation of their bond of friendship, knowing that each would support the other, no matter what. Then Nelwyn spoke again. The words had been in her mind to say for many, many years, and it was finally the time to say them.

"Gaelen, perhaps you should open your heart, and consider that you might not wish to live the rest of your life grieving for Farahin.

There is one who loves you, one who would ease your burden and share your pain. Rogond is true of heart, and he is utterly devoted to you. You need him at your side to aid you. You cannot face this alone."

"Are you going somewhere?" asked Gaelen.

Nelwyn scowled at her. "You know I would never leave you, but I cannot fill this emptiness in your heart. He can." Then she made one final effort to convince her cousin. "What did Ri-Elathan say to you? Did he say anything that might help in guiding your heart? You do not have to repeat it to me, but I would urge you to consider well his words. He was very wise, I'm told."

Gaelen did not reply, as Rogond chose that particular moment to return. Galador and Fima were with him. Nelwyn sighed. Ri-Elathan's words to Gaelen would remain unknown, but she could tell from the look on her cousin's face that it had been a wise course to remind her of them. Only Ri-Elathan could release her from the bonds of grief, only he could help her to see that the joy of her heart would be fulfilled by the one who stood now before her. For although Rogond was mortal, his love for Gaelen would be eternal, though it would endure for an eternity that they could not share.

Ri-Aruin summoned the Company to his private chambers on the following day. He looked careworn as he sat before them; it was obvious that he had not rested and that his mind and heart were troubled. He bade Rogond, Fima, Nelwyn, Galador, Thorndil, and Wellyn to make themselves comfortable, for this would be a war-council and would likely take much of the afternoon. He sent for food and drink so that they might be content, for once closed, the doors to the chamber would remain so except in dire emergency. The King first addressed Rogond, using the common tongue in consideration of Fima and Thorndil, unwittingly offending Fima.

"Let me first summarize the plan as I have understood it, Tuathan, as I must make certain that we are all in agreement before we begin. Through Gaelen, Gorgon will be fed false information that will lure him and his army into a trap. Our people will then attack and finish them, hopefully killing Gorgon and releasing Gaelen from the power of the mirror."

It sounded like an idea that could work, until one began to examine it. The success of the plan depended upon an intricately woven series of events that would entice Gorgon beyond his ability to resist. As Fima had said, one slip and they were all dead, as Gorgon was very clever and wary. He would not hesitate to turn events to his advantage if he grew wise to their deception.

Together with Fima, Galador, and Wellyn, Rogond had put together an irresistible scenario to tempt Gorgon within reach. It would require elaborate staging to lure him in, but it could be done. Gorgon would be allowed to learn that a secret council was being planned to discuss the growing threat of his Black Command and what should be done about it. This council would include two of the most influential Elves in all of Alterra: Ri-Aruin, the King of the Woodland Realm, and Magra, the powerful Èolarin Elf-lord, emissary to Lady Ordath.

Gorgon was probably already aware of the contingent of Elves from Tal-sithian, but Rogond suggested that they represent Oryan as being a person of great importance, emissary to Lord Airan.

Neither Ri-Aruin nor Magra would actually be present at the staging of the "council". Ri-Aruin would be impersonated ably by his son, Wellyn; Magra would be portrayed by Amandir of Tal-sithian, for he resembled Magra to an extent. Not that it really mattered, as they all doubted that Gorgon had ever seen Magra before. He would no doubt be familiar with the appearance of Ri-Aruin however, as they would have to make certain he "overheard" the goings-on of the King's court.

When Gorgon and his army appeared they would expect to come upon the Elves unaware, for Gorgon would expect that the council would be minimally defended. After all, it was secret, and the Elves would have no reason to plan otherwise.

Now the question was where and how to stage the council. Ri-Aruin at first suggested the Greatwood, for it would be easy to vanquish Gorgon within the confines of the Forest Realm. "That is where Gorgon will expect the council to be," said the King.

"True enough, my lord," said Rogond, "but remember that he will not attack such an easily defended location without a very mighty army. He will not be lured in unless he is certain of victory. With all due respect, we must make ourselves more vulnerable. The plan will not succeed unless we can prod him into attacking quickly, before he has the chance to amass a great force. I sense that time is against us, and he is gathering strength even now."

His gaze was drawn to Galador, who had placed a concerned hand upon Nelwyn, as she was obviously disquieted. Her beautiful eyes were wide as she recalled her terrible vision, and she knew that, whatever happened, the conflict must *not* take place in the Greatwood Realm. She rose abruptly to her feet and looked around at all her friends, then spoke to the King in an impassioned voice.

"This cannot happen here…it must not! That creature cannot be allowed anywhere near this fortress. Another way will have to be found!" She was trembling at the memory of her premonition, and Galador rose to his feet, standing beside her.

"Tell them, my love. Tell them of your vision. It's time to make matters plain."

Nelwyn drew a deep breath and told the assembly what she had seen in the Stone. When she finished, those who had not heard the tale before were white-faced and grim.

Galador then addressed the King and the Company, and his words chilled them all.

"Now you know that Nelwyn is right. Much depends upon our ability to coordinate this very elaborate deception. If we fail we must make certain that the realm is secure. We must lure Gorgon to a place where, if we are not victorious, only the few will be lost. We cannot risk the safety of the Elven-hold."

Then he looked Rogond in the eye and spoke the most chilling words of all. "Have any of you considered that Gorgon may already have guessed our plan? Do we know for certain that he has not? What if he witnessed the events with Gaelen in the forest, or overheard Fima accidentally revealing the mirror to her? Do we know that he did not? She tried to take her own life! If he knows this, then he is most certainly suspicious. In that event, we are all planning our own deaths right now." He looked hard at Rogond. "Can you tell me with certainty that Gaelen will not reveal this to him, even unwittingly? So much rests on her shoulders, and they are not as broad as they might be. All she has to do is slip once—look in the wrong direction or say the wrong thing at the wrong time, and we are vanquished."

Rogond's strong jaw was set, and his body was rigid as he regarded his closest friend. "These are words I would have expected from Amandir, not from you," he said. "But of course, you are right…what, then, shall we do? This creature will not relent until he has worked his evil upon your people—your people, Galador, not mine. So shall we stand aside and allow him to gather strength for a massive attack because we are uncertain?"

Galador's face reddened, but he did not look away. "We will not shrink from our task, Rogond, but neither should we engage in folly that cannot result in anything but disaster. We must be fairly certain of ourselves before we proceed."

"There is no time for certainty, Elf of Eádros!" cried Wellyn, rising to his feet. "What of Gaelen? If we do not end this Dark Horror, then what becomes of her? Do we lock her in prison, where she will neither see nor hear anything of use to the creature, until she dies for want of the feel of the air? Do we leave her alone to perish knowing that she will never be free of him?" He turned to Rogond. "Ask her, Tuathan. Ask her whether she has any sense that Gorgon knows. She is very intuitive—ask her! If she is reasonably certain that he has gained little insight, then that is enough for me."

Galador looked around him at the faces of his friends. He closed his eyes for a moment then nodded in agreement. "It is enough for me, as well," he said, returning to his place beside Nelwyn. She took his hand and reassured him; she knew that it had been difficult for him to voice such concerns to Rogond.

"Never mind, my love. These things needed to be said. I know they pained you. It wasn't fair to compare you to Amandir," she whispered.

Ri-Aruin rose and spoke then to all. "I will not enter into this plan unless I have assurance that all of you are willing," said he. "You must choose your path now. Will you support the Tuathan, or no? Provided he receives assurance from Gaelen that the enemy remains unwitting, will you join in this effort? Gorgon will sense your trepidation otherwise. All must be united in their resolve. Choose now."

Each then rose and faced Ri-Aruin, bowed before him, and then turned to Rogond. "I will support Rogond's plan," said Wellyn, who stood first. Rogond liked him more and more every minute. Then Nelwyn, Galador, Fima, Thorndil, and finally the King himself each voiced their affirmation. Ri-Aruin addressed the Company, who stood now united:

"Then let us make our plans. We will await assurance from Gaelen before we proceed with them."

The long afternoon was spent in debate, mostly concerning the proposed location of the "secret council". It could not be held in open country, but would need to take place in a location that was defensible, and where enemies could be seen as they approached. Gorgon would expect nothing less. It would need to be somewhere between Mountain-home and the Elven-hold, yet near enough that they could stage it quickly. Gorgon would be told that the council had been planned since Ri-Aruin had first learned of his existence, back in late winter. Because Gaelen had been both to Mountain-home and the Lake Realm, it would be easy to convince Gorgon that Magra was already on his way. Oryan would be presented as a person of considerable importance: the personal emissary of the Lord and Lady of the Lake.

They obtained a large map of the Lands of Alterra, spreading it out upon the table before the King. Rogond pointed to the Barrens, rugged stone hills that rose beyond the southern borders of the realm. They were surrounded by forest, which would be perfect for concealing an army. This would appeal both to the Woodland army, that would lie in wait, and to Gorgon, who would be able to bring his own forces into proximity undetected. The Barrens were about a hundred miles closer to Mountain-home if the council took place in the easternmost hills; they were nearly in a direct line to the east. "Magra" could "arrive" using the old northern road, staged for Gorgon to witness.

"The Barrens would be the most logical place," said Rogond. "Gorgon is not far away from our southern borders. We need to let him know that the council will take place very soon now, and we cannot afford much travel time, as both our forces and his will need time to make ready."

"But, Rogond," said Nelwyn in a worried tone. "What if he is already taking refuge in the Barrens? What if he is lying in wait? Won't he simply slay us as we appear there?"

Rogond shook his head. "No, Nelwyn. He will want to take *all* of us. Remember his nature—he will not wish to alert any of us by preying on the others. If he is sheltering in the Barrens now, I'll wager he will be gone as soon as he finds out that we're planning the council there. He will want to wait until all are assembled so that he may gain the ultimate victory. Think what killing Ri-Aruin and Magra would mean to one such as Gorgon. He might then plan to march on the Greatwood, as he would sense the dismay and confusion of the Woodland Elves should their King be taken from them."

"The Barrens are well known to many of us," said Ri-Aruin, "for although they are no longer part of our realm, they were once included in the lands of Osgar, my father, before Wrothgar's evil forced us to withdraw our borders."

He drew forth an old but very detailed map of the area, showing several excellent locations for the staging of the council. He pointed with a long, elegant finger at one in particular. The others of the Company nodded in agreement, and the location of the conflict was chosen. Now all that remained was to carefully set the trap.

They would let it be known that there would be a relatively small contingent of guards present at the "secret council', because the Elves did not wish to attract the attention of unfriendly eyes that might be keeping watch on the Barrens. In truth, they wished to tempt Gorgon with the prospect of bringing down Magra and Ri-Aruin with only minimal resistance.

Everyone would have a part to play in the deception and would have to ensure that all went as planned. Gaelen, as Gorgon's "window" into the proceedings, would have to be especially vigilant. She could not be allowed to see or hear anything that would alert Gorgon; all communication with her would have to be strictly orchestrated and controlled. Rogond knew they would have to work quickly to accomplish their ends, as Gaelen would not fare well for long under such conditions. The pressure placed upon her would be horrific. But then, Rogond told himself, so long as she knew the objective of the plan, she would apply herself utterly to it. He gave assurances to his friends that they need not worry. Gaelen would be more than happy to follow any course of action that would lead to the downfall of her enemy and secure her release from his terrible influence.

The Elves of Tal-sithian, who had tracked Gorgon's small army, estimated that it had numbered about thirty, but they did not know how the Ulcas came to be under Gorgon's command in the first place, or whether more would be joining him. The general feeling was that where there were some, there would be others. Once Gorgon knew of the "council", he would work as quickly as he could to add weight to his forces. If given too much time he might very well overcome the Elves of the Greatwood. The trap must be set quickly.

The task of communicating the plan to Gaelen fell to Rogond. It was difficult at first, as Gaelen had to train herself not to look at Rogond as he traced messages slowly and carefully upon her arm. She would then write responses to him on parchment, never looking at them but staring resolutely at something else. It was frustrating, as communicating in this way took so much time and concentration. Gaelen, who was restive by nature, could only stand it for brief periods, though she made a valiant effort.

Rogond was patient with her and tried to cheer her, but it was difficult at times to make her understand, and this taxed them both. As time passed, they became more and more adept, and the process became far less stressful. They took these careful steps because, although they suspected that Gorgon's presence was heralded by Gaelen's cold chills, they could not be certain that it was always so, and they took no chances. The only thing Gorgon would see should he attend these sessions was whatever Gaelen was focusing on, usually the flowing waters of the river. The sound of the rushing, gurgling water and the carefully controlled words of Gaelen and Rogond were all that he would hear.

Rogond had inquired of Gaelen before any further effort was made, and he had looked earnestly into her eyes, tracing carefully his question.

D-O Y-O-U H-A-V-E A-N-Y S-E-N-S-E T-H-A-T G-O-R-G-O-N K-N-O-W-S T-H-A-T W-E A-R-E A-W-A-R-E O-F T-H-E M-I-R-R-O-R? C-O-N-S-I-D-E-R W-E-L-L A-S O-U-R F-A-T-E R-E-S-T-S O-N I-T.

She thought for a moment, and then wrote her response:

I need time to be certain, though I do not believe he is aware at present. I have been concentrating on trying to feel the times when he is making use of the mirror, and to glean what I can of him during those times. I shall apply myself especially to this question until I am reasonably sure.

She continued to gaze at the river as Rogond traced his answer.

T-A-K-E C-O-U-R-A-G-E W-E A-R-E W-I-T-H Y-O-U. W-H-E-N Y-O-U A-R-E C-E-R-T-A-I-N W-E W-I-L-L A-C-T Q-U-I-C-K-L-Y.

Then, almost as an afterthought, he added,

H-I-S T-I-M-E D-R-A-W-S N-E-A-R.

She looked at him and nodded. Then she held him in a gentle embrace, whispering in his ear. "You are so strong, and keen of mind, and faithful. Thaylon, the Trustworthy, I name you. We will prevail over our difficulties, and so long as you stand beside me, I shall not fear."

Then she drew back from him and truly smiled for the first time in a long reckoning, unaware that she had, in naming him Thaylon, given him again the name of his birth, though, of course, he did not know it.

Gaelen went out alone into the forest for the remainder of the day. She intended to apply herself to discerning the extent of Gorgon's awareness, and she thought she knew just how it might be done. Like Rogond, she was keen of mind. Gorgon might well have chosen a different victim had he known then the thoughts turning within her; she would now welcome his intrusions upon her senses, for through them she could attempt to gain insight.

Deep in the Barrens, Gorgon rested in his lair, unaware that Gaelen would turn the use of the mirror to her own purposes as he grasped it in his left hand. He stifled a small cry of pain and shook his head in frustration. She was alone again from the look of things, and was somewhere in the forest. That would not suit his purpose, and he nearly abandoned his effort, but he had learned to wait at least a few minutes before doing so. The pain had usually lessened a bit by then (actually, he just became used to it) and she might yet reveal something. This time he was rewarded, or so he thought, as she began muttering to herself.

"About time someone did something about this horror. After all, we carried the King's message to Lady Ordath ages ago! The Elves of Tal-sithian are behind us, of course, but what of Mountain-home? We shall need their aid. I'm not certain this course of Ri-Aruin's is wise. I wish Nelwyn were here…I would speak of it with her."

Speak of *what* with her? What of Mountain-home, indeed? What did Ri-Aruin intend? Gaelen now had Gorgon's full attention, but he would get nothing more from her this day.

When enough time had passed that he realized this, he broke contact, and when she sensed that he had gone, she nodded her head slowly in satisfaction. She had paid very, very careful attention during this exchange and had detected no hesitation at all from him. There was a feeling of voracious eagerness, as though she could sense his thirst for any information that would aid him in planning some great day of reckoning. She sensed no trepidation, no hint that he knew that she was aware of him.

She rose and stretched her body in a small patch of sunlight, banishing the lingering chill. She would wait until tomorrow to find and report to Rogond; perhaps Gorgon would try again tonight to gain additional insight, and she would again pay careful attention, refining her skills at discerning his mood. The better she became at this, the better it would serve them. Though she was still revolted by his presence, she smiled inwardly as she sensed his cold heart probing and questing for information that he would never receive. He was the victim of the mirror now, though he did not know it.

Having received Gaelen's assurance that Gorgon was unaware of their knowledge of the mirror, the Company now set about the task of setting the trap. This involved a number of carefully staged scenarios in which Gaelen was present. She had perfected a series of signals to let them all know when the now-familiar icy feeling assailed her, and they would then be aware that they were all speaking in the presence of their enemy. They went on their guard immediately if Gaelen alerted them, and they would be extremely careful until she let them know that the feeling had passed.

At such times, Rogond felt a nearly overwhelming urge to take her in his arms and comfort her, for though she concentrated hard on the task before her, her eyes still occasionally betrayed her revulsion and vulnerability. And though Gaelen had professed her faith in him, naming him Thaylon, she still had not responded directly to his declaration of love for her, and he dared not force her decision now. She had warned him of the consequences of doing so. *If you press me, I shall turn from you, do you understand?* He did indeed.

As much as he might want to hold and comfort her, he would have to wait until she came to terms with her own feelings and had decided what her course would be. His future would be in doubt and darkness until then, but there was nothing to be done for it.

For now Rogond was thankful for the difficulty of the task set before them, as it would occupy him completely until it was accomplished, and he would not have to worry so about Gaelen's choice. She could not afford to be distracted by such matters at the moment, anyway. At least he was in his proper place at her side and would remain there until she sent him from her, or until his life's end.

As the intricate plan began to take shape, Ri-Aruin grew concerned, as it carried considerable risk to all who would attend the "council", including his eldest son and heir. He once tried to dissuade Wellyn from taking part, an effort that proved to be a spectacular failure. He then suggested the option of sending a large, well-armed contingent of Elves to directly engage Gorgon's army, but thought better of it, as they did not know his exact location. If Gorgon became alerted to the presence of an army, he would deftly evade them, go into hiding, and emerge at a time of his own choosing. Then he would have had time to increase his forces to the point that they would do serious damage to the Elves of the Greatwood, as Nelwyn had foreseen. No, better to lure him into a situation he was not prepared for and vanquish him before he could gather strength. Summoning Rogond before him, the King prepared for his own part in the plan.

Gaelen was brought to the court, and when they were fairly certain that she was not alone in her perception, they began to set their trap. Ri-Aruin let Gorgon know everything concerning the nature of the "secret council" that would take place in a mere three weeks' time, at the next new moon. He also informed Gorgon that Magra had been sent for long ago and that he would no doubt be attending along with Ri-Aruin himself. Gaelen, Nelwyn, Rogond, and Galador would be sent ahead to scout the Barrens, and to make certain that they were secure. They would be accompanied by a small but doughty host of Wood-elves, who would assist them in clearing the area of hazards and sinister influences. They would also set up the accommodations and amenities that would be provided to their important guests.

Ri-Aruin emphasized the need for concealment; they could not attract attention to this area, as he hoped to engage the emissaries of Mountain-home and Tal-sithian in secrecy. The council would no doubt occupy many days, but they would come to a decision with all speed, for it was the intent of the Elves to quickly prepare to make war upon Gorgon and his army.

Deep in the Barrens, Gorgon's heart leapt with this news, the first news of any real interest in a long time. This, obviously, was the meaning of Gaelen's musings in the forest. He sat with his back to the wall, face twisted with pain, heart pounding, breathing hard and sweating with effort, trying to endure the mirror long enough to learn all that he would. He was rewarded for his pains, as he now had the promise of an opportunity to destroy Magra, Ri-Aruin, and some other very important but as-yet-unnamed Elf, emissary from Tal-sithian.

So! They planned to make war upon him, did they? Well, once he and his army overwhelmed and slew everyone at the council, that plan would be far less likely. He could hardly contain the fire in his heart at the prospect, yet there was doubt. He debated on what the wisest course should be—according to the Elves he had only three weeks to amass an army large enough to ensure that the unfortunate ones attending the council would be easily taken. And first he would have to move from his present location, leaving no trace that he and his contingent of Ulcas had ever occupied this place. It was time to get moving!

He would try to use the mirror more often, especially during the daylight hours, when Ri-Aruin was most likely to hold council. Though it would pain him, he knew it would yield much of interest, and he looked forward to learning more. Yet deep in his heart, he was wary. He knew that he would need a more powerful force to accomplish the havoc he was planning, yet it seemed almost as though the Elves were handing him his heart's desire on a plate. He would need guidance.

First he summoned Kharsh, informing him that the Black Command was to be ready to move on by nightfall. All traces of their presence were to be removed. Gorgon looked up with satisfaction at the gathering storm clouds in the west; a hard rain would wash much of the evidence away. He would move the army farther south until he received additional instructions.

He moved then to a quiet chamber, instructing Kharsh that he was not to be disturbed under any circumstances. Once there, he cleared his mind and sent his thoughts out toward Tûr Dorcha, asking that he be allowed to come into the presence of the Shadowmancer.

Since Lord Wrothgar had first come to him in his need, Gorgon had known that there was a sort of connection between them. Wrothgar seemed to know when Gorgon required guidance; had not Kharsh and the Ulcas been sent at just the right time? It was understandable that he should need aid and counsel in matters such as this, for though Gorgon was powerful and highly intelligent, he still had little understanding of the ways in which people interacted and behaved. After all, he had lived much of his life in solitude. He could not relate to positive emotions of any sort and was susceptible to false promises and flattery. It would be far easier for the Elves to deceive him than he would like to admit.

Now he concentrated hard on re-establishing communication with Wrothgar, for he required a much larger force if he was to attack and destroy Magra and Ri-Aruin, and he was still in some doubt. There were small, uneasy ripplings in his mind. What if, somehow, the Elves had discovered his mirror? Though he knew not how it could be so, he wondered. He had noticed a change, subtle but definitely there, in the way Gaelen carried out her affairs of late. There were differences in the way some of her friends reacted to her, as well.

Could they be aware of his presence? If so, then this was a trap set for him by Ri-Aruin, and he must not fall prey. Yet he had no real evidence, only a gnawing doubt in his mind. Perhaps Wrothgar would be able to discern the truth, as He had great power, and therefore must be very wise.

Had Gorgon but known, his connection with Gaelen was becoming stronger with each time that he invaded her senses. Just as she could, with concentration, make herself at least partly aware of his mood, he was also picking up some impressions of her state of mind. But unlike Gaelen, he was not perceptive enough to make real use of this, and so it resulted in a sort of vague confusion that he could not banish from his thoughts.

Now he sat in silent anticipation, trying to keep his mind clear in expectation of the coming of the Dark Power. All at once his eyelids grew heavy, and the strength seemed to flow out of him as the vision came. He drew himself up, resting his head on his knees, fighting a wave of dizziness that had suddenly come over him, hearing the voice of Wrothgar inside his mind.

Thou hast summoned Me, Elfhunter. What is thy need? What aid dost thou require? Art thou pleased with thy gift, and with the aid I have sent already to thee?

Gorgon knew he was referring to Kharsh and the Black Command. He tried to respond, but a wave of weakness overtook him, and he could not speak.

Wrothgar seemed not to notice. *I sense in thee a need for guidance. What hast thou learned, and what is thy intended course? Speak, Elfhunter, that I may counsel thee.*

Gorgon found the strength to speak at last. "My Lord, I would ask for direction in an important matter. It seems my course should be clear, yet I am in doubt."

Over the next several minutes, Gorgon told Wrothgar of his discovery of the Elves' impending council. He had discerned from their conversations that there would be fewer than one hundred Elves present, including Magra and Ri-Aruin. Gorgon knew the Barrens well enough to feel confident that if he had a larger force under his command, he would overrun the Elves and slay them all. Yet, he held doubt in his mind. He could not explain this to Wrothgar, for he did not fully understand it himself. He just could not seem to avoid the feeling that the council was in fact a trap that had been set for him. Yet Wrothgar was undaunted. He heard what Gorgon would tell, and then answered him.

Most worthy Elfhunter, dispel thy doubt. The opportunity is before thee to eliminate a powerful force in Magra, and to throw the Greatwood into chaos with the death of Ri-Aruin. Our enemies will tremble before thee… do not give in to thoughts of defeat, for thy forces must act with all speed. I will send thee aid; I will empty Tûr Dorcha and send My finest warriors. But they must leave at once and be swift, as thy plans for their use must be made in advance. More than five hundred warriors will move at thy command. Does that ease thy doubt?

Gorgon, who had always worked alone, had difficulty imagining leading a force of five hundred. He had never gone into battle before, and the thought of his force going up against a small force of Elves, who would be taken by surprise, thrilled him. Yet, he wondered.

"Lord, what if this is a trap set to decimate our forces? If the Elves have somehow allowed me to learn of their plan…if they hold the mastery…"

They would have no way of discovering the existence of the mirror. They could not know to set the trap unless they had gained such knowledge. Dispel thy doubt and take thy prize. Bring to Me the head of Magra, along with the King of the Greatwood. I shall have both the gold and the ebony!

Gorgon heard Wrothgar's harsh, malicious laughter as he imagined the heads of the two Elf-lords being carried by their long hair. It was a pleasing thought. Wrothgar hated Magra in particular; the Elf had caused great difficulties during the Third Battle and had historically turned up to combat the Dark Powers when it was most inconvenient. Gorgon knew he would have to go forth despite his doubts. Wrothgar would never let such an opportunity pass.

Strengthen thy resolve, Elfhunter, and go forth to vanquish thy foes. It will be an experience they will not soon forget, and thy name will bring sorrow and dread throughout Alterra. Is that not thy fondest wish? Go forth, now. There is not much time—My warriors will meet thee soon. I will give them armor and weapons the Elves will not withstand. When next I meet thee, bring My tokens that I may rejoice in thy victory. With these words, Wrothgar's voice faded and was heard no more.

Gorgon knew that the "tokens" Wrothgar was referring to were the heads of Magra and Ri-Aruin. He would have the might of the Shadow to aid him, and his doubts seemed to fade away even as Wrothgar's voice had done. They did not return to disquiet him for a long while.

28

The Trap Is Set

Now that the Company had laid their plans to trap Gorgon and his army, the reality of all that needed to be done came down hard upon them. Gaelen, of course, could be party to only those preparations they wanted Gorgon to witness, and it was occasionally quite frustrating staging elaborate displays only to wait, sometimes in vain, for Gorgon to use the mirror. Rogond worried constantly, though he gave no outward sign. They all knew the consequences of failure. Yet they were hopeful, as Gaelen gave no indication that she had received any warning sign from Gorgon. Everything was proceeding according to plan.

Meanwhile, Gorgon and his forces were making preparations of their own. The host of Ulcas sent by Wrothgar had assembled in an area of the forest between Tûr Dorcha and the Barrens. Gorgon had been instructed to rendezvous with them there and to get to know his three new lieutenants. He was glad for Kharsh, who interacted well with them and smoothed over the initial difficulties. They spent some days planning the assault, but in the end it was quite simple.

They would wait until all the Elves were occupied at the council, and after surrounding them the Ulcas would launch their attack, leaving none alive. Gorgon now had many skilled archers and swordsmen at his command, and though he did not reckon that the Elves would be taken without a fight, they would be so surprised and outnumbered that his forces would overwhelm them quickly.

Gorgon inspected his new Company with approval. They were well armed and provisioned with armor that, while not of the same quality as his own, was still formidable. It would be very difficult to see the dull black armor as they moved by dark of night. Still it would be difficult to orchestrate a stealthy approach, as they would be in the close confines of the forest while in full armor, and would be at great risk of being heard. But Gorgon planned to wait until the council was well underway and the Elves' attention was diverted. Hopefully, if there were lookouts, he would learn through Gaelen how many and where they would be found. Then his archers could eliminate them before they could raise the alarm.

It was ten days until the council and just before dawn when Kharsh approached Gorgon as he sat brooding in his temporary headquarters.

"I sense you are troubled, my lord," he said. "We are nearly ready, and the time for the council is not for many days yet. Is not everything proceeding according to your design? Why are you not content?"

Gorgon snarled at him. "And what business is it of yours, Kharsh? My thoughts and plans are my own."

Kharsh bowed low. "Forgive me, lord, I merely want to make certain that we have not caused you to doubt our diligence or our dedication, nothing more. We have great confidence that victory will be ours. If something troubles you, it is of concern to me, for I have learned that your insights are usually quite worthy of attention."

"Flattery will not avail you. I sense that you would have attempted to cut my throat long ago but for fear of the Shadowmancer. Your question, however, shall be answered. I am not content, for I have gained some rather disturbing impressions from my contact with the Elves of late. I cannot explain, as there is nothing definite. I just cannot seem to shake the feeling that they are planning something more than we are expecting."

Kharsh was taken aback. Gorgon had not intimated that he was receiving any but useful insights from the Elves or that anything was amiss until now. "My lord, do you mean to say that you believe this may not go forward as planned? If so, this is fairly serious! Do you think we should proceed if we are uncertain?"

Gorgon drew forth the mirror and held it before Kharsh, who immediately dropped his gaze. "The Shadowmancer expects a return for His gift, and if I do not bring Him that which He desires, I had better have a more compelling reason than a vague impression gleaned from the Elves. We must proceed, or face His wrath. He has made it plain to me that He will not tolerate failure, for He greatly desires the downfall of the Elf-lords. We must proceed, certain or no."

Kharsh nodded. He could certainly relate to Gorgon's point about the Shadowmancer, for he had witnessed the consequences of displeasing Him. The unfortunates involved had begged for death, which came to them not quickly. He shuddered at the memory. He hoped that the misgivings Gorgon was experiencing were just the result of his inexperience in leading a force into open battle.

In a rare, bold moment, Kharsh looked Gorgon in the eye. "I understand. And you are right—we must proceed. I hold hope that your uncertainty will fade as the time draws near, but if not, and the Elves have set a trap for us, let us hope that we do not survive it. Failure will mean death for us all, and given the choice of facing Wrothgar's wrath or falling in battle, I will choose battle! But know that I am your humble servant, my lord, whatever may befall."

"That you are, Kharsh, that you are," growled Gorgon, "whether you would have it or no. We must make certain that our forces are as ready as they can be and that our battle plan is well made. We will prevail; I know the Elves are not expecting a host of this size and ferocity, at any rate. Their pride will assist us, and they will fall. The pride of the Elàni is a thing that I know very much about; long has it been their undoing. But I shall remain vigilant and glean what I may from them until the day of reckoning. We must not assume victory, though we are fairly certain of it."

Gorgon said nothing for a long while, and just as Kharsh assumed that he had finished speaking and turned to leave, Gorgon spoke once more, his voice low, soft, and menacing. "They shall fall before me as blades of grass wither before a flame, and none will remain, save one. I have not yet finished with thee, Gaelen Taldin. But thy choice in the Tuathan will bear no fruit, as he shall be among the first to fall at my hands. All who love thee shall fall."

Kharsh knew then that, regardless of any reservations Gorgon might have, the Black Command would be going to war at the next new moon. The Elves would be thrown into doubt and confusion, and the Shadowmancer would achieve a major victory, even though he was not yet strong.

The eve of departure for the Barrens had come at last. Those chosen to prepare for the council included Rogond and Gaelen, Nelwyn, Galador, Fima and Thorndil, along with a small company of the Elves of the Greatwood. They would carry the provisions necessary to set up the council area, and they would scout the region thoroughly to ensure the safety of the participants. At least, that was the information made available to the Black Command. In reality, they prepared for war. They would be met by others unknown to and unseen by Gorgon, for these preparations would be extensive. They would require a larger force than would the setting up of a simple council chamber.

Rogond had left the Woodland stronghold to walk along the banks of the River Dominglas, mulling over the preparations in his mind. He prayed that they had left nothing undone, no detail overlooked. Had their deception succeeded? They would not know until the confrontation came, he supposed. Of course, if Gorgon had learned of their plans somehow, he might be already awaiting them, and doubtless the advance party would all be killed. Then Gorgon would likely await the arrival of Ri-Aruin, who would oversee the last of the preparations, and he would be slain as well. In anticipation of such a terrible possibility, the Wood-elves had called upon many to serve as lookouts, forming a chain of contact all the way back to the Elven-hold. If the advance party met with disaster, Ri-Aruin would learn of it and be able to prepare.

Rogond had passed by the Narrows to a place where the river calmed and sat down upon a stone, staring at the water as it flowed by. It always relaxed him to look and listen to the river, and he would need to be steady and calm in this effort, as the advance party played an especially important part in ensuring that Gorgon would be well and truly lured in. Gaelen had confided that she was beginning to sense some hesitation when Gorgon was in contact with her, though she could tell that he was still bent on attacking the council. It was a bit of a worry. If Gorgon slipped out of their trap now, the chance would never come again, and Gaelen would be forced to remain in solitude lest she unwittingly play a part in assisting him. She had vowed that no more lives would be taken with her aid.

Rogond's gaze was drawn to a dark object, half washed-up on the rocky riverbank, and he wondered what it could be, as it looked vaguely familiar. He rose and went to retrieve it, then looked down in wonderment. It was Gaelen's blue pouch, though it appeared nearly black in its sodden condition. The strap had broken and it fluttered in the current. Was it too much to hope that the banner of Ri-Elathan, Gaelen's talisman, was still inside? Rogond crouched down beside the waters, reached for the tattered pouch, and lifted it. Then he returned to the stone and sat upon it, gently squeezing the excess water from the old, worn leather. The design could no longer be seen upon it, but inside he found the banner, or what was left of it, and he carefully removed and inspected it.

The pattern was still brilliant; the silk still shimmered. Only about half of the original fabric remained; the rest had been scorched away in the heat of the terrible final confrontation between Ri-Elathan and Wrothgar. This was the first time Rogond had beheld it. He knew of it, of course, having been told about it by Nelwyn, and now he gently fingered the soft silk, imagining the events that it had witnessed. Gaelen's heart was wrapped up in this banner, he knew, and the loss of it had grieved her. It was the first thing she had reached for when she regained her senses after they had pulled her from the river. The look in her eyes when she had realized it was gone had torn at his heart, and he would have given anything in that moment to restore it to her. He often had seen her reach up to hold it in times of stress, and now her fingers searched in vain for it until she remembered that it was lost.

She would be elated at its return, and it gladdened Rogond's heart that he would be the one to bring it back to her and bring her joy. Now he spread the silken remnant upon the warm, soft grass so that it would dry quickly. The pouch was no longer serviceable; it was practically falling to pieces in his hands. Still, he tended it, laying it beside the banner where he could keep an eye on it until he returned to the halls, there to present the banner to his beloved that it might make her glad again.

The advance party would leave at dawn, and all was in readiness. Gaelen was completely focused on the task set before her, and she honed her blades one final time, looking to her bow and quiver as well, for she was going to war. She did not notice Rogond when he first approached her, as he could be quite stealthy if he so wished. He hung back in the shadows for a moment, taking in the sight of his beloved as she held up each arrow-shaft and sighted down it, her bright eyes focused, frowning slightly. She was already dressed for traveling in light garments of dull green and brown, looking small and plain, and very much the rustic hunter-scout. Rogond knew better. She was an eagle in the guise of a sparrow, her heart was fierce and she would see her enemy destroyed. Her eyes burned again with their familiar bright light, but now it was the light of purpose, and she would not turn from it.

He knew that she had come to terms with Gorgon's invasion of her senses, turning it back upon him so that it was almost welcomed, though she still shuddered with revulsion if she allowed herself to think too long of it. There was no longer any risk that she would harm herself, as she was too important in the design of Gorgon's downfall. It was true that she would not allow herself to indulge in her usual pastimes, as she was afraid to relax lest something slip into Gorgon's reckoning.

She kept imagining one of her favorite stories, in which Ri-Aldamar, whom she had never seen but had always imagined as resembling his son, Ri-Elathan, used his incredible fortitude to lead his army over five hundred miles from Tal-elathas in seven days, to come to the aid of his friend Conegal, then Lord of Tuathas, who was besieged. He never gave up hope, so she must not. Her task was small, so she thought, compared with his. Had Ri-Aldamar been privy to her thoughts, he might have disagreed.

Rogond made a sound in his throat to alert Gaelen to his presence and then approached her as she acknowledged him.

"Has everything been made ready? Is there anything else you would have me do?" she asked, her bright eyes alert and willing.

He shook his head. "We are as ready as we will ever be, Gaelen, but there is one thing I would do before we leave tomorrow. Nelwyn told me of Ri-Elathan's banner that you wore as your talisman. She said he never went forth without it, and so you should not. I have come to return that which was lost." So saying, he drew forth the banner, carefully folded, and offered it to her.

Gaelen could not breathe for a moment. She looked into his eyes and read his honest, loving nature in their calm, grey depths. She longed to take the banner from him, but she did not. Instead, she took his hand, folding his fingers gently over the soft silk.

"Ri-Elathan came to me on the shores of the Dark Sea that leads to the Eternal Realm. He told me that I should grieve no more for him, that I should open my heart. I believe that he took the banner from me so that I might realize that my life does have meaning without him. Life does continue, though we may not have it so."

Rogond sorrowed for her in that moment, for the longing in her eyes was still there, though she tried to deny it. He took her arm. Y-O-U G-O T-O W-A-R T-O-M-O-R-R-O-W T-A-K-E I-T. Then he spoke. "He would want you to have it next to your heart. Take it." He offered it again to her. "He meant for me to find it, that I might restore it to you. Take it, please."

"No, Rogond. You found it, not I. He did not return it to me, and therefore he does not wish for me to have it any longer. You found it. You keep it."

He looked into her eyes and saw the depth of her conviction there. She honestly believed that Farahin had given the banner to Rogond. Finally, she took his hand, which was still holding the banner, in both of her own. Then she spoke softly.

"This has passed on, Thaylon. You will have more need of it than I, for you are my protector now."

Then she turned abruptly and left him before he could react. He knew better than to pursue her, but stood alone, fingering the soft silken folds of the banner before tucking it away next to his heart.

At dawn the Company departed for the Barrens, bearing their provisions. A second, much larger group of Elves left the following day, carrying armaments and other supplies that would be needed for battle. They would rendezvous in the appointed place in eight days' time, after traveling well over two hundred miles from the Woodland stronghold, but this would present no difficulty, as they were mounted. Ri-Aruin, who would need to be "seen" by Gorgon, would arrive two days after that. Then he would remain until the arrival of "Magra" and Oryan.

Once Gorgon was aware of Ri-Aruin's presence the King would return to the safety of the stronghold, leaving Wellyn to assume his role. Wellyn resembled his father quite strongly, save that he was a bit more finely made. They would disguise this, however, and Rogond felt that Gorgon would not detect the deception. So long as Wellyn did not speak, all would be well, for his voice was softer than and not as deep as Ri-Aruin's.

On the night of the new moon, the Elves would stage a heated debate in the council-chamber, which was actually a large silken tent erected upon a great, bowl-like plateau that capped the summit of the highest hill. None without wings would be able to view this area, and because it was such a logical place to hold the council, Gorgon would make for it immediately. In addition, so long as Gaelen remained there, the sunken plateau would prevent her from accidentally viewing the battle-preparations. Gorgon would most likely attack when the Elves were most distracted, and Gaelen would be set at the doorway of the silken tent, where she would hear all of the debate, but she would not look directly at Wellyn or Amandir. It would not do to allow Gorgon to have close visual scrutiny of either of them, lest he realize that they were not Ri-Aruin or Magra.

They had but one objective in this confrontation, and that was to kill Gorgon Elfhunter. They did not yet know the extent of his army, but a few skilled hunter-scouts had been sent to occupy posts to the south of the Barrens, where they would catch first sight of the Black Command and return quickly with the information.

Two days prior to the council, Oryan and the Elves of Tal-sithian arrived. Oryan was treated as an honored guest, emissary to the Lake-realm. The appearance of "Magra" had been staged the day before, as he and his small retinue made their way in from the east. Gaelen made certain that Gorgon knew "Lord Magra" had arrived, but she made certain to view him only at a distance, as Gorgon might recognize Amandir and thus see through his disguise. Now the Black Command would be aware that all the Elves planning to attend the council were present, and Gorgon would no doubt begin moving his army north, preparing his assault upon them. The Company anxiously awaited news from their scouts to the south, and they were not disappointed.

Two of the scouts arrived just before dawn of the following day to report that Gorgon's army was approaching. They were dismayed, their faces drawn with anxiety, and they had made all speed in returning with their news. Their tidings were grim—more than five hundred well-armed and armored Ulcas made their way steadily toward the Barrens. Ri-Aruin, Rogond, and Wellyn heard all the scouts would tell, and they wondered how Gorgon could have put such a force together so quickly. The challenge of defeating him would be greater than anticipated, and it was a sobering thought. But Ri-Aruin was not dismayed, and he spoke quickly to Rogond and Wellyn.

"Our forces are gathering to the north even now. I will leave at once, so that I may lead them. I will make certain that our army will be large enough to overwhelm Gorgon. You, my son, will have to hold him at bay long enough for our host to surround him and move in. Are you confident that your defenses will hold?"

Wellyn looked sidelong at Rogond, who had been a bit disillusioned at the thought of five hundred fierce enemies attacking; his last accounting of Gorgon's forces had numbered closer to thirty. The Ranger looked into the eyes of the son of Ri-Aruin, lifted his chin, and nodded.

"They will hold. However, it will not disappoint me if your forces move with all haste once we are attacked."

"So they shall, Tuathan. So they shall. I will take my leave of you now and make my way to rendezvous with them. They will be in position by nightfall. All is prepared." He turned to his son and embraced him with some awkwardness. "Lead well, my son, and safeguard your friends and yourself. You will see me again ere this is ended. May the will of Aontar assure us all of victory."

When he had gone, Rogond turned to Wellyn.

"May we all live up to his expectations. Let's go and inspect our defenses once more, as when last I did so I was not anticipating five hundred attackers."

Wellyn smiled ruefully. "Neither was I. But remember that Gorgon will likewise not be expecting the size of the force my father is planning, which, if I know him well, will be nearly a thousand strong. The days of this enemy are numbered, do not fear." Then his cheerful demeanor seemed to fade, and he grew serious. "Our defenses will have to hold until then." They waited until the dawn's light grew a bit stronger, and then went out to inspect their preparations, for the battle would soon be joined.

The rugged hillside had been set about with shallow pits filled with pitch; these would be set afire using flaming arrows as Gorgon's army attempted to ascend. Their light would reveal the Ulcas to the sharp-eyed archers, who would be well protected, concealed around the rim above. The pits had been hidden under large piles of dry brush; when ignited they would flame up quickly and burn for hours. They were also the signal to Ri-Aruin's host, who would be lying in wait just to the north, to circle around until the hill was surrounded, then move in and overwhelm Gorgon's forces. There were nearly invisible snares set near the rocky ground; several of these were strung between piles of rock that were set to slide down upon the ones unlucky enough to stumble upon them.

About forty of the Elves of Tal-sithian and the Greatwood would be stationed as archers, but the archers would not be able to hold off such a number of enemies for long. Thus the rest of their small force would lie in wait until the archers fell back, indicating that the hilltop would soon be breached. Gorgon would no doubt be using the mirror to view the movements of his enemies, which would otherwise be hidden from view.

When the signal came from the lookouts that the enemy had been sighted, Gaelen had been instructed to leave the council and join the archers on the rim. Gorgon would be more hesitant to attack them and risk killing her; she was too important to his future plans. In addition, she would be training her vision on the enemy below her, and he would then learn nothing of the activity on the hilltop. Nelwyn would be there as well, for her skill with a bow was unrivaled.

Each of the archers would have the task of lighting one of the brush-pits, and they had been instructed to wait until the majority of the Ulcas had moved past them. They could not afford to alert Gorgon to the fact that they were expecting him, as he would no doubt retreat and would likely escape to threaten the Greatwood on a later time. Gaelen had vowed that she would die rather than allow Gorgon to escape her.

When the archers fell back before the invading army, they would join the rest of the defenders in hand-to-hand combat with bow and blade. Horses would be of little use except in the center of the plateau, where the terrain was gentler. The area around the steep edges was far too treacherous to go upon mounted, so most of the horses had been moved to the shelter of a large, rocky alcove. Wellyn, Amandir, and Oryan would each stand with a group of defenders. Fima and Rogond would stand with the Elves of the Greatwood, intending to defend Gaelen and Nelwyn the moment they appeared.

Wellyn had estimated that it would take the first wave of Ri-Aruin's army about fifteen minutes to surround the hill, and then another ten or so to reach them on the hilltop. They had been made aware of the location of the traps on the hillside, and thus could avoid them. Rogond and Galador looked hard at one another. These would be very long minutes, but Gorgon's defeat would be assured once the Wood-elves arrived. Until then, their primary task was to prevent him from escaping.

Everything would be set in motion by signals from the four lookouts stationed one on each side of the hill. They would alert the "council" that the attack was imminent, and everyone would then move into position. Gaelen would leave first so that Gorgon could not accidentally observe the others. She would take her place among the archers and scan the empty horizon, looking out toward the forest, giving him no sign.

Wellyn and Rogond surveyed the scene, turning to regard one another in silence. Finally, Rogond spoke. "Will we be able to hold them off, do you think?"

"I don't know," Wellyn replied, "but if all goes according to design, I believe we will stand a good chance. Our folk will move swiftly once they are summoned, and none will evade them. This creature is outmatched; he cannot possibly escape."

Rogond lowered his dark brows, his eyes narrowing slightly as he thought of Gorgon. "You have not yet encountered him, Wellyn. I will assume nothing impossible until he lies dead before us. But I have faith in your folk. I look forward to the end of this, when our task is completed and Gorgon vanquished. And more than seeing him dead, more than safeguarding the Woodland, more even than avenging my friends, I would see Gaelen set free. It is my deepest desire. I know that must seem odd...."

Wellyn shook his head, his long, dark hair lifting gently in the early morning breeze. "It does not seem at all odd to me, Tuathan. Let us return to the council-chamber. You must aid me in making certain that I more closely resemble my father!" Rogond followed him, reflecting on the fact that the council would begin on the morrow, and after that, when darkness fell, the night would be long indeed.

That evening, the defenders were making their final preparations for the council and the events that would follow. The lookouts were stationed, as they were every night, but they raised no alarm. Everyone on the hilltop knew that many would not survive the conflict to come, and they spent what might be their last night of life in contemplation and fellowship.

Galador sat alone, waiting for Nelwyn, who had promised to join him at moonrise. The moon was only a tiny sliver of light, for tomorrow it would be renewed, and the sky would be dark save for the brilliant stars. Gaelen had sensed a change in the air, most likely a weather front, and had noted with regret that they would see no stars on the night of battle. She would be gazing at them now, as would many of the Elves this night. Hearing a small sound behind him Galador turned to regard not Nelwyn, but one of the Elves of Tal-sithian. She approached Galador, asking to sit beside him for a moment, for she would speak with him.

"Do not be concerned, Galador of Eádros, for you are known to me. I have not revealed myself to you, for I was waiting to see whether you would remember my face." Galador looked hard at her, and indeed saw something familiar in her eyes.

"It does not offend me that you don't remember, for it has been long since we have spoken. Yet, if you search your thoughts, you may recall it."

Galador's brow furrowed in concentration, and then a light appeared in his eyes. "Oriana? Beloved of my friend Galwaith...can it be you, after all these ages?"

She nodded, smiling with pleasure that he had remembered. "It has been long, Elf of Eádros, since you were in the favor of the

King. Much has passed since then. I made my way to the Verdant Mountains and eventually to the Realm of Tal-sithian when Eádros fell and Galwaith was slain. He never did forget you, my friend. He wept for your banishment, and even I could not soothe his heart for a long time."

Galador had not thought of his home in Eádros, or of his friend Galwaith, in untold years. He embraced Oriana, embracing his past as he did so, weeping in grief for his friend who was lost and for the loss of all that he had loved so long ago. She comforted him with her gentle voice and hands, though she wept also at the memories brought back in those moments. At last, she dried her tears.

"Do not weep, Galador, truest of friends. You have made a new, happy life for yourself now, even as I have done. Yet I am glad for this time, on the eve of battle, that I might recall the one whose love we both shared. I shall keep a special watch over you tomorrow, for his sake. But now, your beloved is approaching, and I will take my leave. Know this ere I depart—you were missed and mourned by many. There were those who protested your banishment, and they nearly moved the King to relent, but his heart was hardened, and they did not succeed. I was among them." She embraced him one last time before leaving him. He did not see her again until the battle was joined.

Gaelen spent the night in solitude, for she was filled with anxiety and did not wish to risk betraying this to Gorgon. She had been taken by an oppressive sense of foreboding; somehow, Gorgon would slip from her grasp. She climbed the rim of the hilltop, stood silhouetted against the backdrop of brilliant stars, and sang a song of the Light of Elysia. Every Elf in hearing paused and hearkened to it, for the voices of the Sylvan Elves were among the most beautiful to be heard. Not a few bowed their heads in reverence, as they knew that many would soon be journeying to those Far Shores. Five hundred dark warriors would need to be held off for nearly thirty minutes. The task before the Wood-elves was formidable, but their spirits were united in their resolve. Several raised their voices to join Gaelen's then, and the plateau echoed with ethereal harmony. It was carried on the south wind until it reached the ears of Ri-Aruin's forces, away from Gorgon's army, which was just as well.

29

Fire and Rain

Gorgon grimaced as he endured the pain of the mirror, for he had held it nearly constantly upon this day, the final day before the confrontation that he had come to name the "Night of Reckoning". He was still disquieted, still unable to free himself from the feeling that his army had been anticipated. The Elves seemed tense, somehow, and Gorgon had learned to watch Rogond, for he knew that the Ranger, who was normally quite relaxed and confident, would serve as an excellent indicator. If Rogond appeared uneasy or apprehensive, Gorgon would suspect that something was afoot and would pay very close attention until he learned the nature of it.

He had gone over his own attack plans once more with Kharsh and his three other lieutenants, each of whom would command a phalanx of Gorgon's formidable host. Each would attack from a different direction, surrounding the Elves so that none would escape. Kharsh would take the way from the north, which would be the most difficult, as it encompassed a deep ravine before ascending the very steep hillside to the rim. The others would take the eastern, southern and western faces of the hill, first locating and eliminating all lookouts; there would no doubt be several of those.

Gorgon didn't worry too much about the Elves raising the alarm—after all, they would be occupied in council and were not expecting him. At least, that was what his reason told him. His heart, however, remained in doubt. Best take down the lookouts anyway, just as a precaution. Then his forces would move as quietly as they could toward the summit, unless the Elves engaged them, in which case an all-out attack would begin.

The Elves would no doubt station archers immediately, but there was plenty of cover upon the rocky hillside, and Gorgon had instructed his commanders to make use of it. Gorgon himself would wait until the Elves fell back beyond the rim of the summit, then he would move from behind, working his way through to engage them. Their force would be fairly well decimated by then, and he assumed that his risk would be small. He would make certain that none escaped, and when Ri-Aruin and Magra both were dead, he would claim his tokens. Lord Wrothgar would have His prize.

If his doubts were well founded, if the Elves knew of his presence and were prepared, then Gorgon would retreat. He must not fall this night, for he had not yet achieved his vengeance upon the Elàni. Another chance would come; he would simply have to explain to the Shadowmancer. For a moment he wondered whether death in battle might be preferable, but to die at the hands of the Elves was an ignominious fate that he would never accept. He would proceed for now, but he would remain wary, mindful of all that the mirror would tell him.

The council had begun, and the Elves were presently attending to Nelwyn, who was describing events from the finding of Talrodin to the dividing of the Company. Then Gaelen would tell of her experiences in Cós-domhain. Gorgon listened with prideful fascination as she related the horrors she had witnessed. Rogond spoke of the mysterious deaths in the Verdant Mountains, and Thorndil told of his encounter. But it was the tale of the Elves of Tal-sithian that truly mesmerized Gorgon. Here he learned of his mother, Brinneal, and of Amandir, her beloved. He had not known his mother's name until now, nor the tale of her abduction. The Elves of Tal-sithian sorrowed for Gorgon, and they all pitied him, but they knew he would never be brought to the Light. He was thoroughly evil—a creature of pure, black hatred.

"Whatever grace might have been given him has been subverted by the Black Flame. There is no hope of redeeming him and only one course available to us. We must determine how the creature may be killed, and then see it done. He will not sleep until he has brought us all down one by one," said Oryan.

Gorgon bristled and growled through his pain as the Elves revealed their pity for him. And they were right; he would not sleep until he had brought them down. But no longer would he strike his victims one by one. No, indeed! They would all fall before him tonight. He listened to their plan, which was to adjourn for the day and consider what they had heard, gather for a feast in the early evening and reconvene the council afterward. They would talk far into the night, debating his fate.

The pain grew too great for Gorgon to bear, and his strength was leaving him as he thrust the mirror into its pouch again. No matter. He knew now when the attack would come. He hoped the Elves would feast well and merrily, for it would be their last. He would take rest for a brief while, but then he would need to gather his forces for the final approach, so that they would be ready when the time came.

The weather front that Gaelen had sensed earlier finally arrived just after sundown. The wind had picked up, and they could all smell the rain on the air. The Elves hoped that there would be no truly violent weather this night, as sometimes happened in early summer, for it might cause Gorgon to withdraw until conditions were more favorable. No one wanted this to happen, as they all knew that this deception would never succeed a second time. Gaelen had been wearing a brave face, but those close to her perceived that if not soon made free of Gorgon, she would go mad.

She had attended the feast, sitting beside Rogond, but had partaken of little food or drink. She was weary from the nearly constant contact with Gorgon this day, sitting at the council shivering and trying to keep her teeth from chattering. A little wine might have relaxed her, but the wine-goblets were filled with clear water, for all would need their wits. The overall mood was somber, for all thoughts were upon the dark host that would soon engage them. Then, as they resumed the council, the "debate" began. They wanted to appear preoccupied and distracted, and goad Gorgon into attacking. It had now begun to rain, and the west wind was chilly. Out on the rim, Nelwyn and the archers hunkered down under their cloaks, awaiting the signal from the lookouts.

Gorgon had moved his host into position; a group of over a hundred Ulcas now flanked the hillside from every direction. Kharsh's group had descended into the deep ravine to the north. They were making their way back up when they were spotted by the sharp eyes of Kelin, a hunter-scout of the Greatwood who had been stationed as lookout. She gave a signal—a high-pitched, stuttering cry that sounded much like that of a young nighthawk. This was answered by similar cries from the south and west, as the enemy was seen there as well. One of the lookouts set to watch the eastern flank could not reply; he had been seen by Gorgon and now lay dead with an arrow in his throat.

Kelin and the other surviving lookouts now made their way carefully back up to the rim of the hill to join the archers there. Slowly the enemy host crept toward them; some had passed the first set of fire-pits. The archers were now well aware of them, but would not reveal themselves until the Ulcas had come closer. They waited for Nelwyn, who had been elected to send forth the first arrow.

Gorgon didn't like it. His senses were keen and he was extremely wary. Though the rain had blunted his sense of smell, he thought he detected a faint aroma of pitch. The hillside was strewn and littered with stones and brush, but what was the meaning of that pitch-smell? Gorgon was not familiar with the technique of building fire-pits, but he was highly intelligent and knew that the smell of pitch in this place made little sense. Then the wind rose again from the west, the scent faded, and his path forward was clear again.

He took hold of the mirror. Gaelen was still present at the council, where the debate over how best to deal with him was yet raging. The Elves were at fever pitch in anticipation of battle, and this gave passion to their discourse. Gorgon was convinced that the debate was genuine, and he relaxed his vigilance. Now was the time to engage them; they did not appear to be aware of anything other than their foolish argument. Reassured for the moment, Gorgon and his army continued to close in toward their intended prey.

At the signal from the lookouts, those in the council tent were alerted, and Gaelen left for the rim. It took some time to reach it, as the climb was stony and treacherous, but she soon found herself crouching beside Nelwyn, who was trying to keep her arrows dry. All the archers had lit small fires among the rocks; they would ignite the arrows, but would be hidden from view. Wood-elves are masters at concealing a fire after nightfall.

Gaelen stared resolutely at the dark forest surrounding the hill. Nelwyn noticed that she was literally twitching in expectation of battle. She was armed with her long knives, her short sword and longbow, the smaller bow that she used in hunting, and a very large supply of arrows. She alone would not be required to light one of the fire-pits, as she did not know their locations, but she would be among the first to shed the blood of her enemies. The distant thunder that she had noted earlier was drawing nearer, and the flickering light of the approaching storm would aid the Elves in sighting their enemy. Gaelen was keeping watch for Gorgon, as she wanted to ensure that he had moved close enough that he would not turn back when the battle was joined. She closed her eyes, trying to get a sense of him, hoping, for once, that he would look into the mirror.

In the flickering light of the breaking storm, Gorgon caught sight of one of the archers lying in wait along the rim of the hill. So! Perhaps they had anticipated him after all. Or perhaps this was the only protection they had provided for the council, and he still had little to fear. He wavered in his resolve for a moment as he drew forth the mirror again. Gaelen was still staring out at the stormy sky, and it occurred to him that she had quite possibly been making it a point not to look at the archers arranged all around the hilltop on both sides of her. Was she trying to mislead him, to avoid giving something away? Perhaps it would be better to regroup and attack at a later time, when he was more certain. The council would likely go on for several days. Perhaps a temporary retreat would be better… he smelled a trap!

Abruptly, Gaelen galvanized beside Nelwyn, who looked at her with alarm. Nelwyn knew better than to speak to her cousin, for from the look on her face Gorgon was listening at this moment. Gaelen suddenly rose to her feet, her face betraying an anxiety that was nothing short of panic. He was…he was thinking about turning back! She had to stop him. She drew her bow as Nelwyn gave a cry of dismay that she could not prevent.

Gaelen spoke through clenched teeth. "Turn back now, Dark Horror! I know of your power, and I know you can hear me! We have many warriors in our host, and outnumber you greatly! Turn back, or you will be slain. I shall be the first to place an arrow in your hateful heart! Your Dark Master will be disappointed this night!"

Nelwyn stared at her cousin in horror, wondering whether she truly had gone mad. The last thing she thought Gaelen would have wanted was to see Gorgon turn tail and retreat—the entire purpose of this deception had been to lure him into the conflict! Ri-Aruin's army was awaiting the signal, and this chance would never come again. Had Gaelen lost her senses? Had she gone over to the Darkness at last?

Nelwyn's question was answered as Gaelen loosed her bow, sending an arrow straight to the heart of the Ulca that stood beside Gorgon on the eastern face. Nelwyn grabbed Gaelen's arm. "What have you *done?*" she cried.

Gaelen softened for a moment, and she uttered a phrase in the dwarf-tongue that both she and Nelwyn had been taught by Fima, and which Gorgon would not understand. "Norúk-ahi." *Trust me.*

Gaelen's arrow did not penetrate the excellent armor that had come from the forges of the Shadowmancer, as she had used her small hunting bow, and it lacked the necessary power. Gaelen had known that this would be so, which was why she had not used her longbow. She would give courage to her enemy.

Though he was somewhat dismayed to learn that Gaelen was aware of the power of the mirror, Gorgon's face twisted into a smile. She was trying to frighten him into retreating; she knew her people were outnumbered as well as he, and their pitiful weapons were no match for his well-armored host. Though her fortitude was admirable, her actions would serve only to strengthen his resolve. He instructed the Ulcas that they no longer need worry about killing her; she had served her purpose and would be of no further use to him. Nelwyn gave another cry as he roared in challenge, then signaled his forces to charge, dropping low to the ground with their shields before them.

"Send forth your arrows! Light the fires! They are attacking!" Gaelen yelled in a voice Nelwyn did not recognize.

Nelwyn set her arrow aflame, and then sent it into the pit below. The rain had not aided them there; the wet brush would catch slowly, though the pitch was already smoldering into life. The other archers followed suit, and in a few seconds the pits were ignited, though they burned reluctantly, sending up more smoke than flame. The Elves would get little aid from the firelight, and more importantly, the lighting of the pits was to be the signal to Ri-Aruin's army to surround the hill; they would never see it unless the fires burned brightly. Now the challenge was to bring down as many foes as possible before falling back behind the rim. The archers sent volley after volley, taking many of the enemy, but the Ulcas made use of the terrain, evading the Elves' arrows. They were armed with powerful crossbows, and several of the Elven archers fell back, dead or badly wounded.

Though Gorgon was somewhat dismayed to find that at least some of the Elves' arrows would indeed penetrate the Ulcas' armor, he did not waver. If Gaelen had thought to turn him about so easily, she would be disappointed. The Ulcas moved ever closer, and the beleaguered archers now collectively retreated behind the rim of the hill. The Ulcas gave a lusty yell and charged after them. At least a dozen of the archers had been taken, and Gorgon reckoned that his folk would face fewer than one hundred foes on the plateau; in fact, there were about eighty. The attacking force had suffered greater loss in the ascent; in addition to the archers, the rock-slide traps had taken more than a few. But they still numbered nearly four hundred, and the defending force was thus outnumbered five to one. As they approached the rim, Galador winded his horn, sending the warning to the Elves on the plateau, who braced themselves for the assault.

As soon as they crested the rim the Ulcas found themselves amid a storm of arrows. The Black Command surged forward, hoping to overwhelm by sheer numbers, and swords were drawn. But the Elves were well positioned, and ready for them. The Ulcas had not anticipated the skill of their opponents, or the recklessness of Amandir. None who came near him survived his blade for more than a few seconds. He looked around wildly, hoping to see Gorgon among his enemies, but he could not.

Gorgon was overseeing the attack from the rim of the hill, surrounded by a guard made up of his original force of thirty, now reduced to nineteen. Kharsh stood with him. Gorgon was reasonably satisfied; his forces would soon overpower the Elves, and he wondered whether they now doubted the wisdom of holding the council. He had to admit that this hill was defensible, as the intricacy of the rugged terrain made attacking in large groups difficult. The Elves were skilled and had not been taken completely unaware, but they were still outnumbered. Gorgon looked down upon the fray with satisfaction. Things were not going well for them, no indeed! This would take less effort than he had at first predicted.

Without Ri-Aruin, the defenders would surely be overcome. The rain had not been their friend; it threatened to be their undoing, as the signal to Ri-Aruin's forces could barely be seen. Galador had winded his beautiful horn again and again even as he fought, but the sound would be scattered by the pouring rain, and would no longer serve to alert and summon the King.

Rogond and Fima stood together, back to back, as they engaged the enemy with sword and axe. Rogond had cast his spear into the heart of one of the attackers, and there it remained, for he had yet to retrieve it.

One of Gorgon's three lieutenants, large and fierce, leaped upon Rogond, who was hard put to defend himself. The Great Ulca wielded a heavy blade, and he struck a glancing blow to the side of Rogond's head, hard enough that he was knocked to the ground, momentarily dazed.

Fima turned and buried his axe in the Ulca's belly with a terrible cry, and as he withdrew it, he caught a blur of motion behind him. He turned and swung his axe with deadly force at his perceived attacker, only to miss Gaelen by a hair's breadth as she leaped back, breathless.

"Ooh! Sorry!" he exclaimed, as she knelt beside Rogond.

He shook his head, and his eyes focused on her. "I'm all right," he said thickly.

"Relieved to hear it, but we have another problem," said Gaelen as she pulled her head back just in time to avoid a shaft that passed close enough to ruffle her hair. "The rain has soaked our brush piles, and they are not burning as brightly as needed. If we cannot raise the signal to Ri-Aruin, all is lost!"

Fima and Rogond looked at each other. "If he's not already on his way here, I fear we are doomed," said Fima. "But don't fear, little Wood-elf, you shall have your signal. Rogond, do you still have the gift I gave you in Mountain-home?"

Rogond brightened with sudden understanding. "I do indeed. It is still in my pack, in the council-tent."

"Then let's make haste," said Fima, and the three of them made their way there with all speed. Rogond entered as Gaelen and Fima remained outside to defend him. He emerged moments later, his light pack slung over his shoulder, carrying the phial of maglos in his hand.

"Remember, now, keep it from the rain until you are prepared," Fima admonished him. "Where will you ignite it?"

Rogond looked around as Gaelen sent two more arrows into an Ulca that was running toward them, waving its blade and yelling some incoherent battle-cry. It fell instantly. Rogond pointed to the northern edge of the rim, which would be highly visible to Ri-Aruin's army.

Fima frowned and shook his head. "Let's get as much use from this as possible, my friend. Set it off right in the middle of the plateau. I'll wager these Ulcas have never seen anything like it, and will fall back before it. Don't fear—Ri-Aruin will see it! Use only about half for this, I think."

Rogond took the maglos from the phial, leaving only about a third of it behind. He considered his course of action for a moment. Then, with Gaelen and Fima defending him, he made his way close enough to the large crowd of Ulcas battling in the center of the plateau that he could toss the very large and lethal chunk of maglos onto the wet ground at their feet. He yelled to the defenders to retreat, running as fast as he could away from the group of startled Ulcas.

For a moment, nothing happened. Then, the water worked through the thin film of oil that covered the soft, white metal, and the very ground seemed to explode with light. The Ulcas standing nearest were literally set aflame. The others ran shrieking, except for those that were unfortunate enough to turn and stare at the light when it first flared into brilliance. They wandered blind, heads bursting with pain and eyes streaming. They soon fell, pierced by the arrows of the Elves.

Had Gaelen known it, Ri-Aruin's forces were even now surrounding the hill. They had divided into two groups, one of about two hundred that would storm the hill and assist the defenders, and another much larger group that would surround the entire perimeter, cutting off any chance of escape. They had arrived in their encampment the night before and had remained silent and secret, as only Wood-elves at home in the Greatwood can be, awaiting the signal to attack. Ri-Aruin had used Thorndil's glass, the gift of Arialde, and it had proved invaluable in spotting the weak light of the smoldering signal-fires. As he drew near to the hill, Ri-Aruin hoped that the small attack force he was fielding would be able to get to the defenders quickly; the larger force would require time to surround the enemy and close all gaps such that none would escape.

When the maglos was ignited, Ri-Aruin and his folk were amazed, for they had not known of it. Surely, this was yet another signal from their folk that the battle was underway. The King hoped that it was no dark device or devilry, as he rushed now to the aid of his eldest son.

Unfortunately for the Ulcas, this weapon was not of their making, nor had they ever seen the like of it. They reeled back in pain and confusion, blinded by the incredible brilliance of the light, several still bellowing from the burns they had received from being too close. Gorgon had also looked at the light, but only for a moment. It was enough to sear his senses with pain and cast his black heart into a pit of fear. He had not expected this! He could see nothing for a few moments, then only points of light and spots of color and darkness, before his vision finally returned. By then, the flaring maglos had died down, but where it had been there was a blackened crater in the rocky, wet ground that no one would go near. He saw the flaming Ulcas, and the blinded ones falling to the arrows of the Elves, and he was afraid, for he had no force to answer this weapon.

The balance had shifted. At first the Ulcas had greatly outnumbered the Elves, who fought well and with valor but were slowly being overcome. Only about thirty of the defenders still fought; the rest had been wounded or slain. Nearly two hundred Ulcas had remained until the lighting of the maglos, but now the dark host was reduced by nearly one quarter, and Gorgon despaired as he knew that his chief hope of victory lay in superior numbers, for the Elves held the superior skill.

But then, Kharsh appeared at Gorgon's side, and his ancient yellow eyes were filled with dread. "We have spotted a force of Elves making their way up the hill, my lord, and they are dressed for battle. They will be here in a few moments. I fear it may be time to consider retreating, before they can cut off our escape."

Gorgon took Kharsh by the neck and shook him. "We cannot retreat without our prize! You know it. Now, get to work! I will go for Magra. You and your band take the King. Then, when they are dead, we shall withdraw."

Amandir stood near the northern slope, surrounded by defenders. The wind blew his long, wet hair back from his helmeted face, revealing the fury and frustration in his eyes. He had lived the last years of his life in the hope of accomplishing a single purpose, yet he had been denied. When he finally caught sight of Gorgon standing with his guard on the eastern rim of the hill, he began to work his way toward him, but the Ulcas were too many, and they drove him back. Now the Elves dwindled; if Ri-Aruin did not appear in the next few minutes Gorgon would prevail. Amandir knew that, whatever else befell, he would not leave the field of battle until Gorgon was dead. He had saved enough of his strength for that.

He had taken a small but painful wound to his right shoulder; it burned incessantly as he swung his blade. He caught sight of Gaelen, now wielding her short sword, slashing and ducking as she faced one of the armored Ulcas. The Ulca fell dead with an arrow in its eye, sent from Nelwyn's bow, just as Gaelen's short sword dealt another fatal blow beneath the left arm. Gaelen had spent her arrows and had not had time to glean more. One of her long knives was buried in the throat of an Ulca that now lay under several of its fellows, but she still had the other. She looked around, despairing at the number of remaining defenders and enemies, and then briefly made eye contact with Amandir. They held their gaze for only a few seconds, but much passed between them.

You must bring him down. No matter what else happens, we must work together to bring him down.

I will see it done. Look to the defense of your friends. I misjudged you—I regret that I did not know you on a happier time.

Amandir returned to the business of working his way toward Gorgon, as Gaelen then ran to Rogond and Fima. She did not take notice of him again until several minutes later, after the maglos had done its work, when Gorgon finally decided that the Lord Magra would soon breathe his last.

It was Gorgon's plan to kill Magra and Ri-Aruin, then take his tokens and retreat, leaving the remainder of his army to face the attacking Wood-elves. He must not fail Wrothgar, and he would not. Amandir felt the presence of Gorgon as he worked his way near to where he stood with his few comrades, and as the Elf turned to gaze into the eyes of his mighty foe at last, he knew that the time had come.

Galador, Nelwyn, and Thorndil stood together, a formidable force against the enemy. Once drawn, none evaded Nelwyn's bow, and if the Ulcas drew close enough to Galador or Thorndil they would be cut down by keen blades, wielded with skill that was far beyond them. Yet now all three were weary, and Thorndil's blade was notched and growing dull with the constant engagement of his armored foes.

Wellyn battled nearby under the banner of the Greatwood, wearing the crown, robes, and armor of Ri-Aruin. Kharsh made for him, taking two of his most skilled archers, and as they drew closer, they attacked. Two of Wellyn's defenders were taken as he looked around in alarm. Then one of the dark archers shot a second time, and Wellyn fell. Nelwyn and Gaelen both beheld him as he was thrown back to hit the wet ground hard, a black shaft protruding from the breastplate of Ri-Aruin's armor. The curved, dark bows of the Ulcas held great power at close range, and the Wood-elves preferred lightweight armor or none at all, for it allowed them to remain swift and agile.

Gaelen and Nelwyn were both at his side in a matter of moments, along with Galador and Thorndil. They dragged Wellyn into the council-tent. He was still aware, but the impact had taken much of his strength. Galador struggled to remove the armor; Wellyn gave a strangled cry of agony as the breastplate came away, for the shaft came with it.

Kharsh was still under orders to return with the head of "Ri-Aruin", and he now stormed the council-tent with a considerable force behind him. Galador threw the large council-table over, using it to shield Wellyn, Nelwyn, and himself. Thorndil followed his example, crouching with Gaelen behind one of the smaller tables.

The Ulcas found the task of storming the tent more difficult than they had expected. Still, there was little the Company could do against such numbers, and they all realized that their lives would end here. Gaelen had thrown her second dagger, felling her foe, but she had no arrows, and the Ulcas were too many to engage with a blade. Nelwyn sent forth her last shaft, as did Galador, and their enemies closed in around them.

Wellyn turned toward Nelwyn, grimacing as he drew the shaft of the black arrow from the breastplate of his father's armor. He was pale, and his strength was doubtful, but his eyes were clear as he handed it to her. He would heal if tended to, but it would not matter, for Kharsh and his company would be certain to kill them all in a few moments. Wellyn handed the arrow to Nelwyn.

"Send it back to them. Send it from me," he whispered, and closed his eyes.

Gaelen did not know the extent of Wellyn's hurt, and she despaired, for they had been fast friends for nearly all of his life and for much of hers. She knew that she could escape the tent by simply rolling beneath the silken wall, but she could not leave her friends. She would not be able to aid in bringing down Gorgon; she would have to rely on Amandir, Rogond, and Fima. She smiled for a brief moment as she prepared to make her stand, for she had noticed that she could now be at least partly aware of Gorgon's mood whether he held the mirror or not, and she was now sensing his desperation.

She turned to Thorndil. "I will not fall like a cornered animal, Aridan. Will you stand with me?"

Thorndil looked into her bright eyes and nodded. Gaelen gave a cry and charged from her concealment with Thorndil beside her. They rallied around Wellyn, defending him to the last, Nelwyn releasing the black arrow still stained with his blood. Then, as all seemed hopeless, the Ulcas began to fall forward, taken by the sword of Rogond, the axe of Fima, and the bow of Oriana of Eádros.

Oriana had observed the wounding of Wellyn from her place among the rocks, fighting alongside the Elves of Tal-sithian, who had rallied to Oryan. She saw Galador and Nelwyn drag Wellyn into the tent, along with Thorndil and Gaelen, pursued by an impossibly large host of Ulcas led by Kharsh. She knew they would never survive without help, and she despaired, for her comrades were otherwise engaged and could not aid the Company. Then she heard the voice of Rogond through the melee:

"Gaelen! Gaelen! To me! *To me!*"

Oriana knew then that Rogond and Fima would serve, and she left her place of relative safety, making for the Aridan and the dwarf. Fima was holding up admirably for one of his age, considering he had spent the last fifty years in Mountain-home and had seen little of battle. He was hard as iron, but he was growing weary. Rogond was near panic, for he could not see Gaelen and feared that she had fallen.

Oriana ran up to them, breathless. "I know where your Gaelen is, and she is in dire need, as is your friend Galador. Follow me, and bring all the skills you have!"

As they drew nigh the tent, Rogond and Fima looked with dismay upon the large crowd of Ulcas besieging it. They prayed that their friends were not yet slain as they charged forward.

Amandir stood at last before Gorgon, alone upon the rim of the hill. He had led the creature away from the battle, for he knew that Gorgon sought to kill him, in the belief that he was Lord Magra of Mountain-home. His companions had remained behind at his order—this was between Gorgon and himself. Gorgon knew that Magra was a mighty foe. Wrothgar had warned him of it, yet he had seen little evidence of power beyond that of a skilled Elven warrior. That, he could deal with. He faced Amandir with confidence, for he was yet strong, and he perceived that his foe, having spent much of his strength already in the conflict, was flagging and would fall quickly.

"So, the Mighty Lord Magra stands before me, preparing his defense. I had expected more from you, Èolo. Yet it has been so with all your folk that have fallen before me. Only too easy," he taunted. "Prepare yourself, for I will have your head as tribute to the Dark Power. You are vanquished. Why not make your passing easier?"

Amandir then removed the helmet he had been wearing, fully revealing his face to his enemy. I have been prepared, misbegotten monstrosity, since the loss of my beloved gave life to your ill-conceived existence. For I am the one whose heart was bound to Brinneal, your mother."

The storm had risen to its full power, and the rain ran down Gorgon's dark armor in gleaming rivulets. He winced as a bright fork of lightning stung his sensitive eyes, then glared down at Amandir, snarling.

"You are not Magra?"

"Most assuredly not. I am Amandir, the one who will end your miserable life this night. You have been deceived."

Gorgon froze, his confidence draining from him. Though he had been somewhat suspicious of a trap, he had genuinely believed that Magra and Ri-Aruin were present. Now he was momentarily stunned by the news that he had been taken in completely and that Wrothgar would not receive his expected prize. Gorgon then knew that he was probably doomed, despite the outcome of the conflict.

Amandir took advantage of his stunned confusion to launch his attack. Gorgon was hard put to defend himself from the fury that had welled in Amandir, and the lightning flashed in their clashing blades as they slashed at each other with all their skill. Amandir moved with impressive speed, like a deadly dancer. Even one such as Gorgon would have difficulty so long as Amandir's strength held. They battled long upon the rocky pinnacle of the rim, each trying desperately to overcome the other.

Then the two combatants broke apart, panting and glaring, for a few precious seconds. But as they prepared to engage again, Gorgon reached up with his left hand and removed his black helmet, releasing the silken flood of his golden hair, the gift of his mother, and Amandir's grim, silent face broke into a cry of despair.

The assault on the council-tent had been going well for Kharsh until now. Rogond, Fima, and Oriana had charged in from behind, felling the Ulcas as they turned in dismay. They now perceived that they were surrounded by Elves, men, and dwarves, and fought as only trapped Ulcas can. Kharsh remembered his purpose—to retrieve the head of Ri-Aruin, but as he drew closer to Wellyn, he realized that the Elf before him was not the Elven-king. With Ri-Aruin's armor removed, it was apparent that Wellyn was too young and too slight of build. Kharsh could imagine the reaction of his commander to the news that the Elves had deceived him. Cursing, he dove under the loose silk of the tent wall and was gone. Gaelen caught sight of this and cried in dismay:

"He stands at Gorgon's right hand! We must not let him escape!" Yet her cry was in vain, for none could leave the battle to pursue him.

Fima and Oriana had fallen; Rogond, Galador, Thorndil, Gaelen and Nelwyn stood now at bay. The Ulcas had recovered their wits and had rallied against them, and it looked as though the Company would meet with a grim fate, when at last the folk of the Greatwood Realm arrived, blowing their horns and filling their enemies with dread. Many of the Ulcas fled, others fell, and when the conflict in the council-tent finally ended no living enemy remained. Yet there was much of sorrow and grief to the Company.

Galador knelt beside the body of Oriana, who had been cloven from behind even as she sent forth her last arrow. He closed her now-sightless eyes and bowed his head in silent grief for this fair child of Eádros, as Nelwyn stood by, for she did not understand what had occurred.

Rogond was attending to Fima, who had taken a deadly blow that had literally crushed his iron-banded helm. Gaelen anxiously awaited news from the Ranger, who looked up at her in sorrow, shaking his head, and Gaelen knew that the old lore-master would be lost to them. Tears of rage and grief started in her eyes—this was not yet finished! She ran forward, grabbed Fima's axe, which lay where he had dropped it, and ran from the tent as Rogond called after her.

She caught sight of her quarry immediately. Through the clashing swords and whistling arrows of Ulcas and Elves, she made her way toward the rim of the hill, where Amandir and Gorgon were even now engaged in deadly conflict, their hearts full of vengeful hatred. Gorgon had removed his helmet; his long, golden hair was clearly visible, even through the wind and rain. She made her way toward him with all speed, though it was difficult, as the battle still raged around her.

Amandir had been momentarily unmanned at the sight of Gorgon's beautiful hair. He was overcome with grief in that moment for Brinneal, for he knew then that Gorgon truly had taken a part of her, that he was not begotten only of evil. Gorgon perceived that his opponent was weakened, and pressed him hard with both the long sword of Gelmyr, borne in his right hand, and Turantil, borne in his left. Amandir then came to himself, answering with his two curved blades. They were much like Turantil, but slightly longer and heavier, and were worthy weapons.

Amandir fought beyond his strength, for he knew he would not survive this day, whereas Gorgon still held hope of it. He put forth all the power he could summon, and he wounded Gorgon thrice, but in the end his strength flagged, and he fell.

Gorgon disarmed Amandir quickly with a sweeping stroke that knocked the one blade from his hand, and placed his foot upon Amandir's other hand. Then Gorgon placed his other foot upon the neck of the struggling Elf, who knew in that moment that his time had come…and he had failed. Gorgon had no time to toy with his opponent, and he simply crushed the life from him, pausing long enough to snarl down at Amandir as the light faded from his eyes.

Gaelen reached Amandir within moments, but she had come too late to aid him. She gazed into the depths of his unfocused but still-bright eyes, trying to contact him as his spirit fled his body. She took his hands in her own; they were warm and strong. Her spirit called to him, and he answered.

I have failed. All of my purpose has been denied. He must not prevail. You must help me, Elf of the Greatwood, for in you there is the power to defeat him. You must see this done, or perish yourself. You know it! Farewell.

Gaelen wept for him even as she rose to pursue her enemy, though she need not have cried for Amandir, for his spirit was free at last, and Brinneal awaited him.

Gorgon had fled over the rim of the hill to the north. He was going to take the treacherous path through the ravine in hope of escaping the Elves, who even now might be in pursuit. Gaelen had leaped after him, and she would make great speed in this terrain, for she was agile and swift, and her heart burned in her breast. She knew that Amandir was right—she would surely perish if she was not free of Gorgon, and this knowledge gave wings to her pursuit.

As Gorgon made his way with all speed down toward the ravine, he heard a familiar, unpleasant voice inside his mind. He could not see Gelmyr, but the words of his long-vanquished foe could not be ignored.

It's no use trying to run. She is swifter than you are, and she is gaining ground. You may as well turn and fight, though if she does not defeat you, her folk surely will, for they follow her in great numbers. You are undone, O Half-elven Horror.

He laughed in an ill-natured manner. *They deceived you so easily, and the She-elf was behind it all. You certainly underestimated her resolve and fortitude, didn't you? They all had a hand in it, and you fell right into line. Things might have been worth saving had you not gone to Wrothgar, but now you must face Him even if you manage to evade the vengeance of the Elves, which I think unlikely. Ha! Your hour has come at last!*

This time Gorgon would not even reply to Gelmyr, but turned and looked back over his shoulder, trying to catch sight of Gaelen in pursuit.

You may as well stand and fight, O Gullible Calamity, said Gelmyr. *You cannot evade her—she will track you like a hound, and never relent. Stand and fight! At least when the folk of Ri-Aruin overtake you, they will remember your ferocity.* For once, thought Gorgon, the Elf made some sense. He braced himself for the coming conflict, awaiting the arrival of Gaelen. She, at least, would not escape him.

Rogond knelt beside Fima, despairing as he removed what remained of the dwarf's helmet, certain that he would find naught but ruin beneath it. To his surprise, though there was obviously some damage, all was not as he had thought. He was delighted as Fima stirred, moaned, and opened his eyes, which, though dazed and unfocused, were reasonably clear. "How could you have survived such a blow?" Rogond muttered in wonderment. "Any man or Elf would have been crushed to pulp."

Fima apparently heard him, for he stirred again and, to the amazement of Rogond, spoke in a halting, shaky voice: "As I am ever-proud to state, Rogond, I am neither man nor Elf. It takes a mightier blow to lay low the Children of Fior." With those words, he closed his eyes and spoke no more until the conflict had ended.

Rogond patted Fima's shoulder affectionately, then left him in the Wood-elves' care and ran to aid his beloved, who even now approached the powerful, savage enemy that was lying in wait for her.

He spotted the body of Amandir lying alone and forlorn upon the northern rim. The truth became known when he approached and looked upon Amandir closely, observing the manner of his death. There was only one being here large enough to crush the life from Amandir in this manner. Gorgon's tracks led away from the body, down toward the ravine. Gaelen's tracks were present as well, and Rogond knew what he had to do. He whistled and called for Eros, and the great horse came to his aid. Rogond led Eros down the hillside toward the ravine, following the tracks of Gorgon and Gaelen, hoping that he would not be too late. She would never prevail alone.

The storm was beginning to abate, but the rocky landscape still lit up with bright blue-white flashes of lightning, and the hillside still echoed with thunder. Gaelen slid precipitously on the wet stones as the rain still fell around her. She tracked her enemy now for what she hoped would be the last time. Every now and then she caught a brief sight of him, and she knew that the gap was closing, but suddenly the sign seemed to evaporate before her, and she lost the trail. She gave a cry of frustration, searching frantically for any evidence of his passing, and found none.

"No!" she cried, "I will *not* lose you now!"

That you most certainly will not, thought Gorgon, as he crouched upon the ledge above her, preparing to leap down and send her to her doom.

Once the army of the Greatwood had arrived, Gorgon's forces had been quickly overwhelmed. Standing tall upon the plateau, King Ri-Aruin surveyed the scene before him. There were very few of the enemy remaining; most had fled over the rim of the hill when he and his forces had arrived, and those that still fought would be dispatched quickly. He moved to the council-tent, where many of the wounded had been taken, and was met by Nelwyn, who gave him the news that his son had been injured. Ri-Aruin then rushed to the aid of Wellyn, who brightened when he beheld his father, though the King despaired at the pale, pain-weary face of his son.

"What of Gorgon?" asked Wellyn. "Has he fallen before you? We must make certain that he is dead—I fear Gaelen has gone to engage him. You must find her and aid her!" He was so anxious that they all feared he would expend what little strength remained to him.

Ri-Aruin reassured him. "It shall be so; do not fear. I will send our warriors immediately to locate her. Now you must rest and heal yourself." He examined the wound, his face grim but not grave. "This will mend. You have brought pride to our people and to me, my son. Rest well and with honor. I will inform you when Gaelen is found and when the creature lies dead. Rest, now."

Wellyn did so, for he trusted his father. As he turned from his son, Ri-Aruin hoped that his people would in fact be able to aid Gaelen and ensure the death of Gorgon, for he would never betray such an important trust. He went forth to do all he was able to make it so.

Nelwyn and Galador tended to Oriana's body, carrying it from the mud and filth of the battle to place it reverently among the rest of the dead. Thorndil did not offer to aid them, for he knew this was a private matter, and he despaired as he surveyed the vast number of dead that lay now in this place. Of the original defense force of nearly a hundred Elves, fewer than twenty remained alive and with no serious hurt. Sixty-two had died. The toll on the enemy host had been greater. They had already counted several hundred bodies, and there were many more to be included. But Gorgon's was not among them, and Thorndil hoped that he had not escaped. They would never lure him again, and he was far too dangerous an enemy to remain alive any longer.

Thorndil looked around for Rogond, but did not find him, nor could he find Gaelen. Fima had been especially anxious and concerned for her. Thorndil smiled as he thought of the old dwarf, who had proved such a worthy warrior. All were relieved that he would live. But the absence of his two friends disturbed him, for he suspected they were now after Gorgon, and the success or failure of that confrontation would determine whether this Night of Reckoning had passed, or whether it had merely been delayed.

Gaelen was terribly distressed, as she could find no sign of Gorgon's trail. He could not evade her, not now! She took hold of herself, concentrating on sensing him. She closed her eyes, even as Gorgon crouched silently on the ledge above her, preparing to leap down and take her life. She perceived a faint but definite feeling—it was the same feeling that filled her when she stalked game and knew that her prey would be taken. It was a sort of impending triumph, knowing that a goal would be realized. In the case of the hunt, the goal was to bring meat to the tables of the Greatwood Elves. In this case, though....

Gaelen came alive and drew her short sword just as Gorgon sprang upon her. She leaped from under his taut, powerful body just in time, as he roared in frustration at having missed her. She yelled back at him in a voice charged with ferocity.

"Dark Horror! You cannot evade our vengeance! I have had all of you that I intend to bear, and your hour is NOW!" She flew at him, remembering Amandir's plea that he not escape his doom.

They fought for several minutes, each barely managing to thwart the other, Gorgon slashing at Gaelen with powerful strokes while she darted in and out, feinting and ducking. She was a superb in-fighter, and Gorgon soon grew weary of evading her; it was like trying to swat a very annoying and potentially lethal fly. He backed off for a moment, refocusing and collecting himself, allowing Gaelen a much-needed rest. She still grasped Fima's axe in her left hand, and Gorgon recognized it. He smiled his normal, malicious smile.

"The dwarf is dead, isn't he? Otherwise you would not have his axe. I noticed you practicing with it; you have acquired some skill considering who and what you are. I thought about killing him in Cós-domhain, and I could easily have done so, but I was satiated. The Aridan provided plenty of sport, though he whimpered at the end like a child."

Gaelen knew that Gorgon was trying to goad her into attacking before she was rested, and she smiled back at him. "I know the truth of Belegund and his valor, you pathetic creature! I loved Fima as a cherished friend, but I will not allow myself to grieve for him until you are dead. You think I am so easily gulled into attacking before

I am ready. Why, you must think me as easily deceived as yourself! Which," she added, noting the dark look on his face, "I am not."

She might not have chosen those words had she the time to consider the likely consequence of them. Gorgon would not stand to be insulted by one such as Gaelen! The fact that her words were true, that he *had* been deceived, angered him all the more.

"Ready or not, your doom is at hand. Pathetic, am I? Tell me, Gaelen, do you still dream of Ri-Elathan? Was his death at the hands of the Black Flame difficult for you to bear? Is that why you weep when you are alone? Not so handsome at the end, I'll warrant. He went up like a torch... did you know it? He screamed even as his skin blackened and his throat filled with fire. Dream of that, if you will!"

The sound of her own name issuing from Gorgon's lips in his hateful voice was loathsome enough to Gaelen, but at the mention of Ri-Elathan she could keep still no longer. She gripped Fima's axe and her own blade tightly, knowing that despite her resolve, she would never prevail against this terrible foe, not if she faced him alone.

As Gaelen prepared for a final stand against her enemy, Rogond urged Eros down the precarious descent into the dark ravine. Every so often a flash of lightning would illuminate the path before him, and he almost wished that it had not, for it might have been better for his nerves if he had not seen the nearly impossible difficulty of it. He would trust to Eros who, true to his name, flowed like water over the most treacherous terrain. Rogond's worthy mount had never failed him, yet they came to a place in the path where Eros simply would not move forward. Rogond urged him, but the powerful horse shifted anxiously, unwilling to proceed.

The next flash of lightning revealed the cause; a small tree had come uprooted above them and taken part of the path into the valley, bringing a number of large boulders with it. These now blocked the path, looming nearly five feet in height. The width of the pile was unknown.

Rogond could not dismount from Eros to inspect it, as the path was too narrow. There was a precipitous drop on the right, and a sheer face covered with loose gravel on the left. They could not go around. It was too loose and unsteady for Rogond to climb on his own. Besides, if he abandoned Eros he would never make it to the ravine floor in time to aid Gaelen. He faced a difficult choice: he could carefully turn Eros about and find another way down, which would take considerable time, or he could leap the obstacle and pray that there was a reasonable place to land on the other side. The ring of clashing blades in the valley below decided him. He leaned forward and spoke to Eros.

"My friend, always have you borne me safely, though the way is treacherous. I ask you now to trust in me, for we must surmount this hurdle, though neither of us would deem it wise."

Eros shook his head from side to side, his long mane and forelock sodden with rain. He backed obediently and carefully up the path until he stood far enough from the obstacle that he could gain speed in approaching it. Rogond reassured him, patting Eros' neck, though he knew what he asked.

"Please, Eros, Gaelen is in need and we have no time. Fly now, fly for her!"

Eros shot forward, his powerful hindquarters engaging as he flew down toward the looming pile of boulders. Rogond urged him, yelling a battle cry; in truth he was trying to maintain his own courage. Eros checked back only once at the last, but he trusted Rogond, and taking one more powerful stride, he launched his golden body into the air with a grunt of effort, leaping into the dark and the rain. Rogond clung hard to Eros' wet, black mane, trying not to unbalance him, but as they cleared the crest of the stone-pile his heart sank, for the path before them no longer existed for perhaps twenty feet. He knew that Eros would never be able to make such a distance, and that the fall into the ravine would probably kill them both.

"Oh, Eros…sorry…" was all that he had the time to say.

Below, in the dark deeps of the ravine, Gaelen heard Rogond's battle cry as she strove against her mighty foe. Gorgon heard Gelmyr's laughter echoing inside his mind as he swung at her. She was proving more difficult than he had anticipated, and the last thing he needed was that dead Elf distracting him.

Isn't Wrothgar going to be pleased when He finds out that His forces have been obliterated, and you just walked right into the trap! Perhaps you can take

Amandir's head and pass it off as Magra's! Ha! And now, you are having trouble with the lowly Gaelen of Greatwood. You cannot even kill a Wood-elf! Did you hear that cry? It sounded like the Tuathan. You could not kill either of them the last time...and now you shall have another chance at the same failure. So happy to remind you of it. Good hunting, Elfhunter. Ha!

Gorgon broke apart from Gaelen for another few moments, as each took stock of the other. Gaelen's left sleeve was red with blood, and she was shaky and weak. She had managed to inflict a deep wound under Gorgon's left arm, as she had done before, but his armor had served him well, and he was still in fair fighting form. Gorgon's eyes narrowed, and his mouth quirked in a slight smile. It would not be long now before the mirror would be useless. How had the She-elf discovered it? He supposed he would never know, for she rose to her feet with difficulty, and he noted that Fima's heavy axe shook in her hand.

Gaelen hoped that Rogond would arrive soon, as she had very little strength remaining. She felt a surge of pride as she looked upon Gorgon; she had done well to weaken him to this point, and Rogond might well be able to finish him now. The evil creature looked a bit vague and distracted, as though hearing things that weren't there. Gaelen, of course, could not hear the voice of Gelmyr tormenting him. But that did not make it any less real to Gorgon, who grimaced slightly and shook his head, as though trying to banish the scornful laughter that still rang in his ears and haunted his thoughts.

Gaelen took a deep breath, grimacing as her chest expanded, for her ribs were badly bruised. She had only to keep him here long enough for Rogond to arrive. *Hurry, my friend Thaylon, if you would make my death have meaning*, she thought, unaware that Rogond had taken a terrible risk to aid her, and was now facing death himself.

Rogond clung tightly to Eros' black mane as they flew over the huge pile of boulders toward a landing that wasn't there. The horse would surely panic and try to make the landing, but even if he could extend his front feet far enough, the rest would fall, and he would cartwheel backward on top of his rider. Rogond wanted to close his eyes then, but he did not, as he still held some faith in his mount and needed to be aware so that he might aid Eros as far as he could.

Eros and Rogond were, in fact, very much alike. They shared a practical nature, a tendency to view a situation rationally and not panic. This quality was indispensable in battle, or in such situations as the one they now faced. Eros knew that he could not successfully reach the remnant of the path, and he decided to make the most of it. He saw more clearly in the dark than did Rogond. The ravine was not vertical, there was some slope to it, but it was loose and rocky. It would be nearly impossible to negotiate at any speed, but Eros had no choice. As he hurtled down toward the ravine floor, he dropped his hindquarters toward the steep, rocky slope, causing Rogond to grab his neck. He looked like an eagle about to land.

Hang on, tall man, thought Eros as his hind feet hit the slope, catapulting him forward and slamming his forefeet into the ground. Rogond was flipped handily over his head, still clinging to the horse's neck. It took everything they had to stay upright, but if they did not do so, they would meet with a very unpleasant end.

Eros squealed with effort as he put all his strength into bracing his mighty hindquarters while trying to remain balanced with his forelegs. The rocks and loose gravel tore the skin from his hind legs as Rogond clung to him, hanging before Eros' chest, his legs thrown back beneath the horse's belly. Eros sat down on his hindquarters, sliding uncontrollably for a few seconds, and then launched himself down the slope, his flinty hooves striking sparks in the darkness, trying to keep from going end-over-end.

Rogond's feet hit the gravel, and he swung onto Eros' back, trying to help him keep his balance. It was a frantic, reckless nightmare of a descent, but Eros managed somehow to avoid the large stones, pounding down the gravelly, nearly vertical surface, lunging and catching himself just in time as Rogond struggled to stay aboard. Then the slope gentled, the great horse slowed, and it was over.

Eros stood, panting and trembling, sweat running from his flanks. He had injured both of his back legs in the descent; they were raw and bleeding, and would be forever scarred. His left foreleg had taken a bad strain and would bear no weight; Eros would go no farther. Rogond wept as he patted his friend, but he had no time to tend him. Gaelen fought with a monster in this darkness, and he needed to ensure that the sacrifice of her brave, able mount had not been in vain. Taking his weapons, he ran toward the west, where once again the sound of clashing blades could be heard, yet they were slower than before.

Gorgon towered over Gaelen, who prepared herself for the killing blow that would surely come as she lay now before him. Her strength was spent, and Gorgon knew it. Yet he hesitated, though his hatred for her still burned. He needed to ask something of her, and to her surprise he sank to his knees beside her, though he kept enough distance that she could not strike at him.

"How did you learn of my mirror, Elf of Greatwood? Tell me, and I will take away your pain."

Gaelen grimaced and drew herself up slowly from the ground, now kneeling with her right arm holding her bruised ribs, and looked at him in wonderment. He actually expected her to engage in conversation now, upon the hour of her death? Yet she answered him, for by doing so she gained time for Rogond to reach them.

"Many had a hand in the knowledge. You underestimated the skills of your enemies. There are so many things in this world that you will never know, in your dark solitude. I have no time now to explain them, for my strength wanes and I shall soon go to my fate. Yet I will not be alone, even then."

Gorgon was taken by a sudden, undeniable curiosity, and his left hand crept into the leather pouch at his side, hesitating for just a moment. What would it be like to see himself through her eyes? He had never been this close to her while holding the mirror. As much hatred as she held for him, to see himself though Gaelen was tantalizing. A small voice in the back of his mind cautioned him—it would be best to simply kill her and make his escape, and not toy with her. Yet he could not resist, for the ability the mirror gave to him had become almost addictive, and in his heart he did not wish for it to end with the death of Gaelen.

His desire overcame his reason, and he clutched the golden disc tightly in his left hand. The familiar pain assailed him, and even Gaelen drew a sharp breath and swayed as a wave of dizziness threatened to send her into darkness. Her vision swam for a moment; she had never been this close to the mirror before. Gorgon's vision came slowly back into focus as both he and Gaelen shook off the initial wave of pain and bewilderment.

"*Look at me, Elf!*" he shouted at her, and she obliged him, turning and looking into his eager face.

What Gorgon saw then would remain in his mind for the remainder of his days. Gaelen also was affected by it, for something passed between them as they knelt side by side in the rain. She felt, for the first time, the violence and pathos of his life, and he felt the strength and purity of her spirit, and they knew that, but for different circumstances, they might each have shared the fate of the other.

Gorgon saw himself through her eyes, but the sight did not please him, for now as she looked upon him and felt the pain and deprivation he had endured, she wondered what might have been. Her attention was drawn to the evidence of his High-elven heritage: his hair, his tall, straight frame and long legs, and his brilliant, inquisitive mind. And for a fleeting moment, she saw him as Elven, beautiful and whole, and unscarred by hatred and pain.

Then, almost immediately, the vision changed. Her view of him twisted into the familiar scarred, dark figure, but he did not look powerful, or fearsome, or terrible. Through Gaelen's eyes, Gorgon was pathetic, twisted, ugly, and alone. They shared thoughts then, for the mirror had bewildered them both and turned them away from the battle for the moment. Gorgon knew that Gaelen anticipated her death and that she would go to the Far Shores, there to reunite with her beloved. She felt his uncertainty as to his own fate, and he wondered aloud:

"Will I, too, go to the Eternal Realm? What shall be my fate? I have no one awaiting me, and no race will claim me. Where, then, shall I go?"

Gaelen answered him, for she felt pity for him in that moment. "I cannot imagine, Dark Horror, what fate awaits you. But you shall find out soon, for your hour is at hand. You may kill me now, but Rogond is coming, and he will not see you as I do. Prepare yourself, for I cannot imagine that your destiny lies anywhere except in Darkness. I cannot weep for you. None of the Elàni shall weep for you."

Her words enraged him as his pride welled once more. He leaped to his feet, preparing to strike her down, for she was weak and would not resist. He still grasped the mirror, for he wanted to view her last sight as he cut her down. Raising Turantil over his head, he roared at her, relishing the terrible sight of himself standing tall over her. The beautiful, bright sword may have been dwarfed by Gorgon's massive form, but it would cleave her neck all the same.

Gaelen knew that her time had come, but she would take as much of him with her as she could manage. Her gaze darted to Fima's axe lying on the wet ground beside her, and she recalled the words of her beloved friend, who was now lost.

It is well that you would learn the skills of the axe, Gaelen, but have a care as you practice with this weapon, for it will cleave iron. There are not many things that it will not cleave, in fact! Gaelen knew then what she would do.

She grabbed the axe in her right hand, and gathering herself for a last effort she ducked beneath Turantil as Gorgon brought it down upon her, and swung with all her might at his left arm, severing the hand that held the mirror. He roared with pain and dropped the sword, gripping his left forearm and staggering back as he heard the voice of Rogond approaching.

Gaelen grabbed Turantil and the severed hand, and backed away as quickly as she could, while her mighty enemy moaned in his agony.

She wondered whether the mirror still worked, though the hand of Gorgon was separated from his body, and she closed her eyes. She would blind him if she could. Gorgon was terribly confused, as the mirror would indeed hold power over him for a time, and he saw nothing but darkness. He blundered away from her then, for he would be no match for Rogond if he could not see to fight.

Rogond arrived a few moments later, as Gaelen urged him to pursue Gorgon. "Track him, Thaylon, for he is not far away. Track him! You must not let him escape. I will aid you from here, for the influence of the mirror may lessen as Gorgon leaves it farther behind." Rogond looked puzzled, but Gaelen spoke again. "There is no time!" She could sense her connection with Gorgon beginning to wane, and she cautioned Rogond. "Go now, beloved, but be swift and careful. He will see through his own eyes again ere long."

Rogond dropped his leather pack from his shoulders, and carried only his weapons as he left in pursuit.

Gorgon moaned in pain and despair as he beheld Rogond, who was now tracking him. It would be very difficult to evade pursuit, seeing only through Gaelen's eyes. He had heard Gaelen say that the influence of the mirror was fading; he had felt it, too. Yet it was still strong enough to blind him to all else but her visions as he ran, stumbling, into the night.

Gaelen was taken with a sudden feeling that Gorgon might well escape, or even do harm to Rogond, as she sat on the rain-soaked ground with Gorgon's hand in her lap. She stared at the glint of gold visible through Gorgon's thick fingers, wondering what would happen if she took the mirror and gazed into it herself?

She thought better of it, for the mirror frightened her and she dared not test its power. The Stone of Léir had taught her the folly of giving in to her inquisitiveness. But now, she beheld Turantil, and Fima's axe, and her thoughts again turned to vengeance for the hurts Gorgon had caused.

Her eyes strayed to Rogond's pack, and a thought came to her as to how this vengeance could be achieved. She drew forth the remaining maglos from the pack, set the hand in her lap, and opened the phial, flinging the remaining chunk of metal onto the rain-soaked ground not twenty feet from where she was sitting.

She crawled painfully back, knowing that she needed a greater distance from it, when it burst violently into blinding light. She turned her head away, as Rogond both heard the explosion and beheld it when he turned back toward her. He knew at once what she had done and why. He ran toward the light, calling her name, screaming at her to stop, to turn from her course, for he knew what it would do to her.

Gaelen had not much time before the influence of the mirror would fade and the connection would be broken. Turning toward the flaring maglos, she stared directly into its light, willing herself to keep her eyes open despite the pain, as Gorgon shrieked in agony. His light-sensitive brain was incapable of enduring this, and he dropped to the ground, his own pale eyes squeezed tightly shut, to no avail. As he writhed on the wet ground, he heard Gaelen calling in a terrible voice; it was obvious that she was filled with pain herself, but it was a mere shadow of his own suffering.

Talrodin! Halrodin! Gelmyr! Noli! Tibo! Amandir! Belegund! Fima! he heard through the white, flaring agony in his mind, before it faded at last and all was dark again.

Rogond ran back to where Gaelen now sat before the dwindling light. He heard her calling out the names of Gorgon's victims, and as he appeared, she turned toward him. As he knelt beside her he could see that her eyes were strangely blank, and he knew that she could not see him.

"The hold of the mirror has faded—Gorgon will gain no more from it. My vengeance has been achieved," she said, as she sagged sideways, her strength gone at last. He caught her in his arms, holding her gently to him.

She roused herself and spoke to him again. "I have hurt him badly, and he is blind. You may well defeat him now, but be cautious, as he is a wounded animal and will visit as much harm upon you as he can. I can still feel his desperation. You must see him dead before it fades."

Rogond heard her words, but he was still shocked and grieved at her blank gaze and her weak, shaky voice. "Oh, Gaelen…why did you do this? You will have harmed only yourself. His eyes were not burned by the light! Why did you do it?"

A vague, brief smile crossed her face. "I will heal. He cannot, for the image of the light was not in his eyes, but in his mind...in his heart. He will never truly heal." With those words, she sank into darkness, as Rogond held her and despaired.

Galador and Nelwyn had found Eros, still standing where Rogond had left him, and had turned him over to the Wood-elves, who would take him slowly and carefully back to a place where he could be tended. Galador looked in wonder at the evidence of Eros' heroic descent, and he addressed the animal with new respect.

"All is forgiven between us, Eros. Do not fear...I will find Rogond. Go, now, and submit to the kind attentions of the people of the Greatwood."

They had been tracking their friends with the help of Ri-Aruin's folk, and when the maglos flared they had been drawn to it, arriving to find Rogond sitting with Gaelen in his arms. Nelwyn rushed to his side as Galador looked around in alarm.

"Where is Gorgon?" he asked Rogond, looking with some concern at Gaelen's pale face and bloody clothing.

Rogond looked up at him, his face full of pain. "I don't know, and I have not the will to care, but now that you are here I shall track him and make certain that he does not escape the net Ri-Aruin's folk have laid for him. I fear Gaelen is grievously hurt, and I dared not leave her."

Nelwyn bent to examine her cousin. "She is spent, but her heart is still strong and her wounds are not grave. She will be hale again, my friend, do not fear. But we should get her back to a place of healing and make certain she is warm and dry. Eros is being well tended as we speak. Lift up your heart, my dear Rogond." She embraced him as she spoke, for he was a beloved friend.

Rogond knew that Nelwyn was right, that Gaelen would heal, but only he knew the extent of what she had done, and in his heart he wept for her. As he turned now to pursue Gorgon, Rogond noticed the severed hand now lying, nearly invisible, on the muddy ground. He lifted it up, noticing the mirror gripped in the bloodstained palm. The touch of Gorgon's flesh was repulsive, yet Rogond knew the hand and the mirror must be preserved. He did not wish to handle the mirror or remove it without guidance. Tearing the fabric of his cloak, he wrapped the hand in it, and then placed it beside Nelwyn.

"Guard this well. The enemy must not recover it," he cautioned her. Nelwyn stared at the cloth-wrapped hand in morbid fascination as Rogond and Galador fell once more onto the trail of their enemy.

30

The Trail Ends

Gorgon felt his doom approaching as the circle tightened around him. Though his connection with the mirror had faded and his own eyes were now functional, his mind could not perceive the images sent to it in the darkness, and he was blind. If he closed his eyes he saw only the brilliant, searing light of the maglos, and with a cry he would open them again, for he could not bear it.

He had dealt with the problem of his bleeding left arm, for the blood would be a sign for his enemies to follow. He had taken a thong of leather and tied it so tightly around his left wrist that the bleeding stopped. Unfortunately this caused a great deal of pain, and he did not know how long he could withstand it.

He crept carefully along the ravine floor, scenting the wind for his enemies, listening intently. He caught the scent of Rogond and Galador in pursuit, and he called upon all of his considerable skill, climbing carefully up the treacherous, rain-slick wall of the ravine, leaving almost no sign of his passing.

This was made much more difficult by the absence of his left hand. He occasionally forgot the hand was missing and tried to gain purchase with it. This was a mistake, and he grimaced as a throbbing bolt of pain shot up his left arm. There was only one hope for him now, and that was to find a place deep under the hills where he could hide from the wrath of the Wood-elves. Gorgon was accustomed to this; he had perfected the art of remaining nearly inert, sometimes for weeks at a time, subsisting only on the occasional sip of water. He would try to heal himself, though he was in so much pain and was so dispirited that this now seemed doubtful.

The scornful words of Gelmyr echoed in his mind, tormenting him. In addition, he had been humiliated by Gaelen, after she had cut the mirror free. Though she had barely enough strength left to speak, he sensed her smiling at him as he backed away, crying out in pain, right hand grasping his left wrist.

"You said that Belegund whimpered like a child at the end, didn't you? Did he sound half as pitiful as you do right now? I think not!" Then she had crawled back from him and closed her eyes, effectively blinding him.

How had things come so far awry? He had been deceived, and the Elves had won the night, though they paid a terrible price for their victory. And now Gorgon himself would have to pay the price of disappointing Wrothgar and leading his fearsome force to disaster.

Deep in the fortress of Tûr Dorcha, the Shadowmancer surely awaited Gorgon's return. He would eventually learn of the deception of the Elves, but would not know what had befallen Gorgon for a long time after. If Gorgon escaped Ri-Aruin's net, and survived, it would then be up to the Black Flame to decide the fate of his Dark Child. Gorgon knew that whatever else befell, he would have to face this fate, and the thought terrified him.

For a moment he considered engaging Rogond and Galador, effectively taking his own life, for he could not prevail in his blind, one-handed state. At least then he would not have to face the wrath of Wrothgar, and he might accomplish at least one of their deaths, for he would fight like the wounded animal he was. But in the end, he could not face the thought of any Elf accomplishing his end, and so he continued, hoping against all reason that he would be able to find his intended hiding place before Galador and Rogond could reach him.

The warm, moist air that had borne the rain with it had spawned a thick mist that seemed to hang all about the ravine and was especially dense near the floor, where Rogond and Galador tracked Gorgon relentlessly. Far above them, Gorgon could not see the mist, but he could feel it. He rejoiced in his dark heart, for he knew that it would conceal him. The Tuathan and the tall Elf would never find him if he could only reach his goal...and here it was.

Weeks ago he had found this place, when the words of Gelmyr had brought to his mind the vivid image of being murdered by one of his own Ulcas in the dark of night. He had decided then to find a secret place in which he could rest undisturbed, and none of his minions had known of it. He searched with the fingers of his right hand and located the cleft in the rocks, barely large enough for him to slip through. But slip through he did, and he sat upon the cool, damp stone inside the narrow cavern, tears of pain still glistening on his dark, scarred face. He roused himself for one final effort, and groping blindly he found what he was seeking—a stone large enough to block the entrance so that it could not be seen.

Rogond looked up at Galador, who was shaking his head in frustration. "He has not left us much to go on, has he, my friend?"

"Indeed not. For such a large being he can be incredibly light-footed. And now we must contend with this mist, which makes tracking nearly impossible even when there is sign to find. I fear we may have lost him."

Rogond's shoulders dropped as he spoke, for he was dispirited. He did not wish to disappoint Gaelen, but his hope of finding Gorgon was fading.

Galador reassured him. "Don't be dismayed. The people of Ri-Aruin are many and vigilant. Gorgon will not escape their nets. Have hope in your heart, for we have only to await the news that he has fallen to them. Do not fear. Gaelen will understand; she knows what it is to lose his trail."

"If only the wind moved in our favor! I might track him by scent," said Rogond, who was not yet ready to give up the chase.

Galador peered into the mist, clearly uneasy. The thought of an enraged, wounded Gorgon leaping upon them from a place of concealment was unsettling.

"I am not comfortable with this; he could so easily come on us unaware. And though I believe we could prevail, he might inflict grievous hurt on at least one of us. Are you sure that you can find no sign?"

Rogond rose to his feet and shook his head. This left them with little choice, as Galador knew that Rogond was an accomplished tracker. If he could find no sign, then there was none to find. Gorgon had eluded them for now, and there was nothing to do but return to Gaelen and Nelwyn. Though he despaired at having to tell Gaelen that Gorgon still walked free, Rogond brightened a little as he remembered that he could also inform her that her dear friend Fima still lived. He was looking forward to that moment very much indeed.

Kharsh despaired as he cowered among the rocks, hoping not to be noticed. The Wood-elves had arrived and routed what remained of Gorgon's forces utterly. Now Kharsh hoped for escape, but he knew in his old, dark heart that this was unlikely. He had survived many battles in his long life, but never before had he faced the wrath of the Shadowmancer, and he wondered whether it might be better to face death here, where the Elves would take his life quickly. It could have been worse, he thought. Gorgon's methods for dealing with captured enemies, for example, were far less merciful. The Elves did not take captives; they would simply dispatch him with efficiency and add his carcass to the large pile they had amassed in the center of the plateau. The smoke from the fire set to the pile of dead Ulcas might even be seen as far away as Tûr Dorcha, but Kharsh doubted it. Still, the Shadowmancer had many ways of gathering information, and He was probably already aware of the disastrous outcome of the battle.

Kharsh wondered, for a moment, what had befallen Gorgon. His powerful commander probably would not escape the fate the Elves had planned for him, and that was well, for Kharsh knew that Wrothgar would not have treated His wayward creation kindly; not after a failure of this magnitude. Kharsh's ugly, grey face twisted into an expression of resolve, and he drew a final, deep breath as he prepared to charge, a battle-cry on his lips, his curved scimitar in hand. He would end his life as a fearsome warrior, not cringing before the Shadowmancer. He managed to send three of the surprised Elves to their deaths before they took him down.

Gaelen had been taken to the place where the wounded were tended, and Nelwyn had stayed by her side, for Gaelen was exhausted, and did not stir. Galador and Rogond returned not long after with the somewhat disappointing news that they had lost Gorgon's trail, and though they all knew Gaelen would be disheartened, they also knew that she would understand. Ri-Aruin's folk would surely find him; he was blind, wounded, and fairly helpless. Yet he was still crafty enough to elude them, and would be dangerous if cornered. The Elves had best be very, very cautious.

Rogond looked down upon his beloved, who appeared to be at peace for the first time in a long reckoning. She was free of the mirror now, and much of the burden had been lifted from her. The taste of her vengeance had been painful, but sweet. Rogond stroked her hair with a gentle hand as the healers tended her, and then he went in search of Fima.

The old dwarf was giving the healers some trouble, as he was simply bursting with the desire for news and would not remain quiet. He was still a bit muddled and could not yet stand on his legs, but Rogond noticed that his eyes were bright in his lined face.

"What news, Rogond? What of Gaelen and the enemy? You must tell me, for otherwise I cannot rest. Where is our little Wood-elf?" He closed his eyes, for the effort of such an outburst had wearied him.

Rogond sat beside him. "She is being tended…she fought Gorgon in single combat and managed to cut off his left hand…and the mirror with it! He was clutching it for some reason. I have it here." He drew forth the wrapped hand as Fima beheld it in wonderment.

"Hmmm…it must be that he wanted to see himself through Gaelen's eyes—how very morbid! A terrible sight it must have been…I trust it was worth it to him. She still managed to fight him off by herself!" He shook his head. "She is incredibly quick and fairly strong of late; still, he could surely have killed her quickly, but for his own pride and twisted curiosity." He paused, looking sidelong at Rogond. "Both curses of his Elven heritage, you know. Ever have pride and curiosity been the downfall of the Elàni. But now we have the mirror, and so she is free of it. Please tell me that she used my axe to accomplish her victory—I noticed it was missing."

"She did, Master Fima," Rogond chuckled. "And you will be happy to hear that it has been recovered. I wondered why she had shown such an interest in learning the use of it of late. A good thing she did, otherwise she would not have prevailed. Her strength was completely spent."

Fima grew solemn as Rogond then described the events that followed, including the lighting of the maglos. The dwarf would not rest until Rogond had taken him to see Gaelen, who still had not stirred; it would be nearly a day and a night before she would regain her senses. Fima sat by her side, chanting softly in the dwarf-tongue for nearly an hour before returning to his place of healing, where he rested at last. Rogond had assured him that Gorgon would be brought to bay by the folk of Ri-Aruin, even as he prayed it would be so.

Rogond, Fima, and Gaelen would not be the only ones who would be disappointed should Gorgon evade them. Wellyn, son of Ri-Aruin, requested that Rogond be brought to his side as he lay with the rest of the wounded. He was still weak, but would heal quickly, for the ancient lines ran strong within him. He was relieved to learn of the recovery of the mirror.

"So, she is free. That is well, for I don't know how much longer she could have borne that burden," he said, looking earnestly at Rogond. "And what of the remainder of the Company?"

Rogond then recounted the fate of the travelers. Thorndil, Nelwyn, and Galador had survived with only minor wounds. Fima and Gaelen would require healing, but they would recover quickly, for both were made of strong fiber. Only Amandir and Oriana had left them forever. Wellyn turned his pale face away for a moment, an expression of sorrow in his eyes.

"Tuathan, you must come and tell me when the creature has been found and slain. Will you do that for me?"

Rogond nodded. "Of course I will, but I will leave you to rest now, son of Ri-Aruin. I must see to Gaelen, for when she awakens I would be beside her, even though she will not be able to see my face. Rest well, my friend."

Wellyn nodded and closed his eyes. By the time Rogond had risen from beside him and turned to leave, he was asleep. Regrettably, though Rogond had promised to inform Wellyn of the slaying of Gorgon Elfhunter, he never did so, for Ri-Aruin's folk found no trace of him, and they did not know whether he was alive or dead.

As soon as they were strong enough, the wounded were taken back to the Woodland stronghold along with the bodies of the dead. All who had died would be borne with honor, for they had fought valiantly in defense of their homes. Gaelen had given Turantil back to Halrodin's kin, who had stormed the hill with Ri-Aruin. They took the sword reverently as Gaelen wept, partly in lingering grief for the loss of her friend, but mostly with relief that the quest to recover Turantil was finally achieved. She had taken the news that Gorgon had eluded capture surprisingly well. Rogond held her to him, expecting her to weep in frustration, yet she merely sighed and shook her head. She alone knew of the involvement of the Shadowmancer, and that at the last Gorgon had been directed by a power whose evil was vastly deeper than his own. She had sensed Gorgon's fear of Wrothgar when he had first approached the archers on the hill, and, like Kharsh, she thought death in battle might have been preferable.

The King himself escorted Gaelen, Wellyn, and the rest of the Company as they traveled back through the forest under heavy guard. He had been quite impressed with his two hunter-scouts and had given each of them a gift. To Nelwyn he gave a beautiful emerald ring, and he presented Gaelen with a fine new set of knives, for hers had been notched in the battle and had lost their perfect throwing-balance.

"I would wait, Gaelen, until your sight returns before you try them out, however," he said in a deadly serious tone that did not quite conceal the humor behind it.

He drew Rogond aside. "Aridan, you must not be discouraged. Though the creature has not yet fallen, I have little doubt that he is at least weakened to the point that he will not emerge for a long while. Our people are now aware of him, and they will hunt him throughout the lands of Alterra. His power is broken. Your plan was a successful one."

Rogond bowed in respect as he walked beside the King. "I still would have seen his head on a spike, my lord," he muttered under his breath.

Ri-Aruin placed a hand upon his arm. "Stop for a moment and face me," he said gently. "My son has told me much of your heart, Tuathan, at least as he perceives it. I know that I have not welcomed your attentions to Gaelen, for it is not our custom to welcome such unions. However, my son has also informed me that our hunter-scout's heart is closed to Elven-kind and that it will never again be given but to one such as yourself. It is ironic, as I have spent considerable effort keeping her from Wellyn, for I approved even less of a union between Gaelen and my son. It seems I need not have feared. Our worthy Nelwyn has told me that you possess a stone, a gift from the Lady of the Lake. Do you have it with you?"

"Yes, my lord, I carry it always, though it is very small and I am ever-fearful of losing it." Rogond drew forth the stone and handed it to the King, who examined it closely.

"Interesting," said he. "When we return to our stronghold, we will set this in gold for you, that you might never be fearful of losing it. It shall be our gift to you for your aid."

Rogond started to say that, though Ri-Aruin was generous, he needed no thanks from him, but the King held up his hand, and Rogond was silent. "It shall also be a symbol of our acceptance and blessing of the friendship between you and our hunter-scout. Perhaps this will please you?"

Rogond smiled. "The potential fate of that friendship is uncertain, my lord. Yet I welcome your blessing."

"My son has said that her heart was given long ago, yet he does not know the identity of her beloved. I would know of it, if you can enlighten me. I give my word to guard the secret well."

Rogond considered for a moment. It was really not his place to reveal Gaelen's past to anyone, not even the Elven-king. Yet, he thought, it might ease Ri-Aruin's mind, and he knew that the King would be true to his word. He nodded, then reached deep under his tunic and drew forth the banner of Ri-Elathan. The King's eyes grew wide as he beheld it. Rogond smiled a sort of wry smile, and Ri-Aruin drew in a sharp breath, then a moment later his solemn face brightened, and he threw his head back and laughed aloud.

"And I thought she was unworthy of the Prince of the Greatwood Realm! This has been a bit humbling, my friend Rogond. Ah, well, it is said that the Èolar were sometimes lacking in common sense. I shall view her somewhat differently after this day." He smiled at Rogond, who chuckled and shook his head, then grew serious.

"You should view her differently, my lord, but for that which she has accomplished, not because she was chosen by the High King. She has earned your respect, I believe."

Ri-Aruin bowed. "She and Nelwyn have ever had it, Rogond. Yet I still did not want Wellyn consorting with her. Forgive a father's protectiveness of his son."

"Somehow, I do not believe Wellyn would need protection from Gaelen," said Rogond.

The King favored him with another laugh. "Some day, you may find out, Rogond. For now, I shall hope for your happiness. You are ever the friend of Ri-Aruin." With that, he turned and went to see to other matters.

Eros was healing quickly, as well. Rogond led him slowly and carefully, and each night he poulticed Eros' legs with clay, patting him and giving him extra feed.

"For once I believe your spoiling him is justified. What an incredible effort he made! Never has there been a more loyal animal upon feet," said Galador, as Nelwyn nodded in agreement.

Rogond smiled as he walked beside Gaelen, who rode upon her trustworthy Siva, with Fima, as ever, sitting before her. Rogond still did not have Gaelen's answer to his proposal of love, but he would remain beside her, protecting and loving her, for as long as she would have him. The mirror had been given into the care of Lore-master Fima until it could be taken to Mountain-home, where Lady Ordath herself would look after it.

Gorgon would not dare to emerge from his underground sanctuary for many weeks, as the Wood-elves were still searching for him. They turned over every stone, but did not find the hidden way into the cliff-side. More rains had removed what little sign there was of his passing, and he made no sound as he lay alone in the dark. He was still unable to see, though his eyes were undamaged, and still unable to close his eyes for fear of the light of the maglos exploding in his mind. He tried for many days and nights to hold on to his sanity, but in the end the voice of Gelmyr prevailed.

I shall be with you always, Gorgon Elfhunter, for you are vanquished. You have succeeded only in earning the wrath of the Dark Power. Your evasion of the Wood-elves is but a temporary reprieve from your fate at His hands. I expect He doubts now the wisdom of your creation, for you have proven to be a worthless bungler. You have lost the mirror of Dardis, and it is now in the hands of the Elves. I must admit, even I did not expect such a spectacular failure! He laughed at Gorgon then, and his laughter was both loud and long.

Finally, thirst drove Gorgon to remove the huge stone that both blocked and concealed the entrance to his lair. He did not yet know what his course would be, or what his fate would hold. He had been changed forever, and his tortured spirit would seek in vain to regain its purpose. He had thought that there was little to consider in his dark life beyond the hating and slaying of the Elàni, but his connection with Gaelen had shown otherwise.

Despite the fact that they remained the bitterest foes, they were each still somewhat aware of the other, though Gorgon's spirit was now spent to the point that Gaelen could barely sense him. An unwanted but permanent bond had been forged between them, and Gaelen almost welcomed it, though Gorgon did not. If and when he gained strength and ventured forth again, she would know, and would seek to destroy him again. He could never sufficiently avenge the hurt she had done him.

Now he looked up into the night sky, unaware that Gaelen was in that moment doing the same as she traveled back to the Woodland stronghold with Rogond at her side. Her eyes could not see the stars, but her spirit perceived them. Gorgon's eyes were undamaged, and the bright lights could be clearly seen, but within his heart the bright light of Gaelen's vengeance burned forever, and his spirit saw only darkness.

GLOSSARY of NAMES
With aid to pronunciation:

Aincor (INE-cor): Elf of the Èolar, a great scholar and warrior, known as the Fire-heart. He was among the most skilled and passionate of his people, but he was prideful, and his reckless acts bore terrible consequences. It is said that he was incapable of fear. Because of his perceived invincibility in battle, he was appointed the first King of Tal-elathas. It is unflattering to be compared with him in terms of willfulness. He produced two sons, Asgar and Dardis. Name means "fire-heart". (ain-fire, cor-heart)

Airan (EYE-rahn): Lord Airan, Elf of the Eádram that founded the realm of Tal-sithian. From airith (noble).

Alduinar (AL-dwee-nar): Ruler of Tuathas at the time of the Third Uprising. He successfully repelled Kotos' forces, and was a good friend and ally of the High King. His name means "worthy guide".

Alterra (Al-TAIR-ra): The World That Is; the Realm in which these tales take place. From terra (earth) and alta (being).

Amandir (AH-mahn-deer): Elf of Tal-Sithian, spouse of Brinneal. His name means "artful one". From aman (artful).

Ambros (AHM-bros): Great River of Western Alterra, it is formed by the Eros and the Brocca in the north. From ambra (great) and ros (river).

Angael (AHN-gehl): Small but doughty mare ridden by Gaelen in her youth. Name means "valor-mare". From gael (valor, feminine).

Anlon (AHN-lon): Great horse belonging to Gaelen and Nelwyn's uncle Tarmagil. Name means "champion".

Anori (Ah-NOR-ee): Men who dwell in the eastern regions of Alterra. Though they are comprised of many cultures, little is known of them in the West. It is said that there are great eastern civilizations founded by them—strongholds of learning and enlightenment. The Anori are physically smaller than the Tuathar, with golden skin, raven or reddish hair, and dark eyes. They fear the Elves, and many consider them to be evil. The foundation of this belief is not known.

Of particular note among Anori tribes are the Khazhi-folk. These are short, stocky, brown-skinned nomads. As horsemen they are unexcelled, and though they are gentle and hospitable to their friends, they are fierce enemies. From anoir (east).

Aontar (Ay-ON-tar): The One Lord of All, the Creator. Also known as the Lord of Light.

He formed the Lands of Alterra and endowed them with light in the form of stars, sun and moon. To aid and instruct His children, Aontar sent emissaries known as Asari. They played a great role in the growth and enlightenment of the Elves and the men of Tuathas.

Arialde (Ah-ree-AL-deh): Lady Arialde, the Asarla who founded Tal-sithian with Lord Airan. She is one of the only female Asari, and is the keeper of the Stone of Léir. Water is her element. From arialdas (beautiful).

Aridani (Ah-ree-DAHN-ee), sing. Aridan (AH-ree-dahn): Men. One of the mortal races, men have spread into nearly every region of Alterra. Highly variable in appearance and culture, they may be savage or enlightened depending on influence and opportunity. For the most part they are unremarkable, reasonably peaceful folk quietly living their daily lives. They are the farmers, the tradesmen, the fishermen, laborers, and craftsmen. They maintain trade with the Elves and also with the dwarves, providing both goods and services. Men have founded several great realms, which have served as repositories of learning and lore. Most notable among these was Tuathas, but the great cities of Dûn Bennas and Dûn Arian have also stood as fortresses of Light.

Regrettably, men are subject to sickness—their numbers were vastly reduced in the Great Plague of s.r.7216. Known as Tâmo-fuath, the terrible death, this pestilence devastated men in nearly all areas of Alterra; it was spread by the wind and spared very few. The Duathar and the Anori lost nearly eight of ten, and though the northern and western peoples fared a little better, they still lost more than half their number. Only the far southern city of Dûn Arian was spared, and that was only because of her isolation and because the winds in that part of the world prevail from the sea. Name means "those who fade". From aridar (fading).

Artan (AR-tan): River formed by the 2 streams that flow from Monadh-talam.

Aruinnas (Ar-WEE-nas): The Greatwood Forest. From Aruinnas (forest).

Asarla (Ah-SAR-la) pl. Asari (Ah-sah-REE): Ancient magic-users sent to enlighten the children of Aontar. Each was affiliated with one of the four elements—earth, water, air, or fire. Their influence is at the heart of most of the great Elf-realms, as well as the northern realm of men known as Tuathas.

The Asari were never many; it is thought that only twelve were sent by Aontar. Of those, only three are known to remain in the western lands at the time our tales begin. Two are of the light—Lady Arialde of Talsithian, and Lord Shandor of Mountain-home. The other, Lord Kotos, sits at the right hand of Wrothgar and is responsible for much of the corruption of men.

The founders of the Elven-realms of Eádros and Tal-elathas, and of the northern realm of men known as Tuathas, are believed lost. They were called Léiras the far-sighted, Cuimir the beautiful, Baelta the bright, and Duinar the guide.

Three Asari made their way to the far eastern lands; their fate is unknown to Western scholars.

The last two turned to Darkness during the Time of Mystery. Though it is believed that they no longer dwell in Alterra, they were said to have given rise to the Bödvari, the demonic captains of Wrothgar's army.

The powers of the Asari vary according to the gifts given them by Aontar, but all are very learned, and they are capable of exerting their influence to protect their people. The Elven-realms have remained hidden from their enemies largely due to the Asari, who do not stray from them. The exception was Shandor, who actually went forth on several occasions, notably during the Second Uprising.

The climate within their lands is moderated by their benevolent power. Mountain-home, for example, is not locked in the grip of deadly winters despite its location, and the lands of Tuathas did not often suffer from flooding or drought.

The Asari can beget children, though rarely have they done so. These included the Bödvari, who thankfully could not beget children themselves, and Lady Ordath of Mountain-home, daughter of Lord Shandor.

Asgar (ASZ-gar): Elf of the Èolar and elder son of Aincor. Asgar was like Aincor in temperament. After witnessing the disastrous consequences of his father's stubbornness, he declined the throne in favor of his cousin, Ri-Aldamar. His name means "the bold".

Aureth (OW-reth): Maiden of Tal-sithian, friend of Brinneal. From aura (dawn).

Baelta (Bah-EL-tah): Asarla, friend of Kotos, whose dark influence turned him into the unwitting servant of Wrothgar. Baelta so regretted the destruction caused by his deeds that he took his own life. His name means "bright light".

Belegund (BEH-le-gund): Northman, Ranger and friend of Rogond. His name means "noble warrior". From bele- (noble) and gunnar (warrior).

Bödvari, sing Bödvar (BODE-var): Dark servants of Wrothgar, they are the offspring of Dark Asari. They are as black demons that kill their enemies with fire after first paralyzing them with fear. They are terrible enemies in battle. From bödvar (demon).

Brinneal (BRIN-nee-al): Golden-haired Elf of the Èolar, she moved to Tal-sithian after the fall of Tal-elathas. She is the mother of Gorgon Elfhunter and the spouse of Amandir. Name means "beautiful young maid".

Brocca (BRAW-ka): The river in the north that, along with the Eros, gives rise to the Ambros. It is as wild and turbulent as the Eros is smooth and gentle. From broca (restive).

Brunner Aigred (BROO-nair AYE-gred): The cold-spring that flows from the Great Mountains into the Linnefionn. From aigred (cold, High-elven dialect) and brunner (spring).

Brunner Ia (BROO-nair EE-ya): The cold-spring that flows through the Greatwood, eventually entering the Darkmere. From Ia (cold, Sylvan dialect) and brunner (spring).

Capellion (Ka-PELL-lee-on): Master of Horse in the Greatwood realm. His name means "horse master". From capella (horse).

Conegal (Con-eh-GAHL): One of the renowned Lords of Tuathas, he was a great friend of Ri-Aldamar.

Cós-domhain (Coss-Dome-Ha-EEN): Great Dwarf-realm, known as the Realm of Caverns. Ruled by Lord Grundin. From cós (cavern) and domhain (domain). At the time of these tales there are three dwarf-realms in Alterra: they are Cós-domhain, beneath the Great Mountains, Cós-tollan (the Rûm-harnen or Harnian) beneath the Northern Mountains, and Cós-anor, beneath the Eastern Hills. One of the greatest known dwarf-realms, the City of Rûmm, was destroyed by Elves of the Eádram during the War of Betrayal.

Cronan (CRO-nan): Sturdy dark chestnut pack horse belonging to Rogond and Galador.

Cuimir (coo-ee-MEER): Asarla that founded Eádros, the Realm of Light. He was lost during the War of Betrayal. Name means "comely, handsome". From cuimas (handsome).

Cúinar (COO-ee-nar): Sylvan Elves, Wood-elves. Considered to be of lesser stature than High-elves, they did not have the benefit of Asari influence. They are more earthy and innocent, possessing a very deep bond with the forest, and they possess unique abilities. They have a greater empathy with and understanding of other creatures, and form strong bonds with beasts and birds. At the time our tales begin there are two large groups of Cúinar remaining in the west of Alterra—the Elves of the Greatwood under the reign of Ri-Aruin, and those of the Monadh-ailan, the Verdant Mountains. Examples are Gaelen and Nelwyn. From cúin (silent).

Dardis (DAR-dees): The second son of Aincor, Dardis was a highly talented and inventive artisan and lover of learning. Unlike his father, Dardis was of gentle temperament and was revered especially by the dwarves. He was apprenticed to an Asarla named Léiras (the far-sighted), who taught him of the making of things that could be endowed with magical properties. It was Dardis who made the mirror given to Gorgon Elfhunter; he also created the Stone of Léir.

Much of what transpires in Alterra has little to do with magic. The people live and die according to the laws of nature, and are subjected to the hardships of living as in any other world. It was once true that magic played a greater role in the affairs of Alterra, and the scholars state that the waning of magical influences reflects the waning of the Asari. Yet there is still magic at work in the world at the time these tales begin, and Dardis is responsible for much of it.

Léiras instructed Dardis in the making of magical things—blades, rings, mirrors, amulets, armor, and shields. Mirrors made by Dardis could tell an enemy from a friend despite outward appearances; hence it was Dardis who first realized the treachery of Lord Kotos. He was killed on the eve of the Second Uprising.

Dardis was rather plain and disheveled, often spending months in his "chamber of inspiration" as he created some new and wondrous object. Gentle, humble, and unassuming, he was perhaps the most universally beloved of all Elves in Alterra.

Darkmere: Name given to the Great Forest Realm (Greatwood) when Wrothgar took up residence in the Laban Fuath. The Elves refer only to the southern part of the Forest as the Darkmere, but others make no such distinction. See also Dominglas Forest.

Diomar (DYOH-mar): Man of the Tuathar, sire of Rogond. His name means "the proud". From diomas (proud).

Dominglas Forest (DOME-een-glas): The vast woodland occupying approximately one-third of the northern lands of Alterra. Sylvan Elves patrol and maintain the north, but Wrothgar has overtaken a large area in the south. From domhain (domain) and glas (deep green). See also Greatwood, Darkmere, Aruinnas.

Duathar (DOO-ah-thar): These are the men of the south. Like the Anori-folk, they represent a vast array of cultures, but all have been shaped by the harsh desert lands that are their home. Also known as "sutherlings", many Duathar are tribal, and they often war with their neighbors and with each other. Yet there have been some great scholars among them, and when they find themselves in more civilized surroundings there is little that they cannot achieve. They are very fierce fighters, and are skilled horsemen. They have occasionally troubled the area near to Dûn Bennas, but have always been driven back.

Duinar (DOO-ee-nar): Asarla who founded Tuathas, the northern realm of Men. He appeared to be very old, with a long snow-white beard and a lined, weathered face. He was thought slain during the cataclysmic rising of the Fire-mountain that destroyed Tuathas and all lands near it. Earth is his element. Name means "guide".

Dûn Bennas (Doon-ben-NAS): City of Men founded by the Tuathar, located in the southern tip of the Monadh-ailan where the Ambros enters the Sea. It was built by survivors of the ruin of Tuathas, together with men already living in that region, and it has since withstood many assaults upon its gates. Dûn Bennas is a fair city, and has within its walls one of the great libraries of western Alterra; the lore and works contained therein are equaled only by those of Mountain-home and of Dûn Arian. Name means "white fortress". From dûn (fortress) and benna (white).

Dûn Arian (Doon-AH-ree-AHN): Largely unknown City of Men founded by the renowned scholar Salasin, located in the far southern lands. Also known as The Citadel. Name means "fortress of silver". From dûn (fortress) and ariant (silver).

Dwarves: The third of the great races of Alterra, and the least understood, as they tend to keep to themselves. They were also created by Aontar, but they name Him Fior, the Maker. They call themselves Rûmhar, the Delvers. Their tongue, Rûmhul, is known to very few outside their own race, and is among the most difficult languages to master.
Dwarves are arguably the cleverest of all folk, and they make many wonderful devices. They also make things of great beauty and worth, for they are craftsmen matched only by the Èolar. They are diggers and delvers, and they live almost exclusively in underground realms, though they go abroad in daylight quite happily when needed. They are short in stature, but broadly-made and very strong for their size. They are also quite hardy and tolerant of fire, which is a good thing as they work huge forges deep underground.

All dwarves are bearded, and they take great pride in the length and lushness of their beards, thinking it highly amusing that the Elves have none. As with men, they have a limited lifespan, although dwarves live longer. Two hundred years is about average.

Dwim (DWEEM): Dwarf of Cós-domhain.

Eádram (Ay-AH-drahm): High-elves, Elves of the Light. The Eádram founded most of the High-elven Realms of Alterra, together with the Asari. Of these there were four, but only two remain at present. The Realm of Eádros was lost in a terrible conflict known as the War of Betrayal. The other lost realm, Tal-elathas, was the great center of the Èolar. The remaining realms are Tal-sithian, founded by Lord Airan of the Eádram with Arialde of the Asari, and Monadh-talam, or Mountain-home, founded by the Èolar together with Lord Shandor. High Elves are endowed with an inner light; with practice they can call upon it during battle. Examples of High-elves are Galador and Lord Airan of Tal-sithian. From eádra (light).

Eádri (Ay-AH-dree): The Evening Star.

Eádros (Ay-AH-dross): Elven-realm, greatest of the Eádram. It was lost in the War of Betrayal, destroyed by the Dwarves of Rûmm. The complete tale of the War of Betrayal is told by Fima in Ravenshade. From eádra (light).

Elàni (El-LAN-ee): Elves. Immortal and impressive, they do not willingly serve the Darkness, though they may unwittingly do so through pride or deception. They have established some of the greatest realms in Alterra. Because of their very long lives, Elves are highly skilled, and many are quite learned. They make many beautiful things, and are unrivalled as musicians, singers, poets, and artisans. Elves are formidable in battle, and quick to defend their lands from any perceived threat.

Elves are almost universally beautiful, High-elves in particular. They are tall and very well made, with fine, silken hair that is usually worn long and flowing or plaited to keep it out of the way. Their hair may be of any color: silver, flaxen, golden, chestnut, mahogany, or raven. Their elegantly-shaped ears aid in distinguishing them from men. Their eyes are bright, and may also be of any color— the High-elves tend toward blue and grey, the Sylvan Elves green and brown. The males are beardless, which also separates them from men and rather pointedly from dwarves.

Elves enjoy an endless life span, unless they are slain. Their flesh will not fester, and they do not suffer disease. Yet they may be poisoned, killed in battle or by mischance, or even die from grief. Because of their very long lives, they do not often beget children.

They delight in sharing their knowledge and their language; hence most names of places and roots of common speech are in their tongue. Though some Elves can be arrogant and dismissive of other races, they have formed alliances and friendships with men and dwarves. Regrettably, they have also warred with them at times. The War of Betrayal between the Elves of Eádros and the dwarves of Rûmm accounts for much of the remaining enmity between Elves and dwarves.

The magical abilities of the folk of Alterra are held mostly by the Elves and, naturally, by the Asari. The Elves' abilities are varied according to their origins, age, and experience. For example, the High Kings were possessed of supernormal strength in battle. They could exert a sort of inner power, engulfing their enemies with blue-white light, as could certain others among the High-elves. They could prevail over all but the most powerful of enemies. By contrast, the Bödvari also engulfed their opponents, but with fire rather than light.

Many Elves have the gift of foresight and insight, and they sense things over great distances. A rare few can actually see into the hearts and minds of others; some can do this only with living thought, and some can perceive only the final thoughts of the dead.

Some Elves possess powers that assist them in the healing of wounds, though they have little knowledge of or power over the afflictions of men.

The Wood-elves are thought to be less magical than the High-elves, but this is untrue. Their abilities are entirely practical; they are the stealthiest, lightest-footed and most agile beings in Alterra. They sometimes seem to defy the laws of nature, springing up into impossibly high tree-limbs and treading so lightly upon mud or snow that tracking them is difficult. They communicate on a very high level with other good-hearted creatures, especially horses and birds. It is said that an Elf of the Cúinar can tame the most fractious horse in a manner of moments. All Elves are known as Elàni. See "Cuinar", "Eádram", and "Èolar".

Elethorn (EL-eh-thorn): Elf of Monadh-talam, rescued by the Company. His name means "piercing", probably in reference to his bright gaze. From elàn (elf) and thorn (to pierce).

Elwyn (EL-win): Sylvan Elf, mother of Nelwyn. Name means "Elf-maiden". From elàn (elf) and wyn (maid).

Elysia (Eh-LEE-see-ah): Eternal Elven-home that has been provided to house the spirits of the Elàni after death. It is a paradise separate from the afterlife of Men. From elàn (elf). The Elves, being immortal, will not die unless they are slain or they choose to relinquish their spirits. Loved ones who have gone before are sent to conduct them to the Sacred Realm of Elysia, a place of eternal bliss and light that has been set aside only for the Elves—neither man nor dwarf nor Asarla can hope to gain its shores.

Èolar (AY-oh-lahr): High-elves who achieved the highest level of learning and skill, but were deceived by Wrothgar and Lord Kotos. They were mostly lost during the second uprising. The Èolar are but a family of the Eádram, yet they are distinct from them. They of all the Elàni most desired to learn and know all things, and this desire was both their uplifting and their undoing. They designed and wrought many magical devices, and their forges produced what is arguably the finest weaponry ever seen.

Their great realm, Tal-elathas, was lost in the second uprising of Wrothgar, and only a remnant of her people survived. Fortunately, the realm of Mountain-home, founded by the Èolar and Lord Shandor, survives to this day. Examples are Aincor, Dardis, Magra, and Ri-Elathan. From Èolas (knowing).

Eros (EH-rohs): Sturdy, intelligent dun horse of Rogond. Also a smooth-flowing, gentle river that gives rise to the Ambros in the north. From eran (soft, easy).

Falad capell (FAH-lahd ka-PELL): Horse pastures of Tal-sithian. From falad (pasture) and capella (horse).

Farahin (FAH-rah-heen): Given name of Ri-Elathan. Name means "welcome rain", from farath (welcome) and hin (rain).

Farath-talam! (Fah-RATH TAH-lahm): Elvish welcome, it means "you are welcome among us" or "welcome to our realm".

Farin (FAH-rin): Dwarf of Cós-domhain, eminent craftsman and maker of Rogond's ring.
Fiana (Fee-AH-na): Wood-elves' name for the constellation Orion, also the clear stream that flows from the Linnefionn. Name means "huntress".

Fima (FEE-ma): Dwarvish Loremaster, originally of Cós-domhain and now serving Lady Ordath in Monadh-talam, he is a good friend of Rogond.

Fiona (Fee-YO-na): Elvish name for the constellation Orion, it is named after Fiona, the Huntress.

Fior (FYOR): The dwarves' name for Aontar. Name means "The Maker".

First Reckoning: The Reckonings are marked in increments of ten thousand, and the First Reckoning coincides with the beginning of recorded history. We are well into the seventh age of the Second Reckoning at the time our tale begins in the year s.r.7266, thus the Third Reckoning will begin in 2,034 years. The time before the First Reckoning is known simply as the Time of Mystery, and events of that time are known only through oral accounting. As many as could be recorded have been, but there is much of conflict and disagreement in the accounts, and their accuracy is in doubt. A complete summary may be found in the Rûndiam-har, the Book of Mystery.

Gaelen (GEH-lehn): Sylvan Elf of the Greatwood, daughter of Tarfian and Gloranel, cousin of Nelwyn. Name means "daughter of valor". From gael- (valor, feminine).

Galador (GAL-ah-dore): High-elf, formerly of Eádros, beloved of Gwynnyth and later of Nelwyn. Friend of Rogond. From gal- (valor, masculine).

Galwaith (GAL-wyeth): High-elf, friend of Galador and beloved of Oriana. His name means "brave wanderer". From gal-(valor, masculine) and waith (to wander).

Gelmyr (GEL-meer): Èolarin Warrior-elf of Monadh-talam, friend of Magra, slain by Gorgon. From gal- (valor, masculine) and mirys (graceful).

Glomin (GLO-meen): Dwarf of Cós-domhain, who first reveals the secret of Rogond's ring.

Gloranel (GLOR-ah-nel): Sylvan Elf, mother of Gaelen. Name means "Bright tree". From glora (bright light) and nellas (tree).

Gorgon (GORE-gun): Dark but mighty perversion brought into being by Wrothgar, he is also known as the Elfhunter. From gor- (dark) and gundas (horror).

Gorlan (Gor-lahn): Great horse of Ri-Aruin, his name means "dark coated". From gor- (dark) and lanys (wool).

Gryffa (GRIF-fa): Chestnut horse ridden by Nelwyn, his name means "the red".

Grundin (GROON-din): Dwarf-lord, ruler of Cós-domhain. Grundin was very wise and reasonably open-minded, and he could trace his lineage back directly to the Five Founders. Name means "solid-as-stone".

Gwynnyth (GWIN-nith): Beloved mortal woman, lost love of Galador. Her name means "blissful".

Gwyr Farsing (Gweer FAR-sing): Wide grasslands to the west of the Ambros. From gwyr (grass) and farsa (wide).

Halrodin (HAL-roe-din): Hunter-scout of the Greatwood, friend of Gaelen, slain by Gorgon. His name means basically "tall tree". From halla (tall) and rodo (trunk of a tree).

Iduna (Ih-DOO-nah): Mare of Tal-sithian, her name means "the young".

Iolar (Yo-LAHR): Also called Monadh-iolar. Two tall peaks comprising the Iolari Pass, the best way across the Monadh-hin in the region of the Linnefion. Name means "eagle".

Iomar (Yo-MAR): Elf of the Eolar, elder son and heir of Ri-Aldamar, elder brother of Farahin (Ri-Elathan). Iomar was in line to succeed Ri-Aldamar as High King, but he was slain during the Second Uprising. His name means "eagle".

Kelin (KEH-leen): Hunter-scout of the Greatwood. Her name means "slender maid". From kelas (slender).

Kharsh (KARSH): Ulca, venerable and able advisor to Gorgon. The meaning of his name is unknown.

Kotos (KO-tos): Dark Asarla, formerly of Tal-elathas, whose desire for power and to learn all things turned him to the service of Wrothgar. He can see into the hearts and minds of those he encounters. Kotos wore a magical amulet that allowed him to appear benevolent and wise, and he served Wrothgar as his emissary, turning men to his service through deception and promise of reward. His name means "the powerful", but it can also mean "wrathful". He is called "deceiver" by the Elves, and they name him Trachair, the treacherous. At the time of these writings, Kotos can no longer take physical form, but he can inhabit the body (and mind) of any person who wears the amulet.

Laban Fuath (la-Ban foo-ath): The great evil bog surrounding Tûr Dorcha in the south of the Darkmere. Name means "terrible mire". From laban (bog) and fuath (terrible).

Léiras (LEH-ee-ras): Asarla, friend and mentor of Dardis. He instructed Dardis in the making of objects that could be endowed with magical properties. Name means "the far-sighted".

Liathwyn (Lee-ATH-win): Elf of the Eolar, mother of Ordath, espoused to Shandor the Asarla, with whom she founded Monadh-talam. She relinquished her spirit after the Second Uprising. She was kin to the High Kings Ri-Aldamar and Ri-Elathan. Her name means "blue-eyed maiden". From liath (blue).

Lindor (LIN-door): Elf of Tal-sithian.

Linnefionn (Lin-neh-finn): The very large, very deep and very clear Lake in the center of which is located the Elven-realm of Tal-sithian. The Lake is generally shrouded in mist and cannot be seen by unwelcome visitors. Name means "clear lake". From linne (lake) and fionn (crystal-clear).

Maglos (MAG-los): Soft, white metal discovered and refined by the dwarves, it reacts violently when exposed to water. It is most likely akin to sodium or magnesium. Name means "mighty light". From magra (mighty).

Magra (MAH-gra): Èolarin Elf-lord, second-in-command and kinsman of Ri-Elathan. Magra is very tall and strong, and has golden hair. He is related to Liathwyn, and hence to Lady Ordath. His name means "mighty".

Maidrin (MYE-drin): Name given to Gaelen by Gorgon, it means "vixen fox".

Maleck (MAL-eck): Fisherman living along the River Ambros.

Monadh-ailan (Monath-EYE-lan): The Verdant Mountains. Gentle, coastal peaks that run along the sea, they are inhabited by folk of many races, notably the Wood-elves of Tal-ailean. Name means "green-mountains". From monad (mountain) and ailan (green).

Monadh-hin (Monad-HEEN): The Great Mountains, largest of all mountain-ranges in Alterra, they are a daunting obstacle for travelers.

Snow-covered in winter, they are shrouded by clouds year-around. Name means "peaks of rain". From hin (rain).

Monadh-talam (Monath-TAH-lahm): Elven-realm presided over by the Lady Ordath. Hidden among tall peaks of the Monadh-hin, it is also known as Mountain-home. The Sanctuary, a great university founded by Shandor, is located there. Mountain-home is a place of healing, study, and enlightenment, and is home to folk of many races. Name means "mountain-realm". From monad (mountain) and tal- (realm).

Mulafiann: Name given affectionately to Gaelen by Ri-Elathan, it means "little hunter". From mula (small, loveable) and fiana (huntress).

Nachtan (NOCH-tan): Narrow and turbulent cold river that flows to the south and west from Monadh-talam. From nachta- (wild)

Nasülle (Na-SOO-leh): Elf of Monadh-talam.

Nelwyn (NEL-win): Sylvan Elf of the Greatwood, daughter of Turanen and Elwyn, younger cousin of Gaelen. Name means "tree-maiden". From nellas (tree).

Nimo (NEE-mo): Elder dwarf of Cós-domhain, descended of Rûmm.

Noli (NO-lee): Dwarf of the northern Mountains, descended of Rûmm, cousin of Nimo and son of Kino.

Odo (OH-doh): Arguably the most accomplished of all dwarvish scholars, certainly their most renowned lore-master. He wrote the volume given to Fima by Lady Arialde upon their parting. His name means "wealthy".

Ordath (OR-dath): The Lady Ordath, very powerful overseer of Monadh-talam. She is the product of a union between a powerful Asarla (Shandor) and an Elf of the Eolar (Liathwyn). She is a great healer and protector of Monadh-talam. Name means "treasure-of-the-land". From or- (golden, gentle) and –dath (of the land).

Oriana (Oh-ree-AH-na): Elf of Eádros, beloved of Galwaith, friend of Galador. Oriana and Galwaith tried unsuccessfully to advocate for Galador after he was banished from Eádros. Her name means "the golden".

Oryan (ORE-ian): Elf of Tal-sithian who travels with the Company to the Greatwood and aids the Wood-elves in battle. His name means "fine singer". From oran (to sing).

Osgar (OSZ-gar): King of the Greatwood and sire of Ri-Aruin, he was known as "the fierce". Somewhat impulsive and reckless, he was slain during the Third Uprising.

Réalta (ray-AL-ta): Swift and beautiful grey stallion, favored mount of Galador and companion of Eros. His name means "star".

Ri-Aldamar (ree AL-da-mar): Second High King of the Eolar, brother of Liathwyn and sire of Farahin. He was killed by a dragon during the Second Uprising. His name means "majestic noble". From aldos (high, noble) and amar (great, majestic).

Ri-Aruin (ree-AR-oo-een): Ruler of the Sylvan Elves of the Greatwood Realm. His name means "king of the forest". From ri-(ruler) and aruinnas (forest

Ri-Elathan (ree-EL-a-than): Last High-elven King, Ri-Elathan left no one to succeed him. He was arguably the wisest of all the High Kings, and was both feared and beloved, but he lived a very lonely and arduous life. Beloved of Gaelen Taldin, he was killed during the Third Uprising, taken by the Black Flame. His given name was Farahin, but Gaelen simply calls him "Rain". His name means "King of Wisdom". From ri-(ruler) and elathas (wisdom).

Rogond (ROE-gond): Man of the Tuathar, born during the Plague Year and fostered by the Elves of the Verdant Mountains. Name means "treasure within the stone". From oro- (golden, gentle) and gondas (stone).

Rosalin (ROS-a-lin): "River-beauty". Woman descended of Tuathas, mother of Rogond. From Ros-(river) and –aille (beautiful).

Rûmhar (ROOM-har): Dwarves. Their speech is known as Rûmhul. From Rûm (to delve).

Rûmm (RHUM): Ancient and Great Dwarf-realm known as the Deep Delving, which was lost in the War with the Eádram. From Rûm (to delve).

Rûndiam-har (Roon-dee-ahm-HAR): The Book of Mystery, an accounting of what is known of the time before the First Reckoning begins. From rûndiam (deep/hidden mystery).

Sanctuary: Lord Shandor built the Sanctuary so that all free folk of Alterra would have a place to study and learn. It is a huge edifice of white granite, and contains many levels both above and below ground. It represents an enormous repository of written lore—an irreplaceable treasure.

Shadowmancer: Wrothgar, the Dark Power of Alterra. He is thought by many to be an extremely powerful, black sorcerer, hence the name. The name has also been applied to Lord Kotos, but in these tales it refers specifically to Wrothgar.

Shandor (SHAN-dor): Arguably the most powerful of the Asari, he loved Liathwyn, an Elf of the Èolar, and together they founded Mountain-home. He actually challenged Wrothgar in battle and defeated him during the Second Uprising. He is the sire of Lady Ordath. When Liathwyn relinquished her spirit and went to Elysia, Shandor withdrew from the world, eventually seeking refuge in the great stone crystal of Léir, which is presently in the keeping of Lady Arialde, the Asarla of Tal-sithian. Shandor was the only Asarla to leave his protected realm and go forth to war. Physically, Shandor is strikingly handsome, but cold, with silver hair and ice-blue eyes. Air is his element. His name essentially means "great spirit".

Siva (SEE-va): Silver-white horse ridden by Gaelen, her name simply means "grey".

Srath Miadan (Srath mee-ah-DAHN): Meadows to the east of the Ambros and west of the Linnefionn. From srath (riverbank) and miadan (meadow).

Stone of Léir (Stone of Leh-eer): One of the most powerful and renowned magical objects remaining in Alterra, this gigantic crystal is now kept in the realm of Tal-sithian by the Lady Arialde, and she alone governs its use. It was made in Tal-elathas, and was first relocated to Monadh-talam. Originally endowed only with power to behold pleasant visions of the past, it was of limited use until the coming of Shandor.

Lord Shandor founded the realm of Monadh-talam, together with his beloved Lady Liathwyn of the Èolar. When Liathwyn gave up her life

Shandor was so grieved that he sought refuge in the Stone of Léir, hoping to relive his happy memories with her.

He gazed so long into its depths, weeping and calling to his beloved, that his spirit was drawn into the crystal, and now resides there. The Stone was moved to Tal-sithian in s.r.6985, at the onset of the Third Uprising, and has remained there under the watchful eye of Lady Arialde. Because of Shandor's powerful spirit, the Stone is now a mighty object capable of great visions not only of the past, but of the future.

Shandor is bitter and grieved, and he will not suffer anyone to seek his visions outside the grace of the Lady. Many of the things seen in the Stone are disquieting, and if one looks into it without leave Shandor may afflict him with visions so terrible that they will haunt him until the end of his days. Yet the Stone can be of great value in predicting and averting disaster, and it has greatly aided the Lady Arialde in safeguarding her people. From léir (far-sighted).

Sylvan elves: Wood-elves, or Cúinar.

Tal-ailean (Tal-EYE-lee-ahn): Elven-realm located in the Monadh-ailan. It is inhabited by various small, secretive groups of Cúinar known as the Elàni-ailan (green-elves). From tal (realm) and ailan (green).

Taldin (TAl-deen): Name given affectionately to Gaelen by Ri-Elathan, it means "walks unnoticed, stealthy". From taldin (silent-footed).

Tal-elathas (Tal-EL-a-thas): Ancient realm of the Èolar, it was the greatest center of invention and discovery that has ever been. At one time there were no less than three Asari that resided there: Leiras, Baelta, and Kotos. It was destroyed by Wrothgar's army when Kotos betrayed the Elves, aided unwittingly by Baelta. From tal- (realm) and elathas (wisdom).

Talrodin (TAL-roh-deen): Hunter-scout of Greatwood, friend of Nelwyn and brother of Halrodin. He was slain by Gorgon. His name means "pillar of the realm". From tal (realm) and rodos (as the trunk of a tree).

Tal-sithian (SITH-ee-ahn): Green forested island in the Linnefionn; the Elven-realm of the Lord Airan and Lady Arialde. From sithion (deer). It means "realm of deer roaming".

Tarfion (TAR-fee-ohn): Father of Gaelen, spouse of Gloranel, twin brother of Tarmagil and elder brother of Turanen. Tarfion was probably unexcelled as a hunter-scout, and he gained the King's favor upon saving the life of his son, prince Aruin. Name means "hunter of the realm". From fiona (hunter) and tar (of the realm).

Tarmagil (TAR-mah-geel): Fraternal twin brother of Tarfion and favorite uncle of Gaelen and Nelwen. Known for being free-spirited and of good humor, he was slain in the Third Uprising. Name means "strong ally". From tar- (of the realm) and magra (mighty).

Thaldallen (Thall-DAH-len): An enormous, solitary oak in the Greatwood forest. Name means "steadfast oak". From thayla (trust) and dalen (oak).

Thaylon (THAY-lon): Given name of Rogond, it means "trustworthy". From thayla (to trust).

Thorndil (THORN-deel): Northman, ranger, and friend of Rogond, companion of Belegund. His name means "Piercing gaze, eagle-eyed". From thorn- (to pierce).

Tibo (TEE-bo): Dwarf of Grundin's realm. Tibo was known for his love of Elves.

Trachair (TRACH-eye-eer): "The treacherous". Evil Asarla also known as Kotos, Trachair is the name given him by the Elves.

Troll: These unusual beings are found in and around the hilly and mountainous areas of Alterra. If Ulcas do not love sunlight, trolls live in dread of it, for they cannot survive exposure for more than a few moments. Trolls turn to stone if the sun finds them, and hence they are abroad only at night. They are very large, dull-witted, and slow-moving. If caught by them, one should expect to be crushed and then eaten.

They are ancient creatures of unlimited lifespan, and their origin is uncertain. The Rûndiam-har tells that they were formed from the earth itself, and at first they served no one, but Wrothgar subverted them during the Time of Mystery. They have since played a part in all three Uprisings—an army of trolls approaching by night is a fearsome sight. The armies of Light ultimately routed them, though they are very difficult to kill using ordinary weapons. It is a rare blade that will give more than a shallow wound, and arrows will kill them only through the eye or the mouth.

A few speak crude Aridani, though not very well, and they may wear rough clothing, but go about unshod. Slow and stupid they might be, but one should not underestimate them, for they stand three times as tall as a man with ten times the girth, and wield great hammers of stone. They will eat anything they can catch and kill. They have often plagued the dwarves, who hate them with a passion. Most formidable are the trolls that have lived beneath fire-mountains, for those lands are poisoned, and the trolls have grown larger and more dangerous as a result.

Tuathas (TOO-ah-thas): Greatest of all Realms of Men, Tuathas alone possessed an Asarla. Because of this they were more enlightened than other men and were nearly as fair as the Elves. Tuathas was destroyed during an eruption of one of the great Fire-mountains that bounded it, and very little of the realm survived. The cataclysm occurred in the year s.r.6740, and nearly wiped out the entire northern race—the lands remained lifeless until the turning of the Age. From tuath (north).

Tuathar (TOO-ah-thar) sing. Tuathan: Men of the northern Realm of Tuathas, lost in the rising of the Great Fire-mountain. They are tall and comely, hardy and strong. Because of the influence of their Asarla, they are more enlightened than other races of men. They founded not only the realm of Tuathas, but the great cities of Dùn Bennas and Dùn Arian. Examples are Rogond and Thorndil. Name means 'north-man'. From tuath (north) and aridan (man).

Turanen (TOOR-ah-nen): Younger brother of Tarfion and Tarmagil, father of Nelwyn and spouse of Elwyn. An unparalleled archer, he was slain in the third uprising. Name means 'glen-bowman'. From tuag- (bow) and ranen (glen).

Turantil (TOOR-an-TEEL): Sword of Halrodin, prized heirloom stolen by Gorgon. Name means "scourge of the north". From tuath (north) and ranta (scourge).

Tûr Dorcha (Toor DOR-ka): Wrothgar's stronghold in the Darkmere, it means "Dark Tower". The fortress is actually a sickly, pale grey due to the fetid mists of the Laban Fuath, hence it is also called the "Pale Tower". Most of the stronghold is belowground, carved into solid rock. The surrounding bog is entirely unnatural and contains many vile, disgusting perversions of normal creatures. Only the servants of Wrothgar are likely to survive drawing too near to Tûr Dorcha.

Ular (OO-lar): "The longbeard", chief of the Council of Elders in Cósdomhain.

Ulcas (UL-cas), sing. Ulca: Evil servants of Wrothgar. Some are quite formidable in battle, but most can prevail only through sheer numbers. All are ugly. They dislike sunlight and live in dark places, particularly beneath mountains. They lurk in nearly every dark, forsaken place in Alterra, and their numbers have waxed and waned according to the power of their Master. There is some debate among scholars concerning the origin of Ulcas, but it is assumed that they are perversions of existing races, for Wrothgar can create nothing of his own; he can only twist and subvert the creations of Aontar.

There is some speculation that the Elves had a part in the making of the Ulcas, a notion that is most emphatically denied by both the Elves and the Ulcas. The two races hate each other, and they claim no relationship that does not involve the point of a blade. The Elves are quick to point out that Ulcas will not consume their flesh (they will eat nearly anything else), that they are entirely hairless, lacking even eyelashes, and that they will not suffer the touch of objects that are Elven-made, hence they could not share the same forebears.

The prevailing view held by western scholars is that Ulcas were men in the beginning, and that Wrothgar, desiring to make them stronger, infected them with a pestilence. This disease killed the weaker members, and those that survived lived much longer, even to the point of appearing to be immortal. All Ulcas now carry the pestilence, which has changed over generations such that it can no longer infect men. It is passed to the Ulcas before they are born, and it makes them hardy and long-lived, but it also twists and distorts their hairless bodies and makes them intolerant of sunlight. Naturally, the Elves prefer this view, yet it has not been proven.

Ulcas are highly variable in appearance; most are greyish-black in color, but some are pale or mottled, and some are dark as pitch. They are all undeniably ugly, some so ugly as to be hideous. Ulcas typically speak a crude form of Aridani, varied according to the area of origin. Because they do not write or record events, we know little of their history, customs, or culture. Their name simply means "evil, wicked" in the Elven-speech.

They have played a large part in Wrothgar's plans throughout history, swarming down upon their enemies in huge masses during battles. They are terribly weakened by sunlight, hence it is perilous to go abroad at night in any unprotected lands. During daylight they are most often found belowground. They feed primarily upon flesh, scavenging the dead as well as preying upon the living.

Their eyes are well designed for seeing in darkness, with cat-like, vertical pupils. In color they are generally a pale yellow to muddy yellow-brown; blue or grey-eyed Ulcas are almost unknown.

Úlfar (OOL-far): "Fen-serpents", vile, slimy eels with rasping, sucker-like mouths. Arguably the most unpleasant creatures in Alterra, they ensnare wading travelers or animals by miring them in slime and entangling them. Once the prey is brought down into the water, they attach to any hairless area and give an envenomed bite. The venom subdues the victim, whereupon the creatures enter through body orifices and consume it from the inside out. They are normally found in bogs but can travel up fresh waterways for a considerable distance. They cannot live in salt water. Their bite is so septic that a man bitten by an Úlfa is doomed to a very bad death. They are undoubtedly a perversion of normal eels, designed by Wrothgar.

Unvar (OON-vahr): Fisherman, brother of Maleck.

Wellyn (WEL-lin): Son and reluctant heir of Ri-Aruin of the Greatwood, Wellyn is a very dear friend of Gaelen. He has raven-black hair and blue-grey eyes. His name means "courageous, one who is brave".

Wodon: Herd stallion of Tal-sithian. His name means "the hammer".

Wrothgar (ROTH-gar): Evil Being of Alterra, also known as the Shadowmancer or the Black Flame. He was so named because of his ability to summon the dreadful being known as "The Shadow", who can so confuse the soldiers of an enemy army that they turn upon one another. His hallmark is the peculiar dark fire that envelops him when he is engaged in battle—this flame will slowly consume everything it touches.

Wrothgar has arisen thrice at the time these tales begin; first in f.r.3506-3525, second in s.r.2026-2029, and third in s.r.6085-6091.

About C.S. Marks

C.S. Marks has often been described as a Renaissance woman. The daughter of academic parents, she holds a Ph.D. in Biology and has spent the past two decades teaching Biology and Equine Science. She is currently a Full Professor at Saint Mary-of-the-Woods College in west central Indiana.

She began writing shortly after the untimely death of her father, who was a Professor of American Literature at Butler University. A gifted artist, she has produced illustrations and cover art for all three books. She plays and sings Celtic music and a few examples of her songwriting may be found within the pages of Fire-heart. She enjoys archery, and makes hand-crafted longbows using primitive tools.

Horses are her passion, and she is an accomplished horsewoman, having competed in the sport of endurance racing for many years. One of only a handful of Americans to complete the prestigious Tom Quilty Australian national championship hundred-mile ride, she has described this moment as her finest hour.

Website: CSMarks.com
Facebook: Facebook.com/Alterra
CSMarksTwitter: Twitter.com/CSMarks_Alterra
Goodreads: https://www.goodreads.com/author/show/521676.C_S_Marks
C.S. Marks Mailing List Sign Up: http://eepurl.com/st8Vj

Books by C.S. Marks

Tales of Alterra (The Elfhunter Trilogy)

Elfhunter

Fire-heart

Ravenshade

Alterra Histories

The Fire King

Fallen Embers

The Shadow-man

Undiscovered Realms

Outcaste

We hope you've enjoyed reading Elfhunter. Please consider leaving a review on Goodreads and your point of purchase.

Where to Find C.S. Marks

The Author's Website: CSMarks.com

Facebook.com/Alterra.CSMarks

Twitter.com/CSMarks_Alterra

Stay up to date with what's happening with C.S. Marks by joining the mailing list. You will receive exclusive teasers and be the first to know when a new book has been released.

Sign Up For the C.S. Marks Mailing List at CSMarks.com

Made in the USA
Middletown, DE
10 July 2016